ISAAC ASIMOV, one of America's great resources, has by now written more than 330 books. No other writer in history has published so much on such a wide variety of subjects, which range from science fiction and murder novels to books on history, the physical sciences, and Shakespeare. Born in the Soviet Union and raised in Brooklyn, he is married and lives in New York City.

MARTIN H. GREENBERG, who has been called 'the king of anthologists', now has some 130 to his credit. Greenberg is professor of regional analysis and political science at the University of Wisconsin, Green Bay, USA, where he also teaches a course in the history of science fiction.

CHARLES G. WAUGH is professor of psychology and mass communications at the University of Maine at Augusta, USA. He is a leading authority on science fiction and fantasy and has collaborated on more than 80 anthologies and single-author collections with Isaac Asimov, Martin H. Greenberg, and assorted colleagues.

Also available

The Mammoth Book of Classic Science Fiction – Short Novels of the 1930s

The Mammoth Book of Golden Age Science Fiction – Short Novels of the 1940s

The Mammoth Book of Private Eye Stories

The Mammoth Book of Modern Crime Stories

The Mammoth Book of Great Detective Stories

The Mammoth Book of Spy Thrillers

The Mammoth Book of Murder

The Mammoth Book of True Crime

The Mammoth Book of True Crime 2

The Mammoth Book of Short Horror Novels

The Mammoth Book of Ghost Stories

The Mammoth Book of

VINTAGE SCIENCE FICTION

Short Novels of the 1950s

Edited by Isaac Asimov,
Charles G. Waugh and Martin H. Greenberg

Carroll & Graf Publishers, Inc
New York

First pubished in Great Britain 1990
First Carroll & Graf edition 1990

Carroll & Graf Publishers, Inc.
260 Fifth Avenue
New York
NY 10001

ISBN 0-88184-621-X

Printed and bound in Great Britain by
Cox & Wyman Ltd., Reading

CONTENTS

ACKNOWLEDGEMENTS

"Flight to Forever" by Poul Anderson. Copyright 1950 by Poul Anderson; renewed © 1978 by Poul Anderson. Reprinted by permission of the Scott Meredith Literary Agency, Inc., 845 Third Avenue, New York, NY 10022.

"The Martian Way" by Isaac Asimov. Copyright 1952 by Galaxy Publishing Corporation, renewed © 1980 by Isaac Asimov. Reprinted by permission of the author.

"The Alley Man" by Philip Jose Farmer. Copyright © 1959 by Mercury Press, Inc. First appeared in THE MAGAZINE OF FANTASY AND SCIENCE FICTION. Reprinted by permission of the Scott Meredith Literary Agency, Inc., 845 Third Avenue, New York, NY 10022.

"Second Game" by Katherine MacLean and Charles De Vet. Copyright © 1958 by Street & Smith Publications, Inc.; Copyright © 1980 by Robert Silverberg and Martin H. Greenberg. Reprinted by permission of the authors and of Virginia Kidd, Literary Agent.

"Dark Benediction" by Walter M. Miller, Jr. Copyright 1951, renewed © 1979 by Walter M. Miller, Jr. Reprinted by permission of Don Congdon Associates, Inc.

"The Midas Plague" by Frederik Pohl. Copyright 1954 by Galaxy Publishing Corporation; renewed © 1982 by Frederik Pohl. Reprinted by permission of the author.

"The Oceans are Wide" by Frank M. Robinson. Copyright 1954, renewed © 1982 by Frank M. Robinson. Reprinted by permission of Curtis Brown, Ltd.

"And Then There Were None" by Eric Frank Russell. Copyright 1951 by Street & Smith Publications, Inc. Reprinted by permission of the agents for the author's Estate, the Scott Meredith Literary Agency, Inc., 845 Third Avenue, New York, NY 10022.

"Baby is Three" by Theodore Sturgeon. Copyright 1952 by Galaxy Publishing Corporation, renewed © 1980 by Theordore Sturgeon. Reprinted by permission of Kirby McCauley, Ltd.

"Firewater" by William Tenn. Copyright 1952 by Street & Smith Publications, Inc.; renewed © 1980 by William Tenn. Reprinted by permission of the author and the author's agent, Virginia Kidd.

INTRODUCTION

THE AGE OF THE TROIKA

Isaac Asimov

In the 1950's, John W. Campbell, Jr., editor of *Astounding Science Fiction* was still a giant figure in the field of American magazine science fiction. *Astounding* was still the magazine with the highest circulation and the greatest prestige.

However, he was not quite the monolith of the 1940's. He now had competition and there were two other editors, running two other magazines, that gave *Astounding* considerable competition.

In 1949, the *Magazine of Fantasy and Science Fiction* (usually referred to, for convenience's sake, as *F & SF*) had its genesis under the editorship of Anthony Boucher and J. Francis McComas (and later, Boucher alone.) In 1950, *Galaxy Science Fiction* came into being with Horace L. Gold as its editor.

Both editors were top-notch men with experience as science fiction writers and both put out top-notch magazines.

F & SF emphasized literary quality and for many years was the cutting edge of the genre, even though it had smaller circulation figures than the other two.

Galaxy emphasized the human side of science fiction, in contradistinction to Campbell's emphasis on machinery and gadgets. He had waited to start his magazine until he had an initial collection of stories that satisfied him completely. The result was that the magazine burst on the science fiction world like a bombshell. There were many who thought the first three numbers of *Galaxy* were the best three-in-a-row issues ever to be seen in the world of magazine science fiction.

As it happened, Campbell, in the face of this new competition weakened his own position by falling prey to his penchant for iconoclasm. Campbell always felt that orthodox science was too stiff in its orthodoxy and that it needed shaking up. For that reason he championed far-out developments as a matter of principle. His choices, however, were not good. In 1951, he fell in love with Dianetics, and from there went on to other dubious fields and devices such as flying saucers, the Dean Drive, the Hieronymus machine and so on.

He wanted stories that reflected these new interests of his and a number of writers, unwilling to oblige, sought refuge in the other two magazines.

On the whole, Campbell's diminution worked to the benefit of the field. With three major magazines of importance, writers had a broader market, could experiment more freely, while the readers tripled the quantity of reading matter available to them, and enjoyed a distinct improvement in the quality of their reading matter as well.

In the 1950's also, major publishing houses (notably Doubleday and Company) began to publish hard-cover science fiction novels, and the magazines, as a group, began to experience a kind of competition they had not had to face in the 1940's. This also helped bring new young talent into the field.

FLIGHT TO FOREVER

Poul Anderson

That morning it rained, a fine, summery mist blowing over the hills and hiding the gleam of the river and the village beyond. Martin Saunders stood in the doorway letting the cool, wet air blow in his face and wondered what the weather would be like a hundred years from now.

Eve Lang came up behind him and laid a hand on his arm. He smiled down at her, thinking how lovely she was with the raindrops caught in her dark hair like small pearls. She didn't say anything; there was no need for it, and he felt grateful for silence.

He was the first to speak. "Not long now, Eve." And then, realizing the banality of it, he smiled. "Only why do we have this airport feeling? It's not as if I'll be gone long."

"A hundred years," she said.

"Take it easy, darling. The theory is foolproof. I've been on time jaunts before, remember? Twenty years ahead and twenty back. The projector works, it's been proven in practice. This is just a little longer trip, that's all."

"But the automatic machines, that went a hundred years ahcad, never came back—"

"Exactly. Some damn fool thing or other went wrong with them. Tubes blew their silly heads off, or some such thing. That's why Sam and I have to go, to see what went wrong. We can repair our machine. We can compensate for the well-known perversity of vacuum tubes."

"But why the two of you? One would be enough. Sam—"

"Sam is no physicist. He might not be able to find the trouble. On the other hand, as a skilled mechanic he can do things I never could. We supplement each other." Saunders took a deep breath. "Look, darling—"

Sam Hull's bass shout rang out to them. "All set, folks! Any time you want to go, we can ride!"

"Coming." Saunders took his time, bidding Eve a proper farewell, a little in advance. She followed him into the house and down to the capacious underground workshop.

The projector stood in a clutter of apparatus under the white radiance of fluoro-tubes. It was unimpressive from the outside, a metal cylinder some ten feet high and thirty feet long with the unfinished look of all experimental set-ups. The outer shell was simply protection for the battery banks and the massive dimensional projector within. A tiny space in the forward end was left for the two men.

Sam Hull gave them a gay wave. His massive form almost blotted out the gray-smocked little body of MacPherson. "All set for a hundred years ahead," he exclaimed. "Two thousand seventy-three, here we come!"

MacPherson blinked owlishly at them from behind thick lenses. "It all tests out," he said. "Or so Sam here tells me. Personally, I wouldn't know an oscillograph from a klystron. You have an ample supply of spare parts and tools. There should be no difficulty."

"I'm not looking for any, Doc," said Saunders. "Eve here won't believe we aren't going to be eaten by monsters with stalked eyes and long fangs. I keep telling her all we're going to do is check your automatic machines, if we can find them, and make a few astronomical observations, and come back."

"There'll be people in the future," said Eve.

"Oh, well, if they invite us in for a drink we won't say no," shrugged Hull. "Which reminds me—" He fished a pint out of his capacious coverall pocket. "We ought to drink a toast or something, huh?"

Saunders frowned a little. He didn't want to add to Eve's impression of a voyage into darkness. She was worried enough, poor kid, poor, lovely kid. "Hell," he said, "we've been back to nineteen fifty-three and seen the house standing. We've been ahead to nineteen ninety-three and seen the house standing. Nobody home at either time. These jaunts are too dull to rate a toast."

"Nothing," said Hull, "is too dull to rate a drink." He poured and they touched glasses, a strange little ceremony in the utterly prosaic laboratory. "Bon voyage!"

"Bon voyage." Eve tried to smile, but the hand that lifted the glass to her lips trembled a little.

"Come on," said Hull. "Let's go, Mart. Sooner we set out, the sooner we can get back."

"Sure." With a gesture of decision, Saunders put down his glass and swung toward the machine. "Goodbye, Eve, I'll see you in a couple of hours—after a hundred years or so."

"So long—Martin." She made the name a caress.

MacPherson beamed with avuncular approval.

Saunders squeezed himself into the forward compartment with Hull. He was a big man, long-limbed and wide-shouldered, with blunt, homely features under a shock of brown hair and wide-set gray eyes lined with crow's feet from much squinting into the sun. He wore only the plain blouse and slacks of his work, stained here and there with grease or acid.

The compartment was barely large enough for the two of them, and crowded with instruments—as well as the rifle and pistol they had along entirely to quiet Eve's fears. Saunders swore as the guns got in his way, and closed the door. The clang had in it an odd note of finality.

"Here goes," said Hull unnecessarily.

Saunders nodded and started the projector warming up. Its powerful thrum filled the cabin and vibrated in his bones. Needles flickered across gauge faces, approaching stable values.

Through the single porthole he saw Eve waving. He waved back and then, with an angry motion, flung down the main switch.

The machine shimmered, blurred, and was gone. Eve drew a shuddering breath and turned back to MacPherson.

Grayness swirled briefly before them, and the drone of the projectors filled the machine with an enormous song. Saunders watched the gauges, and inched back the switch which controlled their rate of time advancement. A hundred years ahead—less the number of days since they'd sent the first automatic, just so that no dunderhead in the future would find it and walk off with it. . .

He slapped down the switch and the noise and vibration came to a ringing halt.

Sunlight streamed in through the porthole. "No house?" asked Hull.

"A century is a long time," said Saunders. "Come on, let's go out and have a look."

They crawled through the door and stood erect. The machine lay in the bottom of a half-filled pit above which grasses waved. A few broken shards of stone projected from the earth. There was a bright blue sky overhead, with fluffy white clouds blowing across it.

"No automatics," said Hull, looking around.

"That's odd. But maybe the ground-level adjustments—let's go topside." Saunders scrambled up the sloping walls of the pit.

It was obviously the half-filled basement of the old house, which must somehow have been destroyed in the eighty years since his last visit. The ground-level machine in the projector automatically materialized it on the exact surface whenever it emerged. There would be no sudden falls or sudden burials unders risen earth. Nor would there be disastrous materializations inside something solid; mass-sensitive circuits prevented the machine from halting whenever solid matter occupied its own space. Liquid or gas molecules could get out of the way fast enough.

Saunders stood in tall, wind-rippled grass and looked over the serene landscape of upper New York State. Nothing had changed, the river and the forested hills beyond it were the same, the sun was bright and clouds shone in the heavens.

No—no, before God! Where was the village?

House gone, town gone—what had happened? Had people simply moved away, or. . .

He looked back down to the basement. Only a few minutes ago—a hundred years in the past—he had stood there in a tangle of battered apparatus, and Doc and Eve—and now it was a pit with wild grass covering the raw earth. An odd desolation tugged at him.

Was *he* still alive today? Was—Eve? The gerontology of 1973 made it entirely possible, but one never knew. And he didn't want to find out.

"Must'a give the country back to the Indians," grunted Sam Hull.

The prosaic wisecrack restored a sense of balance. After all, any sensible man knew that things changed with time. There would be good and evil in the future as there had been in the past. "—And they lived happily ever after" was pure myth. The important thing was change, an unending flux out of which all could come. And right now there was a job to do.

They scouted around in the grass, but there was no trace of the small automatic projectors. Hull scowled thoughtfully. "You know," he said, "I think they started back and blew out on the way."

"You must be right," nodded Saunders. "We can't have arrived more than a few minutes after their return-point." He started back toward the big machine. "Let's take our observation and get out."

They set up their astronomical equipment and took readings on the declining sun. Waiting for night, they cooked a meal on a camp stove and sat while a cricket-chirring dusk deepened around them.

"I like this future," said Hull. "It's peaceful. Think I'll retire here—or now—in my old age."

The thought of transtemporal resorts made Saunders grin. But—who knew? Maybe!

The stars wheeled grandly overhead. Saunders jotted down figures on right ascension, declination and passage times. From that, they could calculate later, almost to the minute, how far the machine had taken them. They had not moved in space at all, of course, relative to the surface of the earth. "Absolute space" was an obsolete fiction, and as far as the projector was concerned Earth was the immobile center of the universe.

They waded through dew-wet grass back down to the machine. "We'll try ten-year stops, looking for the automatics," said Saunders. "If we don't find 'em that way, to hell with them. I'm hungry."

2063—it was raining into the pit.

2053—sunlight and emptiness.

2043—the pit was fresher now, and a few rotting timbers lay half buried in the ground.

Saunders scowled at the meters. "She's drawing more power than she should," he said.

2023—the house had obviously burned, charred stumps of wood were in sight. And the projector had roared with a skull-cracking insanity of power; energy drained from the batteries like water from a squeezed sponge; a resistor was beginning to glow.

They checked the circuits, inch by inch, wire by wire. Nothing was out of order.

"Let's go." Hull's face was white.

It was a battle to leap the next ten years, it took half an hour of bawling, thundering, tortured labor for the projector to fight backward. Radiated energy made the cabin unendurably hot.

2013—the fire-blackened basement still stood. On its floor lay two small cylinders, tarnished with some years of weathering.

"The automatics got a little farther back," said Hull. "Then they quit, and just lay here."

Saunders examined them. When he looked up from his instruments, his face was grim with the choking fear that was rising within him. "Drained," he said. "Batteries completely dead. They used up all their energy reserves."

"What in the devil is this?" It was almost a snarl from Hull.

"I—don't—know. There seems to be some kind of resistance which increases the further back we try to go—"

"Come on!"

"But—"

"Come on, God damn it!"

Saunders shrugged hopelessly.

It took two hours to fight back five years. Then Saunders stopped the projector. His voice shook.

"No go, Sam. We've used up three quarters of our stored energy—and the farther back we go, the more we use per year. It seems to be some sort of high-order exponential function."

"So—"

"So we'd never make it. At this rate, our batteries will be dead before we get back another ten years." Saunders looked ill. "It's some effect the theory didn't allow for, some accelerating increase in power requirements the farther back into the past we go. For twenty-year hops or less, the energy increases roughly as the square of the number of years traversed. But it must actually be something like an exponential curve, which starts building up fast and furious beyond a certain point. We haven't enough power left in the batteries!"

"If we could recharge them—"

"We don't have such equipment with us. But maybe—"

They climbed out of the ruined basement and looked eagerly towards the river. There was no sign of the village. It must have been torn down or otherwise destroyed still further back in the past at a point they'd been through.

"No help there," said Saunders.

"We can look for a place. There must be people somewhere!"

"No doubt." Saunders fought for calm. "But we could spend a long time looking for them, you know. And—" his voice wavered, "Sam, I'm not sure even recharging at intervals would help. It looks very much to me as if the curve of energy consumption is approaching a vertical asymptote."

"Talk English, will you?" Hull's grin was forced.

"I mean that beyond a certain number of years an infinite amount of energy may be required. Like the Einsteinian concept of light as the limiting velocity. As you approach the speed of light, the energy needed to accelerate increases ever more rapidly. You'd need infinite energy to get beyond the speed of light—which is just a fancy way of saying you can't do it. The same thing may apply to time as well as space."

"You mean—we can't ever get back?"

"I don't know." Saunders looked desolately around at the smiling landscape. "I could be wrong. But I'm horribly afraid I'm right."

Hull swore, "What're we going to do about it?"

"We've got two choices," Saunders said. "One, we can hunt for people, recharge our batteries, and keep trying. Two, we can go into the future."

"The future!"

"Uh-huh. Sometime in the future, they ought to know more about such things than we do. They may know a way to get around this effect. Certainly they could give us a powerful enough engine so that, if energy is all that's needed, we can get back. A small atomic generator, for instance."

Hull stood with bent head, turning the thought over in his mind. There was a meadowlark singing somewhere, maddeningly sweet.

Saunders forced a harsh laugh. "But the very first thing on the agenda," he said, "is breakfast!"

The food was tasteless. They ate in a heavy silence, choking the stuff down. But in the end they looked at each other with a common resolution.

Hull grinned and stuck out a hairy paw. "It's a hell of a roundabout way to get home," he said, "but I'm for it."

Saunders clasped hands with him, wordlessly. They went back to the machine.

"And now where?" asked the mechanic.

"It's two thousand eight," said Saunders. "How about—well—two-thousand five-hundred A.D.?"

"Okay. It's a nice round number. Anchors aweigh!"

The machine thrummed and shook. Saunders was gratified to notice the small power consumption as the years and decades fled by. At that rate, they had energy enough to travel to the end of the world.

Eve, Eve, I'll come back. I'll come back if I have to go ahead to Judgment Day. . .

2500 A.D. The machine blinked into materialization on top of a low hill—the pit had filled in during the intervening centuries. Pale, hurried sunlight flashed through wind-driven rain clouds into the hot interior.

"Come," said Hull. "We haven't got all day."

He picked up the automatic rifle. "What's the idea?" exclaimed Saunders.

"Eve was right the first time," said Hull grimly. "Buckle on that pistol, Mart."

Saunders strapped the heavy weapon to his thigh. The metal was cold under his fingers.

They stepped out and swept the horizon. Hull's voice rose in a shout of glee. "People!"

There was a small town beyond the river, near the site of old Hudson. Beyond it lay fields of ripening grain and clumps of trees. There was no sign of a highway. Maybe surface transportation was obsolete now.

The town looked—odd. It must have been there a long time, the houses were weathered. They were tall peak-roofed buildings, crowding narrow streets. A flashing metal tower reared some five hundred feet into the lowering sky, near the center of town.

Somehow, it didn't look the way Saunders had visualized communities of the future. It had an oddly stunted appearance, despite the high buildings and—sinister? He couldn't say. Maybe it was only his depression.

Something rose from the center of the town, a black ovoid that whipped into the sky and lined out across the river. *Reception committee*, thought Saunders. His hand fell on his pistol butt.

It was an airjet, he saw as it neared, an egg-shaped machine with stubby wings and a flaring tail. It was flying slowly now, gliding groundward toward them.

"Hallo, there!" bawled Hull. He stood erect with the savage wind tossing his flame-red hair, waving. "Hallo, people!"

The machine dove at them. Something stabbed from its nose, a line of smoke—tracers!

Conditioned reflex flung Saunders to the ground. The bullets whined over his head, exploding with a vicious crash behind him. He saw Hull blown apart.

The jet rushed overhead and banked for another assault. Saunders got up and ran, crouching low, weaving back and forth. The line of bullets spanged past him again, throwing up gouts of dirt where they hit. He threw himself down again.

Another try. . . Saunders was knocked off his feet by the bursting of a shell. He rolled over and hugged the ground, hoping the grass would hide him. Dimly, he thought that the jet was too fast for strafing a single man; it overshot its mark.

He heart it whine overhead, without daring to look up. It circled vulture-like, seeking him. He had time for a rising tide of bitter hate.

Sam—they'd killed him, shot him without provocation—Sam, red-haired Sam with his laughter and his comradeship, Sam was dead and they had killed him.

He risked turning over. The jet was settling to earth; they'd hunt him from the ground. He got up and ran again.

A shot wailed past his ear. He spun around, the pistol in his hand, and snapped a return shot. There were men in black uniforms coming out of the jet. It was long range, but his gun was a heavy war model; it carried. He fired again and felt a savage joy at seeing one of the black-clad figures spin on its heels and lurch to the ground.

The time machine lay before him. No time for heroics; he had to get away—fast! Bullets were singing around him.

He burst through the door and slammed it shut. A slug whanged through the metal wall. Thank God the tubes were still warm!

He threw the main switch. As vision wavered, he saw the pursuers almost on him. One of them was aiming something like a bazooka.

They faded into grayness. He lay back, shuddering. Slowly, he grew aware that his clothes were torn and that a metal fragment had scratched his hand.

And Sam was dead. Sam was dead.

He watched the dial creep upward. Let it be 3000 A.D. Five hundred years was not too much to put between himself and the men in black.

He chose night time. A cautious look outside revealed that he was among tall buildings with little if any light. Good!

He spent a few moments bandaging his injury and changing into the extra clothes Eve had insisted on providing—a heavy wool shirt and breeches, boots, and a raincoat that should help make him relatively inconspicuous. The holstered pistol went along, of course, with plenty of extra cartridges. He'd have to leave the machine while he reconnoitered and chance its discovery. At least he could lock the door.

Outside, he found himself standing in a small cobbled courtyard between high houses with shuttered and darkened windows. Over head was utter night, the stars must be clouded, but he saw a vague red glow to the north, pulsing and flickering. After a moment, he squared his shoulders and started down an alley that was like a cavern of blackness.

Briefly, the incredible situation rose in his mind. In less than an hour he had leaped a thousand years past his own age, had seen his friend murdered and now stood in an alien city more alone than man had ever been. *And Eve, will I see you again*?

A noiseless shadow, blacker than the night, slipped past him. The dim light shone greenly from its eyes—an alley cat! At least man still had pets. But he could have wished for a more reassuring one.

Noise came from ahead, a bobbing light flashing around at the doors of houses. He dropped a hand through the slit in his coat to grasp the pistol butt.

Black against the narrowed skyline four men came abreast, filling the street. The rhythm of their footfall was military. A guard of some kind. He looked around for shelter; he didn't want to be taken prisoner by unknowns.

No alleys to the side—he sidled backward. The flashlight beam darted ahead, crossed his body, and came back. A voice shouted something, harsh and peremptory.

Saunders turned and ran. The voice cried again behind him. He heard the slam of boots after him. Someone blew a horn, raising echoes that hooted between the high dark walls.

A black form grew out of the night. Fingers like steel wires closed on his arm, yanking him to one side. He opened his mouth, and a hand slipped across it. Before he could recover balance, he was pulled down a flight of stairs in the street.

"In heah." The hissing whisper was taut in his ear. "Quickly."

A door slid open just a crack. They burst through, and the other man closed it behind them. An automatic lock clicked shut.

"Ih don'tink dey vised use," said the man grimly. "Dey better not ha'!"

Saunders stared at him. The other man was of medium height, with a lithe, slender build shown by the skin-tight gray clothes under his black cape. There was a gun at one hip, a pouch at the other. His face was sallow, with a yellowish tinge, and the hair was shaven. It was a lean, strong face, with high cheekbones and narrow jaw, straight nose with flaring nostrils, dark, slant eyes under Mephistophelean brows. The mouth, wide and self-indulgent, was drawn into a reckless grin that showed sharp white teeth. Some sort of white-Mongoloid half-breed, Saunders guessed.

"Who are *you*?" he asked roughly.

The stranger surveyed him shrewdly. "Belgotai of Syrtis," he said at last. "But yuh don' belong heah."

"I'll say I don't." Wry humor rose in Saunders. "Why did you snatch me that way?"

"Yuh didn' wanna fall into de Watch's hands, did yuh?" asked Belgotai. "Don' ask mih why Ih ressued a stranger. Ih happened to come out, see yuh running, figgered anybody running fro de Watch desuhved help, an' pulled yuh back in." He shrugged. "Of course, if yuh don' wanna be helped, go back upstaiahs."

"I'll stay here, of course," Saunders said. "And—thanks for rescuing me."

"*De nada,*" said Belgotai. "Come, le's ha' a drink."

It was a smoky, low-ceilinged room, with a few scarred wooden tables crowded about a small charcoal fire and big barrels in the rear—a tavern of some sort, an underworld hangout. Saunders reflected that he might have done worse. Crooks wouldn't be as finicky about his antecedents as officialdom might be. He could ask his way around, learn.

"I'm afraid I haven't any money," he said. "Unless—" He pulled a handful of coins from his pocket.

Belgotai looked sharply at them and drew a whistling breath between his teeth. Then his face smoothed into blankness. "Ih'll buy," he said genially. "Come Hennaly, gi' us whissey."

Belgotai drew Saunders into a dark corner seat, away from the others in the room. The landlord brought tumblers of rotgut remotely akin to whiskey, and Saunders gulped his with a feeling of need.

"Wha' name do yuh go by?" asked Belgotai.

"Saunders. Martin Saunders."

"Glad to see yuh. Now—" Belgotai leaned closer, and his voice dropped to a whisper—"Now, Saunders, *when* 're yuh from?"

Saunders started. Belgotai smiled thinly. "Be frank," he said. "Dese're mih frien's heah. Dey'd think nawting of slitting yuh troat and dumping yuh in de alley. But Ih mean well."

With a sudden great weariness, Saunders relaxed. What the hell, it had to come out sometime. "Nineteen hundred seventy-three," he said.

"Eh? De future?"

"No—the past."

"Oh. Diff'ent chronning, den. How far back?"

"One thousand and twenty-seven years."

Belgotai whistled. "Long ways! But Ih were sure yuh mus' be from de past. Nobody eve' came fro' de future."

Sickly: "You mean—it's impossible?"

"Ih do' know." Belgotai's grin was wolfish. "Who'd visit dis era fro' de future, if dey could? But wha's yuh story?"

Saunders bristled. The whiskey was coursing hot in his veins now. "I'll trade information," he said coldly. "I won't give it."

"Faiah enawff. Blast away, Mahtin Saundahs."

Saunders told his story in a few words. At the end, Belgotai nodded gravely. "Yuh ran into de Fanatics, five hundred yeahs ago," he said. "Dey was deat' on time travelers. Or on most people, for dat matter."

"But what's happened? What sort of world is this, anyway?"

Belgotai's slurring accents were getting easier to follow. Pronunciation had changed a little, vowels sounded different, the "r" had shifted to something like that in twentieth-century French or Danish, other consonants were modified. Foreign words, especially Spanish, had crept in. But it was still intelligible. Saunders listened. Belgotai was not too well versed in history, but his shrewd brain had a grasp of the more important facts.

The time of troubles had begun in the twenty-third century with the revolt of the Martian colonists against the increasingly corrupt and tyrannical Terrestrial Directorate. A century later the folk of Earth were on the move, driven by famine, pestilence and civil war, a chaos out of which rose the religious enthusiasm of the Armageddonists—the Fanatics, as they were called later. Fifty years after the massacres on Luna, Huntry was the military dictator of Earth, and the rule of the Armageddonists endured for nearly three hundred years. It was a nominal sort of rule, vast territories were always in revolt and the planetary colonists were building up a power which kept the Fanatics out of space, but wherever they did have control they ruled with utter ruthlessness.

Among other things they forbade was time travel. But it had never been popular with anyone since the Time War, when a defeated Directorate army had leaped from the twenty-third to the twenty-fourth century and wrought havoc before their attempt at conquest was smashed. Time travelers were few anyway, the future was too precarious—they were apt to be killed or enslaved in one of the more turbulent periods.

In the late twenty-seventh century, the Planetary League and the African Dissenters had finally ended Fanatic rule. Out of the postwar confusion rose the Pax Africana, and for two hundred years man had enjoyed an era of comparative peace and progress which was wistfully looked back on as a golden age; indeed, modern chronology dated from the ascension of John Mteza I. Breakdown came through internal decay and the onslaughts of barbarians from the outer planets, the Solar System split into a multitude of small states and even independent cities. It was a hard, brawling period, not without a brilliance of its own, but it was drawing to a close now.

"Dis is one of de city-states," said Belgotai. "Liung-Wei, it's named—founded by Sinese invaders about three centuries ago. It's under de dictatorship of Krausmann now, a stubborn old buzzard who'll no surrender dough de armies of de Atlantic Master're at ouah very gates now. Yuh see de red glow? Dat's deir projectors working on our energy screen. When dey break it down, dey'll take de city and punish it for holding out so long. Nobody looks happily to dat day."

He added a few remarks about himself. Belgotai was of a dying age, the past era of small states who employed mercenaries to fight their battles. Born on Mars, Belgotai had hired out over the whole Solar System. But the little mercenary companies were helpless before the organized levies of the rising nations, and after annihilation of his band Belgotai had fled to Earth where he dragged out a weary existence as thief and assassin. He had little to look forward to.

"Nobody wants a free comrade now," he said ruefully. "If de Watch don't catch me first, Ih'll hang when de Atlantics take de city."

Saunders nodded with a certain sympathy.

Belgotai leaned close with a gleam in his slant eyes. "But yuh can help me, Mahtin Saundahs," he hissed. "And help yuhself too."

"Eh?" Saunders blinked wearily at him.

"Sure, sure. Take me wid yuh, out of dis damned time. Dey can't help yuh here, dey know no more about time travel dan yuh do—most likely dey'll throw yuh in de calabozo and smash yuh machine. Yuh have to go on. Take me!"

Saunders hesitated, warily. What did he really know? How much truth was in Belgotai's story? How far could he trust—

"Set me off in some time when a free comrade can fight again. Meanwhile I'll help. Ih'm a good man wid gun or vibrodagger. Yuh can't go batting alone into de future."

Saunders wondered. But what the hell—it was plain enough that this period was of no use to him. And Belgotai had saved him, even if the Watch wasn't as bad he claimed. And—well—he needed someone to talk to, if nothing else. Someone to help him forget Sam Hull and the gulf of centuries separating him from Eve.

Decision came. "Okay."

"Wonnaful! Yuh'll no be sorry, Mahtin." Belgotai stood up. "Come, le's be blasting off."

"Now?"

"De sooner de better. Someone may find yuh machine. Den it's too late."

"But—you'll want to make ready—say goodbye—"

Belgotai slapped his pouch. "All Ih own is heah." Bitterness underlay his reckless laugh. "Ih've none to say goodbye to, except mih creditors. Come!"

Half dazed, Saunders followed him out of the tavern. This time-hopping was going too fast for him, he didn't have a chance to adjust.

For instance, if he ever got back to his own time he'd have descendants in this age. At the rate at which lines of descent spread, there would be men in each army who had his own and Eve's blood, warring on each other without thought of the tenderness which had wrought their very beings. But then, he remembered wearily, he had never considered the common ancestors he must have with men he'd shot out of the sky in the war he once had fought.

Men lived in their own times, a brief flash of light ringed with an enormous dark, and it was not in their nature to think beyond that little span of years. He began to realize why time travel had never been common.

"Hist!" Belgotai drew him into the tunnel of an alley. They crouched there while four black-caped men of the Watch strode past. In the wan red light, Saunders had a glimpse of high cheekbones, half-Oriental features, the metallic gleam of guns slung over their shoulders.

They made their way to the machine where it lay between lowering houses crouched in a night of fear and waiting. Belgotai laughed again, a soft, joyous ring in the dark. "Freedom!" he whispered.

They crawled into it and Saunders set the controls for a hundred years ahead. Belgotai scowled. "Most like de world'll be very tame and quiet den," he said.

"If I get a way to return," said Saunders, "I'll carry you on whenever you want to go."

"Or yuh could carry me back a hundred years from now," said the warrior. "Blast away, den!"

3100 A.D. A waste of blackened, fused rock. Saunders switched on the Geiger counter and it clattered crazily. Radioactive! Some hellish atomic bomb had wiped Liung-Wei from existence. He leaped another century, shaking.

3200 A.D. The radioactivity was gone, but the desolation remained, a vast vitrified crater under a hot, still sky, dead and lifeless. There was little prospect of walking across it in search of man, nor did Saunders want to get far from the machine. If he should be cut off from it. . .

By 3500, soil had drifted back over the ruined land and a forest was growing. They stood in a drizzling rain and looked around them.

"Big trees," said Saunders. "This forest has stood for a long time without human interference."

"Maybe man went back to de caves?" suggested Belgotai.

"I doubt it. Civilization was just too widespread for a lapse into total savagery. But it may be a long ways to a settlement."

"Let's go ahead, den!" Belgotai's eyes gleamed with interest.

The forest still stood for centuries thereafter. Saunders scowled in worry. He didn't like this business of going farther and farther from his time, he was already too far ahead ever to get back without help. Surely, in all ages of human history—

4100 A.D. They flashed into materialization on a broad grassy sward where low, rounded buildings of something that looked like tinted plastic stood between fountains, statues, and bowers. A small aircraft whispered noiselessly overhead, no sign of motive power on its exterior.

There were humans around, young men and women who wore long colorful capes over light tunics. They crowded forward with a shout. Saunders and Belgotai stepped out, raising hands in a gesture of friendship. But the warrior kept his hands close to his gun.

The language was a flowing, musical tongue with only a baffling hint of familiarity. Had times changed that much?

They were taken to one of the buildings. Within its cool, spacious interior, a grave, bearded man in ornate red robes stood up to greet them. Someone else brought in a small machine reminiscent of an oscilloscope with microphone attachments. The man set it on the table and adjusted its dials.

He spoke again, his own unknown language rippling from his lips. But words came out of the machine—English!

"Welcome, travelers, to this branch of the American College. Please be seated."

Saunders and Belgotai gaped. The man smiled. "I see the psychophone is new to you. It is a receiver of encephalic emissions from the speech centers. When one speaks, the corresponding thoughts are taken by the machine, greatly amplified, and beamed to the brain of the listener, who interprets them in terms of his own language.

"Permit me to introduce myself. I am Hamalon Avard; dean of this branch of the College." He raised bushy gray eyebrows in polite inquiry.

They gave their names and Avard bowed ceremoniously. A slim girl, whose scanty dress caused Belgotai's eyes to widen, brought a tray of sandwiches and a beverage not unlike tea. Saunders suddenly realized how hungry and tired he was. He collapsed into a seat that molded itself to his contours and looked dully at Avard.

Their story came out, and the dean nodded. "I thought you were time travelers," he said. "But this is a matter of great interest. The archeology departments will want to speak to you, if you will be so kind—"

"Can you help us?" asked Saunders bluntly. "Can you fix our machine so it will reverse?"

"Alas, no. I am afraid our physics holds no hope for you. I can consult the experts, but I am sure there has been no change in spatiotemporal theory since Priogan's reformulation. According to it, the energy needed to travel into the past increases tremendously with the period covered. The deformation of world lines, you see. Beyond a period of about seventy years, infinite energy is required."

Saunders nodded dully. "I thought so. Then there's no hope?"

"Not in this time, I am afraid. But science is advancing rapidly. Contact with alien culture in the Galaxy has proved an immense stimulant—"

"Yuh have interstellar travel?" exploded Belgotai. "Yuh can travel to de stars?"

"Yes, of course. The faster-than-light drive was worked out over five hundred years ago on the basis of Priogan's modified relativity theory. It involves warping through higher dimensions—But you have more urgent problems than scientific theories."

"Not Ih!" said Belgotai fiercely. "If Ih can get put among de stars—dere must be wars dere—"

"Alas, yes, the rapid expansion of the frontier has thrown the Galaxy into chaos. But I do not think you could get passage on a spaceship. In fact, the Council will probably order your temporal deportation as unintegrated individuals. The sanity of Sol will be in danger otherwise."

"Why, yuh—" Belgotai snarled and reached for his gun. Saunders clapped a hand on the warrior's arm.

"Take it easy, you bloody fool," he said furiously. We can't fight a whole planet. Why should we? There'll be other ages."

Belgotai relaxed, but his eyes were still angry.

They stayed at the College for two days. Avard and his colleagues were courteous, hospitable, eager to hear what the travelers had to tell of their periods. They provided food and living quarters and much-needed rest. They even pleaded Belgotai's case to the Solar Council, via telescreen. But the answer was inexorable: the Galaxy already had too many barbarians. The travelers would have to go.

Their batteries were taken out of the machine for them and a small atomic engine with nearly limitless energy reserves installed in its place. Avard gave them a psychophone for communication with whoever they met in the future. Everyone was very nice and considerate. But Saunders found himself reluctantly agreeing with Belgotai. He didn't care much for these over-civilized gentlefolk. He didn't belong in this age.

Avard bade them grave goodbye. "It is strange to see you go," he said. "It is a strange thought that you will still be traveling long after my cremation, that you will see things I cannot dream of." Briefly, something stirred in his face. "In a way I envy you." He turned away quickly, as if afraid of the thought. "Goodbye and good fortune."

4300 A.D. The campus buildings were gone, but small, elaborate summerhouses had replaced them. Youths and girls in scanty rainbow-hued dress crowded around the machine.

"You are time travelers?" asked one of the young men, wide-eyed.

Saunders nodded, feeling too tired for speech.

"Time travelers!" A girl squealed in delight.

"I don't suppose you have any means of traveling into the past these days?" asked Saunders hopelessly.

"Not that I know of. But please come, stay for a while, tell us about your journeys. This is the biggest lark we've had since the ship came from Sirius."

There was no denying the eager insistence. The women, in particular, crowded around, circling them in a ring of soft arms, laughing and shouting and pulling them away from the machine. Belgotai grinned. "Let's stay de night," he suggested.

Saunders didn't feel like arguing the point. There was time enough, he thought bitterly. All the time in the world.

It was a night of revelry. Saunders managed to get a few facts. Sol was a Galactic backwater these days, stuffed with mercantile wealth and guarded by nonhuman mercenaries against the interstellar raiders and conquerors. This region was one of many playgrounds for the children of the great merchant families, living for generations off inherited riches. They were amiable kids, but there was a mental and physical softness about them, and a deep inward weariness from a meaningless round of increasingly stale pleasure. Decadence.

Saunders finally sat alone under a moon that glittered with the diamond-points of domed cities, beside a softly lapping artificial lake, and watched the constellations wheel overhead—the far suns that man had conquered without mastering himself. He thought of Eve and wanted to cry, but the hollowness in his breast was dry and cold.

★

Belgotai had a thumping hangover in the morning which a drink offered by one of the women removed. He argued for a while about staying in this age. Nobody would deny him passage this time; they were eager for fighting men out in the Galaxy. But the fact that Sol was rarely visited now, that he might have to wait years, finally decided him on continuing.

"Dis won' go on much longer," he said. "Sol is too tempting a prize, an' mercenaries aren' allays loyal. Sooner or later, dere'll be war on Eart' again."

Saunders nodded dispiritedly. He hated to think of the blasting energies that would devour a peaceful and harmless folk, the looting and murdering and enslaving, but history was that way. It was littered with the graves of pacifists.

The bright scene swirled into grayness. They drove ahead.

4400 A.D. A villa was burning, smoke and flame reaching up into the clouded sky. Behind it stood the looming bulk of a ray-scarred spaceship, and around it boiled a vortex of men, huge bearded men in helmets and cuirasses, laughing as they bore out golden loot and struggling captives. The barbarians had come!

The two travelers leaped back into the machine. Those weapons could fuse it to a glowing mass. Saunders swung the main-drive switch far over.

"We'd better make a longer jump," Saunders said, as the needle crept past the century mark. "Can't look for much scientific progress in a dark age. I'll try for five thousand A.D."

His mind carried the thought on: *Will there ever be progress of the sort we must have? Eve, will I ever see you again*? As if his yearning could carry over the abyss of millennia: *Don't mourn me too long, my dearest. In all the bloody ages of human history, your happiness is all that ultimately matters.*

As the needle approached six centuries, Saunders tried to ease down the switch. Tried!

"What's the matter?" Belgotai leaned over his shoulder.

With a sudden cold sweat along his ribs, Saunders tugged harder. The switch was immobile—the projector wouldn't stop.

"Out of order?" asked Belgotai anxiously.

"No—it's the automatic mass-detector. We'd be annihilated if we emerged in the same space with solid matter. The detector prevents the projector from stopping if it senses such a structure." Saunders grinned savagely. "Some damned idiot must have built a house right where we are!"

The needle passed its limit, and still they droned on through a featureless grayness. Saunders re-set the dial and noted the first half millennium. It was nice, though not necessary, to know what year it was when they emerged.

He wasn't worried at first. Man's works were so horribly impermanent; he thought with a sadness of the cities and civilizations he had seen rise and spend their little hour and sink back into the night and chaos of time. But after a thousand years . . .

Two thousand . . .

Three thousand . . .

Belgotai's face was white and tense in the dull glow of the instrument panel. "How long to go?" he whispered.

"I—don't—know."

Within the machine, the long minutes passed while the projector hummed its song of power and two men stared with hypnotized fascination at the creeping record of centuries.

For twenty thousand years that incredible thing stood. In the year 25,296 A.D., the switch suddenly went down under Saunders' steady tug. The machine flashed into reality, tilted, and slid down a few feet before coming to rest. Wildly, they opened the door.

The projector lay on a stone block big as a small house, whose ultimate slipping from its place had freed them. It was halfway up a pyramid.

A monument of gray stone, a tetrahedron a mile to a side and a half a mile high. The outer casing had worn away, or been removed, so that the tremendous blocks stood naked to the weather. Soil had drifted up onto it, grass and trees grew on its titanic slopes. Their roots, and wind and rain and frost, were slowly crumbling the artificial hill to earth again, but still it dominated the landscape.

A defaced carving leered out from a tangle of brush. Saunders looked at it and looked away, shuddering. No human being had ever carved that thing.

The countryside around was altered; he couldn't see the old river and there was a lake glimmering in the distance which had not been there before. The hills seemed lower, and forest covered them. It was a wild, primeval scene, but there was a spaceship standing near the base, a monster machine with its nose rearing skyward and a sunburst blazon on its hull. And there were men working nearby.

Saunders' shout rang in the still air. He and Belgotai scrambled down the steep slopes of earth, clawing past trees and vines. Men!

No—not all men. A dozen great shining engines were toiling without supervision at the foot of the pyramid—robots. And of the group which turned to stare at the travelers, two were squat, blue-furred, with snouted faces and six-fingered hands.

Saunders realized with an unexpectedly eerie shock that he was seeing extra-terrestial intelligence. But it was to the men that he faced.

They were all tall, with aristocratically refined features and a calm that seemed inbred. Their clothing was impossible to describe, it was like a rainbow shimmer around them, never the same in its play of color and shape. So, thought Saunders, so must the old gods have looked on high Olympus, beings greater and more beautiful than man.

But it was a human voice that called to them, a deep, well-modulated tone in a totally foreign language. Saunders remembered exasperately that he had forgotten the psychophone. But one of the blue-furred aliens were already fetching a round, knob-studded globe out of which the familiar translating voice seemed to come: ". . . time travelers."

"From the very remote past, obviously," said another man. Damn him, damn them all, they weren't any more excited than at the bird which rose, startled, from the long grass. You'd think time travelers would at least be worth shaking by the hand.

"Listen," snapped Saunders, realizing in the back of his mind that his annoyance was a reaction against the awesomeness of the company, "we're in trouble. Our machine won't carry us back, and we have to find a period of time which knows how to reverse the effect. Can you do it?"

One of the aliens shook his animal head. "No," he said. "There is no way known to physics of getting farther back than about seventy years. Beyond that, the required energy approaches infinity and—"

Saunders groaned. "We know it," said Belgotai harshly.

"At least you must rest," said one of the men in a more kindly tone. "It will be interesting to hear your story."

"I've told it to too many people in the last few millennia," rasped Saunders. "Let's hear yours for a change."

Two of the strangers exchanged low-voiced words. Saunders could almost translate them himself: "*Barbarians—childish emotional pattern—well, humor them for a while.*"

"This is an archeological expedition, excavating the pyramid," said one of the men patiently. "We are from the Galactic Institute, Sarlan-sector branch. I am Lord Arsfel of Astracyr, and these are my subordinates. The nonhumans, as you may wish to know, are from the planet Quulhan, whose sun is not visible from Terra."

Despite himself, Saunders' awed gaze turned to the stupendous mass looming over them. "Who built it?" he breathed.

"The Ixchulhi made such structures on planets they conquered, no one knows why. But then, no one knows what they were or where they came from, or where they ultimately went. It is hoped that some of the answers may be found in their pyramids."

The atmosphere grew more relaxed. Deftly, the men of the expedition got Saunders' and Belgotai's stories and what information about their almost prehistoric periods they cared for. In exchange, something of history was offered them.

After the Ixchulhi's ruinous wars the Galaxy had made a surprisingly rapid comeback. New techniques of mathematical psychology made it possible to unite the peoples of a billion worlds and rule them effectively. The Galactic Empire was egalitarian—it had to be, for one of its mainstays was the fantastically old and evolved race of the planet called Vro-Hi by men.

It was peaceful, prosperous, colorful with diversity of races and cultures, expanding in science and the arts. It had already endured for ten thousand years, and there seemed no doubt in Arsfel's calm mind that it could endure forever. The barbarians along the Galactic periphery and out in the Magellanic Clouds? Nonsense! The Empire would get around to civilizing them in due course; meanwhile they were only a nuisance.

But Sol could almost be called one of the barbarian suns, though it lay within the Imperial boundaries. Civilization was concentrated near the center of the Galaxy, and Sol lay in what was actually a remote and thinly starred region of space. A few primitive landsmen still lived on its planets and had infrequent intercourse with the nearer stars, but they hardly counted. The human race had almost forgotten its ancient home.

Somehow the picture was saddening to the American. He thought of old Earth spinning on her lonely way through the emptiness of space, he thought of the great arrogant Empire and of all the mighty dominions which had fallen to dust through the millennia. But when he ventured to suggest that this civilization, too, was not immortal, he was immediately snowed under with figures, facts, logic, the curious paramathematical symbolism of modern mass psychology. It could be shown rigorously that the present set-up was inherently stable—and already ten thousand years of history had given no evidence to upset that science. . .

"I give up," said Saunders. "I can't argue with you."

They were shown through the spaceship's immense interior, the luxurious apartments of the expedition, the looming intricate machinery which did its own thinking. Arsfel tried to show them his art, his recorded music, his psychobooks, but it was no use, they didn't have the understanding.

Savages! Could an Australian aborigine have appreciated Rembrandt, Beethoven, Kant, or Einstein? Could he have lived happily in sophisticated New York society?

"We'd best go," muttered Belgotai. "We don't belong heah."

Saunders nodded. Civilization had gone too far for them, they could never be more than frightened pensioners in its hugeness. Best to get on their way again.

"I would advise you to leap ahead for long intervals," said Arsfel. "Galactic civilization won't have spread out this far for many thousands of years, and certainly whatever native culture Sol develops won't be able to help you." He smiled. "It doesn't matter if you overshoot the time when the process you need is invented. The records won't be lost, I assure you. From here on, you are certain of encountering only peace and enlightenment . . . unless, of course, the barbarians of Terra get hostile, but then you can always leave them behind. Sooner or later, there will be true civilization here to help you."

"Tell me honestly," said Saunders. "Do you think the negative time machine will ever be invented?"

One of the beings from Quulhan shook his strange head. "I doubt it," he said gravely. "We would have had visitors from the future."

"They might not have cared to see your time," argued Saunders desperately. "They'd have complete records of it. So they'd go back to investigate more primitive ages, where their appearance might easily pass unnoticed."

"You may be right," said Arsfel. His tone was disconcertingly like that with which an adult comforts a child by a white lie.

"Le's go!" snarled Belgotai.

In 26,000 A.D. the forests still stood and the pyramid had become a high hill where trees nodded and rustled in the wind.

In 27,000 A.D. a small village of wood and stone houses stood among smiling grain fields.

In 28,000 A.D. men were tearing down the pyramid, quarrying it for stone. But its huge bulk was not gone before 30,000 A.D., and a small city had been built from it.

Minutes ago, thought Saunders grayly, they had been talking to Lord Arsfel of Astracyr, and now he was five thousand years in his grave.

In 31,000, A.D. they materialized on one of the broad lawns that reached between the towers of a high and proud city. Aircraft swarmed overhead and a spaceship, small beside Arsfel's but nonetheless impressive, was standing nearby.

"Looks like de Empire's got heah," said Belgotai.

"I don't know," said Saunders. "But it looks peaceful, anyway. Let's go out and talk to people."

They were received by tall, stately women in white robes of classic lines. It seemed that the Matriarchy now ruled Sol, and would they please conduct themselves as befitted the inferior sex? No, the Empire hadn't ever gotten out here; Sol paid tribute, and there was an Imperial legate at Sirius, but the actual boundaries of Galactic culture hadn't changed for the past three millennia. Solar civilization was strictly home-grown and obviously superior to the alien influence of the Vro-Hi.

No, nothing was known about time theory. Their visit had been welcome and all that, but now would they please go on? They didn't fit in with the neatly regulated culture of Terra.

"I don't like it," said Saunders as they walked back toward the machine. "Arsfel swore the Imperium would keep expanding its actual as well as its nominal sphere of influence. But it's gone static now. Why?"

"Ih tink," said Belgotai, "dat spite of all his fancy mathematics, yuh were right. Nawthing lasts forever."

"But—my God!"

34,000 A.D. The Matriarchy was gone. The city was a tumbled heap of fire-blackened rocks. Skeletons lay in the ruins.

"The barbarians are moving again," said Saunders bleakly. "They weren't here so very long ago, these bones are still fresh, and they've got a long ways to go to dead center. An empire like this one will be many thousands of years in dying. But it's doomed already."

"What'll we do?" asked Belgotai.

"Go on," said Saunders tonelessly. "What else can we do?"

35,000 A.D. A peasant hut stood under huge old trees. Here and there a broken column stuck out of the earth, remnant of the city. A bearded man in coarsely woven garments fled wildly with his woman and brood of children as the machine appeared.

36,000 A.D. There was a village again, with a battered old spaceship standing hard by. There were half a dozen different races, including man, moving about, working on the construction of some enigmatic machine. They were dressed in plain, shabby clothes, with guns at their sides and the hard look of warriors in their eyes. But they didn't treat the new arrivals too badly.

Their chief was a young man in the cape and helmet of an officer of the Empire. But his outfit was at least a century old, and he was simply head of a small troop which had been hired from among the barbarian hordes to protect this part of Terra. Oddly, he insisted he was a loyal vassal of the Emperor.

The Empire! It was still a remote glory, out there among the stars. Slowly it waned, slowly the barbarians encroached while corruption and civil war tore it apart from the inside, but it was still the pathetic, futile hope of intelligent beings throughout the Galaxy. Some day it would be restored. Some day civilization would return to the darkness of the outer worlds, greater and more splendid than ever. Men dared not believe otherwise.

"But we've got a job right here," shrugged the chief. "Tautho of Sirius will be on Sol's necks soon. I doubt if we can stand him off for long."

"And what'll yuh do den?" challenged Belgotai.

The young-old face twisted in a bitter smile. "Die, of course. What else is there to do—these days?"

They stayed overnight with the troopers. Belgotai had fun swapping lies about warlike exploits, but in the morning he decided to go on with Saunders. The age was violent enough, but its hopelessness daunted even his tough soul.

Saunders looked haggardly at the control panel. "We've got to go a long ways ahead," he said. "A hell of a long ways."

50,000 A.D. They flashed out of the time drive and opened the door. A raw wind caught at them, driving thin sheets of snow before it. The sky hung low and gray over a landscape of high rock hills where pine trees stood gloomily between naked crags. There was ice on the river that murmured darkly out of the woods.

Geology didn't work that fast, even fourteen thousand years wasn't a very long time to the slowly changing planets. It must have been the work of intelligent beings, ravaging and scoring the world with senseless wars of unbelievable forces.

A gray stone mass dominated the landscape. It stood enormous a few miles off, its black walls sprawling over incredible acres, its massive crenellated towers reaching gauntly into the sky. And it lay half in ruin, torn and tumbled stone distorted by energies that once made rock run molten, blurred by uncounted millennia of weather—old.

"Dead," Saunders' voice was thin under the hooting wind. "All dead."

"No!" Belgotai's slant eyes squinted against the flying snow. "No, Mahtin, Ih tink Ih see a banner flying."

The wind blew bitterly around them, searing them with its chill. "Shall we go on?" asked Saunders dully.

"Best we go find out wha's happened," said Belgotai. "Dey can do no worse dan kill us, and Ih begin to tink dat's not so bad."

Saunders put on all the clothes he could find and took the psychophone in one chilled hand. Belgotai wrapped his cloak tightly about him. They started toward the gray edifice.

The wind blew and blew. Snow hissed around them, covering the tough gray-green vegetation that hugged the stony ground. Summer on Earth, 50,000 A.D.

As they neared the structure, its monster size grew on them. Some of the towers which still stood must be almost half a mile high, thought Saunders dizzily. But it had a grim, barbaric look; no civilized race had ever built such a fortress.

Two small, swift shapes darted into the air from that cliff-like wall. "Aircraft," said Belgotai laconically. The wind ripped the word from his mouth.

They were ovoidal, without external controls or windows, apparently running on the gravitic forces which had long ago been tamed. One of them hovered overhead, covering the travelers, while the other dropped to the ground. As it landed, Saunders saw that it was old and worn and scarred. But there was a faded sunburst on its side. Some memory of the Empire must still be alive.

Two beings came out of the little vessel and approached the travelers with guns in their hands. One was human, a tall well-built young man with shoulder-length black hair blowing under a tarnished helmet, a patched purple coat streaming from his cuirassed shoulders, a faded leather kit and buskins. The other. . .

He was a little shorter than the man, but immensely broad of chest and limb. Four muscled arms grew from the massive shoulders, and a tufted tail lashed against his clawed feet. His head was big, broad-skulled, with a round half-animal face and cat-like whiskers about the fanged mouth and the split-pupilled yellow eyes. He wore no clothes except a leather harness, but soft blue-gray fur covered the whole great body.

The psychophone clattered out the man's hail: "Who comes?"

"Friends," said Saunders. "We wish only shelter and a little information."

"Where are you from?" There was a harsh, peremptory note in the man's voice. His face—straight, thin-boned, the countenance of a highly bred aristocrat—was gaunt with strain. "What do you want? What sort of spaceship is that you've got down there?"

"Easy, Vargor," rumbled the alien's bass. "That's no spaceship, you can see that."

"No," said Saunders. "It's a time projector."

"Time travelers!" Vargor's intense blue eyes widened. "I heard of such things once, but—time travelers!" Suddenly: "When are you from?" Can you help us?"

"We're from very long ago," said Saunders pityingly. "And I'm afraid we're alone and helpless."

Vargor's erect carriage sagged a little. He looked away. But the other being stepped forward with an eagerness in him. "How far back?" he asked. "Where are you going?"

"We're going to hell, most likely. But can you get us inside? We're freezing."

"Of course. Come with us. You'll not take it amiss if I send a squad to inspect your machine? We have to be careful, you know."

The four squeezed into the aircraft and it lifted with a groan of ancient engines. Vargor gestured at the fortress ahead and his tone was a little wild. "Welcome to the hold of Brontothor! Welcome to the Galactic Empire!"

"The Empire?"

"Aye, this is the Empire, or what's left of it. A haunted fortress on a frozen ghost world, last fragment of the old Imperium and still trying to pretend that the Galaxy is not dying—that it didn't die millennia ago, that there is something left besides wild beasts howling among the ruins." Vargor's throat caught in a dry sob. "Welcome!"

The alien laid a huge hand on the man's shoulder. "Don't get hysterical, Vargor," he reproved gently. "As long as brave beings hope, the Empire is still alive—whatever they say."

He looked over his shoulder at the others. "You really are welcome," he said. "It's a hard and dreary life we lead here. Taury and the Dreamer will both welcome you gladly." He paused. Then, unsurely, "But best you don't say too much about the ancient time, if you've really seen it. We can't bear too sharp a reminder, you know."

The machine slipped down beyond the wall, over a gigantic flagged courtyard to the monster bulk of the—the donjon, Saunders supposed one could call it. It rose up in several tiers, with pathetic little gardens on the terraces, toward a dome of clear plastic.

The walls, he saw, were immensely thick, with weapons mounted on them which he could see clearly through the drifting snow. Behind the donjon stood several long, barrack-like buildings, and a couple of spaceships which must have been held together by pure faith rested near what looked like an arsenal. There were guards on duty, helmeted men with energy rifles, their cloaks wrapped tightly against the wind, and other folk scurried around under the monstrous walls, men and women and children.

"There's Taury," said the alien, pointing to a small group clustered on one of the terraces. "We may as well land right there." His wide mouth opened in an alarming smile. "And forgive me for not introducing myself before. I'm Hunda of Haamigur, general of the Imperial armies, and this is Vargor Alfri, prince of the Empire."

"Yuh crazy?" blurted Belgotai. "What Empire?"

Hunda shrugged. "It's a harmless game, isn't it? At that, you know, we are the Empire—legally. Taury is a direct descendant of Maurco the Doomer, last Emperor to be anointed according to the proper forms. Of course, that was five thousand years ago, and Maurco had only three systems left then, but the law is clear. These hundred or more barbarian pretenders, human and otherwise, haven't the shadow of a real claim to the title."

The vessel grounded and they stepped out. The others waited for them to come up. There were half a dozen old men, their long beards blowing wildly in the gale, there was a being with the face of a long-beaked bird and one that had the shape of a centauroid.

"The court of the Empress Taury," said Hunda.

"Welcome." The answer was low and gracious.

Saunders and Belgotai stared dumbly at her. She was tall, tall as a man, but under her tunic of silver links and her furred cloak she was such a woman as they had dreamed of without ever knowing in life. Her proudly lifted head had something of Vargor's looks, the same clean-lined, high-cheeked face, but it was the countenance of a woman, from the broad clear brow to the wide, wondrously chiseled mouth and the strong chin. The cold had flushed the lovely pale planes of her cheeks. Her heavy bronze-red hair was braided about her helmet, with one rebellious lock tumbling softly toward the level, dark brows. Her eyes, huge and oblique and gray as northern seas, were serene on them.

Saunders found tongue. "Thank you, your majesty," he said in a firm voice. "If it please you, I am Martin Saunders of America, some forty-eight thousand years in the past, and my companion is Belgotai, free companion from Syrtis about a thousand years later. We are at your service for what little we may be able to do."

She inclined her stately head, and her sudden smile was warm and human. "It is a rare pleasure," she said. "Come inside, please. And forget the formality. Tonight let us simply be alive."

They sat in what had been a small council chamber. The great hall was too huge and empty, a cavern of darkness and rustling relics of greatness, hollow with too many memories. But the lesser room had been made livable, hung with tapestries and carpeted with skins. Fluorotubes cast a white light over it, and a fire crackled cheerfully in the hearth. Had it not been for the wind against the windows, they might have forgotten where they were.

"—and you can never go back?" Taury's voice was sober. "You can never get home again?"

"I don't think so,"said Saunders. "From our story, it doesn't look that way, does it?"

"No," said Hunda. "You'd better settle down in some time and make the best of matters."

"Why not with us?" asked Vargor eagerly.

"We'd welcome you with all our hearts," said Taury, "but I cannot honestly advise you to stay. These are evil times."

It was a harsh language they spoke, a ringing metallic tongue brought in by the barbarians. But from her throat, Saunders thought, it was utter music.

"We'll at least stay a few days," he said impulsively. "It's barely possible we can do something."

"I doubt that," said Hunda practically. "We've retrogressed, yes. For instance, the principle of the time projector was lost long ago. But still, there's a lot of technology left which was far beyond your own times."

"I know," said Saunders defensively. "But—well, frankly—we haven't fitted in any other time as well."

"Will there ever be a decent age again?"asked one of the old courtiers bitterly.

The avian from Klakkahar turned his eyes on Saunders. "It wouldn't be cowardice for you to leave a lost cause which you couldn't possibly aid," he said in his thin, accented tones. "When the Anvardi come, I think we will all die."

"What is de tale of de Dreamer?" asked Belgotai. "You've mentioned some such."

It was like a sudden darkness in the room. There was silence, under the whistling wind, and men sat wrapped in their own cheerless thoughts. Finally Taury spoke.

"He is the last of Vro-Hi, counselors of The Empire. That one still lives—the Dreamer. But there can never really be another

Empire, at least not on the pattern of the old one. No other race is intelligent enough to co-ordinate it."

Hunda shook his big head, puzzled. "The Dreamer once told me that might be for the best," he said. "But he wouldn't explain."

"How did you happen to come here—to Earth, of all planets?" Saunders asked.

Taury smiled with a certain grim humor. "The last few generations have been one of the Imperium's less fortunate periods," she said. "In short, the most the Emperor ever commanded was a small fleet. My father had even that shot away from him. He fled with three ships, out toward the Periphery. It occurred to him that Sol was worth trying as a refuge."

The Solar System had been cruelly scarred in the dark ages. The great engineering works which had made the other planets habitable were ruined, and Earth herself had been laid waste. There had been a weapon used which consumed atmospheric carbon dioxide. Saunders, remembering the explanation for the Ice Ages offered by geologists of his own time, nodded in dark understanding. Only a few starveling savages lived on the planet now, and indeed the whole Sirius Sector was so desolated that no conqueror thought it worth bothering with.

It had pleased the Emperor to make his race's ancient home the capital of the Galaxy. He had moved into the ruined fortress of Brontothor, built some seven thousand years ago by the nonhuman Grimmani and blasted out of action a millennium later. Renovation of parts of it, installation of weapons and defensive works, institution of agriculture. . . "Why, he had suddenly acquired a whole planetary system!" said Taury with a half-sad little smile.

She took them down into the underground levels the next day to see the Dreamer. Vargor went along too, walking close beside her, but Hunda stayed topside; he was busy supervising the construction of additional energy screen generators.

They went through immense vaulted caverns hewed out of the rock, dank tunnels of silence where their footfall echoed weirdly and shadows flitted beyond the dull glow of fluorospheres. Now and then they passed a looming monstrous bulk, the corroded hulk of some old machine. The night and loneliness weighed heavily on them, they huddled together and did not speak for fear of rousing the jeering echoes.

"There were slideways here once," remarked Taury as they started, "but we haven't gotten around to installing new ones. There's too much else to do."

Too much else—a civilization to rebuild, with these few broken remnants. How can they dare even to keep trying in the face of the angry gods? What sort of courage is it they have?

Taury walked ahead with the long, swinging stride of a warrior, a red lioness of a woman in the wavering shadows. Her gray eyes caught the light with a supernatural brilliance. Vargor kept pace, but he lacked her steadiness, his gaze shifted nervously from side to side as they moved down the haunted, booming length of the tunnels. Belgotai went cat-footed, his own restless eyes had merely the habitual wariness of his hard and desperate lifetime. Again Saunders thought, what a strange company they were, four humans from the dawn and the dusk of human civilization, thrown together at the world's end and walking to greet the last of the gods. His past life, Eve, MacPherson, the world of his time, were dimming in his mind, they were too remote from his present reality. It seemed as if he had never been anything but a follower of the Galactic Empress.

They came at last to a door. Taury knocked softly and swung it open—yes, they were even back to manual doors now.

Saunders had been prepared for almost anything, but nonetheless the appearance of the Dreamer was a shock. He had imagined a grave white-bearded man, or a huge-skulled spider-thing, or a naked brain pulsing in a machine-tended case. But the last of the Vro-Hi was—a monster.

No—not exactly. Not when you discarded human standards, then he even had a weird beauty of his own. The gross bulk of him sheened with iridescence, and his many seven-fingered hands were supple and graceful, and the eyes—the eyes were huge pools of molten gold, lambent and wise, a stare too brilliant to meet directly.

He stood up on his stumpy legs as they entered, barely four feet high though the head-body unit was broad and massive. His hooked beak did not open, and the psychophone remained silent, but as the long delicate feelers pointed toward him Saunders thought he heard words, a deep organ voice rolling soundless through the still air: "Greeting, your majesty. Greeting your highness. Greeting, men out of time, and welcome!"

Telepathy—direct telepathy—so that was how it felt!

"Thank you . . . sir." Somehow, the thing rated the title, rated an awed respect to match his own grave formality. "But I thought you were in a trance of concentration till now. How did you know—" Saunders' voice trailed off and he flushed with sudden distaste.

"No, traveler, I did not read your mind as you think. The Vro-Hi always respected privacy and did not read any thoughts save those contained in speech addressed solely to them. But my induction was obvious."

"What were you thinking about in the last trance?" asked Vargor. His voice was sharp with strain. "Did you reach any plan?"

"No, your highness," vibrated the Dreamer. "As long as the factors involved remain constant, we cannot logically do otherwise than we are doing. When new data appear, I will reconsider immediate necessities. No, I was working further on the philosophical basis which the Second Empire must have."

"What Second Empire?" sneered Vorgar bitterly.

"The one which will come—some day," answered Taury quietly.

The Dreamer's wise eyes rested on Saunders and Belgotai. "With your permission," he thought, "I would like to scan your complete memory patterns, conscious, subconscious, and cellular. We know so little of your age." As they hesitated: "I assure you, sirs, that a nonhuman being half a million years old can keep secrets, and certainly does not pass moral judgments. And the scanning will be necessary anyway if I am to teach you the present language."

Saunders braced himself. "Go ahead" he said distastefully.

For a moment he felt dizzy, a haze passed over his eyes and there was an eerie thrill along every nerve of him. Taury laid an arm about his waist, bracing him.

It passed. Saunders shook his head, puzzled. "Is that *all*?"

"Aye, sir. A Vro-Hi brain can scan an indefinite number of units simultaneously." With a faint hint of a chuckle: "But did you notice what tongue you just spoke in?"

"I—eh—huh?" Saunders looked wildly at Taury's smiling face. The hard, open-voweled syllables barked from his mouth: "I—by the gods—I can speak Stellarian now!"

"Aye," thought the Dreamer. "The language centers are peculiarly receptive, it is easy to impress a pattern on them. The method of instruction will not work so well for information involving other faculties, but you must admit it is a convenient and efficient way to learn speech."

"Blast off wit me, den," said Belgoti cheerfully. "Ih allays was a dumkoff at languages."

When the Dreamer was through, he thought: "You will not take it amiss if I tell all that I what I saw in both your minds was good—brave and honest, under the little neuroses which all beings at your level of evolution cannot help accumulating. I will be pleased to remove those for you, if you wish."

"No, thanks," said Belgotai. "I like my little neuroses."

"I see that you are debating staying here," went on the Dreamer. "You will be valuable, but you should be fully warned of the desperate position we actually are in. This is not a pleasant age in which to live."

"From what I've seen," answered Saunders slowly, "golden ages are only superficially better. They may be easier on the surface, but there's death in them. To travel hopefully, believe me, is better than to arrive."

"That has been true in all past ages, aye. It was the great mistake of the Vro-Hi. We should have known better, with ten million years of civilization behind us." There was a deep and tragic note in the rolling thought-pulse. "But we thought that since we had achieved a static physical state in which the new frontiers and challenges lay within our own minds, all beings at all levels of evolution could and should have developed in them the same idea.

"With our help, and with the use of scientific psychodynamics and the great cybernetic engines, the co-ordination of a billion planets became possible. It was perfection, in a way—but perfection is death to imperfect beings, and even the Vro-Hi had many shortcomings. I cannot explain all the philosophy to you; it involves concepts you could not fully grasp, but you have seen the workings of the great laws in the rise and fall of cultures. I have proved rigorously that permanence is a self-contradictory concept. There can be no goal to reach, not ever."

"Then the Second Empire will have no better hope than decay and chaos again?" Saunders grinned humorlessly. "Why the devil do you want one?"

Vargor's harsh laugh shattered the brooding silence. "What indeed does it matter?" he cried. "What use to plan the future of the universe, when we are outlaws on a forgotten planet? The Anvardi are coming!" He sobered, and there was a set to his jaw which Saunders liked. "They're coming, and there's little we can do to stop it," said Vargor. "But we'll give them a fight. We'll give them such a fight as the poor old Galaxy never saw before!"

"Oh, no—oh no—oh no—"

The murmur came unnoticed from Vargor's lips, a broken cry of pain as he stared at the image which flickered and wavered on the great interstellar communiscreen. And there was horror in the eyes of Taury, grimness to the set of Hunda's mighty jaws, a sadness of many hopeless centuries in the golden gaze of the Dreamer.

After weeks of preparation and waiting, Saunders realized matters were at last coming to a head.

"Aye, your majesty," said the man in the screen. He was haggard, exhausted, worn out by strain and struggle and defeat. "Aye, fifty-four shiploads of us, and the Anvardian fleet in pursuit."

"How far behind?" rapped Hunda.

"About half a light-year, sir, and coming up slowly. We'll be close to Sol before they can overhaul us."

"Can you fight them?" rapped Hunda.

"No, sir," said the man. "We're loaded with refugees, women and children and unarmed peasants, hardly a gun on a ship— Can't you help us?" It was a cry, torn by the ripping static that filled the interstellar void. "Can't you help us, your majesty? They'll sell us for slaves!"

"How did it happen?" asked Taury wearily.

"I don't know, your majesty. We heard you were at Sol through your agents, and secretly gathered ships. We don't want to be under the Anvardi, Empress; they tax the life from us and conscript our men and take our women and children. . . We only communicated by ultrawave; it can't be traced, and we only used the code your agents gave us. But as we passed Canopus, they called on us to surrender in the name of their king—and they have a whole war fleet after us!"

"How long before they get here?" asked Hunda.

"At this rate, sir, perhaps a week," answered the captain of the ship. Static snarled through his words.

"Well, keep on coming this way," said Taury wearily. "We'll send ships against them. You may get away during the battle. Don't go to Sol, of course, we'll have to evacuate that. Our men will try to contact you later."

"We aren't worth it, you majesty. Save all your ships."

"We're coming," said Taury flatly, and broke the circuit.

She turned to the others, and her red head was still lifted. "Most of our people can get away," she said. "They can flee into the Arlath cluster; the enemy won't be able to find them in that wilderness." She smiled, a tired little smile that tugged at one corner of her mouth. "We all know what to do, we've planned against this day. Munidor, Falz, Mico, start readying for evacuation. Hunda, you and I will have to plan our assault. We'll want to make it as effective as possible, but use a minimum of ships."

"Why sacrifice fighting strength uselessly?" asked Belgotai.

"It won't be useless. We'll delay the Anvardi, and give those refugees a chance to escape."

"If we had weapons," rumbled Hunda. His huge fists clenched. "By the gods, if we had decent weapons!"

The Dreamer stiffened. And before he could vibrate it, the same thought had leaped into Saunders' brain, and they stared at each other, man and Vro-Hian, with a sudden wild hope. . .

Space glittered and flared with a million stars, thronging against the tremendous dark, the Milky Way foamed around the sky in a rush of cold silver, and it was shattering to a human in its utter immensity. Saunders felt the loneliness of it as he had never felt it on the trip to Venus—for Sol was dwindling behind them, they were rushing out into the void between the stars.

There had only been time to install the new weapon on the dreadnought, time and facilities were so cruelly short, there had been no chance even to test it in maneuvers. They might, perhaps, have leaped back into time again and again, gaining weeks, but the shops of Terra could only turn out so much material in the one week they did have.

So it was necessary to risk the whole fleet and the entire fighting strength of Sol on this one desperate gamble. If the old *Vengeance* could do her part, the outnumbered Imperials would have their chance. But if they failed. . .

Saunders stood on the bridge, looking out at the stellar host, trying to discern the Anvardian fleet. The detectors were far over scale, the enemy was close, but you couldn't visually detect something that outran its own image.

Hunda was at the control central, bent over the cracked old dials and spinning the corroded signal wheels, trying to coax another centimeter per second from a ship more ancient than the Pyramids had been in Saunders' day. The Dreamer stood quietly in a corner, staring raptly out at the Galaxy. The others at the court were each in charge of a squadron, Saunders had talked to them over the inter-ship visiscreen—Vargor white-lipped and tense, Belgotai blasphemously cheerful, the rest showing only cool reserve.

"In a few minutes," said Taury quietly. "In just a few minutes, Martin."

She paced back from the viewport, lithe and restless as a tigress. The cold white starlight glittered in her eyes. A red cloak swirled about the strong, deep curves of her body, a Sunburst helmet sat proudly on her bronze-bright hair. Saunders thought how beautiful she was—by all the gods, how beautiful!

She smiled at him. "It is your doing, Martin," she said. "You came from the past just to bring us hope. It's enough to make one believe in destiny." She took his hand. "But of course it's not the hope you wanted. This won't get you back home."

"It doesn't matter," he said.

"It does, Martin. But—may I say it? I'm still glad of it. Not only for the sake of the Empire, but—"

A voice rattled over the bridge communicator: "Ultrawave to bridge. The enemy is sending us a message, your majesty. Shall I send it up to you?"

"Of course." Taury switched on the bridge screen.

A face leaped into it, strong and proud and ruthless, the Sunburst shining in the green hair. "Greeting, Taury of Sol," said the Anvardian. "I am Ruulthan, Emperor of the Galaxy."

"I know who you are," said Taury thinly, "but I don't recognize your assumed title."

"Our detectors report your approach with a fleet approximately one-tenth the size of ours. You have one Supernova ship, of course, but so do we. Unless you wish to come to terms, it will mean annihilation."

"What are your terms?"

"Surrender, execution of the criminals who led the attacks on Anvardian planets, and your own pledge of allegiance to me as Galactic Emperor." The voice was clipped, steel-hard.

Taury turned away in disgust. Saunders told Ruulthan in explicit language what to do with his terms, and then cut off the screen.

Taury gestured to the newly installed time-drive controls. "Take them, Martin," she said. "They're yours, really." She put her hands in his and looked at him with serious gray eyes. "And if we should fail in this—goodbye, Martin."

"Goodbye," he said thickly.

He wrenched himself over the panel and sat down before its few dials. *Here goes nothing!*

He waved one hand, and Hunda cut off the hyperdrive. At low intrinsic velocity, the *Vengeance* hung in space while the invisible ships of her fleet flushed past toward the oncoming Anvardi.

Slowly then, Saunders brought down the time-drive switch. And the ship roared with power, atomic energy flowed into the mighty circuits which they had built to carry her huge mass through time—the lights dimmed, the giant machine throbbed and pulsed, and a featureless grayness swirled beyond the ports.

He took her back three days. They lay in empty space, the Anvardi were still fantastic distances away. His eyes strayed to the brilliant yellow spark of Sol. Right there, this minute, he was sweating his heart out installing the time projector which had just carried him back. . .

But no, that was meaningless, simultaneity was arbitrary. And there was a job to do right now.

The chief astrogator's voice came with a torrent of figures. They had to find the exact position in which the Anvardian flagship would be in precisely seventy-two hours. Hunda rang the signals to the robots in the engine room, and slowly, ponderously, the *Vengeance* slid across five million miles of space.

"All set," said Hunda. "Let's go!"

Saunders smiled, a mirthless skinning of teeth, and threw his main switch in reverse. Three days forward in time. . .

To lie alongside the Anvardian dreadnought!

Frantically Hunda threw the hyperdrive back in, matching translight velocities. They could see the ship now, it loomed like a metal mountain against the stars. And every gun in the *Vengeance* cut loose!

Vortex cannon—blasters—atomic shell and torpedoes—gravity snatchers—all the hell which had ever been brewed in the tortured centuries of history vomited against the screens of the Anvardian flagship.

Under that monstrous barrage, filling space with raving energy till it seemed its very structure must boil, the screens went down, a flare of light searing like another nova. And through the solid matter of her hull those weapons bored, cutting, blasting, disintegrating. Steel boiled into vapor, into atoms, into pure devouring energy that turned on the remaining solid material. Through and through the hull that fury raged, a waste of flame that left not even ash in its track.

And now the rest of the Imperial fleet drove against the Anvardi. Assaulted from outside, with a devouring monster in its very midst, the Anvardian fleet lost the offensive, recoiled and broke up into desperately fighting units. War snarled between the silent white stars.

Still the Anvardi fought, hurling themselves against the ranks of the Imperials, wrecking ships and slaughtering men even as they went down. They still had the numbers, if not the organization, and they had the same weapons and the same bitter courage as their foes.

The bridge of the *Vengeance* shook and roared with the shock of battle. The lights darkened, flickered back, dimmed again. The riven air was sharp with ozone, and the intolerable energies loosed made her interior a furnace. Reports clattered over the communicator: "—Number Three screen down—Compartment Number Five doesn't answer–Vortex turret Five Hundred Thirty Seven out of action—"

Still she fought, still she fought, hurling metal and energy in an unending storm, raging and rampaging among the ships of the Anvardi. Saunders found himself manning a gun, shooting out at vessels he couldn't see, getting his aim by sweat-blinded glances at the instruments—and the hours dragged away in flame and smoke and racking thunder. . ."

"They're fleeing!"

The exuberant shout rang through every remaining compartment of the huge old ship. *Victory, victory, victory*—She had not heard such cheering for five thousand weary years.

Saunders staggered drunkenly back onto the bridge. He could see the scattered units of the Anvardi now that he was behind them, exploding out into the Galaxy in wild search of refuge, hounded and harried by the vengeful Imperial fleet.

And now the Dreamer stood up, and suddenly he was not a stump-legged little monster but a living god whose awful thought leaped across space, faster than light, to bound and roar through the skulls of the barbarians. Saunders fell to the floor under the impact of that mighty shout, he lay numbly staring at the impassive stars while the great command rang in his shuddering brain:

"Soldiers of the Anvardi, your false emperor is dead and Taury the Red, Empress of the Galaxy, has the victory. You have seen her power. Do not resist it longer, for it is unstoppable.

"Lay down your arms. Surrender to the mercy of the Imperium. We pledge you amnesty and safe-conduct. And bear this word back to your planets:

"Taury the Red calls on all the chiefs of the Anvardian Confederacy to pledge fealty to her and aid her in restoring the Galactic Empire!"

They stood on a balcony of Brontothor and looked again at old Earth for the first time in almost a year and the last time, perhaps, in their lives.

It was strange to Saunders, this standing again on the planet which had borne him after those months in the many and alien worlds of a Galaxy huger than he could really imagine. There was an odd little tug at his heart, for all the bright hope of the future. He was saying goodbye to Eve's world.

But Eve was gone, she was part of a past forty-eight thousand years dead, and he had *seen* those years rise and die, his one year of personal time was filled and stretched by the vision of history until

Eve was a remote, lovely dream. God keep her, wherever her soul had wandered in these millennia—God grant she had had a happy life—but as for him, he had his own life to live, and a mightier task at hand than he had ever conceived.

The last months rose in his mind, a bewilderment of memory. After the surrender of the Anvardian fleet, the Imperials had gone under their escort directly to Canopus and thence through the Anvardian empire. And chief after chief, now that Ruulthan was dead and Taury had shown she could win a greater mystery than his, pledged allegiance to her.

Hunda was still out there with Belgotai, fighting a stubborn Anvardian earl. The Dreamer was in the great Polarian System, toiling at readjustment. It would be necessary, of course, for the Imperial capital to move from isolated Sol to central Polaris, and Taury did not think she would ever have time or opportunity to visit Earth again.

And so she had crossed a thousand starry light-years to the little lonely sun which had been her home. She brought ships, machines, troops. Sol would have a military base sufficient to protect it. Climate engineers would drive the glacial winter of Earth back to its poles and begin the resettlement of the other planets. There would be schools, factories, civilization, Sol would have cause to remember its Empress.

Saunders came along because he couldn't quite endure the thought of leaving Earth altogether without farewell. Vargor, grown ever more silent and moody, joined them, but otherwise the old comradeship of Brontothor was dissolving in the sudden fury of work and war and complexity which claimed them.

And so they stood again in the old ruined castle, Saunders and Taury, looking out at the night of Earth.

It was late, all others seemed to be asleep. Below the balcony, the black walls dropped dizzily to the gulf of night that was the main courtyard. Beyond it, a broken section of outer wall showed snow lying white and mystic under the moon. The stars were huge and frosty, flashing and glittering with cold crystal light above the looming pines, grandeur and arrogance and remoteness wheeling enormously across the silent sky. The moon rode high, its scarred old face the only familiarity from Saunders' age, its argent radiance flooding down on the snow to shatter in a million splinters.

It was quiet, quiet, sound seemed to have frozen to death in the bitter windless cold. Saunders had stood alone, wrapped in furs with his breath shining ghostly from his nostrils, looking out on the silent winter world and thinking his own thoughts. He had heard a soft footfall and turned to see Taury approaching.

"I couldn't sleep," she said.

She came out onto the balcony to stand beside him. The moonlight was white on her face, shimmering faintly from her eyes and hair. She seemed a dim goddness of the night.

"What were you thinking, Martin?" she asked after a while.

"Oh—I don't know," he said. "Just dreaming a little, I suppose. It's a strange thought to me, to have left my own time forever and now to be leaving even my own world."

She nodded gravely. "I know. I feel the same way." Her low voice dropped to a whisper. "I didn't have to come back in person, you know. They need me more at Polaris. But I thought I deserved this last farewell to the days when we fought with our own hands, and fared between the stars, when we were a small band of sworn comrades whose dreams outstripped our strength. It was hard and bitter, yes, but I don't think we'll have time for laughter any more. When you work for a million stars, you don't have a chance to see one peasant's wrinkled face light with a deed of kindness you did, or hear him tell you what you did wrong—the world will all be strangers to us—"

For another moment, silence under the far cold stars, then, "Martin—I am so lonely now."

He took her in his arms. Her lips were cold against his, cold with the cruel silent chill of the night, but she answered him with a fierce yearning.

"I think I love you, Martin," she said after a very long time. Suddenly she laughed, a clear and lovely music echoing from the frosty towers of Brontothor. "Oh, Martin, I shouldn't have been afraid. We'll never be lonely, not ever again—"

The moon had sunk far toward the dark horizon when he took her back to her rooms. He kissed her goodnight and went down the booming corridor toward his own chambers.

His head was awhir—he was drunk with the sweetness and wonder of it, he felt like singing and laughing aloud and embracing the whole starry universe. Taury, Taury, Taury!

"Martin."

He paused. There was a figure standing before his door, a tall slender form wrapped in a dark cloak. The dull light of a fluoroglobe threw the face into sliding shadow and tormented highlights. Vargor.

"What is it?" he asked.

The prince's hand came up, and Saunders saw the blunt muzzle of a stun pistol gaping at him. Vargor smiled, lopsidedly and sorrowfully. "I'm sorry, Martin," he said.

Saunders stood paralyzed with unbelief. Vargor—why, Vargor had fought beside him; they'd saved each other's lives, laughed and worked and lived together—Vargor!

The gun flashed. There was a crashing in Saunders' head and he tumbled into illimitable darkness.

He awoke very slowly, every nerve tingling with the pain of returning sensation. Something was restraining him. As his vision cleared, he saw that he was lying bound and gagged on the floor of his time projector.

The time machine—he'd all but forgotten it, left it standing in a shed while he went out to the stars, he'd never thought to have another look at it. The time machine!

Vargor stood in the open door, a fluoroglobe in one hand lighting his haggard face. His hair fell in disarray past his tired, handsome features, and his eyes were as wild as the low words that spilled from his mouth.

"I'm sorry, Martin, I am. I like you, and you've done the Empire such a service as it can never forget, and this is as low a trick as one man can ever play on another. But I have to. I'll be haunted by the thought of this night all my life, but I have to."

Saunders tried to move, snarling incoherently through his gag. Vargor shook his head. "Oh, no, Martin, I can't risk letting you make an outcry. If I'm to do evil, I'll at least do a competent job of it.

"I love Taury, you see. I've loved her ever since I first met her, when I came from the stars with a fighting fleet to her father's court and saw her standing there with the frost crackling through her hair and those gray eyes shining at me. I love her so it's like a pain in me. I can't be away from her, I'd pull down the cosmos for her sake. And I thought she was slowly coming to love me.

"And tonight I saw you two on the balcony, and knew I'd lost. Only I can't give up! Our breed has fought the Galaxy for a dream, Martin—it's not in us ever to stop fighting while life is in us. Fighting by any means, for whatever is dear and precious—but fighting!"

Vargor made a gesture of deprecation. "I don't want power, Martin, believe me. The consort's job will be hard and unglamorous, galling to a man of spirit—but if that's the only way to have her, then so be it. And I do honestly believe, right or wrong, that I'm better for her and for the Empire than you. You don't really belong here, you know. You don't have the tradition, the feeling, the training—you don't even have the biological heritage of five thousand years. Taury may care for you now, but think twenty years ahead!"

Vargor smiled wryly. "I'm taking a chance, of course. If you do find a means of negative time travel and come back here, it will be disgrace and exile for me. It would be safer to kill you. But I'm not quite that much of a scoundrel, I'm giving you your chance. At worst, you should escape into the time when the Second Empire is in its glorious bloom, a happier age than this. And if you do find a means to come back—well, remember what I said about your not belonging, and try to reason with clarity and kindness. Kindness to Taury, Martin."

He lifted the fluoroglobe, casting its light over the dim interior of the machine. "So it's goodbye, Martin, and I hope you won't hate me too much. It should take you several thousand years to work free and stop the machine. I've equipped it with weapons, supplies, everything I think you may need for any eventuality. But I'm sure you'll emerge in a greater and more peaceful culture, and be happier there."

His voice was strangely tender, all of a sudden. "Goodbye, Martin my comrade. And—good luck!"

He opened the main-drive switch and stepped out as the projector began to warm up. The door clanged shut behind him.

Saunders writhed on the floor, cursing with a brain that was a black cauldron of bitterness. The great drone of the projector rose, he was on his way—*oh no—stop the machine, God, set me free before it's too late!*

The plastic cords cut his writs. He was lashed to a stanchion, unable to reach the switch with any part of his body. His groping fingers slid across the surface of a knot, the nails clawing for a hold. The machine roared with full power, driving ahead through the vastness of time.

Vargor had bound him skillfully. It took him a long time to get free. Toward the end he went slowly, not caring, knowing with a dull knowledge that he was already more thousands of irretrievable years into the future than his dials would register.

He climbed to his feet, plucked the gag from his mouth, and looked blankly out at the faceless gray. The century needle was hard against its stop. He estimated vaguely that he was some ten thousand years into the future already.

Ten thousand years!

He yanked down the switch with a raging burst of savagery.

It was dark outside. He stood stupidly for a moment before he saw water seeping into the cabin around the door. Water—he was under water—short circuits! Frantically, he slammed the switch forward again.

He tasted the water on the floor. It was salt. Sometime in that ten thousand years, for reasons natural or artificial, the sea had come in and covered the site of Brontothor.

A thousand years later he was still below its surface. Two thousand, three thousand, ten thousand. . .

Taury, Taury! For twenty thousand years she had been dust on an alien planet. And Belgotai was gone with his wry smile, Hunda's staunchness, even the Dreamer must long ago have descended into darkness. The sea rolled over dead Brontothor, and he was alone.

He bowed his head on his arms and wept.

For three million years the ocean lay over Brontothor's land. And Saunders drove onward.

He stopped at intervals to see if the waters had gone. Each time the frame of the machine groaned with pressure and the sea poured in through the crack of the door. Otherwise he sat dully in the throbbing loneliness, estimating time covered by his own watch and the known rate of the projector, not caring any more about dates or places.

Several times he considered stopping the machine, letting the sea burst in and drown him. There would be peace in its depths, sleep and forgetting. But no, it wasn't in him to quit that easily. Death was his friend, death would always be there waiting for his call.

But Taury was dead.

Time grayed to its end. In the four millionth year, he stopped the machine and discoverd that there was dry air around him.

He was in a city. But it was not such a city as he had ever seen or imagined, he couldn't follow the wild geometry of the titanic structures that loomed about him and they were never the same. The place throbbed and pulsed with incredible forces, it wavered and blurred in a strangely unreal light. Great devastating energies flashed and roared around him—lightning come to Earth. The air hissed and stung with their booming passage.

The thought was a shout filling his skull, blazing along his nerves, too mighty a thought for his stunned brain to do more than grope after meaning:

CREATURE FROM OUT OF TIME, LEAVE THIS PLACE AT ONCE OR THE FORCES WE USE WILL DESTROY YOU!

Through and through him that mental vision seared, down to the very molecules of his brain, his life lay open to Them in a white flame of incandescence.

Can you help me? he cried to the gods. *Can you send me back through time?*

MAN, THERE IS NO WAY TO TRAVEL FAR BACKWARD IN TIME, IT IS INHERENTLY IMPOSSIBLE. YOU MUST GO ON TO THE VERY END OF THE UNIVERSE, AND BEYOND THE END, BECAUSE THAT WAY LIES—

He screamed with the pain of unendurably great thought and concept filling his human brain.

GO ON, MAN, GO ON! BUT YOU CANNOT SURVIVE IN THAT MACHINE AS IT IS. I WILL CHANGE IT FOR YOU . . . GO!

The time projector started again by itself. Saunders fell forward into a darkness that roared and flashed.

Grimly, desperately, like a man driven by demons, Saunders hurtled into the future.

There could be no gainsaying the awful word which had been laid on him. The mere thought of the gods had engraven itself on the very tissue of his brain. Why he should go on to the end of time, he could not imagine, nor did he care. But go on he must!

The machine had been altered. It was airtight now, and experiment showed the window to be utterly unbreakable. Something had been done to the projector so that it hurled him forward at an incredible rate, millions of years passed while a minute or two ticked away within the droning shell.

But what had the gods been?

He would never know. Beings from beyond the Galaxy, beyond the very universe—the ultimately evolved descendants of man—something at whose nature he could not even guess—there was no way of telling. This much was plain: whether it had become extinct or had changed into something else, the human race was gone. Earth would never feel human tread again.

I wonder what became of the Second Empire? I hope it had a long and good life. Or—could that have been its unimaginable end product?

The years reeled past, millions, billions mounting on each other while Earth spun around her star and the Galaxy aged. Saunders fled onward.

He stopped now and then, unable to resist a glimpse of the world and its tremendous history.

A hundred million years in the future, he looked out on great sheets of flying snow. The gods were gone. Had they too died, or abandoned Earth—perhaps for an altogether different plane of existence? He would never know.

There was a being coming through the storm. The wind flung the snow about him in whirling, hissing clouds. Frost was in his gray fur. He moved with a lithe, unhuman grace, carrying a curved staff at whose tip was a blaze like a tiny sun.

Saunders hailed him through the psychophone, letting his amplified voice shout through the blizzard: "Who are you? What are you doing on Earth?"

The being carried a stone axe in one hand and wore a string of crude beads about his neck. But he stared with bold yellow eyes at the machine and the psychophone brought his harsh scream: "You must be from the far past, one of the earlier cycles."

"They told me to go on, back almost a hundred million years ago. They told me to go to the end of time!"

The psychophone hooted with metallic laughter. "If *They* told you so—then go!"

The being walked on into the storm.

Saunders flung himself ahead. There was no place on Earth for him anymore, he had no choice but to go on.

A billion years in the future there was a city standing on a plain where grass grew that was blue and glassy and tinkled with a high crystalline chiming as the wind blew through it. But the city had never been built by humans, and it warned him away with a voice he could not disobey.

Then the sea came, and for a long time thereafter he was trapped within a mountain, he had to drive onward till it had eroded back to the ground.

The sun grew hotter and whiter as the hydrogen-helium cycle increased its intensity. Earth spiraled slowly closer to it, the friction of gas and dust clouds in space taking their infinitesimal toll of its energy over billions of years.

How many intelligent races had risen on Earth and had their day, and died, since the age when man first came out of the jungle? *At least*, he thought tiredly, *we were the first*.

A hundred billion years in the future, the sun had used up its last reserves of nuclear reactions. Saunders looked out on a bare mountain scene, grim as the Moon—but the Moon had long ago fallen back toward its parent world and exploded into a meteoric rain. Earth faced its primary now; its day was as long as its year. Saunders saw part of the sun's huge blood-red disc shining wanly.

So goodbye, Sol, he thought. *Goodbye, and thank you for many million years of warmth and light. Sleep well, old friend.*

Some billions of years beyond, there was nothing but the elemental dark. Entropy had reached a maximum, the energy sources were used up, the universe was dead.

The universe was dead!

He screamed with the graveyard terror of it and flung the machine onward. Had it not been for the gods' command, he might have let it hang there, might have opened the door to airlessness and absolute zero to die. But he had to go on. He had reached the end of all things, but he had to go on. *Beyond the end of time—*

Billions upon billions of years fled. Saunders lay in his machine, sunk into an apathetic coma. Once he roused himself to eat, feeling the sardonic humor of the situation—the last living creature, the last free energy in all the cindered cosmos, fixing a sandwich.

Many billions of years in the future, Saunders paused again. He looked out into blackness. But with a sudden shock he discerned a far faint glow, the vaguest imaginable blur of light out in the heavens.

Trembling, he jumped forward another billion years. The light was stronger now, a great sprawling radiance swirling inchoately in the sky.

The universe was reforming.

It made sense, thought Saunders, fighting for self-control. Space had expanded to some kind of limit, now it was collapsing in on itself to start the cycle anew—the cycle that had been repeated none knew how many times in the past. The universe was mortal, but it was a phoenix which would never really die.

But he was disturbingly mortal, and suddenly he was free of his death wish. At the very least he wanted to see what the next time around looked like. But the universe would, according to the best theories of twentieth-century cosmology, collapse to what was virtually a point-source, a featureless blaze of pure energy out of which the primal atoms would be reformed. If he wasn't to be devoured in that raging furnace, he'd better leap a long ways ahead. A hell of a long ways!

He grinned with sudden reckless determination and plunged the switch forward.

Worry came back. How did he know that a planet would be formed under him? He might come out in open space, or in the heart of a sun. . . Well, he'd have to risk that. The gods must have foreseen and allowed for it.

He came out briefly—and flashed back into time-drive. The planet was still molten!

Some geological ages later, he looked out at a spuming gray rain, washing with senseless power from a hidden sky, covering naked rocks with a raging swirl of white water. He didn't go out; the atmosphere would be unbreathable until plants had liberated enough oxygen.

On and on! Sometimes he was under seas, sometimes on land. He saw strange jungles like overgrown ferns and mosses rise and wither in the cold of a glacial age and rise again in altered life-form.

A thought nagged at him, tugging at the back of his mind as he rode onward. It didn't hit him for several million years, then: *The moon! Oh, my God, the moon!*

His hands trembled too violently for him to stop the machine. Finally, with an effort, he controlled himself enough to pull the switch. He skipped on, looking for a night of full moon.

Luna. The same old face—*Luna!*

The shock was too great to register. Numbly, he resumed his journey. And the world began to look familiar, there were low forested hills and a river shining in the distance . . .

He didn't really believe it till he saw the village. It was the same—Hudson, New York.

He sat for a moment, letting his physicist's brain consider the tremendous fact. In Newtonian terms, it meant that every particle newly formed in the Beginning had exactly the same position and velocity as every corresponding particle formed in the previous cycle. In more acceptable Einsteinian language, the continuum was spherical in all four dimensions. In any case—if you traveled long enough, through space or time, you got back to your starting point.

He could go home!

He ran down the sunlit hill, heedless of his foreign garments, ran till the breath sobbed in raw lungs and his heart seemed about to burst from the ribs. Gasping, he entered the village, went into a bank, and looked at the tear-off calendar and the wall clock.

June 17, 1936, 1:30 p.m. From that, he could figure his time of arrival in 1973 to the minute.

He walked slowly back, his legs trembling under him, and started the time machine again. Grayness was outside—for the last time.

1973.

Martin Saunders stepped out of the machine. Its moving in space, at Brontothor, had brought it outside MacPherson's house; it lay halfway up the hill at the top of which the rambling old building stood.

There came a flare of soundless energy. Saunders sprang back in alarm and saw the machine dissolve into molten metal—into gas—into a nothingness that shone briefly and was gone.

The gods must have put some annihilating device into it. They didn't want its devices from the future loose in the twentieth century.

But there was no danger of that, thought Saunders as he walked slowly up the hill through the rain-wet grass. He had seen too much of war and horror ever to give men knowledge they weren't ready for. He and Eve and MacPherson would have to suppress the story of his return around time—for that would offer a means of travel into the past, remove the barrier which would keep man from too much use of the machine for murder and oppression. The Second Empire and the Dreamer's philosophy lay a long time in the future.

He went on. The hill seemed strangely unreal, after all that he had seen from it, the whole enormous tomorrow of the cosmos. He would never quite fit into the little round of days that lay ahead.

Taury—her bright lovely face floated before him, he thought he heard her voice whisper in the cool wet wind that stroked his hair like her strong, gentle hands.

"Goodbye," he whispered into the reaching immensity of time. "Goodbye, my dearest."

He went slowly up the steps and in the front door. There would be Sam to mourn. And then there would be the carefully censored thesis to write, and a life spent in satisfying work with a girl who was sweet and kind and beautiful even if she wasn't Taury. It was enough for a mortal man.

He walked into the living room and smiled at Eve and MacPherson. "Hello," he said. "I guess I must be a little early."

THE MARTIAN WAY

Isaac Asimov

1

From the doorway of the short corridor between the only two rooms in the travel-head of the spaceship, Mario Esteban Rioz watched sourly as Ted Long adjusted the video dials painstakingly. Long tried a touch clockwise, then a touch counter. The picture was lousy.

Rioz knew it would stay lousy. They were too far from Earth and at a bad position facing the Sun. But then Long would not be expected to know that. Rioz remained standing in the doorway for an additional moment, head bent to clear the upper lintel, body turned half sidewise to fit the narrow opening. Then he jerked into the galley like a cork popping out of a bottle.

"What are you after?" he asked.

"I thought I'd get Hilder," said Long.

Rioz propped his rump on the corner of a table shelf. He lifted a conical can of milk from the companion shelf just above his head. Its point popped under pressure. He swirled it gently as he waited for it to warm.

"What for?" he said. He upended the cone and sucked noisily.

"Thought I'd listen."

"I think it's a waste of power."

Long looked up, frowning. "It's customary to allow free use of personal video sets."

"Within reason," retorted Rioz.

Their eyes met challengingly. Rioz had the rangy body, the gaunt, cheek-sunken face that was almost the hallmark of the Martian Scavenger, those Spacers who patiently haunted the space routes between Earth and Mars. Pale blue eyes were set keenly in the brown, lined face which, in turn, stood darkly out against the white surrounding syntho-fur that lined the up-turned collar of his leathtic space jacket.

Long was altogether paler and softer. He bore some of the marks of the Grounder, although no second-generation Martian could be a Grounder in the sense that Earthmen were. His own collar was thrown back and his dark brown hair freely exposed.

"What do you call within reason?" demanded Long.

Rioz's thin lips grew thinner. He said, "Considering that we're not even going to make expenses this trip, the way it looks, any power drain at all is outside reason."

Long said, "If we're losing money, hadn't you better get back to your post? It's your watch."

Rioz grunted and ran a thumb and forefinger over the stubble on his chin. He got up and trudged to the door, his soft, heavy boots muting the sound of his steps. He paused to look at the thermostat, then turned with a flare of fury.

"I *thought* it was hot. Where do you think you are?"

Long said, "Forty degrees isn't excessive."

"For you it isn't, maybe. But this is space, not a heated office at the iron mines." Rioz swung the thermostat control down to minimum with a quick thumb movement. "Sun's warm enough."

"The galley isn't on Sunside."

"It'll percolate through, damn it."

Rioz stepped through the door and Long stared after him for a long moment, then turned back to the video. He did not turn up the thermostat.

The picture was still flickering badly, but it would have to do. Long folded a chair down out of the wall. He leaned forward waiting through the formal announcement, the momentary pause before the slow dissolution of the curtain, the spotlight picking out the well-known bearded figure which grew as it was brought forward until it filled the screen.

The voice, impressive even through the flutings and croakings induced by the electron storms of twenty millions of miles, began:

"Friends! My fellow citizens of Earth . . ."

2

Rioz's eye caught the flash of the radio signal as he stepped into the pilot room. For one moment, the palms of his hands grew clammy when it seemed to him that it was a radar pip; but that was only his guilt speaking. He should not have left the pilot room while on duty theoretically, though all Scavengers did it. Still, it was the standard nightmare, this business of a strike turning up during just those five minutes when one knocked off for a quick coffee because it seemed certain that space was clear. And the nightmare had been known to happen, too.

Rioz threw in the multi-scanner. It was a waste of power, but while he was thinking about it, he might as well make sure.

Space was clear except for the far-distant echoes from the neighboring ships on the scavenging line.

He hooked up the radio circuit, and the blond, long-nosed head of Richard Swenson, co-pilot of the next ship on the Marsward side, filled it.

"Hey, Mario," said Swenson.

"Hi. What's new?"

There was a second and a fraction of pause between that and Swenson's next comment, since the speed of electromagnetic radiation is not infinite.

"What a day I've *had*."

"Something happened?" Rioz asked.

"I had a strike."

"Well, good."

"Sure, if I'd roped it in," said Swenson morosely.

"What happened?"

"Damn it, I headed in the wrong direction."

Rioz knew better than to laugh. He said, "How did you do that?"

"It wasn't my fault. The trouble was the shell was moving way out of the ecliptic. Can you imagine the stupidity of a pilot that can't work the release maneuver decently? How was I to know? I got the distance of the shell and let it go at that. I just assumed its orbit was in the usual trajectory family. Wouldn't you? I started along what I thought was a good line of intersection and it was five minutes before I noticed the distance was still going up. The pips were taking their sweet time returning. So then I took the angular projections of the thing, and it was too late to catch up with it."

"Any of the other boys getting it?"

"No. It's 'way out of the ecliptic and'll keep on going forever. That's not what bothers me so much. It was only an inner shell. But I hate to tell you how many tons of propulsion I wasted getting up speed and then getting back to station. You should have heard Canute."

Canute was Richard Swenson's brother and partner.

"Mad, huh?" said Rioz.

"Mad? Like to have killed me! But then we've been out five months now and it's getting kind of sticky. You know."

"I know."

"How are you doing, Mario?"

Rioz made a spitting gesture. "About that much this trip. Two shells in the last two weeks and I had to chase each one for six hours."

"Big ones?"

"Are you kidding? I could have scaled them down to Phobos by hand. This is the worst trip I've ever had."

"How much longer are you staying?"

"For my part, we can quit tomorrow. We've only been out two months and it's got so I'm chewing Long out all the time."

There was a pause over and above the electromagnetic lag.

Swenson said, "What's he like, anyway? Long, I mean."

Rioz looked over his shoulder. He could hear the soft, crackly mutter of the video in the galley. "I can't make him out. He says to me about a week after the start of the trip, 'Mario, why are you a Scavenger?' I just look at him and say, 'To make a living. Why do you suppose?' I mean, what the hell kind of a question is that? Why is anyone a Scavenger?

"Anyway, he says, 'That's not it, Mario.' *He's* telling *me*, you see. He says, 'You're a Scavenger because this is part of the Martian way.' "

Swenson said, "And what did he mean by that?"

Rioz shrugged. "I never asked him. Right now he's sitting in there listening to the ultra-microwave from Earth. He's listening to some Grounder called Hilder."

"Hilder? A Grounder politician, an Assemblyman or something, isn't he?"

"That's right. At least, I think that's right. Long is always doing things like that. He brought about fifteen pounds of books with him, all about Earth. Just plain dead weight, you know."

"Well, he's your partner. And talking about partners, I think I'll get back on the job. If I miss another strike, there'll be murder around here."

He was gone and Rioz leaned back. He watched the even green line that was the pulse scanner. He tried the multi-scanner a moment. Space was still clear.

He felt a little better. A bad spell is always worse if the Scavengers all about you are pulling in shell after shell; if the shells go spiraling down to the Phobos scrap forges with everyone's brand welded on except your own. Then, too, he had managed to work off some of his resentment toward Long.

It was a mistake teaming up with Long. It was always a mistake to team up with a tenderfoot. They thought what you wanted was conversation, especially Long, with his eternal theories about Mars and its great new role in human progress. That was the way he said it—Human Progress: the Martian Way; the New Creative Minority. And all the time what Rioz wanted wasn't talk, but a strike, a few shells to call their own.

At that, he hadn't any choice, really. Long was pretty well known down on Mars and made good pay as a mining engineer. He was a friend of Commissioner Sankov and he'd been out on one or two short scavenging missions before. You can't turn a fellow down flat before a tryout, even though it did look funny. Why should a mining engineer with a comfortable job and good money want to muck around in space?

Rioz never asked Long that question. Scavenger partners are forced too close together to make curiosity desirable, or sometimes even safe. But Long talked so much that he answered the question.

"I had to come out here, Mario," he said. "The future of Mars isn't in the mines; it's in space."

Rioz wondered how it would be to try a trip alone. Everyone said it was impossible. Even discounting lost opportunities when one man had to go off watch to sleep or attend to other things, it was well known that one man alone in space would become intolerably depressed in a relatively short while.

Taking a partner along made a six-month trip possible. A regular crew would be better, but no Scavenger could make money on a ship large enough to carry one. The capital it would take in propulsion alone!

Even two didn't find it exactly fun in space. Usually you had to change partners each trip and you could stay out longer with some than with others. Look at Richard and Canute Swenson. They teamed up every five or six trips because they were brothers. And yet whenever they did, it was a case of constantly mounting tension and antagonism after the first week.

Oh well. Space was clear. Rioz would feel a little better if he went back in the galley and smoothed down some of the bickering with Long. He might as well show he was an old spacehand who took the irritations of space as they came.

He stood up, walked the three steps necessary to reach the short, narrow corridor that tied together the two rooms of the spaceship.

3

Once again Rioz stood in the doorway for a moment, watching. Long was intent on the flickering screen.

Rioz said gruffly, "I'm shoving up the thermostat. It's all right—we can spare the power."

Long nodded. "If you like."

Rioz took a hesitant step forward. Space was clear, so to hell with sitting and looking at a blank, green, pipless line. He said, "What's the Grounder been talking about?"

"History of space travel mostly. Old stuff, but he's doing it well. He's giving the whole works—color cartoons, trick photography, stills from old films, everything."

As if to illustrate Long's remarks, the bearded figure faded out of view, and a cross-sectional view of a spaceship flitted onto the screen. Hilder's voice continued, pointing out features of interest that appeared in schematic color. The communications system of the ship outlined itself in red as he talked about it, the storerooms, the proton micropile drive, the cybernetic circuits . . .

Then Hilder was back on the screen. "But this is only the travel-head of the ship. What moves it? What gets it off the Earth?"

Everyone knew what moved a spaceship, but Hilder's voice was like a drug. He made spaceship propulsion sound like the secret of the ages, like an ultimate revelation. Even Rioz felt a slight tingling of suspense, though he had spent the greater part of his life aboard ship.

Hilder went on. "Scientists call it different names. They call it the Law of Action and Reaction. Sometimes they call it Newton's Third Law. Sometimes they call it Conservation of Momentum. But we don't have to call it any name. We can just use our common sense. When we swim, we push water backward and move forward ourselves. When we walk, we push back against the ground and move forward. When we fly a gyro-flivver, we push air backward and move forward.

"Nothing can move forward unless something else moves backward. It's the old principle of 'You can't get something for nothing.'

"Now imagine a spaceship that weighs a hundred thousand tons lifting off Earth. To do that, something else must be moved downward. Since a spaceship is extremely heavy, a great deal of material must be moved downward. So much material, in fact, that there is no place to keep it all aboard ship. A special compartment must be built behind the ship to hold it."

Again Hilder faded out and the ship returned. It shrank and a truncated cone appeared behind it. In bright yellow, words appeared within it: MATERIAL TO BE THROWN AWAY.

"But now,"said Hilder, "the total weight of the ship is much greater. You need still more propulsion and still more."

The ship shrank enormously to add on another larger shell and still another immense one. The ship proper, the travel-head, was a little dot on the screen, a glowing red dot.

Rioz said, "Hell, this is kindergarten stuff."

"Not to the people he's speaking to, Mario," replied Long. "Earth isn't Mars. There must be billions of Earth people who've never even seen a spaceship; don't know the first thing about it."

Hilder was saying, "When the material inside the biggest shell is used up, the shell is detached. It's thrown away, too."

The outermost shell came loose, wobbled about the screen.

"Then the second one goes," said Hilder, "and then, if the trip is a long one, the last is ejected."

The ship was just a red dot now, with three shells shifting and moving, lost in space.

Hilder said, "These shells represent a hundred thousand tons of tungsten, magnesium, aluminum, and steel. They are gone forever from Earth. Mars is ringed by Scavengers, waiting along the routes of space travel, waiting for the cast-off shells, netting and branding them, saving them for Mars. Not one cent of payment reaches Earth for them. They are salvage. They belong to the ship that finds them."

Rioz said, "We risk our investment and our lives. If we don't pick them up, no one gets them. What loss is that to Earth?"

"Look," said Long, "he's been talking about nothing but the drain that Mars, Venus, and the Moon put on Earth. This is just another item of loss."

"They'll get their return. We're mining more iron every year."

"And most of it goes right back into Mars. If you can believe his figures, Earth has invested two hundred billion dollars in Mars and received back about five billion dollars' worth of iron. It's put five hundred billion dollars into the Moon and gotten back a little over twenty-five billion dollars of magnesium, titanium, and assorted light metals. It's put fifty billion dollars into Venus and gotten back nothing. And that's what the taxpayers of Earth are really interested in—tax money out; nothing in."

The screen was filled, as he spoke, with diagrams of the Scavengers on the route to Mars; little, grinning caricatures of ships, reaching out wiry, tenuous arms that groped for the tumbling, empty shells, seizing and snaking them in, branding them MARS PROPERTY in glowing letters, then scaling them down to Phobos.

Then it was Hilder again. "They tell us eventually they will return it all to us. Eventually! Once they are a going concern! We don't know when that will be. A century from now? A thousand years? A million? 'Eventually.' Let's take them at their word. Someday they will give us back all our metals. Someday they will grow their own food, use their own power, live their own lives.

"But one thing they can never return. Not in a hundred million years. *Water!*

"Mars has only a trickle of water because it is too small. Venus has no water at all because it is too hot. The Moon has none because it is too hot and too small. So Earth must supply not only drinking water and washing water for the Spacers, water to run their industries, water for the hydroponic factories they claim to be setting up—but even water to throw away by the millions of tons.

"What is the propulsive force that spaceships use? What is it they throw out behind so that they can accelerate forward? Once it was the gases generated from explosives. That was very expensive. Then the proton micropile was invented—a cheap power source that could heat up any liquid until it was a gas under tremendous pressure. What is the cheapest and most plentiful liquid available? Why, water, of course.

"Each spaceship leaves Earth carrying nearly a million tons—not pounds, *tons*—of water, for the sole purpose of driving it into space so that it may speed up or slow down.

"Our ancestors burned the oil of Earth madly and wilfully. They destroyed its coal recklessly. We despise and condemn them for that, but at least they had this excuse—they thought that when the need arose, substitutes would be found. And they were right. We have our plankton farms and our proton micropiles.

"But there is no substitute for water. None! There never can be. And when our descendants view the desert we will have made of Earth, what excuse will they find for us? When the droughts come and grow—"

Long leaned forward and turned off the set. He said, "That bothers me. The damn fool is deliberately—What's the matter?"

Rioz had risen uneasily to his feet. "I ought to be watching the pips."

"The hell with the pips." Long got up likewise, followed Rioz through the narrow corridor, and stood just inside the pilot room. "If Hilder carries this through, if he's got the guts to make a real issue out of it—*Wow!*"

He had seen it too. The pip was a Class A, racing after the outgoing signal like a greyhound after a mechanical rabbit.

Rioz was babbling, "Space was clear, I tell you, *clear*. For Mars' sake, Ted, don't just freeze on me. See if you can spot it visually."

Rioz was working speedily and with an efficiency that was the result of nearly twenty years of scavenging. He had the distance in two minutes. Then, remembering Swenson's experience, he measured the angle of declination and the radial velocity as well.

He yelled at Long, "One point seven six radians. You can't miss it, man."

Long held his breath as he adjusted the vernier. "It's only half a radian off the Sun. It'll only be crescent-lit."

He increased magnification as rapidly as he dared, watching for the one "star" that changed position and grew to have a form, revealing itself to be no star.

"I'm starting, anyway," said Rioz. "We can't wait."

"I've got it. I've got it." Magnification was still too small to give it a definite shape, but the dot Long watched was brightening and dimming rhythmically as the shell rotated and caught sunlight on cross sections of different sizes.

"Hold on."

The first of many fine spurts of steam squirted out of the proper vents, leaving long trails of micro-crystals of ice gleaming mistily in the pale beams of the distant Sun. They thinned out for a hundred miles or more. One spurt, then another, then another, as the Scavenger ship moved out of its stable trajectory and took up a course tangential to that of the shell.

"It's moving like a comet at perihelion!" yelled Rioz. "Those damned Grounder pilots knock the shells off that way on purpose. I'd like to—"

He swore his anger in a frustrated frenzy as he kicked steam backward and backward recklessly, till the hydraulic cushioning of his chair had soughed back a full foot and Long had found himself all but unable to maintain his grip on the guard rail.

"Have a heart," he begged.

But Rioz had his eye on the pips. "If you can't take it, man, stay on Mars!" The steam spurts continued to boom distantly.

The radio came to life. Long managed to lean forward through what seemed like molasses and closed contact. It was Swenson, eye glaring.

Swenson yelled, "Where the hell are you guys going? You'll be in my sector in ten seconds."

Rioz said, "I'm chasing a shell."

"In *my* sector?"

"It started in mine and you're not in position to get it. Shut off that radio, Ted."

The ship thundered through space, a thunder that could be heard only within the hull. And then Rioz cut the engines in stages large enough to make Long flail forward. The sudden silence was more ear-shattering than the noise that had preceded it.

Rioz said, "All right. Let me have the 'scope."

They both watched. The shell was a definite truncated cone now, tumbling with slow solemnity as it passed along among the stars.

"It's a Class A shell, all right," said Rioz with satisfaction. A giant among shells, he thought. It would put them into the black.

Long said, "We've got another pip on the scanner. I think it's Swenson taking after us."

Rioz scarcely gave it a glance. "He won't catch us."

The shell grew larger still, filling the visiplate.

Rioz's hands were on the harpoon lever. He waited, adjusted the angle microscopically twice, played out the length allotment. Then he yanked, tripping the release.

For a moment, nothing happened. Then a metal mesh cable snaked out onto the visiplate, moving toward the shell like a striking cobra. It made contact, but it did not hold. If it had, it would have snapped instantly like a cobweb strand. The shell was turning with a rotational momentum amounting to thousands of tons. What the cable did do was to set up a powerful magnetic field that acted as a brake on the shell.

Another cable and another lashed out. Rioz sent them out in an almost heedless expenditure of energy.

"I'll get this one! By Mars, I'll get this one!"

With some two dozen cables stretching between ship and shell, he desisted. The shell's rotational energy, converted by breaking into heat, had raised its temperature to a point where its radiation could be picked up by the ship's meters.

Long said, "Do you want me to put our brand on?"

"Suits me. But you don't have to if you don't want to. It's my watch."

"I don't mind."

Long clambered into his suit and went out the lock. It was the surest sign of his newness to the game that he could count the number of times he had been out in space in a suit. This was the fifth time.

He went out along the nearest cable, hand over hand, feeling the vibration of the mesh against the metal of his mitten.

He burned their serial number in the smooth metal of the shell. There was nothing to oxidize the steel in the emptiness of space. It simply melted and vaporized, condensing some feet away from the energy beam, turning the surface it touched into a gray, powdery dullness.

Long swung back toward the ship.

Inside again, he took off his helmet, white and thick with frost that collected as soon as he had entered.

The first thing he heard was Swenson's voice coming over the radio in this almost unrecognizable rage: ". . . straight to the Commissioner. Damn it, there are rules to this game!"

Rioz sat back, unbothered. "Look, it hit my sector. I was late spotting it and I chased it into yours. You couldn't have gotten it with Mars for a backstop. That's all there is to it—You back, Long?"

He cut contact.

The signal button raged at him, but he paid no attention.

"He's going to the Commissioner?" Long asked.

"Not a chance. He just goes on like that because it breaks the monotony. He doesn't mean anything by it. He knows it's our shell. And how do you like that hunk of stuff, Ted?"

"Pretty good."

"Pretty good? It's terrific! Hold on. I'm setting it swinging."

The side jets spat steam and the ship started a slow rotation about the shell. The shell followed it. In thirty minutes, they were a gigantic bolo spinning in emptiness. Long checked the *Ephemeris* for the position of Deimos.

At a precisely calculated moment, the cables released their magnetic field and the shell went streaking off tangentially in a trajectory that would, in a day or so, bring it within pronging distance of the shell stores on the Martian satellite.

Rioz watched it go. He felt good. He turned to Long. "This is one fine day for us."

"What about Hilder's speech?" asked Long.

"What? Who? Oh, that. Listen, if I had to worry about every thing some damned Grounder said, I'd never get any sleep. Forget it."

"I don't think we should forget it."

"You're nuts. Don't bother me about it, will you? Get some sleep instead."

4

Ted Long found the breadth and height of the city's main thoroughfare exhilarating. It had been two months since the Commissioner had declared a moratorium on scavenging and had pulled all ships out of space, but this feeling of a stretched-out vista had not stopped thrilling Long. Even the thought that the moratorium was called pending a decision on the part of Earth to enforce its new insistence on water economy, by deciding upon a ration limit for scavenging, did not cast him entirely down.

The roof of the avenue was painted a luminous light blue, perhaps as an old-fashioned imitation of Earth's sky. Ted wasn't sure. The walls were lit with the store windows that pierced it.

Off in the distance, over the hum of traffic and the sloughing noise of people's feet passing him, he could hear the intermittent blasting as new channels were being bored into Mars' crust. All his life he remembered such blastings. The ground he walked on had been part of solid, unbroken rock when he was born. The city was growing and would keep on growing—if Earth would only let it.

He turned off at a cross street, narrower, not quite as brilliantly lit, shop windows giving way to apartment houses, each with its row of lights along the front façade. Shoppers and traffic gave way to slower-paced individuals and to squawling youngsters who had as yet evaded the maternal summons to the evening meal.

At the last minute, Long remembered the social amenities and stopped off at a corner water store.

He passed over his canteen. "Fill 'er up."

The plump storekeeper unscrewed the cap, cocked an eye into the opening. He shook it a little and let it gurgle. "Not much left," he said cheerfully.

"No," agreed Long.

The storekeeper trickled water in, holding the neck of the canteen close to the hose tip to avoid spillage. The volume gauge whirred. He screwed the cap back on.

Long passed over the coins and took his canteen. It clanked against his hip now with a pleasing heaviness. It would never do to visit a family without a full canteen. Among the boys, it didn't matter. Not as much, anyway.

He entered the hallway of No.27, climbed a short flight of stairs, and paused with his thumb on the signal.

The sound of voices could be heard quite plainly.

One was a woman's voice, somewhat shrill. "It's all right for you to have your Scavenger friends here, isn't it? I'm supposed to be thankful you manage to get home two months a year. Oh, it's quite enough that you spend a day or two with me. After that, it's the Scavengers again."

"I've been home for a long time now," said a male voice, "and this is business. For Mars' sake, let up, Dora. They'll be here soon."

Long decided to wait a moment before signaling. It might give them a chance to hit a more neutral topic.

"What do I care if they come?" retorted Dora. "Let them hear me. And I'd just as soon the Commissioner kept the moratorium on permanently. You hear me?"

"And what would we live on?" came the male voice hotly. "You tell me that."

"I'll tell you. You can make a decent, honorable living right here on Mars, just like everybody else. I'm the only one in this apartment house that's a Scavenger widow. That's what I am—a widow. I'm worse than a widow, because if I were a widow, I'd at least have a chance to marry someone else—What did you say?"

"Nothing. Nothing at all."

"Oh, I know what you said. Now listen here, Dick Swenson—"

"I only said," cried Swenson, "that now I know why Scavengers usually don't marry."

"You shouldn't have either. I'm tired of having every person in the neighborhood pity me and smirk and ask when you're coming home. Other people can be mining engineers and administrators and even tunnel borers. At least tunnel borers' wives have a decent home life and their children don't grow up like vagabonds. Peter might as well not have a father—"

A thin boy-soprano voice made its way through the door. It was somewhat more distant, as though it were in another room. "Hey, Mom, what's a vagabond?"

Dora's voice rose a notch. "Peter! You keep you mind on your homework."

Swenson said in a low voice, "It's not right to talk this way in front of the kid. What kind of notions will he get about me?"

"Stay home then and teach him better notions."

Peter's voice called out again. "Hey, Mom, I'm going to be a Scavenger when I grow up."

Footsteps sounded rapidly. There was a momentary hiatus in the sounds, then a piercing, "Mom! Hey, Mom! Leggo my ear! What did I do?" and a snuffling silence.

Long seized the chance. He worked the signal vigorously. Swenson opened the door, brushing down his hair with both hands.

"Hello, Ted," he said in a subdued voice. Then loudly, "Ted's here, Dora. Where's Mario, Ted?"

Long said, "He'll be here in a while."

Dora came bustling out of the next room, a small, dark woman with a pinched nose, and hair, just beginning to show touches of gray, combed off the forehead.

"Hello, Ted. Have you eaten?"

"Quite well, thanks. I haven't interrupted you, have I?"

"Not at all. We finished ages ago. Would you like some coffee?"

"I think so." Ted unslung his canteen and offered it.

"Oh, goodness, that's all right. We've plenty of water."

"I insist."

"Well, then—"

Back into the kitchen she went. Through the swinging door, Long caught a glimpse of dishes sitting in Secoterg, the "waterless cleaner that soaks up and absorbs grease and dirt in a twinkling. One ounce of water will rinse eight square feet of dish surface clean as clean. Buy Secoterg. Secoterg just cleans it right, makes your dishes shiny bright, does away with water waste—"

The tune started whining through his mind and Long crushed it with speech. He said, "How's Pete?"

"Fine, fine. The kid's in the fourth grade now. You know I don't get to see him much. Well, sir, when I came back last time, he looked at me and said . . ."

It went on for a while and wasn't too bad as bright sayings of bright children as told by dull parents go.

The door signal burped and Mario Rioz came in, frowning and red.

Swenson stepped to him quickly. "Listen, don't say anything about shell-snaring. Dora still remembers the time you fingered a Class A shell out of my territory and she's in one of her moods now."

"Who the hell wants to talk about shells?" Rioz slung off a fur-lined jacket, threw it over the back of the chair, and sat down.

Dora came through the swinging door, viewed the newcomer with a synthetic smile, and said, "Hello, Mario. Coffee for you, too?"

"Yeah," he said, reaching automatically for his canteen.

"Just use some more of my water, Dora," said Long quickly. "He'll owe it to me."

"Yeah," said Rioz.

"What's wrong, Mario?" asked Long.

Rioz said heavily, "Go on. Say you told me so. A year ago when Hilder made that speech, you told me so. Say it."

Long shrugged.

Rioz said, "They've set up the quota. Fifteen minutes ago the news came out."

"Well?"

"Fifty thousand tons of water per trip."

"What?" yelled Swenson, burning. "You can't get off Mars with fifty thousand!"

"That's the figure. It's a deliberate piece of gutting. No more scavenging."

Dora came out with the coffee and set it down all around.

"What's all this about no more scavenging?" She sat down very firmly and Swenson looked helpless.

"It seems," said Long, "that they're rationing us at fifty thousand tons and that means we can't make any more trips."

"Well, what of it?" Dora sipped her coffee and smiled gaily. "If you want my opinion, it's a good thing. It's time all you Scavengers found yourselves a nice, steady job here on Mars. I mean it. It's no life to be running all over space—"

"Please, Dora," said Swenson.

Rioz came close to a snort.

Dora raised her eyebrows. "I'm just giving my opinions."

Long said, "Please feel free to do so. But I would like to say something. Fifty thousand is just a detail. We know that Earth—or at least Hilder's party—wants to make political capital out of a campaign for water economy, so we're in a bad hole. We've got to get water somehow or they'll shut us down altogether, right?"

"Well, sure," said Swenson.

"But the question is how, right?"

"If it's only getting water," said Rioz in a sudden gush of words, "there's only one thing to do and you know it. If the Grounders won't give us water, we'll take it. The water doesn't belong to them just because their fathers and grandfathers were too damned sick-yellow ever to leave their fat planet. Water belongs to people wherever they are. We're people and the water's ours, too. We have a right to it."

"How do you propose taking it?" asked Long.

"Easy! They've got oceans of water on Earth. They can't post a guard over every square mile. We can sink down on the night side of the planet any time we want, fill our shells, then get away. How can they stop us?"

"In half a dozen ways, Mario. How do you spot shells in space up to distances of a hundred thousand miles? One thin metal shell in all that space. How? By radar. Do you think there's no radar on Earth? Do you think that if Earth ever gets the notion we're engaged in waterlegging, it won't be simple for them to set up a radar network to spot ships coming in from space?"

Dora broke in indignantly. "I'll tell you one thing, Mario Rioz. My husband isn't going to be part of any raid to get water to keep up his scavenging with."

"It isn't just scavenging," said Mario. "Next they'll be cutting down on everything else. We've got to stop them now."

"But we don't need their water, anyway," said Dora. "We're not the Moon or Venus. We pipe enough water down from the polar caps for all we need. We have a water tap right in this apartment. There's one in every apartment on this block."

Long said, "Home use is the smallest part of it. The mines use water. And what do we do about the hydroponic tanks?"

"That's right," said Swenson. "What about the hydroponic tanks, Dora? They've got to have water and it's about time we arranged to grow our own fresh food instead of having to live on the condensed crud they ship us from Earth."

"Listen to him," said Dora scornfully. "What do you know about fresh food? You've never eaten any."

"I've eaten more than you think. Do you remember those carrots I picked up once?"

"Well, what was so wonderful about them? If you ask me, good baked protomeal is much better. And healthier, too. It just seems to be the fashion now to be talking fresh vegetables because they're increasing taxes for these hydroponics. Besides, all this will blow over."

Long said, "I don't think so. Not by itself, anyway. Hilder will probably be the next Co-ordinator, and then things may really get bad. If they cut down on food shipments, too—"

"Well, then," shouted Rioz, "what do we do? I still say take it! Take the water!"

"And I say we can't do that, Mario. Don't you see that what you're suggesting is the Earth way, the Grounder way? You're trying to hold on to the umbilical cord that ties Mars to Earth. Can't you get away from that? Can't you see the Martian way?"

"No, I can't. Suppose you tell me."

"I will, if you'll listen. When we think about the Solar System, what do we think about? Mercury, Venus, Earth, Moon, Mars, Phobos, and Deimos. There you are—seven bodies, that's all. But that doesn't represent one per cent of the Solar System. We Martians are right at the edge of the other ninety-nine per cent. Out there, farther from the Sun, there's unbelievable amounts of water!"

The others stared.

Swenson said uncertainly, "You mean the layers of ice on Jupiter and Saturn?"

"Not that specifically, but it *is* water, you'll admit. A thousand-mile-thick layer of water is a lot of water."

But it's all covered up with layers of ammonia or—or something, isn't it?" asked Swenson. "Besides, we can't land on the major planets."

"I know that," said Long, "but I haven't said that was the answer. The major planets aren't the only objects out there. What about the asteroids and the satellites? Vesta is a two-hundred-mile-diameter asteroid that's hardly more than a chunk of ice. One of the moons of Saturn is mostly ice. How about that?"

Rioz said, "Haven't you ever been in space, Ted?"

"You know I have. Why do you ask?"

"Sure, I know you have, but you still talk like a Grounder. Have you thought of the distances involved? The average asteroid is a hundred twenty million miles from Mars at the closest. That's twice the Venus-Mars hop and you know that hardly any liners do even that in one jump. They usually stop off at Earth or the Moon. After all, how long do you expect anyone to stay in space, man?"

"I don't know. What's your limit?"

"You know the limit. You don't have to ask me. It's six months. That's handbook data. After six months, if you're still in space, you're psychotherapy meat. Right, Dick?"

Swenson nodded.

"And that's just the asteroids," Rioz went on. "From Mars to Jupiter is three hundred thirty million miles, and to Saturn it's seven hundred million. How can anyone handle that kind of distance? Suppose you hit standard velocity or, to make it even, say you get up to good two hundred kilomiles an hour. It would take you—let's see, allowing time for acceleration and deceleration—about six or seven months to get to Jupiter and nearly a year to get to Saturn. Of course, you could hike the speed to a million miles an hour, theoretically, but where would you get the water to do that?"

"Gee," said a small voice attached to a smutty nose and round eyes. "Saturn!"

Dora whirled in her chair. "Peter, march right back into your room!"

"Aw, Ma."

"Don't 'Aw, Ma' me." She began to get out of the chair, and Peter scuttled away.

Swenson said, "Say, Dora, why don't you keep him company for a while? It's hard to keep his mind on homework if we're all out here talking."

Dora sniffed obstinately and stayed put. "I'll sit right here until I find out what Ted Long is thinking of. I tell you right now I don't like the sound of it."

Swenson said nervously, "Well, never mind Jupiter and Saturn. I'm sure Ted isn't figuring on that. But what about Vesta? We could make it in ten or twelve weeks there and the same back. And two hundred miles in diameter. That's four million cubic miles of ice!"

"So what?" said Rioz. "What do we do on Vesta? Quarry the ice? Set up mining machinery? Say, do you know how long that would take?"

Long said, "I'm talking about Saturn, not Vesta."

Rioz addressed an unseen audience. "I tell him seven hundred million miles and he keeps on talking."

"All right," said Long, "suppose you tell me how you know we can only stay in space six months, Mario?"

"It's common knowledge, damn it."

"Because it's in the *Handbook of Space Flight*. It's data compiled by Earth scientists from experience with Earth pilots and spacemen.

You're still thinking Grounder style. You won't think the Martian way."

"A Martian may be a Martian, but he's still a man."

"But how can you be so blind? How many times have you fellows been out for over six months without a break?"

Rioz said, "That's different."

"Because you're Martians? Because you're professional Scavengers?"

"No. Because we're not on a flight. We can put back for Mars any time we want to."

"But you *don't* want to. That's my point. Earthmen have tremendous ships with libraries of films, with a crew of fifteen plus passengers. Still, they can only stay out six months maximum. Martian Scavengers have a two-room ship with only one partner. But we can stick it out more than six months."

Dora said, "I suppose you want to stay in a ship for a year and go to Saturn."

"Why not, Dora?" said Long. "We can do it. Don't you see we can? Earthmen can't. They've got a real world. They've got open sky and fresh food, all the air and water they want. Getting into a ship is a terrible change for them. More than six months is too much for them for that very reason. Martians are different. We've been living on a ship our entire lives.

"That's all Mars is—a ship. It's just a big ship forty-five hundred miles across with one tiny room in it occupied by fifty thousand people. It's closed in like a ship. We breathe packaged air and drink packaged water, which we repurify over and over. We eat the same food rations we eat aboard ship. When we get into a ship, it's the same thing we've known all our lives. We can stand it for a lot more than a year if we have to."

Dora said, "Dick, too?"

"We all can."

"Well, Dick can't. It's all very well for you, Ted Long, and this shell stealer here, this Mario, to talk about jaunting off for a year. You're not married. Dick is. He has a wife and he has a child and that's enough for him. He can just get a regular job right here on Mars. Why, my goodness, suppose you go to Saturn and find there's no water there. How'll you get back? Even if you had water left, you'd be out of food. It's the most ridiculous thing I ever heard of."

"No. Now listen," said Long tightly. "I've thought this thing out. I've talked to Commissioner Sankov and he'll help. But we've got to have ships and men. I can't get them. The men won't listen to me.

I'm green. You two are known and respected. You're veterans. If you back me, even if you don't go yourselves, if you'll just help me sell this thing to the rest, get volunteers—"

"First," said Rioz grumpily, "you'll have to do a lot more explaining. Once we get to Saturn, where's the water?"

"That's the beauty of it," said Long. "That's why it's got to be Saturn. The water there is just floating around in space for the taking."

5

When Hamish Sankov had come to Mars, there was no such thing as a native Martian. Now there were two-hundred-odd babies whose grandfathers had been born on Mars—native in the third generation.

When he had come as a boy in his teens, Mars had been scarcely more than a huddle of grounded spaceships connected by sealed underground tunnels. Through the years, he had seen buildings grow and burrow widely, thrusting blunt snouts up into the thin, unbreathable atmosphere. He had seen huge storage depots spring up into which spaceships and their loads could be swallowed whole. He had seen the mines grow from nothing to a huge gouge in the Martian crust, while the population of Mars grew from fifty to fifty thousand.

It made him feel old, these long memories—they and the even dimmer memories induced by the presence of this Earthman before him. His visitor brought up those long-forgotten scraps of thought about a soft-warm world that was as kind and gentle to mankind as the mother's womb.

The Earthman seemed fresh from that womb. Not very tall, not very lean; in fact, distinctly plump. Dark hair with a neat little wave in it, a neat little mustache, and neatly scrubbed skin. His clothing was right in style and as fresh and neatly turned as plastek could be.

Sankov's own clothes were of Martian manufacture, serviceable and clean, but many years behind the times. His face was craggy and lined, his hair was pure white, and his Adam's apple wobbled when he talked.

The Earthman was Myron Digby, member of Earth's General Assembly. Sankov was Martian Commissioner.

Sankov said, "This all hits us hard, Assemblyman."

"It's hit most of us hard, too, Commissioner."

"Uh-huh. Can't honestly say then that I can make it out. Of course, you understand, I don't make out that I can understand Earth ways, for all that I was born there. Mars is a hard place to live, Assemblyman, and you have to understand that. It takes a lot of shipping space just to bring us food, water, and raw materials so we can live. There's not much room left for books and news films. Even video programs can't reach Mars, except for about a month when Earth is in conjunction, and even then nobody has much time to listen.

"My office gets a weekly summary film from Planetary Press. Generally, I don't have time to pay attention to it. Maybe you'd call us provincial, and you'd be right. When something like this happens, all we can do is kind of helplessly look at each other."

Digby said slowly, "You can't mean that your people on Mars haven't heard of Hilder's anti-Waster campaign."

"No, can't exactly say that. There's a young Scavenger, son of a good friend of mine who died in space"—Sankov scratched the side of his neck doubtfully—"who makes a hobby out of reading up on Earth history and things like that. He catches video broadcasts when he's out in space and he listened to this man Hilder. Near as I can make out, that was the first talk Hilder made about Wasters.

"The young fellow came to me with that. Naturally, I didn't take him very serious. I kept an eye on the Planetary Press films for a while after that, but there wasn't much mention of Hilder and what there was made him out to look pretty funny."

"Yes, Commissioner," said Digby, "it all seemed quite a joke when it started."

Sankov stretched out a pair of long legs to one side of his desk and crossed them at the ankles. "Seems to me it's still pretty much of a joke. What's his argument? We're using up water. Has he tried looking at some figures? I got them all here. Had them brought to me when this committee arrived.

"Seems that Earth has four hundred million cubic miles of water in its oceans and each cubic mile weighs four and a half billion tons. That's a lot of water. Now we use some of that heap in space flight. Most of the thrust is inside Earth's gravitational field, and that means the water thrown out finds its way back to the oceans. Hilder doesn't figure that in. When he says a million tons of water is used up per flight, he's a liar. It's less than a hundred thousand tons.

"Suppose, now, we have fifty thousand flights a year. We don't, of course; not even fifteen hundred. But let's say there are fifty thousand. I figure there's going to be considerable expansion as time goes on. With fifty thousand flights, one cubic mile of water would be lost to space each year. That means that in a million years, Earth would lose *one quarter of 1 per cent* of its total water supply!"

Digby spread his hands, palms upward, and let them drop. "Commissioner, Interplanetary Alloys has used figures like that in their campaign against Hilder, but you can't fight a tremendous, emotion-filled drive with cold mathematics. This man Hilder has invented a name, 'Wasters'. Slowly he has built this name up into a gigantic conspiracy; a gang of brutal, profit-seeking wretches raping Earth for their own immediate benefit.

"He has accused the government of being riddled with them, the Assembly of being dominated by them, the press of being owned by them. None of this, unfortunately, seems ridiculous to the average man. He knows all too well what selfish men can do to Earth's resources. He knows what happened to Earth's oil during the Time of Troubles, for instance, and the way topsoil was ruined.

"When a farmer experiences a drought, he doesn't care that the amount of water lost in space flight isn't a droplet in a fog as far as Earth's over-all water supply is concerned. Hilder has given him something to blame and that's the strongest possible consolation for disaster. He isn't going to give that up for a diet of figures."

Sankov said, "That's where I get puzzled. Maybe it's because I don't know how things work on Earth, but it seems to me that there aren't just droughty farmers there. As near as I could make out from the news summaries, these Hilder people are a minority. Why is it Earth goes along with a few farmers and some crackpots that egg them on?"

"Because, Commissioner, there are such things as worried human beings. The steel industry sees that an era of space flight will stress increasingly the light, nonferrous alloys. The various miners' unions worry about extraterrestrial competition. Any Earthman who can't get aluminum to build a prefab is certain that it is because the aluminum is going to Mars. I know a professor of archaeology who's an anti-Waster because he can't get a government grant to cover his excavations. He's convinced that all government money is going into rocketry research and space medicine and he resents it."

Sankov said, "That doesn't sound like Earth people are much different from us here on Mars. But what about the General Assembly? Why do they have to go along with Hilder?"

Digby smiled sourly. "Politics isn't pleasant to explain. Hilder introduced this bill to set up a committee to investigate waste in space flight. Maybe three-fourths or more of the General Assembly was against such an investigation as an intolerable and useless extension of bureaucracy—which it is. But then how could any legislator be against a mere investigation of waste? It would sound as though he had something to fear or to conceal. It would sound as though he were himself profiting from waste. Hilder is not in the least afraid of making such accusations, and whether true or not, they would be a powerful factor with the voters in the next election. The bill passed.

"And then there came the question of appointing the members of the committee. Those who were against Hilder shied away from membership, which would have meant decisions that would be continually embarrassing. Remaining on the side lines would make that one that much less a target for Hilder. The result is that I am the only member of the committee who is outspokenly anti-Hilder and it may cost me re-election."

Sankov said, "I'd be sorry to hear that, Assemblyman. It looks as though Mars doesn't have as many friends as we thought we had. We wouldn't like to lose one. But if Hilder wins out, what's he after, anyway?"

"I should think," said Digby, "that that is obvious. He wants to be the next Global Co-ordinator."

"Think he'll make it?"

"If nothing happens to stop him, he will."

"And then what? Will he drop this Waster campaign then?"

"I can't say. I don't know if he's laid his plans past the Co-ordinacy. Still, if you want my guess, he couldn't abandon the campaign and maintain his popularity. It's gotten out of hand."

Sankov scratched the side of his neck. "All right. In that case, I'll ask you for some advice. What can we folks on Mars do? You know Earth. You know the situation. We don't. Tell us what to do."

Digby rose and stepped to the window. He looked out upon the low domes of other buildings; red, rocky, completely desolate plain in between; a purple sky and a shrunken sun.

He said, without turning, "Do you people really like it on Mars?"

Sankov smiled. "Most of us don't exactly know any other world, Assemblyman. Seems to me Earth would be something queer and uncomfortable to them."

"But wouldn't Martians get used to it? Earth isn't hard to take after this. Wouldn't your people learn to enjoy the privilege of breathing air under an open sky? You once lived on Earth. You remember what it was like."

"I sort of remember. Still, it doesn't seem to be easy to explain. Earth is just there. It fits people and people fit it. People take Earth the way they find it. Mars is different. It's sort of raw and doesn't fit people. People got to make something out of it. They got to *build* a world, and not take what they find. Mars isn't much yet, but we're building, and when we're finished, we're going to have just what we like. It's sort of a great feeling to know you're building a world. Earth would be kind of unexciting after that."

The Assemblyman said, "Surely the ordinary Martian isn't such a philosopher that he's content to live this terribly hard life for the sake of a future that must be hundreds of generations away."

"No-o, not just like that." Sankov put his right ankle on his left knee and cradled it as he spoke. "Like I said, Martians are a lot like Earthmen, which means they're sort of human beings, and human beings don't go in for philosophy much. Just the same, there's something to living in a growing world, whether you think about it much or not.

"My father used to send me letters when I first came to Mars. He was an accountant and he just sort of stayed an accountant. Earth wasn't much different when he died from what it was when he was born. He didn't see anything happen. Every day was like every other day, and living was just a way of passing time until he died.

"On Mars, it's different. Every day there's something new—the city's bigger, the ventilation system gets another kick, the water lines from the poles get slicked up. Right now, we're planning to set up a news-film association of our own. We're going to call it Mars Press. If you haven't lived when things are growing all about you, you'll never understand how wonderful it feels.

"No, Assemblyman, Mars is hard and tough and Earth is a lot more comfortable, but seems to me if you take our boys to Earth, they'll be unhappy. They probably wouldn't be able to figure out why, most of them, but they'd feel lost; lost and useless. Seems to me lots of them would never make the adjustment."

Digby turned away from the window and the smooth, pink skin of his forehead was creased into a frown. "In that case, Commissioner, I am sorry for you. For all of you."

"Why?"

"Because I don't think there's anything your people on Mars can do. Or the people on the Moon or Venus. It won't happen now; maybe it won't happen for a year or two, or even for five years. But pretty soon you'll all have to come back to Earth, unless—"

Sankov's white eyebrows bent low over his eyes. "Well?"

"Unless you can find another source of water besides the planet Earth."

Sankov shook his head. "Don't seem likely, does it?"

"Not very."

"And except for that, seems to you there's no chance?"

"None at all."

Digby said that and left, and Sankov stared for a long time at nothing before he punched a combination of the local communiline.

After a while, Ted Long looked out at him.

Sankov said, "You were right, son. There's nothing they can do. Even the ones that mean well see no way out. How did you know?"

"Commissioner," said Long, "when you've read all you can about the Time of Troubles, particularly about the twentieth century, nothing political can come as a real surprise."

"Well, maybe. Anyway, son, Assemblyman Digby is sorry for us, quite a piece sorry, you might say, but that's all. He says we'll have to leave Mars—or else get water somewhere else. Only he thinks that we can't get water somewhere else."

"You know we can, don't you, Commissioner?"

"I know we *might*, son. It's a terrible risk."

"If I find enough volunteers, the risk is our business."

"How is it going?"

"Not bad. Some of the boys are on my side right now. I talked Mario Rioz into it, for instance, and you know he's one of the best."

"That's just it—the volunteers will be the best men we have. I hate to allow it."

"If we get back, it will be worth it."

"If! It's a big word, son."

"And a big thing we're trying to do."

"Well, I gave my word that if there was no help on Earth, I'll see that the Phobos water hole lets you have all the water you'll need. Good luck."

6

Half a million miles above Saturn, Mario Rioz was cradled on nothing and sleep was delicious. He came out of it slowly and for a while, alone in his suit, he countd the stars and traced lines from one to another.

At first, as the weeks flew past, it was scavenging all over again, except for the gnawing feeling that every minute meant an additional number of thousands of miles away from all humanity. That made it worse.

They had aimed high to pass out of the ecliptic while moving through the Asteroid Belt. That had used up water and had probably been unnecessary. Although tens of thousands of worldlets look as thick as vermin in two-dimensional projection upon a photographic plate, they are nevertheless scattered so thinly through the quadrillions of cubic miles that make up their conglomerate orbit that only the most ridiculous of coincidences would have brought about a collision.

Still, they passed over the Belt and someone calculated the chances of collision with a fragment of matter large enough to do damage. The value was so low, so impossibly low, that it was perhaps inevitable that the notion of the "space-float" should occur to someone.

The days were long and many, space was empty, only one man was needed at the controls at any one time. The thought was a natural.

First, it was a particularly daring one who ventured out for fifteen minutes or so. Then another who tried half an hour. Eventually, before the asteroids were entirely behind, each ship regularly had its off-watch member suspended in space at the end of a cable.

It was easy enough. The cable, one of those intended for operations at the conclusion of their journey, was magnetically attached at both ends, one to the space suit to start with. Then you clambered out the lock onto the ship's hull and attached the other end there. You paused awhile, clinging to the metal skin by the electromagnets in your boots. Then you neutralized those and made the slightest muscular effort.

Slowly, ever so slowly, you lifted from the ship and even more slowly the ship's larger mass moved an equivalently shorter distance downward. You floated incredibly, weightlessly, in solid, speckled black. When the ship had moved far enough away from you, your gauntleted hand, which kept touch upon the cable, tightened its grip slightly. Too tightly, and you would begin moving back toward the ship and it toward you. Just tightly enough, and friction would halt you. Because your motion was equivalent to that of the ship, it seemed as motionless below you as though it had been painted against an impossible background while the cable between you hung in coils that had no reason to straighten out.

It was a half-ship to your eye. One half was lit by the light of the feeble Sun, which was still too bright to look at directly without the heavy protection of the polarized space-suit visor. The other half was black on black, invisible.

Space closed in and it was like sleep. Your suit was warm, it renewed its air automatically, it had food and drink in special containers from which it could be sucked with a minimal motion of the head, it took care of wastes appropriately. Most of all, more than anything else, there was the delightful euphoria of weightlessness.

You never felt so well in your life. The days stopped being too long, they weren't long enough, and there weren't enough of them.

They had passed Jupiter's orbit at a spot some 30 degrees from its then position. For months, it was the brightest object in the sky, always excepting the glowing white pea that was the Sun. At its brightest, some of the Scavengers insisted they could make out Jupiter as a tiny sphere, one side squashed out of true by the night shadow.

Then over a period of additional months it faded, while another dot of light grew until it was brighter than Jupiter. It was Saturn, first as a dot of brilliance, then as an oval, glowing splotch.

("Why oval?" someone asked, and after a while, someone else said, "The rings, of course," and it was obvious.)

Everyone space-floated at all possible times toward the end, watching Saturn incessantly.

("Hey, you jerk, come on back in, damn it. You're on duty." "Who's on duty? I've got fifteen minutes more by my watch." "You set your watch back. Besides, I gave you twenty minutes yesterday." "You wouldn't give two minutes to your grandmother." "Come on in, damn it, or I'm coming out anyway." "All right, I'm coming. Holy howlers, what a racket over a lousy minute." But no quarrel could possibly be serious, not in space. It felt too good.)

Saturn grew until at last it rivaled and then surpassed the Sun. The rings, set at a broad angle to their trajectory of approach, swept grandly about the planet, only a small portion being eclipsed. Then, as they approached, the span of the rings grew still wider, yet narrower as the angle approach constantly decreased.

The larger moons showed up in the surrounding sky like serene fireflies.

Mario Rioz was glad he was awake so that he could watch again.

Saturn filled half the sky, streaked with orange, the night shadow cutting it fuzzily nearly one quarter of the way in from the right. Two round little dots in the brightness were shadows of the moons. To the left and behind him (he could look over his left shoulder to see, and as he did so, the rest of his body inched slightly to the right to converse angular momentum) was the white diamond of the Sun.

Most of all he liked to watch the rings. At the left, they emerged from behind Saturn, a tight, bright triple band of orange light. At the right, their beginnings were hidden in the night shadow, but showed up closer and broader. They widened as they came, like the flare of a horn, growing hazier as they approached, until, while the eye followed them, they seemed to fill the sky and lose themselves.

From the position of the Scavenger fleet just inside the outer rim of the outermost ring, the rings broke up and assumed their true identity as a phenomenal cluster of solid fragments rather than the tight, solid band of light they seemed.

Below him, or rather in the direction his feet pointed, some twenty miles away, was one of the ring fragments. It looked like a large, irregular splotch, marring the symmetry of space, three quarters in brightness and the night shadow cutting it like a knife. Other fragments were farther off, sparkling like star dust, dimmer and thicker, until, as you followed them down, they became rings once more.

The fragments were motionless, but that was only because the ships had taken up an orbit about Saturn equivalent to that of the outer edge of the rings.

The day before, Rioz reflected, he had been on that nearest fragment, working along with more than a score of others to mold it into the desired shape. Tomorrow he would be at it again.

Today—today he was space-floating.

"Mario?" The voice that broke upon his earphones was questioning.

Momentarily Rioz was flooded with annoyance. Damn it, he wasn't in the mood for company.

"Speaking," he said.

"I thought I had your ship spotted. How are you?"

"Fine. That you, Ted?"

"That's right," said Long.

"Anything wrong on the fragment?"

"Nothing. I'm out here floating."

"You?"

"It gets me, too, occasionally. Beautiful, isn't it?"

"Nice," agreed Rioz.

"You know, I've read Earth books—"

"Grounder books, you mean." Rioz yawned and found it difficult under the circumstances to use the expression with the proper amount of resentment.

"—and sometimes I read descriptions of people lying on grass," continued Long. "You know that green stuff like thin, long pieces of paper they have all over the ground down there, and they look up at the blue sky with clouds in it. Did you ever see any films of that?"

"Sure. It didn't attract me. It looked cold."

"I suppose it isn't, though. After all, Earth is quite close to the Sun, and they say their atmosphere is thick enough to hold the heat. I must admit that personally I would hate to be caught under open sky with nothing on but clothes. Still, I imagine they like it."

"Grounders are nuts!"

"They talk about the trees, big brown stalks, and the winds, air movements, you know."

"You mean drafts. They can keep that, too."

"It doesn't matter. The point is they describe it beautifully, almost passionately. Many times I've wondered, 'What's it really like? Will I ever feel it or is this something only Earthmen can possibly feel?' I've felt so often that I was missing something vital. Now I know what it must be like. It's this. Complete peace in the middle of a beauty-drenched universe."

Rioz said, "They wouldn't like it. The Grounders, I mean. They're so used to their own lousy little world they wouldn't appreciate what it's like to float and look down on Saturn." He flipped his body slightly and began swaying back and forth about his center of mass, slowly, soothingly.

Long said, "Yes, I think so too. They're slaves to their planet. Even if they come to Mars, it will only be their children that are free. There'll be starships someday; great, huge things that can carry thousands of people and maintain their self-contained equilibrium for decades, maybe centuries. Mankind will spread through the whole Galaxy. But people will have to live their lives out on shipboard until new methods of inter-stellar travel are developed, so it will be Martians, not planet-bound Earthmen, who will colonize the Universe. That's inevitable. It's got to be. It's the Martian way."

But Rioz made no answer. He had dropped off to sleep again, rocking and swaying gently, half a million miles above Saturn.

7

The work shift of the ring fragment was the tail of the coin. The weightlessness, peace, and privacy of the space-float gave place to something that had neither peace nor privacy. Even the weightlessness, which continued, became more a purgatory than a paradise under the new conditions.

Try to manipulate an ordinarily non-portable heat projector. It could be lifted despite the fact that it was six feet high and wide and almost solid metal, since it weighed only a fraction of an ounce. But its inertia was exactly what it had always been, which meant that if it wasn't moved into position very slowly, it would just keep on going, taking you with it. Then you would have to hike the pseudo-grav field of your suit and come down with a jar.

Keralski had hiked the field a little too high and he came down a little too roughly, with the projector coming down with him at a dangerous angle. His crushed ankle had been the first casualty of the expedition.

Rioz was swearing fluently and nearly continuously. He continued to have the impulse to drag the back of his hand across his forehead in order to wipe away the accumulating sweat. The few times that he had succumbed to the impulse, metal had met silicone with a clash that rang loudly inside his suit, but served no useful purpose. The desiccators within the suit were sucking at maximum and, of course, recovering the water and restoring ion-exchanged liquid, containing a careful proportion of salt, into the appropriate receptacle.

Rioz yelled, "Damn it, Dick, wait till I give the word, will you?"

And Swenson's voice rang in his ears, "Well, how long am I supposed to sit here?"

"Till I say," replied Rioz.

He strengthened pseudo-grav and lifted the projector a bit. He released pseudo-grav, insuring that the projector would stay in place for minutes even if he withdrew support altogether. He kicked the cable out of the way (it stretched beyond the close "horizon" to a power source that was out of sight) and touched the release.

The material of which the fragment was composed bubbled and vanished under its touch. A section of the lip of the tremendous cavity he had already carved into its substance melted away and a roughness in its contour had disappeared.

"Try it now," called Rioz.

Swenson was in the ship that was hovering nearly over Rioz's head.

Swenson called, "All clear?"

"I told you to go ahead."

It was a feeble flicker of steam that issued from one of the ship's forward vents. The ship drifted down toward the ring fragment. Another flicker adjusted a tendency to drift sidewise. It came down straight.

A third flicker to the rear slowed it to a feather rate.

Rioz watched tensely. "Keep her coming. You'll make it. You'll make it."

The rear of the ship entered the hole, nearly filling it. The bellying walls came closer and closer to its rim. There was a grinding vibration as the ship's motion halted.

It was Swenson's turn to curse. "It doesn't fit," he said.

Rioz threw the projector groundward in a passion and went flailing up into space. The projector kicked up a white crystalline dust all about it, and when Rioz came down under pseudo-grav, he did the same.

He said, "You went in on the bias, you dumb Grounder."

"I hit it level, you dirt-eating farmer."

Backward-pointing side jets of the ship were blasting more strongly than before, and Rioz hopped to get out of the way.

The ship scraped up from the pit, then shot into space half a mile before forward jets could bring it to a halt.

Swenson said tensely, "We'll spring half a dozen plates if we do this once again. Get it right, will you?"

"I'll get it right. Don't worry about it. Just you come in right."

Rioz jumped upward and allowed himself to climb three hundred yards to get an over-all look at the cavity. The gouge marks of the ship were plain enough. They were concentrated at one point halfway down the pit. He would get that.

It began to melt outward under the blaze of the projector.

Half an hour later the ship snuggled neatly into its cavity, and Swenson, wearing his space suit, emerged to join Rioz.

Swenson said, "If you want to step in and climb out of the suit, I'll take care of the icing."

"It's all right," said Rioz. "I'd just as soon sit here and watch Saturn."

He sat down at the lip of the pit. There was a six-foot gap between it and the ship. In some places about the circle, it was two feet; in a few places, even merely a matter of inches. You couldn't expect a better fit out of handwork. The final adjustment would be made by steaming ice gently and letting it freeze into the cavity between the lip and the ship.

Saturn moved visibly across the sky, its vast bulk inching below the horizon.

Rioz said, "How many ships are left to put in place?"

Swenson said, "Last I heard, it was eleven. We're in now, so that means only ten. Seven of the ones that are placed are iced in. Two or three are dismantled."

"We're coming along fine."

"There's plenty to do yet. Don't forget the main jets at the other end. And the cables and the power lines. Sometimes I wonder if we'll make it. On the way out, it didn't bother me so much, but just now I was sitting at the controls and I was saying, 'We won't make it. We'll sit out here and starve and die with nothing but Saturn over us.' It makes me feel—"

He didn't explain how it made him feel. He just sat there.

Rioz said, "You think too damn much."

"It's different with you," said Swenson. "I keep thinking of Pete – and Dora."

"What for? She said you could go, didn't she? The Commissioner gave her that talk on patriotism and how you'd be a hero and set for life once you got back, and she said you could go. You didn't sneak out the way Adams did."

"Adams is different. That wife of his should have been shot when she was born. Some women can make hell for a guy, can't they? She didn't want him to go—but she'd probably rather he didn't come back if she can get his settlement pay."

"What's your kick, then? Dora wants you back, doesn't she?"

Swenson sighed. "I never treated her right."

"You turned over your pay, it seems to me. I wouldn't do that for any woman. Money for value received, not a cent more."

"Money isn't it. I get to thinking out here. A woman likes company. A kid needs his father. What am I doing 'way out here?"

"Getting set to go home."

"Ah-h, you don't understand."

8

Ted Long wandered over the ridged surface of the ring fragment with his spirits as icy as the ground he walked on. It had all seemed perfectly logical back on Mars, but that was Mars. He had worked it out carefully in his mind in perfectly reasonable steps. He could still remember exactly how it went.

It didn't take a ton of water to move a ton of ship. It was not mass equals mass, but mass times velocity equals mass times velocity. It didn't matter, in other words, whether you shot out a ton of water at a mile a second or a hundred pounds of water at twenty miles a second. You got the same final velocity out of the ship.

That meant the jet nozzles had to be made narrower and the steam hotter. But then drawbacks appeared. The narrower the nozzle, the more energy was lost in friction and turbulence. The hotter the steam, the more refractory the nozzle had to be and the shorter its life. The limit in that direction was quickly reached.

Then, since a given weight of water could move considerably more than its own weight under the narrow-nozzle conditions, it paid to be big. The bigger the water-storage space, the larger the size of the actual travel-head, even in proportion. So they started to make liners heavier and bigger. But then the larger the shell, the heavier the bracings, the more difficult the weldings, the more exacting the engineering requirements. At the moment, the limit in that direction had been reached also.

And then he had put his finger on what had seemed to him to be the basic flaw—the original unswervable conception that the fuel had to be placed *inside* the ship; the metal had to be built to encircle a million tons of water.

Why? Water did not have to be water. It could be ice, and ice could be shaped. Holes could be melted into it. Travel-heads and jets could be fitted into it. Cables could hold travel-heads and jets stiffly together under the influence of magnetic field-force grips.

Long felt the trembling of the ground he walked on. He was at the head of the fragment. A dozen ships were blasting in and out of sheaths carved in its substance, and the fragment shuddered under the continuing impact.

The ice didn't have to be quarried. It existed in proper chunks in the rings of Saturn. That's all the rings were—pieces of nearly pure ice, circling Saturn. So spectroscopy stated and so it had turned out to be. He was standing on one such piece now, over two miles long, nearly one mile thick. It was almost half a billion tons of water, all in one piece, and he was standing on it.

But now he was face to face with the realities of life. He had never told the men just how quickly he had expected to set up the fragment as a ship, but in his heart, he had imagined it would be two days. It was a week now and he didn't dare to estimate the remaining time. He no longer even had any confidence that the task was a possible one. Would they be able to control jets with enough delicacy through leads slung across two miles of ice to manipulate out of Saturn's dragging gravity?

Drinking water was low, though they could always distill more out of the ice. Still, the food stores were not in a good way either.

He paused, looked up into the sky, eyes straining. *Was* the object growing larger? He ought to measure its distance. Actually, he lacked the spirit to add that trouble to the others. His mind slid back to greater immediacies.

Morale, at least, was high. The men seemed to enjoy being out Saturn-way. They were the first humans to penetrate this far, the first to pass the asteroids, the first to see Jupiter like a glowing pebble to the naked eye, the first to see Saturn—like that.

He didn't think fifty practical, case-hardened, shell-snatching Scavengers would take time to feel that sort of emotion. But they did. And they were proud.

Two men and a half-buried ship slid up the moving horizon as he walked.

He called crisply, "Hello, there!"

Rioz answered, "That you, Ted?"

"You bet. Is that Dick with you?"

"Sure. Come on, sit down. We were just getting ready to ice in and we were looking for an excuse to delay."

"I'm not," said Swenson promptly. "When will we be leaving, Ted?"

"As soon as we get through. That's no answer, is it?"

Swenson said dispiritedly, "I suppose there isn't any other answer."

Long looked up, staring at the irregular bright splotch in the sky.

Rioz followed his glance. "What's the matter?"

For a moment, Long did not reply. The sky was black otherwise and the ring fragments were an orange dust against it. Saturn was more than three-fourths below the horizon and the rings were going with it. Half a mile away a ship bounded past the icy rim of the planetoid into the sky, was orange-lit by Saturn-light, and sank down again.

The ground trembled gently.

Rioz said, "Something bothering you about the Shadow?"

They called it that. It was the nearest fragment of the rings, quite close considering that they were at the outer rim of the rings, where the pieces spread themselves relatively thin. It was perhaps twenty miles off, a jagged mountain, its shape clearly visible.

"How does it look to you?" asked Long.

Rioz shrugged. "Okay, I guess. I don't see anything wrong."

"Doesn't it seem to be getting larger?"

"Why should it?"

"Well, doesn't it?" Long insisted.

Rioz and Swenson stared at it thoughtfully.

"It does look bigger," said Swenson.

"You're just putting the notion into our minds," Rioz argued. "If it were getting bigger, it would be coming closer."

"What's impossible about that?"

"These things are on stable orbits."

"They were when we came here," said Long. "There, did you feel that?"

The ground had trembled again.

Long said, "We've been blasting this thing for a week now. First, twenty-five ships landed on it, which changed its momentum right there. Not much, of course. Then we've been melting parts of it away and our ships have been blasting in and out of it—all at one end, too. In a week, we may have changed its orbit just a bit. The two fragments, this one and the Shadow, might be converging."

"It's got plenty of room to miss us in." Rioz watched it thoughtfully. "Besides, if we can't even tell for sure that it's getting bigger, how quickly can it be moving? Relative to us, I mean."

"It doesn't have to be moving quickly. Its momentum is as large as ours, so that, however gently it hits, we'll be nudged completely out of our orbit, maybe in toward Saturn, where we don't want to go. As a matter of fact, ice has a very low tensile strength, so that both planetoids might break up into gravel."

Swenson rose to his feet. "Damn it, if I can tell how a shell is moving a thousand miles away, I can tell what a mountain is doing twenty miles away." He turned toward the ship.

Long didn't stop him.

Rioz said, "There's a nervous guy."

The neighboring planetoid rose to zenith, passed overhead, began sinking. Twenty minutes later, the horizon opposite that portion behind which Saturn had disappeared burst into orange flame as its bulk began lifting again.

Rioz called into his radio, "Hey, Dick, are you dead in there?"

"I'm checking," came the muffled response.

"Is it moving?" asked Long.

"Yes."

"Toward us?"

There was a pause. Swenson's voice was a sick one. "On the nose, Ted. Intersection of orbits will take place in three days."

"You're crazy!" yelled Rioz.

"I checked four times," said Swenson.

Long thought blankly, What do we do now?

9

Some of the men were having trouble with the cables. They had to be laid precisely; their geometry had to be very nearly perfect for the magnetic field to attain maximum strength. In space, or even in air, it wouldn't have mattered. The cables would have lined up automatically once the juice went on.

Here it was different. A gouge had to be plowed along the planetoid's surface and into it the cable had to be laid. If it were not lined up within a few minutes of arc of the calculated direction, a torque would be applied to the entire planetoid, with consequent loss of energy, none of which could be spared. The gouges then had to be redriven, the cables shifted and iced into the new positions.

The men plodded wearily through the routine.

And then the word reached them:

"All hands to the jets!"

Scavengers could not be said to be the type that took kindly to discipline. It was a grumbling, growling, muttering group that set about disassembling the jets of the ships that yet remained intact, carrying them to the tail end of the planetoid, grubbing them into position, and stringing the leads along the surface.

It was almost twenty-four hours before one of them looked into the sky and said, "Holy jeepers!" followed by something less printable.

His neighbor looked and said, "I'll be damned!"

Once they noticed, all did. It became the most astonishing fact in the Universe.

"Look at the Shadow!"

It was spreading across the sky like an infected wound. Men looked at it, found it had doubled its size, wondered why they hadn't noticed that sooner.

Work came to a virtual halt. They besieged Ted Long.

He said, "We can't leave. We don't have the fuel to see us back to Mars and we don't have the equipment to capture another planetoid. So we've got to stay. Now the Shadow is creeping in on us because our blasting has thrown us out of orbit. We've got to change that by continuing the blasting. Since we can't blast the front end any more without endangering the ship we're building, let's try another way."

They went back to work on the jets with a furious energy that received impetus every half hour when the Shadow rose again over the horizon, bigger and more menacing than before.

Long had no assurance that it would work. Even if the jets would respond to the distant controls, even if the supply of water, which depended upon a storage chamber opening directly into the icy body of the planetoid, with built-in heat projectors steaming the propulsive fluid directly into the driving cells, were adequate, there was still no certainty that the body of the planetoid without a magnetic cable sheathing would hold together under the enormously disruptive stresses.

"Ready!" came the signal in Long's receiver.

Long called, "Ready!" and depressed the contact.

The vibration grew about him. The star field in the visiplate trembled.

In the rearview, there was a distant gleaming spume of swiftly moving ice crystals.

"It's blowing!" was the cry.

It kept on blowing. Long dared not stop. For six hours, it blew, hissing, bubbling, steaming into space; the body of the planetoid converted to vapour and hurled away.

The Shadow came closer until men did nothing but stare at the mountain in the sky, surpassing Saturn itself in spectacularity. Its every groove and valley was a plain scar upon its face. But when it passed through the planetoid's orbit, it crossed more than half a mile behind its then position.

The steam jet ceased.

Long bent in his seat and covered his eyes. He hadn't eaten in two days. He could eat now, though. Not another planetoid was close enough to interrupt them, even if it began an approach that very moment.

Back on the planetoid's surface, Swenson said, "All the time I watched that damned rock coming down, I kept saying to myself, 'This can't happen. We can't let it happen.' "

"Hell," said Rioz, "we were all nervous. Did you see Jim Davis? He was green. I was a little jumpy myself."

"That's not it. It wasn't just—dying, you know. I was thinking—I know it's funny, but I can't help it—I was thinking that Dora warned me I'd get myself killed, she'll never let me hear the last of it. Isn't that a crummy sort of attitude at a time like that?"

"Listen," said Rioz, "you wanted to get married, so you got married. Why come to me with your troubles?"

10

The flotilla, welded into a single unit, was returning over its mighty course from Saturn to Mars. Each day it flashed over a length of space it had taken nine days outward.

Ted Long had put the entire crew on emergency. With twenty-five ships embedded in the planetoid taken out of Saturn's rings and unable to move or maneuver independently, the co-ordination of their power sources into unified blasts was a ticklish problem. The jarring that took place on the first day of travel nearly shook them out from under their hair.

That, at least, smoothed itself out as the velocity raced upward under the steady thrust from behind. They passed the one-hundred-thousand-mile-an-hour mark late on the second day, and climbed steadily toward the million-mile mark and beyond.

Long's ship, which formed the needle point of the frozen fleet, was the only one which possessed a five-way view of space. It was an uncomfortable position under the circumstances. Long found himself watching tensely, imagining somehow that the stars would slowly begin to slip backward, to whizz past them, under the influence of the multi-ship's tremendous rate of travel.

They didn't, of course. They remained nailed to the black backdrop, their distance scorning with patient immobility any speed mere man could achieve.

The men complained bitterly after the first few days. It was not only that they were deprived of the space-float. They were burdened by much more than the ordinary pseudo-gravity field of the ships, by the effects of the fierce acceleration under which they were living. Long himself was weary to death of the relentless pressure against hydraulic cushions.

They took to shutting off the jet thrusts one hour out of every four and Long fretted.

It had been just over a year that he had last seen Mars shrinking in an observation window from this ship, which had then been an independent entity. What had happened since then? Was the colony still there?

In something like a growing panic, Long sent out radio pulses toward Mars daily, with the combined power of twenty-five ships behind it. There was no answer. He expected none. Mars and Saturn were on opposite sides of the Sun now, and until he mounted high enough above the ecliptic to get the Sun well beyond the line connecting himself and Mars, solar interference would prevent any signal from getting through.

High above the outer rim of the Asteroid Belt, they reached maximum velocity. With short spurts of power from first one side jet, then another, the huge vessel reversed itself. The composite jet in the rear began its mighty roaring once again, but now the result was deceleration.

They passed a hundred million miles over the Sun, curving down to intersect the orbit of Mars.

A week out of Mars, answering signals were heard for the first time, fragmentary, ether-torn, and incomprehensible, but they were coming from Mars. Earth and Venus were at angles sufficiently different to leave no doubt of that.

Long relaxed. There were still humans on Mars, at any rate.

Two days out of Mars, the signal was strong and clear and Sankov was at the other end.

Sankov said, "Hello, son. It's three in the morning here. Seems like people have no consideration for an old man. Dragged me right out of bed."

"I'm sorry, sir."

"Don't be. They were following orders. I'm afraid to ask, son. Anyone hurt? Maybe dead?"

"No deaths, sir. Not one."

"And—and the water? Any left?"

Long said, with an effort at nonchalance, "Enough."

"In that case, get home as fast as you can. Don't take any chances, of course."

"There's trouble, then."

"Fair to middling. When will you come down?"

"Two days. Can you hold out that long?"

"I'll hold out."

Forty hours later Mars had grown to a ruddy-orange ball that filled the ports and they were in the final planet-landing spiral.

"Slowly," Long said to himself, "slowly." Under these conditions, even the thin atmosphere of Mars could do dreadful damage if they moved through it too quickly.

Since they came in from well above the ecliptic, their spiral passed from north to south. A polar cap shot whitely below them, then the much smaller one of the summer hemisphere, the large one again, the small one, at longer and longer intervals. The planet approached closer, the landscape began to show features.

"Prepare for landing!" called Long.

11

Sankov did his best to look placid, which was difficult considering how closely the boys had shaved their return. But it had worked out well enough.

Until a few days ago, he had no sure knowledge that they had survived. It seemed more likely—inevitable, almost—that they were nothing but frozen corpses somewhere in the trackless stretches from Mars to Saturn, new planetoids that had once been alive.

The Committee had been dickering with him for weeks before the news had come. They had insisted on his signature to the paper for the sake of appearances. It would look like an agreement, voluntarily and mutually arrived at. But Sankov knew well that, given complete obstinacy on his part, they would act unilaterally and be damned with appearances. It seemed fairly certain that Hilder's election was secure now and they would take the chance of arousing a reaction of sympathy for Mars.

So he dragged out the negotiations, dangling before them always the possibility of surrender.

And then he heard from Long and concluded the deal quickly.

The papers had lain before him and he had made a last statement for the benefit of the reporters who were present.

He said, "Total imports of water from Earth are twenty million tons a year. This is declining as we develop our own piping system. If I sign this paper agreeing to an embargo, our industry will be paralyzed, any possibilities of expansion will halt. It looks to me as if that can't be what's in Earth's mind, can it?"

Their eyes met his and held only a hard glitter. Assemblyman Digby had already been replaced and they were unanimous against him.

The Committee Chairman impatiently pointed out, "You have said all this before."

"I know, but right now I'm kind of getting ready to sign and I want it clear in my head. Is Earth set and determined to bring us to an end here?"

"Of course not. Earth is interested in conserving its irreplaceable water supply, nothing else."

"You have one and a half quintillion tons of water on Earth."

The Committee Chairman said, "We cannot spare water."

And Sankov had signed.

That had been the final note he wanted. Earth had one and a half quintillion tons of water and could spare none of it.

Now, a day and a half later, the Committee and the reporters waited in the spaceport dome. Through thick, curving windows, they could see the bare and empty grounds of Mars Spaceport.

The Committee Chairman asked with annoyance, "How much longer do we have to wait? And, if you don't mind, what are we waiting for?"

Sankov said, "Some of our boys have been out in space, out past the asteroids."

The Committee Chairman removed a pair of spectacles and cleaned them with a snowy-white handkerchief. "And they're returning?"

"They are."

The Chairman shrugged, lifted his eyebrows in the direction of the reporters.

In the smaller room adjoining, a knot of women and children clustered about another window. Sankov stepped back a bit to cast a glance toward them. He would much rather have been with them, been part of their excitement and tension. He, like them, had waited over a year now. He, like them, had thought, over and over again, that the men must be dead.

"You see that?" said Sankov, pointing.

"Hey!" cried a reporter. "It's a ship!"

A confused shouting came from the adjoining room.

It wasn't a ship so much as a bright dot obscured by a drifting white cloud. The cloud grew larger and began to have form. It was a double streak against the sky, the lower ends billowing out and upward again. As it dropped still closer, the bright dot at the upper end took on a crudely cylindrical form.

It was rough and craggy, but where the sunlight hit, brilliant high lights bounced back.

The cylinder dropped toward the ground with the ponderous slowness characteristic of space vessels. It hung suspended on those blasting jets and settled down upon the recoil of tons of matter hurling downward like a tired man dropping into his easy chair.

And as it did so, a silence fell upon all within the dome. The women and children in one room, the politicians and reporters in the other remained frozen, heads craned incredulously upward.

The cylinder's landing flanges, extending far below the two rear jets, touched ground and sank into the pebbly morass. And then the ship was motionless and the jet action ceased.

But the silence continued in the dome. It continued for a long time.

Men came clambering down the sides of the immense vessel, inching down, down the two-mile trek to the ground, with spikes on their shoes and ice axes in their hands. They were gnats against the blinding surface.

One of the reporters croaked, "What is it?"

"That," said Sankov calmly, "happens to be a chunk of matter that spent its time scooting around Saturn as part of its rings. Our boys fitted it out with travel-head and jets and ferried it home. It just turns out the fragments in Saturn's rings are made up out of ice."

He spoke into a continuing deathlike silence. "That thing that looks like a spaceship is just a mountain of hard water. If it were standing like that on Earth, it would be melting into a puddle and maybe it would break under its own weight. Mars is colder and has less gravity, so there's no such danger.

"Of course, once we get this thing really organized, we can have water stations on the moons of Saturn and Jupiter and on the asteroids. We can scale in chunks of Saturn's rings and pick them up and send them on at the various stations. Our Scavengers are good at that sort of thing.

"We'll have all the water we need. That one chunk you see is just under a cubic mile—or about what Earth would send us in two hundred years. The boys used quite a bit of it coming back from Saturn. They made it in five weeks, they tell me, and used up about a hundred million tons. But, Lord, that didn't make any dent at all in that mountain. Are you getting all this, boys?"

He turned to the reporters. There was no doubt they were getting it.

He said, "Then get this, too. Earth is worried about its water supply. It only has one and a half quintillion tons. It can't spare us a single ton out of it. Write down that we folks on Mars are worried about Earth and don't want anything to happen to Earth people. Write down that we'll sell water to Earth. Write down that we'll let them have million-ton lots for a reasonable fee. Write down that in ten years, we figure we can sell it in cubic-mile lots. Write down that Earth can quit worrying because Mars can sell it all the water it needs and wants."

The Committee Chairman was past hearing. He was feeling the future rushing in. Dimly he could see the reporters grinning as they wrote furiously.

Grinning.

He could hear the grin become laughter on Earth as Mars turned the tables so neatly on the anti-Wasters. He could hear the laughter thunder from every continent when word of the fiasco spread. And he could see the abyss, deep and black as space, into which would drop forever the political hopes of John Hilder and of every opponent of space flight left on Earth—his own included, of course.

In the adjoining room, Dora Swenson screamed with joy, and Peter, grown two inches, jumped up and down, calling, "Daddy! Daddy!"

Richard Swenson had just stepped off the extremity of the flange and, face showing clearly through the clear silicone of the headpiece, marched toward the dome.

"Did you ever see a guy look so happy?" asked Ted Long. "Maybe there's something in this marriage business."

"Ah, you've just been out in space too long," Rioz said.

SECOND GAME

Charles V. De Vet

and Katherine MacLean

The sign was big, with black letters that read: I'LL BEAT YOU THE SECOND GAME.

I eased myself into a seat behind the play board, straightened the pitchman's cloak about my shoulders, took a final deep breath, let it out—and waited.

A nearby Fair visitor glanced at the sign as he hurried by. His eyes widened with anticipated pleasure and he shifted his gaze to me, weighing me with the glance.

I knew I had him.

The man changed direction and came over to where I sat. "Are you giving any odds?" he asked.

"Ten to one," I answered.

"A dronker." He wrote on a blue slip with a white stylus, dropped it at my elbow, and sat down.

"We play the first game for feel," I said. "Second game pays."

Gradually I let my body relax. Its weight pulled at the muscles of my back and shoulders, and I slouched into a half-slump. I could feel my eyelids droop as I released them, and the corners of my mouth pulled down. I probably appeared tired and melancholy. Or like a man operating in a gravity heavier than was normal for him. Which I was.

I had come to this world called Velda two weeks earlier. My job was to find why its humanlike inhabitants refused all contacts with the Federation.

Earth's colonies had expanded during the last several centuries until they now comprised a loose alliance known as The Ten Thousand Worlds. They were normally peaceful—and wanted peace with Velda. But you cannot talk peace with a people who won't talk back. Worse, they had obliterated the fleet bringing our initial peace overtures. As a final gesture I had been smuggled in—in an attempt to breach that stand-off stubbornness. This booth at their Fair was my best chance—as I saw it—to secure audience with the men in authority. And with luck it would serve a double purpose.

Several Veldians gathered around the booth and watched with interest as my opponent and I chose colors. He took the red; I the black. We arranged our fifty-two pieces on their squares and I nodded to him to make the first move.

He was an anemic oldster with an air of nervous energy, and he played the same way, with intense concentration. By the fourth move I knew he would not win. On each play he had to consult the value board suspended between us before deciding what his next move would be. On a play board with one hundred and sixty-nine squares, each with a different value—in fact one set of values for offense, and another for defense—only a brilliant player could keep them all in mind. But no man without that ability was going to beat me.

I let him win the first game. Deliberately. The "second game counts" gimmick was not only to attract attention, but to give me a chance to test a player's strength—and find his weakness.

At the start of the second game, the oldster moved his front row center pukt three squares forward and one left oblique. I checked it with an end pukt, and waited.

The contest was not going to be exacting enough to hold my complete attention. Already an eidetic portion of my mind—which I always thought of as a small machine, ticking away in one corner of my skull, independent of any control or direction from me—was moving its interest out to the spectators around my booth.

It caught a half-completed gesture of admiration at my last move from a youth directly ahead of me. And with the motion, and the glimpse of the youth's face, something slipped into place in my memory. Some subconscious counting finished itself, and I knew that there had been too many of these youths, with faces like this one, finely boned and smooth, with slender delicate necks and slim hands and movements that were cool and detached. Far too many to be a normal number in a population of adults and children.

As if drawn, my glance went past the forms of the watchers around the booth and plumbed the passing crowd to the figure of a man; a magnificent masculine type of the Veldian race, thick shouldered and strong, thoughtful in motion, yet with something of the swagger of a gladiator, who, as he walked, spoke to the woman who held his arm, leaning toward her cherishingly as if he protected a great prize.

She was wearing a concealing cloak, but her face was beautiful, her hair semi-long, and in spite of the cloak I could see that her body was full-fleshed and almost voluptuously feminine. I had seen few such women on Velda.

Two of the slim, delicately built youths went by arm in arm, walking with a slight defiant sway of bodies, and looked at the couple as they passed, with a pleasure in the way the man's fascinated attention clove to the woman, and looked at the beauty of the woman possessively without lust, and passed by, their heads held higher in pride as if they shared a secret triumph with her. Yet they were strangers.

I had an answer to my counting. The "youths" with the large eyes and smooth delicate heads, with the slim straight asexual bodies, thought of themselves as women. I had not seen them treated with the subdued attraction and conscious avoidance one sex gives another, but by numbers . . . My memory added the number of these "youths" to the numbers of figures and faces that had been obviously female. It totaled to almost half the population I had seen. No matter what the biological explanation, it seemed reasonable that half . . .

I bent my head, to not see the enigma of the boy-woman face watching me, and braced my elbow to steady my hand as I moved. For two weeks I had been on Velda and during the second week I had come out of hiding and passed as a Veldian. It was incredible that I had been operating under a misunderstanding as to which were women, and which men, and not blundered openly. The luck that had saved me had been undeserved.

Opposite me, across the board, the bleach-skinned hand of the oldster was beginning to waver with indecision as each pukt was placed. He was seeing defeat, and not wishing to see it.

In eight more minutes I completed the rout of his forces and closed out the game. In winning I had lost only two pukts. The other's defeat was crushing, but my ruthlessness had been deliberate. I wanted my reputation to spread.

My sign, and the game in progress, by now had attracted a line of challengers, but as the oldster left the line broke and most of them shook their heads and moved back, then crowded around the booth and good-naturedly elbowed their way to positions of better vantage.

I knew then that I had set my lure with an irresistible bait. On a world where the Game was played from earliest childhood—was in fact a vital aspect of their culture—my challenge could not be ignored. I pocketed the loser's blue slip and nodded to the first in line of the four men who still waited to try me.

This second man played a better game than the old one. He had a fine tight-knit offensive, with a good grasp of values, but his weakness showed early in the game when I saw him hesitate before making a simple move in a defensive play. He was not skilled in the strategy of retreat and defense, or not suited to it by temperament. He would be unable to cope with a swift forward press, I decided.

I was right.

Some of the challengers bet more, some less, all lost on the second game. I purchased a nut and fruit confection from a passing food vender and ate it for a sparse lunch while I played through the late afternoon hours.

By the time Velda's distant sun had begun to print long shadows across the Fair grounds, I was certain that word of my booth had spread well.

The crowd about the railing of my stand was larger—but the players were fewer. Sometimes I had a break of several minutes before one made a decision to try his skill. And there were no more challenges from ordinary players. Still the results were the same. None had sufficient adroitness to give me more than a passing contest.

Until Caertin Vlosmin made his appearance.

Vlosmin played a game intended to be impregnably defensive, to remain untouchable until an opponent made a misplay or an overzealous drive, of which he would then take advantage. But his mental prowess was not quite great enough to be certain of a sufficiently concealed or complex weakness in the approach of an adversary, and he would not hazard an attack on an uncertainty. Excess caution was his weakness.

During our play I sensed that the crowd about us was very intent and still. On the outskirts, newcomers inquiring cheerfully were silenced by whispered exclamations.

Though it required all my concentration the game was soon over. I looked at Vlosmin as he rose to his feet, and noted with surprise that a fine spotting of moisture brightened his upper lip. Only then did I recognize the strain and effort he had invested into the attempt to defeat me.

"You are an exceptional craftsman," he said. There was a grave emphasis he put on the "exceptional" which I could not miss, and I saw that his face was whiter.

His formal introduction of himself earlier as Caertin Vlosmin had meant something more than I had realized at the time.

I had just played against, and defeated, one of the Great Players!

The sun set a short time later and floating particles of light-reflecting air-foam drifted out over the Fair grounds. Some way they were held suspended above the ground while air currents tossed them about and intermingled them in the radiance of vari-hued spotlights. The area was still as bright as day, but filled with pale, shifting, shadows that seemed to heighten the byplay of sound and excitement coming from the Fair visitors.

Around my booth all was quiet; the spectators were subdued—as though waiting for the next act in a tense drama. I was very tired now, but I knew by the tenseness I observed around me that I did not have much longer to wait.

By the bubbles' light I watched new spectators take their positions about my booth. And as time went by I saw that some of them did not move on, as my earlier visitors had done.

The weight that rode my stomach muscles grew abruptly heavier. I had set my net with all the audacity of a spider waiting for a fly, yet I knew that when my anticipated victim arrived he would more likely resemble a spider hawk. Still the weight was not caused by fear: It was excitement—the excitement of the larger game about to begin.

I was playing an opponent of recognizably less ability than Vlosmin when I heard a stirring and murmuring in the crowd around my stand. The stirring was punctuated by my opponent rising to his feet.

I glanced up.

The big man who had walked into my booth was neither arrogant nor condescending, yet the confidence in his manner was like an aura of strength. He had a deep reserve of vitality, I noted as I studied him carefully, but it was a leashed, controlled vitality. Like most of the men of the Veldian race he wore a uniform, cut severely plain, and undecorated. No flowing robes or tunics for these men. They were a warrior race, unconcerned with the aesthetic touches of personal dress, and left that strictly to their women.

The newcomer turned to my late opponent. His voice was impressive, controlled. "Please finish your game," he said courteously.

The other shook his head. "The game is already as good as over. My sword is broken. You are welcome to my place."

The tall man turned to me. "If you don't mind?"

"My pleasure," I answered. "Please be seated."

This was it.

My visitor shrugged his close-wrapped cloak back from his shoulders and took the chair opposite me. "I am Kalin Trobt," he said. As if he knew I had been expecting him.

In reply I came near to telling him my correct name. But Robert O. Lang was a name that would have been alien to Velda. Using it would have been as good as a confession. "Claustil Anteer," I said, giving a name I had invented earlier.

We played the first game as children play it, taking each other's pukts as the opportunity presented, making no attempt at finesse. Trobt won, two up. Neither of us had made mention of a wager. There would be more than money involved in this Game.

I noticed, when I glanced up before the second game, that the spectators had been cleared from around the booth. Only the inner, unmoving ring I had observed earlier remained now. They watched calmly—professionally.

Fortunately I had no intention of trying to escape.

During the early part of the second game Trobt and I tested each other carefully, as skilled swordsmen, probing, feinting, and shamming attack, but never actually exposing ourselves. I detected what could have been a slight tendency to gamble in Trobt's game, but there was no concrete situation to confirm it.

My first moves were entirely passive. Alertly passive. If I had judged correctly the character of the big man opposite me, I had only to ignore the bait he offered to draw me out, to disregard his openings and apparent—too apparent—errors, until he became convinced that I was unshakably cautious, and not to be tempted into making the first thrusts. For this was his weakness as I had guessed it: That his was a gambling temperament—that when he saw an opportunity he would strike—without the caution necessary to insure safety.

Pretending to move with timidity, and pausing with great deliberation over even the most obvious plays, I maneuvered only to defend. Each time Trobt shifted to a new position of attack I covered—until finally I detected the use of slightly more arm force than necessary when he moved a pukt. It was the only sign of impatience he gave, but I knew it was there.

Then it was that I left one—thin—opening.

Trobt streaked a pukt through and cut out one of my middle defenders.

Instead of making the obvious counter of taking his piece, I played a pukt far removed from his invading man. He frowned in concentration, lifted his arm—and his hand hung suspended over the board.

Suddenly his eyes widened. His glance swept upward to my face and what he saw there caused his expression to change to one of mingled dismay and astonishment. There was but one move he could make. When he made it his entire left flank would be exposed. He had lost the game.

Abruptly he reached forward, touched his index finger to the tip of my nose, and pressed gently.

After a minute during which neither of us spoke, I said, "You know?"

He nodded. "Yes," he said. "You're a Human."

There was a stir and rustle of motion around me. The ring of spectators had leaned forward a little as they heard his words. I looked up and saw that they were smiling, inspecting me with curiosity and something that could have been called admiration. In the dusk the clearest view was the ring of teeth, gleaming—the view a rabbit might get of a circle of grinning foxes. Foxes might feel friendly toward rabbits, and admire a good big one. Why not?

I suppressed an ineffectual impulse to deny what I was. The time was past for that. "How did you find out?" I asked Trobt.

"Your Game. No one could play like that and not be well known. And now your nose."

"My nose?" I repeated.

"Only one physical difference between a Human and a Veldian is apparent on the surface. The nose cartilage. Yours is split—mine is single." He rose to his feet. "Will you come with me, please?"

It was not a request.

My guards walked singly and in couples, sometimes passing Trobt and myself, sometimes letting us pass them, and sometimes lingering at a booth, like any other walkers, and yet, unobtrusively they held me encircled, always in the center of the group. I had already learned enough of the Veldian personality to realize that this was simply a habit of tact. Tact to prevent an arrest from being conspicuous, so as not to add the gaze of his fellows to whatever punishment would be decided for a culprit's offense. Apparently they considered humiliation too deep a punishment to use indiscriminately.

At the edge of the Fair grounds some of the watchers bunched around me while others went to get the tricars. I stood and looked across the park to The City. That was what it was called, The City, The Citadel, The Hearthplace, the home place where one's family is kept safe, the sanctuary whose walls have never been pierced. All those connotations had been in the name and the use of the name; in the voices of those who spoke it. Sometimes they called it The Hearth, and sometimes The Market, always *The* as if it were the only one.

Though the speakers lived in other places and named them as the homes of their ancestors, most of the Veldians were born here. Their history was colored, I might say even shaped, by their long era of struggle with the dleeth, a four-footed, hairy carnivora, physically little different from the big cats of Earth, but intelligent. They had battled the Veldians in a struggle for survival from the Veldians' earliest memories until a couple of centuries before my visit. Now the last few surviving dleeth had found refuge in the frigid region of the north pole. With their physical superiority they probably would have won the struggle against the Veldians, except that their instincts had been purely predatory, and they had no hands and could not develop technology.

The City had been the one strong point that the dleeth had never been able to breach. It had been held by one of the stronger clans, and there was seldom unity among the tribes, yet any family about to bear a child was given sanctuary within its walls.

The clans were nomads—made so by the aggression of the dleeth—but they always made every effort to reach The City when childbirth was imminent. This explained, at least partly, why even strangers from foreign areas regarded The City as their home place.

I could see the Games Building from where I stood. In the walled city called Hearth it was the highest point. Big and red, it towered above the others, and the city around it rose to it like a wave, its consort of surrounding smaller buildings matched to each other in size and shape in concentric rings. Around each building wound the ramps of elevator runways, harmonious and useful, each of different colored stone, lending variety and warmth. Nowhere was there a clash of either proportion or color. Sometimes I wondered if the Veldians did not build more for the joy of creating symmetry than because of utilitarian need.

I climbed into Trobt's three-wheeled car as it stopped before me, and the minute I settled into the bucket seat and gripped the bracing handles, Trobt spun the car and it dived into the highway and rushed toward the city. The vehicle seemed unstable, being about the width of a motorbike, with side car in front, and having nothing behind except a metal box that must have housed a powerful battery, and a shaft with the rear wheel that did the steering. It was an arrangement that made possible sudden wrenching turns that were battering to any passenger as unused to it as I. To my conditioning it seemed that the Veldians on the highway drove like madmen, the traffic rules were incomprehensible or non-existent, and all drivers seemed determined to drive only in gull-like sweeping lines, giving no obvious change of course for other such cars, brushing by tricars from the opposite direction with an inch or less of clearance.

Apparently the maneuverability of the cars and the skill of the drivers were enough to prevent accidents, and I had to force my totally illogical driver's reflexes to relax and stop tensing against the non-existent peril.

I studied Trobt as he drove, noting the casual way he held the wheel, and the assurance in the set of his shoulders. I tried to form a picture in my mind of the kind of man he was, and just what were the motivations that would move or drive him.

Physically he was a long-faced man, with a smooth muscular symmetry, and an Asiatic cast to his eyes. I was certain that he excelled at whatever job he held. In fact I was prepared to believe that he would excel at anything he tried. He was undoubtedly one of those amazing men for whom the exceptional was mere routine. If he were to be cast in the role of my opponent: be the person in whom the opposition of this race would be actualized—as I now anticipated—I would not have wanted to bet against him.

The big skilled man was silent for several minutes, weaving the tricar with smooth swerves through a three-way tangle at an intersection, but twice he glanced at my expression with evident curiosity. Finally, as a man would state an obvious fact he said, "I presume you know you will be executed."

Trobt's face reflected surprise at the shock he must have read in mine. I had known the risk I would be taking in coming here, of course, and of the very real danger that it might end in my death. But this had come up on me too fast. I had not realized that the affair had progressed to the point where my death was already assured. I had thought that there would be negotiations, consultations, and perhaps ultimatums. But only if they failed did I believe that the repercussions might carry me along to my death.

However, there was the possibility that Trobt was merely testing my courage. I decided on boldness. "No," I said. "I do not expect to be executed."

Trobt raised his eyebrows and slowed, presumably to gain more time to talk. With a sudden decision he swung the tricar from the road into one of the small parks spread at regular intervals along the highway.

"Surely you don't think we would let you live? There's a state of war between Velda and your Ten Thousand Worlds. You admit that you're Human, and obviously you are here to spy. Yet when you're captured, you do not expect to be executed?"

"Was I captured?" I asked, emphasizing the last word.

He pondered on that a moment, but apparently did not come up with an answer that satisfied him. "I presume your question means something," he said.

"If I had wanted to keep my presence here a secret, would I have set up a booth at the Fair and invited inspection?" I asked.

He waved one hand irritably, as though to brush aside a picayune argument. "Obviously you did it to test yourself against us, to draw the great under your eye, and perhaps become a friend, treated as an equal with access to knowledge of our plans and weapons. Certainly! Your tactic drew two members of the Council into your net before it was understood. If we had accepted you as a previously unknown Great, you would have won. You are a gambling man, and you played a gambler's hand. You lost."

Partly he was right.

"My deliberate purpose was to reach you," I said, "or someone else with sufficient authority to listen to what I have to say."

Trobt pulled the vehicle deeper into the park. He watched the cars of our escort settling to rest before and behind us. I detected a slight unease and rigidity in his stillness as he said, "Speak then. I'm listening."

"I've come to negotiate," I told him.

Something like a flash of puzzlement crossed his features before they returned to tighter immobility. Unexpectedly he spoke in *Earthian*, my own language. "Then why did you choose this method? Would it not have been better simply to announce yourself?"

This was the first hint he had given that he might have visited our Worlds before I visited his. Though we had suspected before I came that some of them must have. They probably knew of our existence years before we discovered them.

Ignoring his change of language, I replied, still speaking Veldian, "Would it have been that simple? Or would some minor official, on capturing me, perhaps have had me imprisoned, or tortured to extract information?"

Again the suppressed puzzlement in the shift of position as he looked at me. "They would have treated you as an envoy, representing your Ten Thousand Worlds. You could have spoken to the Council immediately." He spoke in Veldian now.

"I did not know that," I said. "You refused to receive our fleet envoys; why should I expect you to accept me any more readily?"

Trobt started to speak, stopped, and turned in his seat to regard me levelly and steadily, his expression unreadable. "Tell me what you have to say then. I will judge whether or not the Council will listen."

"To begin with—" I looked away from the expressionless eyes, out the windshield, down the vistas of brown short trees that grew between each small park and the next. "Until an exploring party of ours found signs of extensive mining operations on a small metal-rich planet, we knew nothing of your existence. We were not even aware that another race in the galaxy had discovered faster-than-light space travel. But after the first clue we were alert for other signs, and found them. Our discovery of your planet was bound to come. However, we did not expect to be met on our first visit with an attack of such hostility as you displayed."

"When we learned that you had found us," Trobt said, "we sent a message to your Ten Thousand Worlds, warning them that we wanted no contact with you. Yet you sent a fleet of spaceships against us."

I hesitated before answering. "That phrase, 'sent against us,' is hardly the correct one," I said. "The fleet was sent for a diplomatic visit, and was not meant as an aggressive action." I thought, *But obviously the display of force was intended 'diplomatically' to frighten you people into being polite.* In diplomacy the smile, the extended hand—and the big stick visible in the other hand—had obviated many a war, by giving the stranger a chance to choose a hand, in full understanding of the alternative. *We showed our muscle to your little planet—you showed your muscle. And now we are ready to be polite.*

I hoped these people would understand the face-saving ritual of negotiation, the disclaimers of intent, that would enable each side to claim that there had been no war, merely accident.

"We did not at all feel that you were justified in wiping the fleet from space," I said. "But it was probably a legitimate misunderstanding—"

"You had been warned!" Trobt's voice was grim, his expression not inviting of further discussion. I thought I detected a bunching of the muscles in his arms.

For a minute I said nothing, made no gesture. Apparently

this angle of approach was unproductive—and probably explosive. Also, trying to explain and justify the behavior of the Federation politicos could possibly become rather taxing.

"Surely you don't intend to postpone negotiations indefinitely?" I asked tentatively. "One planet cannot conquer the entire Federation."

The bunched muscles of his arms strained until they pulled his shoulders, and his lips whitened with the effort of controlling some savage anger. Apparently my question had impugned his pride.

This, I decided quickly, was not the time to make an enemy. "I apologize if I have insulted you," I said in Earthian. "I do not yet always understand what I am saying, in your language."

He hesitated, made some kind of effort, and shifted to Earthian. "It is not a matter of strength, or weakness," he said, letting his words ride out on his released breath, "but of behavior, courtesy. We would have left you alone, but now it is too late. We will drive your faces into the ground. I am certain that we can, but if we could not, still we would try. To imply that we would not try, from fear, seems to me words to soil the mouth, not worthy of a man speaking to a man. We are converting our ships of commerce to war. Your people will see soon that we will fight."

"It is too late for negotiation?" I asked.

His forehead wrinkled into a frown and he stared at me in an effort of concentration. When he spoke it was with a considered hesitation. "If I make a great effort I can feel that you are sincere, and not speaking to mock or insult. It is strange that beings who look so much like ourselves can"—he rubbed a hand across his eyes—"pause a moment. When I say 'yag loogt'-n'balt' what does it mean to you in Earthish?"

"I must play." I hesitated as he turned one hand palm down, signifying that I was wrong. "I must duel," I said, finding another meaning in the way I had heard the phrase expressed. It was a strong meaning, judging by the tone and inflection the speaker had used. I had mimicked the tone without full understanding. The verb was perhaps stronger than *must*, meaning something inescapable, fated, but I could find no Earthian verb for it. I understood why Trobt dropped his hand to the seat without turning it palm up to signify that I was correct.

"There may be no such thought on the Human worlds," he said resignedly. "I have to explain as to a child or a madman. I cannot explain in Veldian, for it has no word to explain what needs no explanation."

He shifted to Earthian, his controlled voice sounding less controlled when moving with the more fluid inflections of my own tongue. "We said we did not want further contact. Nevertheless you sent the ships—deliberately in disregard of our expressed desire. That was an insult, a deep insult, meaning we have not strength to defend our word, meaning we are so helpless that we can be treated with impoliteness, like prisoners, or infants.

"Now we must show you which of us is helpless, which is the weakling. Since you would not respect our wishes, then in order to be no further insulted we must make of your people a captive or a child in helplessness, so that you will be without power to affront us another time."

"If apologies are in order—"

He interrupted with raised hand, still looking at me very earnestly with forehead wrinkled, thought half turned inward in difficult introspection of his own meaning, as well as a grasping for my viewpoint.

"The insult of the fleet can only be wiped out in the blood of testing—of battle—and the test will not stop until one or the other shows that he is too weak to struggle. There is no other way."

He was demanding total surrender!

I saw it was a subject that could not be debated. The Federation had taken on a bearcat this time!

"I stopped because I wanted to understand you," Trobt resumed. "Because the others will not understand how you could be an envoy—how your Federation could send an envoy—except as an insult. I have seen enough of Human strangeness to be not maddened by the insolence of an emissary coming to us, or by your people expecting us to exchange words when we carry your first insult still unwashed from our face. I can even see how it could perhaps be considered *not* an insult, for I have seen your people living on their planets and they suffered insult from each other without striking, until finally I saw that they did not know when they were insulted, as a deaf man does not know when his name is called."

I listened to the quiet note of his voice, trying to recognize the attitude that made it different from his previous tones—calm and slow and deep. Certainty that what he was saying was important . . . conscious tolerance . . . generosity.

Trobt turned on the tricar's motor and put his hands on the steering shaft. "You are a man worthy of respect," he said, looking down the dark empty road ahead. "I wanted you to understand us. To see the difference between us. So that you will not think us without justice." The car began to move.

"I wanted you to understand why you will die."

I said nothing—having nothing to say. But I began immediately to bring my report up to date, recording the observations during the games, and recording with care this last conversation, with the explanation it carried of the Veldian reactions that had been previously obscure.

I used nerve-twitch code, "typing" on a tape somewhere inside myself the coded record of everything that had passed since the last time I brought the report up to date. The typing was easy, like flexing a finger in code jerks, but I did not know exactly where the recorder was located. It was some form of transparent plastic which would not show up on x-ray. The surgeons had imbedded it in my flesh while I was unconscious, and had implanted a mental block against my noticing which small muscle had been linked into the contrivance for the typing.

If I died before I was able to return to Earth, there were several capsuled chemicals buried at various places in my body, that intermingled, would temporarily convert my body to a battery for a high powered broadcast of the tape report, destroying the tape and my body together. This would go into action only if my temperature fell fifteen degrees below the temperature of life.

I became aware that Kalin Trobt was speaking again, and that I had let my attention wander while recording and taping some subjective material. The code twitches easily became an unconscious accompaniment to memory and thought, and this was the second time I had found myself recording more than necessary.

Trobt watched the dark road, threading among buildings and past darkened vehicles. His voice was thoughtful. "In the early days, Miklas of Danlee, when he had the Ornan family surrounded and outnumbered, wished not to destroy them, for he needed good warriors, and in another circumstance they could have been his friends. Therefore he sent a slave to them with an offer of terms of peace. The Ornan family had the slave skinned while alive, smeared with salt and grease so that he would not bleed, and sent back, tied in a bag of his own skin, with a message of no. The chroniclers agree that since the Ornan family was known to be honorable, Miklas should not have made the offer.

"In another time and battle, the Cheldos were offered terms of surrender by an envoy. Nevertheless they won against superior forces, and gave their captives to eat a stew whose meat was the envoy of the offer to surrender. Being given to eat their own words as you'd say in Earthish. Such things are not done often, because the offer is not given."

He wrenched the steering post sideways and the tricar turned almost at right angles, balanced on one wheel for a dizzy moment, and fled up a great spiral ramp winding around the outside of the red Games Building.

Trobt still looked ahead, not glancing at me. "I understand, from observing them, that you Earthians will lie without soiling the mouth. What are you here for, actually?"

"I came from interest, but I intend, given the opportunity, to observe and to report my observations back to my government. They should not enter a war without knowing anything about you."

"Good." He wrenched the car around another abrupt turn into a red archway in the side of the building, bringing it to a stop inside. The sound of the other tricars entering the tunnel echoed hollowly from the walls and died as they came to a stop around us. "You are a spy then."

"Yes," I said, getting out. I had silently resigned my commission as envoy some five minutes earlier. There was little point in delivering political messages, if they have no result except to have one skinned or made into a stew.

A heavy door with the seal of an important official engraved upon it opened before us. In the forepart of the room we entered, a slim-bodied creature with the face of a girl sat with crossed legs on a platform like a long coffee table, sorting vellum marked with the dots and dashes, arrows and pictures, of the Veldian language.

She had green eyes, honeyed-olive complexion, a red mouth, and purple-black hair. She stopped to work an abacus, made a notation on one of the stiff sheets of vellum, then glanced up to see who had come in. She saw us, and glanced away again, as if she had coolly made a note of our presence and gone back to her work, sorting the vellum sheets and stacking them in thin shelves with quick, graceful motions.

"Kalin Trobt of Pagael," a man on the far side of the room said, a man sitting cross-legged on a dais covered with brown fur and scattered papers. He accepted the hand Trobt extended and they gripped wrists in a locked gesture of friendship. "And how survive the other sons of the citadel of Pagael?"

"Well, and continuing in friendship to the house of Lyagin," Trobt replied carefully. "I have seen little of my kin. There are many farlanders all around us, and between myself and my hearthfolk swarm the adopted."

"It is not like the old days, Kalin Trobt. In a dream I saw a rock sink from the weight of sons, and I longed for the sight of a land that is without strangers."

"We are all kinfolk now, Lyagin."

"My hearth pledged it."

Lyagin put his hand on a stack of missives which he had been considering, his face thoughtful, sparsely fleshed, mostly skull and tendon, his hair bound back from his face, and wearing a short white cotton dress beneath a light fur cape.

He was an old man, already in his senility, and now he was lost in a lapse of awareness of what he had been doing a moment before. By no sign did Trobt show impatience, or even consciousness of the other's lapse.

Lyagin raised his head after a minute and brought his rheumy eyes into focus on us. "You bring someone in regard to an inquiry?" he asked.

"The one from the Ten Thousand Worlds," Trobt replied.

Lyagin nodded apologetically. "I received word that he would be brought," he said. "How did you capture him?"

"He came."

The expression must have had some connotation that I did not recognize for the official let his glance cross mine, and I caught one slight flicker of interest in his eyes. "You say these Humans lie?" he asked Trobt.

"Frequently. It is considered almost honorable to lie to an enemy in circumstances where one may profit by it."

"You brought back from his worlds some poison which insures their speaking the truth, I believe?"

"Not a poison, something they call drugs, which affects one like strong drink, dulling a man and changing what he might do. Under its influence he loses his initiative of decision."

"You have this with you?"

"Yes." Trobt was going to waste no time getting from me anything I had that might be of value to them.

"It will be interesting having an enemy co-operate," Lyagin said. "If he finds no way to kill himself, he can be very useful to us." So far my contact with the Veldians had not been going at all as I had hoped and planned.

The boy-girl at the opposite side of the room finished a problem on the abacus, noted the answer, and glanced directly at my face, at my expression, then locked eyes with me for a brief moment.

When she glanced down to the vellum again it was as if she had seen whatever she had looked up to see, and was content. She sat a little straighter as she worked, and moved with an action that was a little less supple and compliant.

I believe she had seen me as a man.

During the questioning I made no attempt to resist the drug's influence. I answered truthfully—but literally. Many times my answers were undecidable—because I knew not the answers, or I lacked the data to give them. And the others were cloaked under a full literal subtlety that made them useless to the Veldians. Questions such as the degree of unity existing between the Worlds: I answered—truthfully—that they were united under an authority with supreme power of decision. The fact that that authority had no actual force behind it; that it was subject to the whims and fluctuations of sentiment and politics of intra-alliances; that it had deteriorated into a mere supernumerary body of impractical theorists that occupied itself, in a practical sphere, only with picayune matters, I did not explain. It was not asked of me.

Would our Worlds fight? I answered that they would fight to the death to defend their liberty and independence. I did not add that that will to fight would evidence itself first in internecine bickering, procrastinations, and jockeying to avoid the worst thrusts of the enemy—before it finally resolved itself into a united front against attack.

By early morning Trobt could no longer contain his impatience. He stepped closer. "We're going to learn one thing," he said, and his voice was harsh. "Why did you come here?"

"To learn all that I could about you," I answered.

"You came to find a way to whip us!"

It was not a question and I had no necessity to answer.

"Have you found the way?"

"No."

"If you do, and you are able, will you use that knowledge to kill us?"

"No."

Trobt's eyebrows raised. "No?" he repeated. "Then why do you want it?"

"I hope to find a solution that will not harm either side."

"But if you found that a solution was not possible, you would be willing to use your knowledge to defeat us?"

"Yes."

"Even if it meant that you had to exterminate us—man, woman, and child?"

"Yes."

"Why? Are you so certain that you are right, that you walk with God, and that we are knaves?"

"If the necessity to destroy one civilization or the other arose, and the decision were mine to make, I would rule against you because of the number of sentient beings involved."

Trobt cut the argument out from under me. "What if the situation were reversed, and your side was in the minority? Would you choose to let them die?"

I bowed my head as I gave him the truthful answer. "I would choose for my own side, no matter what the circumstances."

The interrogation was over.

On the drive to Trobt's home I was dead tired, and must have slept for a few minutes with my eyes open. With a start I heard Trobt say, ". . . that a man with ability enough to be a games—chess—master is given no authority over his people, but merely consulted on occasional abstract questions of tactics."

"It is the nature of the problem." I caught the gist of his comment from his last words and did my best to answer it. I wanted nothing less than to engage in conversation, but I realized that the interest he was showing now was just the kind I had tried to guide him to, earlier in the evening. If I could get him to understand us better, our motivations and ideals, perhaps even our frailties, there would be more hope for a compatible meeting of minds. "Among peoples of such mixed natures, such diverse histories and philosophies, and different ways of life, most administrative problems are problems of a choice of whims, of changing and conflicting goals; not *how* to do what a people want done, but *what* they want done, and whether their next generation will want it enough to make work on it, now, worthwhile."

"They sound insane," Trobt said. "Are your administrators supposed to serve the flickering goals of demented minds?"

"We must weigh values. What is considered good may be a matter of viewpoint, and may change from place to place, from generation to generation. In determining what people feel and what their unvoiced wants are, a talent of strategy, and an impatience with the illogic of others, are not qualifications."

"The good is good, how can it change?" Trobt asked. "I do not understand."

I saw that truly he could not understand, since he had seen nothing of the clash of philosophies among a mixed people. I tried to think of ways it could be explained; how to show him that a people who let their emotions control them more than their logic, would unavoidably do many things they could not justify or take pride in—but that that emotional predominance was what had enabled them to grow, and spread throughout their part of the galaxy—and be, in the main, happy.

I was tired, achingly tired. More, the events of the long day, and Velda's heavier gravity had taken me to the last stages of exhaustion. Yet I wanted to keep that weakness from Trobt. It was possible that he, and the other Veldians, would judge the Humans by what they observed in me.

Trobt's attention was on his driving and he did not notice that I followed his conversation only with difficulty. "Have you had only the two weeks of practice in the Game, since you came?" he asked.

I kept my eyes open with an effort and breathed deeply. Velda's one continent, capping the planet on its upper third, merely touched what would have been a temperate zone. During its short summer its mean temperature hung in the low sixties. At night it dropped to near freezing. The cold night air bit into my lungs and drove the fog of exhaustion from my brain.

"No," I answered Trobt's question. "I learned it before I came. A chess adept wrote me, in answer to an article on chess, that a man from one of the outworlds had shown him a game of greater richness and flexibility than chess, with much the same feeling to the player, and had beaten him in three games of chess after only two games to learn it, and had said that on his own planet this chesslike game was the basis for the amount of authority with which a man is invested. The stranger would not name his planet.

"I hired an investigating agency to learn the whereabouts of this planet. There was none in the Ten Thousand Worlds. That meant that the man had been a very ingenious liar, or—that he had come from Velda."

"It was I, of course," Trobt acknowledged.

"I realized that from your conversation. The sender of the letter," I resumed, "was known to me as a chess champion of two Worlds. The matter tantalized my thoughts for weeks, and finally I decided to try to arrange a visit to Velda. If you had this game, I wanted to try myself against your skilled ones."

"I understand that desire very well," Trobt said. "The same temptation caused me to be indiscreet when I visited your Worlds. I have seldom been able to resist the opportunity for an intellectual gambit."

"It wasn't much more than a guess that I would find the Game on Velda," I said. "But the lure was too strong for me to pass it by."

"Even if you came intending to challenge, you had little enough time to learn to play as you have—against men who have spent lifetimes learning. I'd like to try you again soon, if I may."

"Certainly." I was in little mood or condition to welcome any further polite conversation. And I did not appreciate the irony of his request—to the best of my knowledge I was still under a sentence of early death.

Trobt must have caught the bleakness in my reply for he glanced quickly over his shoulder at me. "There will be time," he said, gently for him. "Several days at least. You will be my guest." I knew that he was doing his best to be kind. His decision that I must die had not been prompted by any meanness of nature: to him it was only—inevitable.

The next day I sat at one end of a Games table in a side wing of his home while Trobt leaned against the wall to my left. "Having a like nature I can well understand the impulse that brought you here," he said. "The supreme gamble. Playing—with your life the stake in the game. Nothing you've ever experienced can compare with it. And even now—when you have lost, and will die—you do not regret it, I'm certain."

"I'm afraid you're overestimating my courage, and misinterpreting my intentions," I told him, feeling instinctively that this would be a good time to again present my arguments. "I came because I hoped to reach a better understanding. We feel that an absolutely unnecessary war, with its resulting death and destruction, would be foolhardy. And I fail to see your viewpoint. Much of it strikes me as stupid racial pride."

Trobt ignored the taunt. "The news of your coming is the first topic of conversation in the City," he said. "The clans understand that you have come to challenge; one man against a nation. They greatly admire your audacity."

"Look," I said, becoming angry and slipping into Earthian. "I don't know whether you consider me a damn fool or not. But if you think I came here expecting to die, that I'm looking forward to it with pleasure—"

He stopped me with an idle gesture of one hand. "You deceive yourself if you believe what you say," he commented. "Tell me this: would you have stayed away if you had known just how great the risk was to be?"

I was surprised to find that I did not have a ready answer to his question.

"Shall we play?" Trobt asked.

We played three games; Trobt with great skill, employing diversified and ingenious attacks. But he still had that bit too much audacity in his execution. I won each time.

"You're undoubtedly a Master," Trobt said at the end of the third game. "But that isn't all of it. Would you like me to tell you why I can't beat you?"

"Can you?' I asked.

"I think so," he said. "I wanted to try against you again and again, because each time it did not seem that you had defeated me, but only that I had played badly, made childish blunders, and that I lost each game before we ever came to grips. Yet when I entered the duel against you a further time, I'd begin to blunder again."

He shoved his hands more deeply under his weapons belt, leaning back and observing me with his direct inspection. "My blundering then has to do with you, rather than myself," he said. "Your play is excellent, of course, but there is more beneath the surface than above. This is your talent: you lose the first game to see an opponent's weakness—and play it against him."

I could not deny it. But neither would I concede it. Any small advantage I might hold would be sorely needed later.

"I understand Humans a little," Trobt said. "Enough to know that very few of them would come to challenge us without some other purpose. They have no taste for death, with glory or without."

Again I did not reply.

"I believe," Trobt said, "that you came here to challenge in your own way, which is to find any weakness we might have, either in our military, or in some odd way, in our very selves."

Once again—with a minimum of help from me—he had arrived in his reasoning at a correct answer. From here on—against this man—I would have to walk a narrow line.

"I think," Trobt said more slowly, glancing down at the board between us, then back at my expression, "that this may be the First Game, and that you are more dangerous than you seem, that you are accepting the humiliation of allowing yourself to be thought of as weaker than you are, in actuality. You intend to find our weakness, and you expect somehow to tell your states what you find."

I looked across at him without moving. "What weakness do you fear I've seen?" I countered.

Trobt placed his hands carefully on the board in front of him and rose to his feet. Before he could say what he intended a small boy pulling something like a toy riding-horse behind him came into the game room and grabbed Trobt's trouser leg. He was the first blond child I had seen on Velda.

The boy pointed at the swords on the wall. "Da," he said beseechingly, making reaching motions. "Da."

Trobt kept his attention on me. After a moment a faint humorless smile moved his lips. He seemed to grow taller, with the impression a strong man gives when he remembers his strength. "You will find no weakness," he said. He sat down again and placed the child on his lap.

The boy grabbed immediately at the abacus hanging on Trobt's belt and began playing with it, while Trobt stroked his hair. All the Veldians dearly loved children, I had noticed.

"Do you have any idea how many of our ships were used to wipe out your fleet?" he asked abruptly.

As I allowed myself to show the interest I felt he put a hand on the boy's shoulder and leaned forward. "One," he said.

I very nearly called Trobt a liar—one ship obliterating a thousand— before I remembered that Veldians were not liars, and that Trobt obviously was not lying. Somehow this small under-populated planet had developed a science of weapons that vastly exceeded that of the Ten Thousand Worlds.

I had thought that perhaps my vacation on this Games-mad planet would result in some mutual information that would bring quick negotiation or conciliation: that players of a chesslike game would be easy to approach; that I would meet men intelligent enough to see the absurdity of such an ill-fated war against the overwhelming odds of the Ten Thousand Worlds Federation. Intelligent enough to foresee the disaster that would result from such a fight. It began to look as if the disaster might be to the Ten Thousand and not to the one.

Thinking, I walked alone in Trobt's roof garden.

Walking in Velda's heavy gravity took more energy than I cared to expend, but too long a period without exercise brought a dull ache to the muscles of my shoulders and at the base of my neck.

This was my third evening in the house. I had slept at least ten hours each night since I arrived, and found myself exhausted at day's end, unless I was able to take a nap or lie down during the afternoon.

The flowers and shrubbery in the garden seemed to feel the weight of gravity also, for most of them grew low, and many sent creepers out along the ground. Overhead strange formations of stars clustered thickly and shed a glow on the garden very like Earth's moonlight.

I was just beginning to feel the heavy drag in my leg tendons when a woman's voice said, "Why don't you rest a while?" It spun me around as I looked for the source of the voice.

I found her in a nook in the bushes, seated on a contour chair that allowed her to stretch out in a half-reclining position. She must have weighed near to two hundred—Earth-weight—pounds.

But the thing that had startled me more than the sound of her voice was that she had spoken in the universal language of the Ten Thousand Worlds. And without accent!

"You're—?" I started to ask.

"Human," she finished for me.

"How did you get here?" I inquired eagerly.

"With my husband." She was obviously enjoying my astonishment. She was a beautiful woman, in a gentle bovine way, and very friendly. Her blonde hair was done up in tight ringlets.

"You mean . . . Trobt?" I asked.

"Yes." As I stood trying to phrase my wonderment into more questions, she asked, "You're the Earthman, aren't you?"

I nodded. "Are you from Earth?"

"No," she answered. "My home world is Mandel's Planet, in the Thumb group."

She indicated a low hassock of a pair, and I seated myself on the lower and leaned an elbow on the higher, beginning to smile. It would have been difficult not to smile in the presence of anyone so contented. "How did you meet Trobt?" I asked.

"It's a simple love story. Kalin visited Mandel—without revealing his true identity of course—met, and courted me. I learned to love him, and agreed to come to his world as his wife."

"Did you know that he wasn't . . . That he . . ." I stumbled over just how to phrase the question. And wondered if I should have started it.

Her teeth showed white and even as she smiled. She propped a pillow under one plump arm and finished my sentence for me. ". . . That he wasn't Human?" I was grateful for the way she put me at ease—almost as though we had been old friends.

I nodded.

"I didn't know." For a moment she seemed to draw back into her thoughts, as though searching for something she had almost forgotten. "He couldn't tell me. It was a secret he had to keep. When I arrived here and learned that his planet wasn't a charted world, was not even Human, I was a little uncertain and lonesome. But not frightened. I knew Kalin would never let me be hurt. Even my lonesomeness left quickly. Kalin and I love each other very deeply. I couldn't be more happy than I am now."

She seemed to see I did not consider that my question had been answered—completely. "You're wondering still if I mind that he isn't Human, aren't you?" she asked. "Why should I? After all, what does it mean to be 'Human'? It is only a word that differentiates one group of people from another. I seldom think of the Veldians as being different—and certainly never that they're beneath me."

"Does it bother you—if you'll pardon this curiosity of mine—that you will never be able to bear Kalin's children?"

"The child you saw the first morning is my son," she answered complacently.

"But that's impossible," I blurted.

"Is it?" she asked. "You saw the proof."

"I'm no expert at this sort of thing," I said slowly, "but I've always understood that the possibility of two separate species producing offspring was a million to one."

"Greater than that, probably," she agreed. "But whatever the odds, sooner or later the number is bound to come up. This was it."

I shook my head, but there was no arguing a fact. "Wasn't it a bit unusual that Kalin didn't marry a Veldian woman?"

"He has married—two of them," she answered. "I'm his third wife."

"Then they do practice polygamy," I said. "Are you content with such a marriage?"

"Oh, yes," she answered. "You see, besides being very much loved, I occupy a rather enviable position here. I, ah . . ." She grew slightly flustered. "Well . . . the other women—the Veldian women—can bear children only once every eight years, and during the other seven . . ." She hesitated again and I saw a tinge of red creep into her cheeks. She was obviously embarrassed, but she laughed and resolutely went on.

"During the other seven, they lose their feminine appearance, and don't think of themselves as women. While I . . ." I watched with amusement as her color deepened and her glance dropped. "I am always of the same sex, as you might say, always a woman. My husband is the envy of all his friends."

After her first reticence she talked freely, and I learned then the answer to the riddle of the boy-girls of Velda. And at least one reason for their great affection for children.

One year of fertility in eight . . .

Once again I saw the imprint of the voracious dleeth on this people's culture. In their age-old struggle with their cold planet and its short growing seasons—and more particularly with the dleeth—the Veldian women had been shaped by evolution to better fit their environment. The women's strength could not be spared for frequent childbearing—so childbearing had been limited. Further, one small child could be carried in the frequent flights from the dleeth, but not more than one. Nature had done its best to cope with the problem: in the off seven years she tightened the women's flesh, atrophying glands and organs—making them non-functional—and changing their bodies to be more fit to labor and survive—and to fight, if necessary. It was an excellent adaptation—for a time and environment where a low birth rate was an asset to survival.

But this adaptation had left only a narrow margin for race perpetuation. Each woman could bear only four children in her lifetime. That, I realized as we talked, was the reason why the Veldians had not colonized other planets, even though they had space flight—and why they probably never would, without a drastic change in their biological make-up. That left so little ground for a quarrel between them and the Ten Thousand Worlds. Yet here we were, poised to spring into a death struggle.

"You are a very unusual woman." My attention returned to Trobt's wife. "In a very unusual situation."

"Thank you," she accepted it as a compliment. She made ready to rise. "I hope you enjoy your visit here. And that I may see you again before you return to Earth."

I realized then that she did not know of my peculiar position in her home. I wondered if she knew even of the threat of war between us and her adopted people. I decided not, or she would surely have spoken of it. Either Trobt had deliberately avoided telling her, perhaps to spare her the pain it would have caused, or she had noted that the topic of my presence was disturbing to him and had tactfully refrained from inquiring. For just a moment I wondered if I should explain everything to her, and have her use the influence she must have with Trobt. I dismissed the idea as unworthy—and useless.

"Good night," I said.

★

The next evening as we rode in a tricar Trobt asked if I would like to try my skill against a better Games player.

"I had assumed you were the best," I said.

"Only the second best," he answered. "It would be interesting to compare your game with that of our champion. If you can whip him, perhaps we will have to revise our opinion of you Humans."

He spoke as though in jest, but I saw more behind his words than he intended me to see. Here at last might be a chance to do a positive service for my side. "I would be happy to play," I said.

Trobt parked the tricar on a side avenue and we walked perhaps a hundred yards. We stopped at the door of a small one-story stone house and Trobt tapped with his fingernails on a hollow gong buried in the wood.

After a minute a curtain over the door glass was drawn back and an old woman with straggly gray hair peered out at us. She recognized Trobt and opened the door.

We went in. Neither Trobt nor the old woman spoke. She turned her back after closing the door and went to stir embers in a stone grate.

Trobt motioned with his head for me to follow and led the way into a back room.

"Robert O. Lang," he said, "I would like you to meet Yondtl."

I looked across the room in the direction Trobt had indicated. My first impression was of a great white blob, propped up on a couch and supported by the wall at its back.

Then the thing moved. Moved its eyes. It was alive. Its eyes told me also that it was a man. If I could call it a man.

His head was large and bloated, with blue eyes, washed almost colorless, peering out of deep pouches of flesh. He seemed to have no neck; almost as though his great head were merely an extension of the trunk, and separated only by puffy folds of fat. Other lappings of flesh hung from his body in great thick rolls.

It took another minute of fascinated inspection before I saw that he had no arms, and that no legs reached from his body to the floor. The entire sight of him made me want to leave the room and be sick.

"Robert O. Lang is an Earthian who would challenge you sir," Trobt addressed the monstrosity.

The other gave no sign that I could see but Trobt went to pull a Games table at the side of the room over toward us. "I will serve as his hands," Trobt said.

The pale blue eyes never left my face.

I stood without conscious thought until Trobt pushed a chair under me. Mentally I shook myself. With unsteady hands—I had to do something with them—I reached for the pukts before me. "Do you . . . do you have a choice . . . of colors, sir?" I stammered, trying to make up for my earlier rudeness of staring.

The lips of the monstrosity quivered, but he made no reply.

All this while Trobt had been watching me with amusement. "He is deaf and speechless," Trobt said. "Take either set. I will place the other before him."

Absently I pulled the red pieces toward me and placed them on their squares.

"In deference to you as a visitor, you will play 'second game counts,'" Trobt continued. He was still enjoying my consternation. "He always allows his opponent the first move. You may begin when you are ready."

With an effort I forced myself to concentrate on the playing board. My start, I decided, must be orthodox. I had to learn something of the type of game this . . . Yondtl . . . played. I moved the first row right hand pukt its two oblique and one left squares.

Yondtl inclined his head slightly. His lips moved. Trobt put his hand to a pukt and pushed it forward. Evidently Trobt read his lips. Very probably Yondtl could read ours also.

We played for almost an hour with neither of us losing a man.

I had tried several gambits; gambits that invited a misplay on Yondtl's part. But he made none. When he offered I was careful to make no mistakes of my own. We both played as though this first game were the whole contest.

Another hour went by. I deliberately traded three pukts with Yondtl, in an attempt to trick him into a misplay. None came.

I tried a single decoy gambit, and when nothing happened, followed with a second decoy. Yondtl countered each play. I marveled that he gave so little of his attention to the board. Always he seemed to be watching me. I played. He played. He watched me.

I sweated.

Yondtl set up an overt side pass that forced me to draw my pukts back into the main body. Somehow I received the impression that he was teasing me. It made me want to beat him down.

I decided on a crossed-force, double decoy gambit. I had never seen it employed. Because, I suspect, it is too involved, and open to error by its user. Slowly and painstakingly I set it up and pressed forward.

The Caliban in the seat opposite me never paused. He matched me play for play. And though Yondtl's features had long since lost the power of expression, his pale eyes seemed to develop a blue luster. I realized, almost with a shock of surprise, that the fat monstrosity was happy—intensely happy.

I came out of my brief reverie with a start. Yondtl had made an obvious play. I had made an obvious counter. I was startled to hear him sound a cry somewhere between a muffled shout and an idiot's laugh, and my attention jerked back to the board. I had lost the game!

My brief moment of abstraction had given Yondtl the opportunity to make a pass too subtle to be detected with part of my faculties occupied elsewhere.

I pushed back my chair. "I've had enough for tonight," I told Trobt. If I were to do the Humans a service, I would need rest before trying Yondtl in the second game.

We made arrangements to meet again the following evening, and let ourselves out. The old woman was nowhere in sight.

The following evening when we began play I was prepared to give my best. I was rested and eager. And I had a concrete plan. Playing the way I had been doing I would never beat Yondtl, I'd decided after long thought. A stand-off was the best I could hope for. Therefore the time had come for more consummate action. I would engage him in a triple decoy gambit!

I had no illusion that I could handle it—the way it should be handled. I doubt that any man, Human or Veldian, could. But at least I would play it with the greatest skill I had, giving my best to every move, and push the game up the scale of reason and involution—up and up—until either Yondtl or I became lost in its innumerable complexities, and fell.

As I attacked, the complexes and complications would grow gradually more numerous, become more and more difficult, until they embraced a span greater than one of us had the capacity to encompass, and the other would win.

The Game began and I forced it into the pattern I had planned. Each play, and each maneuver, became all important, and demanding of the greatest skill I could command. Each pulled at the core of my brain, dragging out the last iota of sentient stuff that writhed there. Yondtl stayed with me, complex gambit through complex gambit.

When the strain became too great I forced my mind to pause, to rest, and to be ready for the next clash. At the first break I searched the annotator. It was working steadily, with an almost smooth throb of efficiency, keeping the position of each pukt—and its value—strong in the forefront of visualization. But something was missing!

A minute went by before I spotted the fault. The move of each pukt involved so many possibilities, so many avenues of choice, that no exact answer was predictable on any one. The number and variation of gambits open on every play, each subject to the multitude of Yondtl's counter moves, stretched the possibilities beyond prediction. The annotator was a harmonizing perceptive force, but not a creative, initiating one. It operated in a statistical manner, similar to a computer, and could not perform effectively where a crucial factor or factors were unknown, or concealed, as they were here.

My greatest asset was negated.

At the end of the third hour I began to feel a steady pain in my temples, as though a tight metal band pressed against my forehead and squeezed it inward. The only reaction I could discern in Yondtl was that the blue glint in his eyes had become brighter. All his happiness seemed gathered there.

Soon my pauses became more frequent. Great waves of brain weariness had to be allowed to subside before I could play again.

And at last it came.

Suddenly, unexpectedly, Yondtl threw a pukt across the board and took my second decoy—and there was no way for me to retaliate! Worse, my entire defense was smashed.

I felt a kind of calm dismay. My shoulders sagged and I pushed the board away from me and slumped in my chair.

I was beaten.

The next day I escaped from Trobt. It was not difficult. I simply walked away.

For three days I followed the wall of the City, looking for a way out. Each gate was guarded. I watched unobserved and saw that a permit was necessary when leaving. If I found no other way I would make a run for it. The time of decision never came.

Meanwhile to obtain food I was forced into some contact with the City's people, and learned to know them better. Adding this new knowledge to the old I decided that I liked them.

Their manners and organization—within the framework of their culture—was as simple and effective as their architecture. There was a strong emphasis on pride, on strength and honor, on skill, and on living a dangerous life with a gambler's self-command, on rectitude, on truth, and the unbreakable bond of loyalty among family and friends. Lying, theft, and deceit were practically unknown.

I did detect what might have been a universal discontent in their young men. They had a warrior heritage and nature which, with the unity of the tribes and the passing of the dleeth—and no one to fight except themselves—had left them with an unrecognized futility of purpose. They had not quite been able to achieve a successful sublimation of their post-warrior need to fight in the Games. Also, the custom of polygamy—necessary in the old days, and desired still by those able to attain it—left many sexually frustrated.

I weighed all these observations in my reactions to the Veldians, and toward the end a strange feeling—a kind of wistfulness—came as I observed. I felt kin to them, as if these people had much in common with myself. And I felt that it was too bad that life was not fundamentally so simple that one could discard the awareness of other ways of life, of other values and philosophies that bid against one another, and against one's attention, and make one cynical of the philosophy one lives by, and dies for. Too bad that I could not see and take life as that direct, and as that simple.

The third day I climbed a spiral ramp to the top of a tower that rose above the walls of Hearth and gazed out over miles of swirling red sand. Directly beneath me stretched a long concrete ribbon of road. On the road were dozens of slowly crawling vehicles that might have been caterpillar trucks of Earth!

In my mind the pattern clicked into place. Hearth was not typical of the cities of Velda!

It was an anachronism, a revered Homeplace, a symbol of their past, untainted by the technocracy that was pursued elsewhere. This was the capital city, from which the heads of the government still ruled, perhaps for sentimental reasons, but it was not typical.

My stay in Hearth was cut short when I descended from the tower and found Trobt waiting for me.

As I might have expected, he showed no sign of anger with me for having fled into the City. His was the universal Veldian viewpoint. To them all life was the Game. With the difference that it was played on an infinitely larger board. Every man, and every woman, with whom the player had contact, direct or indirect, were pukts on the Board. The player made his decisions, and his plays, and how well he made them determined whether he won or lost. His every move, his every joining of strength with those who could help him, his every maneuver against those who would oppose him, was his choice to make, and he rose or fell on the wisdom of the choice. Game, in Velda, means Duel, means struggle and the test of man against the opponent, Life. I had made my escape as the best play as I saw it. Trobt had no recriminations.

The evening of the next day Trobt woke me. Something in his constrained manner brought me to my feet. "Not what you think," he said, "but we must question you again. We will try our own methods this time."

"Torture?"

"You will die under the torture, of course. But for the questioning it will not be necessary. You will talk."

The secret of their method was very simple. Silence. I was led to a room within a room within a room. Each with very thick walls. And left alone. Here time meant nothing.

Gradually I passed from boredom to restlessness, to anxiety, briefly through fear, to enervating frustration, and finally to stark apathy.

When Trobt and his three accompanying guardsmen led me into the blinding daylight I talked without hesitation or consideration of consequences.

"Did you find any weakness in the Veldians?"

"Yes."

I noted then a strange thing. It was the annotator—the thing in my brain that was a part of me, and yet apart from me—that had spoken. It was not concerned with matters of emotion; with sentiments of patriotism, loyalty, honor, and self-respect. It was interested only in my—and its own—survival. Its logic told it that unless I gave the answers my questioner wanted I would die. That, it intended to prevent.

I made one last desperate effort to stop that other part of my mind from assuming control—and sank lower into my mental impotence.

"What is our weakness?"

"Your society is doomed." With the answer I realized that the annotator had arrived at another of its conclusions.

"Why?"

"There are many reasons."

"Give one."

"Your culture is based on a need for struggle, for combat. When there is no one to fight it must fall."

Trobt was dealing with a familiar culture now. He knew the questions to ask.

"Explain that last statement."

"Your culture is based on its impetuous need to battle . . . it is armed and set against dangers and the expectation of danger . . . fostering the pride of courage under stress. There is no danger now . . . nothing to fight, no place to spend your overaggressiveness, except against each other in personal duels. Already your decline is about to enter the bloody circus and religion stage, already crumbling in the heart while expanding at the outside. And this is your first civilization . . . like a boy's first love . . . you have no experience of a fall in your history before to have recourse to—no cushioning of philosophy to accept it . . ."

For a time Trobt maintained a puzzled silence. I wondered if he had the depth of understanding to accept the truth and significance of what he had heard. "Is there no solution?" he asked at last.

"Only a temporary one." Now it was coming.

"Explain."

"War with the Ten Thousand Worlds."

"Explain."

"Your willingness to hazard, and eagerness to battle is no weakness when you are armed with superior weapons, and are fighting against an opponent as disorganized, and as incapable of effective organization as the Ten Thousand Worlds, against your long-range weapons and subtle traps."

"Why do you say the solution is only temporary?"

"You cannot win the war. You will seem to win, but it will be an illusion. You will win the battles, kill billions, rape Worlds, take slaves, and destroy ships and weapons. But after that you will be forced to hold the subjection. Your numbers will not be expendable. You will be spread thin, exposed to other cultures that will influence you, change you. You will lose skirmishes, and in the end you will be forced back. Then will come a loss of old ethics, corruption and opportunism will replace your honor and you will know unspeakable shame and dishonor . . . your culture will soon be weltering back into a barbarism and disorganization which in its corruption and despair will be nothing like the proud tribal primitive life of its first barbarism. You will be aware of the difference and unable to return."

I understood Trobt's perplexity as I finished. He could not accept what I told him because to him winning was only a matter of a military victory, a victory of strength; Velda had never experienced defeat as a weakness from within. My words made him uneasy, but he did not understand. He shrugged. "Do we have any other weakness?" he asked.

"Your women."

"Explain."

"They are 'set' for the period when they greatly out-numbered their men. Your compatible ratio is eight women to one man. Yet now it is one to one. Further, you produce too few children.. Your manpower must ever be in small supply. Worse, your shortage of women sponsors a covert despair and sadism in your young men . . . a hunger and starvation to follow instinct, to win women by courage and conquest and battle against danger . . . that only a war can restrain.

"The solution?"

"Beat the Federation. Be in a position to have free access to their women."

Came the final ingnominy. "Do you have a means of reporting back to the Ten Thousand Worlds?"

"Yes. Buried somewhere inside me is a nerve-twitch tape. Flesh pockets of chemicals are stored there also. When my body temperature drops fifteen degrees below normal the chemicals will be activated and will use the tissues of my body for fuel and generate sufficient energy to transmit the information on the tape back to the Ten Thousand Worlds."

That was enough.

"Do you still intend to kill me?" I asked Trobt the next day as we walked in his garden.

"Do not fear," he answered. "You will not be cheated of an honorable death. All Velda is as eager for it as you."

"Why?" I asked. "Do they see me as a madman?"

"They see you as you are. They cannot conceive of one man challenging a planet, except to win himself a bright and gory death on a page of history, the first man to deliberately strike and die in the coming war—not an impersonal clash of battleships, but a *man* declaring personal battle against men. We would not deprive you of that death. Our admiration is too great. We want the symbolism of your blood now just as greatly as you want it yourself. Every citizen is waiting to watch you die—gloriously."

I realized now that all the while he had interpreted my presence here in this fantastic way. And I suspected that I had no arguments to convince him differently.

Trobt had hinted that I would die under torture. I thought of the old histories of Earth that I had read. Of the warrior race of North American Indians. A captured enemy must die. But if he had been an honorable enemy he was given an honorable death. He was allowed to die under the stress most familiar to them. Their strongest ethic was a cover-up for the defeated, the universal expressionless suppressal of reaction in conquering or watching conquest, so as not to shame the defeated. Public torture—with the women, as well as warriors, watching—the chance to exhibit fortitude, all the way to the breaking point, and beyond. That was considered the honorable death, while it was a shameful trick to quietly slit a man's throat in his sleep without giving him a chance to fight—to show his scorn of flinching under the torture.

Here I was the Honorable Enemy who had exhibited courage. They would honor me, and satisfy their hunger for an Enemy, by giving me the breaking point test.

But I had no intention of dying!

"You will not kill me," I addressed Trobt. "And there will be no war."

He looked at me as though I had spoken gibberish.

My next words, I knew, would shock him. "I'm going to recommend unconditional surrender," I said.

Trobt's head, which he had turned away, swiveled sharply back to me. His mouth opened and he made several motions to speak before succeeding. "Are you serious?"

"Very," I answered.

Trobt's face grew gaunt and the skin pressed tight against his cheekbones—almost as though he were making the surrender rather than I. "Is this decision dictated by your logic," he asked dryly, "or by faintness of heart?"

I did not honor the question enough to answer.

Neither did he apologize. "You understand that unconditional surrender is the only kind we will accept?"

I nodded wearily.

"Will they agree to your recommendation?"

"No," I answered. "Humans are not cowards, and they will fight—as long as there is the slightest hope of success. I will not be able to convince them that their defeat is inevitable. But I can prepare them for what is to come. I hope to shorten the conflict immeasurably."

"I can do nothing but accept," Trobt said after a moment of thought. "I will arrange transportation back to Earth for you tomorrow." He paused and regarded me with expressionless eyes. "You realize that an enemy who surrenders without a struggle is beneath contempt?"

The blood crept slowly into my cheeks. It was difficult to ignore his taunt. "Will you give me six months before you move against us?" I asked. "The Federation is large. I will need time to bring my message to all."

"You have your six months." Trobt was still not through with me, personally. "On the exact day that period ends I will expect your return to Velda. We will see if you have any honor left."

"I will be back," I said.

During the next six months I spread my word throughout the Ten Thousand Worlds. I met disbelief everywhere. I had not expected otherwise. The last day I returned to Velda.

Two days later Velda's Council acted. They were going to give the Humans no more time to organize counteraction. I went in the same spaceship that carried Trobt. I intended to give him any advice he needed about the Worlds. I asked only that his first stop be at the Jason's Fleece fringe.

Beside us sailed a mighty armada of warships, spaced in a long line that would encompass the entire portion of the galaxy occupied by the Ten Thousand Worlds. For an hour we moved ponderously forward, then the stars about us winked out for an instant. The next moment a group of Worlds became visible on the ship's vision screen. I recognized them as Jason's Fleece.

One World expanded until it appeared the size of a baseball. "Quagman," Trobt said.

Quagman, the trouble spot of the Ten Thousand Worlds. Dominated by an unscrupulous clique that ruled by vendetta, it had been the source of much trouble and vexation to the other Worlds. Its leaders were considered little better than brigands. They had received me with much apparent courtesy. In the end they had even agreed to surrender to the Veldians—when and if they appeared. I had accepted their easy concurrence with suspicion, but they were my main hope.

Two Veldians left our ship in a scooter. We waited ten long, tense hours. When word finally came back it was from the Quagmans themselves. The Veldian envoys were being held captive. They would be released upon the delivery of two billion dollars—in the currency of any recognized World—and the promise of immunity.

The fools!

Trobt's face remained impassive as he received the message.

We waited several more hours. Both Trobt and I watched the green mottled baseball on the vision screen. It was Trobt who first pointed out a small, barely discernible, black spot on the upper lefthand corner of Quagman.

As the hours passed, and the black spot swung slowly to the right as the planet revolved, it grew almost imperceptibly larger. When it disappeared over the edge of the world we slept.

In the morning the spot appeared again, and now it covered half the face of the planet. Another ten hours and the entire planet became a blackened cinder.

Quagman was dead.

The ship moved next to Mican.

Mican was a sparsely populated prison planet. Criminals were usually sent to newly discovered Worlds on the edge of the Human expansion circle, and allowed to make their own adjustments toward achieving a stable government. Men with the restless natures that made them criminals on their own highly civilized Worlds made the best pioneers. However, it always took them several generations to work their way up from anarchy to a co-operative government. Mican had not yet had that time. I had done my best in the week I spent with them to convince them to organize, and to be prepared to accept any terms the Veldians might offer. The gesture, I feared, was useless but I had given all the arguments I knew.

A second scooter left with two Veldian representatives. When it returned Trobt left the control room to speak with them.

He returned, and shook his head. I knew it was useless to argue.

Mican died.

At my request Trobt agreed to give the remaining Jason's Fleece Worlds a week to consider—on the condition that they made no offensive forays. I wanted them to have time to fully assess what had happened to the other two Worlds—to realize that that same stubbornness would result in the same disaster for them.

At the end of the third twenty-four hour period the Jason's Fleece Worlds surrendered—unconditionally. They had tasted blood; and recognized futility when faced with it. That had been the best I had been able to hope for, earlier.

Each sector held off surrendering until the one immediately ahead had given in. But the capitulation was complete at the finish. No more blood had had to be shed.

The Veldians' terms left the Worlds definitely subservient, but they were neither unnecessarily harsh, nor humiliating. Velda demanded specific limitations on Weapons and war-making potentials; the obligation of reporting all technological and scientific progress; and colonial expansion only by prior consent.

There was little actual occupation of the Federation Worlds, but the Veldians retained the right to inspect any and all functions of the various governments. Other aspects of social and economic methods would be subject only to occasional checks and investigation. Projects considered questionable would be supervised by the Veldians at their own discretion.

The one provision that caused any vigorous protest from the Worlds was the Veldian demand for Human women. But even this was a purely emotional reaction, and died as soon as it was more fully understood. The Veldians were not barbarians. They used no coercion to obtain our women. They only demanded the same right to woo them as the citizens of the Worlds had. No woman would be taken without her free choice. There would be no valid protest to that.

In practice it worked quite well. On nearly all the Worlds there were more women than men, so that few men had to go without mates because of the Veldians' inroads. And—by human standards—they seldom took our most desirable women. Because the acquiring of weight was corollary with the Veldian women becoming sexually attractive, their men had an almost universal perference for fleshy women. As a result many of our women who would have had difficulty securing human husbands found themselves much in demand as mates of the Veldians.

Seven years passed after the Worlds' surrender before I saw Kalin Trobt again.

The pact between the Veldians and the Worlds had worked out well, for both sides. The demands of the Veldians involved little sacrifice by the Federation, and the necessity of reporting to a superior authority made for less wrangling and jockeying for advantageous position among the Worlds themselves.

The fact that the Veldians had taken more than twenty million of our women—it was the custom for each Veldian to take a Human woman for one mate—caused little dislocation or discontent. The number each lost did less than balance the ratio of the sexes.

For the Veldians the pact solved the warrior-set frustrations, and the unrest and sexual starvation of their males. Those men who demanded action and adventure were given supervisory posts on the Worlds as an outlet for their drives. All could now obtain mates; mates whose biological make-up did not necessitate an eight to one ratio.

Each year it was easier for the Humans to understand the Veldians and to meet them on common grounds socially. Their natures became less rigid, and they laughed more—even at themselves, when the occasion demanded.

This was especially noticeable among the younger Veldians, just reaching an adult status. In later years when the majority of them would have a mixture of human blood, the difference between us would become even less pronounced.

Trobt had changed little during those seven years. His hair had grayed some at the temples, and his movements were a bit less supple, but he looked well. Much of the intensity had left his aquiline features, and he seemed content.

We shook hands with very real pleasure. I led him to chairs under the shade of a tree in my front yard and brought drinks.

"First, I want to apologize for having thought you a coward," he began, after the first conventional pleasantries. "I know now I was very wrong. I did not realize for years, however, just what had happened." He gave his wry smile. "You know what I mean, I presume?"

I looked at him inquiringly.

"There was more to your decision to capitulate than was revealed. When you played the Game your forte was finding the weakness of an opponent. And winning the second game. You made no attempt to win the first. I see now, that as on the board, your surrender represented only the conclusion of the first game. You were keeping our weakness to yourself, convinced that there would be a second game. And that your Ten Thousand Worlds would win it. As you have."

"What would you say your weakness was?" By now I suspected he knew everything, but I wanted to be certain.

"Our desire and need for Human women, of course."

There was no need to dissemble further. "The solution first came to me," I explained, "when I remembered a formerly independent Earth country named China. They lost most of their wars, but in the end they always won."

"Through their women?"

"Indirectly. Actually it was done by absorbing their conquerors. The situation was similar between Velda and the Ten Thousand Worlds. Velda won the war, but in a thousand years there will be no Veldians—racially."

"That was my first realization," Trobt said. "I saw immediately then how you had us hopelessly trapped. The marriage of our men to your women will blend our bloods until—with your vastly greater numbers—in a dozen generations there will be only traces of our race left.

"And what can we do about it?" Trobt continued. "We can't kill our beloved wives—and our children. We can't stop further acquisition of human women without disrupting our society. Each generation the tie between us will become closer, our blood thinner, yours more dominant, as the intermingling continues. We cannot even declare war against the people who are doing this to us. How do you fight an enemy that has surrendered unconditionally?"

"You do understand that for your side this was the only solution to the imminent chaos that faced you?" I asked.

"Yes." I watched Trobt's swift mind go through its reasoning. I was certain he saw that Velda was losing only an arbitrary distinction of race, very much like the absorbing of the early clans of Velda into the family of the Danlee. Their dislike of that was very definitely only an emotional consideration. The blending of our bloods would benefit both; the resultant new race would be better and stronger because of that blending.

With a small smile Trobt raised his glass. "We will drink to the union of two great races," he said. "And to you—the winner of the Second Game!"

DARK BENEDICTION

Walter M. Miller, Jr.

Always fearful of being set upon during the night, Paul slept uneasily despite his weariness from the long trek southward. When dawn broke, he rolled out of his blankets and found himself still stiff with fatigue. He kicked dirt over the remains of the campfire and breakfasted on a tough forequarter of cold boiled rabbit which he washed down with a swallow of earthy-tasting ditchwater. Then he buckled the cartridge belt about his waist, leaped the ditch, and climbed the embankment to the trafficless four-lane highway whose pavement was scattered with blown leaves and unsightly debris dropped by a long-departed throng of refugees whose only wish had been to escape from one another. Paul, with characteristic independence, had decided to go where the crowds had been the thickest—to the cities—on the theory that they would now be deserted, and therefore noncontagious.

The fog lay heavy over the silent land, and for a moment he paused groping for cognisance of direction. Then he saw the stalled car on the opposite shoulder of the road—a late model convertible, but rusted, flat-tired, with last year's license plates, and most certainly out of fuel. It obviously had been deserted by its owner during the exodus, and he trusted in its northward heading as he would have trusted the reading of a compass. He turned right and moved south on the empty highway. Somewhere just ahead in the gray vapor lay the outskirts of Houston. He had seen the high skyline before the setting of yesterday's sun, and knew that his journey would soon be drawing to a close.

Occasionally he passed a deserted cottage or a burned-out roadside tavern, but he did not pause to scrounge for food. The exodus would have stripped such buildings clean. Pickings should be better in the heart of the metropolitan area, he thought—where the hysteria had swept humanity away quickly.

Suddenly Paul froze on the highway, listening to the fog. Footsteps in the distance—footsteps and a voice singing an absent-minded ditty to itself. No other sounds penetrated the sepulchral silence which once had growled with the life of a great city. Anxiety caught him with clammy hands. An old man's voice it was, crackling and tuneless. Paul groped for his holster and brought out the revolver he had taken from a deserted police station.

"Stop where you are, dermie!" he bellowed at the fog. "I'm armed."

The footsteps and the singing stopped. Paul strained his eyes to penetrate the swirling mist-shroud. After a moment, the oldster answered: "Sure foggy, ain't it, sonny? Can't see ya. Better come a little closer. I ain't no dermie."

Loathing choked in Paul's throat. "The hell you're not. Nobody else'd be crazy enough to sing. Get off the road! I'm going south, and if I see you I'll shoot. Now move!"

"Sure, sonny. I'll move. But I'm no dermie. I was just singing to keep myself company. I'm past caring about the plague. I'm heading north, where there's people, and if some dermie hears me a'singing . . . why, I'll tell him t'come jine in. What's the good o' being healthy if yer alone?"

While the old man spoke, Paul heard his sloshing across the ditch and climbing through the brush. Doubt assailed him. Maybe the old crank wasn't a dermie. An ordinary plague victim would have whimpered and pleaded for satisfaction of his strange craving—the laying-on of hands, the feel of healthy skin beneath moist gray palms. Nevertheless, Paul meant to take no chances with the oldster.

"Stay back in the brush while I walk past!" he called.

"Okay, sonny. You go right by. I ain't gonna touch you. You aiming to scrounge in Houston?"

Paul began to advance. "Yeah, I figure people got out so fast that they must have left plenty of canned goods and stuff behind."

"Mmmm, there's a mite here and there," said the cracked voice in a tone that implied understatement. "Course, now, you ain't the first to figure that way, y'know."

Paul slacked his pace, frowning. "You mean . . . a lot of people are coming back?"

"Mmmm, no—not a lot. But you'll bump into people every day or two. Ain't my kind o'folks. Rough characters, mostly—don't take chances, either. They'll shoot first, then look to see if you was a dermie. Don't never come busting out of a doorway without taking a peek at the street first. And if two people come around a corner in opposite directions, somebody's gonna die. The few that's there is trigger happy. Just thought I'd warn ya."

"Thanks."

"D'mention it. Been good t'hear a body's voice again, tho I can't see ye."

Paul moved on until he was fifty paces past the voice. Then he stopped and turned. "Okay, you can get back on the road now. Start walking north. Scuff your feet until you're out of earshot."

"Taking no chances, are ye?" said the old man as he waded the ditch. "All right, sonny." The sound of his footsteps hesitated on the pavement. "A word of advice—your best scrounging'll be around the warehouses. Most of the stores are picked clean. Good luck!"

Paul stood listening to the shuffling feet recede northward. When they became inaudible, he turned to continue his journey. The meeting had depressed him, reminded him of the animal-level to which he and others like him had sunk. The oldster was obviously healthy; but Paul had been chased by three dermies in as many days. And the thought of being trapped by a band of them in the fog left him unnerved. Once he had seen a pair of the grinning, maddened compulsives seize a screaming young child while each of them took turns caressing the youngster's arms and face with the gray and slippery hands that spelled certain contraction of the disease—if disease it was. The dark pall of neuroderm was unlike any illness that Earth had ever seen.

The victim became the eager ally of the sickness that gripped him. Caught in its demoniac madness, the stricken human searched hungrily for healthy comrades, then set upon them with no other purpose than to paw at the clean skin and praise the virtues of the blind compulsion that drove him to do so. One touch, and infection was insured. It was as if a third of humanity had become night-prowling maniacs, lurking in the shadows to seize the unwary, working in bands to trap the unarmed wanderer. And two-thirds of humanity found itself fleeing in horror from the mania, seeking the frigid northern climates where, according to rumor, the disease was less infectious. The normal functioning of civilization had been dropped like a hot potato within six months after the first alarm. When the man at the next lathe might be hiding gray discolorations beneath his shirt, industrial society was no place for humanity.

Rumor connected the onslaught of the plague with an unpredicted swarm of meteorites which had brightened the sky one October evening two weeks before the first case was discovered. The first case was, in fact, a machinist who had found one of the celestial cannon balls, handled it, weighed it, estimated its volume by fluid-displacement, then cut into it on his lathe because its low density suggested that it might be hollow. He claimed to have found a pocket of frozen jelly, still rigid from deep space, although the outer shell had been heated white-hot by atmospheric friction. He said he let the jelly thaw, then fed it to his cat because it had an unpleasant fishy odor. Shortly thereafter, the cat disappeared.

Other meteorites had been discovered and similarly treated by university staffs before there was any reason to blame them for the plague. Paul, who had been an engineering student at Texas U at the time of the incident, had heard it said that the missiles were purposefully manufactured by parties unknown, that the jelly contained micro-organisms which under the microscope suggested a cross between a sperm-cell (because of a similar tail) and a Pucini Corpuscle (because of a marked resemblance to nerve tissue in subcellular detail).

When the meteorites were connected with the new and mushrooming disease, some people started a panic by theorizing that the meteor-swarm was a pre-invasion artillery attack by some space-horde lurking beyond telescope range, and waiting for their biological bombardment to wreck civilization before they moved in upon Earth. The government had immediately labeled all investigations "top-secret", and Paul had heard no news since the initial speculations. Indeed, the government might have explained the whole thing and proclaimed it to the country for all he knew. One thing was certain: the country had not heard. It no longer possessed channels of communication.

Paul thought that if any such invaders were coming, they would have already arrived—months ago. Civilization was not truly wrecked; it had simply been discarded during the crazed flight of the individual away from the herd. Industry lay idle and unmanned, but still intact. Man was fleeing from Man. Fear had destroyed the integration of his society, and had left him powerless before any hypothetical invaders. Earth was ripe for plucking, but it remained unplucked and withering. Paul, therefore, discarded the invasion hypothesis, and searched for nothing new to replace it. He accepted the fact of his own existence as best he could. It proved to be a full-time job, with no spare time for theorizing.

Life was a rabbit scurrying over a hill. Life was a warm blanket, and a secluded sleeping place. Life was ditchwater, and an unbloated can of corned beef, and a suit of clothing looted from a deserted cottage. Life, above all else, was an avoidance of other human beings. For no dermie had the grace to cry "unclean!" to the unsuspecting. If the dermie's discolorations were still in the concealable stage, then concealed they would be, while the lost creature deliberately sought to infect his wife, his children, his friends—whoever would not protest an idle touch of the hand. When the grayness touched the face and the backs of the hands, the creature became a feverish night wanderer, subject to strange hallucinations and delusions and desires.

The fog began to part toward mid-morning as Paul drove deeper into the outskirts of Houston. The highway was becoming a commercial subcenter, lined with businesses and small shops. The sidewalks were showered with broken glass from windows kicked in by looters. Paul kept to the center of the deserted street, listening and watching cautiously for signs of life. The distant barking of a dog was the only sound in the once-growling metropolis. A flight of sparrows winged down the street, then darted in through a broken window to an inside nesting place.

He searched a small grocery store, looking for a snack, but the shelves were bare. The thoroughfare had served as a main avenue of escape, and the fugitives had looted it thoroughly to obtain provisions. He turned onto a side street, then after several blocks turned again to parallel the highway, moving through an old residential section. Many houses had been left open, but few had been looted. He entered one old frame mansion and found a can of tomatoes in the kitchen. He opened it and sipped the tender delicacy from the container, while curiosity sent him prowling through the rooms.

He wandered up the first flight of stairs, then halted with one foot on the landing. A body lay sprawled across the second flight—the body of a young man, dead quite a while. A well-rusted pistol had fallen from his hand. Paul dropped the tomatoes and bolted for the street. Suicide was a common recourse, when a man learned that he had been touched.

After two blocks, Paul stopped running. He sat panting on a fire hydrant and chided himself for being overly cautious. The man had been dead for months; and infection was achieved only through contact. Nevertheless, his scalp was still tingling. When he had rested briefly, he continued his plodding course toward the heart of the city. Toward noon, he saw another human being.

The man was standing on the loading dock of a warehouse, apparently enjoying the sunlight that came with the dissolving of the fog. He was slowly and solemnly spooning the contents of a can into a red-lipped mouth while his beard bobbled with appreciative chewing. Suddenly he saw Paul who had stopped in the center of the street with his hand on the butt of his pistol. The man backed away, tossed the can aside, and sprinted the length of the platform. He bounded off the end, snatched a bicycle away from the wall, and pedalled quickly out of sight while he bleated shrill blasts on a police whistle clenched between his teeth.

Paul trotted to the corner, but the man had made another turn. His whistle continued bleating. A signal? A dermie summons to a touching orgy? Paul stood still while he tried to overcome an urge to break into panicked flight. After a minute, the clamor ceased; but the silence was ominous.

If a party of cyclists moved in, he could not escape on foot. He darted toward the nearest warehouse, seeking a place to hide. Inside, he climbed a stack of boxes to a horizontal girder, kicked the stack to topple it, and stretched out belly-down on the steel eye-beam to command a clear shot at the entrances. He lay for an hour, waiting quietly for searchers. None came. At last he slid down a vertical support and returned to the loading platform. The street was empty and silent. With weapon ready, he continued his journey. He passed the next intersection without mishap.

Halfway up the block, a calm voice drawled a command from behind him: "Drop the gun, dermie. Get your hands behind your head."

He halted, motionless. No plague victim would hurl the dermie-charge at another. He dropped the pistol and turned slowly. Three men with drawn revolvers were clambering from the back of a stalled truck. They were all bearded, wore blue jeans, blue neckerchiefs, and green woolen shirts. He suddenly recalled that the man on the loading platform had been similarly dressed. A uniform?

"Turn around again!" barked the speaker.

Paul turned, realizing that the men were probably some sort of self-appointed quarantine patrol. Tow ropes suddenly skidded out from behind and came to a stop near his feet on the pavement—a pair of lariat loops.

"One foot in each loop, dermie!" the speaker snapped.

When Paul obeyed, the ropes were jerked taut about his ankles, and two of the men trotted out to the sides, stood thirty feet apart, and pulled his legs out into a wide straddle. He quickly saw that any movement would cost him his balance.

"Strip to the skin."

"I'm no dermie," Paul protested as he unbuttoned his shirt.

"We'll see for ourselves, Joe," grunted the leader as he moved around to the front. "Get the top off first. If your chest's okay, we'll let your feet go."

When Paul had undressed, the leader walked around him slowly, making him spread his fingers and display the soles of his feet. He stood shivering and angry in the chilly winter air while the men satisfied themselves that he wore no gray patches of neuroderm.

"You're all right, I guess," the speaker admitted; then as Paul stooped to recover his clothing, the man growled, "Not those! Jim, get him a probie outfit."

Paul caught a bundle of clean clothing, tossed to him from the back of the truck. There were jeans, a woolen shirt, and a kerchief, but the shirt and kerchief were red. He shot an inquiring glance at the leader, while he climbed into the welcome change.

"All newcomers are on two weeks probation," the man explained. "If you decide to stay in Houston, you'll get another exam next time the uniform code changes. Then you can join our outfit, if you don't show up with the plague. In fact, you'll have to join if you stay."

"What is the outfit?" Paul asked suspiciously.

"It just started. Schoolteacher name of Georgelle organized it. We aim to keep dermies out. There's about six hundred of us now. We guard the downtown area, but soon as there's enough of us we'll move out to take in more territory. Set up road blocks and all that. You're welcome, soon as we're sure you're clean . . . and can take orders."

"Whose orders?"

"Georgelle's. We got no room for goof-offs, and no time for argument. Anybody don't like the set-up, he's welcome to get out. Jim here'll give you a leaflet on the rules. Better read it before you go anywhere. If you don't, you might make a wrong move. Make a wrong move, and you catch a bullet."

The man called Jim interrupted, "Reckon you better call off the other patrols, Digger?" he said respectfully to the leader.

Digger nodded curtly and turned to blow three short blasts and a long with his whistle. An answering short-long-short came from several blocks away. Other posts followed suit. Paul realized that he had been surrounded by a ring of similar ambushes.

"Jim, take him to the nearest water barrel, and see that he shaves," Digger ordered, then: "What's your name, probie? Also your job, if you had one."

"Paul Harris Oberlin. I was a mechanical engineering student when the plague struck. Part-time garage mechanic while I was in school."

Digger nodded and jotted down the information on a scratchpad. "Good, I'll turn your name in to the registrar. Georgelle says to watch for college men. You might get a good assignment, later. Report to the Esperson Building on the seventeenth. That's inspection day. If you don't show up, we'll come looking for you. All loose probies'll get shot. Now Jim here's gonna see to it that you shave. Don't shave again until your two-weeker. That way, we can estimate how long you been in town—by looking at your beard. We got other ways that you don't need to know about. Georgelle's got a system worked out for everything, so don't try any tricks."

"Tell me, what do you do with dermies?"

Digger grinned at his men. "You'll find out, probie."

Paul was led to a rain barrel, given a basin, razor, and soap. He scraped his face clean while Jim sat at a safe distance, munching a quid of tobacco and watching the operation with tired boredom. The other men had gone.

"May I have my pistol back?"

"Uh-uh! Read the rules. No weapons for probies."

"Suppose I bump into a dermie?"

"Find yourself a whistle and toot a bunch of short blasts. Then run like hell. We'll take care of the dermies. Read the rules."

"Can I scrounge wherever I want to?"

"Probies have their own assigned areas. There's a map in the rules."

"Who wrote the rules, anyhow?"

"Jeezis!" the guard grunted disgustedly. "Read 'em and find out."

When Paul finished shaving, Jim stood up, stretched, then bounded off the platform and picked up his bicycle.

"Where do I go from here?" Paul called.

The man gave him a contemptuous snort, mounted the bike, and pedalled leisurely away. Paul gathered that he was to read the rules. He sat down beside the rain barrel and began studying the mimeographed leaflet.

Everything was cut and dried. As a probie, he was confined to an area six blocks square near the heart of the city. Once he entered it, a blue mark would be stamped on his forehead. At the two-week inspection, the indelible brand would be removed with a special solution. If a branded probie were caught outside his area, he would be forcibly escorted from the city. He was warned against attempting to impersonate permanent personnel, because a system of codes and passwords would ensnare him. One full page of the leaflet was devoted to propaganda. Houston was to become a "Bulwark of health in a stricken world, and the leader of a glorious recovery." The paper was signed by Dr. Georgelle, who had given himself the title of Director.

The pamphlet left Paul with a vague uneasiness. The uniforms—they reminded him of neighborhood boys' gangs in the slums, wearing special sweaters and uttering secret passwords, whipping intruders and amputating the tails of stray cats in darkened garages. And, in another way, it made him think of frustrated little people, gathering at night in brown shirts around a bonfire to sing the *Horst Wessel Leid* and listen to grandiose oratory about glorious destinies. *Their* stray cats had been an unfavored race.

Of course, the dermies were not merely harmless alley prowlers. They were a real menace. And maybe Georgelle's methods were the only ones effective.

While Paul sat with the pamphlet on the platform, he had been gazing absently at the stalled truck from which the men had emerged. Suddenly it broke upon his consciousness that it was a diesel. He bounded off the platform, and went to check its fuel tank, which had been left uncapped.

He knew that it was useless to search for gasoline, but diesel fuel was another matter. The exodus had drained all existing supplies of high octane fuel for the escaping motorcade, but the evacuation had been too hasty and too fear-crazed to worry with out-of-the-ordinary methods. He sniffed the tank. It smelled faintly of gasoline. Some unknowing fugitive had evidently filled it with ordinary fuel, which had later evaporated. But if the cylinders had not been damaged by the trial, the truck might be useful. He checked the engine briefly, and decided that it had not been tried at all. The starting battery had been removed.

He walked across the street and looked back at the warehouse. It bore the sign of a trucking firm. He walked around the block, eyeing the streets cautiously for other patrolmen. There was a fueling platform on the opposite side of the block. A fresh splash of oil on the concrete told him that Georgelle's crew was using the fuel for some purpose—possibly for heating or cooking. He entered the building and found a repair shop, with several dismantled engines lying about. There was a rack of batteries in the corner, but a screwdriver placed across the terminals brought only a weak spark.

The chargers, of course, drew power from the city's electric service, which was dead. After giving the problem some thought, Paul connected five of the batteries in series, then placed a sixth across the total voltage, so that it would collect the charge that the others lost. Then he went to carry buckets of fuel from the pumps to the truck. When the tank was filled, he hoisted each end of the truck with a roll-under jack and inflated the tires with a hand-pump. It was a long and laborious job.

Twilight was gathering by the time he was ready to try it. Several times during the afternoon, he had been forced to hide from cyclists who wandered past, lest they send him on to the probie area and use the truck for their own purposes. Evidently they had long since decided that automotive transportation was a thing of the past.

A series of short whistle-blasts came to his ears just as he was climbing into the cab. The signals were several blocks away, but some of the answering bleats were closer. Evidently another newcomer, he thought. Most new arrivals from the north would pass through the same area on their way downtown. He entered the cab, closed the door softly, and ducked low behind the dashboard as three cyclists raced across the intersection just ahead.

Paul settled down to wait for the all-clear. It came after about ten minutes. Apparently the newcomer had tried to run instead of hiding. When the cyclists returned, they were moving leisurely, and laughing among themselves. After they had passed the intersection, Paul stole quietly out of the cab and moved along the wall to the corner, to assure himself that all the patrolmen had gone. But the sound of shrill pleading came to his ears.

At the end of the building, he clung close to the wall and risked a glance around the corner. A block away, the nude figure of a girl was struggling between taut ropes held by green-shirted guards. She was a pretty girl, with a tousled mop of chestnut hair and clean white limbs—clean except for her forearms, which appeared dipped in dark stain. Then he saw the dark irregular splotch across her flank, like a splash of ink not quite washed clean. She was a dermie.

Paul ducked close to the ground so that his face was hidden by a clump of grass at the corner. A man—the leader of the group—had left the girl, and was advancing up the street toward Paul, who prepared to roll under the building out of sight. But in the middle of the block, the man stopped. He lifted a manhole cover in the pavement, then went back for the girl's clothing, which he dragged at the end of a fishing pole with a wire hook at its tip. He dropped the clothing, one piece at a time into the manhole. A cloud of white dust arose from it, and the man stepped back to avoid the dust. Quicklime, Paul guessed.

Then the leader cupped his hands to his mouth and called back to the others. "Okay, drag her on up here!" He drew his revolver and waited while they tugged the struggling girl toward the manhole.

Paul felt suddenly ill. He had seen dermies shot in self-defense by fugitives from their deathly gray hands, but here was cold and efficient elimination. Here was Dachau and Buchenwald and the nameless camps of Siberia. He turned and bolted for the truck.

The sound of its engine starting brought a halt to the disposal of the pest-girl. The leader appeared at the intersection and stared uncertainly at the truck, as Paul nosed it away from the building. He fidgeted with his revolver doubtfully, and called something over his shoulder to the others. Then he began walking out into the street and signaling for the truck to stop. Paul let it crawl slowly ahead, and leaned out the window to eye the man questioningly.

"How the hell you get that started?" the leader called excitedly. He was still holding the pistol, but it dangled almost unnoticed in his hand. Paul suddenly fed fuel to the diesel and swerved sharply toward the surprised guardsman.

The leader yelped and dived for safety, but the fender caught his hips, spun him off balance, and smashed him down against the pavement. As the truck thundered around the corner toward the girl and her captors, he glanced in the mirror to see the hurt man weakly trying to crawl out of the street. Paul was certain that he was not mortally wounded.

As the truck lumbered on, the girl threw herself prone before it, since the ropes prevented any escape. Paul swerved erratically, sending the girl's captors scurrying for the alley. Then he aimed the wheels to straddle her body. She glanced up, screamed, then hugged the pavement as the behemoth thundered overhead. A bullet ploughed a furrow across the hood. Paul ducked low in the seat and jammed the brake pedal down, as soon as he thought she was clear.

There were several shots, but apparently they were shooting at the girl. Paul counted three seconds, then gunned the engine again. If she hadn't climbed aboard, it was just tough luck, he thought grimly. He shouldn't have tried to save her anyway. But continued shooting told him that she had managed to get inside. The trailer was heaped with clothing, and he trusted the mound of material to halt the barrage of bullets. He heard the explosion of a blowout as he swung around the next corner, and the trailer lurched dangerously. It swayed from side to side as he gathered speed down the wide and trafficless avenue. But the truck had double wheels, and soon the dangerous lurching ceased.

He roared on through the metropolitan area, staying on the same street and gathering speed. An occasional scrounger or cyclist stopped to stare, but they seemed too surprised to act. And they could not have known what had transpired a few blocks away.

Paul could not stop to see if he had a passenger, or if she was still alive. She was more dangerous than the gunmen. Any gratitude she might feel toward her rescuer would be quickly buried beneath her craving to spread the disease. He wished fervently that he had let the patrolmen kill her. Now he was faced with the problem of getting rid of her. He noticed, however, that mirrors were mounted on both sides of the cab. If he stopped the truck, and if she climbed out, he could see, and move away again before she had a chance to approach him. But he decided to wait until they were out of the city.

Soon he saw a highway marker, then a sign that said "Galveston—58 miles." He bore ahead, thinking that perhaps the island-city would provide good scrounging, without the regimentation of Doctor Georgelle's efficient system with its plans for "glorious recovery".

Twenty miles beyond the city limits, he stopped the truck, let the engine idle, and waited for his passenger to climb out. He locked the doors and laid a jack-handle across the seat as an added precaution. Nothing happened. He rolled down the window and shouted toward the rear.

"All passengers off the bus! Last stop! Everybody out!"

Still the girl did not appear. Then he heard something—a light tap from the trailer, and a murmur . . . or a moan. She was there all right. He called again, but she made no response. It was nearly dark outside.

At last he seized the jack-handle, opened the door, and stepped out of the cab. Wary of a trick, he skirted wide around the trailer and approached it from the rear. One door was closed, while the other swung free. He stopped a few yards away and peered inside. At first he saw nothing.

"Get out, but keep away or I'll kill you."

Then he saw her move. She was sitting on the floor, leaning back against a heap of clothing, a dozen feet from the entrance. He stepped forward cautiously and flung open the other door. She turned her head to look at him peculiarly, but said nothing. He could see that she had donned some of the clothing, but one trouser-leg was rolled up, and she had tied a rag tightly about her ankle.

"Are you hurt?"

She nodded. "Bullet . . ." She rolled her head dizzily and moaned.

Paul went back to the cab to search for a first aid kit. He found one, together with a flashlight and spare batteries in the glove compartment. He made certain that the cells were not corroded and that the light would burn feebly. Then he returned to the trailer, chiding himself for a prize fool. A sensible human would haul the dermie out at the end of a towing chain and leave her sitting by the side of the road.

"If you try to touch me, I'll brain you!" he warned, as he clambered into the trailer.

She looked up again. "Would you feel . . . like enjoying anything . . . if you were bleeding like this?" she muttered weakly. The flashlight beam caught the glitter of pain in her eyes, and accentuated the pallor of her small face. She was a pretty girl—scarcely older than twenty—but Paul was in no mood to appreciate pretty women, especially dermies.

"So that's how you think of it, eh? Enjoying yourself!"

She said nothing. She dropped her forehead against her knee and rolled it slowly.

"Where are you hit? Just the foot?"

"Ankle . . ."

"All right, take the rag off. Let's see."

"The wound's in back."

"All right, lie down on your stomach, and keep your hands under your head."

She stretched out weakly, and he shone the light over her leg, to make certain its skin was clear of neuroderm. Then he looked at the ankle, and said nothing for a time. The bullet had missed the joint, but had neatly severed the Achilles' tendon just above the heel.

"You're a plucky kid," he grunted, wondering how she had endured the self-torture of getting the shoe off and clothing herself.

"It was cold back here—without clothes," she muttered.

Paul opened the first aid packet and found an envelope of sulfa powder. Without touching her, he emptied it into the wound, which was beginning to bleed again. There was nothing else he could do. The tendon had pulled apart and would require surgical stitching to bring it together until it could heal. Such attention was out of the question.

She broke the silence. "I . . . I'm going to be crippled, aren't I?"

"Oh, not crippled," he heard himself telling her. "If we can get you to a doctor, anyway. Tendons can be sutured with wire. He'll probably put your foot in a cast, and you might get a stiff ankle from it."

She lay breathing quietly, denying his hopeful words by her silence.

"Here!" he said. "Here's a gauze pad and some tape. Can you manage it yourself?"

She started to sit up. He placed the first aid pack beside her, and backed to the door. She fumbled in the kit, and whimpered while she taped the pad in place.

"There's a tourniquet in there, too. Use it if the bleeding's worse."

She looked up to watch his silhouette against the darkening evening sky. "Thanks . . . thanks a lot, mister. I'm grateful. I promise not to touch you. Not if you don't want me to."

Shivering, he moved back to the cab. Why did they always get that insane idea that they were doing their victims a favor by giving them the neural plague? *Not if you don't want me to.* He shuddered as he drove away. She felt that way now, while the pain robbed her of the craving, but later—unless he got rid of her quickly—she would come to feel that she owed it to him—as a favor. The disease perpetuated itself by arousing such strange delusions in its bearer. The micro-organisms' methods of survival were indeed highly specialized. Paul felt certain that such animalicules had not evolved on Earth.

A light gleamed here and there along the Alvin-Galveston highway—oil lamps, shining from lonely cottages whose occupants had not felt the pressing urgency of the crowded city. But he had no doubt that to approach one of the farmhouses would bring a rifle bullet as a welcome. Where could he find help for the girl? No one would touch her but another dermie. Perhaps he could unhitch the trailer and leave her in downtown Galveston, with a sign hung on the back—"Wounded dermie inside." The plague victims would care for their own—if they found her.

He chided himself again for worrying about her. Saving her life didn't make him responsible for her . . . did it? After all, if she lived, and the leg healed, she would only prowl in search of healthy victims again. She would never be rid of the disease, nor would she ever die of it—so far as anyone knew. The death rate was high among dermies, but the cause was usually a bullet.

Paul passed a fork in the highway and knew that the bridge was just ahead. Beyond the channel lay Galveston Island, once brightly lit and laughing in its role as seaside resort—now immersed in darkness. The wind whipped at the truck from the southwest as the road led up onto the wide causeway. A faint glow in the east spoke of a moon about to rise. He saw the wide structure of the drawbridge just ahead.

Suddenly he clutched at the wheel, smashed furiously down on the brake, and tugged the emergency back. The tires howled ahead on the smooth concrete, and the force threw him forward over the wheel. Dusty water swirled far below where the upward folding gates of the drawbridge had once been. He skidded to a stop ten feet from the end. When he climbed out, the girl was calling weakly from the trailer, but he walked to the edge and looked over. Someone had done a job with dynamite.

Why, he wondered. To keep islanders on the island, or to keep mainlanders off? Had another Doctor Georgelle started his own small nation in Galveston? It seemed more likely that the lower island dwellers had done the demolition.

He looked back at the truck. An experienced truckster might be able to swing it around all right, but Paul was doubtful. Nevertheless, he climbed back in the cab and tried it. Half an hour later he was hopelessly jammed, with the trailer twisted aside and the cab wedged near the sheer drop to the water. He gave it up and went back to inspect his infected cargo.

She was asleep, but moaning faintly. He prodded her awake with the jack-handle. "Can you crawl, kid? If you can, come back to the door."

She nodded, and began dragging herself toward the flashlight. She clenched her lip between her teeth to keep from whimpering, but her breath came as a voiced murmur . . . *nnnng* . . . *nnnng*. . .

She sagged weakly when she reached the entrance, and for a moment he thought she had fainted. Then she looked up. "What next, skipper?" she panted.

"I . . . I don't know. Can you let yourself down to the pavement?"

She glanced over the edge and shook her head. "With a rope, maybe. There's one back there someplace. If you're scared of me, I'll try to crawl and get it."

"Hands to yourself?" he asked suspiciously; then he thanked the darkness for hiding the heat of shame that crawled to his face.

"I won't . . ."

He scrambled into the trailer quickly and brought back the rope. "I'll climb up on top and let it down in front of you. Grab hold and let yourself down."

★

A few minutes later she was sitting on the concrete causeway looking at the wrecked draw. "Oh!" she muttered as he scrambled down from atop the trailer. "I thought you just wanted to dump me here. We're stuck, huh?"

"Yeah! We might swim it, but doubt if you could make it."

"I'd try . . ." She paused, cocking her head slightly. "There's a boat moored under the bridge. Right over there."

"What makes you think so?"

"Water lapping against wood. Listen." Then she shook her head. "I forgot. You're not hyper."

"I'm not what?" Paul listened. The water sounds seemed homogeneous.

"Hyperacute. Sharp senses. You know, it's one of the symptoms."

He nodded, remembering vaguely that he'd heard something to that effect—but he'd chalked it up as hallucinatory phenomenon. He walked to the rail and shone his light toward the water. The boat was there—tugging its rope taut from the mooring as the tide swirled about it. The bottom was still fairly dry, indicating that a recent rower had crossed from the island to the mainland.

"Think you can hold onto the rope if I let you down?" he called.

She gave him a quick glance, then picked up the end she had previously touched and tied a loop about her waist. She began crawling toward the rail. Paul fought down a crazy urge to pick her up and carry her; plague be damned. But he had already left himself dangerously open to contagion. Still, he felt the drumming charges of conscience . . . *depart from me, ye accursed, for I was sick and you visited me not . . .*

He turned quickly away, and began knotting the end of the rope about the rail. He reminded himself that any sane person would desert her at once, and swim on to safety. Yet, he could not. In the oversized clothing she looked like a child, hurt and helpless. Paul knew the demanding arrogance that could possess the wounded—*help me, you've got to help me, you damn merciless bastard!*. . . No, don't touch me there, damn you! Too many times, he had heard the sick curse the physician, and the injured curse the rescuer. Blind aggression, trying to strike back at pain.

But the girl made no complaint except the involuntary hurt sounds. She asked nothing, and accepted his aid with a wide-eyed gratitude that left him weak. He thought that it would be easier to leave her if she would only beg, or plead, or demand.

"Can you start me swinging a little?" she called as he lowered her toward the water.

Paul's eyes probed the darkness below, trying to sort the shadows, to make certain which was the boat. He used both hands to feed out the rope, and the light laid on the rail only seemed to blind him. She began swinging herself pendulum-wise somewhere beneath him.

"When I say 'ready', let me go!" she shrilled.

"You're not going to drop!"

"Have to! Boat's out further. Got to swing for it. I can't swim, really."

"But you'll hurt your—"

"Ready!"

Paul still clung to the rope. "I'll let you down into the water and you can hang onto the rope. I'll dive, and then pull you into the boat."

"Uh-uh! You'd have to touch me. You don't want that, do you? Just a second now . . . one more swing . . . ready!"

He let the rope go. With a clatter and a thud, she hit the boat. Three sharp cries of pain clawed at him. Then—muffled sobbing.

"Are you all right?"

Sobs. She seemed not to hear him.

"Jeezis!" He sprinted for the brink of the drawbridge and dived out over the deep channel. How far . . . down . . . down. . . . Icy water stung his body with sharp whips, then opened to embrace him. He fought to the surface and swam toward the dark shadow of the boat. The sobbing had subsided. He grasped the prow and hauled himself dripping from the channel. She was lying curled in the bottom of the boat.

"Kid . . . you all right, kid?"

"Sorry . . . I'm such a baby," she gasped, and dragged herself back to the stern.

Paul found a paddle, but no oars. He cast off and began digging water toward the other side, but the tide tugged them relentlessly away from the bridge. He gave it up and paddled toward the distant shore. "You know anything about Galveston?" he called—mostly to reassure himself that she was not approaching him in the darkness with the death-gray hands.

"I used to come here for the summer, I know a little about it."

Paul urged her to talk while he plowed toward the island. Her name was Willie, and she insisted that it was for Willow, not for Wilhelmina. She came from Dallas, and claimed she was a salesman's daughter who was done in by a traveling farmer. The farmer, she explained, was just a wandering dermie who had caught her napping by the roadside. He had stroked her arms until she awoke, then had run away, howling with glee.

"That was three weeks ago," she said. "If I'd had a gun, I'd have dropped him. Of course, I know better now."

Paul shuddered and paddled on. "Why did you head south?"

"I was coming here."

"Here? To Galveston?"

"Uh-huh. I heard someone say that a lot of nuns were coming to the island. I thought maybe they'd take me in."

The moon was high over the lightless city, and the tide had swept the small boat far east from the bridge by the time Paul's paddle dug into the mud beneath the shallow water. He bounded out and dragged the boat through thin marsh grass onto the shore. Fifty yards away, a ramshackle fishing cottage lay sleeping in the moonlight.

"Stay here, Willie," he grunted. "I'll find a couple of boards or something for crutches."

He rummaged about through a shed behind the cottage and brought back a wheelbarrow. Moaning and laughing at once, she struggled into it, and he wheeled her to the house, humming a verse of *Rickshaw Boy*.

"You're a funny guy, Paul. I'm sorry . . ." She jiggled her tousled head in the moonlight, as if she disapproved of her own words.

Paul tried the cottage door, kicked it open, then walked the wheelbarrow up three steps and into a musty room. He struck a match, found an oil lamp with a little kerosene, and lit it. Willie caught her breath.

He looked around. "Company," he grunted.

The company sat in a fragile rocker with a shawl about her shoulders and a shotgun between her knees. She had been dead at least a month. The charge of buckshot had sieved the ceiling and spattered it with bits of gray hair and brown blood.

"Stay here," he told the girl tonelessly. "I'll try to get a dermie somewhere—one who knows how to sew a tendon. Got any ideas?"

She was staring with a sick face at the old woman. "Here? With—"

"She won't bother you," he said as he gently disentangled the gun from the corpse. He moved to a cupboard and found a box of shells behind an orange teapot. "I may not be back, but I'll send somebody."

She buried her face in her plague-stained hands, and he stood for a moment watching her shoulders shiver. "Don't worry . . . I will send somebody." He stepped to the porcelain sink and pocketed a wafer-thin sliver of dry soap.

"What's that for?" she muttered, looking up again.

He thought of a lie, then checked it. "To wash you off of me," he said truthfully. "I might have got too close. Soap won't do much good, but I'll feel better." He looked at the corpse coolly. "Didn't do her much good. Buckshot's the best antiseptic all right."

Willie moaned as he went out the door. He heard her crying as he walked down to the waterfront. She was still crying when he waded back to shore, after a thorough scrubbing. He was sorry he'd spoken cruelly, but it was such a damned relief to get rid of her . . .

With the shotgun cradled on his arm, he began putting distance between himself and the sobbing. But the sound worried his ears, even after he realized that he was no longer hearing her.

He strode a short distance inland past scattered fishing shanties, then took the highway toward the city whose outskirts he was entering. It would be at least an hour's trek to the end of the island where he would be most likely to encounter someone with medical training. The hospitals were down there, the medical school, the most likely place for any charitable nuns—if Willie's rumor was true. Paul meant to capture a dermie doctor or nurse and force the amorous-handed maniac at gun-point to go to Willie's aid. Then he would be done with her. When she stopped hurting, she would start craving—and he had no doubt that he would be the object of her manual affections.

The bay was wind-chopped in the moonglow, no longer glittering from the lights along 61st Street. The oleanders along Broadway were choked up with weeds. Cats or rabbits rustled in the tousled growth that had been a carefully tended parkway.

Paul wondered why the plague had chosen Man, and not the lower animals. It was true that an occasional dog or cow was seen with the plague, but the focus was upon humanity. And the craving to spread the disease was Man-directed, even in animals. It was as if the neural entity deliberately sought out the species with the most complex nervous system. Was its onslaught really connected with the meteorite swarm? Paul believed that it was.

In the first place, the meteorites had not been predicted. They were not a part of the regular cosmic bombardment. And then there was the strange report that they were *manufactured* projectiles, teeming with frozen micro-organisms which came alive upon thawing. In these days of tumult and confusion, however, it was hard. Nevertheless Paul believed it. Neuroderm had no first cousins among Earth diseases.

What manner of beings, then, had sent such a curse? Potential invaders? If so, they were slow in coming. One thing was generally agreed upon by the scientists: the missiles had not been "sent" from another solar planet. Their direction upon entering the atmosphere was wrong. They could conceivably have been fired from an interplanetary launching ship, but their velocity was about equal to the theoretical velocity which a body would obtain in falling sunward from the near-infinite distance. This seemed to hint the projectiles had come from another star.

Paul was startled suddenly by the flare of a match from the shadow of a building. He stopped dead still in the street. A man was leaning against the wall to light a cigarette. He flicked the match out, and Paul watched the cigarette-glow make an arc as the man waved at him.

"Nice night, isn't it?" said the voice from the darkness.

Paul stood exposed in the moonlight, carrying the shotgun at the ready. The voice sounded like that of an adolescent, not fully changed to its adult timbre. If the youth wasn't a dermie, why wasn't he afraid that Paul might be one? And if he was a dermie, why wasn't he advancing in the hope that Paul might be as yet untouched?

"I said, 'Nice night, isn't it?' Whatcha carrying the gun for? Been shooting rabbits?"

Paul moved a little closer and fumbled for his flashlight. Then he threw its beam on the slouching figure in the shadows. He saw a young man, perhaps sixteen, reclining against the wall. He saw the pearl-gray face that characterized the final and permanent stage of neuroderm! He stood frozen to the spot a dozen feet away from the youth, who blinked perplexedly into the light. The kid was assuming automatically that he was another dermie! Paul tried to keep him blinded while he played along with the fallacy.

"Yeah, it's a nice night. You got any idea where I can find a doctor?"

The boy frowned. "Doctor? You mean you don't know?"

"Know what? I'm new here."

"New? Oh . . ." the boy's nostrils began twitching slightly, as if he were sniffing at the night air. "Well, most of the priests down at Saint Mary's were missionaries. They're all doctors. Why? You sick?"

"No, there's a girl . . . But never mind. How do I get there? And are any of them dermies?"

The boy's eyes wandered peculiarly, and his mouth fell open, as if he had been asked why a circle wasn't square. "You are new, aren't you? They're all dermies, if you want to call them that. Wh—" Again the nostrils were flaring. He flicked the cigarette away suddenly and inhaled a slow draught of the breeze. "I . . . I smell a nonhyper," he muttered.

Paul started to back away. His scalp bristled a warning. The boy advanced a step toward him. A slow beam of anticipation began to glow in his face. He bared his teeth in a wide grain of pleasure.

"You're not a hyper yet," he hissed, moving forward. "I've never had a chance to touch a nonhyper . . ."

"Stay back, or I'll kill you!"

The lad giggled and came on, talking to himself. "The padre says it's wrong, but . . . you smell so . . . so . . . ugh . . ." He flung himself forward with a low throaty cry.

Paul sidestepped the charge and brought the gun barrel down across the boy's head. The dermie sprawled howling in the street. Paul pushed the gun close to his face, but the youth started up again. Paul jabbed viciously with the barrel, and felt it strike and tear. "I don't want to have to blow your head off—"

The boy howled and fell back. He crouched panting on his hands and knees, head hung low, watching a dark puddle of blood gather on the pavement from a deep gash across his cheek. "Whatcha wanta do that for?" he whimpered. "I wasn't gonna hurt you." His tone was that of a wronged and rejected suitor.

"Now, where's Saint Mary's? Is that one of the hospitals? How do I get there?" Paul had backed to a safe distance and was covering the youth with the gun.

"Straight down Broadway . . . to the Boulevard . . . you'll see it down that neighborhood. About the fourth street, I think." The boy looked up, and Paul saw the extent of the gash. It was deep and ragged, and the kid was crying.

"Get up! You're going to lead me there."

Pain had blanketed the call of the craving. The boy struggled to his feet, pressed a handkerchief against the wound, and with an angry glance at Paul, he set out down the road. Paul followed ten yards behind.

"If you take me through any dermie traps, I'll kill you."

"There aren't any traps," the youth mumbled.

Paul snorted unbelief, but did not repeat the warning. "What made you think I was another dermie?" he snapped.

"Because there's no nonhypers in Galveston. This is a hyper colony. A nonhyper used to drift in occasionally, but the priests had the bridge dynamited. The nonhypers upset the colony. As long as there aren't any around to smell, nobody causes any trouble. During the day, there's a guard out on the causeway, and if any hypers come looking for a place to stay, the guard ferries them across. If nonhypers come, he tells them about the colony, and they go away."

Paul groaned. He had stumbled into a rat's nest. Was there no refuge from the gray curse? Now he would have to move on. It seemed a hopeless quest. Maybe the old man he met on his way to Houston had arrived at the only possible hope for peace: submission to the plague. But the thought sickened him somehow. He would have to find some barren island, find a healthy mate, and go to live a savage existence apart from all traces of civilization.

"Didn't the guard stop you at the bridge?" the boy asked. "He never came back today. He must be still out there."

Paul grunted "no" in a tone that warned against idle conversation. He guessed what had happened. The dermie guard had probably spotted some healthy wanderers; and instead of warning them away, he rowed across the drawbridge and set out to chase them. His body probably lay along the highway somewhere, if the hypothetical wanderers were armed.

When they reached 23rd Street, a few blocks from the heart of the city, Paul hissed at the boy to stop. He heard someone laugh. Footsteps were wandering along the sidewalk, overhung by trees. He whispered to the boy to take refuge behind a hedge. They crouched in the shadows several yards apart while the voices drew nearer.

"Brother James had a nice tenor," someone said softly. "But he sings his Latin with a western drawl. It sounds . . . well . . . peculiar, to say the least. Brother John is a stickler for pronunciation. He won't let Fra James solo. Says it gives a burlesque effect to the choir. Says it makes the sisters giggle."

The other man chuckled quietly and started to reply. But his voice broke off suddenly. The footsteps stopped a dozen feet from Paul's hiding place. Paul, peering through the hedge, saw a pair of brown-robed monks standing on the sidewalk. They were looking around suspiciously.

"Brother Thomas, do you smell—"

"Aye, I smell it."

Paul changed his position slightly, so as to keep the gun pointed toward the pair of plague-stricken monastics. They stood in embarrassed silence, peering into the darkness, and shuffling their feet uneasily. One of them suddenly pinched his nose between thumb and forefinger. His companion followed suit.

"Blessed be God," quavered one.

"Blessed be His Holy Name," answered the other.

"Blessed be Jesus Christ, true God and true Man."

"Blessed be . . ."

Gathering their robes high about their shins, the two monks turned and scurried away, muttering the Litany of the Divine Praises as they went. Paul stood up and stared after them in amazement. The sight of dermies running from a potential victim was almost beyond belief. He questioned his young guide. Still holding the handkerchief against his bleeding face, the boy hung his head.

"Bishop made a ruling against touching nonhypers," he explained miserably. "Says it's a sin, unless the nonhyper submits of his own free will. Says even then it's wrong, except in the ordinary ways that people come in contact with each other. Calls it fleshly desire, and all that."

"Then why did you try to do it?"

"I ain't so religious."

"Well, sonny, you better get religious until we come to the hospital. Now, let's go."

They marched on down Broadway encountering no other pedestrians. Twenty minutes later, they were standing in the shadows before a hulking brick building, some of whose windows were yellow with lamplight. Moonlight bathed the statue of a woman standing on a ledge over the entrance, indicating to Paul that this was the hospital.

"All right, boy. You go in and send out a dermie doctor. Tell him somebody wants to see him, but if you say I'm not a dermie, I'll come in and kill you. Now move. And don't come back. Stay to get your face fixed."

The youth stumbled toward the entrance. Paul sat in the shadow of a tree, where he could see twenty yards in all directions and guard himself against approach. Soon a black-clad priest came out of the emergency entrance, stopped on the sidewalk, and glanced around.

"Over here!" Paul hissed from across the street.

The priest advanced uncertainly. In the center of the road he stopped again, and held his nose. "Y-you're a nonhyper," he said, almost accusingly.

"That's right, and I've got a gun, so don't try anything."

"What's wrong? Are you sick? The lad said—"

"There's a dermie girl down the island. She's been shot. Tendon behind her heel is cut clean through. You're going to help her."

"Of course, but . . ." The priest paused. "You? A nonhyper? Helping a so-called dermie?" His voice went high with amazement.

"So I'm a sucker!" Paul barked. "Now get what you need, and come on."

"The Lord bless you," the priest mumbled in embarrassment as he hurried away.

"Don't stick any of your maniacs on me!" Paul called after him. "I'm armed."

"I'll have to bring a surgeon," the cleric said over his shoulder.

Five minutes later, Paul heard the muffled grunt of a starter. Then an engine coughed to life. Startled, he scurried away from the tree and sought safety in a clump of shrubs. An ambulance backed out of the driveway and into the street. It parked at the curb by the tree, engine running. A pallid face glanced out curiously toward the shadows. "Where are you?" it called, but it was not the priest's voice.

Paul stood up and advanced a few steps.

"We'll have to wait on Father Mendelhaus," the driver called. "He'll be a few minutes."

"You a dermie?"

"Of course. But don't worry. I've plugged my nose and I'm wearing rubber gloves. I can't smell you. The sight of a nonhyper arouses some craving, of course. But it can be overcome with a little will power. I won't infect you, although I don't understand why you nonhypers fight so hard. You're bound to catch it sooner or later. And the world can't get back to normal until everybody has it."

Paul avoided the startling thought. "You the surgeon?"

"Uh, yes. Father Williamson's the name. I'm not really a specialist, but I did some surgery in Korea. How's the girl's condition? Suffering shock?"

"I wouldn't know."

They fell silent until Father Mendelhaus returned. He came across the street carrying a bag in one hand and a brown bottle in the other. He held the bottle by the neck with a pair of tongs and Paul could see the exterior of the bottle steaming slightly as the priest passed through the beam of the ambulance's headlights. He placed the flask on the curb without touching it, then spoke to the man in the shadows.

"Would you step behind the hedge and disrobe, young man? Then rub yourself thoroughly with this oil."

"I doubt it," Paul snapped. "What is it?"

"Don't worry, it's been in the sterilizer. That's what took me so long. It may be a little hot for you, however. It's only an antiseptic and deodorant. It'll kill your odor, and it'll also give you some protection against picking up stray micro-organisms."

After a few moments of anxious hesitation, Paul decided to trust the priest. He carried the hot flask into the brush, undressed, and bathed himself with the warm aromatic oil. Then he slipped back into his clothes and reapproached the ambulance.

"Ride in back," Mendelhaus told him. "And you won't be infected. No one's been in there for several weeks, and as you probably know, the micro-organisms die after a few hours exposure. They have to be transmitted from skin to skin, or else an object has to be handled very soon after a hyper has touched it."

Paul warily climbed inside. Mendelhaus opened a slide and spoke through it from the front seat. "You'll have to show us the way."

"Straight out Broadway. Say, where did you get the gasoline for this wagon."

The priest paused. "That has been something of a secret. Oh well . . . I'll tell you. There's a tanker out in the harbor. The people left town too quickly to think of it. Automobiles are scarcer than fuel in Galveston. Up north, you find them stalled everywhere. But since Galveston didn't have any through-traffic, there were no cars running out of gas. The ones we have are the ones that were left in the repair shop. Something wrong with them. And we don't have any mechanics to fix them."

Paul neglected to mention that he was qualified for the job. The priest might get ideas. He fell into gloomy silence as the ambulance turned onto Broadway and headed down-island. He watched the back of the priests' heads, silhouetted against the headlighted pavement. They seemed not at all concerned about their disease. Mendelhaus was a slender man, with a blond crew cut and rather bushy eyebrows. He had a thin, aristocratic face—now plague-gray—but jovial enough. It might be the face of an ascetic, but for the quick blue eyes that seemed full of lively interest rather than inward-turning mysticism. Williamson, on the other hand, was a rather plain man, with a stolid tweedy look, despite his black cassock.

"What do you think of our plan here?" asked Father Mendelhaus.

"What plan?" Paul grunted.

"Oh, didn't the boy tell you? We're trying to make the island a refuge for hypers who are willing to sublimate their craving and turn their attentions toward reconstruction. We're also trying to make an objective study of this neutral condition. We have some good scientific minds, too—Doctor Relmone of Fordham, Father Seyes of Notre Dame, two biologists from Boston College. . ."

"Dermies trying to cure the plague?" Paul gasped.

Mendelhaus laughed merrily. "I didn't say cure it, son. I said 'study it'."

"Why?"

"To learn how to live with it, of course. It's been pointed out by our philosophers that things become evil only through human misuse. Morphine, for instance, is a product of the Creator; it is therefore good when properly used for relief of pain. When mistreated by an addict, it becomes a monster. We bear this in mind as we study neuroderm."

Paul snorted contemptuously. "Leprosy is evil, I suppose, because Man mistreated bacteria?"

The priest laughed again. "You've got me there. I'm no philosopher. But you can't compare neuroderm with leprosy."

Paul shuddered. "The hell I can't! It's worse."

"Ah? Suppose you tell me what makes it worse? List the symptoms for me."

Paul hesitated, listing them mentally. They were: discoloration of the skin, low fever, hallucinations, and the insane craving to infect others. They seemed bad enough, so he listed them orally. "Of course, people don't die of it," he added. "But which is worse, insanity or death?"

The priest turned to smile back at him through the porthole. "Would you call me insane? It's true that victims have frequently lost their minds. But that's not a direct result of neuroderm. Tell me, how would you feel if everyone screamed and ran when they saw you coming, or hunted you down like a criminal? How long would your sanity last?"

Paul said nothing. Perhaps the anathema was a contributing factor. . . .

"Unless you were of very sound mind to begin with, you probably couldn't endure it."

"But the craving . . . and thc hallucinations . . ."

"True," murmured the priest thoughtfully. "The hallucinations. Tell me something else, if all the world was blind save one man, wouldn't the world be inclined to call that man's sight a hallucination? And the man with eyes might even come to agree with the world."

Again Paul was silent. There was no arguing with Mendelhaus, who probably suffered the strang delusions and thought them real.

"And the craving," the priest went on. "It's true that the craving can be a rather unpleasant symptom. It's the condition's way of perpetuating itself. Although we're not certain how it works, it seems able to stimulate erotic sensations in the hands. We do know the micro-organisms get to the brain, but we're not yet sure what they do there."

"What facts have you discovered?" Paul asked cautiously.

Mendelhaus grinned at him. "Tut! I'm not going to tell you, because I don't want to be called a 'crazy dermie'. You wouldn't believe me, you see."

Paul glanced outside and saw that they were approaching the vicinity of the fishing cottage. He pointed out the lamplit window to the driver, and the ambulance turned onto a side road. Soon they were parked behind the shanty. The priests scrambled out and carried the stretcher toward the light, while Paul skulked to a safer distance and sat down in the grass to watch. When Willie was safe in the vehicle, he meant to walk back to the bridge, swim across the gap, and return to the mainland.

Soon Mendelhaus came out and walked toward him with a solemn stride, although Paul was sitting quietly in the deepest shadow—invisible, he had thought. He arose quickly as the priest approached. Anxiety tightened his throat. "Is she . . . is Willie . . .?"

"She's irrational," Mendelhaus murmured sadly. "Almost . . . less than sane. Some of it may be due to high fever, but . . ."

"Yes?"

"She tried to kill herself. With a knife. Said something about buckshot being the best way, or something . . ."

"Jeezis! Jeezis!" Paul sank weakly in the grass and covered his face with his hands.

"Blessed be His Holy Name," murmured the priest by way of turning the oath aside. "She didn't hurt herself badly, though. Wrist's cut a little. She was too weak to do a real job of it. Father Will's giving her a hypo and a tetanus shot and some sulfa. We're out of penicillin."

He stopped speaking and watched Paul's wretchedness for a moment. "You love the girl, don't you?"

Paul stiffened. "Are you crazy? Love a little tramp dermie? Jeezis . . ."

"Blessed be—"

"Listen! Will she be all right? I'm getting out of here!" He climbed unsteadily to his feet.

"I don't know, son. Infection's the real threat, and shock. If we'd got to her sooner, she'd have been safer. And if she was in the ultimate stage of neuroderm, it would help."

"Why?"

"Oh, various reasons. You'll learn, someday. But listen, you look exhausted. Why don't you come back to the hospital with us? The third floor is entirely vacant. There's no danger of infection up there, and we keep a sterile room ready just in case we get a nonhyper case. You can lock the door inside, if you want to, but it wouldn't be necessary. Nuns are on the floor below. Our male staff lives in the basement. There aren't any laymen in the building. I'll guarantee that you won't be bothered."

"No, I've got to go," he growled, then softened his voice: "I appreciate it though, Father."

"Whatever you wish. I'm sorry, though. You might be able to provide yourself with some kind of transportation if you waited."

"Uh-uh! I don't mind telling you, your island makes me jumpy."

"Why?"

Paul glanced at the priest's gray hands. "Well . . . you still feel the craving, don't you?"

Mendelhaus touched his nose. "Cotton plugs, with a little camphor. I can't smell you." He hesitated. "No, I won't lie to you. The urge to touch is still there to some extent."

"And in a moment of weakness, somebody might—"

The priest straightened his shoulders. His eyes went chilly. "I have taken certain vows, young man. Sometimes when I see a beautiful woman, I feel desire. When I see a man eating a thick steak on a fast-day, I feel envy and hunger. When I see a doctor earning large fees, I chafe under the vow of poverty. But by denying desire's demands, one learns to make desire useful in other ways. Sublimation, some call it. A priest can use it and do more useful work thereby. I am a priest."

He nodded curtly, turned on his heel and strode away. Halfway to the cottage, he paused. "She's calling for someone named Paul. Know who it might be? Family perhaps?"

Paul stood speechless. The priest shrugged and continued toward the lighted doorway.

"Father, wait . . ."

"Yes?"

"I—I am a little tired. The room . . . I mean, will you show me where to get transportation tomorrow?"

"Certainly."

Before midnight, the party had returned to the hospital. Paul lay on a comfortable mattress for the first time in weeks, sleepless, and staring at the moonlight on the sill. Somewhere downstairs, Willie was lying unconscious in an operating room, while the surgeon tried to repair the torn tendon. Paul had ridden back with them in the ambulance, sitting a few feet from the stretcher, avoiding her sometimes wandering arms, and listening to her delirious moaning.

Now he felt his skin crawling with belated hypochondria. What a fool he had been—touching the rope, the boat, the wheelbarrow, riding in the ambulance. There were a thousand ways he could have picked up a few stray micro-organisms lingering from a dermie's touch. And now, he lay here in this nest of disease. . .

But strange—it was the most peaceful, the sanest place he'd seen in months. The religious orders simply accepted the plague—with masochistic complacency perhaps—but calmly. A cross, or a penance, or something. But no, they seemed to accept it almost gladly. Nothing peculiar about that. All dermies went wild-eyed with happiness about the "lovely desire" they possessed. The priests weren't wild-eyed.

Neither was normal man equipped with socially-shaped sexual desire. Sublimation?

"Peace," he muttered, and went to sleep.

A knocking at the door awoke him at dawn. He grunted at it disgustedly and sat up in bed. The door, which he had forgotten to lock, swung open. A chubby nun with a breakfast tray started into the room. She saw his face, then stopped. She closed her eyes, wrinkled her nose, and framed a silent prayer with her lips. Then she backed slowly out.

"I'm sorry, sir!" she quavered through the door. "I—I knew there was a patient in here, but I didn't know . . . you weren't a hyper. Forgive me."

He heard her scurrying away down the hall. Somehow, he began to feel safe. But wasn't that exactly what they wanted him to feel! He realized suddenly that he was trapped. He had left the shotgun in the emergency room. What was he—guest or captive? Months of fleeing from the gray terror had left him suspicious.

Soon he would find out. He arose and began dressing. Before he finished, Mendelhaus came. He did not enter, but stood in the hallway beyond the door. He smiled a faint greeting, and said, "So you're Paul?"

He felt heat rising in his face. "She's awake, then?" he asked gruffly.

The priest nodded. "Want to see her?"

"No, I've got to be going."

"It would do her good."

He coughed angrily. Why did the black-cassocked dermie have to put it that way? "Well it wouldn't do me any good!" he snarled. "I've been around too many gray-leather hides already!"

Mendelhaus shrugged, but his eyes bore a hint of contempt. "As you wish. You may leave by the outside stairway—to avoid disturbing the sisters."

"To avoid being touched, you mean!"

"No one will touch you."

Paul finished dressing in silence. The reversal of attitudes disturbed him. He resented the seeming "tolerance" that was being extended him. It was like asylum inmates being "tolerant" of the psychiatrist.

"I'm ready!" he growled.

Mendelhaus led him down the corridor and out onto a sunlit balcony. They descended a stone stairway while the priest talked over his shoulder.

"She's still not fully rational, and there's some fever. It wouldn't be anything to worry about two years ago, but now we're out of most of the latest drugs. If sulfa won't hold the infection, we'll have to amputate, of course. We should know in two or three days."

He paused and looked back at Paul, who had stopped on the stairway. "Coming?"

"Where is she?" Paul asked weakly. "I'll see her."

The priest frowned. "You don't have to, son. I'm sorry if I implied any obligation on your part. Really, you've done enough. I gather that you saved her life. Very few nonhypers would do a thing like that. I—"

"Where is she?" he snapped angrily.

The priest nodded. "Downstairs. Come on."

As they re-entered the building on the ground floor, the priest cupped his hands to his mouth and called out, "Nonhyper coming! Plug your noses, or get out of the way! Avoid circumstances of temptation!"

When they moved along the corridor, it was Paul who felt like the leper. Mendelhaus led him into the third room.

Willie saw him enter and hid her gray hands beneath the sheet. She smiled faintly, tried to sit up, and failed. Williamson and a nun-nurse who had both been standing by the bedside turned to leave the room. Mendelhaus followed them out and closed the door.

There was a long, painful pause. Willie tried to grin. He shuffled his feet.

"They've got me in a cast," she said conversationally.

"You'll be all right," he said hastily. "It won't be long before you'll be up. Galveston's a good place for you. They're all dermies here."

She clenched her eyes tightly shut. "God! God! I hope I never hear that word again. After last night . . . that old woman in the rocking chair . . . I stayed there all alone . . . and the wind'd start the chair rocking. Ooh!" She looked at him with abnormally bright eyes. "I'd rather die than touch anybody now . . . after seeing that. Somebody touched her, didn't they, Paul? That's why she did it, wasn't it?"

He squirmed and backed toward the door. "Willie . . . I'm sorry for what I said. I mean—"

"Don't worry, Paul! I wouldn't touch you now." She clenched her hands and brought them up before her face, to stare at them with glittering hate. "I loathe myself!" she hissed.

What was it Mendelhaus had said, about the dermie going insane because of being an outcast rather than because of the plague? But she wouldn't be an outcast here. Only among nonhypers, like himself . . .

"Get well quick, Willie," he muttered, then hurriedly slipped out into the corridor. She called his name twice, then fell silent.

"That was quick," murmured Mendelhaus, glancing at his pale face.

"Where can I get a car?"

The priest rubbed his chin. "I was just speaking to Brother Matthew about that. Uh . . . how would you like to have a small yacht instead?"

Paul caught his breath. A yacht would mean access to the seas, and to an island. A yacht was the perfect solution. He stammered gratefully.

"Good," said Mendelhaus. "There's a small craft in dry dock down at the basin. It was apparently left there because there weren't any dock crews around to get her afloat again. I took the liberty of asking Brother Matthew to find some men and get her in the water."

"Dermies?"

"Of course. The boat will be fumigated, but it isn't really necessary. The infection dies out in a few hours. It'll take a while, of course, to get the boat ready. Tomorrow . . . next day, maybe. Bottom's cracked; it'll need some patching."

Paul's smile weakened. More delay. Two more days of living in the gray shadow. Was the priest really to be trusted? Why should he even provide the boat? The jaws of an invisible trap, slowly closing.

Mendelhaus saw his doubt. "If you'd rather leave now, you're free to do so. We're really not going to as much trouble as it might seem. There are several yachts at the dock; Brother Matthew's been preparing to clean one or two up for our own use. And we might as well let you have one. They've been deserted by their owners. And . . . well . . . you helped the girl when nobody else would have done so. Consider the boat as our way of returning the favor, eh?"

A yacht. The open sea. A semitropical island, uninhabited, on the brink of the Caribbean. And a woman, of course—chosen from among the many who would be willing to share such an escape. Peculiarly, he glanced at Willie's door. It was too bad about her. But she'd get along okay. The yacht . . . if he were only certain of Mendelhaus' intentions . . .

The priest began frowning at Paul's hesitation. "Well?"

"I don't want to put you to any trouble. . ."

"Nonsense! You're still afraid of us! Very well, come with me. There's someone I want you to see." Mendelhaus turned and started down the corridor.

Paul lingered. "Who . . . what—"

"Come on!" the priest snapped impatiently.

Reluctantly, Paul followed him to the stairway. They descended to a gloomy basement and entered a smelly laboratory through a double-door. Electric illumination startled him; then he heard the sound of a gasoline engine and knew that the power was generated locally.

"Germicidal lamps," murmured the priest, following his ceilingward gaze. "Some of them are. Don't worry about touching things. It's sterile in here."

"But it's not sterile for your convenience," growled an invisible voice. "And it won't be sterile at all if you don't stay out! Beat it, preacher!"

Paul looked for the source of the voice, and saw a small, short-necked man bending his shaggy gray head over a microscope at the other end of the lab. He had spoken without glancing up at his visitors.

"This is Doctor Seevers, of Princeton, son," said the priest, unruffled by the scientist's ire. "Claims he's an atheist, but personally I think he's a puritan. Doctor, this is the young man I was telling you about. Will you tell him what you know about neuroderm?"

Seevers jotted something on a pad, but kept his eye to the instrument. "Why don't we just give it to him, and let him find out for himself?" the scientist grumbled sadistically.

"Don't frighten him, you heretic! I brought him here to be illuminated."

"Illuminate him yourself. I'm busy. And stop calling me names. I'm not an atheist; I'm a biochemist."

"Yesterday you were a biophysicist. Now, entertain my young man." Mendelhaus blocked the doorway with his body. Paul, with his jaw clenched angrily, had turned to leave.

"That's all I can do, preacher," Seevers grunted. "Entertain him. I know nothing. Absolutely nothing. I have some observed data. I have noticed some correlations. I have seen things happen. I have traced the patterns of the happenings and found some probable common denominators. And that is all! I admit it. Why don't you preachers admit it in your racket?"

"Seevers, as you can see, is inordinately proud of his humility—if that's not a paradox," the priest said to Paul.

"Now, Doctor, this young man—"

Seevers heaved a resigned sigh. His voice went sour-sweet. "All right, sit down, young man. I'll entertain you as soon as I get through counting free nerve-endings in this piece of skin."

Mendelhaus winked at his guest. "Seevers calls it masochism when we observe a fast-day or do penance. And there he sits, ripping off patches of his own hide to look at through his peeping glass. Masochism—heh!"

"Get out, preacher!" the scientist bellowed.

Mendelhaus laughed mockingly, nodded Paul toward a chair, and left the lab. Paul sat uneasily watching the back of Seevers' lab jacket.

"Nice bunch of people really—these black-frocked yahoos," Seevers murmured conversationally. "If they'd just stop trying to convert me."

"Doctor Seevers, maybe I'd better—"

"Quiet! You bother me. And sit still, I can't stand to have people running in and out of here. You're in; now stay in."

Paul fell silent. He was uncertain whether or not Seevers was a dermie. The small man's lab jacket bunched up to hide the back of his neck, and the sleeves covered his arms. His hands were rubber-gloved, and a knot of white cord behind his head told Paul that he was wearing a gauze mask. His ears were bright pink, but their color was meaningless; it took several months for the gray coloring to seep to all areas of the skin. But Paul guessed he was a dermie—and wearing the gloves and mask to keep his equipment sterile.

He glanced idly around the large room. There were several glass cages of rats against the wall. They seemed airtight, with ducts for forced ventilation. About half the rats were afflicted with neuroderm in its various stages. A few wore shaved patches of skin where the disease had been freshly and forcibly inflicted. Paul caught the fleeting impression that several of the animals were staring at him fixedly. He shuddered and looked away.

He glanced casually at the usual maze of laboratory glassware, then turned his attention to a pair of hemispheres, suspended like a trophy on the wall. He recognized them as the twin halves of one of the meteorites, with the small jelly-pocket in the center. Beyond it hung a large picture frame containing several typewritten sheets. Another frame held four pictures of bearded scientists from another century, obviously clipped from magazine or textbook. There was nothing spectacular about the lab. It smelled of clean dust and sour things. Just a small respectable workshop.

Seevers' chair creaked suddenly. "It checks," he said to himself. "It checks again. Forty per cent increase." He threw down the stub pencil and whirled suddenly. Paul saw a pudgy round face with glittering eyes. A dark splotch of neuroderm had crept up from the chin to split his mouth and cover one cheek and an eye, giving him the appearance of a black and white bulldog with a mixed color muzzle.

"It checks," he barked at Paul, then smirked contentedly.

"What checks?"

The scientist rolled up a sleeve to display a patch of adhesive tape on a portion of his arm which had been discolored by the disease. "Here," he grunted. "Two weeks ago this area was normal. I took a centimeter of skin from right next to this one, and counted the nerve endings. Since that time, the derm's crept down over the area. I took another square centimeter today, and recounted. Forty per cent increase."

Paul frowned with disbelief. It was generally known that neuroderm had a sensitizing effect, but new nerve endings . . . No. He didn't believe it.

"Third time I've checked it," Seevers said happily. "One place ran up to sixty-five per cent. Heh! Smart little bugs, aren't they? Inventing new somesthetic receptors that way!"

Paul swallowed with difficulty. "What did you say?" he gasped.

Seevers inspected him serenely. "So you're a nonhyper, are you? Yes, indeed, I can smell that you are. Vile, really. Can't understand why sensible hypers would want to paw you. But then, I've insured myself against such foolishness."

He said it so casually that Paul blinked before he caught the full impact of it. "Y-y-you've done what?"

"What I said. When I first caught it, I simply sat down with a velvet-tipped stylus and located the spots on my hands that gave rise to pleasurable sensations. Then I burned them out with an electric needle. There aren't many of them, really—one or two points per square centimeter." He tugged off his gloves and exhibited pick-marked palms to prove it. "I didn't want to be bothered with such silly urges. Waste of time, chasing nonhypers—for me it is. I never learned what it's like, so I've never missed it." He turned his hands over and stared at them. "Stubborn little critters keep growing new ones, and I keep burning them out."

Paul leaped to his feet. "Are you trying to tell me that the plague causes new nerve cells to grow?"

Seevers looked up coldly. "Ah, yes. You came here to be illoooominated, as the padre put it. If you wish to be de-idiotized, please stop shouting. Otherwise, I'll ask you to leave."

Paul, who had felt like leaving a moment ago, now subsided quickly. "I'm sorry," he snapped, then softened his tone to repeat: "I'm, sorry."

Seevers took a deep breath, stretched his short meaty arms in an unexpected yawn, then relaxed and grinned. "Sit down, sit down, m'boy. I'll tell you what you want to know, if you really want to know anything. Do you?"

"Of course!"

"You don't! You just want to know how you—whatever your name is—will be affected by events. You don't care about understanding for its own sake. Few people do. That's why we're in this mess. The padre now, he cares about understanding events—but not for their own sake. He cares, but for his flock's sake and for his God's sake—which is, I must admit, a better attitude than that of the common herd, whose only interest is in their own safety. But if people would just want to understand events for the understanding's sake, we wouldn't be in such a pickle."

Paul watched the professor's bright eyes and took the lecture quietly.

"And so, before I illuminate you, I want to make an impossible request."

"Yes, sir."

"I ask you to be completely objective," Seevers continued, rubbing the bridge of his nose and covering his eyes with his hand. "I want you to forget you ever heard of neuroderm while you listen to me. Rid yourself of all preconceptions, especially those connected with fear. Pretend these are purely hypothetical events that I'm going to discuss." He took his hands down from his eyes and grinned sheepishly. "It always embarrasses me to ask for that kind of co-operation when I know damn well I'll never get it."

"I'll try to be objective, sir."

"Bah!" Seevers slid down to sit on his spine, and hooked the base of his skull over the back of the chair. He blinked thoughtfully at the ceiling for a moment, then folded his hands across his small paunch and closed his eyes.

When he spoke again, he was speaking to himself: "Assume a planet, somewhat earthlike, but not quite. It has carboniferous life forms, but not human. Warm blooded, probably, and semi-intelligent. And the planet has something else—it has an over-abundance of parasite forms. Actually, the various types of parasites are the dominant species. The warm blooded animals are the parasites' vegetables, so to speak. Now, during two billion years, say, of survival contests between parasite species, some parasites are quite likely to develop some curious methods of adaption. Methods of insuring the food supply—animals, who must have been taking a beating."

Seevers glanced down from the ceiling. "Tell me, youngster, what major activity did Man invent to secure his vegetable food supply?"

"Agriculture?"

"Certainly. Man is a parasite, as far as vegetables are concerned. But he learned to eat his cake and have it, too. He learned to perpetuate the species he was devouring. A very remarkable idea, if you stop to think about it. Very!"

"I don't see—"

"Hush! Now, let's suppose that one species of microparasites on our hypothetical planet learned, through long evolutionary processes, to stimulate regrowth in the animal tissue they devoured. Through exuding controlled amounts of growth hormone, I think. Quite an advancement, eh?"

Paul had begun leaning forward tensely.

"But it's only the first step. It let the host live longer, although not pleasantly, I imagine. The growth control would be clumsy at first. But soon, all parasite-species either learned to do it, or died out. Then came the contest for the best kind of control. The parasites who kept their hosts in the best physical condition naturally did a better job of survival—since the parasite-ascendancy had cut down on the food supply, just as Man wastes his own resources. And since animals were contending among themselves for a place in the sun, it was to the parasite's advantage to help insure the survival of his host-species—through growth control."

Seevers winked solemnly. "Now begins the downfall of the parasites—their decadence. They concentrated all their efforts along the lines of . . . uh . . . scientific farming, you might say. They began growing various sorts of defense and attack weapons for their hosts—weird biodevices, perhaps. Horns, swords, fangs, stingers, poison-throwers—we can only guess. But eventually, one group of parasites hit upon—what?"

Paul, who was beginning to stir uneasily, could only stammer. Where was Seevers getting all this?

"Say it!" the scientist demanded.

"The . . . nervous system?"

"That's right. You don't need to whisper it. The nervous system. It was probably an unsuccessful parasite at first, because nerve tissue grows slowly. And it's a long stretch of evolution between a microspecies which could stimulate nerve growth and one which could direct and utilize that growth for the host's advantage—and for its own. But at last, after a long struggle, our little species gets there. It begins sharpening the host's senses, building up complex senses from aggregates of old style receptors, and increasing the host's intelligence within limits."

Seevers grinned mischievously. "Comes a planetary shake-up of the first magnitude. Such parasites would naturally pick the host species with the highest intelligence to begin with. With the extra boost, this brainy animal quickly beats down its own enemies, and consequently the enemies of its microbenefactor. It puts itself in much the same position that Man's in on Earth—lord it over the beasts, divine right to run the place, and all that. Now understand—it's the animal who's become intelligent, not the parasites. The parasites are operating on complex instinct patterns, like a hive of bees. They're wonderful neurological engineers—like bees are good structural engineers; blind instinct, accumulated through evolution."

He paused to light a cigarette. "If you feel ill, young man, there's drinking water in that bottle. You look ill."

"I'm all right!"

"Well, to continue: the intelligent animal became master of his planet. Threats to his existence were overcome—unless he was a threat to himself, like we are. But now, the parasites had found a safe home. No new threats to force readaption. They sat back and sighed and became stagnant—as unchanging as horseshoe crabs or amoeba or other Earth ancients. They kept right on working in their neurological beehives, and now they became cultivated by the animal, who recognized their benefactors. They didn't know it, but they were no longer the dominant species. They had insured their survival by leaning on their animal prop, who now took care of them with godlike charity—and selfishness. The parasites had achieved biological heaven. They kept on working, but they stopped fighting. The host was their welfare state, you might say. End of a sequence."

He blew a long breath of smoke and leaned forward to watch Paul, with casual amusement. Paul suddenly realized that he was sitting on the edge of his chair and gaping. He forced a relaxation.

"Wild guesswork," he breathed uncertainly.

"Some of it's guesswork," Seevers admitted. "But none of it's wild. There is supporting evidence. It's in the form of a message."

"Message?"

"Sure. Come, I'll show you." Seevers arose and moved toward the wall. He stopped before the two hemispheres. "On second thought, you better show yourself. Take down that sliced meteorite, will you? It's sterile."

Paul crossed the room, climbed unsteadily upon a bench, and brought down the globular meteorite. It was the first time he had examind one of the things, and he inspected it curiously. It was a near-perfect sphere, about eight inches in diameter, with a four-inch hollow in the center. The globe was made up of several concentric shells, tightly fitted, each apparently of a different metal. It was not seemingly heavier than aluminum, although the outer shell was obviously of tough steel.

"Set it face down," Seevers told him. Both halves. Give it a quick little twist. The shells will come apart. Take out the center shell—the hard, thin one between the soft protecting shells."

"How do you know their purposes?" Paul growled as he followed instructions. The shells came apart easily.

"Envelopes are to protect messages," snorted Seevers.

Paul sorted out the hemispheres, and found two mirror-polished shells of paper-thin tough metal. They bore no inscription, either inside or out. He gave Seevers a puzzled frown.

"Handle them carefully while they're out of the protectors. They're already a little blurred . . ."

"I don't see any message."

"There's a small bottle of iron filings in that drawer by your knee. Sift them carefully over the outside of the shells. That powder isn't fine enough, really, but it's the best I could do. Felger had some better stuff up at Princeton, before we all got out. This business wasn't my discovery, incidentally."

Baffled, Paul found the iron filings and dusted the mirror-shells with the powder. Delicate patterns appeared—latitudinal circles, etched in iron dust and laced here and there with diagonal lines. He gasped. It looked like the map of a planet.

"I know what you're thinking," Seevers said. "That's what we thought too, at first. Then Felger came up with this very fine dust. Fine as they are, those lines are rows of pictograph symbols. You can make them out vaguely with a good reading glass, even with this coarse stuff. It's magnetic printing—like two-dimensional wire-recording. Evidently, the animals that printed it had either very powerful eyes, or a magnetic sense."

"Anyone understand it?"

"Princeton staff was working on it when the world went crazy. They figured out enough to guess at what I've just told you. They found five different shell-messages among a dozen or so spheres. One of them was a sort of a key. A symbol equated to a diagram of a carbon atom. Another symbol equated to a 'pi' in binary numbers. Things like that—about five hundred symbols, in fact. Some we couldn't figure. Then they defined other symbols by what amounted to blank-filling quizzes. Things like—'A star is . . .' and there would be the unknown symbol. We would try to decide whether it meant 'hot', 'white', 'huge', and so forth."

"And you managed it?"

"In part. The ruthless way in which the missiles were opened destroyed some of the clarity. The senders were guilty of their own brand of anthropomorphism. They projected their own psychology on us. They expected us to open the things shell by shell, cautiously, and figure out the text before we went further. Heh! What happens? Some machinist grabs one, shakes it, weighs it, sticks it on a lathe, and—brrrrrr! Our curiosity is still rather apelike. Stick our arm in a gopher hole to see if there's a rattlesnake inside."

There was a long silence while Paul stood peering over the patterns on the shell. "Why haven't people heard about this?" he asked quietly.

"Heard about it!" Seevers roared. "And how do you propose to tell them about it?"

Paul shook his head. It was easy to forget that Man had scurried away from his presses and his broadcasting stations and his railroads, leaving his mechanical creatures to sleep in their own rust while he fled like a bee-stung bear before the strange terror.

"What, exactly, do the patterns say, Doctor?"

"I've told you some of it—the evolutionary origin of the neuroderm parasites. We also pieced together their reasons for launching the missiles across space—several thousand years ago. Their sun was about to flare into a supernova. They worked out a theoretical space-drive, but they couldn't fuel it—needed some element that was scarce in their system. They could get to their outer planet, but that wouldn't help much. So they just cultured up a batch of their parasite-benefactors, rolled them into these balls, and fired them like charges of buckshot at various stars. Interception-course, naturally. They meant to miss just a little, so that the projectiles would swing into long elliptical orbits around the suns—close enough in to intersect the radiational 'life-belt' and eventually cross paths with planets whose orbits were near-circular. Looks like they hit us on the first pass."

"You mean they weren't aiming at Earth in particular?"

"Evidently not. They couldn't know we were here. Not at a range like that. Hundreds of light-years. They just took a chance on several stars. Shipping off their pets was sort of a last ditch stand against extinction—symbolic, to be sure—but a noble gesture, as far as they were concerned. A giving away of part of their souls. Like a man writing his will and leaving his last worldly possession to some unknown species beyond the stars. Imagine them standing there—watching the projectiles being fired out toward deep space. There goes their inheritance, to an unknown heir, or perhaps to no one. The little creatures that brought them up from beasthood."

Seevers paused, staring up at the sunlight beyond the high basement window. He was talking to himself again, quietly: "You can see them turn away and silently go back . . . to wait for their collapsing sun to reach the critical point, the detonating point. They've left their last mark—a dark and uncertain benediction to the cosmos."

"You're a fool, Seevers," Paul grunted suddenly.

Seevers whirled, whitening. His hand darted out forgetfully toward the young man's arm, but he drew it back as Paul sidestepped.

"You actually regard this thing as desirable, don't you?" Paul asked. "You can't see that you're under its effect. Why does it affect people that way? And you say I can't be objective."

The professor smiled coldly. "I didn't say it's desirable. I was simply pointing out that the beings who sent it saw it as desirable. They were making some unwarranted assumptions."

"Maybe they just didn't care."

"Of course they cared. Their fallacy was that we would open it as they would have done—cautiously. Perhaps they couldn't see how a creature could be both brash and intelligent. They meant for us to read the warning on the shells before we went further."

"Warning . . .?"

Seevers smiled bitterly. "Yes, warning. There was one group of oversized symbols on all the spheres. See that pattern on the top ring? It says, in effect—'Finder-creatures, you who destroy your own people—if you do this thing, then destroy this container without penetrating deeper. If you are self-destroyers, then the contents will only help to destroy you.' "

There was a frigid silence.

"But somebody would have opened one anyway," Paul protested.

Seevers turned his bitter smile on the window. "You couldn't be more right. The senders just didn't foresee our monkey-minded species. If they saw Man digging out the nuggets, braying over them, chortling over them, cracking them like walnuts, then turning tail to run howling for the forests—well, they'd think twice before they fired another round of their celestial buckshot."

"Doctor Seevers, what do you think will happen now? To the world, I mean?"

Seevers shrugged. "I saw a baby born yesterday—to a woman down the island. It was fully covered with neuroderm at birth. It has some new sensory equipment—small pores in the finger tips, with taste buds and olfactory cells in them. Also a nodule above each eye sensitive to infra-red."

Paul groaned.

"It's not the first case. Those things are happening to adults, too, but you have to have the condition for quite a while. Brother Thomas has the finger pores already. Hasn't learned to use them yet, of course. He gets sensations from them, but the receptors aren't connected to olfactory and taste centers of the brain. They're still linked with the somesthetic interpretive centers. He can touch various substances and get different perceptive combinations of heat, pain, cold, pressure, and so forth. He says vinegar feels ice-cold, quinine sharp-hot, cologne warm-velvet-prickly, and . . . he blushes when he touches a musky perfume."

Paul laughed, and the hollow sound startled him.

"It may be several generations before we know all that will happen," Seevers went on. "I've examined sections of rat brain and found the micro-organisms. They may be working at rerouting these new receptors to proper brain areas. Our grandchildren—if Man's still on Earth by then—can perhaps taste analyze substances by touch, qualitatively determine the contents of a test tube by sticking a finger in it. See a warm radiator in a dark room—by infra-red. Perhaps there'll be some ultraviolet sensitization. My rats are sensitive to it."

Paul went to the rat cages and stared in at three gray-pelted animals that seemed larger than the others. They retreated against the back wall and watched him warily. They began squeaking and exchanging glances among themselves.

"Those are third-generation hypers," Seevers told him. "They've developed a simple language. Not intelligent by human standards, but crafty. They've learned to use their sensory equipment. They know when I mean to feed them, and when I mean to take one out to kill and dissect. A slight change in my emotional odor, I imagine. Learning's a big hurdle, youngster. A hyper with finger pores gets sensations from them, but it takes a long time to attach meaning to the various sensations—through learning. A baby gets visual sensations from his untrained eyes—but the sensation is utterly without significance until he associates milk with white, mother with a face shape, and so forth."

"What will happen to the brain?" Paul breathed.

"Not too much, I imagine. I haven't observed much happening. The rats show an increase in intelligence, but not in brain size. The intellectual boost apparently comes from an ability to perceive things in terms of more senses. Ideas, concepts, precepts—are made of memory collections of past sensory experiences. An apple is red, fruity-smelling, sweet-acid flavored—that's your sensory idea of an apple. A blind man without a tongue couldn't form such a complete idea. A hyper, on the other hand, could add some new adjectives that you couldn't understand. The fully-developed hyper—I'm not one yet—has more sensory tools with which to grasp ideas. When he learns to use them, he'll be mentally more efficient. But there's apparently a hitch.

"The parasite's instinctive goal is to insure the host's survival. That's the substance of the warning. If Man has the capacity to work together, then the parasites will help him shape his environment. If Man intends to keep fighting with his fellows, the parasite will help him do a better job of that, too. Help him destroy himself more efficiently."

"Men have worked together—"

"In small tribes," Seevers interrupted. "Yes, we have group spirit. Ape-tribe spirit, not race spirit."

Paul moved restlessly toward the door. Seevers had turned to watch him with a cool smirk.

"Well, you're illuminated, youngster. Now what do you intend to do?"

Paul shook his head to scatter the confusion of ideas. "What can anyone do? Except run. To an island, perhaps."

Seevers hoisted a cynical eyebrow. "Intend taking the condition with you? Or will you try to stay nonhyper?"

"Take . . . are you crazy? I mean to stay healthy!"

"That's what I thought. If you were objective about this, you'd give yourself the condition and get it over with. I did. You remind me of a monkey running away from a hypodermic needle. The hypo has serum health-insurance in it, but the needle looks sharp. The monkey chatters with fright."

Paul stalked angrily to the door, then paused. "There's a girl upstairs, a dermie. Would you—"

"Tell her all this? I always brief new hypers. It's one of my duties around this ecclesiastical leper ranch. She's on the verge of insanity, I suppose. They all are, before they get rid of the idea that they're damned souls. What's she to you?"

Paul strode out into the corridor without answering. He felt physically ill. He hated Seevers' smug bulldog face with a violence that was unfamiliar to him. The man had given the plague to himself! So he said. But was it true? Was any of it true? To claim that the hallucinations were new sensory phenomena, to pose the plague as possibly desirable—Seevers had no patent on those ideas. Every dermie made such claims; it was a symptom. Seevers had simply invented clever rationalizations to support his delusions, and Paul had been nearly taken in. Seevers was clever. *Do you mean to take the condition with you when you go?* Wasn't that just another way of suggesting, "Why don't you allow me to touch you?" Paul was shivering as he returned to the third floor room to recoat himself with the pungent oil. Why not leave now? he thought.

But he spent the day wandering along the waterfront, stopping briefly at the docks to watch a crew of monks scrambling over the scaffolding that surrounded the hulls of two small sea-going vessels. The monks were caulking split seams and trotting along the platforms with buckets of tar and paint. Upon inquiry, Paul learned which of the vessels was intended for his own use. And he put aside all thoughts of immediate departure.

She was a fifty-footer, a slender craft with a weighted fin-keel that would cut too deep for bay navigation. Paul guessed that the colony wanted only a flat-bottomed vessel for hauling passengers and cargo across from the mainland. They would have little use for the trim seaster with the lines of a baby destroyer. Upon closer examination, he guessed that it had been a police boat, or Coast Guard craft. There was a gun-mounting on the forward deck, minus the gun. She was built for speed, and powered by diesels, and she could be provisioned for a nice long cruise.

Paul went to scrounge among the warehouses and locate a stock of supplies. He met an occasional monk or nun, but the gray-skinned monastics seemed only desirous of avoiding him. The dermie desire was keyed principally by smell, and the deodorant oil helped preserve him from their affections. Once he was approached by a wild-eyed layman who startled him amidst a heap of warehouse crates. The dermie was almost upon him before Paul heard the footfall. Caught without an escape route, and assailed by startled terror, he shattered the man's arm with a shotgun blast, then fled from the warehouse to escape the dermie's screams.

Choking with shame, he found a dermie monk and sent him to care for the wounded creature. Paul had shot at other plague victims when there was no escape, but never with intent to kill. The man's life had been spared only by hasty aim.

"It was self-defense," he reminded himself.

But defense against what? Against the inevitable?

He hurried back to the hospital and found Mendelhaus outside the small chapel. "I better not wait for your boat," he told the priest. "I just shot one of your people. I better leave before it happens again."

Mendelhaus' thin lips tightened. "You shot—"

"Didn't kill him," Paul explained hastily. "Broke his arm. One of the brothers is bringing him over. I'm sorry, Father, but he jumped me."

The priest glanced aside silently, apparently wrestling against anger. "I'm glad you told me," he said quietly. "I suppose you couldn't help it. But why did you leave the hospital? You're safe here. The yacht will be provisioned for you. I suggest you remain in your room until it's ready. I won't vouch for your safety any farther than the building." There was a tone of command in his voice, and Paul nodded slowly. He started away.

"The young lady's been asking for you," the priest called after him.

Paul stopped. "How is she?"

"Over the crisis, I think. Infection's down. Nervous condition not so good. Deep depression. Sometimes she goes a little hysterical." He paused, then lowered his voice. "You're at the focus of it, young man. Sometimes she gets the idea that she touched you, and then sometimes she raves about how she wouldn't do it."

Paul whirled angrily, forming a protest, but the priest continued: "Seevers talked to her, and then a psychologist—one of our sisters. It seemed to help some. She's asleep now. I don't know how much of Seevers' talk she understood, however. She's dazed—combined effects of pain, shock, infection, guilt feelings, fright, hysteria—and some other things. Morphine doesn't make her mind any clearer. Neither does the fact that she thinks you're avoiding her."

"It's the plague I'm avoiding!" Paul snapped. "Not her."

Mendelhaus chuckled mirthlessly. "You're talking to me, aren't you?" He turned and entered the chapel through a swinging door. As the door fanned back and forth, Paul caught a glimpse of a candlelit altar and a stark wooden crucifix, and a sea of monk-robes flowing over the pews, waiting for the celebrant priest to enter the sanctuary and begin the Sacrifice of the Mass. He realized vaguely that it was Sunday.

Paul wandered back to the main corridor and found himself drifting toward Willie's room. The door was ajar, and he stopped short lest she see him. But after a moment he inched forward until he caught a glimpse of her dark mass of hair unfurled across the pillow. One of the sisters had combed it for her, and it spread in dark waves, gleaming in the candlelight. She was still asleep. The candle startled him for an instant—suggesting a deathbed and the sacrament of the dying. But a dog-eared magazine lay beneath it; someone had been reading to her.

He stood in the doorway, watching the slow rise of her breathing. Fresh, young, shapely—even in the crude cotton gown they had given her, even beneath the blue-white pallor of her skin—soon to become gray as a cloudy sky in a wintery twilight. Her lips moved slightly, and he backed a step away. They paused, parted moistly, showing thin white teeth. Her delicately carved face was thrown back slightly on the pillow. There was a sudden tightening of her jaw.

A weirdly pitched voice floated unexpectedly from down the hall, echoing the semi-singing of Gregorian chant: *"Asperges me, Domine, hyssopo, et mundabor . . ."* The priest was beginning Mass.

As the sound came, the girl's hands clenched into rigid fists beneath the sheet. Her eyes flared open to stare wildly at the ceiling. Clutching the bedclothes, she pressed the fists up against her face and cried out: "No! Noooo! God, I won't!"

Paul backed out of sight and pressed himself against the wall. A knot of desolation tightened in his stomach. He looked around nervously. A nun, hearing the outcry, came scurrying down the hall, murmuring anxiously to herself. A plump mother hen in a dozen yards of starched white cloth. She gave him a quick challenging glance and waddled inside.

"Child, my child, what's wrong! Nightmares again?"

He heard Willie breathe a nervous moan of relief. Then her voice, weakly—"They . . . they made me . . . touch . . . Ooo, God! I want to cut off my hands!"

Paul fled, leaving the nun's sympathetic reassurance to fade into a murmur behind him.

He spent the rest of the day and the night in his room. On the following day, Mendelhaus came with word that the boat was not yet ready. They needed to finish caulking and stock it with provisions. But the priest assured him that it should be afloat within twenty-four hours. Paul could not bring himself to ask about the girl.

A monk brought his food—unopened cans, still steaming from the sterilizer, and on a covered tray. The monk wore gloves and mask, and he had oiled his own skin. There were moments when Paul felt as if he were the diseased and contagious patient from whom the others protected themselves. Like Omar, he thought, wondering—"which is the Potter, pray, and which the Pot?"

Was Man, as Seevers implied, a terrorized ape-tribe fleeing illogically from the gray hands that only wanted to offer a blessing? How narrow was the line dividing blessing from curse, god from demon! The parasites came in a devil's mask, the mask of disease. "Diseases have often killed me," said Man. "All disease is therefore evil." But was that necessarily true? Fire had often killed Man's club-bearing ancestors, but later came to serve him. Even diseases had been used to good advantage—artificially induced typhoid and malaria to fight venereal infections.

But the gray skin . . . taste buds in the fingertips . . . alien micro-organisms tampering with the nerves and the brain. Such concepts caused his scalp to bristle. Man—made over to suit the tastes of a bunch of supposedly beneficent parasites—was he still Man, or something else? Little bacteriogical farmers imbedded in the skin, raising a crop of nerve cells—eat one, plant two, sow an olfactor in a new field, reshuffle the feeder-fibers to the brain.

Monday brought a cold rain and stiff wind from the Gulf. He watched the water swirling through littered gutters in the street. Sitting in the window, he watched the gloom and waited, praying that the storm would not delay his departure. Mendelhaus smiled politely, through his doorway once. "Willie's ankle seems healing nicely," he said. "Swelling's gone down so much we had to change casts. If only she would—"

"Thanks for the free report, Padre," Paul growled irritably.

The priest shrugged and went away.

It was still raining when the sky darkened with evening. The monastic dock-crew had certainly been unable to finish. Tomorrow . . . perhaps.

After nightfall, he lit a candle and lay awake watching its unflickering yellow tongue until drowsiness lolled his head aside. He snuffed it out and went to bed.

Dreams assailed him, tormented him, stroked him with dark hands while he lay back, submitting freely. Small hands, soft, cool, tender—touching his forehead and his cheeks, while a voice whispered caresses.

He awoke suddenly to blackness. The feel of the dream-hands was still on his face. What had aroused him? A sound in the hall, a creaking hinge? The darkness was impenetrable. The rain had stopped—perhaps its cessation had disturbed him. He felt curiously tense as he lay listening to the humid, musty corridors. A . . . faint . . . rustle . . . and . . .

Breathing! The sound of soft breathing was in the room with him!

He let out a hoarse shriek that shattered the unearthly silence. A high-pitched scream of fright answered him! From a few feet away in the room. He groped toward it and fumbled against a bare wall. He roared curses, and tried to find first matches, then the shotgun. At last he found the gun, aimed at nothing across the room, and jerked the trigger. The explosion deafened him. The window shattered, and a sift of plaster rustled to the floor.

The brief flash had illuminated the room. It was empty. He stood frozen. Had he imagined it all? But no, the visitor's startled scream had been real enough.

A cool draft fanned his face. The door was open. Had he forgotten to lock it again? A tumult of sound was beginning to arise from the lower floors. His shot had aroused the sleepers. But there was a closer sound—sobbing in the corridor, and an irregular creaking noise.

At last he found a match and rushed to the door. But the tiny flame revealed nothing within its limited aura. He heard a doorknob rattle in the distance; his visitor was escaping via the outside stairway. He though of pursuit and vengeance. But instead, he rushed to the washbasin and began scrubbing himself thoroughly with harsh brown soap. Had his visitor touched him—or had the hands been only dream-stuff? He was frightened and sickened.

Voices were filling the corridor. The light of several candles was advancing toward his doorway. He turned to see monks' faces peering anxiously inside. Father Mendelhaus shouldered his way through the others, glanced at the window, the wall, then at Paul.

"What—"

"Safety, eh?" Paul hissed. "Well, I had a prowler! A woman! I think I've been touched."

The priest turned and spoke to a monk. "Go to the stairway and call for the Mother Superior. Ask her to make an immediate inspection of the sisters' quarters. If any nuns have been out of their rooms—"

A shrill voice called from down the hallway: "Father, Father! The girl with the injured ankle! She's not in her bed! She's gone!"

"Willie!" Paul gasped.

A small nun with a candle scurried up and panted to recover her breath for a moment. "She's gone, Father. I was on night duty. I heard the shot, and I went to see if it disturbed her. She wasn't there!"

The priest grumbled incredulously. "How could she get out? She can't walk with that cast."

"Crutches, Father. We told her she could get up in a few days. While she was still irrational, she kept saying they were going to amputate her leg. We brought the crutches in to prove she'd be up soon. It's my fault, Father. I should have—"

"Never mind! Search the building for her."

Paul dried his wet skin and faced the priest angrily. "What can I do to disinfect myself?" he demanded.

Mendelhaus called out into the hallway where a crowd had gathered. "Someone please get Doctor Seevers."

"I'm here, preacher," grunted the scientist. The monastics parted ranks to make way for his short chubby body. He grinned amusedly at Paul. "So, you decided to make your home here after all, eh?"

Paul croaked an insult at him. "Have you got any effective—"

"Disinfectants? Afraid not. Nitric acid will do the trick on one or two local spots. Where were you touched?"

"I don't know. I was asleep."

Seevers' grin widened. "Well, you can't take a bath in nitric acid. We'll try something else, but I doubt if it'll work for a direct touch."

"That oil—"

"Uh-uh! That'll do for exposure-weakened parasites you might pick up by handling an object that's been touched. But with skin to skin contact, the bugs're pretty stout little rascals. Come on downstairs, though, we'll make a pass at it."

Paul followed him quickly down the corridor. Behind him, a soft voice was murmuring: "I just can't understand why nonhypers are so . . ." Mendelhaus said something to Seevers, blotting out the voice. Paul chafed at the thought that they might consider him cowardly.

But with the herds fleeing northward, cowardice was the social norm. And after a year's fight, Paul had accepted the norm as the only possible way to fight.

Seevers was emptying chemicals into a tub of water in the basement when a monk hurried in to tug at Mendelhaus' sleeve. "Father, the sisters report that the girl's not in the building."

"What? Well, she can't be far! Search the grounds. If she's not there, try the adjoining blocks."

Paul stopped unbuttoning his shirt. Willie had said some mournful things about what she would rather do than submit to the craving. And her startled scream when he had cried out in the darkness—the scream of someone suddenly awakening to reality—from a daze-world.

The monk left the room. Seevers sloshed more chemicals into the tub. Paul could hear the wind whipping about the basement windows and the growl of an angry surf not so far away. Paul rebuttoned his shirt.

"Which way's the ocean?" he asked suddenly. He backed toward the door.

"No, you fool!" roared Seevers. "You're not going to—*get him*, preacher!"

Paul sidestepped as the priest grabbed for him. He darted outside and began running for thc stairs. Mendelhaus bellowed for him to stop.

"Not me!" Paul called back angrily. "Willie!"

Moments later, he was racing across the sodden lawn and into the street. He stopped on the corner to get his bearings. The wind brought the sound of the surf with it. He began running east and calling her name into the night.

The rain had ceased, but the pavement was wet and water gurgled in the gutters. Occasionally the moon peered throught the thinning veil of clouds, but its light failed to furnish a view of the street ahead. After a minute's running, he found himself standing on the seawall. The breakers thundered a stone's throw across the sand. For a moment they became visible under the coy moon, then vanished again in blackness. He had not seen her.

"Willie!"

Only the breakers' growl responded. And a glimmer of phosphorescence from the waves.

"*Willie!*" he slipped down from the seawall and began feeling along the jagged rocks that lay beneath it. She could not have gotten down without falling. Then he remembered a rickety flight of steps just to the north, and he trotted quickly toward it.

The moon came out suddenly. He saw her, and stopped. She was sitting motionless on the bottom step, holding her face in her hands. The crutches were stacked neatly against the handrail. Ten yards across the sand slope lay the hungry, devouring surf. Paul approached her slowly. The moon went out again. His feet sucked at the rainsoaked sand.

He stopped by the handrail, peering at her motionless shadow. "Willie?"

A low moan, then a long silence. "I did it, Paul," she muttered miserably. "It was like a dream at first, but then . . . you shouted . . . and . . ."

He crouched in front of her, sitting on his heels. Then he took her wrists firmly and tugged her hands from her face.

"Don't . . ."

He pulled her close and kissed her. Her mouth was frightened. Then he lifted her—being cautious of the now-sodden cast. He climbed the steps and started back to the hospital. Willie, dazed and weary and still uncomprehending, fell asleep in his arms. Her hair blew about his face in the wind. It smelled warm and alive. He wondered what sensation it would produce to the finger-pore receptors. "Wait and see," he said to himself.

The priest met him with a growing grin when he brought her into the candlelit corridor. "Shall we forget the boat, son?"

Paul paused. "No . . . I'd like to borrow it anyway."

Mendelhaus looked puzzled.

Seevers snorted at him: "Preacher, don't you know any reasons for traveling besides running away?"

Paul carried her back to her room. He meant to have a long talk when she awoke. About an island—until the world sobered up.

THE MIDAS PLAGUE

Frederik Pohl

And so they were married.

The bride and groom made a beautiful couple, she in her twenty-yard frill of immaculate white, he in his formal gray ruffled blouse and pleated pantaloons.

It was a small wedding—the best he could afford. For guests, they had only the immediate family and a few close friends. And when the minister had performed the ceremony, Morey Fry kissed his bride and they drove off to the reception. There were twenty-eight limousines in all (though it is true that twenty of them contained only the caterer's robots) and three flower cars.

"Bless you both," said old man Elon sentimentally. "You've got a fine girl in our Cherry, Morey." He blew his nose on a ragged square of cambric.

The old folks behaved very well, Morey thought. At the reception, surrounded by the enormous stacks of wedding gifts, they drank the champagne and ate a great many of the tiny, delicious canapés. They listened politely to the fifteen-piece orchestra, and Cherry's mother even danced one dance with Morey for sentiment's sake, though it was clear that dancing was far from the usual pattern of her life. They tried as hard as they could to blend into the gathering, but all the same, the two elderly figures in severely simple and probably rented garments were dismayingly conspicuous in the quarter-acre of tapestries and tinkling fountains that was the main ballroom of Morey's country home.

When it was time for the guests to go home and let the newlyweds begin their life together Cherry's father shook Morey by the hand and Cherry's mother kissed him. But as they drove away in their tiny runabout their faces were full of foreboding.

It was nothing against Morey as a person, of course. But poor people should not marry wealth.

Morey and Cherry loved each other, certainly. That helped. They told each other so, a dozen times an hour, all of the long hours they were together, for all of the first months of their marriage. Morey even took time off to go shopping with his bride, which endeared him to her enormously. They drove their shopping carts through the immense vaulted corridors of the supermarket, Morey checking off the items on the shopping list as Cherry picked out the goods. It was fun.

For a while.

Their first fight started in the supermarket, between Breakfast Foods and Floor Furnishings, just where the new Precious Stones department was being opened.

Morey called off from the list, "Diamond lavaliere, costume rings, earbobs."

Cherry said rebelliously, "Morey, I *have* a lavaliere. Please, dear!"

Morey folded back the pages of the list uncertainly. The lavaliere was on there, all right, and no alternative selection was shown.

"How about a bracelet?" he coaxed. "Look, they have some nice ruby ones there. See how beautifully they go with your hair, darling!" He beckoned a robot clerk, who bustled up and handed Cherry the bracelet tray. "Lovely," Morey exclaimed as Cherry slipped the largest of the lot on her wrist.

"And I don't have to have a lavaliere?" Cherry asked.

"Of course not." He peeked at the tag. "Same number of ration points exactly!" Since Cherry looked only dubious, not convinced, he said briskly, "And now we'd better be getting along to the shoe department. I've got to pick up some dancing pumps."

Cherry made no objection, neither then nor throughout the rest of their shopping tour. At the end, while they were sitting in the supermarket's ground-floor lounge waiting for the robot accountants to tote up their bill and the robot cashiers to stamp their ration books, Morey remembered to have the shipping department save out the bracelet.

"I don't want that sent with the other stuff, darling," he explained. "I want you to wear it right now. Honestly, I don't think I ever saw anything looking so *right* for you."

Cherry looked flustered and pleased. Morey was delighted with himself; it wasn't everybody who knew how to handle these little domestic problems just right!

He stayed self-satisfied all the way home, while Henry, their companion-robot, regaled them with funny stories of the factory in which it had been built and trained. Cherry wasn't used to Henry by a long shot, but it was hard not to like the robot. Jokes and funny stories when you needed amusement, sympathy when you were depressed, a never-failing supply of news and information on any subject you cared to name—Henry was easy enough to take. Cherry even made a special point of asking Henry to keep them company through dinner, and she laughed as thoroughly as Morey himself at its droll anecdotes.

But later, in the conservatory, when Henry had considerately left them alone, the laughter dried up.

Morey didn't notice. He was very conscientiously making the rounds: turning on the tri-D, selecting their afterdinner liqueurs, scanning the evening newspaper.

Cherry cleared her throat self-consciously, and Morey stopped what he was doing. "Dear," she said tentatively, "I'm feeling kind of restless tonight. Could we—I mean do you think we could just sort of stay home and—well, relax?"

Morey looked at her with a touch of concern. She lay back wearily, eyes half closed. "Are you feeling all right?" he asked.

"Perfectly. I just don't want to go out tonight, dear. I don't feel up to it."

He sat down and automatically lit a cigarette. "I see," he said. The tri-D was beginning a comedy show; he got up to turn it off, snapping on the tape-player. Muted strings filled the room.

"We had reservations at the club tonight," he reminded her.

Cherry shifted uncomfortably. "I know."

"And we have the opera tickets that I turned last week's in for. I hate to nag, darling, but we haven't used *any* of our opera tickets."

"We can see them right here on the tri-D," she said in a small voice.

"That has nothing to do with it, sweetheart. I—I didn't want to tell you about it, but Wainwright, down at the office, said something to me yesterday. He told me he would be at the circus last night and as much as said he'd be looking to see if we were there, too. Well, we weren't there. Heaven knows what I'll tell him next week."

He waited for Cherry to answer, but she was silent.

He went on reasonably, "So if you *could* see your way clear to going out tonight—"

He stopped, slack-jawed. Cherry was crying, silently and in quantity.

"Darling!" he said inarticulately.

He hurried to her, but she fended him off. He stood helpless over her, watching her cry.

"Dear, what's the matter?" he asked.

She turned her head away.

Morey rocked back on his heels. It wasn't exactly the first time he'd seen Cherry cry—there had been that poignant scene when they Gave Each Other Up, realizing that their backgrounds were too far apart for happiness, before the realization that they *had* to have each other, no matter what. . . But it was the first time her tears had made him feel guilty.

And he did feel guilty. He stood there staring at her.

Then he turned his back on her and walked over to the bar. He ignored the ready liqueurs and poured two stiff highballs, brought them back to her. He set one down beside her, took a long drink from the other.

In quite a different tone, he said, "Dear, what's the *matter?*"

No answer.

"Come on. What is it?"

She looked up at him and rubbed at her eyes. Almost sullenly, she said, "Sorry."

"I know you're sorry. Look, we love each other. Let's talk this thing out."

She picked up her drink and held it for a moment, before setting it down untasted. "What's the use, Morey?"

"Please. Let's try."

She shrugged.

He went on remorselessly, "You aren't happy, are you? And it's because of—well, all this." His gesture took in the richly furnished conservatory, the thick-piled carpet, the host of machines and contrivances for their comfort and entertainment that waited for their touch. By implication it took in twenty-six rooms, five cars, nine robots. Morey said, with an effort, "It isn't what you're used to, is it?"

"I can't help it," Cherry said. "Morey, you know I've tried. But back home—"

"Dammit," he flared, "*this* is your home. You don't live with your father any more in that five-room cottage; you don't spend your evenings hoeing the garden or playing cards for matchsticks. You live here, with me, your husband! You knew what you were getting into. We talked all this out long before we were married—"

The words stopped, because words were useless. Cherry was crying again, but not silently.

Through her tears, she wailed: "Darling, I've tried. You don't *know* how I've tried! I've worn all those silly clothes and I've played all those silly games and I've gone out with you as much as I *possibly* could and—I've eaten all that terrible food until I'm actually getting fa-fa-*fat!* I thought I could stand it. But I just can't go on like this; I'm not used to it. I—I love you, Morey, but I'm going crazy, living like this. I can't help it, Morey—*I'm tired of being poor!*"

Eventually the tears dried up, and the quarrel healed, and the lovers kissed and made up. But Morey lay awake that night, listening to his wife's gentle breathing from the suite next to his own, staring into the darkness as tragically as any pauper before him had ever done.

Blessed are the poor, for they shall inherit the Earth.

Blessed Morey, heir to more worldly goods than he could possibly consume.

Morey Fry, steeped in grinding poverty, had never gone hungry a day in his life, never lacked for anything his heart could desire in the way of food, or clothing, or a place to sleep. In Morey's world, no one lacked for these things; no one could.

Malthus was right—for a civilization without machines, automatic factories, hydroponics and food synthesis, nuclear breeder plants, ocean-mining for metals and minerals . . .

And a vastly increasing supply of labor . . .

And architecture that rose high in the air and dug deep in the ground and floated far out on the water on piers and pontoons . . . architecture that could be poured one day and lived in the next . . .

And robots.

Above all, robots . . . robots to burrow and haul and smelt and fabricate, to build and farm and weave and sew.

What the land lacked in wealth, the sea was made to yield and the laboratory invented the rest . . . and the factories became a pipeline of plenty, churning out enough to feed and clothe and house a dozen worlds.

Limitless discovery, infinite power in the atom, tireless labor of humanity and robots, mechanization that drove jungle and swamp and ice off the Earth, and put up office buildings and manufacturing centers and rocket ports in their place . . .

The pipeline of production spewed out riches that no king in the time of Malthus could have known.

But a pipeline has two ends. The invention and power and labor pouring in at one end must somehow be drained out at the other.

Lucky Morey, blessed economic-consuming unit, drowning in the pipeline's flood, striving manfully to eat and drink and wear out his share of the ceaseless tide of wealth.

Morey felt far from blessed, for the blessings of the poor are always best appreciated from afar.

Quotas worried his sleep until he awoke at eight o'clock the next morning, red-eyed and haggard, but inwardly resolved. He had reached a decision. He was starting a new life.

There was trouble in the morning mail. Under the letterhead of the National Ration Board, it said:

"We regret to advise you that the following items returned by you in connection with your August quotas as used and no longer serviceable have been inspected and found insufficiently worn." The list followed—a long one, Morey saw to his sick disappointment. "Credit is hereby disallowed for these and you are therefore given an additional consuming quota for the current month in the amount of 435 points, at least 350 points of which must be in the textile and home-furnishing categories."

Morey dashed the letter to the floor. The valet picked it up emotionlessly, creased it and set it on his desk.

It wasn't fair! All right, maybe the bathing trunks and beach umbrellas hadn't been *really* used very much—though how the devil, he asked himself bitterly, did you go about using up swimming gear when you didn't have time for such leisurely pursuits as swimming? But certainly the hiking slacks were used! He'd worn them for three whole days and part of a fourth; what did they expect him to do, go around in *rags?*

Morey looked belligerently at the coffee and toast that the valet-robot had brought in with the mail, and then steeled his resolve. Unfair or not, he had to play the game according to the rules. It was for Cherry, more than for himself, and the way to begin a new way of life was to begin it.

Morey was going to consume for two.

He told the valet-robot, "Take that stuff back. I want cream and sugar with the coffee—*lots* of cream and sugar. And besides the toast, scrambled eggs, fried potatoes, orange juice—no, make it half a grape-fruit. *And* orange juice, come to think of it."

"Right away, sir," said the valet. "You won't be having breakfast at nine then, will you, sir?"

"I certainly will," said Morey virtuously. "Double portions!" As the robot was closing the door, he called after it, "Butter and marmalade with the toast!"

He went to the bath; he had a full schedule and no time to waste. In the shower, he carefully sprayed himself with lather three times. When he had rinsed the soap off, he went through the whole assortment of taps in order: three lotions, plain talcum, scented talcum and thirty seconds of ultra-violet. Then he lathered and rinsed again, and dried himself with a towel instead of using the hot-air drying jet. Most of the miscellaneous scents went down the drain with the rinse water, but if the Ration Board accused him of waste, he could claim he was experimenting. The effect, as a matter of fact, wasn't bad at all.

He stepped out, full of exuberance. Cherry was awake, staring in dismay at the tray the valet had brought. "Good morning, dear," she said faintly. "Ugh."

Morey kissed her and patted her hand. "Well!" he said, looking at the tray with a big, hollow smile. "Food!"

"Isn't that a *lot* for just the two of us?"

"Two of us?" repeated Morey masterfully. "Nonsense, my dear, I'm going to eat it all by myself!"

"Oh, Morey!" gasped Cherry, and the adoring look she gave him was enough to pay for a dozen such meals.

Which, he thought as he finished his morning exercises with the sparring-robot and sat down to his *real* breakfast, it just about had to be, day in and day out, for a long, long time.

Still, Morey had made up his mind. As he worked his way through the kippered herring, tea and crumpets, he ran over his plans with Henry. He swallowed a mouthful and said, "I want you to line up some appointments for me right away. Three hours a week in an exercise gym—pick one with lots of reducing equipment, Henry. I think I'm going to need it. And fittings for some new clothes—I've had these for weeks. And, let's see, doctor, dentist—say, Henry, don't I have a psychiatrist's date coming up?"

"Indeed you do, sir!" it said warmly. "This morning, in fact. I've already instructed the chauffeur and notified your office."

"Fine! Well, get started on the other things, Henry."

"Yes, sir," said Henry, and assumed the curious absent look of a robot talking on its TBR circuits—the "Talk Between Robots" radio—as it arranged the appointments for its master.

Morey finished his breakfast in silence, pleased with his own virtue, at peace with the world. It wasn't so hard to be a proper, industrious consumer if you *worked* at it, he reflected. It was only the malcontents, the ne'er-do-wells and the incompetents who simply could not adjust to the world around them. Well, he thought with distant pity, someone had to suffer; you couldn't break eggs without making an omelet. And his proper duty was not to be some sort of wild-eyed crank, challenging the social order and beating his breast about injustice, but to take care of his wife and his home.

It was too bad he couldn't really get right down to work on consuming today. But this was his one day a week to hold a *job*—four of the other six days were devoted to solid consuming—and, besides, he had a group therapy session scheduled as well. His analysis, Morey told himself, would certainly take a sharp turn for the better, now that he had faced up to his problems.

Morey was immersed in a glow of self-righteousness as he kissed Cherry goodbye (she had finally got up, all in a confusion of delight at the new regime) and walked out the door to his car. He hardly noticed the little man in enormous floppy hat and garishly ruffled trousers who was standing almost hidden in the shrubs.

"Hey, Mac." The man's voice was almost a whisper.

"Huh? Oh—what is it?"

The man looked around furtively. "Listen, friend," he said rapidly, "you look like an intelligent man who could use a little help. Times are tough; you help me, I'll help you. Want to make a deal on ration stamps? Six for one. One of yours for six of mine, the best deal you'll get anywhere in town. Naturally, my stamps aren't exactly the real McCoy, but they'll pass, friend, they'll pass—"

Morey blinked at him. "No!" he said violently, and pushed the man aside. Now it's racketeers, he thought bitterly. Slums and endless sordid preoccupation with rations weren't enough to inflict on Cherry; now the neighborhood was becoming a hangout for people on the shady side of the law. It was not, of course, the first time he had ever been approached by a counterfeit ration-stamp hoodlum, but never at his own front door!

Morey thought briefly, as he climbed into his car, of calling the police. But certainly the man would be gone before they could get there; and, after all, he had handled it pretty well as it was.

Of course, it would be nice to get six stamps for one.

But very far from nice if he got caught.

"Good morning, Mr. Fry," tinkled the robot receptionist. "Won't you go right in?" With a steel-tipped finger, it pointed to the door marked GROUP THERAPY.

Someday, Morey vowed to himself as he nodded and complied, he would be in a position to afford a private analyst of his own. Group therapy helped relieve the infinite stresses of modern living, and without it he might find himself as badly off as the hysterical mobs in the ration riots, or as dangerously anti-social as the counterfeiters. But it lacked the personal touch. It was, he thought, too public a performance of what should be a private affair, like trying to live a happy married life with an interfering, ever-present crowd of robots in the house—

Morey brought himself up in panic. How had *that* thought crept in? He was shaken visibly as he entered the room and greeted the group to which he was assigned.

There were eleven of them: four Freudians, two Reichians, two Jungians, a Gestalter, a shock therapist and the elderly and rather quiet Sullivanite. Even the members of the majority groups had their own individual differences in technique and creed, but, despite four years with this particular group of analysts, Morey hadn't quite been able to keep them separate in his mind. Their names, though, he knew well enough.

"Morning, Doctors," he said. "What is it today?"

"Morning," said Semmelweiss morosely. "Today you come into the room for the first time looking as if something is really bothering you, and yet the schedule calls for psychodrama. Dr. Fairless," he appealed, "can't we change the schedule a little bit? Fry here is obviously under a strain; *that's* the time to start digging and see what he can find. We can do your psychodrama next time, can't we?"

Fairless shook his gracefully bald old head. "Sorry, Doctor. If it were up to me, of course—but you know the rules."

"Rules, rules," jeered Semmelweiss. "Ah, what's the use? Here's a patient in an acute anxiety state if I ever saw one—and believe me, I saw plenty—and we ignore it because the *rules* say ignore it. Is that professional? Is that how to cure a patient?"

Little Blaine said frostily, "If I may say so, Dr. Semmelweiss, there have been a great many cures made without the necessity of departing from the rules. I myself, in fact—"

"You yourself!" mimicked Semmelweiss. "You yourself never handled a patient alone in your life. When you going to get out of a group, Blaine?"

Blaine said furiously, "Dr. Fairless, I don't think I have to stand for this sort of personal attack. Just because Semmelweiss has seniority and a couple of private patients one day a week, he thinks—"

"Gentlemen," said Fairless mildly. "Please, let's get on with the work. Mr. Fry has come to us for help, not to listen to us losing our tempers."

"Sorry," said Semmelweiss curtly. "All the same, I appeal from the arbitrary and mechanistic ruling of the chair."

Fairless inclined his head. "All in favor of the ruling of the chair? Nine, I count. That leaves only you opposed, Dr. Semmelweiss. We'll proceed with the psychodrama, if the recorder will read us the notes and comments of the last session."

The recorder, a pudgy, low-ranking youngster named Sprogue, flipped back the pages of his notebook and read in a chanting voice, "Session of twenty-fourth May, subject, Morey Fry; in attendance, Doctors Fairless, Bileck, Semmelweiss, Carrado, Weber—"

Fairless interrupted kindly, "Just the last page, if you please, Dr. Sprogue."

"Um—oh, yes. After a ten-minute recess for additional Rorschachs and an electro-encephalogram, the group convened and conducted rapid-fire word association. Results were tabulated and compared with standard deviation patterns, and it was determined that subject's major traumas derived from, respectively—"

Morey found his attention waning. Therapy was *good*; everybody knew that, but every once in a while he found it a little dull. If it weren't for therapy, though, there was no telling what might happen. Certainly, Morey told himself, he had been helped considerably—at least he hadn't set fire to his house and shrieked at the fire-robots, like Newell down the block when his eldest daughter divorced her husband and came back to live with him, bringing her ration quota along, of course. Morey hadn't even been *tempted* to do anything as outrageously, frighteningly immoral as *destroy* things or *waste* them—well, he admitted to himself honestly, perhaps a little tempted, once in a great while. But never anything important enough to worry about; he was sound, perfectly sound.

He looked up, startled. All the doctors were staring at him. "Mr. Fry," Fairless repeated, "will you take your place?"

"Certainly," Morey said hastily. "Uh—where?"

Semmelweiss guffawed. "*Told* you. Never mind, Morey; you didn't miss much. We're going to run through one of the big scenes in your life, the one you told us about last time. Remember? You were fourteen years old, you said. Christmas time. Your mother had made you a promise."

Morey swallowed. "I remember," he said unhappily. "Well, all right. Where do I stand?"

"Right here," said Fairless. "You're you, Carrado is your mother, I'm your father. Would the doctors not participating mind moving back? Fine. Now, Morey, here we are on Christmas morning. Merry Christmas, Morey!"

"Merry Christmas," Morey said half-heartedly. "Uh—Father dear, where's my—uh—my puppy that Mother promised me?"

"Puppy!" said Fairless heartily. "Your mother and I have something much better than a puppy for you. Just take a look under the tree there—it's a *robot!* Yes, Morey, your very own robot—a full-size thirty-eight-tube fully automatic companion robot for you! Go ahead, Morey, go right up and speak to it. Its name is Henry. Go on, boy."

Morey felt a sudden, incomprehensible tingle inside the bridge of his nose. He said shakily, "But I—I didn't *want* a robot."

"Of course you want a robot," Carrado interrupted. "Go on, child, play with your nice robot."

Morey said violently, "I *hate* robots!" He looked around him at the doctors, at the gray-paneled consulting room. He added defiantly, "You hear me, all of you? I *still* hate robots!"

There was a second's pause; then the questions began.

It was half an hour before the receptionist came in and announced that time was up.

In that half hour, Morey had got over his trembling and lost his wild, momentary passion, but he had remembered what for thirteen years he had forgotten.

He hated robots.

The surprising thing was not that young Morey had hated robots. It was that the Robot Riots, the ultimate violent outbreak of flesh against metal, the battle to the death between mankind and its machine heirs . . . never happened. A little boy hated robots, but the man he became worked with them hand in hand.

And yet, always and always before, the new worker, the competitor for the job, was at once and inevitably outside the law. The waves swelled in—the Irish, the Negroes, the Jews, the Italians. They were squeezed into their ghettoes, where they encysted, seethed and struck out, until the burgeoning generations became indistinguishable.

For the robots, that genetic relief was not in sight. And still the conflict never came. The feed-back circuits aimed the anti-aircraft guns and, reshaped and newly planned, found a place in a new sort of machine—together with a miraculous trail of cams and levers, an indestructible and potent power source and a hundred thousand parts and sub-assemblies.

And the first robot clanked off the bench.

Its mission was its own destruction; but from the scavenged wreck of its pilot body, a hundred better robots drew their inspiration. And the hundred went to work, and hundreds more, until there were millions upon untold millions.

And still the riots never happened.

For the robots came bearing a gift and the name of it was "Plenty".

And by the time the gift had shown its own unguessed ills the time for a Robot Riot was past. Plenty is a habit-forming drug. You do not cut the dosage down. You kick it if you can; you stop the dose entirely. But the convulsions that follow may wreck the body once and for all.

The addict craves the grainy white powder; he doesn't hate it, or the runner who sells it to him. And if Morey as a little boy could hate the robot that had deprived him of his pup, Morey the man was perfectly aware that the robots were his servants and his friends.

But the little Morey inside the man—*he* had never been convinced.

Morey ordinarily looked forward to his work. The one day a week at which he *did* anything was a wonderful change from the dreary consume, consume, consume grind. He entered the bright-lit drafting room of the Bradmoor Amusements Company with a feeling of uplift.

But as he was changing from street garb to his drafting smock, Howland from Procurement came over with a knowing look. "Wainwright's been looking for you," Howland whispered. "Better get right in there."

Morey nervously thanked him and got. Wainwright's office was the size of a phone booth and as bare as Antarctic ice. Every time Morey saw it, he felt his insides churn with envy. Think of a desk with nothing on it but work surface—no calendar-clock, no twelve-color pen rack, no dictating machines!

He squeezed himself in and sat down while Wainwright finished a phone call. He mentally reviewed the possible reasons why Wainwright would want to talk to him in person instead of over the phone, or by dropping a word to him as he passed through the drafting room.

Very few of them were good.

Wainwright put down the phone and Morey straightened up. "You sent for me?" he asked.

Wainwright in a chubby world was aristocratically lean. As General Superintendent of the Design & Development Section of the Bradmoor Amusements Company, he ranked high in the upper section of the well-to-do. He rasped, "I certainly did. Fry, just what the hell do you think you're up to now?"

"I don't know what you m-mean, Mr. Wainwright," Morey stammered, crossing off the list of possible reasons for the interview all of the good ones.

Wainwright snorted. "I guess you don't. Not because you weren't told, but because you don't want to know. Think back a whole week. What did I have you on the carpet for then?"

Morey said sickly, "My ration book. Look, Mr. Wainwright, I know I'm running a little bit behind, but—"

"But nothing! How do you think it looks to the Committee, Fry? They got a complaint from the Ration Board about you. Naturally they passed it on to me. And naturally I'm going to pass it right along to you. The question is, what are you going to do about it? Good God, man, look at these figures—textiles, fifty-one per cent; food, sixty-seven per cent; amusements and entertainment, *thirty* per cent! You haven't come up to your ration in anything for months!"

Morey stared at the card miserably. "We—that is, my wife and I—just had a long talk about that last night, Mr. Wainwright. And, believe me, we're going to do better. We're going to buckle right down and get to work and—uh—do better," he finished weakly.

Wainwright nodded, and for the first time there was a note of sympathy in his voice. "Your wife. Judge Elon's daughter, isn't she? Good family. I've met the Judge many times." Then, gruffly, "Well, nevertheless, Fry, I'm warning you. I don't care how you straighten this out, but *don't let the Committee mention this to me again*."

"No, sir."

"All right. Finished with the schematics on the new K- 50?"

Morey brightened. "Just about, sir! I'm putting the first section on tape today. I'm very pleased with it, Mr. Wainwright, honestly I am. I've got more than eighteen thousand moving parts in it now, and that's without—"

"Good. Good." Wainwright glanced down at his desk. "Get back to it. And straighten out this other thing. You can do it, Fry. Consuming is everybody's duty. Just keep that in mind."

Howland followed Morey out of the drafting room, down to the spotless shops. "Bad time?" he inquired solicitously. Morey grunted. It was none of Howland's business.

Howland looked over his shoulder as he was setting up the programing panel. Morey studied the matrices silently, then got busy reading the summary tapes, checking them back against the schematics, setting up the instructions on the programing board. Howland kept quiet as Morey completed the set-up and ran off a test tape. It checked perfectly; Morey stepped back to light a cigarette in celebration before pushing the *start* button.

Howland said, "Go on, run it. I can't go until you put it in the works."

Morey grinned and pushed the button. The board lighted up; within it, a tiny metronomic beep began to pulse. That was all. At the other end of the quarter-mile shed, Morey knew, the automatic sorters and conveyers were fingering through the copper reels and steel ingots, measuring hoppers of plastic powder and colors, setting up an intricate weaving path for the thousands of individual components that would make up Bradmoor's new K-50 Spin-a-Game. But from where they stood, in the elaborately muraled programing room, nothing showed. Bradmoor was an ultra-modernized plant; in the manufacturing end, even robots had been dispensed with in favor of machines that guided themselves.

Morey glanced at his watch and logged in the starting time while Howland quickly counter-checked Morey's raw-material flow program.

"Checks out," Howland said solemnly, slapping him on the back. "Calls for a celebration. Anyway, it's your first design, isn't it?"

"Yes. First all by myself, at any rate."

Howland was already fishing in his private locker for the bottle he kept against emergency needs. He poured with a flourish. "To Morey Fry," he said, "our most favorite designer, in whom we are much pleased."

Morey drank. It went down easily enough. Morey had conscientiously used his liquor rations for years, but he had never gone beyond the minimum, so that although liquor was no new experience to him, the single drink immediately warmed him. It warmed his mouth, his throat, the hollows of his chest; and it settled down with a warm glow inside him. Howland, exerting himself to be nice, complimented Morey fatuously on the design and poured another drink. Morey didn't utter any protest at all.

Howland drained his glass. "You may wonder," he said formally, "why I am so pleased with you, Morey Fry. I will tell you why this is."

Morey grinned. "Please do."

Howland nodded. "I will. It's because I am pleased with the world, Morey. My wife left me last night."

Morey was as shocked as only a recent bridegroom can be by the news of a crumbling marriage. "That's too ba—I mean is that a fact?"

"Yes, she left my beds and board and five robots, and I'm happy to see her go." He poured another drink for both of them. "Women. Can't live with them and can't live without them. First you sigh and pant and chase after 'em—you like poetry?" he demanded suddenly.

Morey said cautiously, "Some poetry."

Howland quoted: "'How long, my love, shall I behold this wall between our gardens—yours the rose, and mine the swooning lily.' Like it? I wrote it for Jocelyn—that's my wife—when we were first going together."

"It's beautiful," said Morey.

"She wouldn't talk to me for two days." Howland drained his drink. "Lots of spirit, that girl. Anyway, I hunted her like a tiger. And then I caught her. *Wow!*"

Morey took a deep drink from his own glass. "What do you mean, *wow?*" he asked.

"*Wow.*" Howland pointed his finger at Morey. "*Wow*, that's what I mean. We got married and I took her home to the dive I was living in, and *wow* we had a kid, and *wow* I got in a little trouble with the Ration Board—nothing serious, of course, but there was a mixup—and *wow* fights.

"Everything was a fight," he explained. "She'd start with a little nagging, and naturally I'd say something or other back, and *bang* we were off. Budget, budget, budget; I hope to die if I ever hear the word 'budget' again. Morey, you're a married man; you know what it's like. Tell me the truth, weren't you just about ready to blow your top the first time you caught your wife cheating on the budget?"

"Cheating on the budget?" Morey was startled. "Cheating how?"

"Oh, lots of ways. Making your portions bigger than hers. Sneaking extra shirts for you on her clothing ration. You know."

"Damn it, I do *not* know!" cried Morey. "Cherry wouldn't do anything like that!"

Howland looked at him opaquely for a long second. "Of course not," he said at last. "Let's have another drink."

Ruffled, Morey held out his glass. Cherry wasn't the type of girl to *cheat*. Of course she wasn't. A fine, loving girl like her—a pretty girl, of a good family; she wouldn't know how to begin.

Howland was saying, in a sort of chant, "No more budget. No more fights. No more 'Daddy never treated me like this.' No more nagging. No more extra rations for household allowance. No more—Morey, what do you say we go out and have a few drinks? I know a place where—"

"Sorry, Howland," Morey said. "I've got to get back to the office, you know."

Howland guffawed. He held out his wristwatch. As Morey, a little unsteadily, bent over it, it tinkled out the hour. It was a matter of minutes before the office closed for the day.

"Oh," said Morey. "I didn't realize—Well, anyway, Howland, thanks, but I can't. My wife will be expecting me."

"She certainly will," Howland sniggered. "Won't catch *her* eating up your rations and hers tonight."

Morey said tightly, "Howland!"

"Oh, sorry, sorry." Howland waved an arm. "Don't mean to say anything against *your* wife, of course. Guess maybe Jocelyn sourced me on women. But honest, Morey, you'd like this place. Name of Uncle Piggotty's, down in the Old Town. Crazy bunch hangs out there. You'd like them. Couple nights last week they had—I mean, you understand, Morey, I don't go there as often as all that, but I just happened to drop in and—"

Morey interrupted firmly. "Thank you, Howland. Must go home. Wife expects it. Decent of you to offer. Good night. Be seeing you."

He walked out, turned at the door to bow politely, and in turning back cracked the side of his face against the door jamb. A sort of pleasant numbness had taken possession of his entire skin surface, though, and it wasn't until he perceived Henry chattering at him sympathetically that he noticed a trickle of blood running down the side of his face.

"Mere flesh wound," he said with dignity. "Nothing to cause you *least* conshter—consternation, Henry. Now kindly shut your ugly face. Want to think."

And he slept in the car all the way home.

It was worse than a hangover. The name is "holdover". You've had some drinks; you've started to sober up by catching a little sleep.

Then you are required to be awake and to function. The consequent state has the worst features of hangover and intoxication; your head thumps and your mouth tastes like the floor of a bear-pit, but you are nowhere near sober.

There is one cure. Morey said thickly, "Let's have a cocktail, dear."

Cherry was delighted to share a cocktail with him before dinner. Cherry, Morey thought lovingly, was a wonderful, wonderful, wonderful—

He found his head nodding in time to his thoughts and the motion made him wince.

Cherry flew to his side and touched his temple. "Is it bothering you, darling?" she asked solicitously. "Where you ran into the door, I mean?"

Morey looked at her sharply, but her expression was open and adoring. He said bravely, "Just a little. Nothing to it, really."

The butler brought the cocktails and retired. Cherry lifted her glass. Morey raised his, caught a whiff of the liquor and nearly dropped it. He bit down hard on his churning insides and forced himself to swallow.

He was surprised but grateful: it stayed down. In a moment, the curious phenomenon of warmth began to repeat itself. He swallowed the rest of the drink and held out his glass for a refill. He even tried a smile. Oddly enough, his face didn't fall off.

One more drink did it. Morey felt happy and relaxed, but by no means drunk. They went in to dinner in fine spirits. They chatted cheerfully with each other and Henry, and Morey found time to feel sentimentally sorry for poor Howland, who couldn't make a go of his marriage, when marriage was obviously such an easy relationship, so beneficial to both sides, so warm and relaxing . . .

Startled, he said, "What?"

Cherry repeated, "It's the cleverest scheme I ever heard of. Such a funny little man, dear. All kind of *nervous*, if you know what I mean. He kept looking at the door as if he was expecting someone, but of course that was silly. None of his friends would have come to *our* house to see him."

Morey said tensely, "Cherry, *please!* What was that you said about ration stamps?"

"But I told you, darling! It was just after you left this morning. This funny little man came to the door; the butler said he wouldn't give any name. Anyway, I talked to him. I thought he might be a neighbor and I certainly would *never* be rude to any neighbor who might come to call, even if the neighborhood was—"

"The ration stamps!" Morey begged. "Did I hear you say he was peddling phony ration stamps?"

Cherry said uncertainly, "Well, I suppose that in a *way* they're phony. The way he explained it, they weren't the regular official kind. But it was four for one, dear—four of his stamps for one of ours. So I just took out our household book and steamed off a couple of weeks' stamps and—"

"How many?" Morey bellowed.

Cherry blinked. "About—about two weeks' quota," she said faintly. "Was that wrong, dear?"

Morey closed his eyes dizzily. "A couple of weeks' stamps," he repeated. "Four for one—you didn't even get the regular rate."

Cherry wailed, "How was I supposed to know? I never had anything like this when I was *home!* We didn't have food riots and slums and all these horrible robots and filthy little revolting men coming to the door!"

Morey stared at her woodenly. She was crying again, but it made no impression on the case-hardened armor that was suddenly thrown around his heart.

Henry made a tentative sound that, in a human, would have been a preparatory cough, but Morey froze him with a white-eyed look.

Morey said in a dreary monotone that barely penetrated the sound of Cherry's tears, "Let me tell you just what it was you did. Assuming, at best, that these stamps you got are at least average good counterfeits, and not so bad that the best thing to do with them is throw them away before we get caught with them in our possession, you have approximately a two-month supply of funny stamps. In case you didn't know it, those ration books are not merely ornamental. They have to be turned in every month to prove that we have completed our consuming quota for the month.

"When they are turned in, they are spot-checked. Every book is at least glanced at. A big chunk of them are gone over very carefully by the inspectors, and a certain percentage are tested by ultra-violet, infra-red, X-ray, radio-isotopes, bleaches, fumes, paper chromatography and every other damned test known to Man." His voice was rising to an uneven crescendo. "*If* we are lucky enough to get away with using any of these stamps at all, we daren't—we simply *dare* not—use more than one or two counterfeits to every dozen or more real stamps.

"That means, Cherry, that what you bought is not a two-month supply, but maybe a two-*year* supply—and since, as you no doubt have never noticed, the things have expiration dates on them, there is probably no chance in the world that we can ever hope to use more than half of them." He was bellowing by the time he pushed back his chair and towered over her. "Moreover," he went on, "right *now*, right as of this *minute*, we have to make up the stamps you gave away, which means that at the very best we are going to be on double rations for two weeks or so.

"And that says nothing about the one feature of this whole grisly mess that you seem to have thought of least, namely that counterfeit stamps are against the *law!* I'm poor, Cherry; I live in a slum, and I know it; I've got a long way to go before I'm as rich or respected or powerful as your father, about whom I am beginning to get considerably tired of hearing. But poor as I may be, I can tell you *this* for sure: Up until now, at any rate, I have been *honest*."

Cherry's tears had stopped entirely and she was bowed white-faced and dry-eyed by the time Morey had finished. He had spent himself; there was no violence left in him.

He stared dismally at Cherry for a moment, then turned wordlessly and stamped out of the house.

Marriage! he thought as he left.

He walked for hours, blind to where he was going.

What brought him back to awareness was a sensation he had not felt in a dozen years. It was not, Morey abruptly realized, the dying traces of his hangover that made his stomach feel so queer. He was hungry—actually hungry.

He looked about him. He was in the Old Town, miles from home, jostled by crowds of lower-class people. The block he was on was as atrocious a slum as Morey had ever seen—Chinese pagodas stood next to rococo imitations of the chapels around Versailles; gingerbread marred every facade; no building was without its brilliant signs and flarelights.

He saw a blindingly overdecorated eating establishment called Billie's Budget Busy Bee and crossed the street toward it, dodging through the unending streams of traffic. It was a miserable excuse for a restaurant, but Morey was in no mood to care. He found a seat under a potted palm, as far from the tinkling fountains and robot string ensemble as he could manage, and ordered recklessly, paying no attention to the ration prices. As the waiter was gliding noiselessly away, Morey had a sickening realization: He'd come out without his ration book. He groaned out loud; it was too late to leave without causing a disturbance. But then, he thought rebelliously, what difference did one more unrationed meal make, anyhow?

Food made him feel a little better. He finished the last of his *profiterole au chocolat*, not even leaving on the plate the uneaten one-third that tradition permitted, and paid his check. The robot cashier reached automatically for his ration book. Morey had a moment of grandeur as he said simply, "No ration stamps."

Robot cashiers are not equipped to display surprise, but this one tried. The man behind Morey in line audibly caught his breath, and less audibly mumbled something about *slummers*. Morey took it as a compliment and strode outside feeling almost in good humor.

Good enough to go home to Cherry? Morey thought seriously of it for a second; but he wasn't going to pretend he was wrong and certainly Cherry wasn't going to be willing to admit that *she* was at fault.

Besides, Morey told himself grimly, she was undoubtedly asleep. That was an annoying thing about Cherry at best: she never had any trouble getting to sleep. Didn't even use her quota of sleeping tablets, though Morey had spoken to her about it more than once. Of course, he reminded himself, he had been so polite and tactful about it, as befits a newlywed, that very likely she hadn't even understood that it was a complaint. Well, *that* would stop!

Man's man Morey Fry, wearing no collar ruff but his own, strode determinedly down the streets of the Old Town.

"Hey, Joe, want a good time?"

Morey took one unbelieving look. "You again!" he roared.

The little man stared at him in genuine surprise. Then a faint glimmer of recognition crossed his face. "Oh, yeah," he said. "This morning, huh?" He clucked commiseratingly. "Too bad you wouldn't deal with me. Your wife was a lot smarter. Of course, you got me a little sore, Jack, so naturally I had to raise the price a little bit."

"You skunk, you cheated my poor wife blind! You and I are going to the local station house and talk this over."

The little man pursed his lips. "We are, huh?"

Morey nodded vigorously. "Damn right! And let me tell you—" He stopped in the middle of a threat as a large hand cupped around his shoulder.

The equally large man who owned the hand said, in a mild and cultured voice, "Is this gentleman disturbing you, Sam?"

"Not so far," the little man conceded. "He might want to, though, so don't go away."

Morey wrenched his shoulder away. "Don't think you can strong-arm me. I'm taking you to the police."

Sam shook his head unbelievingly. "You mean you're going to call the law in on this?"

"I certainly am!"

Sam sighed regretfully. "What do you think of that, Walter? Treating his wife like that. Such a nice lady, too."

"What are you talking about?" Morey demanded, stung on a peculiarly sensitive spot.

"I'm talking about your wife," Sam explained. "Of course, I'm not married myself. But it seems to me that if I was, I wouldn't call the police when my wife was engaged in some kind of criminal activity or other. No, sir, I'd try to settle it myself. Tell you what," he advised, "why don't you talk this over with her? Make her see the error of—"

"Wait a minute," Morey interrupted. "You mean you'd involve my wife in this thing?"

The man spread his hands helplessly. "It's not me that would involve her, Buster," he said. "She already involved her own self. It takes two to make a crime, you know. I sell, maybe; I won't deny it. But after all, I can't sell unless somebody buys, can I?"

Morey stared at him glumly. He glanced in quick speculation at the large-sized Walter; but Walter was just as big as he'd remembered, so that took care of that. Violence was out; the police were out; that left no really attractive way of capitalizing on the good luck of running into the man again.

Sam said, "Well, I'm glad to see that's off your mind. Now, returning to my original question, Mac, how would you like a good time? You look like a smart fellow to me; you look like you'd be kind of interested in a place I happen to know of down the block."

Morey said bitterly, "So you're a dive-steerer, too. A real talented man."

"I admit it," Sam agreed. "Stamp business is slow at night, in my experience. People have their minds more on a good time. And, believe me, a good time is what I can show 'em. Take this place I'm talking about, Uncle Piggotty's is the name of it, it's what I would call an unusual kind of place. Wouldn't you say so, Walter?"

"Oh, I agree with you entirely," Walter rumbled.

But Morey was hardly listening. He said, "Uncle Piggotty's, you say?"

"That's right," said Sam.

Morey frowned for a moment, digesting an idea. Uncle Piggotty's sounded like the place Howland had been talking about back at the plant; it might be interesting, at that.

While he was making up his mind, Sam slipped an arm through his on one side and Walter amiably wrapped a big hand around the other. Morey found himself walking.

"You'll like it," Sam promised comfortably. "No hard feelings about this morning, sport? Of course not. Once you get a look at Piggotty's, you'll get over your mad, anyhow. It's something special. I swear, on what they pay me for bringing in customers, I wouldn't do it unless I *believed* in it."

"Dance, Jack?" the hostess yelled over the noise at the bar. She stepped back, lifted her flounced skirts to ankle height and executed a tricky nine-step.

"My name is Morey," Morey yelled back. "And I don't want to dance, thanks."

The hostess shrugged, frowned meaningfully at Sam and danced away.

Sam flagged the bartender. "First round's on us," he explained to Morey. "Then we won't bother you any more. Unless you want us to, of course. Like the place?" Morey hesitated, but Sam didn't wait. "Fine place," he yelled, and picked up the drink the bartender left him. "See you around."

He and the big man were gone. Morey stared after them uncertainly, then gave it up. He was here, anyhow; might as well at least have a drink. He ordered and looked around.

Uncle Piggotty's was a third-rate dive disguised to look, in parts of it at least, like one of the exclusive upper-class country clubs. The bar, for instance, was treated to resemble the clean lines of nailed wood; but underneath the surface treatment, Morey could detect the intricate laminations of plyplastic. What at first glance appeared to be burlap hangings were in actuality elaborately textured synthetics. And all through the bar the motif was carried out.

A floor show of sorts was going on, but nobody seemed to be paying much attention to it. Morey, straining briefly to hear the master of ceremonies, gathered that the wit was on a more than mildly vulgar level. There was a dispirited string of chorus beauties in long ruffled pantaloons and diaphanous tops; one of them, Morey was almost sure, was the hostess who had talked to him just a few moments before.

Next to him a man was declaiming to a middle-aged woman:

Smote I the monstrous rock, yahoo!
Smote I the turgid tube, Bully Boy!
Smote I the cankered hill—

"Why, Morey!" he interrupted himself. "What are you doing here?"

He turned farther around and Morey recognized him. "Hello, Howland," he said. "I—uh—I happened to be free tonight, so I thought—"

Howland sniggered. "Well, guess your wife is more liberal than mine was. Order a drink, boy."

"Thanks, I've got one," said Morey.

The woman, with a tigerish look at Morey, said, "Don't stop, Everett. That was one of your most beautiful things."

"Oh, Morey's heard my poetry," Howland said. "Morey, I'd like you to meet a very lovely and talented young lady, Tanaquil Bigelow. Morey works in the office with me, Tan."

"Obviously," said Tanaquil Bigelow in a frozen voice, and Morey hastily withdrew the hand he had begun to put out.

The conversation stuck there, impaled, the woman cold, Howland relaxed and abstracted, Morey wondering if, after all, this had been such a good idea. He caught the eye-cell of the robot bartender and ordered a round of drinks for the three of them, politely putting them on Howland's ration book. By the time the drinks had come and Morey had just got around to deciding that it wasn't a very good idea, the woman had all of a sudden become thawed.

She said abruptly, "You look like the kind of man who *thinks*, Morey, and I like to talk to that kind of man. Frankly, Morey, I just don't have any patience at all with the stupid, stodgy men who just work in their offices all day and eat all their dinners every night, and gad about and consume like mad and where does it all get them, anyhow? That's right, I can see you understand. Just one crazy rush of consume, consume from the day you're born *plop* to the day you're buried *pop!* And who's to blame if not the robots?"

Faintly, a tinge of worry began to appear on the surface of Howland's relaxed calm. "Tan," he chided, "Morey may not be very interested in politics."

Politics, Morey thought; well, at least that was a clue. He'd had the dizzying feeling, while the woman was talking, that he himself was the ball in the games machine he had designed for the shop earlier that day. Following the woman's conversation might, at that, give his next design some valuable pointers in swoops, curves and obstacles.

He said, with more than half truth, "No, please go on, Miss Bigelow. I'm very much interested."

She smiled; then abruptly her face changed to a frightening scowl. Morey flinched, but evidently the scowl wasn't meant for him. "Robots!" she hissed. "Supposed to work for us, aren't they? Hah! We're their slaves, slaves for every moment of every miserable day of our lives. Slaves! Wouldn't you like to join us and be free, Morey?"

Morey took cover in his drink. He made an expressive gesture with his free hand—expressive of exactly what, he didn't truly know, for he was lost. But it seemed to satisfy the woman.

She said accusingly, "Did you know that more than three-quarters of the people in this country have had a nervous breakdown in the past five years and four months? That more than half of them are under the constant care of psychiatrists for psychosis—not just plain ordinary neurosis like my husband's got and Howland here has got and you've got, but psychosis. Like I've got. Did you know that? Did you know that forty per cent of the population are essentially manic depressive, thirty-one per cent are schizoid, thirty-eight per cent have an assortment of other unfixed psychogenic disturbances and twenty-four—"

"Hold it a minute, Tan," Howland interrupted critically. "You've got too many per cents there. Start over again."

"Oh, the hell with it," the woman said moodily. "I wish my husband were here. He expresses it so much better than I do." She swallowed her drink. "Since you've wriggled off the hook," she said nastily to Morey, "how about setting up another round—on my ration book this time?"

Morey did; it was the simplest thing to do in his confusion. When that was gone, they had another on Howland's book.

As near as he could figure out, the woman, her husband and quite possibly Howland as well belonged to some kind of anti-robot group. Morey had heard of such things; they had a quasi-legal status, neither approved nor prohibited, but he had never come into contact with them before. Remembering the hatred he had so painfully relived at the psychodrama session, he thought anxiously that perhaps he belonged with them. But, question them though he might, he couldn't seem to get the principles of the organization firmly in mind.

The woman finally gave up trying to explain it, and went off to find her husband while Morey and Howland had another drink and listened to two drunks squabble over who bought the next round. They were at the Alphonse-Gaston stage of inebriation; they would regret it in the morning; for each was bending over backward to permit the other to pay the ration points. Morey wondered uneasily about his own points; Howland was certainly getting credit for a lot of Morey's drinking tonight. Served him right for forgetting his book, of course.

When the woman came back, it was with the large man Morey had encountered in the company of Sam, the counterfeiter, steerer and general man about Old Town.

"A remarkably small world, isn't it?" boomed Walter Bigelow, only slightly crushing Morey's hand in his. "Well, sir, my wife has told me how interested you are in the basic philosophical drives behind our movement, and I should like to discuss them further with you. To begin with, sir, have you considered the principle of Twoness?"

Morey said, "Why—"

"Very good," said Bigelow courteously. He cleared his throat and declaimed:

Han-headed Cathay saw it first,
Bright as brightest solar burst;
Whipped it into boy and girl,
The blinding spiral-sliced swirl:
Yang
And Yin.

He shrugged deprecatingly. "Just the first stanza," he said. "I don't know if you got much out of it."

"Well, no," Morey admitted.

"Second stanza," Bigelow said firmly:

Hegal saw it, saw it clear;
Jackal Marx drew near, drew near:
O'er his shoulder saw it plain,
Turned it upside down again:
Yang
And Yin.

There was an expectant pause. Morey said, "I—uh—"

"Wraps it all up, doesn't it?" Bigelow's wife demanded. "Oh, if only others could see it as clearly as you do! The robot peril *and* the robot savior. Starvation *and* surfeit. Always twoness, always!"

Bigelow patted Morey's shoulder. "The next stanza makes it even clearer," he said. "It's really very clever—I shouldn't say it, of course, but it's Howland's as much has it's mine. He helped me with the verses." Morey darted a glance at Howland, but Howland was carefully looking away. "Third stanza," said Bigelow. "This is a hard one, because it's long, so pay attention."

Justice, tip your sightless scales;
One pan rises, one pan falls.

"Howland," he interrupted himself, "are you *sure* about that rhyme? I always trip over it. Well, anyway:

Add to A and B grows less;
A's B's partner, nonetheless.
Next, the Twoness that there be
In even electricity.
Chart the current as it's found:
Sine the hot lead, line the ground.
The wild sine dances, soars and falls,
But only to figures the zero calls.
Sine wave, scales, all things that be
Share a reciprocity.
Male and female, light and dark:
Name the numbers of Noah's Ark!
Yang
And Yin!

"Dearest!" shrieked Bigelow's wife. "You've never done it better!" There was a spatter of applause, and Morey realized for the first time that half the bar had stopped its noisy revel to listen to them. Bigelow was evidently quite a well-known figure here.

Morey said weakly, "I've never heard anything like it."

He turned hesitantly to Howland, who promptly said, "Drink! What we all need right now is a drink."

They had a drink on Bigelow's book.

Morey got Howland aside and asked him, "Look, level with me. Are these people nuts?"

Howland showed pique. "No. Certainly not."

"Does that poem mean anything? Does this whole business of twoness mean anything?"

Howland shrugged. "If it means something to them, it means something. They're philosophers, Morey. They see deep into things. You don't know what a privilege it is for me to be allowed to associate with them."

They had another drink. On Howland's book, of course.

Morey eased Walter Bigelow over to a quiet spot. He said, "Leaving twoness out of it for the moment, what's this about the robots?"

Bigelow looked at him round-eyed. "Didn't you understand the poem?"

"Of course I did. But diagram it for me in simple terms so I can tell my wife."

Bigelow beamed. "It's about the dichotomy of robots," he explained. "Like the little salt mill that the boy wished for: it ground out salt and ground out salt and ground out salt. He had to have salt, but not *that* much salt. Whitehead explains it clearly—"

They had another drink on Bigelow's book.

Morey wavered over Tanaquil Bigelow. He said fuzzily, "Listen. Mrs. Walter Tanaquil Strongarm Bigelow. Listen."

She grinned smugly at him. "Brown hair," she said dreamily.

Morey shook his head vigorously. "Never mind hair," he ordered. "Never mind poem. Listen. In *pre-cise* and el-e-*men*-ta-ry terms, explain to me what is wrong with the world today."

"Not enough brown hair," she said promptly.

"Never mind hair!"

"All right," she said agreeably. "Too many robots. Too many robots make too much of everything."

"Ha! Got it!" Morey exclaimed triumphantly. "Get rid of robots!"

"Oh, no. No! No! No. We wouldn't eat. Everything is mechanized. Can't get rid of them, can't slow down production—slowing down is dying, stopping is quicker dying. Principle of twoness is the concept that clarifies all these—"

"No!" Morey said violently. "What should we *do*?"

"Do? I'll tell you what we should do, if that's what you want. I can tell you."

"Then tell me."

"What we should do is—" Tanaquil hiccupped with a look of refined consternation—"have another drink."

They had another drink. He gallantly let her pay, of course. She ungallantly argued with the bartender about the ration points due her.

Though not a two-fisted drinker, Morey tried. He really worked at it.

He paid the price, too. For some little time before his limbs stopped moving, his mind stopped functioning. Blackout. Almost a blackout, at any rate, for all he retained of the late evening was a kaleidoscope of people and places and things. Howland was there, drunk as a skunk, disgracefully drunk, Morey remembered thinking as he stared up at Howland from the floor. The Bigelows were there. His wife, Cherry, solicitous and amused, was there. And oddly enough, Henry was there.

It was very, very hard to reconstruct. Morey devoted a whole morning's hangover to the effort. It was *important* to reconstruct it, for some reason. But Morey couldn't even remember what the reason was; and finally he dismissed it, guessing that he had either solved the secret of twoness or whether Tanaquil Bigelow's remarkable figure was natural.

He did, however, know that the next morning he had waked in his own bed, with no recollection of getting there. No recollection of anything much, at least not of anything that fit into the proper chronological order or seemed to mesh with anything else, after the dozenth drink when he and Howland, arms around each other's shoulders, composed a new verse on twoness and, plagiarizing an old marching tune, howled it across the boisterous bar-room:

A twoness on the scene much later
Rests in your refrigerator.
Heat your house and insulate it.
Next your food: Refrigerate it.
Frost will damp your Freon coils,
So flux in nichrome till it boils.
See the picture? Heat in cold
In heat in cold, the story's told!
Giant-writ the sacred scrawl:
Oh, the twoness of it all!
Yang
And Yin!

It had, at any rate, seemed to mean something at the time.

If alcohol opened Morey's eyes to the fact that there *was* a twoness, perhaps alcohol was what he needed. For there was.

Call it a dichotomy, if the word seems more couth. A kind of two-pronged struggle, the struggle of two unwearying runners in an immortal race. There is the refrigerator inside the house. The cold air, the bubble of heated air that is the house, the bubble of cooled air that is the refrigerator, the momentary bubble of heated air that defrosts it. Call the heat Yang, if you will. Call the cold Yin. Yang overtakes Yin. Then Yin passes Yang. Then Yang passes Yin. Then—

Give them other names. Call Yin a mouth; call Yang a hand.

If the hand rests, the mouth will starve. If the mouth stops, the hand will die. The hand, Yang, moves faster.

Yin may not lag behind.

Then call Yang a robot.

And remember that a pipeline has two ends.

Like any once-in-a-lifetime lush, Morey braced himself for the consequences—and found startledly that there were none.

Cherry was a surprise to him. "You were so funny," she giggled. "And, honestly, so *romantic*."

He shakily swallowed his breakfast coffee.

The office staff roared and slapped him on the back. "Howland tells us you're living high, boy!" they bellowed more or less in the same words. "Hey, listen to what Morey did—went on the town for the night of a lifetime *and didn't even bring his ration book along to cash in*!"

They thought it was a wonderful joke.

But, then, everything was going well. Cherry, it seemed, had reformed out of recognition. True, she still hated to go out in the evening and Morey never saw her forcing herself to gorge on unwanted food or play undesired games. But, moping into the pantry one afternoon, he found to his incredulous delight that they were well ahead of their ration quotas. In some items, in fact, they were *out*—a month's supply and more was gone ahead of schedule!

Nor was it the counterfeit stamps, for he had found them tucked behind a bain-marie and quietly burned them. He cast about for ways of complimenting her, but caution prevailed. She was sensitive on the subject; leave it be.

And virtue had its reward.

Wainwright called him in, all smiles. "Morey, great news! We've all appreciated your work here and we've been able to show it in some more tangible way then compliments. I didn't want to say anything till it was definite, but—your status has been reviewed by Classification and the Ration Board. You're out of Class Four Minor, Morey!"

Morey said tremulously, hardly daring to hope, "I'm a full Class Four?"

"Class Five, Morey. *Class Five*! When we do something, we do it right. We asked for a special waiver and got it—you've skipped a whole class." He added honestly, "Not that it was just our backing that did it, of course. Your own recent splendid record of consumption helped a lot. I told you you could do it!"

Morey had to sit down. He missed the rest of what Wainwright had to say, but it couldn't have mattered. He escaped from the office, side-stepped the knot of fellow-employees waiting to congratulate him, and got to a phone.

Cherry was as ecstatic and inarticulate as he. "Oh, darling!" was all she could say.

"And I couldn't have done it without you," he babbled. "Wainwright as much as said so himself. Said if it wasn't for the way we—well, *you* have been keeping up with the rations, it never would have got by the Board. I've been meaning to say something to you about that, dear, but I just haven't known how. But I do appreciate it. I—Hello?" There was a curious silence at the other end of the phone. "Hello?" he repeated worriedly.

Cherry's voice was intense and low. "Morey Fry, I think you're mean. I wish you hadn't spoiled the good news." And she hung up.

Morey stared slack-jawed at the phone.

Howland appeared behind him, chuckling. "Women," he said. "Never try to figure them. Anyway, congratulations, Morey."

"Thanks," Morey mumbled.

Howland coughed and said, "Uh—by the way, Morey, now that you're one of the big shots, so to speak, you won't—uh—feel obliged to—well, say anything to Wainwright, for instance, about anything I may have said while we—"

"Excuse me," Morey said, unhearing, and pushed past him. He thought wildly of calling Cherry back, of racing home to see just what he'd said that was wrong. Not that there was much doubt, of course. He'd touched her on her sore point.

Anyhow, his wristwatch was chiming a reminder of the fact that his psychiatric appointment for the week was coming up.

Morey sighed. The day gives and the day takes away. Blessed is the day that gives only good things.

If any.

The session went badly. Many of the sessions had been going badly, Morey decided; there had been more and more whispering in knots of doctors from which he was excluded, poking and probing in the dark instead of the precise psychic surgery he was used to. Something was wrong, he thought.

Something was. Semmelweiss confirmed it when he adjourned the group session. After the other doctor had left, he sat Morey down for a private talk. On his own time—too—he didn't ask for his usual ration fee. That told Morey how important the problem was.

"Morey," said Semmelweiss, "you're holding back."

"I don't mean to, Doctor," Morey said earnestly.

"Who knows what you 'mean' to do? Part of you 'means' to. We've dug pretty deep and we've found some important things. Now there's something I can't put my finger on. Exploring the mind, Morey, is like sending scouts through cannibal territory. You can't see the cannibals—until it's too late. But if you send a scout through the jungle and he doesn't show up on the other side, it's a fair assumption that something obstructed his way. In that case, we would label the obstruction 'cannibals.' In the case of the human mind, we label the obstruction a 'trauma.' What the trauma is, or what its effects on behavior will be, we have to find out, once we know that it's there."

Morey nodded. All of this was familiar; he couldn't see what Semmelweiss was driving at.

Semmelweiss sighed. "The trouble with healing traumas and penetrating psychic blocks and releasing inhibitions—the trouble with everything we psychiatrists do, in fact, is that we can't afford to do it too well. An inhibited man is under a strain. We try to relieve the strain. But if we succeed completely, leaving him with no inhibitions at all, we have an outlaw, Morey. Inhibitions are often socially necessary. Suppose, for instance, that an average man were not inhibited against blatant waste. It could happen, you know. Suppose that instead of consuming his ration quota in an orderly and responsible way, he did such things as set fire to his house and everything in it or dumped his food allotment in the river.

"When only a few individuals are doing it, we treat the individuals. But if it were done on a mass scale, Morey, it would be the end of society as we know it. Think of the whole collection of anti-social actions that you see in every paper. Man beats wife; wife turns into a harpy; junior smashes up windows; husband starts a black-market stamp racket. And every one of them traces to a basic weakness in the mind's defenses against the most important single anti-social phenomenon—failure to consume."

Morey flared, "That's not fair, Doctor! That was weeks ago! We've certainly been on the ball lately. I was just commended by the Board, in fact—"

The doctor said mildly, "Why so violent, Morey? I only made a general remark."

"It's just natural to resent being accused."

The doctor shrugged. "First, foremost and above all, we do *not* accuse patients of things. We try to help you find things out." He lit his end-of-session cigarette. "Think about it, please. I'll see you next week."

Cherry was composed and unapproachable. She kissed him remotely when he came in. She said, "I called Mother and told her the good news. She and Dad promised to come over here to celebrate."

"Yeah," said Morey. "Darling, what did I say wrong on the phone?"

"They'll be here about six."

"Sure. But what did I say? Was it about the rations? If you're sensitive, I swear I'll never mention them again."

"I *am* sensitive, Morey."

He said despairingly, "I'm sorry. I just—"

He had a better idea. He kissed her.

Cherry was passive at first, but not for long. When he had finished kissing her, she pushed him away and actually giggled. "Let me get dressed for dinner."

"Certainly. Anyhow, I was just—"

She laid a finger on his lips.

He let her escape and, feeling much less tense, drifted into the library. The afternoon papers were waiting for him. Virtuously, he sat down and began going through them in order. Midway through the *World-Telegram-Sun-Post-and-News*, he rang for Henry.

Morey had read clear through to the drama section of the *Times-Herald-Tribune-Mirror* before the robot appeared. "Good evening," it said politely.

"What took you so long?" Morey demanded. "Where are all the robots?"

Robots do not stammer, but there was a distinct pause before Henry said, "Belowstairs, sir. Did you want them for something?"

"Well, no. I just haven't seen them around. Get me a drink."

It hesitated. "Scotch, sir?"

"*Before* dinner? Get me a Manhattan."

"We're all out of Vermouth, sir."

"All out? Would you mind telling me how?"

"It's all used up, sir."

"Now that's just ridiculous," Morey snapped. "We have never run out of liquor in our whole lives and you know it. Good heavens, we just got our allotment in the other day and I certainly—"

He checked himself. There was a sudden flicker of horror in his eyes as he stared at Henry.

"You certainly what, sir?" the robot prompted.

Morey swallowed. "Henry, did I—did I do something I shouldn't have?"

"I'm sure I wouldn't know, sir. It isn't up to me to say what you should and shouldn't do."

"Of course not," Morey agreed grayly.

He sat rigid, staring hopelessly into space, remembering. What he remembered was no pleasure to him at all.

"Henry," he said. "Come along, we're going belowstairs. Right now!"

It had been Tanaquil Bigelow's remark about the robots. *Too many robots—make too much of everything.*

That had implanted the idea; it germinated in Morey's home. More than a little drunk, less than ordinarily inhibited, he had found the problem clear and the answer obvious.

He stared around him in dismal worry. His own robots, following his own orders, given weeks before . . .

Henry said, "It's just what you *told* us to do, sir."

Morey groaned. He was watching a scene of unparalleled activity, and it sent shivers up and down his spine.

There was the butler-robot, hard at work, his copper face expressionless. Dressed in Morey's own sports knickers and golfing shoes, the robot solemnly hit a ball against the wall, picked it up and teed it, hit it again, over and again, with Morey's own clubs. Until the ball wore ragged and was replaced; and the shifts of the clubs leaned out of true; and the close-stitched seams in the clothing began to stretch and abrade.

"My God!" said Morey hollowly.

There were the maid-robots, exquisitely dressed in Cherry's best, walking up and down in the delicate, slim shoes, sitting and rising and bending and turning. The cook-robots and the serving-robots were preparing Dionysian meals.

Morey swallowed. "You—you've been doing this right along," he said to Henry. "That's why the quotas have been filled."

"Oh, yes, sir. Just as you told us."

Morey had to sit down. One of the serving-robots politely scurried over with a chair, brought from upstairs for their new chores.

Waste.

Morey tasted the word between his lips.

Waste.

You never wasted things. You *used* them. If necessary, you drove yourself to the edge of breakdown to use them; you made every breath a burden and every hour a torment to use them, until through diligent consuming and/or occupational merit, you were promoted to the next higher class, and were allowed to consume less frantically. But you didn't wantonly destroy or throw out. You *consumed*.

Morey thought fearfully: When the Board finds out about this . . .

Still, he reminded himself, the Board hadn't found out. It might take some time before they did, for humans, after all, never entered robot quarters. There was no law against it, not even a sacrosanct custom. But there was no reason to. When breaks occurred, which was infrequently, maintenance robots or repair squads came in and put them back in order. Usually the humans involved didn't even know it had happened, because the robots used their own TBR radio circuits and the process was next thing to automatic.

Morey said reprovingly, "Henry, you should have told—well, I mean reminded me about this."

"But, sir!" Henry protested. "'Don't tell a living soul,' you said. You made it a direct order."

"Umph. Well, keep it that way. I—uh—I have to go back upstairs. Better get the rest of the robots started on dinner."

Morey left, not comfortably.

The dinner to celebrate Morey's promotion was difficult. Morey liked Cherry's parents. Old Elon, after the pre-marriage inquisition that father must inevitably give to daughter's suitor, had buckled right down to the job of adjustment. The old folks were good about not interfering, good about keeping their superior social status to themselves, good about helping out on the budget—at least once a week, they could be relied on to come over for a hearty meal, and Mrs. Elon had more than once remade some of Cherry's new dresses to fit herself, even to the extent of wearing all the high-point ornamentation.

And they had been wonderful about the wedding gifts, when Morey and their daughter got married. The most any member of Morey's family had been willing to take was a silver set or a few crystal table pieces. The Elons had come through with a dazzling promise to accept a car, a bird-bath for their garden and a complete set of living-room furniture! Of course, they could afford it—they had to consume so little that it wasn't much strain for them even to take gifts of that magnitude. But without their help, Morey knew, the first few months of matrimony would have been even tougher consuming than they were.

But on this particular night it was hard for Morey to like anyone. He responded with monosyllables; he barely grunted when Elon proposed a toast to his promotion and his brilliant future. He was preoccupied.

Rightly so. Morey, in his deepest, bravest searching, could find no clue in his memory as to just what the punishment might be for what he had done. But he had a sick certainty that trouble lay ahead.

Morey went over his problem so many times that an anesthesia set in. By the time dinner was ended and he and his father-in-law were in the den with their brandy, he was more or less functioning again.

Elon, for the first time since Morey had known him, offered him one of *his* cigars. "You're Grade Five—can afford to smoke somebody else's now, hey?"

"Yeah," Morey said glumly.

There was a moment of silence. Then Elon as punctilious as any companion-robot, coughed and tried again. "Remember being peaked till I hit Grade Five," he reminisced meaningfully. "Consuming keeps a man on the go, all right. Things piled up at the law office, couldn't be taken care of while ration points piled up, too. And consuming comes first, of course—that's a citizen's prime duty. Mother and I had our share of grief over that, but a couple that wants to make a go of marriage and citizenship just pitches in and does the job, hey?"

Morey repressed a shudder and managed to nod.

"Best thing about upgrading," Elon went on, as if he had elicited a satisfactory answer, "don't have to spend so much time consuming, give more attention to work. Greatest luxury in the world, work. Wish I had as much stamina as you young fellows. Five days a week in court are about all I can manage. Hit six for a while, relaxed first time in my life, but my doctor made me cut down. Said we can't overdo pleasures. You'll be working two days a week now, hey?"

Morey produced another nod.

Elon drew deeply on his cigar, his eyes bright as they watched Morey. He was visibly puzzled, and Morey, even in his half-daze, could recognize the exact moment at which Elon drew the wrong inference. "Ah, everything okay with you and Cherry?" he asked diplomatically.

"Fine!" Morey exclaimed. "Couldn't be better!"

"Good, good." Elon changed the subject with almost an audible wrench. "Speaking of court, had an interesting case the other day. Young fellow—year or two younger than you, I guess—came in with a Section Ninety-seven on him. Know what that is? Breaking and entering!"

"Breaking and entering," Morey repeated wonderingly, interested in spite of himself. "Breaking and entering what?"

"Houses. Old term; law's full of them. Originally applied to stealing things. Still does, I discovered."

"You mean he *stole* something?" Morey asked in bewilderment.

"Exactly! He *stole*. Strangest thing I ever came across. Talked it over with one of his bunch of lawyers later; new one on him, too. Seems this kid had a girl friend, nice kid but a little, you know, plump. She got interested in art."

"There's nothing wrong with that," Morey said.

"Nothing wrong with her, either. She didn't do anything. She didn't like him too much, though. Wouldn't marry him. Kid got to thinking about how he could get her to change her mind and—well, you know that big Mondrian in the Museum?"

"I've never been there," Morey said, somewhat embarrassed.

"Um. Ought to try it some day, boy. Anyway, comes closing time at the Museum the other day, this kid sneaks in. He steals the painting. That's right—*steals* it. Takes it to give to the girl."

Morey shook his head blankly. "I never heard of anything like that in my life."

"Not many have. Girl wouldn't take it, by the way. Got scared when he brought it to her. She must've tipped off the police, I guess. Somebody did. Took 'em three hours to find it, even when they knew it was hanging on a wall. Pretty poor kid. Forty-two room house."

"And there was a *law* against it?" Morey asked. "I mean it's like making a law against breathing."

"Certainly was. Old law, of course. Kid got set back two grades. Would have been more but, my God, he was only a Grade Three as it was."

"Yeah," said Morey, wetting his lips. "Say, Dad—"

"Um?"

Morey cleared his throat. "Uh—I wonder—I mean what's the penalty, for instance, for things like—well, misusing rations or anything like that?"

Elon's eyebrows went high. "Misusing rations?"

"Say you had a liquor ration, it might be, and instead of drinking it, you—well, flushed it down the drain or something . . ."

His voice trailed off. Elon was frowning. He said, "Funny thing, seems I'm not as broadminded as I thought I was. For some reason, I don't find that amusing."

"Sorry," Morey croaked.

And he certainly was.

It might be dishonest, but it was doing him a lot of good, for days went by and no one seemed to have penetrated his secret. Cherry was happy. Wainwright found occasion after occasion to pat Morey's back. The wages of sin were turning out to be prosperity and happiness.

There was a bad moment when Morey came home to find Cherry in the middle of supervising a team of packing-robots; the new house, suitable to his higher grade, was ready, and they were expected to move in the next day. But Cherry hadn't been belowstairs, and Morey had his household robots clean up the evidences of what they had been doing before the packers got that far.

The new house was, by Morey's standards, pure luxury.

It was only fifteen rooms. Morey had shrewdly retained one more robot than was required for a Class Five, and had been allowed a compensating deduction in the size of his house.

The robot quarters were less secluded than in the old house, though, and that was a disadvantage. More than once Cherry had snuggled up to him in the delightful intimacy of their one bed in their single bedroom and said, with faint curiosity, "I wish they'd stop that noise." And Morey had promised to speak to Henry about it in the morning. But there was nothing he could say to Henry, of course, unless he ordered Henry to stop the tireless consuming through each of the day's twenty-four hours that kept them always ahead, but never quite far enough ahead, of the inexorable weekly increment of ration quotas.

But, though Cherry might once in a while have a moment's curiosity about what the robots were doing, she was not likely to be able to guess at the facts. Her upbringing was, for once, on Morey's side—she knew so little of the grind, grind, grind of consuming that was the lot of the lower classes that she scarcely noticed that there was less of it.

Morey almost, sometimes, relaxed.

He thought of many ingenious chores for robots, and the robots politely and emotionlessly obeyed.

Morey was a success.

It wasn't all gravy. There was a nervous moment for Morey when the quarterly survey report came in the mail. As the day for the Ration Board to check over the degree of wear on the turned-in discards came due, Morey began to sweat. The clothing and furniture and household goods the robots had consumed for him were very nearly in shreds. It had to look plausible, that was the big thing—no normal person would wear a hole completely through the knee of a pair of pants, as Henry had done with his dress suit before Morey stopped him. Would the Board question it?

Worse, was there something about the *way* the robots consumed the stuff that would give the whole show away? Some special wear point in the robot anatomy, for instance, that would rub a hole where no human's body could, or stretch a seam that should normally be under no strain at all?

It was worrisome. But the worry was needless. When the report of survey came, Morey let out a long-held breath. *Not a single item disallowed*!

Morey was a success—and so was his scheme!

To the successful man come the rewards of success. Morey arrived home one evening after a hard day's work at the office and was alarmed to find another car parked in his drive. It was a tiny two-seater, the sort affected by top officials and the very well-to-do.

Right then and there Morey learned the first half of the embezzler's lesson: Anything different is dangerous. He came uneasily into his own home, fearful that some high officer of the Ration Board had come to ask questions.

But Cherry was glowing. "Mr. Porfirio is a newspaper feature writer and he wants to write you up for their 'Consumers of Distinction' page! Morey, I *couldn't* be more proud!"

"Thanks," said Morey glumly. "Hello."

Mr. Porfirio shook Morey's hand warmly. "I'm not exactly from a newspaper," he corrected. "Trans-video Press is what it is, actually. We're a news wire service; we supply forty-seven hundred papers with news and feature material. Every one of them," he added complacently, "on the required consumption list of Grades One through Six inclusive. We have a Sunday supplement self-help feature on consuming problems and we like to—well, give credit where credit is due. You've established an enviable record, Mr. Fry. We'd like to tell our readers about it."

"Um," said Morey. "Let's go in the drawing room."

"Oh, no!" Cherry said firmly. "I want to hear this. He's so modest, Mr. Porfirio, you'd really never know what kind of a man he is just to listen to him talk. Why, my goodness, I'm his wife and I swear *I* don't know how he does all the consuming he does. He simply—"

"Have a drink, Mr. Porfirio," Morey said, against all etiquette. "Rye? Scotch? Bourbon? Gin-and-tonic? Brandy Alexander? Dry Manha—I mean what would you like?" He became conscious that he was babbling like a fool.

"Anything," said the newsman. "Rye is fine. Now, Mr. Fry, I notice you've fixed up your place very attractively here and your wife says that your country home is just as nice. As soon as I came in, I said to myself, 'Beautiful home. Hardly a stick of furniture that isn't absolutely necessary. Might be a Grade Six or Seven.' And Mrs. Fry says the other place is even barer."

"She does, does she?" Morey challenged sharply. "Well, let me tell you, Mr. Porfirio, that every last scrap of my furniture allowance is accounted for! I don't know what you're getting at, but—"

"Oh, I certainly didn't mean to imply anything like *that*! I just want to get some information from you that I can pass on to our readers. You know, to sort of help them do as well as yourself. How *do* you do it?"

Morey swallowed. "We—uh—well, we just keep after it. Hard work, that's all."

Porfirio nodded admiringly. "Hard work," he repeated, and fished a triple-folded sheet of paper out of his pocket to make notes on. "Would you say," he went on, "that anyone could do as well as you simply by devoting himself to it—setting a regular schedule, for example, and keeping to it very strictly?"

"Oh, yes," said Morey.

"In other words, it's only a matter of doing what you have to do every day?"

"That's it exactly. I handle the budget in my house—more experience than my wife, you see—but no reason a woman can't do it."

"Budgeting," Porfirio recorded approvingly. "That's our policy, too."

The interview was not the terror it had seemed, not even when Porfirio tactfully called attention to Cherry's slim waistline ("So many housewives, Mrs. Fry, find it difficult to keep from being—well, a little plump") and Morey had to invent endless hours on the exercise machines, while Cherry looked faintly perplexed, but did not interrupt.

From the interview, however, Morey learned the second half of the embezzler's lesson. After Porfirio had gone, he leaped in and spoke more than a little firmly to Cherry. "That business of exercise, dear. We really have to start doing it. I don't know if you've noticed it, but you *are* beginning to get just a trifle heavier and we don't want that to happen, do we?"

In the following grim and unnecessary sessions on the mechanical horses, Morey had plenty of time to reflect on the lesson. Stolen treasures are less sweet than one would like, when one dare not enjoy them in the open.

But some of Morey's treasures were fairly earned.

The new Bradmoor K-50 Spin-a-Game, for instance, was his very own. His job was design and creation, and he was a fortunate man in that his efforts were permitted to be expended along the line of greatest social utility—namely, to increase consumption.

The Spin-a-Game was a well-nigh perfect machine for the purpose. "Brilliant," said Wainwright, beaming, when the pilot machine had been put through its first tests. "Guess they don't call me the Talent-picker for nothing. I knew you could do it, boy!"

Even Howland was lavish in his praise. He sat munching on a plate of petits-fours (he was still only a Grade Three) while the tests were going on, and when they were over, he said enthusiastically, "It's a beauty, Morey. That series-corrupter—sensational! Never saw a prettier piece of machinery."

Morey flushed gratefully.

Wainwright left, exuding praise, and Morey patted his pilot model affectionately and admired its polychrome gleam. The looks of the machine, as Wainwright had lectured many a time, were as important as its function: "You have to make them *want* to play it, boy! They won't play it if they don't *see* it!" And consequently the whole K series was distinguished by flashing rainbows of light, provocative strains of music, haunting scents that drifted into the nostrils of the passerby with compelling effect.

Morey had drawn heavily on all the old masterpieces of design—the one-arm bandit, the pinball machine, the juke box. You put your ration book in the hopper. You spun the wheels until you selected the game you wanted to play against the machine. You punched buttons or spun dials or, in any of 325 different ways, you pitted your human skill against the magnetic-taped skills of the machine.

And you lost. You had a chance to win, but the inexorable statistics of the machine's setting made sure that if you played long enough, you had to lose.

That is to say, if you risked a ten-point ration stamp—showing, perhaps, that you had consumed three six-course meals—your statistic return was eight points. You might hit the jackpot and get a thousand points back, and thus be exempt from a whole freezerful of steaks and joints and prepared vegetables; but it seldom happened. Most likely you lost and got nothing.

Got nothing, that is, in the way of your hazarded ration stamps. But the beauty of the machine, which was Morey's main contribution, was that, win or lose, you *always* found a pellet of vitamin-drenched, sugar-coated antibiotic hormone gum in the hopper. You played your game, won or lost your stake, popped your hormone gum into your mouth and played another. By the time that game was ended, the gum was used up, the coating dissolved; you discarded it and started another.

"That's what the man from the NRB liked," Howland told Morey confidentially. "He took a set of schematics back with him; they might install it on *all* new machines. Oh, you're the fair-haired boy, all right!"

It was the first Morey had heard about a man from the National Ration Board. It was good news. He excused himself and hurried to phone Cherry the story of his latest successes. He reached her at her mother's, where she was spending the evening, and she was properly impressed and affectionate. He came back to Howland in a glowing humor.

"Drink?" said Howland diffidently.

"Sure," said Morey. He could afford, he thought, to drink as much of Howland's liquor as he liked; poor guy, sunk in the consuming quicksands of Class Three. Only fair for somebody a little more successful to give him a hand once in a while.

And when Howland, learning that Cherry had left Morey a bachelor for the evening, proposed Uncle Piggotty's again, Morey hardly hesitated at all.

The Bigelows were delighted to see him. Morey wondered briefly if they *had* a home; certainly they didn't seem to spend much time in it.

It turned out they did, because when Morey indicated virtuously that he'd only stopped in at Piggotty's for a single drink before dinner, and Howland revealed that he was free for the evening, they captured Morey and bore him off to their house.

Tanaquil Bigelow was haughtily apologetic. "I don't suppose this is the kind of place Mr. Fry is used to," she observed to her husband, right across Morey, who was standing between them. "Still, we call it home."

Morey made an appropriately polite remark. Actually, the place nearly turned his stomach. It was an enormous glaringly new mansion, bigger even than Morey's former house, stuffed to bursting with bulging sofas and pianos and massive mahogany chairs and tri-D sets and bedrooms and drawing rooms and breakfast rooms and nurseries.

The nurseries were a shock to Morey; it had never occurred to him that the Bigelows had children. But they did and, though the children were only five and eight, they were still up, under the care of a brace of robot nursemaids, doggedly playing with their overstuffed animals and miniature trains.

"You don't know what a comfort Tony and Dick are," Tanaquil Bigelow told Morey. "They consume *so* much more than their rations. Walter says that every family ought to have at least two or three children to, you know, help out. Walter's so intelligent about these things, it's a pleasure to hear him talk. Have you heard his poem, Morey? The one he calls *The Twoness of—*"

Morey hastily admitted that he had. He reconciled himself to a glum evening. The Bigelows had been eccentric but fun back at Uncle Piggotty's. On their own ground, they seemed just as eccentric, but painfully dull.

They had a round of cocktails, and another, and then the Bigelows no longer seemed so dull. Dinner was ghastly, of course; Morey was nouveau-riche enough to be a snob about his relatively Spartan table. But he minded his manners and sampled, with grim concentration, each successive course of chunky protein and rich marinades. With the help of the endless succession of table wines and liqueurs, dinner ended without destroying his evening or his strained digestive system.

And afterward, they were a pleasant company in the Bigelow's ornate drawing room. Tanaquil Bigelow, in consultation with the children, checked over their ration books and came up with the announcement that they would have a brief recital by a pair of robot dancers, followed by string music by a robot quartet. Morey prepared himself for the worst, but found before the dancers were through that he was enjoying himself. Strange lesson for Morey: When you didn't *have* to watch them, the robot entertainers were fun!

"Good night, dears," Tanaquil Bigelow said firmly to the children when the dancers were done. The boys rebelled, naturally, but they went. It was only a matter of minutes, though, before one of them was back, clutching at Morey's sleeve with a pudgy hand.

Morey looked at the boy uneasily, having little experience with children. He said, "Uh—what is it, Tony?"

"Dick, you mean," the boy said. "Gimme your autograph." He poked an engraved pad and a vulgarly jeweled pencil at Morey.

Morey dazedly signed and the child ran off, Morey staring after him. Tanaquil Bigelow laughed and explained, "He saw your name in Porfirio's column. Dick *loves* Porfirio, reads him every day. He's such an intellectual kid, really. He'd always have his nose in a book if I didn't keep after him to play with his trains and watch tri-D."

"That was quite a nice write-up," Walter Bigelow commented—a little enviously, Morey thought. "Bet you make Consumer of the Year. I wish," he sighed, "that we could get a little ahead on the quotas the way you did. But it just never seems to work out. We eat and play and consume like crazy, and somehow at the end of the month we're always a little behind in something—everything keeps piling up—and then the Board sends us a warning, and they call me down and, first thing you know, I've got a couple of hundred added penalty points and we're worse off than before."

"Never you mind," Tanaquil replied staunchly. "Consuming isn't everything in life. You have your work."

Bigelow nodded judiciously and offered Morey another drink. Another drink, however, was not what Morey needed. He was sitting in a rosy glow, less of alcohol than of sheer contentment with the world.

He said suddenly, "Listen."

Bigelow looked up from his own drink. "Eh?"

"If I tell you something that's a *secret*, will you keep it that way?"

Bigelow rumbled, "Why, I guess so, Morey."

But his wife cut in sharply, "Certainly we will, Morey. Of course! What is it?" There was a gleam in her eye, Morey noticed. It puzzled him, but he decided to ignore it.

He said, "About that write-up. I—I'm not such a hot-shot consumer, really, you know. In fact—" All of a sudden, everyone's eyes seemed to be on him. For a tortured moment, Morey wondered if he was doing the right thing. A secret that two people know is compromised, and a secret known to three people is no secret. Still—

"It's like this," he said firmly. "You remember what we were talking about at Uncle Piggotty's that night? Well, when I went home I went down to the robot quarters, and I—"

He went on from there.

Tanaquil Bigelow said triumphantly, "I *knew* it!"

Walter Bigelow gave his wife a mild, reproving look. He declared soberly, "You've done a big thing, Morey. A mighty big thing. God willing, you've pronounced the death sentence on our society as we know it. Future generations will revere the name of Morey Fry." He solemnly shook Morey's hand.

Morey said dazedly, "I *what*?"

Walter nodded. It was a valedictory. He turned to his wife. "Tanaquil, we'll have to call an emergency meeting."

"Of course, Walter," she said devotedly.

"And Morey will have to be there. Yes, you'll have to, Morey; no excuses. We want the Brotherhood to meet you. Right, Howland?"

Howland coughed uneasily. He nodded noncommittally and took another drink.

Morey demanded desperately, "What are you talking about? Howland, you tell me!"

Howland fiddled with his drink. "Well," he said, "it's like Tan was telling you that night. A few of us, well, politically mature persons have formed a little group. We—"

"*Little* group!" Tanaquil Bigelow said scornfully. "Howland, sometimes I wonder if you really catch the spirit of the thing at all! It's everybody, Morey, everybody in the world. Why, there are eighteen of us right here in Old Town! There are *scores more* all over the world! I knew you were up to something like this, Morey. I told Walter so the morning after we met you. I said, 'Walter, mark my words, that man Morey is up to something.' But I must say," she admitted worshipfully, "I didn't know it would have the *scope* of what you're proposing now! Imagine—a whole world of consumers, rising as one man, shouting the name of Morey Fry, fighting the Ration Board with the Board's own weapon—the robots. What poetic justice!"

Bigelow nodded enthusiastically. "Call Uncle Piggotty's, dear," he ordered. "See if you can round up a quorum right now! Meanwhile, Morey and I are going belowstairs. Let's go, Morey—let's get the new world started!"

Morey sat there open-mouthed. He closed it with a snap. "Bigelow," he whispered, "do you mean to say that you're going to spread this idea around through some kind of subversive organization?"

"Subversive?" Bigelow repeated stiffly. "My dear man, *all* creative minds are subversive, whether they operate singly or in such a group as the Brotherhood of Freemen. I scarcely like—"

"Never mind what you like," Morey insisted. "You're going to call a meeting of this Brotherhood and you want *me* to tell them what I just told you. Is that right?"

"Well—yes."

Morey got up. "I wish I could say it's been nice, but it hasn't. Good night!"

And he stormed out before they could stop him.

Out on the street, though, his resolution deserted him. He hailed a robot cab and ordered the driver to take him on the traditional time-killing ride through the park while he made up his mind.

The fact that he had left, of course, was not going to keep Bigelow from going through with his announced intention. Morey remembered, now, fragments of conversation from Bigelow and his wife at Uncle Piggotty's, and cursed himself. They had, it was perfectly true, said and hinted enough about politics and purposes to put him on his guard. All that nonsense about twoness had diverted him from what should have been perfectly clear: they were subversives indeed.

He glanced at his watch. Late, but not too late; Cherry would still be at her parents' home.

He leaned forward and gave the driver their address. It was like beginning the first of a hundred-shot series of injections: you know it's going to cure you, but it hurts just the same.

Morey said manfully: "And that's it, sir. I know I've been a fool. I'm willing to take the consequences."

Old Elon rubbed his jaw thoughtfully. "Um," he said.

Cherry and her mother had long passed the point where they could say anything at all; they were seated side by side on a couch across the room, listening with expressions of strain and incredulity.

Elon said abruptly, "Excuse me. Phone call to make." He left the room to make a brief call and returned. He said over his shoulder to his wife, "Coffee. We'll need it. Got a problem here."

Morey said, "Do you think—I mean what should I do?"

Elon shrugged, then, surprisingly, grinned. "What can you do?" he demanded cheerfully. "Done plenty already, I'd say. Drink some coffee. Call I made," he explained, "was to Jim, my law clerk. He'll be here in a minute. Get some dope from Jim, then we'll know better."

Cherry came over to Morey and sat beside him. All she said was, "Don't worry," but to Morey it conveyed all the meaning in the world. He returned the pressure of her hand with a feeling of deepest relief. Hell, he said to himself, why *should* I worry? Worst they can do to me is drop me a couple of grades and what's so bad about that?

He grimaced involuntarily. He had remembered his own early struggles as a Class One and what *was* so bad about that.

The law clerk arrived, a smallish robot with a battered stainless-steel hide and dull coppery features. Elon took the robot aside for a terse conversation before he came back to Morey.

"As I thought," he said in satisfaction. "No precedent. No laws prohibiting. Therefore no crime."

"Thank heaven!" Morey said in ecstatic relief.

Elon shook his head. "They'll probably give you a reconditioning and you can't expect to keep your Grade Five. Probably call it anti-social behavior. Is, isn't it?"

Dashed, Morey said, "Oh." He frowned briefly, then looked up. "All right, Dad, if I've got it coming to me, I'll take my medicine."

"Way to talk," Elon said approvingly. "Now go home. Get a good night's sleep. First thing in the morning, go to the Ration Board. Tell 'em the whole story, beginning to end. They'll be easy on you." Elon hesitated. "Well, fairly easy," he amended. "I hope."

The condemned man ate a hearty breakfast.

He had to. That morning, as Morey awoke, he had the sick certainty that he was going to be consuming triple rations for a long, long time to come.

He kissed Cherry goodbye and took the long ride to the Ration Board in silence. He even left Henry behind.

At the Board, he stammered at a series of receptionist robots and was finally brought into the presence of a mildly supercilious young man named Hachette.

"My name," he started, "is Morey Fry. I—I've come to—talk over something I've been doing with—"

"Certainly, Mr. Fry," said Hachette. "I'll take you in to Mr. Newman right away."

"Don't you want to know what I did?" demanded Morey.

Hachette smiled. "What makes you think we don't know?" he said, and left.

That was Surprise Number One.

Newman explained it. He grinned at Morey and ruefully shook his head. "All the time we get this," he complained. "People just don't take the trouble to learn anything about the world around them. Son," he demanded, "what do you think a robot is?"

Morey said, "Huh?"

"I mean how do you think it operates? Do you think it's just a kind of a man with a tin skin and wire nerves?"

"Why, no. It's a machine, of course. It isn't *human*."

Newman beamed. "Fine!" he said. "It's a machine. It hasn't got flesh or blood or intestines—or a brain. Oh—" he held up a hand—"robots are *smart* enough. I don't mean that. But an electronic thinking machine, Mr. Fry, takes about as much space as the house you're living in. It has to. Robots don't carry brains around with them; brains are too heavy and much too bulky."

"Then how do they think?"

"With their brains, of course."

"But you just said—"

"I said they didn't *carry* them. Each robot is in constant radio communication with the Master Control on its TBR circuit—the 'Talk Between Robots' radio. Master Control gives the answer, the robot acts."

"I see," said Morey. "Well, that's very interesting, but—"

"But you still don't see," said Newman. "Figure it out. If the robot gets information from Master Control, do you see that Master Control in return necessarily gets information from the robot?"

"Oh," said Morey. Then, louder, "Oh! You mean that all my robots have been—" The words wouldn't come.

Newman nodded in satisfaction. "Every bit of information of that sort comes to us as a matter of course. Why, Mr. Fry, if you hadn't come in today, we would have been sending for you within a very short time."

That was the second surprise. Morey bore up under it bravely. After all, it changed nothing, he reminded himself.

He said, "Well, be that as it may, sir, here I am. I came in of my own free will. I've been using my robots to consume my ration quotas—"

"Indeed you have," said Newman.

"—and I'm willing to sign a statement to that effect any time you like. I don't know what the penalty is, but I'll take it. I'm guilty; I admit my guilt."

Newman's eyes were wide. "Guilty?" he repeated. "Penalty?"

Morey was startled. "Why, yes," he said. "I'm not denying anything."

"Penalties," repeated Newman musingly. Then he began to laugh. He laughed, Morey thought, to considerable excess; Morey saw nothing he could laugh at, himself, in the situation. But the situation, Morey was forced to admit, was rapidly getting completely incomprehensible.

"Sorry," said Newman at last, wiping his eyes, "but I couldn't help it. Penalties! Well, Mr. Fry, let me set your mind at rest. I wouldn't worry about the penalties if I were you. As soon as the reports began coming through on what you had done with your robots, we naturally assigned a special team to keep observing you, and we forwarded a report to the national headquarters. We made certain—ah—recommendations in it and—well, to make a long story short, the answers came back yesterday.

"Mr. Fry, the National Ration Board is delighted to know of your contribution toward improving our distribution problem. Pending a further study, a tentative program has been adopted for setting up consuming-robot units all over the country based on your scheme. Penalties? Mr. Fry, you're a *hero*!"

A hero has responsibilities. Morey's were quickly made clear to him. He was allowed time for a brief reassuring visit to Cherry, a triumphal tour of his old office, and then he was rushed off to Washington to be quizzed. He found the National Ration Board in a frenzy of work.

"The most important job we've ever done," one of the high officers told him. "I wouldn't be surprised if it's the last one we ever have! Yes, sir, we're trying to put ourselves out of business for good and we don't want a single thing to go wrong."

"Anything I can do to help—" Morey began diffidently.

"You've done fine, Mr. Fry. Gave us just the push we've been needing. It was there all the time for us to see, but we were too close to the forest to see the trees, if you get what I mean. Look, I'm not much on rhetoric and this is the biggest step mankind has taken in centuries and I can't put it into words. Let me show you what we've been doing."

He and a delegation of other officials of the Ration Board and men whose names Morey had repeatedly seen in the newspapers took Morey on an inspection tour of the entire plant.

"It's a closed cycle, you see," he was told, as they looked over a chamber of industriously plodding consumer-robots working off a shipment of shoes. "Nothing is permanently lost. If you want a car, you get one of the newest and best. If not, your car gets driven by a robot until it's ready to be turned in and a new one gets built for next year. We don't lose the metals—they can be salvaged. All we lose is a little power and labor. And the Sun and the atom give us all the power we need, and the robots give us more labor than we can use. Same thing applies, of course, to all products."

"But what's in it for the robots?" Morey asked.

"I beg your pardon?" one of the biggest men in the country said uncomprehendingly.

Morey had a difficult moment. His analysis had conditioned him against waste and this decidedly was sheer destruction of goods, no matter how scientific the jargon might be.

"If the consumer is just using up things for the sake of using them up," he said doggedly, realizing the danger he was inviting, "we could use wear-and-tear machines instead of robots. After all why waste *them*?"

They looked at each other worriedly.

"But that's what *you* were doing," one pointed out with a faint note of threat.

"Oh, no!" Morey quickly objected. "I built in satisfaction circuits—my training in design, you know. Adjustable circuits, of course."

"Satisfaction circuits?" he was asked. "Adjustable?"

"Well, sure. If the robot gets no satisfaction out of using up things—"

"Don't talk nonsense," growled the Ration Board official. "Robots aren't human. How do you make them feel satisfaction? And adjustable satisfaction at that!"

Morey explained. It was a highly technical explanation, involving the use of great sheets of paper and elaborate diagrams. But there were trained men in the group and they became even more excited than before.

"Beautiful!" one cried in scientific rapture. "Why, it takes care of every possible moral, legal and psychological argument!"

"What does?" the Ration Board official demanded. "How?"

"You tell him, Mr. Fry."

Morey tried and couldn't. But he could *show* how his principle operated. The Ration Board lab was turned over to him, complete with more assistants than he knew how to give orders to, and they built satisfaction circuits for a squad of robots working in a hat factory.

Then Morey gave his demonstration. The robots manufactured hats of all sorts. He adjusted the circuits at the end of the day and the robots began trying on the hats, squabbling over them, each coming away triumphantly with a huge and diverse selection. Their metalic features were incapable of showing pride or pleasure, but both were evident in the way they wore their hats, their fierce possessiveness . . . and their faster, neater, more intensive, more *dedicated* work to produce a still greater quantity of hats . . . which they also were allowed to own.

"You see?" an engineer exclaimed delightedly. "They can be adjusted to *want* hats, to wear them lovingly, to wear the hats to pieces. And not just for the sake of wearing them out—the hats are an incentive for them!"

"But how can we go on producing just hats and more hats?" the Ration Board man asked puzzledly. "Civilization does not live by hats alone."

"That," said Morey modestly, "is the beauty of it. Look."

He set the adjustment of the satisfaction circuit as porter robots brought in skids of gloves. The hat-manufacturing robots fought over the gloves with the same mechanical passion as they had for hats.

"And that can apply to anything we—or the robots—produce," Morey added. "Everything from pins to yachts. But the point is that they get satisfaction from possession, and the craving can be regulated according to the glut in various industries, and the robots show their appreciation by working harder." He hesitated. "That's what I did for my servant-robots. It's a feedback, you see. Satisfaction leads to more work—and *better* work—and that means more goods, which they can be made to want, which means incentive to work, and so on, all around."

"Closed cycle," whispered the Ration Board man in awe. "A *real* closed cycle this time!"

And so the inexorable laws of supply and demand were irrevocably repealed. No longer was mankind hampered by inadequate supply or drowned by overproduction. What mankind needed was there. What the race did not require passed into the insatiable—and adjustable—robot maw. Nothing was wasted.

For a pipeline has two ends.

Morey was thanked, complimented, rewarded, given a ticker-tape parade through the city, and put on a plane back home. By that time, the Ration Board had liquidated itself.

Cherry met him at the airport. They jabbered excitedly at each other all the way to the house.

In their own living room, they finished the kiss they had greeted each other with. At last Cherry broke away, laughing.

Morey said, "Did I tell you I'm through with Bradmoor? From now on I work for the Board as civilian consultant. *And*," he added impressively, "starting right away, I'm a Class Eight!"

"My!" gasped Cherry, so worshipfully that Morey felt a twinge of conscience.

He said honestly, "Of course, if what they were saying in Washington is so, the classes aren't going to mean much pretty soon. Still, it's quite an honor."

"It certainly is," Cherry said staunchly. "Why, Dad's only a Class Eight himself and he's been a judge for I don't know *how* many years."

Morey pursed his lips. "We can't all be fortunate," he said generously. "Of course, the classes still will count for *something*—

that is, a Class One will have so much to consume in a year, a Class Two will have a little less, and so on. But each person in each class will have robot help, you see, to do the actual consuming. The way it's going to be, special facsimile robots will—"

Cherry flagged him down. "I know, dear. Each family gets a robot duplicate of every person in the family."

"Oh," said Morey, slightly annoyed. "How did you know?"

"Ours came yesterday," she explained. "The man from the Board said we were the first in the area—because it was your idea, of course. They haven't even been activated yet. I've still got them in the Green Room. Want to see them?"

"Sure," said Morey buoyantly. He dashed ahead of Cherry to inspect the results of his own brainstorm. There they were, standing statue-still against the wall, waiting to be energized to begin their endless tasks.

"Yours is real pretty," Morey said gallantly. "But—say, is that thing supposed to look like me?" He inspected the chromium face of the man-robot disapprovingly.

"Only roughly, the man said." Cherry was right behind him. "Notice anything else?"

Morey leaned closer, inspecting the features of the facsimile robot at a close range. "Well, no," he said. "It's got a kind of squint that I don't like, but—Oh, you mean *that*!" He bent over to examine a smaller robot, half hidden between the other pair. It was less than two feet high, big-headed, pudgy-limbed, thick-bellied. In fact, Morey thought wonderingly, it looked almost like—

"My God!" Morey spun around, staring wide-eyed at his wife. "You mean—"

"I mean," said Cherry, blushing slightly.

Morey reached out to grab her in his arms.

"Darling!" he cried. "Why didn't you *tell* me?"

THE OCEANS ARE WIDE

Frank M. Robinson

1

When we talk of voyages and the planting of colonies, Junius, what interests me is not the ones that fail, for after all the oceans are wide and the Fates can frown upon you with a thousand faces. But, ah, the ones that succeed—what manner of men must lead them!

DIALOGUES OF LYKOS

They found Matty late that living period, a scant half hour before the Director died. They had searched the regions of weightlessness and inspected the empty holds on the twenty-fifth level before they finally found him in one of the abandoned gun blisters that projected out beyond the hull.

They should have looked there first. Of all the holds and compartments in the *Astra,* Matty liked the plastic blisters the best. The guns had long since gone to Metals Reduction so the blisters were empty and he could lie alone in the darkness and make noises with the stringed sound box that Nurse Margaret had given him.

He floated slowly through the blister, strumming the sound box in the darkness and drifting among the millions of stars that flared and burned seemingly mere inches away from him, just beyond the plastic. He liked to sneak up to the blisters and play the sound box; in the darkened, star-lit hemispheres there were none of the other children of Executives around to tease him.

He bumped into the other side of the blister, twisted so the universe whirled about him in a giddy circle, then pushed off with frail legs and drifted slowly back. Halfway across, the blister suddenly exploded with blinding light and the plastic faded to an opaque gray.

"What the blazes are you doing up here, Kendrick? Your father's dying!"

A softer voice. "Don't be harsh with him, Seth! He's frail and . . ."

"Well?"

The question was harsh and threatening. One of the Executives of the *Astra*, his uncle Seth, a Manager in Air Control, was framed in the open air-lock between blister and hull. He was a thin-lipped, hawk-nosed man with a cruel streak that showed in the set of his lips and the coldness of his eyes. With him was Matty's nurse, a fat, fluttery-looking woman.

"Come here, Kendrick," his uncle repeated, a little softer but with the threat of punishment running just beneath the surface.

Matty spread-eagled himself against the plastic, frightened and trembling, unable to move. The sound box floated a few feet away.

"He's a coward!" a shrill voice suddenly interrupted. "A coward!" The leering face of Matty's cousin, Jeremiah Paulson, peered around his uncle's legs. Matty felt his fear almost vanish in the face of hatred for his cousin—a cousin who was bigger and stronger and far more favored among his relatives.

"I know," Seth sneered, the words cutting like a lash. "An effeminate one at that." He launched himself into the blister, the purple loincloth of Management flapping about his spare frame. He braked just before he reached the plastic, then clutched Matty's arm in a bone-wrenching grip.

"I said your father was dying, boy. You, of all people, should be there. Or have you forgotten that you're of Kendrick blood?"

"I didn't know he was dying," Matty mumbled tearfully. "Nobody told me!"

His nurse, looking heavy and awkward in her flowing robes, floated up and grasped the sound box. "We kept it from him. He's so young and . . ."

"You're the one we have to thank for what he is!" Seth snarled. He glared at her contemptuously. "You didn't do him any favor by shielding him from death. Now, maybe it will come all too soon for him—and perhaps for you, as well."

Jeremiah, half-hidden behind the lock, made a face. Matty started to tremble uncontrollably and his uncle pushed him harshly towards the lock.

"It will be worth your life if you start crying, Kendrick. When you go below, remember only one thing: you're the Director's son. And if you don't act like it, nothing in the *Astra* or Outside will be able to help you!"

The small infirmary was crowded with Executives and their children, clustered about the cushioned dais on which the Director lay. They had been talking in low whispers. When Matty and his uncle came in, the conversation died and the Executives reluctantly made a narrow opening for them.

Matty stayed close to Seth, feeling the hostility of the crowd, and followed him silently up to the dais. The man who lay on the cushions was yellowed and shrunken, a thin froth on his lips and his weak chest pumping slowly in and out and sounding like a leak in an air tube. Matty felt no emotion for the man who lay there; his father was a stranger to him. The first he had known his father was dying was when Seth had told him in the gun blister. And all the way down from the upper levels he had thought about it and wondered what it was like to die . . .

The yellowed lids suddenly flickered open and a gasp, half of awe and half of consternation, swept the compartment. The sunken eyes fixed on Matty and a withered hand pointed feebly at him.

The Directorship goes to a weakling," his father whispered bitterly. "You're your mother's son—too good, too weak." He paused and his breath rattled in his throat. "You won't last long, Matty . . ." The hand relaxed, the eyes closed, and the thin chest went back to pumping the last few gasps of life.

Matty flushed with shame at his father's words and he knelt woodenly in front of the dais. He could feel the impatience in the crowd and guessed correctly that if he hadn't been there, somebody would have strangled the dying man to save the waiting.

He looked at those in the compartment from under lowered lids. There was an aunt, Reba Saylor of Hydroponics, a thin, hungry-looking woman dressed in the flowing woman's smock that hid the sharp angles of her body but couldn't hide the sharpness in her face. She was staring at him with a peculiar look. And there was Junius Shroeder, a Department Head in Engineers. A fat, guileless man with a thoughtful expression. Between them stood Jeremiah, his cousin and their favorite. He was heavier, thicker in the shoulders, and far more self-assured. Matty hated him and knew that Jeremiah returned it. And Jeremiah, being bigger and stronger, did more about it.

And there were others in the room. Alvah Hendron of Security—a plump, haughty man. And there was Nahum Kessler, Asaph Whitney, and all the Kendricks. All of them wore looks that were almost evenly split between hatred and pity.

There was a sudden moan and convulsive shudder from the body that lay on the cushions, and then it was still, the chest no longer heaving. A priest came forward from the rear of the compartment and started chanting in Latin. When he was through, other attendants cloaked the body with a sheet and carried it quickly away.

"The Director is dead," Reba Saylor said in a flat voice. She bowed mockingly to Matty. "Hail the Director-to-be!"

The others grudgingly bowed low and then Reba pointed a gaunt arm at Seth. "The boy, Seth! Remember?"

Seth took Matty by the shoulder. "Come with me, Kendrick. We have to discuss something private here." Matty felt puzzled by the change in tone of his uncle's voice but willingly followed him into a small anteroom filled with medical equipment. "You'll wait here, boy, until we call for you."

Matty roamed idly about the compartment, inspecting the neat, glassed-in racks of gleaming surgical tools that walled the room and reading the labels on the vials of medicine in the closed cabinets. The minutes lengthened and Seth did not return. Matty tried the hatch to the infirmary. It was tightly secured, as was the one that led to the passageway. He began to feel the first prickle of fear.

What did they have to discuss in the infirmary that was so important he could not remain to listen, although his cousin Jere Paulson could? Unless it was that they were discussing him?

He pressed his ear to the infirmary hatch. He could make out the sounds of argument and over all, Reba's strident voice.

"Do you want a ten-year-old milksop as Director? If we're going to prevent it, then we'll have to do something about it now!"

There was a silken voice that he couldn't place.

"If the brat should die or come to grief in other ways, then a new Director would have to be selected from among our number, wouldn't he?"

Seth's voice.

"You're a pack of fools! Do you think nobody would guess?"

For a moment Matty thought his uncle was trying to shield him. The next sentence quickly dashed his hopes.

"We'll have to think of something more subtle than that."

Reba's demanding voice suddenly cut in.

"How many, besides those of us in this compartment, know the boy on sight?"

There was a low murmur, then Nahum's husky tones.

"With the exception of his nurse, possibly no one. What's your plan?"

Shrewdly.

"If the nurse were removed, then there would be no one who knew the boy. And it doesn't have to be Mathew Kendrick who is presented to the colonists as the Director's son!"

Matty could feel fear clutch at his heart and the sound of its pounding filled his ears. That was why his cousin Jeremiah had stayed behind; to take his place after he had been—murdered.

"What about the Predict?"

The voices from the infirmary were suddenly silent.

"The Predict doesn't interfere with the internal affairs of the ship. And who's seen him in the last generation?"

The mumble of conversation started up again.

"What do we do with Kendrick?"

Reba was indifferent.

"Poison or strangling. It doesn't matter which."

Seth's smooth voice.

"Who's going to strangle the boy, Reba? You?"

Reba laughed.

"Squeamish, aren't you, Seth? But it shouldn't be difficult and there's no reason to procrastinate. Get the boy!"

Matty crouched by the hatch, half-paralyzed with fear. There was no place to hide, no one who could help him. And he could hear footsteps approaching the hatch from the other side.

He glanced frantically about the compartment, then ran over to one of the cabinets that lined the bulkheads and tore down a heavy surgery mallet. Back to the hatch, where he quickly smashed the glass eye that opened it when the locks were removed. He had a few minutes now; even with the locks off, the hatch was jammed shut.

The hatch that opened out into the passageway took longer. He placed his palms against it and tried to push it back without success. There were no projections to get a grip on, and even if there had been, he was too small and too weak to work it. There were angry noises inside the infirmary now—it wouldn't be more than a few moments more before the Executives thought of entry from the passageway.

He tried the hatch again, then seized a heavy bone chisel, shoved it in the small crack between bulkhead and hatch and leaned his weight against it. The locks suddenly snapped and he was racing down the corridor.

There were no sounds of pursuit. He breathed a little easier, rounded a corner, and was suddenly snatched up by a thick heavy arm that drew him quickly into a small compartment. He shivered and closed his eyes, waiting for the fingers to fasten tightly around his throat.

"Matty, look at me."

His nurse was standing there, holding a small bundle of freshly washed waist cloths and his sound box. Her face was tense and troubled.

"There is no one who will turn a hand to help you, Matty. They are all against you. And you cannot hide from them forever."

He suddenly burst into tears, partly from relief that it was Nurse Margaret who had snatched him from the corridor and partly from the realization that he had only postponed the inevitable.

The nurse wiped his face and lifted his chin. "You are neither a coward nor a weakling, Matty. But be thankful they misjudged you on that score." Her manner became brisk. "And it isn't hopeless. You'll have to take refuge with the Predict, that's all."

He shivered again. The Predict, the stranger who lived up in the forward part of the *Astra*. The immortal man whom nobody had seen—the stories went—for the last twenty-five years. And there were some who said that he didn't exist at all, that he was only a legend.

"Would he give me refuge, Margaret?"

She quickly masked the doubt in her eyes. "Of course he would, Matty."

"He doesn't know me," Matty went on. "He doesn't know what happened." He was dangerously close to crying again.

"The Predict knows all about you," Margaret said with firm conviction. "The Predict knows everything!"

Matty didn't argue but accepted it as true because she said so. "How will I go there? My uncle and the others will kill me on sight!"

"They won't recognize you, child." She stripped off his cloth of purple and knotted one of common white about his waist. Then she took a kit from under her voluminous robes and quickly changed his blond hair to black and subtly broadened the shape of his naturally narrow face. Last, she moulded loose coils of soft, flesh-colored plastic to his chest and arms, adding pounds in appearance to his slight build.

When she was finished, she opened the hatch and peered cautiously out. There was no one in sight. She turned back to the boy.

"Good-bye, Matty."

He wanted to cry and bury his face in her skirts, but he knew the last time he would ever do that had passed a few moments before. He pressed his fingers lightly to her lips, then took the bundle of cloths and his sound box and started down the passageway.

The passageway fed into another which led down to the huge central cavern that ran the full length of the *Astra*. He stepped on the slow-moving Walk and hunkered down on its soft surface. It took him through the Shops area where red-faced workmen labored at forges and lathes to turn out parts for machines that had broken down and to manufacture the farming tools that had recently been decreed necessary. The commercial district was next with the stores fronting right on the Walk and the phosphorescent adsigns staring down from every bulkhead. Then the commercial district gave way to the Engineering compartments, expansive living quarters where there were only two families to a cabin.

He stopped for lunch at one of the Walkway Restaurants in the huge Hydroponics section. The menu was standard—yeasty-meat and tomatoes, with flavored water as a beverage. A bronzed worker in the green-colored waist cloth of Hydroponics watched him curiously.

"It's too bad you're not skinnier, half-grown."

Matty managed to control his face so no flicker of fear showed. "Why?"

"There's a big reward in Cash offered for a half-grown your age. Security just passed the description over the speakers a little while ago. Supposed to be an illegitimate."

Matty caught his breath. The *Astra* had been designed to support a static number of colonists. Birth slips were handed out to couples when somebody died or reached the official euthanasia age of sixty. But the discovery of an illegitimate meant that some family wouldn't get a birth slip—if the person were allowed to live. So conviction as an unaccepted illegitimate automatically meant the public strangler.

"I have parents," Matty said, desperately trying to hide the tremble in his voice. He held up the ident chain that Margaret had slipped around his neck. "See?"

"Sure—but you don't have to act so scared about it."

The eyes that had been only curious before were suspicious now. Matty hurried with his meal, then slid off the stool and took the Walk again.

The hydroponics tubs stretched through compartment after compartment, and by the time he had ridden through the last of them, he felt tired and a little sweaty from the ultraviolet lamps set high in the overhead. He worried that his sweating might have loosened the plastic moulded to him.

Several times he passed Executives on the return Walk who had been present when his father died. None of them recognized him though some glanced sharply at the sound box. He thought for a moment of discarding it, then decided against it. Outside of his nurse, it had been the only friend he had ever had; he was willing to take some risk for it.

Toward the forward part of the *Astra*, the number of people on the Walk decreased sharply and then the Walk itself ended. Matty felt nervous. This part of the ship was almost deserted except for the wandering Security patrols. If anybody should stop him, he knew he'd have a difficult time explaining why he was there.

The compartments and passageways had disappeared entirely now and he was in a world of catwalks suspended over the Engineering chasms that fell off hundreds of feet below. He crept along one of the walks, then suddenly stopped and hid behind a large metal warning plate. Up ahead, patrolling the catwalk that bridged the chasms to the Predict's compartment, were two of the younger members of Management.

Reba and the others had guessed where he would go, Matty thought sickly. His journey and disguise had been in vain; they had sent representatives there ahead of him. His courage started to ebb and then he recalled Reba's threatening face and strong, powerful hands. He felt along the oil-slicked catwalk, then ran his hands over the warning plate. A bolt was loose in it, a bolt he could easily turn with his fingers. He worked it loose, then threw it in the chasm below.

The noise of the falling bolt drew the two men over to the rail.

"You hear something?"

"Sure—same thing you did. Somebody's down there."

The chasm was poorly lit and the shadows were deceptive.

"I thought I saw something—next level down!"

"Well, let's go! You know the Cash they're offering!"

They climbed down a metal ladder to the next lower level and Matty dashed silently across the catwalk. A moment later he was standing outside the section of the *Astra* that was carefully sealed off from the colonist's quarters. The single hatch bore the brass nameplate *"Joseph Smith. Predict."*

Matty hesitated, his heart thumping painfully in his chest. It might not open. Despite what Margaret had said, there was a chance that he wouldn't be granted refuge. Then he took his courage in his hands and quickly covered the cell with his palm. The hatch slid back and he suddenly felt dizzy with relief.

He was safe.

2

Thou preparest a table before me in the
presence of my enemies;
thou anointest my head with oil, my
cup overflows.
Surely goodness and mercy shall follow me
all the days of my life;
and I shall dwell in the house of the LORD
for ever.

THE 23RD PSALM, REVISED STANDARD VERSION

There was nobody beyond the hatch. Matty started to enter, then hesitated when his feet touched something warm and soft instead of the usual cold hardness of metal. He went on in. The Predict, he soon realized, didn't live as did others on board the *Astra*. All the decks were covered with this soft, warm material and instead of a single cabin, he had several of them—all to himself.

Matty glanced through the living compartments, then stepped inside one that he took to be an office. It was luxury beyond anything he had ever dreamed of. The soft material covered the deck from bulkhead to bulkhead and the desk and chairs were of practically legendary *wood*. A calendar hung on one of the bulkheads and he stared at it for a moment. The curling cardboard was five hundred years out of date.

In the bulkhead just behind the desk there was a large, square porthole and . . . He gasped. The porthole was *open* and he was looking down a wide street, flanked with what he knew were houses and trees and green lawns. Bright blue sky and an occasional wisp of cloud peeped through the gaps in the trees. There were two strips of white cloth hanging in front of the porthole and these moved slowly in a warm wind that rustled the leaves and brushed across the grass. A few people walked slowly down the street; some of them looked up and waved politely at the port. Matty stared, fascinated. It took him a minute to notice that it was the same people who kept walking down the street and the identical few who each time waved to him.

The port suddenly faded to blankness.

"That's a moving solidograph, Matty," a voice behind him said. "It was taken back on Earth."

Matty whirled. The man who stood behind him was tall, as tall as Seth, dressed in the type of rough brown garment called a *suit* that Matty had seen pictured in history books. He was, perhaps, thirty. His face was smooth and unwrinkled with high cheekbones and thin, colorless lips. Black hair was combed neatly back and shone with an oily luster. He was smiling—smiling with everything but his cold gray eyes. To Matty, the eyes looked impossibly old.

"I've been expecting you, Matty. Sit down." He had been smoking a pipe—something prohibited to everybody on board the *Astra,* even the Management—and gestured with the stem towards a chair.

Matty sat down—gingerly—on the very edge.

"Earth is our birth planet," the tall man continued. "The planet we left five hundred years ago." He passed a hand over a row of lights on the desk and a large plastic cube on a stand in the corner glowed and darkened and finally showed a small, green planet, obscured with trailing layers of cloud, against a starry background.

Matty finally found his voice. "I've heard songs about Earth," he said timidly.

"Do you know why we left it?"

The boy slowly shook his head, almost hypnotized by his surroundings and the quiet man behind the desk.

"We couldn't stay, Matty—our race was dying. We had fought wars and poisoned the atmosphere; those of us who were chosen had to leave."

The picture in the cube changed to the velvet blackness of space, with a handful of small, red streaks showing among the stars. Of all the streaks, only one still glowed with a pulsing, red light; the others looked dead and dull.

"Fourteen ships left Earth," the tall man mused. "The *Astra* is the only one left. The *Star-Rover*, *Man's Hope*, the *Aldebaran*—all gone now. Tube trouble or pile blow-ups or else hulled by meteors. Any number of reasons." His voice lowered and Matty caught a tinge of sadness to it. "Kenworthy, Tucker, Reynolds—they're all gone, too."

He was silent for a moment, staring at the cube, then looked up at Matty. "Out of four billion human beings five centuries ago, there's only the few thousand of us on board who remain. And all our lives depend on the man at the top—the Director. He has to be a strong man, Matty."

"That's why they wanted to kill me, isn't it?" Matty asked. "I wouldn't have made a strong Director. And Jere Paulson would."

The Predict shook his head. "You're wrong. You see, power is a queer thing. Those who have it usually want more of it. Seth and Reba and the others, for example. They wanted to kill you and make Jeremiah the Director-to-be, not because he could be a strong man but because he would be a weak one. He would owe his Directorship to those who had helped him get it, and a man who owes his position to others is both a weak man and a fool. That's why the Directorship was designed to be hereditary; so that the person who held it would owe nothing to his friends but hold it by virtue solely of his birth."

He noticed Matty's sound box, seemingly for the first time, and suddenly changed the subject. "Do you play music?"

"A—little."

Joseph Smith relaxed in his chair.

"Play me something."

Matty strummed the wires of the sound box in an embarrassed fashion. Finally he decided on a tune and commenced singing in a soft, boyish voice.

"Among the years of night black sky
That fills the Universe,
Among the miles of velvet dusk
That hopes and ships traverse,
There spins a world forever lost
The world that saw Man's birth,
A world no man shall see again
The small green globe of Earth."

The music died and Matty's voice drifted off to silence. The Predict applauded admiringly, bringing a faint flush of pleasure to the boy's cheeks.

"That was very nice playing, Matty. A little unusual—we had a different tonal system back on Earth; one where the interval was longer."

"I made this one up," Matty said shyly.

"Do you know anything else? Something not so sad?"

Matty nodded and let his fingers dance across the wires.

"Listen to the throbbing of the Ship!

Harken to the meaning of the Trip!
Drink in all the wonders of the Stars,
Listen to the legends of Old Mars,
Dream of Earth and sky we called our Home,
But learn to live in worlds of steel and chrome!"

Joseph Smith leaned back in his chair and looked at the boy for a long moment, actually seeing him for the first time. He was a slightly built lad—the size of his wrists and ankles had given away the plastic at first glance—with a thin face graced with a strong chin and Roman nose. His eyebrows were blond, almost white, his hair—under the black dye—probably only slightly darker. It was a face that would not find it easy to be deceitful or cruel. It was more the face of an honest poet than a politician.

"Wouldn't you like to be a minstrel, Matty—a singer of songs and poems? They're quite important in our world, you know. They'll be even more important when we land. And you can do a lot of things for people. You can make them happy or you can make them cry, if you wish."

Matty considered it for a moment, then thought of what his father had said just before he died, the Executives who had tried to kill him, and Jeremiah Paulson leering at him in contempt and derision.

"I want to be Director," he said steadily.

The Predict frowned. "Are you sure you've thought it over? Remember that everything you do will have to be done with an eye to the good of the ship. And you'll have problems. We'll be landing in less than twenty years. You'll have the problems of colonization to deal with. And you'll find out that the privileges and honors of being a Director are pretty hollow; the worries and troubles are almost infinitely great."

"I wouldn't change my mind," Matty said firmly. "Ever."

Joseph Smith looked at him thoughtfully. "You might make a good one at that, Matty. You're quick-witted—you survived long enough to make it up here, which is proof enough of that. You'll owe your position to no one and you're young enough to be taught." He paused. "I've been around a long time, over five hundred years. I know people rather well. I advise them and make predictions as to the results of their actions. I'll advise you—and everything I'll tell you will be true—but you may have to take it on faith to begin with. Think you could?"

Matty nodded. The thoughtful look on Joseph Smith's face faded and it chilled into an expression that looked as if it had been cast in steel.

"To begin with, there are few things you must learn. The first is that the ship and the colonists on it have one purpose and one purpose only. We are to colonize a planet and establish a civilization there. Everything we do must be directed towards that one end. Do you understand that?"

The intensity in his voice made Matty nervous. "Yes, sir, I understand."

The Predict's voice softened slightly and he reached for his pipe. "Even though you're missing, as long as your body isn't found as proof of death, the Directorship will be held open to your eighteenth birthday. But in the meantime we can't allow the *Astra* to go without an Acting Director. I'll have to appoint one now." He leaned back in his chair and puffed contentedly. "Any suggestions?"

Matty understood that the selection of an Acting Director would be limited to the Executives. But there were none that he could think of who hadn't been in on the attempt to kill him, none whom he felt he could trust.

"You don't limit your decisions to those you personally like," the Predict said slowly, guessing his thoughts. "If you want to be a good Director, Matty, you appoint people solely on the basis of ability and loyalty to you. Now who do you think would be a capable man for Acting Director, everything else aside?"

Matty found it difficult to say but at last he forced the name out. "Seth," he said reluctantly. "The Manager of Air Control."

"A very good choice. One that I had thought of myself."

"But he wouldn't be loyal," Matty objected strenuously. He had sudden visions of Seth in a position of importance, a position where Seth might yet succeed in killing him.

The Predict looked amused.

"For one thing, he won't even know who you are. So until you're eighteen, his loyalty actually doesn't matter. But there is another consideration. The next few years will be very difficult ones for a Director. We have to set up organization lines for when we land. There will be no more jobs for Air Control, obviously, and the importance of Engineers and the sanitary corps will decrease sharply. Once landed, the living situation will be entirely different than it is now. We have to prepare people for that now, or else we would have an impossible task when we land.

"There will, of course, be resentment at the changes." He smiled slightly. "The resentment will be directed towards Seth, as Acting

Director, not against you. Once you assume office, if you want to you could send Seth to the public strangler and there wouldn't be a single dissenting voice. And that's a point you must never forget, Matty. If there are unpleasant duties to perform, never do them yourself. Assign them to subordinates—preferably those who are already disliked."

He riffled through some cards on his desk.

"We'll have a doctor up here to alter your eye-prints and features in a moment. For the next few years you'll have to keep out of the way of Management. Once they locate you, your life will be worth nothing." He found the card he wanted and jerked it out of the box.

"You'll be registered as an acceptable illegitimate." They were the ones who were spared because of exceptional traits and abilities. "You'll live with the Reynolds family—Hydroponics. They're a good family; they can give you a lot."

He paused and picked up Matty's sound box and ran a thumb harshly across the wires. "As a Director-to-be, Matty, you can do nothing that appears frivolous or effeminate. You have to appear, let us say, as a man among men."

He held up the sound box.

"A sound box is fine for a minstrel. It is fine for a talented young man who is known for his prowess in other fields. But what do people think of *you* playing the sound box, Matty?"

Matty licked dry lips. He knew what was coming.

"They think it's kind of . . . kind of childish."

"Then it has to go, doesn't it?"

Matty nodded miserably and the Predict brought the sound box sharply against the side of the desk. The wires twanged and the plastic box itself shattered into a thousand pieces.

3

And youth is cruel, and has no remorse
And smiles at situations which it cannot see.

PORTRAIT OF A LADY, T.S. ELIOT

It was a warm, spring day. The woods were alive with the rustle of trees and the quiet noises of small living things. A caterpillar inched slowly down the tree behind which Mathew Reynolds was hiding, while high up in the branches a small, red squirrel scampered eagerly about the business of collecting nuts and scraps of bark.

Matty pressed himself into the shadows and took only shallow breaths, doing his best to become a part of the landscape. His eyes were riveted on the small valley that spread out just beyond the trees. There were clumps of weeds and small hillocks throughout the valley and it was these that he watched in particular. There was life there; life which in a minute would show itself.

He could feel the sweat gather on his shoulders and underneath his arms but he didn't move. If he did, he knew he would lose the game and it would probably go to Sylvanus by default. His eyes moved slightly in his head and he caught a glimpse of his half-brother out of the corner of them. Sylvanus was hiding in another section of the L-shaped forest, in the leg that stretched away to his left. Silly was as quiet and unmoving as he himself was, Matty thought, but it would take more than a forest to hide his flame-red hair.

His eyes swiveled back to the valley. There had been a slight movement there. He silently fitted an arrow to his bow and drew back on the thin length of synthetic gut. There was another whisper of motion and he let the shaft sly. Two other arrows thudded into the far clump of weeds and a small, gray shape leaped high in the air, a trickle of red showing where a feathered shaft had buried itself near the hind-quarters.

Matty dashed out of the woods. "It's mine, I saw it hit!"

Sylvanus, thin and gawky-awkward, joined him. He was unhappy. "It has to be yours, Matt—mine didn't even come close."

Matty picked up the small animal and started to tug on the arrow.

"It isn't yours at all," a small, cool voice said. "It's mine."

Matty turned in indignation, ready to reply with hot words of possession, then stopped short. She was no older than his own fifteen years, thin with just the faint swellings of maturity to come. But the features of her face were finely chiseled and there was something about her that made him suddenly aware of his own sixty-four muscular kilos and taller than average height. He inflated his chest slightly without even knowing that he was doing it.

"I watch my arrows carefully," he said, with just a trace of haughtiness. "I don't claim animals that I'm not certain I've hit."

"I never miss," she said, equally as proud. "I never have before and I haven't now."

That such a small girl should have such a large conceit was just too much. Matty disdainfully held out the animal. "So I'm wrong," he said, making his voice as condescending as possible. "Here, take it."

"You don't need to be nice to me," she said, reddening. "I hit it and I can prove it!" She turned towards the forest behind them. "Huntsman!"

The sun faded to just an average fluorescent glow, the breeze died down, the small living things in the woods suddenly became silent, and the electronic caterpillar and squirrel stopped in mid-movement. Further off, the backdrops of the end of the valley and the depths of the forest faded and were replaced by the squarish outlines of a large hold.

An old man in the red waist cloth of a huntsman stepped out of the control booth and hobbled over. "What's the matter?"

The girl handed him the mechanical rabbit with the punctured dye-sac. "Who killed it, Peter?"

The huntsman laughed, a high-pitched old man's cackle. "Can't rightly say anybody killed it since it was never alive. But just a minute and I'll tell you who hit it." He twisted the arrow expertly, pulled it out, and read the number on the metal tip. "Number three. Lemme see, can't remember . . ." He took some custody tags out of a pocket pouch. "That must be yours, Karen—see the writing . . ."

She turned to Matty triumphantly. "You see! It was mine after all!"

He flushed and stared at the ground, digging his toes in the artificial turf. "I must have been off. Anybody coulda hit it . . ."

Her hand touched his and he looked up at her. She was smiling. "I was just lucky this time—I'm really not that good."

After she had gone, the old huntsman puttered about the compartment, hiding another mechanical rabbit behind one of the hillocks and resetting the solidograph projectors for the benefit of the next class. Matty and Sylvanus started for the hatch.

"All three of you did right well," the huntsman called after them. "You'll make good colonists, mark my words!"

Matty didn't even hear him.

He toyed with his food that night, not feeling especially hungry.

"That's good protein, Matty," Alice Reynolds said, frowning. "If you don't eat it tonight, you won't be able to make it up tomorrow, you know."

"I'm not hungry," Matty mumbled.

His foster-mother looked over at her husband. "What ails the boy, Jeff?"

Jefferey Reynolds, a big, bluff man increasingly worried by the fear that they wouldn't make planet landing before his sixtieth—and legally last—birthday, looked up from his wax-slate newspaper, annoyed. "How the blazes should I know?" Why women could be so worried over trifles when there were far more important things to worry about was something he could never understand.

"He's in love," Sylvanus said callously.

Matty glared at him. His parents looked interested. "What's her name?"

"None of anybody's business!" Matty said, angered.

Sylvanus maliciously furnished the information. "Karen West."

"I never heard of her," Alice Reynolds mused, slightly disappointed. She had fond hopes of her two boys marrying into Management, though Matty being an illegitimate—even an accepted one—made that almost impossible.

Matty felt a trust betrayed. "You better watch out, Silly, or you'll end up even uglier than you already are!"

His foster parents gave each other a raised-eyebrow look and dropped the subject.

Matty went to bed early that night period, curling up on his flat pad of sponge rubber in a corner of the small compartment and falling asleep almost instantly.

"Matt!"

He jerked awake. Sylvanus was bending over in the darkness, motioning to the passageway. Matty glanced around. The Reynoldses were snoring quietly behind their curtained-off section of the compartment. He followed Sylvanus out to the corridor. The attendant from the local gymnasium—a small, gnarled man with a face that had always been too professionally poker-faced for Matty's taste—was waiting for them.

Low, confiding voice: "There's a tournament of *slit* up a no-weight, Matt. Good players from all over the ship."

Sylvanus dug him in the ribs, eagerly. "We could go and watch if nothing else, Matt."

He hesitated. He had never played opposite strangers from other parts of the ship and he had no idea of methods of play different from his own region.

"You're favored from this section, Matt," the attendant urged. "Hydroponics has a thousand Cash bet on you."

The Cash wasn't an unusually large sum—Hydro had undoubtedly hedged their bets—but the local bet swelled his pride and he felt that he would be doing his section a disservice if he didn't play.

He ducked back into the compartment and came out with the green cloth of Hydroponics tied around his waist. "Let's go."

Sylvanus slapped him on the back and the attendant grinned. "I've got five of my own bet on you, Matt. Good luck!"

Matty and Sylvanus drifted through the upper levels along with other figures floating in the shadowy gloom. On the twenty-fifty, a gang of toughs quickly searched them down—a ridiculously short task—and asked for the password. Matty gave it, realizing the precautions were necessary since *slit* games were banned by Security and there was always the danger of official spies.

They finally came out in a large, brilliantly lit hold aft of the gun blisters and towards the tube section of the *Astra*. Both sides of the long hold were crowded with spectators while the stretch in the middle was left open for the contestants.

Sylvanus looked around uneasily. "There's a lot of people here, Matt. Too many. This looks like a sponsored event."

"What do you mean?"

"Somebody's been advertising it. There's a lot of people here who never came to *slit* games before."

Matty shrugged it off and they drifted towards one end of the compartment where the contestants were waiting for their match to come up. He paid for a handle from the Keeper—a young Shops man with a withered arm—and inspected it carefully. It was short, made out of plastic, in one end of which was inserted a piece of razor blade half a centimeter long.

He stripped off his waist cloth and Sylvanus started rubbing him down with the thick, antiseptic grease.

"The players look pretty good, Matt."

He grunted and turned his attention to the present battle. The two contestants were about his own age and evenly matched as to skill. Each bore two long, red gashes on their bodies that dripped red, the drops slowly floating to the deck. He felt mildly interested. The match was close; one more slash would determine the winner.

The contestants backed up to the opposite bulkheads, then lunged and floated swiftly towards each other. They met in the middle, grappled briefly for a moment, their hands slipping on the grease that covered their bodies, then their initial momentum tore them apart. There was a sigh of disappointment from the closely packed spectators. No score. They crouched at the opposing bulkheads again, faces shining with grease and sweat, and dove towards each other once more. They met in the middle with a quick, convulsive movement, and when they separated one of them bore the bloody slash across chest and arm that marked him as the loser.

There was a *"Hah!"* of appreciation from the crowd.

Both winner and loser were immediately swabbed with collodion and quick-heal ointments by infirmary assistants who hired out for a modest fee to the *slit* players. Then the lights dimmed while enterprising hucksters with hand projectors flashed colorful adsigns on the overhead. The crowd laughed and gossiped good-naturedly while waiting for the next match, exchanging the small, aluminium Cash disks to settle their debts.

". . . that short one, the one from Shops, ten Cash he gets in three straight . . ."

". . . and I'm fifty-seven now and you know as well as I we won't make planet-landing before I'm sixty . . ."

". . . got to leave, you know, there's none this far up and even if there was it wouldn't do any good . . ."

". . . that half-grown there Reba, the one who came in wearing the Hydroponic green . . ."

". . . if Security ever raids this hold they'll get some mighty big fish believe . . ."

". . . don't think so, he's too heavy for Kendrick, but Jere knows what to do . . ."

". . . wonder if they know what fools they really are, but when I was their age . . ."

Matty was perspiring when it came his turn. There was little ventilation and the sweating of the crowd and participants had fouled the air. He got the nod from the games master and buckled on the plastic shields that protected his loins and face.

Sylvanus squeezed his arm. "Good luck, Matt."

His first opponent was a swarthy youngster from Engineers; a husky half-grown well knotted with muscles and marked with *slit* scars that stamped him as a veteran of the game. Matty clutched his knife in one hand, gathered his legs under him, and pushed off on signal. They met in the middle, Matty twisted and whirled in the bright light, then felt the sharp sting of the razor and drifted away with a streak of red on his thigh.

"Hah!"

The next time his opponent clumsily left an opening and Matty inflicted a slashing wound of his own. Then it was even up and Matty surprisingly won the match with a light arm wound.

The games wore on, the losers retired to the spectators side, and the odds juggled back and forth as the compartment filled with the clink of passing coin. Much to Matty's surprise, he went as far as the finals and ended up matched against a husky youth wearing a tight black mask. Masks were not unusual—*slit* games were prohibited by Security and some contestants from well-known families didn't want to be recognized—but there was something about the youth that struck Matty as being familiar.

"He's dangerous," Sylvanus warned. "I've seen him play before— but you can take him, Matt!" Matty looked at him affectionately. Sylvanus, thin and somewhat undersized, had a bad case of hero-worship—or maybe it was just that he saw himself in there during the bouts.

The signal was given and the bout was on. Matty lunged out into the light, grappled briefly, and then hesitated with shock as his opponent said distinctly in a voice he would have known anywhere: *"Coward!"* The hesitation cost him the point and he drifted away with a thin slash on his wrist.

"Hah!"

He wheeled at the bulkhead and came in again, trembling with a sudden weakness that he was ashamed of. He knew his opponent was Jeremiah and it was hard to shake off the feeling of inferiority that he had carried with him for so long. He lost the second point as well. The spectators from Hydroponics set up a low wail.

"Hah! Matty! Matty!"

Jeremiah left himself open and Matty took the next point, fighting in determined silence. On the following lunge, Jeremiah slipped and that point went to Matty, too. The match was even up. On his third try, Matty caught a glimpse of a familiar face in the crowd and once again almost lost the match. Reba Saylor, her bony figure cloaked in a disguise of common white! There was a howl from the crowd and his mind slipped back to the fight. He grabbed for Jeremiah, missed, and then the compartment was plunged into darkness.

"Scatter! Security! Security!"

The darkened compartment was suddenly jammed with scurrying figures. Somebody grabbed Matty's wrist and Sylvanus's voice yelled *"This way!"* in his ear. They squeezed through the after hatch and then Matty was diving down the long passageways, silently dodging Security's light beams. Then he felt the short hairs rise on the back of his neck. It wasn't Security who was after him. The lights were sticking with him too long, they were too persistent. Usually, Security's only aim was to break up the game, not to capture and hold for trial all those who had attended.

He banked at the next bulkhead, gathered his legs under him, and dove down a vertical through shaft, starting the long fall towards the center of the ship. He caught at the hand-holds of a ledge a dozen decks down and swung himself onto another level, quietly avoiding making noise. Nobody was following him.

It was then that he became aware Sylvanus wasn't with him. The idea that something must have happened to Silly didn't occur to him; he concluded that Sylvanus had taken another through shaft and had probably beat him to the home compartment. He started walking down the passageway.

The red light was winking on the speak-box just above his sponge-rubber pallet. Matty noticed with a slight stirring of fear that Sylvanus wasn't back yet, then turned the box on low so it wouldn't waken the Reynolds.

The speaker rasped with the voice of the Predict. *"Come into the office, Matty. I want to talk with you."*

He hesitated, then let his face slip into a defiant expression and took the Walk down to the Predict's compartment.

The Predict stood behind the desk, dressed in his old lounging robe and what he called pajamas, tapping the tobacco in his pipe. Matty expected a minor dressing-down, then praise of his prowess in the *slit* games, as was customary for other contestants to receive when their parents apprehended them.

Joseph Smith's face was grim and distant. He looked at Matty with disgust, then reached behind the desk and threw him a rag. "Wipe the grease off." He followed it up with a small plastic bottle of alcohol. "That's the last time you'll be wearing grease for a *slit* game so do a good job." Matty rubbed in the alcohol with a growing feeling of anxiety; he winced when it burned in his cuts.

"How old are *slit* players?" the Predict suddenly asked.

"My own age," Matty mumbled, not caring to meet the tall man's cold eyes.

"Do you know why they're your own age and no older?"

"No sir."

"Because only the very young and very foolish play *slit*. It draws spectators because it's a good betting game, and people have always liked to gamble. And it amuses people to watch others slice themselves to ribbons. But perhaps you're too young to know the difference between entertainment and amusement."

Matty flushed. The biting sarcasm was worse than any punishment that could have been levied.

Joseph Smith fell silent for a moment, watching Matty work with the rag and the alcohol. Some of the cuts had started to bleed again, but beyond a slight wince, the boy gave no sign that he felt them.

"I've tried to stamp the game out, Matty. Regardless of the actions of the infirmary assistants, it's still a dangerous pastime." He paused. "I don't suppose I'll ever succeed. Children"—Matty reddened at the word—"your age have always done foolish and dangerous things for as long as I can remember. But it isn't going to help when you become Director and the younger colonists recall you as a famous *slit* player."

He abruptly changed the subject.

"How are your studies coming?"

"Not very good," Matty answered sullenly.

Joseph Smith's voice grew harder. "I know. You're poor in maths, you're poor in science, you're poor in danger drills. You're good in sports, you're good in hunting. Maybe it's my fault because I've emphasized the physical too much—but you had such a long way to go to catch up."

Matty stared at the deck and said nothing.

"Perhaps you think that all that's necessary to be Director is to know how to play *slit* and glove-ball?"

"No sir, I don't think that."

"Then starting the next living period you're going to devote more of your time to books. And you'll do your best to become familiar with the administration of the *Astra*; you'll attend Judgings, you'll find out how Security works."

"I'll do anything you say, sir," Matty said, chastened.

Some of the hardness went out of the Predict's voice. "Did you recognize anybody at the *slit* game?"

"Reba Saylor," Matty said in a sudden rush of memory.

"Reba wasn't the only one," Joseph Smith said quietly. "There was Junius Shroeder and Nahum Kessler and quite a number of others. Do you know why they were there?" He didn't wait for an answer. "Watch this." He toyed with a plastic and bone handle such as Matty had used in the *slit* game. Suddenly the half centimeter of razor imbedded in the end sprouted to a full twelve of shining steel. "Jeremiah Paulson could have killed you at any time—probably *would* have killed you—if Security hadn't broken the game up. And it was sheer luck that you managed to get away afterwards."

Matty blanched.

"Your friends in Management haven't given up," the Predict continued in a deadly serious tone of voice. "With you out of the way it would be a simple matter for your cousin Jeremiah to be elected to the Directorship when your eighteenth birthday comes up. And if you were more observant than you are, you would know it wouldn't be an unpopular choice. Jeremiah has many friends, among the colonists as well as the Executives."

Matty digested it for a moment. It was true. He had been busy—playing. And Jeremiah had been busy acquiring a reputation. He had sponsored games, he had put in time entertaining the pile workers who were down with radiation sickness in the infirmaries, he had been a heavy favorite in the more legitimate games.

Then, suddenly, the full meaning of events broke on him.

"Then I'm through," he said dully. "They know who I am."

"No—they don't. They're suspicious but they're not positive. And I've arranged for a decoy. A young illegitimate your age that Security turned in the other period. When we're done he'll look like Matthew Kendrick would have looked at fifteen. And then we'll stake him out for the wolves." Matty shivered. The Predict said it, knowing he was condemning the youth to death, with all the casualness of a man ordering breakfast at a Walkway Restaurant.

"I'm not worth bothering about," Matty said, feeling sorry for himself.

"I bother with you for a very simple reason," the Predict said bluntly. "Because I can trust you. Because you'll do what I say." He paused. "You might be interested to know that the *slit* game was all arranged beforehand. The attendant from the locker room was the steerer. The youngster from Engineers and your other opponents were paid to lose so you would eventually be matched against Jeremiah. And Jeremiah—who is still your superior in strength and agility—would have slit your throat for third point and escaped with the others in the confusion."

Matty felt both furious and curiously hollow, all at the same time. He clenched his fists and tried to blink back the sudden tears in his eyes.

"This isn't a game we're playing. This is for keeps. If you lose, it won't be my neck that will be stretched, it'll be yours. And your worst enemy will be your own conceit. It's nice to excel in things, but to be conceited is bad, for conceit can blind a man and make him do foolish and dangerous things."

Matty was only half listening. He wanted desperately to leave the cabin, to hide his tears of rage and shame.

"One more thing," the Predict continued, almost as an afterthought. "You pay for every stupid thing you do. If not directly, then through somebody else. In this case, your foster brother Sylvanus. He didn't get away. Security found his body up in no-weight a few minutes ago."

4

The hungry judges soon the sentence sign,
And wretches hang that jurymen dine.
THE RAPE OF THE LOCK, ALEXANDER POPE

The Judging compartment was slowly filling up with spectators. Matty found himself a seat and waited for the proceedings to begin.

A few minutes after he was seated, there was a commotion down the row and a thin, red-faced worker wearing the gaudy red-and-yellow waist cloth of Shops worked his way up and sat next to him. The man glanced curiously around then thrust a plastic sack under Matty's nose.

"Wanna sandwich? Better than the stuff the hawkers sell; wife made them up special."

Matty hesitated, then shook his head. "No, thanks." He paused. "You watch these things very often on your lunch period?"

The man nodded between mouthfuls of bread and yeasty-meat. "Sure, all the time. Lots of us do. It's a lotta fun." He looked at Matty curiously. "This the first time you ever been to a Judging?"

Matty said yes and the man from Shops leaned close, anxious to be helpful and explain the operations of the court to a novice. "Not much to it, actually. The Accusing Attorney comes in and states the case, then the witnesses. Then the Defense Attorney comes in and states his side, then his witnesses. The panel"—he pointed to ten colonists laughing and joking at the front of the compartment—"sets the punishment. Had the same panel for the last week now—most popular panel they had. Death sentence every time."

"Who presides over the court?" Matty asked curiously.

His companion found another sandwich and let the greasy crust fall to the deck. "An Executive. Junius Shroeder this time. Good man; never overruled a panel yet."

The compartment was filled now, the trial was ready to begin. Shroeder, white-haired and grossly fat, waddled in and took his place behind the Judging bench.

"There's three things you can get death for,"the man from Shops whispered to Matty. "Thefts, murders, and Negligence of Duty. That's the worst of the lot and that's what we got now." He nudged Matty in the ribs. "You can always tell by the size of the crowds."

There was a *"Shhh!"* from behind them and the worker shut up, edging forward in his chair so he would be sure not to miss anything.

Matty listened intently. The case was simple. A middle-aged woman assigned to Diet had been negligent and unsanitary in her duties at a Walkway restaurant, with the result that thirteen workers from Shops had become seriously ill. During the length of time elapsed between their sickness and the start of the Judging, all thirteen had recovered. They filed to the witness stand one by one and described with flying gestures and much emotion the pain they had experienced and the ensuing sickness.

Their stories drew much sympathetic response from the packed compartment but Matty withheld judgement. None of the witnesses had struck him as being of good character and he waited impatiently for the defendant to take the chair. When she did, Matty felt his heart suddenly sink. The woman on the stand, slightly older than when she had given him his sound box and waist cloths and sent him to see the Predict five years before, was his old nurse, Margaret.

"She's guilty!" the Shops man said in a low voice. "You can see it in her face from here!"

"Shhh!"

Matty watched the remainder of the trial sick at heart. The Judging went as the Shops man had intentionally predicted right at the very beginning. The thirteen workers refused to change their testimony and most produced medical certificates to verify that they had—as testified—suffered food poisoning. The efforts of the Defense to introduce proof that they had actually been working on the days they claimed they were sick was openly sneered at by Junius Shroeder. He likewise refused to admit—and instructed the panel to ignore—evidence that there was a legitimate doubt as to the validity of the medical records introduced.

Matty's head was aching. It would do no good for him to challenge the court; he had no authority and it was far too late to get the Predict to intercede in her behalf, even if he would. There was nothing he could do but sit there and watch.

There was a short intermission, during which hawkers roamed the aisles selling sandwiches and colored drinks. A few minutes later, the panel rendered the expected verdict of guilty.

The Shops man, along with most of the others in the compartment, jumped on the chair to watch. "Can't miss this . . ."

Matty shuddered and hid his face while the public strangler did his duty. When it was over, the audience filed out, joking and finishing off the last of their lunch.

Matty's friend enthusiastically started comparing the trial and its results with the others he had seen, then caught the look on Matty's face. He looked contemptuous. "Maybe a half-grown like you shouldn't come to these, especially if you got a weak gut."

"That's right," Matty said bitterly. "It made me sick."

He drifted around the ship the remainder of that living period, desultorily going through an emergency hulling drill, then finally went to the Predict's compartment. He told the tall man all about it, including how he had felt and what he had wanted to do about it.

"Do you believe the witnesses?"

"They were lying. Anybody could have seen that."

"You've got opinions on it, Matty. Let's hear them."

"She helped me a long time ago," Matty said slowly. "I think that was part of it. And I think that by killing her they were trying to get to me."

"The noose is drawing tighter," Joseph Smith agreed. "They're reasonably sure that you're alive, even if they don't know who you are. They're trying to isolate you. One, you'll be harder to identify when you try to claim the directorship. And two, you'll be easier to handle if and when you do become Director."

"And there's nothing we can do about it, is there?"

"They're too smart, Matty. They're experts at covering their tracks. Even when you become Director, you're going to have a difficult time pinning anything on them."

Matty idly ran his knuckles across the backs of the books in the wall cabinet. "It didn't mean anything to the people who were watching," he said in a dull voice. "It was just more entertainment. Something to do during their lunch period, something to watch between sandwiches."

"If you're going to be Director," Joseph Smith said curtly, "you've got to get used to things like that."

"I don't think I ever will," Matty said stubbornly.

"Then maybe you better start trying."

For the first time it occurred to Matty that the Predict didn't feel concerned, that he didn't care, that the murders of Sylvanus and Margaret had been insignificant incidents in the ephemeral life of the colonists. The man had no feelings, no emotions. Maybe five hundred years had made him contemptuous of life, had filled his veins with ice.

He gave the Predict a long, cold look and felt a sudden hatred towards the man to whom Death meant so little.

"All right. I'll try."

When he was sixteen, Matty became an apprentice. Though almost every duty on board the *Astra* was a father-son arrangement, there were always youths whose family jobs had been eliminated who were apprenticed out to other sections on their sixteenth birthday. As an accepted illegitimate, Matty went along.

The fat, stocky assignment man read off the list, and as each name was called out, foremen from the section broke away from the group at the far end of the compartment and came forward to get their men.

"Avery, Hydroponics. Banks, Engineers. Dowd, Medical . . ." The line dwindled. "Reynolds."

Matty stepped forward.

"Shops."

One of the foremen came over to Matty. He held out his hand in the familiar greeting gesture.

"Name's Olson—guess I'm your boss now."

Matty took the hand and gave it a single, solemn shake. The man was big and solid-looking, with thick wrists and a bull neck and a blunt, honest-looking face.

"Isn't much to tell you, Reynolds. We got a good group and everybody gets along. We'll expect an honest period's work out of you." He said it as if he expected an argument.

"I expect to work," Matty said simply.

Olson's big, homely face split into a smile. "Then you and me will get along just fine."

Matty followed the big man back to his department in Shops.

"Meet Matt Reynolds, gang!" Matty went down the line. Askelund, the old man with stooped shoulders who ran a lather, Martin, Wagner—too many to remember. And finally the man with whom he'd work.

"This is Dion West, Matt. You'll work with him at the start."

Matty froze. Dion West was young, his age, with a familiar-looking face. A wide, not-too-handsome face, with an almost abnormal expanse of forehead and ice-blue eyes set on either side of a thin, narrow nose. A sour-looking face, an unfriendly face, but one that he had seen before. Then Matty saw the withered arm and into his mind flashed the picture of the young Shops man who had issued the razor-handles at the *slit* game the year before. After Olson had left, Matty said quietly: "You were at the *slit* game when Security raided it, weren't you?"

Dion West's pale face was a perfect blank.

"I don't know what you're talking about, Reynolds."

Matty gave him a searching look, wondering why he should deny it, then shrugged his shoulders. "Have it your way, West."

That living period he was promptly indoctrinated into the back-breaking labor of foundry work and the forging and machining of metal parts. In the weeks that followed he came to like the feel of sweat rolling down his back and the pleasure of creation as tools and parts took shape under his hands.

He got along with everybody but Dion West. And Dion West was liked by no one. He was a cold, quiet youth whose crippled arm had turned him into a social misfit. It was almost two years before Matty discovered the human being that lay beneath the silent exterior.

He was coming home from a *slit* game—as a spectator—and was riding the Walk through the darkened Shops area. He was almost through it and could make out the dark greenness of Hydroponics far ahead when a sudden small noise made him turn and glance back. There was a brief burst of light from one of the machine shops and then darkness again.

Matty felt for the long knife hidden in the folds of his waist cloth, then crept silently back. He quietly tried the locks of the hatch, then suddenly threw it open. West had his back toward the hatch, bent over a workbench. He twisted around awkwardly as the hatch banged open.

"You're working late, aren't you, West?"

"It's not your business, is it?"

"There's laws against it."

"There's laws against everything, Reynolds."

Matty felt irritated, then let curiosity get the better of him.

"What were you doing?"

West shrugged. "You wouldn't be interested."

"Try me."

The cripple stared at him for a minute, then stepped aside. "Take a look if you want."

There was nothing on the bench but a thin wire, held in the opposing jaws of a strength-test machine. A rather simple arrangement, too simple. Then Matty looked at the kilo-pull registered on the machine. It was at its maximum, an impossible pull for the wire to have withstood.

"Where did you get this?"

"I made it—a special alloy." There was a note of pride in West's voice.

Matty was suddenly intensely interested. "You do know a lot about science, don't you? You've done a lot of inventing, haven't you?"

West flushed. "A little. I guess I've got a knack for it."

"I'd like to see more of it," Matty said sincerely.

West hesitated, half refusing to believe that somebody was honestly interested in his work.

"I've got more—at home."

Matty followed him out of the Shops area to the residential compartments. West had somehow managed to bribe the housing authority to let him have a compartment all to himself; a compartment that, Matty discovered later, he shared with his sister.

Working models of inventions almost filled one end of the compartment. There were two that interested Matty the most. One was a heat-gun, looking more like a flashlight, that quickly turned a circle of the compartment bulkhead a cherry red when Matty pointed the gun and pressed the button. It was effective, but the workmanship was crude and it looked as if it had been laid aside with little attempt to improve on it.

The other invention looked like an old-fashioned crossbow that Matty had seen pictures of. It was ingeniously machined out of West's alloy with springs and wires of the same material that could be tightened to an impossible degree-of-tension. Unlike the heat-gun, it showed that an immense amount of time and work had been spent on it.

"I can hurtle a metal shaft clean through the bulkhead of this compartment," West said quietly.

"I don't understand," Matty said, puzzled. "Why all the time spent on something so primitive and practically none on the heat-gun?"

Dion West shook his head. "We won't be able to support the technology we have on board once we land, Reynolds. We'll be an expanding society, for one thing, and we probably couldn't find the necessary raw materials, for another. And within a few generations the knowledge of how to make a complicated heat-gun would probably be lost. But it'll be hard to forget something simple, like a crossbow."

Matty thought about it and silently agreed. It was for the same reason that so many of their techniques in working metal and machining in the Shops were primitive. What they did and what they worked with was purposely kept on a primitive level. Once they landed and the long slide towards barbarism started, perhaps they wouldn't slide so far . . .

"I wish I had your ability in science, Dion," Matty said enviously.

West relaxed on the sponge-rubber mat in the corner. "I'm not actually interested in science," he said calmly. "I play around with it for lack of anything else to do—and because I'm good at it. But it isn't what I actually want."

Matty looked at him curiously. "Just what is it you want?"

West's face glistened in the soft light from the overhead glow lamp. "I want what everybody else has, Reynolds. I'd like to play games, I'd like to be a good *slit* player, I'd like to be admired, I'd like to be accepted by people, I'd like to know that girls want to sleep with me." The sweat was dripping off his forehead, his face was tense. "I'd like to be so big, so powerful, that people would forget that I'm a damned cripple!"

Matty felt embarrassed.

"You'll never get what you want by feeling sorry for yourself," a voice said.

Matty whirled, his hand flashing towards his long knife.

"It's only my sister, Reynolds," West said dryly.

Karen West, Matty thought, his mind racing. He should have known. She walked in with a sound box under her arm and Matty reflected that any resemblance between her and the thin, rather plain-looking girl of a few years before was purely accidental. She had filled out, the finely chiseled, somewhat jutting cheekbones had receded so her face was simpler in line and more pensive, and the stringy black hair had thickened and waved until it fell in loose rolls over her shoulders.

She stared at Matty in frank curiosity, then smiled. "I remember you. You're the boy who never claims animals that he's not certain he's hit."

"He's our guest," Dion West explained curtly. "Prepare something to eat."

She looked at Matty and gave the faintest shrug to her shoulders, then moved over to the electric plate and began preparations for a late evening meal. Matty watched her in silence, fascinated by the grace of her movements. When the meal was over, she moved to the far corner of the compartment and softly ran her fingers across the sound box. The wires whispered and a moment later her clear voice was singing the familiar sad song of the *Astra*'s voyage through space.

When she had finished, Matty applauded warmly. Her eyes sparkled their thanks and she handed the sound box to him. "You play, don't you?"

He fondled the instrument reluctantly. "How could you tell?"

"I could tell by the look in your eyes when I was playing," she said softly.

Dion West snorted. Matty ignored him and let his fingers stray across the wire strands. Then he suddenly gave the instrument back to her. "Sound boxes are for minstrels and women," he said sharply. "I have no use for them."

He started for the hatch, then suddenly looked back at Dion West. He was still reclining on the mat; expressionless eyes looking out of an almost inhumanly intelligent face.

"You gave Jeremiah Paulson the trick razor handle, didn't you?"

The ice-blue eyes didn't even blink. "Yes."

"Why?"

The stooped shoulders shrugged casually. "They never told me what it was. And they offered Cash for it—a lot of Cash."

"Would you testify to that at a Judging?"

Thin lips curled sarcastically. "You don't honestly think I would live long enough to testify, do you, Reynolds?"

5

I certainly think it is better to be impetuous than cautious, for fortune is a woman and it is necessary . . . to conquer her by force.

THE PRINCE, NICCOLO MACHIAVELLI

The stars never changed, Matty thought. They blazed and burned beyond the plastic just as harshly as they had eight years before; small pinpoints of blinding light that to the average eye never moved, never varied. He floated quietly in the darkness, then gradually became aware that he was not alone. There was another shadow inside the blister, obscuring the stars a few yards away.

"The observatory is further aft," Matty said. "It's better for star-gazing than the gun blisters."

Joseph Smith's voice was easy and quiet in the dark. "I like to watch the stars from here. I have more of a detached view-point." He paused. "That small yellow one out there—that's where we're going. We'll be there in a few years."

Matty only half listened, then his mind raced back to the words. Only a few years.

"How many know this besides you?"

"A few. The Planning Board, for one."

The Planning Board. Reba Saylor and Asaph Whitney and Junius Shroeder. And that was all. He filed the information for future reference and turned his attention back to the stars.

"How many planets does it have?"

"An even dozen. Spectroscopic evidence indicates that three will be habitable—if we're lucky."

If we're lucky, Matty thought. But only part of it was luck. When they landed, the rest would lie with the Director.

"You'll be Director in a few hours," the Predict mused. "Management is holding a meeting to nominate Jeremiah for it—in expectation of your failure to show up to claim it."

"I know."

"You know what to do?"

Matty hesitated. "I think so."

The Predict's voice turned businesslike. "Have you made any plans for your own protection, Matty? Once you're out in the open, it'll be open season on assassination."

"I'm not worried."

"I'm sorry you feel that way. I was hoping that you would have made plans to protect yourself."

"I can always have bodyguards."

Joseph Smith laughed curtly. "They're just more people whose loyalty you'll have to worry about. The only way you'll save yourself is to get at the root of the trouble."

"How?"

Hesitation. "I could tell you but I'd rather you thought of it yourself."

They floated in silence for a moment, watching the motionless stars outside.

"There's a Dion West on board," Matty said suddenly. "He's a scientific—genius."

"I know. I have his record."

"He's also a misfit. A social outcast. Somebody ought to help him."

"You?"

"Maybe."

Joseph Smith sighed. "Your intentions are good—but don't do it."

"Why not?"

"Because he's more valuable to the ship the way he is. You see, if you relieve West of his social frustrations, you also relieve the compulsion that makes him try to excel in things scientific. That isn't always the case, of course, but in this instance you'd gain—if you succeeded—one normal, happy individual. And lose a most talented scientist of the type that we desperately need right now."

"Doesn't West, as an individual, mean anything?"

"The individual never means anything."

Matty digested that in silence.

"How well do you like Karen West?"

Matty stiffened.

"That's my personal life."

"As the Director-to-be, you have no personal life."

Reluctantly. "I like her very much."

"I wouldn't advise marrying her."

"That's my business."

"No—it isn't. Marriage is nothing to be entered into lightly. In your case, doubly so. Marriage is too valuable, politically. If you marry now you throw away what could be of great advantage to you in the future."

Matty realized with sudden insight that he hated the Predict. He hated the remorseless logic, the constant denial of self for ship.

"When I'm Director, I'll do as I damn well please."

Coldly. "No, you won't. You're my creation, Matty, just as surely as if I were a sculptor and had carved you out of marble. You owe me your life, you'll owe me your Directorship. You'll do exactly as I say and nothing else. I made you and if necessary, I wouldn't hesitate to break you."

It wasn't primarily a threat; it was a cold recital of fact.

"You're saving me for something. What?"

And then, for the first time, he heard uncertainty.

"I'm not sure."

Matty watched the proceedings over a viewscreen in the Shops compartment. The screen showed the huge banquet hall crowded with the purple waist cloths and smocks of Management: Managers and Department Heads and Foremen eating and drinking and waiting for Jeremiah Paulson to be proclaimed Director so they could all pledge faith and fealty to him.

It was pretty much as Matty expected. A pageant that began with solidgraphs of the death of the old Director and comments about his only son who had disappeared the same period as the death of his father. There was even—as Matty knew there would be—a solidograph of himself at the age of ten. A blond-haired, rather thin, wide-eyed youngster with a sound box tucked under his arm.

The announcer's voice was unctuous. "*. . . all bereaved with the disappearance of young Mathew Kendrick at the age of ten. It is thought that the boy was murdered by persons still unknown or was the victim of amnesia, though to this period it has been hoped among official circles that he would turn up . . .*"

There was a stir in the crowd in Shops as people edged closer to get a better view of the youngster on the screen.

In the slight stir nobody saw Matty slip away. They had done it perfectly, he thought. Just enough hypocrisy with which to hang themselves . . .

He found an empty washroom near the banquet compartment and quickly slipped out of his waist cloth. To dye his hair back to its original yellow took but a moment. His eye-prints had already been altered back by the Predict's doctor and enforced diet had thinned him down to what an eighteen-year-old Mathew Kendrick could be expected to look like. He surveyed himself in the three-D reflecting mirror and was satisfied with the results. He looked the part, now he had only to act it.

He eased himself into the rear of the banquet compartment and waited. Reba and Junius shared the head table with Jeremiah and his sister. Matty watched them closely. Reba, thin-faced and shrewd-eyed, almost glowing with the knowledge that eight years of plotting was about to pay off. Junius, fat and wattle-faced, almost dozing under the steady barrage of speeches and comments. Julia Paulson, a little too fleshy, a little uncomfortable, shy and somewhat frightened. There had been, Matty reflected honestly, nothing but good to be said about Jeremiah's younger sister. A shy, retiring personality, quiet and unassuming—and dull.

His attention switched to his cousin. Jeremiah, handsome, athletic, professionally friendly—with just a trace of weakness showing in a somewhat too-small chin and watery brown eyes. Not too intelligent —probably because with Reba around, he didn't need to be.

Jeremiah was, Matty decided coldly and without prejudice to himself, not fit to be Director.

The speeches wore on and then the climatic moment came. Reba got to her feet and motioned for absolute silence. This was the dramatic moment, the moment that had colonists all over the *Astra* holding their breath while they drank in the pageantry.

"To all the *Astra*—I give you your new Director, Jeremiah Paulson!"

Between the end of any dramatic statement and the thunder of applause that follows, there is the briefest, tiniest moment of absolute silence. Matty took advantage of it, using a low-pitched voice but one with enough volume to fill the entire compartment.

"Since when can you give away a hereditary Directorship, Reba, when the inheritor is still alive?"

Reba didn't hear and the thunder of applause started at the far ends of the compartment. But those around Matty stared at him and suddenly grew silent. The silence slowly spread throughout the compartment and the applause slackened. Matty could sense the colonists in the corridor outside and throughout the *Astra* frown and look questioningly at each other. It was what he wanted, what he needed—an audience of colonists that would be watching every move that was made.

Reba seemed puzzled by the deepening, embarrassing silence, then her sharp eyes picked out Matty solemnly approaching down one of the aisles. Her face mirrored a moment of shocked surprise, then her agile mind quickly sized up the situation.

"Security—seize that imposter!"

The Security men stationed around the bulkheads hesitated. The man was a dead ringer for what Kendrick would look like at this age and what was far more important, he *acted* like he was Kendrick. And if they laid hands on him . . .

Matty walked up the stairs to the platform and casually took the cushioned chair that Jeremiah had been about to sit in, as part of the pageantry. Jeremiah reddened, Reba grew pale.

"Nobody would be fool enough to act as an imposter," Matty said evenly. "Everybody knows it would mean the public strangler."

Reba's eyes were narrow slits. "Why should we believe you?"

"My eye-prints match, so do the skeletal X-rays."

"They can be forged."

Matty helped himself to a small bunch of grapes from the banquet table and leaned back in the chair.

"Memories can't, Reba—do you want to try me?"

The question hung there. Matty pushed his luck and stared at her critically. "You were younger the last time I saw you, Reba. Somewhat prettier and a good deal more respectful. I remember at the time you said 'Hail the Director-to-be!' Or have you forgotten?"

"If you really are Kendrick," Reba asked in a silken voice, "what happened to you, why did you disappear?"

It was one of the questions that Matty hoped she would ask. He turned slightly so he was facing the viewscreen operator; his words, he knew, would reach the entire ship.

"I wanted to get to know the colonists," he said slowly and distinctly. "I wanted to live among them because I knew, when I became Director, that I would be their Director as well as Director of the Executives. I've lived with the Reynolds family in Hydroponics"—he had a sudden vision of Alice Reynolds's awestruck face—"and I've worked with the men in Shops. I *know* them—far better than I would have if I had been raised in the Management."

It was a propaganda statement—he knew it and knew that Reba was aware of it, but that would in no way diminish its effectiveness.

Reba was almost strangling on her suddenly fading hopes, realizing her error in allowing the statement to be broadcast. She recovered her poise and gave an abrupt signal to the viewscreen operator to cut the broadcast. The cut broadcast could be laid to "technical difficulties" later on.

When she was certain she was off the screens, she gave an imperceptible nod to Jeremiah. Two Executives jerked Matty suddenly to his feet while Jeremiah hastily pulled his arms behind him and tied them with a napkin. Matty offered no resistance.

"Security!"

The men who lined the bulkheads were up on the stage now, their initial hesitation forgotten.

"How old are you, Reba?"

It was a loud question so all those in the compartment could hear. Fear suddenly showed on Reba's face. Out of the corner of his eyes Matty could see the viewscreen operator, sensing what was coming, silently flick the machine back on.

"Why don't you tell them, Reba?"

There were cries from the audience now, purple-clothed old men and women were staring at Reba in sudden suspicion.

"You carry your age well," Matty continued. "But the records show that you're sixty-one!"

There was pandemonium in the audience now. Old men and women who had drawn close to their sixtieth birthday and automatic euthanasia were screaming curses and fighting with the Security guards, furiously trying to reach the platform and the woman who had defied the age edicts.

"It's a lie!" Reba screamed.

Matty smiled. She was right. It was an outright lie. But it was a lie that would be easily believed and almost impossible to deny, particularly now.

"It doesn't matter," Matty said loudly and distinctly. "I think it's time to tell them now."

The uproar below him suddenly quieted. There were cries of "*Tell what?*" Somebody slashed the cloth that bound his arms and Matty raised them overhead in a sign of triumph.

"The Planning Board hasn't seen fit to tell you," he said, "but we make planet-fall in two years!"

A dead silence. The minds of the younger Executives were filled with nothing but thoughts of the adventure to come. But older people counted on their fingers and then groaned inwardly. Two years more would cheat them of ten or twenty. They would be sixty before they landed, but once landed there would be no need to limit the population . . .

"I think," Matty continued quietly, "that there is no further reason to keep the euthanasia laws. We will need every colonist we can muster, and we will have desperate need for those among us who are older and more experienced . . ."

The older Executives suddenly shouted and cried with laughter, the older colonists rioted in the corridors.

It gradually quieted down. Matty looked around then found the one face he wanted to see.

"I have still to be confirmed as your Director," he said slowly.

A man stood up in the crowd and Matty knew that he had won.

"As Acting Director," Seth said loudly, "I acknowledge you as the Director of the *Astra*!"

There was nothing hypocritical about it; Matty thought. Of all the words he had ever heard spoken, these were by far the most sincere. And they stemmed from the one fact that he had been sure of when he had slipped into the banquet compartment an hour before.

Seth was fifty-nine years old.

6

The actions of a successful ruler are of three types, Junius. There are the things he can do, which are few. There are the things he cannot do, which are many. And then there are the things he must do, and they are legion.

DIALOGUES OF LYKOS

There was one prime characteristic of being Director, Matty discovered. And that was the fact that he was busy. There were appointments to be made, official functions to attend, and most important of all—there was the re-education program that the colonists were currently going through preparatory to planet landing. There were regular classes to be scheduled and the showing of solidograph films . . .

His second in command, a young Executive named Uriah, brought him the list of solidographs to be shown. Matty ran his eye down the sheet, then picked out three for the first program. *Farming in Solids, Hunting and Fishing*, and *First Aid*.

Uriah frowned. "Why the last?"

"Because they'll need to know it," Matty said bluntly. "On board the *Astra*, wherever you are, you're only a short distance from an aid station. Once landed, a colonist may be miles away from professional help." He scooted the list back across the desk. "Anything else?"

Uriah bit his lip. "I probably shouldn't say this . . ."

"If you shouldn't, then don't. If you should, then it must be important and I ought to know it. What is it?"

"There's been some talk . . ." Uriah started, having difficulty finding the words.

"About what?"

Hastily. "Nothing more than rumors. That your health isn't too good and it might be better if the Directorship were in other hands."

Matty started to laugh, and then abruptly fell silent. He was in excellent health, but how many people actually saw him each day and could verify it? A few Executives and that was all. And he could almost guess the lines the rumors would take. Frail to begin with as a child, and now the strain and overwork of Director . . .

"Whose hands?"

Uriah looked uncomfortable.

"Jeremiah Paulson's."

"Thanks for telling me. On your way out, tell Alvah Hendron to come in." He stopped the young Executive at the hatch. "One thing more, Uriah. Don't hesitate to tell me things of that nature that you think are important. Don't forget that if I go down, you'll be right there with me. You've been far too closely associated with me to escape."

Uriah paled, nodded and disappeared.

It was an hour before Alvah Hendron came in. Matty let him stand for a few minutes while he studied him. Hendron was in his forties, well fed, just a trifle plump, and with a somewhat superior air about him. Finally, Matty told him the essence of what he had just heard, neglecting to mention the name of his informant.

Hendron laughed. "Nothing to it, nothing at all. If there was anything to back it up, Security would have discovered it."

Matty wasn't quite so sure.

"You have any suggestions on how to quiet the rumors?"

Hendron looked nettled. "Certainly. What about an inspection tour of the ship? You're due to make one in the near future anyways; a lot of colonists could see you and make up their own minds."

"What time do you recommend?"

"The next living period would be as good as any."

Matty mentally rearranged his schedule and agreed.

The small compartments back near the after tubes were dark and practically deserted.

"This is a long way back, Hendron."

Hendron smiled, somewhat uneasily. "Nobody's been back here for a long time; that's why I thought it would be a good place to begin."

There was a turn in the passageway and Matty stopped short. A small group of Executives blocked the corridor a few short yards ahead. Reba Saylor, hawk-faced and imperious as always, Junius Shroeder, looking fat and somewhat unhappy, and, as usual, among a backdrop of more minor figures, Jeremiah Paulson, fierce and determined looking—the handsome figurehead of the revolutionary movement.

Reba bowed slightly. "Hail the new Director!"

Matty grasped the situation in an instant. Alvah Hendron, naturally, had been in on it. And he, fool that he was, had fallen for it. And he had gone off with Hendron alone, disregarding the Predict's warning of some time ago that once he became Director, it would be open season on assassinations. Once the colonists became used to his Directorship, it would be increasingly difficult to remove him. But now, while his administration and its policies were still in a state of flux . . .

He started to back down the passageway . . .

Jeremiah rasped, "I wouldn't, Kendrick."

One of the young Executives made a movement and Matty found himself staring at something he had seen once before: a glistening crossbow machined from shiny metal. Dion West's invention had been stolen from him or, more likely, West himself had sold it. He was unstable, neurotic, frustrated—it had probably taken very little to buy his brains and soul.

"What do you want?"

"My Directorship," Jeremiah said slowly. "The one I was raised for."

"You should have done better for foster parents than Reba and Junius. Anybody else would have told you it is hereditary."

"You deserted it!"

Matty grinned. "I had to. It was getting to be unhealthy." He paused. "What do you intend to do?"

Reba smiled. "Surely you can guess, Kendrick. And remember that we're the only witnesses."

Matty kept looking at his cousin. "You know the penalty for murder, Jeremiah. It's not too late to change your mind. You're well-liked, you're a valuable man, we'll need you when we land. And once landed, there will be important positions open."

He threw out the bait and waited for Jeremiah to take it. The handsome, rugged face with the weak chin wavered a moment.

"He doesn't mean it!" Reba snarled. "He's trying to fool you!"

It was no use, Matty thought quickly. Reba's will was Jeremiah's backbone. He suddenly whirled, pinioned Hendron's arms behind him, and thrust the man in front as a shield. Then he backed down the corridor, still keeping his unwilling victim in front of him.

Reba gave a signal and the young Executive with the cross-bow pulled back on the wire gut.

Hendron squirmed. *"Don't . . ."*

"You've been a fool, Alvah," Reba said quietly.

There was the musical *twang* of the wire and Hendron quietly sagged in Matty's arms, a bloody froth at his chest. Matty dropped the body and leaped around the corner. There was a *whirr* behind him and a metal shaft buried itself in the opposing bulkhead.

He dove for a through shaft, then violently twisted to one side at a sudden breath of air that marked the near-miss of a metal arrow. There was no escape down below and he would have to go *up*. He wadded up his purple waist cloth and threw it into the shaft; in the dark shaft it would be difficult to tell the difference between it and a person. An arrow sped up the shaft, tearing through the loose cloth, then the cloth was below the next level and the missiles were aimed downward.

Matty leaped diagonally across the open shaft, upwards, towards the next level. Over the edge—and a thin metal shaft sheared through the fleshy part of his thigh.

He winced with pain and the sudden gout of blood, then hobbled swiftly down the level, doing his best to favor the one leg. He could hear pursuit on the level below; it wouldn't be a moment before they searched the next level up.

The passageway narrowed and then came to a dead end except for a small hatch that gave access to the tubes—a hatch that now would open on the cold and vacuum of space. There was an air vent a few feet overhead. The screen that covered it was not bolted in place but pushed upward in a frame. He leaped for it and pushed upward with the palms of his hands. It buckled and moved an inch. He pushed it a few more inches. On the third leap he managed to hang on with one hand in the opening and work on the screen with the other.

Far down the corridor there was a muffled sound of bare feet slapping on metal. He worked frantically at the screen. He got it all the way up, worked his legs in the opening, then hung for a brief instant on the black inside of the chute. The screen slid down on the outside and banged on his knuckles. He hung there and tried to feel for a ledge or deck beneath him. There was nothing but empty space. Then a sudden cry from the passageway made him jerk his fingers loose.

It was like falling in a through shaft, only a through shaft that was pitch black and thick with dust. There were no handholds along the sides and no way to brake himself on the smooth, metal surface. It would end at the center of the *Astra*, he thought. Straight down, with the knife edges of fan blades or a thick mesh screen at the bottom.

There was a sudden pressure of metal against his left side and he knew with a sudden hope that the air vent was curving out towards another outlet. He spread his legs and arms and tried to grip the sides of the shaft. Then his sweating, bloody body hit a vent screen, tore it from its frame, and he was catapulted into a Shops storeroom.

He lay there for a moment, feeling sick and dizzy, the warm blood from his torn thigh muscles trickling down his leg. He'd have to get to an aid station, he thought thickly.

And then he'd have to do something about Reba.

★

Seth showed his age, even more than he had at the Management banquet. The man was still spare, still tall, but shrunken and a little waxy. His hair was white and the thin, aquiline nose seemed thinner and more prominent than ever. The life in Seth's spare frame, Matty thought, had receded like a tide, leaving two small pools behind in the man's sharp eyes.

"With Alvah Hendron's murder, it becomes necessary to appoint a new Security head. You're it, Seth."

His uncle looked at him shrewdly. "Why choose me? How can you be so sure that I'll remain loyal?"

"I haven't the faintest doubt as to your loyalty," Matty said calmly. "Now, or at any time in the future. You see, your life rests quite securely in the palm of my hand. Ever since the Reorganization you're hardly what I would call the most popular man on board. I'm quite sure that there are several hundred colonists who would volunteer for the duties of public strangler—as long as you stood accused. And any panel would only be too happy to condemn you. You follow me?"

Seth managed the slight bow of acknowledgement without his eyes betraying any feelings whatsoever.

"I have something in mind," Matty continued, "that I want acted on right away."

Seth kept his mask of impassivity. "Yes?"

"I don't think it's any secret," Matty said slowly, "that some of the Executives on board would be happier if I were eliminated from the scheme of things. They've had their chance and failed. Now I think it's my turn. I want Security to find evidence—evidence that I can use at a Judging."

"You can testify yourself—that's all that's necessary."

Matty shook his head. "I don't want to seem like a dictator. I want evidence in writing, something you can point to as exhibits A and B."

Seth digested this in silence, then: "Who did you have in mind?"

Matty handed him a list. "You know the names. Reba Saylor, Junius Shroeder, Nahum Kessler, Jeremiah Paulson . . . they're all down there."

Seth fingered the list hesitantly, then looked at Matty somewhat critically. "I don't like to give advice, but these people are hardly stupid enough to leave evidence behind." His tone of voice belied his words and indicated that he wasn't at all adverse to giving advice, particularly to his nephew.

Matty leaned back in his chair and casually studied his uncle. Like so may old men, Seth was unwilling to admit that time had passed, that the ten-year-old milksop he had once planned to kill so long ago was neither ten years old nor a milksop now.

"I didn't ask for your advice, Seth."

"Jeremiah is too popular among the colonists; it will make you enemies."

"I'm not concerned."

Hesitation, then growing stubbornness. "Evidence will be hard to find."

Matty laughed.

"Finding evidence is your problem, Seth. I don't care whether it actually exists or whether you have to buy it, whether you find it or whether you plant it. Such minor difficulties shouldn't bother a man with your background and abilities. Just so long as the evidence you present holds up at a Judging, that's all that matters."

Seth bowed much lower this time and when he straightened up his face looked even older than when he had come in.

"You've changed, Kendrick."

"If I have," Matty said slowly, "it's because I had to."

After Seth had left, Matty took a crumpled piece of paper from his desk and spread it out and re-read the note he had received at the start of that living period.

To Mathew Kendrick:

Niccolo Machiavelli once said that a man who wished to make a profession of goodness in everything would come to grief among so many who were not good. That it was necessary for a prince who wished to maintain himself to learn how not to be good, and to use this knowledge when necessary. It's necessary. There is no doubt in my mind if you do not eliminate Reba, she will eliminate you.

Joseph Smith

The Judgings were a popular success. Seth had done a good job. He had planted evidence, he had bought witnesses, he had done a thorough job of packing the panel with colonists who had been hurt by the defendants in the past. Crowds of colonists came to watch, bringing their lunches and dragging their children. It was covered on the ship's viewscreens and regular reports of the proceedings were posted on all bulletin boards.

Matty attended one of the Judgings, sitting far back in the compartment. It sickened him. The seemingly endless parade of bought-and-paid-for witnesses, the trumped-up stories of perjury, the avid lust of the audience waiting for the penalty they knew would be extracted . . .

And the defendants themselves. Reba Saylor, an old and cringing woman, afraid of the Panel, afraid of the court, afraid for her life. Junius Shroeder, fat and trembling, sweating in the docks . . .

One by one they went to the public strangler, with the exception of Jeremiah. Jeremiah was too popular, too handsome, to be killed. He was acquitted and Matty reflected that it would have been better to pardon him and to have made an attempt to win him over. As it was, he would always be a focal point of opposition.

And then it was Dion West's turn. He calmly told the panel his own part in the actual plot. Yes, he had sold crossbows to an agent of Reba Saylor's. Didn't he know the weapons were prohibited on board? Yes, he had known it. Then why had he done it? For so many of the aluminum money disks.

And for the self-importance it would bring him, Matty thought grimly. For the knowledge that he had at least tried to revolt against a society that had refused to accept him.

The panel suspended judgment for one period and in the interim, Matty received a visitor in the Director's quarters, the spacious compartment with the viewscreen of the stars set in the bulkheads.

She seemed frail and thin, paler than he could remember, and the cheekbones in her face jutted out as they had when she had been a child. But her face was still the face he dreamt about.

"I came to see about Dion."

"It's out of my hands."

"You're the Director. You can do anything you want."

That's what he had told the Predict once, he thought. When he became Director he would do as he damned well pleased.

"Don't you think it would be rather foolish if I did, Karen? He's amoral, he's not a stable personality. His mind is for sale to the highest bidder. Admitted he's a genius but I'm not sure we can afford his type of genius."

"I would make him promise. I would watch him."

Faintly amused. "For the rest of his life?"

She stood up and walked over to the viewscreen, staring out at the blazing stars.

"I've always wondered what people would be like if they had power. All the power they wanted—the power of life and death. Now I know. And I wish I didn't."

He spun her around so she was facing him.

"Do you think I like being Director?"

"Don't you?"

"No—I don't. I'm free game for anybody on board—like your brother—who doesn't happen to like the color of my waistcloth. I have all of the worries and none of the benefits of life. I can't do what I want—I never have—because I have to do what I think is best for the ship. Like power? I only wish that somebody else had it, that somebody else had to do the job!"

His fingers dug into her arms for a moment more, then he let her go and turned away.

She touched him on the shoulder for a moment, the soft coolness of her hands making his flesh ache.

"I'm sorry." She started for the hatch.

"I can give him a Director's pardon," Matty said suddenly. "He didn't know what he was doing."

She turned. "You don't need to. And I couldn't—guarantee him."

"That's all right. We need him and a pardon will make the Director look magnanimous." He smiled crookedly. "And it's for the good of the ship."

7

Not what we would, but what we must.
THE COUNTRY LIFE, RICHARD HENRY STODDARD

Matty lay on his foam-rubber mat, still half-asleep. Something was wrong, something . . . He snapped wide-awake. The clangor of the emergency alarm filled the compartment. A drill, he thought—but there were no drills scheduled. He counted the peals of the bell, then raced through the adjoining compartment and up the ladder to the huge control cabin. Hulled, the *Astra* had been hulled!

Sleepy-eyed technicians were already manning their posts, blaring out orders to the repair parties in different sections of the ship. Matty took his place at the central control board and quickly plugged in the circuits that connected him with the different nerve centers of the vessel. The light from Engineers was flashing impatiently and he flicked the switch sharply up.

"Meteor hulling on the twenty-fifth level. Level evacuated, hatches automatically secured in hold fourteen. Air pressure zero. Space plates being bought up from the central storeroom."

"Serious?"

The voice at the other end was noncommital. *"Can't tell extent of physical damage. There's been rumors that a* slit *game was going on in the hold. Don't know how many were there."*

Somebody in the compartment said, "My God, my son might have been there!"

Matty swore quietly over the circuit. "I'll check."

He plugged into Personnel.

"Hulling on the twenty-fifth level. Possibility of *slit* game players and spectators being sealed off. Want a personnel check within an hour."

"Right!"

Uriah, his second in command, was now manning the other half of the board. Matty turned to him. "Take over. I'm going up."

He caught an up through shaft and a moment later clutched the hand rails at the twenty-fifth level and swung out of the shaft. The level was confusion. Rescue workers and technicians fought with the mob of colonists who filled the passageway.

Matty struggled viciously to get through, then collared an almost helpless man in the blue waist cloth of Security.

"Who are these people and why aren't they at their drill posts?"

The man wiped a sweating brow, the drops flying off and floating through the gravity-less level. "They think their kids were up here for the *slit* game; probably couldn't locate them right away and came up."

All the colonists on board the *Astra* would end up jammed in the one small passageway, Matty thought, if something wasn't done.

"Get your reserves!" Matty bawled over the noise in the corridor. "Clear these people out of here and post a cordon at the shaft! All colonists who desert their emergency posts will draw a mandatory death penalty—see that it's publicized!"

It was moments before Security reserves swarmed into the passageway, ousted the distraught colonists, and blocked off the corridor. Down at the other end of the passageway, a group of men were clustered about the hatch. It had already been cut into and a temporary air-lock installed. The Boss in charge was Olson, Matty's old foreman in the Shops.

"How's it look?"

"How the hell do you think?" Olson snarled, then recognized Matty and brought up his arm in sharp salute. "We're doing the best we can, sir. As soon as the lock is in position, we'll send a man in with plates and a welding torch."

"Who's going in?"

"Warren—one of the Engineers. He's handled this in drills."

The men finished welding in the air-lock and a moment later a man in a bulky suit came through the cordon at the end of the passageway. His kit of tools was buckled to his side; the helmet he wore was a space-welding helmet, opaque except for the small colored strip through which he looked.

His voice was muffled. "What's the pressure?"

Olson shook his head. "There ain't none. If your suit gives, that'll be it."

The bulky figure nodded. Matty couldn't see the face but he imagined the lines of strain that were written on it. There hadn't been a hulling since the Trip began and the suits had never been used. They had been frequently tested, but there was always the chance that the testers, assuming that since they hadn't been used chances were they never would be, had been careless. And if they had, then Warren would face the chance of a blow-up in the after compartment.

The figure huddled in the air-lock and the hatch was slammed shut. There was silence while the air-pressure gauge fell to zero, then the lights glimmered in the signal that meant Warren was through the other half of the lock and in the compartment.

The built in radio pick-up and amplifier on the bulkhead broadcast Warren's comments while he was on the inside.

"*Bad. Bigger than I thought—and the plates around it are buckled. Send in the welding outfit and the largest of the plates.*"

They were fed in through the air-lock and then there was silence as Warren went to work. The minutes passed and no word from inside. The men in the repair crew began to look at each other with worried expressions on their faces. If something had happened to Warren . . .

Olson ordered another suit brought up. "If Warren doesn't come out within twenty minutes, I'll go in after him."

The bulkhead amplifier suddenly hummed.

"*It's patched—airtight as far as I can make it. I'm inspecting for further leaks.*" There was a long silence and suddenly the amplifier broke in again. Even with the muffled tones, Matty could sense the horror that lay underneath. "*I'm in hold fourteen. People here—dead—must be close to a hundred. I'll get the names before you open up the hatch. Pretty much of a mess but heat and air would make it worse.*" He hesitated a moment and Matty could imagine he was searching the bodies for their ident chains. "*Arnold Sampson, Marcia Dawdet, Caleb Olson . . .*"

The Shops foreman suddenly groaned and held his head in his hands. Matty remembered his son—half-grown, a little too smart and a little too wild for his own good. Rumor had it that he had been a champion in the sub-rosa *slit* tournaments held up on the upper levels.

The list of dead droned on and a man from Personnel started taking down the names. There was utter silence in the passageway as the repair crew tried to catch the names as they were read. Occasionally one of them would groan.

The voice finally ceased and a glance at the pressure gauge told Matty that Warren was coming out. The outer air-lock hatch clanged open and then the figure of Warren was in the passageway and anxious hands were helping him off with his suit. When the helmet was off the repair crew and the cordon of Security broke into cheers.

"*Jere! Jere Paulson!*"

Jeremiah stood there for a moment, the sweat rolling down his hard-hewn face, then turned to Matty. "Warren was sick; he couldn't make it up."

There were a hundred other men who could have taken Warren's place, Matty thought. A hundred others who would have volunteered. But Jeremiah had to show up. From honest motives or because it was a ready-made opportunity to be a hero? Matty didn't know and it didn't matter. Jeremiah was beyond all laws, beyond all authority now. He had become a public hero.

"Congratulations," Matty said dryly.

The moon hung low over the hill and the wind from the west was soft and warm. It was early evening, the stars just beginning to brighten in the sky. Matty was lying on the grass in a low meadow, grass that was sweet and smelled heavy with clover. Behind him the woods stretched away into shadows that were black and almost threatening. The only sound was that of the crickets and the quiet noises of small animals moving about in the brush . . .

And the sound of Karen playing the sound box. She was seated against the tree a few yards away, on the top of a slight rise. Matty could see her outline against the darkening sky, an outline that showed the tilt of her head and the mass of curls at her neck and the thrust of her fine breasts against the stars.

She finished the tune and laid the sound box aside.

"I wish the moon was higher," she said.

Matty felt around in the grass by his side and located the dial. He gave it a twist. The night perceptibly darkened, the stars blazed, and the moon obligingly leaped higher in the night sky.

"How's that?"

"Fine."

They sat in silence for a while, listening to the sounds around them. Finally Karen said, "Do you think the world we land on will be anything like this one?"

"I don't know. It might be." He laughed in the darkness. "I don't think the moon will be quite as obliging—if there is one."

"There might be more than one. There might be two or three—a whole dozen of them. Think how confusing the world would be for lovers then!"

"You mean like saying 'I'll meet you when the moon is full' and they pick different moons?"

"Something like that."

The conversation died. Matty searched in his mind for the means of telling her what he had to do, but could find no way of doing it. And—very slowly—the fact that they were alone and would not be disturbed was driving the importance of it from his mind.

"What will be the first things we'll have to do when we land, Matty?"

He stirred. "Set up a stockade of some kind against whatever life there must be on this planet. Start farming immediately. Build shelters against the weather. That sort of thing."

"Can't we live in the ship?"

"We could," he admitted. "But I don't think you'd want to. We've been cooped up, as a race, for too long. It'd be too wonderful to live under the open sky and stars once more. I suppose it would be a lot like this compartment here—but the grass would be real, the animals wouldn't be robots, and there wouldn't be bulkheads just behind the forest or over the hill."

"I don't know if I'd like it or not," she said slowly. "And I think a lot of people have gotten used to living on board. I think you might find it hard to get them to change."

She was standing against the tree, leaning back against it—a mere shadow in the night.

He walked over to where she stood. He suddenly wanted her in the worst way, a way that made his very bones ache. He put his hands on her slender waist.

"Why did you ask me to come here, Matty?"

His hands fell away. "Can't you guess?"

"You wanted to tell me something, didn't you? Something unpleasant."

He sat on a boulder on the hill's crest. "All right," he said harshly. "You've got a right to know. I'm in a struggle to hold the Directorship, Karen. I may not succeed."

"Jeremiah?"

He nodded. "Jeremiah. He's well-liked— he's worked hard enough at it. And he's more capable than I thought. And there's still the opinion that Jeremiah was somehow cheated out of the Directorship, that by disappearing when I was young, I automatically relinquished all claim to it." He paused. "And there's some talk of making the Directorship an elected office."

"Would that be bad?"

"Some years from now, after we've landed and settled down, it might not. It would now."

"Why?"

"Because," he said simply, "I know the reason for the ship, the purpose for the Trip. I'll see that it's carried out—I couldn't do anything else. But I'm not at all sure that somebody else would do the same. Reba would have thought only of herself. So would Jeremiah, I'm afraid. He's a brave man, a capable man—but what has that to do with it? I *know* what I will do; I'm not at all sure what he would do."

"The indispensable man, Matty?"

"Maybe."

It was getting colder in the compartment; the small-animal noises quieted.

"You've changed," Karen mused. "I remember when I first met you in this compartment. You were a young boy and so different then. I think—at least a part of you—is the same person. But it's in the bottom of a big pit where the bulkheads are duty and purpose and Joseph Smith." She paused. "What did you want to tell me?"

Matty took a breath. "I can't kill Jeremiah, I can't fight him. In a way, I'll have to join him." He felt like he was tearing himself to small shreds. "He has a sister named Julia. I'm going to marry her."

Silence.

"Well, aren't you going to say something? You've got a right to. Go ahead, say what you're thinking!"

"I can't say anything, Matty. I feel too sorry for you."

Then he was alone on the artificial hill, with only the synthetic moon and stars for company.

8

And here were gardens bright with sinuous rills,
Where blossomed many an incense-bearing tree,
And here were forests ancient as the hills,

Enfolding sunny spots of greenery.
KUBLA KHAN, S. T. COLERIDGE

The green, white-flecked globe swung slowly beneath them—a thousand miles below. Matty watched it in the viewscreen, searching for the speck that was the research rocket. There was a tiny flare of light on the screen and he bent closer to watch it. He couldn't be mistaken—there was a tiny flight moving from the globe below to the *Astra* high up in the stratosphere.

A few moments later there was a clang against the metal deck in the vast hold. Matty watched over the viewscreen in the control cabin. The deck split down the middle and silently folded downward. The small research rocket rose slowly into view balancing delicately on its bottom jets, then the deck folded back into place, the jets splashed red against the metal for an instant, and the rocket was safely housed.

Olson and Murphy, a young and promising colonist Matty had seen fit to elevate to the Management, came directly to the cabin.

"It's perfect!" Olson said, his eyes sparkling with excitement. "If Earth was anything like this, it must have been paradise. Warm—a little over eighty Fahrenheit at the landing site—composition of air almost the same as what we've been used to, a little high on the oxygen."

"Let's see the report sheet."

Olson handed it over and Matty scanned it quickly. The biologists had okayed the world—with reservations. "It's about right," he said slowly. "Everything that should be there is." He looked over at Murphy. "Any life?"

The thin, bespectacled Executive was as enthusiastic as Olson." All kinds of vegetation. Animal life—the planet is teeming—but no signs of intelligent life that we could see, and we circled the globe an even dozen times. No cities, no villages, no signs of industrial activity."

"That doesn't mean there isn't any," Matty said thoughtfully. "There could be cities beneath the seas for all we know."

He took another look at the report sheet, then turned to his second in command. "What do you think, Uriah?"

Uriah shrugged, trying to mask his eagerness. "There's no sense in waiting; we might as well send down the landing parties now as ever."

Matty punched the button that connected him to Diet. "Send up ten gallons of coffee and sandwiches to Central Control." Then he flipped the switch that put him out over all the *Astra's* speakers.

"*All hands—landing Stations*!"

It was going to be a long grind, he thought. The five thousand colonists would have to be ferried down by the research rocket and the lifeboats, and then the equipment and supplies. The *Astra* itself could never take a planet landing; its own vast bulk would crush it.

They were the last to go down in the lifeboats, leaving only a skeleton crew behind. Matty nervously watched through the plastic port. Far below, he caught glimpses of the rushing planet as the clouds moved slowly across it, hiding it for a moment and then revealing a glimpse of blue and green that might have been sea and land but for which they were still too high up to tell.

The clouds came steadily closer and then they were sinking down through billows of white. The white clouds seemed almost blinding drifting past the port. They gave Matty a peculiar feeling—he had been used to the quiet blackness of space, broken only by the blazing stars. The drifting shreds of white cleared away and they were over what seemed to be a rolling, blue sea; from their height the waves looked like ripples.

They moved over the sea and approached a large land mass in the distance. The land came closer—they were flying over a smooth, broad beach against which the waves of the blue sea washed. They moved inland, settling closer to the land. There was vegetation now—stately forests and green meadows and valleys carpeted with purple flowers.

The lifeboat dipped, dropped closer to the *Astra*'s temporary camp, and settled slowly towards the edge of the clearing. The throbbing sounds of the rockets died.

The Trip was over.

The following day, Matty and Olson took the small lifeboat for a planetary survey. Uriah was left in charge, along with Murphy, to start the building of a more permanent small village.

The pilot—a young Engineer named Silas Pollard—guided the rocket over a small grove of trees, then steadily gained altitude. Olson sat close to the ports, enthusiastically watching the scenery they passed over.

"We couldn't have picked a better planet, Matt. It's perfect!"

"It looks pretty good," Matty mused, reserving most of his opinion. "We probably won't be able to appreciate it for a year or so, though. We've got a lot of work to do. We'll have to start farming, locate metals, things like that."

Olson only half heard him. "Sure, it'll be a lot of work. But my God, Matt, what a world!"

It was a paradise, Matty silently agreed. It was far more than they had any right to expect. He moved closer to the port and looked out.

The small valley near which they had originally landed was a fair sample of the entire planet. Lush, almost semitropical vegetation that would signify a young planet—but the mountains were dulled and blunted and the valleys were filled, which would mean an old one. But that was a problem for the geologists.

They passed over rivers and low mountains and across continents and oceans. They passed through showers but no storms, through gentle drifts of snow in the northern reaches of the land but through no blizzards. Even slight variations in climate would seem drastic to the colonists, used to the static atmosphere control on board the *Astra*, Matty thought, but they had seen nothing to match the solidographs showing the changes of weather back on Earth.

They spent the first night sleeping in the open on the grass in the lea of the lifeboat. The night was warm and mild and the turf was soft and spongy; Matty fell asleep almost at once.

"*Matt!*"

He jerked awake. Olson was shaking him by the shoulder.

"What's wrong?"

"Listen!"

He strained his ears. There was a small, crunching sound not more than a dozen yards away, to his left.

"It's probably nothing," he whispered uneasily. "Night noises, like the kind they used to have in the Training Room."

"I'll bet it isn't," Olson said slowly. His big face was damp with sweat. "Probably some . . . carnivore."

Pollard was awake now. "Just a minute."

Matty could hear the pilot feeling around in the dark, then there was a brilliant flare of light as the young Engineer found the portable sudden-flash. Their carnivore squatted near a small bush. He was a small, gray animal, not more than two feet high with saucerlike nocturnal eyes that blinked, frightened, in the glare of the light. Little bits of turf and bush shoots hung from a small, bow-like mouth.

Matty laughed. "There's your man-eater, Olson!"

"Well—it coulda been," the foreman mumbled, red-faced.

Matty lay back on the turf. "No," he said sleepily, "it's not that kind of a world. It's a friendly world." And then, for no reason at all, he wondered if it was too friendly.

They stayed out a week completing a rough survey of the world and getting the feel of the geography, then flew back to the colonist camp.

It had moved nearer to the ocean's edge, a collection of nondescript tents and plastic-sided housing cubes.

The lifeboat grounded and Matty got out. Uriah wasn't there to meet him. Neither was anybody else. He walked down to the camp and looked around. There were plastic-enclosed working rooms set up for Shop machinery—but nobody was running the machines. There was no power, there were no stockades. People were working at small household tasks but there was a certain lassitude in their actions.

A few of the passing colonists nodded respectfully and Matty stopped one of them. "Where's the Executive Uriah?"

The man shrugged. "Don't know, sir. Maybe down at the beach."

He walked down to the strip of white sand and watched the bathers. He located Uriah and his family splashing in the surf and caught the young man's eye. Uriah hastened over.

"There isn't much being done, is there?" Matty commented mildly.

Uriah shrugged. "People have been cooped up for a long time, Matt. You can't blame them if they want to relax for a few days."

"There's no farming," Matty said, more concerned. "With an expanding population we can't expect the hydroponics tubs to supply us forever."

Uriah grinned. "That's the beauty of it. We won't have to plant much. It grows wild around here—the trees are loaded, even the grass is edible. We ran tests on some of the wild vegetables in this area and it's just as nourishing as what we grow in Hydroponics, some of it even more so."

Matty relaxed. That had been his biggest worry.

"We should stick to our schedule," he said, only slightly worried. "We'll fall behind."

"We're a little late on it," Uriah admitted. His voice grew more confident. "We'll get back to it in about a week."

But they didn't get back to the schedule that week. Nor that month. In six weeks, the schedule was forgotten.

It was early morning, the sun had just risen and the colonists were still asleep. Matty walked aimlessly down the beach, kicking at small pebbles with his toe. He rounded a small hill of sedge that grew down almost to the water's edge, then stopped.

A man in a brown suit was idly picking flat stones off the sand and skipping them across the low waves.

"Good morning, Matt. Care for a walk?" Matty nodded and they walked in silence along the beach until they were out of earshot of the camp. Joseph Smith asked quietly, "How many men could you count on—I really mean count on if it were a matter of life and death? Men who would follow you into hell itself."

Matty thought for a moment. "Maybe fifty. Why?"

"Because we're not staying here. And those fifty are going to have to help us leave."

Matty stared at him blankly.

"Where are we going to go?"

"Next planet out."

Matty stopped, the incoming tide wetting his feet and ankles. "Why?"

"How long have we been here?"

"Six weeks."

"Any progress being made? Any work being done?"

"It'll change."

Joseph Smith laughed curtly. "Not while we remain here. People do things because they have to, not always because they want to." He paused. "What's the purpose of the Trip?"

"To establish a civilization."

The Predict looked moodily out at the ocean.

"That's right—to establish a civilization. But it isn't going to happen here. Civilizations usually arise in response to a challenge, either from nature or from marauding tribes. And people huddle in towns and villages for mutual protection—that's another incentive for civilization. But here there isn't any threat from nature, or from other forms of life. And people aren't huddling—they're leaving. Do you know how many slipped away to the brush already?"

Reluctantly. "No."

"Close to three hundred—almost a tenth of the ship. If we stay here, within a generation we'll have degenerated to little scattered groups of savages. Within three we'll have forgotten our science, we'll probably even have forgotten where we came from. And why."

Matty sat down on a clump of sedge.

"You mentioned the next planet out. What do you know about it?"

"It's livable—but not like this. The average temperature is lower, food is plentiful but we'll have to work for it. And there's an intelligent life. A low form but it will probably give us trouble. They won't like it if we drop in." He seemed oddly satisfied at the somewhat foreboding picture he had drawn.

"How do we sell everybody on leaving here?" Matty asked slowly. "They won't want to exchange this for what you've just described. They're not going to pack up and live in hell just because we want them to."

Joseph Smith juggled a few pebbles aimlessly in his hand.

"That's more your trouble than mine. That's why I asked you how many men you could count on to help. You couldn't convince the colonists to leave voluntarily." He paused. "Maybe you'll have to get them to leave involuntarily."

"*Hah! Matty! Matty!*"

He lifted a glass and got to his feet. It was dusk but the rigged lights from the lifeboats glittered over hundreds of tables loaded with meat and vegetables and bowls of fermented roots and berries. The colonists sprawled on benches and on the white sand.

"*Are you happy?*"

The crowd roared back in a half-drunken voice. Matty felt cold sober.

"*Do you like it here?*"

They did. Matty felt sick.

"*Then I give you—the new Earth!*"

They toasted him and laughed, some started to sing, others danced on the sands. The party was a success, Matty thought. Everybody was there, even most of the stragglers who had built houses in the brush country had come back for it. There was food and drink, most if it native, a lot of it from the raided hydroponic tubs on the *Astra*.

The party roared on and Matty leaned back in his crude chair and waited. There weren't so many celebrating now; quite a few were sprawled silently on the ground, asleep. It wouldn't be too long before the drugged food and drink hit the others.

An hour later there was only silence on the beaches, except for the quiet work of fifty men clearing away the tables and transferring the colonists to the lifeboats. Olson watched the first one take off, then walked back to Matty.

"I don't like this. It'll take us a while to get them all in the *Astra*—think they'll be out that long?"

"They'll be out forty-eight hours," Matty said in a tired voice. "That'll be time enough."

He left on the last boat just as dawn was breaking on the littered beach. Olson and the personnel checker were waiting for him at the *Astra*'s air-lock.

The checker touched a hand to his forehead. "We're three short, sir. Raymond Jeffries, Alice Scott, and Herbert Shippen."

Matty rubbed his chin thoughtfully. "Jeffries is a good Engineer and Shippen is the best tub man in Hydroponics—but we can't stay and look for them. We can't waste the time." He started for the main control cabin. "Where did you put the colonists?"

"Most of them are in the main salon and the compartments. None of them showed signs of coming out of it."

"Olson?"

"Yes, sir."

"What do you think the colonists' reaction will be when they wake up?"

"They aren't going to like it."

Grimly. "That's my opinion. Take a detachment of men and collect all the knives in Diet and anything in Shops that might be used as weapons. Then bring our families in to central control and see that there's food and water enough to last. We'll barricade the hatches from the inside. It'll take us six periods to reach the next planet out. For the last four we're going to be in trouble."

A few minutes later, the families filed in. The last one to enter was Joseph Smith. He didn't look at Matty but sat at one of the ports in the rear of the cabin, an inconspicuous figure in brown.

Matty turned to a white-faced Uriah. "Go ahead and lift."

He walked to the port and looked out. There was the familiar throbbing feel of the rear tubes beginning to fire, then the floating globe below them started to dwindle.

It was a farewell to paradise, Matty thought. A good-bye to Eden.

The mob howled outside the hatch, venting their fury on the inert steel and trying to force their way in. They had tried to storm the pile room and disable the pile machinery until some of the cooler heads reminded the others that then they'd be stranded forever—in space.

It was quiet on the inside. Matty watched the others in the compartment. Nobody had gotten panicky, nobody had had hysterics. And one of the calmest of all was Julia. Julia . . .

He went into a brown study. She was generous, kind-hearted, and she loved him. Whether or not he loved her, he hadn't yet decided. But he no longer saw Karen's face when he looked at her . . .

"They'll get us when we land," Olson said gloomily. "The public strangler or the hangman."

Matty grunted. "You afraid of dying?"

"I'm not afraid of death," Olson said curtly. "Just the method by which it's achieved."

There was silence for the next few hours and Matty morosely watched the planet swim closer in the plate. He had seen the report that the Predict had compiled on it and had a rough picture of what it would be like. It would be livable—there might even be a few times when it would be pleasant. But compared to the world they had just left, it would be living hell.

The hours dragged slowly by but the clamor outside the hatch didn't die. One thousand miles up, the *Astra* went into an orbit.

"What do we do now?" Olson asked sarcastically. "Who's going to volunteer to go out and load them into the lifeboats?"

There was a hesitant silence and then a voice said: "We don't load them in the lifeboats. We're going down in the *Astra*."

Joseph Smith stepped forward, a tall, thin figure in outlandish clothes, and took the pilot's seat at the control board.

There was dead silence while fear battled superstitious awe in the minds of the others in the compartment. The silence was broken by shouted protests. Olson was livid, his eyes thin slits in his beefy face.

"We'll never make it! The *Astra* was built and assembled in space—it can't take a planet landing! We'd wreck it, we'd never be able to leave!"

"That's right," Joseph Smith said calmly. "We wouldn't be able to leave. Ever."

Olson started for him. "I say we're not going down!"

The Predict turned, something small and blue shining in his fist. "Don't come any nearer, Olson." There was no mistaking the intent in his voice.

Uneasy silence. Anxious eyes looked at the Predict, then turned to Matty.

"Well, Matt," Joseph Smith said softly. "Are we going down?"

Matty looked at him, his eyes dueling with the cold gray eyes of the man who had saved his life at ten and whose word had been law ever since. There was no pity, there was no sympathy in those eyes—there was only the calm determination to do what was necessary. Matty's own eyes fell.

"We're going down," he said huskily.

Olsen went white. "We'll never reach the surface alive!"

Matty ignored him and flipped the switch to the ship's speaker. "*All hands man emergency landing stations twelfth level and above! Evacuate all other levels!*"

The clamor in the passageway outside the control cabin suddenly died and a low moan of terror swept the colonists. Then there was only the sound of Uriah calling out orders to the pile crew.

Julia came over and stood close by Matty at one of the ports. The world below started to swell up. They were dropping steadily, the mottled continents and seas rushing rapidly at them. The thin air of the atmosphere screamed past them and they were at storm level. Shrieking winds tore and buffeted the huge vessel and it pitched sharply, throwing those in the compartment towards the after bulkhead. Matty grabbed Julia with one arm and clung to the port railing with the other.

The whipping rains cleared for a moment and the *Astra* settled towards a wooded ridge. The ship touched the top, smashing the timber growth, grazed the ground and kept right on going. The sides of the ridge exploded outward in a burst of shattered granite and flying dirt. At the same time, the bottom plates of the *Astra* buckled and crumpled in a dozen spots, spewing out stores and equipment and colonists who were unlucky enough to be trappped in the bottom sections.

The crumpling motion stopped. Matty staggered to the hatch, threw it open, and stumbled down the passageway. He found an open access lock near ground level and dropped the few feet to the ground. The others who had been in the control cabin followed him.

It was cold, the sky dull and clouded. A drizzle of rain coated the ship and ran down the sides to collect in the thick red mud at the base. Further back from the sides of the ship, at the end of the space of smashed timber, was the start of black, unfriendly forest.

Joseph Smith limped over. There were bruises on his face and blood was running down a cheek. The expression on his face was one of accomplishment.

"The colonists will never leave the ship for something like this!" Matty cried above the roar of the wind.

"They already are!"

Matty turned. Flames were spouting from the cracked and broken sides of the *Astra* far down near the tube section. Tiny figures dropped from the ports and hatches or crawled through the torn hull.

"It won't be a total loss," Joseph Smith mused. "We can salvage a lot later on."

Matty didn't reply but stared in horror at the scene. There must have been tens killed in the landing alone. Tens more would perish in the shooting flames.

How much would people take? he thought. And what penalties would they exact from the ones they held responsible?

9

A day will come when beings . . . shall stand upon this earth as one stands upon a footstool, and shall laugh and reach out their hands amid the stars.

"THE DISCOVERY OF THE FUTURE", H. G. WELLS

★

It has been thirty days since the vessel Astra crash-landed on this world. Ninety-eight souls were killed in the landing and one hundred six perished in the flames that consumed the ship shortly afterwards. We have labored hard and long with primitive tools and have erected a stockade and log houses for the survivors. Hunting has proved excellent, though dangerous, and farming appears possible though not as easy as we had hoped. There have been no defections from the group and hard work and danger has only improved the morale of the colonists. There is every prospect for a permanent civilization here, although the world and the small primitive humanoids that inhabit it are hostile.

As expected, the colonists have rightly held their leadership responsible for the situation they are now in. The larger picture is one that only their historians will appreciate. At present, they consider that we have stolen their paradise and substituted hell . . .'

There were footsteps outside. Matty put down his pen and hastily secreted the few scraps of paper in a crack in the rough-hewn floor. The board door suddenly flew open and the small cabin was filled with bearded colonists dressed in stiff and foul-smelling skins.

He and the other prisoners were jerked roughly to their feet and hustled outside. It was still cool in the early morning but the sun had split the overhanging clouds and shone fitfully on the cleared assembly area in the center of the stockade. Most of the colonists had gathered there, crowded about a wooden platform on which Jeremiah Paulson and his aides sat.

Matty blinked in the bright sunlight, then stole a glance down the line of other accused. Olson, big and threatening, his alert eyes watching for a break—any break—on the part of the guards. Uriah, white-faced but firm in the knees. Murphy, trembling . . . A dozen others.

He was pushed out in front of the platform, his hands trussed behind his back, the thongs cutting deep into his flesh. He stretched and felt the warm sunlight on his back and neck, the neck that would so soon feel the tightening of fingers that he had escaped from fifteen years before . . .

Jeremiah started reading the charge.

"That in as much as Mathew Kendrick be accused of illegally and in a premeditated fashion crashing and stranding the star-ship *Astra* on a cruel and inhospitable world and . . . eh?"

One of his advisors had nudged him in the ribs and Jeremiah bent down to listen. Matty watched in disgust. The advisors who had sprung up to guide Jeremiah had almost uniformly been a shifty and lazy lot. And Jeremiah listened . . .

". . . yes . . . and stand accused of setting the fires after landing . . ."

There was more but Matty wasn't listening. He was thinking of the *Astra,* half-buried in the valley a mile away. It was rusting now, birds nesting in the shattered ports. A few more generations and the ship would have crumpled and there would be left only stories and myth . . .

"How do you plead to the charge, Mathew Kendrick?"

The cold voice cut into his reverie and he jerked awake. Jeremiah was going through the Judging process automatically, even though it was a foregone conclusion what the result would be.

"Well?"

It was the moment he had waited for, the moment when his greatest decision would have to be made. His mind felt like glue. He was not afraid of death for himself but it was obvious that it wouldn't stop with him. It would go on. Olson, Uriah, Murphy, Silas Pollard—and their families. The terror would consume them and then strike among the other colonists, searching out those who had helped any of the accused in the past or who had been so lacking in foresight that they had been friends of the accused. It would sow hate and fear and eventually crush the colony, if Jeremiah didn't crush it first through his own stupidity . . .

"I plead innocent," he said slowly. "And so are these others."

There was a burst of angry cries from the crowded colonists. Matty suddenly whirled, facing Joseph Smith, a tall, thin figure in brown standing at the edge of the crowd. The Predict had been convicted with the others as an accomplice and then immediately absolved by the court. And Matty had originally refused to testify against him.

"The guilty man is Joseph Smith, your Predict."

There was dead silence and Matty talked on. He could feel the shock in the colonists' faces, sense the contemptuous look on Olson's. His testimony lasted an hour. Some of it was true, some of it was false, and all of it was damning. Towards the end, Matty could feel the mood of the crowd change. Joseph Smith had become the God that had failed, the idol with the feet of clay . . .

And Joseph Smith did not deny it.

Matty unlocked the door and entered. It was dark and foul smelling on the inside and there was the scamper of little things across the floor. He felt for the table, set down the lamp, and lit it. It flickered, then grew to a steady glow that cast a yellow light throughout the room.

The man in the corner was dirty, with matted beard and a brown suit that was rumpled and covered with filth. Matty studied him for a moment. The face was haggard and gaunt, but, everything considered, it looked much the same as when he had first seen it. The gray eyes were still alert and unsmiling—and cold.

"How are you?"

"All right." Pause. "I understand that you're Director again."

Matty felt uncomfortable. "That's right. It wasn't difficult to get it back. The responsibility was . . . too much for Jeremiah."

The Predict nodded. "When's my time up?"

"It isn't. The public strangler has been abolished. In your case, you'll get exile—that was the best I could do. I've had your trunk brought up; you'll leave tomorrow."

Silence. The man in brown picked a small moving thing off his wrist and crushed it between his fingers.

"You hate me a great deal, don't you, Matty?"

Slowly. "I don't think I hate anybody. Let's say I don't understand you, I don't understand the reasons for some of the things you've done." He paused. "The Director is a manufactured personality, isn't he? You pull the environmental strings, so to speak, so the Director ends up as a willing pawn."

"You wanted the Directorship."

"Does a ten-year-old boy know what he wants? But that isn't answering my question."

The Predict leaned back in the corner, watching Matty curiously. "All right, you're correct. The Director is manufactured—as much as anything can be manufactured."

Matty suddenly wondered how much of his life had been left to chance, and how much had been planned by the Predict. Whether, for example, the Executives had been entirely responsible for the persecution that had driven him to the arms of Joseph Smith . . .

"Why?"

"The Predict is a man apart, Matty. He lives longer than the colonists, his own roots are in a culture that the colonists know nothing about, for the most part haven't even heard of. The Predict acts through the Director." He paused. "You won't understand the allusion, Matty, but the Directors play Trilby to my Svengali. I'm not always successful, of course. Your father was an ignorant stupid man over whom I had little control. You . . . were much better."

"Why is there a Predict in the first place?"

"Predict isn't exactly the right word. Psychologist would be more exact—it's the title I started out with, anyways." Musing. "Five hundred years, twenty generations, is a long time. People forget things. They forget where they're going, they forget why. And they forget the necessity. Somebody had to go along to see that the purpose of the Trip was carried out."

Matty thought about it for a moment.

"It was an insane culture on board ship. I've never realized it until the last thirty days when it's been—different."

"It was a Machiavellian culture on board," Joseph Smith said slowly. "It didn't start out that way, though, it just grew. We didn't organize the ship on military lines; we were afraid of what might happen after a few hundred years had passed. So we ran it like a business, trying to preserve as much of our culture as we could. The Executives of each department made up Management, and at the head of that was the Director. It didn't turn out as we hoped. You take a race that's used to a whole planet to live on and coop them up in a steel cell a few miles long and a thousand yards wide and you might be surprised at the result. The individuals stay sane, but the culture itself goes mad."

"You could have made it different."

The Predict looked up, surprised.

"A democracy?"

"Why not?"

The Predict shook his head. "The *Astra* couldn't have been a democracy under any conditions. Democracies are run by men who agree among themselves as to their course of collective action. The colonists weren't free agents. A civilization that had died a long time ago had already decided what they were going to do. If the *Astra* was a democracy they would have voted to stay behind on the first planet we landed on. And that would have been the end of the Trip and the end of the hopes of . . . the people I knew."

It was cold in the cabin and the man in the corner shivered slightly. He looked tired.

"We were to establish a civilization, Matty, not run loose like a lot of savages and start the long climb from the very bottom. Everything I did was done with that in mind. I've acted under the orders of four billion people who died five centuries ago—and I've been a blackguard, a murderer and a dictator to carry them out. I've twisted people's lives, I've seen them unhappy, I've seen them die, and I haven't given it a second thought. I've played God—or the devil, if you want to look at it that way. And if I had it to do all over again, I would do it the same way!"

He suddenly twisted and faced the wall, holding his head in his hands. Matty stood there for a moment more, then quietly left.

It was morning of a bright, warm day. The colonists were already up and about the village, drawing water, airing linen, making up hunting parties, and the farm workers were getting ready to go out for the day. All of them were equipped with the crossbows that Dion West had invented and Matty congratulated himself for the hundredth time on having spared his life the years before.

He stopped at the cabin, knocked, then pushed the door open and walked in.

Joseph Smith—washed and shaved and looking considerably better than he had the night before—was busy, arms deep in the trunk that Matty had had delivered earlier. He was sorting out items and slowly piling them up on the table. Matty looked at them curiously. held several up to the light streaming through the doorway, then paused—puzzled—over a long slender rod of metal.

"That was what you call a raincoat and hip boots you had there, Matty. These are blankets and wool socks and a canvas pack. The rod you have in your hand is what we used to call a fly-rod. Good for fishing." He took some more clothing out of the box and methodically packed it away in the canvas sack. "Fishing should be good here. Nobody's ever tried it. I've got a shotgun down there, too. Works on a chemical explosive basis—you wouldn't know the theory."

"You don't need to go too far away," Matty said suddenly. "If you hid out in the woods, Julia and I could bring you food. See that you weren't—lonely."

Joseph Smith laughed—a hollow, bitter laugh. "For five hundred years I've lived with the human race. I know everything there is to know about people, I've enjoyed all the pleasures that can possibly be extracted from their companionship. I've lived with them for five centuries and the only thing that's changed have been the faces. I'm tired of it—Lord, I'm tired of it!"

He rolled up a few more woolen shirts and stuffed them in the almost full pack.

"Matty, exile isn't a punishment for me—it's something I've looked forward to for a long time."

He tightened the buckles and adjusted the pack to his back. He wore boots and a leather jacket and a red hat; the "shotgun" was tied in with the pack. He took a last look in the bottom of his trunk, then took out a small box.

"Why did you denounce me at the trial, Matty? To save your own life?"

Matty looked him in the eyes. "I've never regarded my own life so highly that I would be willing to sacrifice somebody else's to save it. I had my choice of two alternatives. I think I made the right decision. To a large extent, your purpose had been accomplished. You were expendable."

"Cold, aren't you?"

Matty shrugged. "Maybe."

Joseph Smith nodded slowly. "I meant you to be. Ever since you were ten, I've tried to teach you one thing. The hardest thing there is to do is to make decisions for something as abstract as an ideal and do it on an impersonal basis. Whether those decisions hurt you personally, or those you know, can't enter in. I thought of the same solution as you did—but I couldn't offer myself to the mob, it wouldn't have been convincing. But it had to be done. I would satisfy them, I was an important enough figure. I was hoping you would do what you did, Matt. When you did—I realized you were Predict material."

He gave the box to Matty.

"They need another Predict here more than they need a Director. We're not in the ship anymore and we'll have to have a different type of culture. A culture that, perhaps, should be fashioned by a poet and a sound-box player. And there has to be somebody around with the long view—somebody to see that the colonists don't forget why they left Earth in the first place, that this time it has to be played differently."

He paused briefly at the door. "Good luck, Matty."

He turned and strode through the clearing and out the open gate of the stockade, disappearing for a moment in the slope of the valley, then coming into view as he climbed the ridges towards the hills beyond. He grew smaller, dwindled, and then was gone.

Nobody would ever see him again, Matty thought. Perhaps someday somebody in the far future would find a pile of bleached bones on some mountain ledge or by some fish stream. And then, nearby, there would be a rotting canvas bag and a rusting shotgun . . .

He turned back to the table and opened the small box. There was a small plastic bottle of clear, colorless liquid and a hypodermic needle whose bluish contents sparkled in the sunlight. The contents of the hypodermic, he realized, was all the difference there was between a Predict and a colonist.

He swabbed his arm with alcohol, then took the needle and slowly pushed the plunger home.

AND THEN THERE WERE NONE

Eric Frank Russell

The Battleship was eight hundred feet in diameter and slightly more than one mile long. Mass like that takes up room and makes a dent. The one sprawled right across one field and halfway through the next. Its weight made a rut twenty feet deep which would be there for keeps.

On board were two thousand people divisible into three distinct types. The tall, lean, crinkly-eyed ones were the crew. The crop-haired, heavy-jowled ones were the troops. Finally, the expressionless, balding and myopic ones were the cargo of bureaucrats.

The first of these types viewed this world with the professional but aloof interest of people everlastingly giving a planet the swift once-over before chasing along to the next. The troops regarded it with a mixture of tough contempt and boredom. The bureaucrats peered at it with cold authority. Each according to his lights.

This lot were accustomed to new worlds, had dealt with them by the dozens and reduced the process to mere routine. The task before them would have been nothing more than repetition of well-used, smoothly operating technique but for one thing: the entire bunch were in a jam and did not know it.

Emergence from the ship was in strict order of precedence. First, the Imperial Ambassador. Second, the battleship's captain. Third, the officer commanding the ground forces. Fourth, the senior civil servant.

Then, of course, the next grade lower, in the same order: His Excellency's private secretary, the ship's second officer, the deputy commander of troops, the penultimate pen pusher.

Down another grade, then another, until there was left only His Excellency's barber, boot wiper and valet, crew members with the lowly status of O.S.—Ordinary Spaceman—the military nonentities in the ranks, and a few temporary ink-pot fillers dreaming of the day when they would be made permanent and given a desk of their own. This last collection of unfortunates remained aboard to clean ship and refrain from smoking, by command.

Had this world been alien, hostile and well-armed, the order of exit would have been reversed, exemplifying the Biblical promise that the last shall be first and the first shall be last. But this planet, although officially new, unofficially was not new and certainly was not alien. In ledgers and dusty files some two hundred light-years away it was recorded as a cryptic number and classified as a ripe plum long overdue for picking. There had been considerable delay in the harvesting due to a super-abundance of other still riper plums elsewhere.

According to the records, this planet was on the outermost fringe of a huge assortment of worlds which had been settled immediately following the Great Explosion. Every school child knew all about the Great Explosion, which was no more than the spectacular name given to the bursting outward of masses of humanity when the Blieder drive superseded atomic-powered rockets and practically handed them the cosmos on a platter.

At that time, between three and five hundred years ago, every family, group, cult or clique that imagined it could do better some place else had taken to the star trails. The restless, the ambitious, the malcontents, the eccentrics, the antisocial, the fidgety and the just plain curious, away they had roared by the dozens, the hundred, the thousands.

Some two hundred thousand had come to this particular world, the last of them arriving three centuries back. As usual, ninety percent of the mainstream had consisted of friends, relatives or acquaintances of the first-comers, people persuaded to follow the bold example of Uncle Eddie or Good Old Joe.

If they had since doubled themselves six or seven times over, there now ought to be several millions of them. That they had increased far beyond their original strength had been evident during the approach, for while no great cities were visible there were many medium to smallish towns and a large number of villages.

His Excellency looked with approval at the turf under his feet, plucked a blade of it, grunting as he stooped. He was so constructed that this effort approximated to an athletic feat and gave him a crick in the belly.

"Earth-type grass. Notice that, captain? Is it just a coincidence, or did they bring seed with them?"

"Coincidence, probably," thought Captain Grayder. "I've come across four grassy worlds so far. No reason why there shouldn't be others."

"No, I suppose not." His Excellency gazed into the distance, doing it with pride of ownership. "Looks like there's someone plowing over there. He's using a little engine between a pair of fat wheels. They can't be so backward. Hm-m-m!" He rubbed a couple of chins. "Bring him here. We'll have a talk, find out where it's best to get started."

"Very well." Captain Grayder turned to Colonel Shelton, boss of the troops. "His Excellency wishes to speak to that farmer." He pointed to the faraway figure.

"The farmer," said Shelton to Major Hame. "His Excellency wants him at once."

"Bring that farmer here," Hame ordered Lieutenant Deacon. "Quickly!"

"Go get that farmer," Deacon told Sergeant major Bidworthy. "And hurry—His Excellency is waiting!"

The sergeant major, a big, purple-faced man, sought around for a lesser rank, remembered that they were all cleaning ship and not smoking. He, it seemed, was elected.

Tramping across four fields and coming within hailing distance of his objective, he performed a precise military halt and released a barracks-square bellow of, "Hi, you!" He waved urgently.

The farmer stopped, wiped his forehead, looked around. His manner suggested that the mountainous bulk of the battleship was a mirage such as are dime a dozen around these parts. Bidworthy waved again, making it an authoritative summons. The farmer calmly waved back, got on with his plowing.

Sergeant Major Bidworthy employed an expletive which—when its flames had died out—meant, "Dear me!" and marched fifty paces nearer. He could now see that the other was bushy-browed and leather-faced.

"*Hi*!"

Stopping the plow again, the farmer leaned on a shaft, picked his teeth.

Struck by the notion that perhaps during the last three centuries the old Earth-language had been dropped in favor of some other lingo, Bidworthy asked, "Can you understand me?"

"Can any person understand another?" inquired the farmer, with clear diction. He turned to resume his task.

Bidworthy was afflicted with a moment of confusion. Recovering, he informed hurriedly, "His Excellency, the Earth Ambassador, wishes to speak with you at once."

"So?" The other eyed him speculatively. "How come that he is excellent?"

"He is a person of considerable importance," said Bidworthy, unable to decide whether the other was being funny at his expense or alternatively was what is known as a character. A good many of these isolated planet-scratchers liked to think of themselves as characters.

"Of considerable importance," echoed the farmer, narrowing his eyes at the horizon. He appeared to be trying to grasp an alien concept. After a while, he inquired, "What will happen to your home world when this person dies?"

"Nothing," Bidworthy admitted.

"It will roll on as usual?"

"Of course."

"Then," declared the farmer, flatly, "he cannot be important." With that, his little engine went *chuff-chuff* and the wheels rolled forward and the plow plowed.

Digging his nails into the palms of his hands, Bidworthy spent half a minute gathering oxygen before he said, in hoarse tones, "I cannot return without at least a message for His Excellency."

"Indeed?" The other was incredulous. "What is to stop you?" Then, noting the alarming increase in Bidworthy's color, he added with compassion, "Oh, well, you may tell him that I said"—he paused while he thought it over—"God bless you and goodbye!"

Sergeant Major Bidworthy was a powerful man who weighed two-twenty pounds, had hopped around the cosmos for twenty years, and feared nothing. He had never been known to permit the shiver of one hair—but he was trembling all over by the time he got back to the ship.

His Excellency fastened a cold eye upon him and demanded, "Well?"

"He won't come." Bidworthy's veins stood out on his forehead. "And, sir, if only I could have him in my field company for a few months I'd straighten him up and teach him to move at the double."

"I don't doubt that, Sergeant Major," soothed His Excellency. He continued in a whispered aside to Colonel Shelton. "He's a good fellow but no diplomat. Too abrupt and harsh voiced. Better go yourself and fetch that farmer. We can't sit here forever waiting to find out where to begin."

"Very well, your Excellency." Colonel Shelton trudged across the fields, caught up with the plow. Smiling pleasantly, he said, "Good morning, my man!"

Stopping his plow, the farmer sighed as if it were another of those days one has sometimes. His eyes were dark-brown, almost black, as they looked at the other.

"What makes you think I'm *your* man?" he inquired.

"It is a figure of speech," explained Shelton. He could see what was wrong now. Bidworthy had fallen foul of an irascible type. Two dogs snarling at one another. Shelton went on, "I was only trying to be courteous."

"Well," meditated the farmer, "I reckon that's something worth trying for."

Pinking a little, Shelton continued with determination. "I am commanded to request the pleasure of your company at the ship."

"Think they'll get any pleasure out of my company?" asked the other, disconcertingly bland.

"I'm sure of it," said Shelton.

"You're a liar," said the farmer.

His color deepening, Colonel Shelton snapped, "I do not permit people to call me a liar."

"You've just permitted it," the other pointed out.

Letting it pass, Shelton insisted, "Are you coming to the ship or are you not?"

"I am not."

"Why not?"

"Myob!" said the farmer.

"What was that?"

"Myob!" he repeated. It smacked of a mild insult.

Colonel Shelton went back.

He told the ambassador, "That fellow is one of these too-clever types. All I could get out of him at the finish was 'myob', whatever that means."

"Local slang," chipped in Captain Grayder. "An awful lot of it develops over three or four centuries. I've come across one or two worlds where there's been so much of it that one almost had to learn a new language."

"He understood your speech?" asked the ambassador, looking at Shelton.

"Yes, your Excellency. And his own is quite good. But he won't come away from his plowing." He reflected briefly, then suggested, "If it were left to me, I'd bring him in by force, under an armed escort."

"That would encourage him to give essential information," commented the ambassador, with open sarcasm. He patted his stomach, smoothed his jacket, glanced down at his glossy shoes. "Nothing for it but to go speak to him myself."

Colonel Shelton was shocked. "Your Excellency, you can't do *that*!"

"Why can't I?"

"It would be undignified."

"I am aware of it," said the ambassador, dryly. "Can you suggest an alternative?"

"We can send out a patrol to find someone more co-operative."

"Someone better informed, too," Captain Grayder offered. "At best we wouldn't get much out of one surly hayseed. I doubt whether he knows a quarter of what we require to learn."

"All right." His Excellency abandoned the notion of doing his own chores. "Organize a patrol and let's have some results."

"A patrol," said Colonel Shelton to Major Hame. "Nominate one immediately."

"Call out a patrol," Hame ordered Lieutenant Deacon. "At once."

"Parade a patrol immediately, Sergeant Major," said Deacon.

Bidworthy went to the ship, climbed a ladder, stuck his head in the lock and bawled, "Sergeant Gleed, out with your squad, and make it snappy!" He gave a suspicious sniff and went farther into the lock. His voice gained several more decibels. "Who's been smoking? By the Black Sack, if I catch—"

Across the fields something quietly went *chuff-chuff* while balloon tires crawled along.

The patrol formed by the right in two ranks of eight men each, turned at a barked command, marched off noseward. Their boots thumped in unison, their accoutrements clattered and the orange-colored sun made sparkles on their metal.

Sergeant Gleed did not have to take his men far. They had got one hundred yards beyond the battleship's nose when he noticed a man ambling across the field to his right. Treating the ship with utter indifference, the newcomer was making toward the farmer still plowing far over to the left.

"Patrol, right wheel!" yelled Gleed. Marching them straight past the wayfarer, he gave them a loud about-turn and followed it with the high-sign.

Speeding up its pace, the patrol opened its ranks, became a double file of men tramping at either side of the lone pedestrian. Ignoring his suddenly acquired escort, the latter continued to plod straight ahead like one long convinced that all is illusion.

"Left wheel!" Gleed roared, trying to bend the whole caboodle toward the waiting ambassador.

Swiftly obedient, the double file headed leftward, one, two, three, hup! It was neat, precise execution, beautiful to watch. Only one thing spoiled it: the man in the middle maintained his self-chosen orbit and ambled casually between numbers four and five of the right-hand file.

That upset Gleed, especially since the patrol continued to thump ambassadorwards for lack of a further order. His Excellency was being treated to the unmilitary spectacle of an escort dumbly boot-beating one way while its prisoner airily mooched another. Colonel Shelton would have plenty to say about it in due course, and anything he forgot Bidworthy would remember.

"Patrol!" roared Gleed, pointing an outraged finger at the escapee, and momentarily dismissing all regulation commands from his mind. "Get that yimp!"

Breaking ranks, they moved at the double and surrounded the wanderer too closely to permit further progress. Perforce, he stopped.

Gleed came up, said somewhat breathlessly, "Look, the Earth Ambassador wants to speak to you—that's all."

The other said nothing, merely gazed at him with mild blue eyes. He was a funny looking bum, long overdue for a shave, with a fringe of ginger whiskers sticking out all around his pan. He resembled a sunflower.

"Are you going to talk with His Excellency?" Gleed persisted.

"Naw." The other nodded toward the farmer. "Going to talk with Pete."

"The ambassador first," retorted Gleed, toughly. "He's a big noise."

"I don't doubt that," remarked the sunflower.

"Smartie Artie, eh?" said Gleed, pushing his face close and making it unpleasant. He gave his men a gesture. "All right—shove him along. We'll show him!"

Smartie Artie sat down. He did it sort of solidly, giving himself the aspect of a statue anchored for aeons. The ginger whiskers did nothing to lend grace to the situation. But Sergeant Gleed had handled sitters before, the only difference being that this one was cold sober.

"Pick him up," ordered Gleed, "and carry him."

They picked him up and carried him, feet first, whiskers last. He hung limp and unresisting in their hands, a dead weight. In this inauspicious manner he arrived in the presence of the Earth Ambassador where the escort plonked him on his feet.

Promptly he set out for Pete.

"Hold him, damn it!" howled Gleed.

The patrol grabbed and clung tight. His Excellency eyed the whiskers with well-bred concealment of distaste, coughed delicately, and spoke.

"I am truly sorry that you had to come to me in this fashion."

"In that case," suggested the prisoner, "you could have saved yourself some mental anguish by not permitting it to happen."

"There was no other choice. We've got to make contact somehow."

"I don't see it." said Ginger Whiskers. "What's so special about this date?"

"The date?" His Excellency frowned in puzzlement. "Where does that come in?"

"That's what I'd like to know."

"The point eludes me." The ambassador turned to Colonel Shelton. "Do you get what he's aiming at?"

"I could hazard a guess, your Excellency. I think he is suggesting that since we've left them without contact for more than three hundred years, there's no particular urgency about making it today." He looked at the sunflower for confirmation.

That worthy rallied to his support by remarking, "You're doing pretty well for a half-wit."

Regardless of Shelton's own reaction, this was too much for Bidworthy purpling nearby. His chest came up and his eyes caught fire. His voice was an authoritative rasp.

"Be more respectful while addressing high-ranking officers!"

The prisoner's mild blue eyes turned upon him in childish amazement, examined him slowly from feet to head and all the way down again. The eyes drifted back to the ambassador.

"Who is this preposterous person?"

Dismissing the question with an impatient wave of his hand, the ambassador said, "See here, it is not our purpose to bother you from sheer perversity, as you seem to think. Neither do we wish to detain you any longer than is necessary. All we—"

Pulling at his face-fringe as if to accentuate its offensiveness, the other interjected, "It being you, of course, who determines the length of the necessity?"

"On the contrary, you may decide that yourself," said the ambassador, displaying admirable self-control. "All you need do is tell—"

"Then I've decided it right now," the prisoner chipped in. He tried to heave himself free of his escort. "Let me go talk to Pete."

"All you need do," the ambassador persisted, "is to tell us where we can find a local official who can put us in touch with your central government." His gaze was stern, commanding, as he added, "For instance, where is the nearest police post?"

"Myob!" said the other.

"The same to you," retorted the ambassador, his patience starting to evaporate.

"That's precisely what I'm trying to do," assured the prisoner, enigmatically. "Only you won't let me."

"If I may make a suggestion, your Excellency," put in Colonel Shelton, "let me—"

"I require no suggestions and I won't let you," said the ambassador, rapidly becoming brusque. "I have had enough of all this tomfoolery. I think we've landed at random in an area reserved for imbeciles and it would be as well to recognize the fact and get out of it with no more delay."

"Now you're talking," approved Ginger Whiskers. "And the farther the better."

"I'm not thinking of leaving this planet if that's what is in your incomprehensible mind," asserted the ambassador, with much sarcasm. He stamped a proprietory foot on the turf. "This is part of the Earth Empire. As such, it is going to be recognized, charted and organized."

"*Heah, heah*!" put in the senior civil servant, who aspired to honors in elocution.

His Excellency threw a frown behind, went on, "We'll move the ship to some other section where brains are brighter." He signed to the escort. "Let him go. Doubtless he is in a hurry to borrow a razor."

They released their grips. Ginger Whiskers at once turned toward the still-plowing farmer, much as if he were a magnetized needle irresistibly drawn Peteward. Without a word he set off at his original mooching pace. Disappointment and disgust showed on the faces of Gleed and Bidworthy as they watched him go.

"Have the vessel shifted at once," the ambassador instructed Captain Grayder. "Plant it near a suitable town—not out in the wilds where every hayseed views strangers as a bunch of gyps."

He marched importantly up the gangway. Captain Grayder followed, then Colonel Shelton, then the elocutionist. Next, their successors in due order of precedence. Lastly, Gleed and his men.

The gangway rolled inward. The lock closed. Despite its immense bulk, the ship shivered briefly from end to end and soared without deafening uproar or spectacular display of flame.

Indeed, there was silence save for the plow going *chuff-chuff* and the murmurings of the two men walking behind it. Neither bothered to turn his head to observe what was happening.

"Seven pounds of prime tobacco is a whale of a lot to give for one case of brandy," Ginger Whiskers was protesting.

"Not for my brandy," said Pete. "It's stronger than a thousand Gands and smoother than an Earthman's downfall."

The great battleship's second touchdown was made on a wide flat one mile north of a town estimated to hold twelve to fifteen thousand people. Captain Grayder would have preferred to survey the place from low altitude before making his landing, but one cannot maneuver an immense space-going job as if it were an atmospheric tug. Only two things can be done so close to a planetary surface—the ship is taken up or brought down with no room for fiddling betweentimes.

So Grayder bumped his ship in the best spot he could find when finding is a matter of split-second decisions. It made a rut only twelve feet deep, the ground being harder and on a rock bed. The gangway was shoved out; the procession descended in the same order as before.

His Excellency cast an anticipatory look toward the town, registered disappointment and remarked, "Something's badly out of kilter here. There's the town. Here's us in plain view, with a ship like a metal mountain. A thousand people at least must have seen us even if the rest are holding seances behind drawn curtains or playing pinochle in the cellars. Are they excited?"

"It doesn't seem so," admitted Colonel Shelton, pulling an eyelid for the sake of feeling it spring back.

"I wasn't asking you. I was telling you. They are not excited. They are not surprised. In fact, they are not even interested. One would almost think they've had a ship here before and it was full of smallpox, or sold them a load of gold bricks, or something like that. What is wrong with them?"

"Possibly they lack curiosity," Shelton offered.

"Either that or they're afraid. Or maybe the entire gang of them are crackers. A good many worlds were appropriated by woozy groups who wanted some place where their eccentricities could run loose. Nutty notions become conventional after three hundred years of undisturbed continuity. It's then considered normal and proper to nurse the bats out of your grandfather's attic. That, and generations of inbreeding, can create some queer types. But we'll cure 'em!"

"Yes, your Excellency, most certainly we will."

"You don't look so balanced yourself, chasing that eye around your pan," reproved the ambassador. He pointed southeast as Shelton stuck the fidgety hand firmly into a pocket. "There's a road over there. Wide and well-built by the looks of it. Get that patrol across it. If they don't bring in a willing talker within reasonable time, we'll send a battalion into the town itself."

"A patrol," repeated Colonel Shelton to Major Hame.

"Call out the patrol," Hame ordered Lieutenant Deacon.

"That patrol again, Sergeant Major," said Deacon.

Bidworthy raked out Gleed and his men, indicated the road, barked a bit, shooed them on their way.

They marched, Gleed in the lead. Their objective was half a mile and angled slightly nearer the town. The left-hand file, who had a clear view of the nearest suburbs, eyed them wistfully, wished Gleed in warmer regions with Bidworthy stoking beneath him.

Hardly had they reached their goal than a customer appeared. He came from the town's outskirts, zooming along at fast pace on a contraption vaguely resembling a motorcycle. It ran on a pair of big rubber balls and was pulled by a caged fan. Gleed spread his men across the road.

The oncomer's machine suddenly gave forth a harsh, penetrating sound that vaguely reminded them of Bidworthy in the presence of dirty boots.

"Stay put," warned Gleed. "I'll skin the guy who gives way and leaves a gap."

Again the shrill metallic warning. Nobody moved. The machine slowed, came up to them at a crawl and stopped. Its fan continued to spin at low rate, the blades almost visible and giving out a steady hiss.

"What's the idea?" demanded the rider. He was lean-featured, in his middle thirties, wore a gold ring in his nose and had a pigtail four feet long.

Blinking incredulously at this get-up, Gleed managed to jerk an indicative thumb toward the iron mountain and say, "Earth ship."

"Well, what d'you expect me to do about it?"

"Co-operate," said Gleed, still bemused by the pigtail. He had never seen one before. It was in no way effeminate, he decided. Rather did it lend a touch of ferocity like that worn—according to the picture books—by certain North American aborigines of umpteen centuries ago.

"Co-operation," mused the rider. "Now there is a beautiful word. You know what it means, of course?"

"I ain't a dope."

"The precise degree of your idiocy is not under discussion at the moment," the rider pointed out. His nose-ring waggled a bit as he spoke. "We are talking about co-operation. I take it you do quite a lot of it yourself?"

"You bet I do," Gleed assured. "And so does everyone else who knows what's good for him."

"Let's keep to the subject, shall we? Let's not sidetrack and go rambling all over the map." He revved up his fan a little then let it slow down again. "You are given orders and you obey them?"

"Of course. I'd have a rough time if—"

"That is what you call co-operation?" put in the other. He shrugged his shoulders, indulged a resigned sigh. "Oh, well, it's nice to check the facts of history. The books *could* be wrong." His fan flashed into a circle of light and the machine surged forward. "Pardon me."

The front rubber ball barged forcefully between two men, knocking them sidewise without injury. With a high whine, the machine shot down the road, its fan-blast making the rider's plaited hairdo point horizontally backward.

"You dumb galoots!" raged Gleed as his fallen pair got up and dusted themselves. "I ordered you to stand fast. What d'you mean, letting him run out on us like that?"

"Didn't have much choice about it, sarge," answered one, giving him a surly look.

"I want none of your back-chat. You could have busted a balloon if you'd had your weapons ready. That would have stopped him."

"You didn't tell us to have guns ready."

"Where was your own, anyway?" added a voice.

Gleed whirled round on the others and bawled, "Who said that?" His irate eyes raked a long row of blank, impassive faces. It was impossible to detect the culprit. "I'll shake you up with the next quota of fatigues," he promised. "I'll see to it—"

"The Sergeant Major's coming," one of them warned.

Bidworthy was four hundred yards away and making martial progress toward them. Arriving in due time, he cast a cold, contemptuous glance over the patrol.

"What happened?"

Giving a brief account of the incident, Gleed finished aggrievedly, "He looked like a Chickasaw with an oil well."

"What's a Chickasaw?" Bidworthy demanded.

"I read about them somewhere once when I was a kid," explained Gleed, happy to bestow a modicum of learning. "They had long haircuts, wore blankets and rode around in gold-plated automobiles."

"Sounds crazy to me," said Bidworthy. "I gave up all that magic-carpet stuff when I was seven. I was deep in ballistics before I was twelve and military logistics at fourteen." He sniffed loudly, gave the other a jaundiced eye. "Some guys suffer from arrested development."

"They actually existed," Gleed maintained. "They—"

"So did fairies," snapped Bidworthy. "My mother said so. My mother was a good woman. She didn't tell me a lot of tomfool lies—often." He spat on the road. "Be your age!" Then he scowled at the patrol. "All right, get out your guns, assuming that you've got them and know where they are and which hand to hold them in. Take orders from me. I'll deal personally with the next one along."

He sat on a large stone by the roadside and planted an expectant gaze on the town. Gleed posed near him, slightly pained. The patrol remained strung across the road, guns held ready. Half an hour crawled by without anything happening.

One of the men said, "Can we have a smoke, Sergeant Major?"

"No."

They fell into lugubrious silence, watching the town, licking their lips and thinking. They had plenty to think about. A town—any town of human occupation—had desirable features not found elsewhere in the cosmos. Lights, company, freedom, laughter, all the makings of life. And one can go hungry too long.

Eventually a large coach came from the outskirts, hit the high road, came bowling toward them. A long, shiny, streamlined job, it rolled on twenty balls in two rows of ten, gave forth a whine similar to but louder than that of its predecessor, but had no visible fans. It was loaded with people.

At a point two hundred yards from the road block a loud-speaker under the vehicle's bonnet blared an urgent, "Make way! Make way!"

"This is it," commented Bidworthy, with much satisfaction. "We've got a dollop of them. One of them is going to chat or I leave the service." He got off his rock, stood in readiness.

"Make way! Make way!"

"Bust his bags if he tries to bull his way through," Bidworthy ordered the men.

It wasn't necessary. The coach lost pace, stopped with its bonnet a yard from the waiting file. Its driver peered out the side of his cab. Other faces snooped farther back.

Composing himself and determined to try the effect of fraternal cordiality, Bidworthy went up to the driver and said, "Good morning."

"Your time-sense is shot to pot," observed the other. He had a blue jowl, a broken nose, cauliflower ears, looked the sort who usually drives with others in hot and vengeful pursuit. "Can't you afford a watch?"

"Huh?"

"It isn't morning. It's late afternoon."

"So it is," admitted Bidworthy, forcing a cracked smile. "Good afternoon."

"I'm not so sure about that," mused the driver, leaning on his wheel and moodily picking his teeth. "It's just another one nearer the grave."

"That may be," agreed Bidworthy, little taken with that ghoulish angle. "But I have other things to worry about, and—"

"Not much use worrying about anything, past or present," advised the driver. "Because there are lots bigger worries to come."

"Perhaps so," Bidworthy said, inwardly feeling that this was no time or place to contemplate the darker side of existence. "But I prefer to deal with my own troubles in my own time and my own way."

"Nobody's troubles are entirely their own, nor their time, nor their methods," remarked the tough looking oracle. "Are they now?"

"I don't know and I don't care," said Bidworthy, his composure thinning down as his blood pressure built up. He was conscious of Gleed and the patrol watching, listening, and probably grinning inside themselves. There was also the load of gaping passengers. "I think you are chewing the fat just to stall me. You might as well know now that it won't work. The Earth Ambassador is waiting—"

"So are we," remarked the driver, pointedly.

"He wants to speak to you," Bidworthy went on, "and he's going to speak to you!"

"I'd be the last to prevent him. We've got free speech here. Let him step up and say his piece so's we can get on our way."

"*You*," Bidworthy informed, "are going to *him*." He signed to the rest of the coach. "And your load as well."

"Not me," denied a fat man, sticking his head out of a side window. He wore thick-lensed glasses that gave him eyes like poached eggs. Moreover, he was adorned with a high hat candy-striped in white and pink. "Not me," repeated this vision, with considerable firmness.

"Me, neither," indorsed the driver.

"All right." Bidworthy registered menace. "Move this birdcage an inch, forward or backward, and we'll shoot your pot-bellied tires to thin strips. Get out of that cab."

"Not me. I'm too comfortable. Try fetching me out."

Bidworthy beckoned to his nearest six men. "You heard him—take him up on that."

Tearing open the cab door, they grabbed. If they had expected the victim to put up a futile fight against heavy odds, they were disappointed. He made no attempt to resist. They got him, lugged together, and he yielded with good grace, his body leaning sidewise and coming halfway out of the door.

That was as far as they could get him.

"Come on," urged Bidworthy, displaying impatience. "Show him who's who. He isn't a fixture."

One of the men climbed over the body, poked around inside the cab, and said, "He is, you know."

"What d'you mean?"

"He's chained to the steering column."

"Eh? Let me see." He had a look, found that it was so. A chain and a small but heavy and complicated padlock linked the driver's leg to his coach. "Where's the key?"

"Search me," invited the driver, grinning.

They did just that. The frisk proved futile. No key.

"Who's got it?"

"Myob!"

"Shove him back into his seat," ordered Bidworthy, looking savage. "We'll take the passengers. One yap's as good as another so far as I'm concerned." He strode to the doors, jerked them open. "Get out and make it snappy."

Nobody budged. They studied him silently and with varied expressions, not one of which did anything to help his ego. The fat man with the candy-striped hat mooned at him sardonically. Bidworthy decided that he did not like the fat man and that a stiff course of military calisthenics might thin him down a bit.

"You can come out on your feet," he suggested to the passengers in general and the fat man in particular, "or on your necks. Whichever you prefer. Make up your minds."

"If you can't use your head you can at least use your eyes," commented the fat man. He shifted in his seat to the accompaniment of metallic clanking noises.

Bidworthy did as suggested, leaning through the doors to have a gander. Then he got right into the vehicle, went its full length and studied each passenger. His florid features were two shades darker when he came out and spoke to Sergeant Gleed.

"They're all chained. Every one of them." He glared at the driver. "What's the big idea, manacling the lot?"

"Myob!" said the driver, airily.

"Who's got the keys?"

"Myob!"

Taking a deep breath, Bidworthy said to nobody in particular, "Every so often I hear of some guy running amok and laying 'em out by the dozens. I always wonder why—but now I know." He gnawed his knuckles, then added to Gleed, "We can't run this contraption to the ship with that dummy blocking the driver's seat. Either we must find the keys or get tools and cut them loose."

"Or you could wave us on our way and go take a pill," offered the driver.

"Shut up! If I'm stuck here another million years I'll see to it that—"

"The colonel's coming," muttered Gleed, giving him a nudge.

Colonel Shelton arrived, walked once slowly and officiously around the outside of the coach, examining its construction and its occupants. He flinched at the striped hat whose owner leered at him through the glass. Then he came over to the disgruntled group.

"What's the trouble this time, Sergeant Major?"

"They're as crazy as the others, sir. They give a lot of lip and say, 'Myob!' and couldn't care less about his excellency. They don't want to come out and we can't get them out because they're chained to their seats."

"Chained?" Shelton's eyebrows shot upward. "What for?"

"I don't know, sir. They're linked in like a load of lifters making for the pen, and—"

Shelton moved off without waiting to hear the rest. He had a look for himself, came back.

"You may have something there, Sergeant Major. But I don't think they are criminals."

"No, sir?"

"No." He threw a significant glance toward the colorful headgear and several other sartorial eccentricities, including a ginger-haired man's foot-wide polka-dotted bow. "It is more likely that they're a bunch of whacks being taken to a giggle emporium. I'll ask the driver." Going to the cab, he said, "Do you mind telling me your destination?"

"Yes," responded the other.

"Very well, where is it?"

"Look," said the driver, "are we talking the same language?"

"Huh?"

"You asked me if I minded and I said yes." He made a gesture. "I do mind."

"You refuse to tell?"

"Your aim's improving, sonny."

"Sonny?" put in Bidworthy, vibrant with outrage. "Do you realize you are speaking to a colonel?"

"Leave this to me," insisted Shelton, waving him down. His expression was cold as he returned his attention to the driver. "On your way. I'm sorry you've been detained."

"Think nothing of it," said the driver, with exaggerated politeness. "I'll do as much for you some day."

With that enigmatic remark, he let his machine roll forward. The patrol parted to make room. The coach built up its whine to top note, sped down the road, diminished into the distance.

"By the Black Sack!" swore Bidworthy, staring purple-faced after it. "This planet has got more punks in need of discipline than any this side of—"

"Calm yourself, Sergeant Major," advised Shelton. "I feel the same way as you—but I'm taking care of my arteries. Blowing them full of bumps like seaweed won't solve any problems."

"Maybe so, sir, but—"

"We're up against something mighty funny here," Shelton went on. "We've got to find out exactly what it is and how best to cope with it. That will probably mean new tactics. So far, the patrol has achieved nothing. It is wasting its time. We'll have to devise some other and more effective method of making contact with the powers-that-be. March the men back to the ship, Sergeant Major."

"Very well, sir." Bidworthy saluted, swung around, clicked his heels, opened a cavernous mouth. "Patro-o-ol! . . . right form!"

The conference lasted well into the night and halfway through the following morning. During these argumentative hours various oddments of traffic, mostly vehicular, passed along the road, but nothing paused to view the monster spaceship, nobody approached for a friendly word with its crew. The strange inhabitants of this world seemed to be afflicted with a peculiar form of mental blindness, unable to see a thing until it was thrust into their faces and then surveying it squint-eyed.

One passer-by in midmorning was a truck whining on two dozen rubber balls and loaded with girls wearing colorful head-scarves. The girls were singing something about one little kiss before we part, dear. Half a dozen troops lounging near the gang-way came eagerly to life, waved, whistled and yoohooed. The effort was wasted, for the singing continued without break or pause and nobody waved back.

To add to the discomfiture of the love-hungry, Bidworthy stuck his head out of the lock and rasped, "If you monkeys are bursting with surplus energy, I can find a few jobs for you to do—nice dirty ones." He seared them one at a time before he withdrew.

Inside, the top brass sat around a horseshoe table in the chartroom near the bow and debated the situation. Most of them were content to repeat with extra emphasis what they had said the previous evening, there being no new points to bring up.

"Are you certain," the Earth Ambassador asked Captain Grayder, "that this planet has not been visited since the last emigration transport dumped the final load three hundred years back?"

"Positive, your Excellency. Any such visit would have been recorded."

"If made by an Earth ship. But what about others? I feel it in my bones that at sometime or other these people have fallen foul of one or more vessels calling unofficially and have been leery of spaceships ever since. Perhaps somebody got tough with them, tried to muscle in where he wasn't wanted. Or they've had to beat off a gang of pirates. Or they were swindled by some unscrupulous fleet of traders."

"Quite impossible, your Excellency," declared Grayder. "Emigration was so scattered over so large a number of worlds that even today every one of them is under-populated, only one-hundredth developed, and utterly unable to build spaceships of any kind, even rudimentary ones. Some may have the techniques but not the facilities, of which they need plenty."

"Yes, that's what I've always understood."

"All Blieder-drive vessels are built in the Sol system, registered as Earth ships and their whereabouts known. The only other ships in existence are eighty or ninety antiquated rocket jobs bought at scrap price by the Epsilon system for haulage work between their fourteen closely-planned planets. An old-fashioned rocket job couldn't reach this place in a hundred years."

"No, of course not."

"Unofficial boats capable of this range just don't exist," Grayder assured. "Neither do space buccaneers, for the same reason. A Blieder-job takes so much that a would-be pirate has to become a billionaire to become a pirate."

"Then," said the ambassador, heavily, "back we go to my original theory—that something peculiar to this world plus a lot of inbreeding has made them nutty."

"There's plenty to be said for that notion," put in Colonel Shelton. "You should have seen the coach load I looked over. There was a mortician wearing odd shoes, one brown, one yellow. And a moon-faced gump sporting a hat made from the skin of a barber's pole, all stripy. Only thing missing was his bubble pipe—and probably he'll be given that where he was going."

"Where was he going?"

"I don't know, your Excellency. They refused to say."

Giving him a satirical look, the ambassador remarked, "Well, that is a valuable addition to the sum total of our knowledge. Our minds are now enriched by the thought that an anonymous individual may be presented with a futile object for an indefinable purpose when he reaches his unknown destination."

Shelton subsided, wishing that he had never seen the fat man or, for that matter, the fat man's cockeyed world.

"Somewhere they've got a capital, a civic seat, a center of government wherein function the people who hold the strings," the ambassador asserted. "We've got to find that place before we can take over and reorganize on up-to-date lines whatever setup they've got. A capital is big by the standards of its own administrative area. It's never an ordinary, nondescript place. It has certain physical features lending it importance above the average. It should be easily visible from the air. We must make a search for it—in fact, that's what we ought to have done in the first place. Other planets' capital cities have been found without trouble. What's the hoodoo on this one?"

"See for yourself, your Excellency." Captain Grayder poked a couple of photographs across the table. "There are the two hemispheres as recorded by us when coming in. They reveal nothing resembling a superior city. There isn't even a town conspicuously larger than its fellows or possessing outstanding features setting it apart from the others."

"I don't place great faith in pictures, particularly when taken at long distance. The naked eye sees more. We have got four lifeboats capable of scouring the place from pole to pole. Why not use them?"

"Because, your Excellency, they were not designed for such a purpose."

"Does that matter so long as they get results?"

Grayder said, patiently, "They were designed to be launched in space and hit up forty thousand. They are ordinary, old-style rocket jobs, for emergencies only. You could not make efficient ground-survey at any speed in excess of four hundred miles per hour. Keep the boats down to that and you're trying to run them at landing-speed, muffling the tubes, balling up their efficiency, creating a terrible waste of fuel, and inviting a crash which you're likely to get before you're through."

"Then it's high time we had Blieder-drive lifeboats on Blieder-drive ships."

"I agree, your Excellency. But the smallest Blieder engine has an Earth mass of more than three hundred tons—far too much for little boats." Picking up the photographs, Grayder slid them into a drawer. "What we need is an ancient, propeller-driven airplane. They could do something we can't do—they could go slow."

"You might as well yearn for a bicycle," scoffed the ambassador, feeling thwarted.

"We have a bicycle," Grayder informed. "Tenth Engineer Harrison owns one."

"And he has brought it with him?"

"It goes everywhere with him. There is a rumor that he sleeps with it."

'A spaceman toting a bicycle!" The ambassador blew his nose with a loud honk. "I take it that he is thrilled by the sense of immense velocity it gives him, an ecstatic feeling of rushing headlong through space?"

"I wouldn't know, your Excellency."

"Hm-m-m! Bring this Harrison in to me. We'll set a nut to catch a nut."

Grayder blinked, went to the caller board, spoke over the ship's system. "Tenth Engineer Harrison wanted in the chartroom immediately."

Within ten minutes Harrison appeared. He had walked fast three-quarters of a mile from the Blieder room. He was thin and wiry, with dark, monkeylike eyes, and a pair of ears that cut out the pedaling with the wind behind him. The ambassador examined him curiously, much as a zoologist would inspect a pink giraffe.

"Mister, I understand that you possess a bicycle."

Becoming wary, Harrison said, "There's nothing against it in the regulations, sir, and therefore—"

"Damn the regulations!" The ambassador made an impatient gesture. "We're stalled in the middle of a crazy situation and we're turning to crazy methods to get moving."

"I see, sir."

"So I want you to do a job for me. Get out your bicycle, ride down to town, find the mayor, sheriff, grand panjandrum, supreme galootie, or whatever he's called, and tell him he's officially invited to evening dinner along with any other civic dignitaries he cares to bring and, of course, their wives."

"Very well, sir."

"Informal attire," added the ambassador.

Harrison jerked up one ear, drooped the other, and said, "Beg pardon, sir?"

"They can dress how they like."

"I get it. Do I go right now, sir?"

"At once. Return as quickly as you can and bring me the reply."

Saluting sloppily, Harrison went out. His Excellency found an easy-chair, reposed in it at full length and ignored the others' stares.

"As easy as that!" He pulled out a long cigar, carefully bit off its end. "If we can't touch their minds, we'll appeal to their bellies." He cocked a knowing eye at Grayder. "Captain, see that there is plenty to drink. Strong stuff. Venusian cognac or something equally potent. Give them an hour at a well-filled table and they'll talk plenty. We won't be able to shut them up all night." He lit the cigar, puffed luxuriously. "That is the tried and trusted technique of diplomacy—the insidious seduction of the distended gut. It always works—you'll see."

Pedaling briskly down the road, Tenth Engineer Harrison reached the first street on either side of which were small detached houses with neat gardens front and back. A plump, amiable looking woman was clipping a hedge halfway along. He pulled up near to her, politely touched his cap.

"'Scuse me, ma'am, I'm looking for the biggest man in town."

She half-turned, gave him no more than a casual glance, pointed her clipping-shears southward. "That'd be Jeff Baines. First on the right, second on the left. It's a small delicatessen."

"Thank you."

He moved on, hearing the *snip-snip* resume behind him. First on the right. He curved around a long, low, rubber-balled truck parked by the corner. Second on the left. Three children pointed at him and yelled shrill warnings that his back wheel was going round. He found the delicatessen, propped a pedal on the curb, gave his machine a reassuring pat before be went inside and had a look at Jeff.

There was plenty to see. Jeff had four chins, a twenty-two-inch neck, and a paunch that stuck out half a yard. An ordinary mortal could have got into either leg of his pants without taking off a diving suit. He weighed at least three hundred and undoubtedly *was* the biggest man in town.

"Wanting something?" inquired Jeff, lugging it up from far down.

"Not exactly." Tenth Engineer Harrison eyed the succulent food display, decided that anything unsold by nightfall was not given to the cats. "I'm looking for a certain person."

"Are you now? Usually I avoid that sort—but every man to his taste." He's the most certain man I know." He plucked at a fat lip while he mused a moment, then suggested, "Try Sid Wilcock over on Dane Avenue. He's the most certain man I know."

"I didn't mean it that way," said Harrison. "I meant I was searching for somebody particular."

"Then why the dub didn't you say so?" Jeff Baines worked over the new problem, finally offered, "Tod Green ought to fit that bill. You'll find him in the shoeshop end of this road. He's particular enough for anyone. He's downright finicky."

"You misunderstand me," Harrison explained. "I'm hunting a big-wig so's I can invite him to a feed."

Resting himself on a high stool which he overlapped by a foot all round, Jeff Baines eyed him peculiarly and said, "There's something lopsided about this. In the first place, you're going to use up a considerable slice of your life finding a guy who wears a wig, especially if you insist on a big one. And where's the point of dumping an ob on him just because he uses a bean-blanket?"

"Huh?"

"It's plain common sense to plant an ob where it will cancel an old one out, isn't it?"

"Is it?" Harrison let his mouth hang open while his mind moiled around the strange problem of how to plant an ob.

"So you don't know?" Jeff Baines massaged a plump chop and sighed. He pointed at the other's middle. "Is that a uniform you're wearing?"

"Yes."

"A genuine, pukka, dyed-in-the-wool uniform?"

"Of course."

"Ah!" said Jeff. "That's where you've fooled me—coming in by yourself, on your ownsome. If there had been a gang of you dressed identically the same, I'd have known at once it was a uniform. That's what uniform means—all alike. Doesn't it?"

"I suppose so," agreed Harrison, who had never given it a thought.

"So you're off that ship, I ought to have guessed it in the first place. I must be slow on the uptake today. But I didn't expect to see one, just one, messing around on a pedal contraption. It goes to show, doesn't it?"

"Yes," said Harrison, glancing around to make sure that no confederate had swiped his bicycle while he was detained in conversation. The machine was still there. "It goes to show."

"All right, let's have it—what have you come here for?"

"I've been trying to tell you all along. I've been sent to—"

"Been sent?" Jeff's eyes widened a little. "Mean to say you actually let yourself be *sent*?"

Harrison gaped at him. "Of course. Why not?"

"Oh, I get it now," said Jeff Baines, his puzzled features suddenly clearing. "You confuse me with the queer way you talk. You mean you planted an ob on someone?"

Desperately, Harrison said, "What's an ob?"

"He doesn't know," commented Jeff Baines, looking prayerfully at the ceiling. "He doesn't even know that!" He gave out a resigned sigh. "You hungry by any chance?"

"Going on that way."

"O.K. I could tell you what an ob is, but I'll do something better—I'll show you." Heaving himself off the stool, he waddled to a door at back. "Don't know why I should bother to try educate a uniform. It's just that I'm bored. C'mon, follow me."

Obediently, Harrison went behind the counter, paused to give his bicycle a reassuring nod, trailed the other through a passage and into a yard.

Jeff Baines pointed to a stack of cases. "Canned goods." He indicated an adjacent store. "Bust 'em open and pile the stuff in there. Stack the empties outside. Please yourself whether you do it or not. That's freedom, isn't it?" He lumbered back into the shop.

Left by himself, Harrison scratched his ears and thought it over. Somewhere, he felt, there was an obscure sort of gag. A candidate named Harrison was being tempted to qualify for his sucker certificate. But if the play was beneficial to its organizer it might be worth learning because the trick could then be passed on. One must speculate in order to accumulate.

So he dealt with the cases as required. It took him twenty minutes of brisk work, after which he returned to the shop.

"Now," explained Baines, "you've done something for me. That means you've planted an ob on me. I don't thank you for what you've done. There's no need to. All I have to do is get rid of the ob."

"Ob?"

"Obligation. Why use a long word when a short one is good enough? An obligation is an ob. I shift it this way: Seth Warburton, next door but one, has got half a dozen of my obs saddled on him. So I get rid of mine to you and relieve him of one of his to me by sending you around for a meal." He scribbled briefly on a slip of paper. "Give him this."

Harrison stared at it. In casual scrawl, it read, "Feed this bum. Jeff Baines."

Slightly dazed, he wandered out, stood by the bicycle and again eyed the paper. Bum, it said. He could think of several on the ship who would have exploded with wrath over that. His attention drifted to the second shop farther along. It had a window crammed with comestibles and two big words on the sign-strip above: *Seth's Gulper*.

Coming to a decision which was encouraged by his innards, he went into Seth's still holding the paper as if it were a death warrant. Inside there was a long counter, some steam and a clatter of crockery. He chose a seat at a marble-topped table occupied by a gray-eyed brunette.

"Do you mind?" he inquired politely, as he lowered himself into a chair.

"Mind what?" she examined his ears as if they were curious

phenomena. "Babies, dogs, aged relations or going out in the rain?"

"Do you mind me being here?"

"I can please myself whether or not I endure it. That's freedom, isn't it?"

"Yeah," said Harrison. "Sure it is." He fidgeted in his seat, feeling somehow that he'd made a move and promptly lost a pawn. He sought around for something else to say and at that point a thin-featured man in a white coat dumped before him a plate loaded with fried chicken and three kinds of unfamiliar vegetables.

The sight unnerved him. He couldn't remember how many years it was since he last saw fried chicken, nor how many months since he'd had vegetables in other than powder form.

"Well," said the waiter, mistaking his fascinated gaze upon the food. "Doesn't it suit you?"

"Yes." Harrison handed over the slip of paper. "You bet it does."

Glancing at the note, the other called to someone semivisible in the steam at one end of the counter, "You've killed another of Jeff's." He went away, tearing the slip into small pieces.

"That was a fast pass," commented the brunette, nodding at the loaded plate. "He dumps a feed-ob on you and you bounce it straight back, leaving all quits. I'll have to wash dishes to get rid of mine, or kill one Seth has got on somebody else."

"I stacked a load of canned stuff." Harrison picked up knife and fork, his mouth watering. There were no knives and forks on the ship. They weren't needed for powders and pills. "Don't give you any choice here, do they? You take what you get."

"Not if you've got an ob on Seth," she informed. "In that case, he's got to work it off best way he can. You should have put that to him instead of waiting for fate and complaining afterward."

"I'm not complaining."

"It's your right. That's freedom, isn't it?" She mused a bit, went on, "Isn't often I'm a plant ahead of Seth, but when I am I scream for iced pineapple and he comes running. When *he's* a plant ahead, *I* do the running." Her gray eyes narrowed in sudden suspicion, and she added, "You're listening like it's all new to you. Are you a stranger here?"

He nodded, his mouth full of chicken. A little later he managed, "I'm off that spaceship."

"Good grief!" She froze considerably. "An Antigand! I wouldn't have thought it. Why, you look almost human."

"I've long taken pride in that similarity," his wit rising along with his belly. He chewed, swallowed, looked around. The white-coated man came up. "What's to drink?" Harrison asked.

"Dith, double-dith, shemak or coffee."

"Coffee. Big and black."

"Shemak is better," advised the brunette as the waiter went away. "But why should I tell you?"

The coffee came in a pint-sized mug. Dumping it, the waiter said, "It's your choice seeing Seth's working one off. What'll you have for after—apple pie, yimpik delice, grated tarfelsoufers or canimelon in syrup?"

"Iced pineapple."

"Ugh!" The other blinked at Harrison, gave the brunette an accusing stare, went away and got it.

Harrison pushed it across. "Take the plunge and enjoy yourself."

"It's yours."

"Couldn't eat it if I tried." He dug up another load of chicken, stirred his coffee, began to feel at peace with the world. "Got as much as I can manage right here." He made an inviting motion with his fork. "G'wan, be greedy and forget about the waistline."

"No." Firmly she pushed the pineapple back at him. "If I got through that, I'd be loaded with an ob."

"So what?"

"I don't let strangers plant obs on me."

"Quite right, too. Very proper of you," approved Harrison. "Strangers often have strange notions."

"You've been around," she agreed. "Only I don't know what's strange about the notions."

"Dish washer!"

"Eh?"

"Cynic," he translated. "One washes dishes in a cynic." The pineapple got another pass in her direction. "If you feel I'll be dumping an ob which you'll have to pay off, you can do it in seemly manner right here. All I want is some information. Just tell me where I can put my finger on the ripest cheese in the locality."

"That's an easy one. Go round to Alec Peters' place, middle of Tenth Street." With that, she dug into the dish.

"Thanks. I was beginning to think everyone was dumb or afflicted with the funnies."

He carried on with his own meal, finished it, lay back expansively. Unaccustomed nourishment got his brain working a bit more dexterously, for after a minute an expression of deep suspicion clouded his face and he inquired, "Does this Peters run a cheese warehouse?"

"Of course." Emitting a sigh of pleasure, she put aside her empty dish.

He groaned low down, then informed, "I'm chasing the mayor."

"What is that?"

"Number one. The big boss. The sheriff, pohanko, or whatever you call him."

"I'm no wiser," she said, genuinely puzzled.

"The man who runs this town. The leading citizen."

"Make it a little clearer," she suggested, trying hard to help him. "Who or what should this citizen be leading?"

"You and Seth and everyone else." He waved a hand to encompass the entire burg.

Frowning, she said, "Leading us *where*?"

"Wherever you're going."

She gave up, beaten, and signed the white-coated waiter to come to her assistance.

"Matt, are we going any place?"

"How should I know?"

"Well, ask Seth then."

He went away, came back with, "Seth says he's going home at six o'clock and what's it to you?"

"Anyone leading him there?" she inquired.

"Don't be daft," Matt advised. "He knows his own way and he's cold sober."

Harrison chipped in with, "Look, I don't see why there should be so much difficulty about this. Just tell me where I can find an official, any official—the police chief, the city treasurer, the mortuary keeper or even a mere justice of the peace."

"What's an official?" asked Matt, openly puzzled.

"What's a justice of the peace?" added the brunette.

His mind side-slipped and did a couple of spins. It took him quite a while to reassemble his thoughts and try another tack.

"Supposing," he said to Matt, "this joint catches fire. What would you do?"

"Fan it to keep it going," responded Matt, fed up and making no effort to conceal the fact. He returned to the counter with the air of one who has no time to waste on half-wits.

"He'd put it out," informed the brunette. "What else would you expect him to do?"

"Supposing he couldn't?"

"He'd call in others to help him."

"And would they?"

"Of course," she assured, surveying him with pity. "They'd jump at the chance. They'd be planting a nice crop of strong obs, wouldn't they?"

"Yes, I guess so." He began to feel stalled, but made a last shot at the problem. "What if the fire were too big and fast for passers-by to tackle?"

"Seth would summon the fire squad."

Defeat receded. A touch of triumph replaced it.

"Ah, so there is a fire squad! That's what I meant by something official. That's what I've been after all along. Quick, tell me where I can find the depot."

"Bottom end of Twelfth. You can't miss it."

"Thanks." He got up in a hurry. "See you again sometime." Going out fast, he grabbed his bicycle, shoved off from the curb.

The fire depot was a big place holding four telescopic ladders, a spray tower and two multiple pumps, all motorized on the usual array of fat rubber balls. Inside, Harrison came face to face with a small man wearing immense plus fours.

"Looking for someone?" asked the small man.

"The fire chief," said Harrison

"Who's he?"

By this time prepared for that sort of thing, Harrison spoke as one would to a child. "See here, mister, this is a fire-fighting outfit. Somebody bosses it. Somebody organizes the shebang, fills forms, presses buttons, recommends promotions, kicks the shiftless, take all the credit, transfers all the blame and generally lords it around. He's the most important guy in the bunch and everybody knows it." His forefinger tapped the other's chest. "And he's the fella I'm going to talk to if it's the last thing I do."

"Nobody's any more important than anyone else. How can they be? I think you're crazy."

"You're welcome to think what you like, but I'm telling you that—"

A shrill bell clamored, cutting off the sentence. Twenty men appeared as if by magic, boarded a ladder and a multi-pump, roared into the street.

Squat, basin-shaped helmets were the crews' only item of common attire. Apart from these, they plumbed the depths of sartorial iniquity. The man with the plus fours, who had gained the pump in one bold leap, was whirled out standing between a fat firefighter wearing a rainbow-hued cummerbund and a thin one sporting a canary yellow kilt. A latecomer decorated with earrings shaped like little bells hotly pursued the pump, snatched at its tailboard, missed, disconsolately watched the outfit disappear from sight. He walked back, swinging his helmet in one hand.

"Just my lousy luck," he informed the gaping Harrison. "The sweetest call of the year. A big brewery. The sooner they get there the bigger the obs they'll plant on it." He licked his lips at the thought, sat on a coil of canvas hose. "Oh, well, maybe it's all for the good of my health."

"Tell me something," Harrison insisted. "How do you get a living?"

"There's a hell of a question. You can see for yourself. I'm on the fire squad."

"I know. What I mean is, who pays you?"

"Pays me?"

"Gives you money for all this."

"You talk kind of peculiar. What is money?"

Harrison rubbed his cranium to assist the circulation of blood through the brain. What is money? Yeouw. He tried another angle.

"Supposing your wife needs a new coat, how does she get it?"

"Goes to a store saddled with fireobs, of course. She kills one or two for them."

"But what if no clothing store has had a fire?"

"You're pretty ignorant, brother. Where in this world do you come from?" His ear bells swung as he studied the other a moment, then went on, "Almost all stores have fire-obs. If they've any sense, they allocate so many per month by way of insurance. They look ahead, just in case, see? They plant obs on us, in a way, so that when we rush to the rescue we've got to kill off a dollop of theirs before we can plant any new ones of our own. That stops us overdoing it and making hogs of ourselves. Sort of cuts down the stores' liabilities. It makes sense, doesn't it?"

"Maybe, but—"

"I get it now," interrupted the other, narrowing his eyes. "You're from that spaceship. You're an Antigand."

"I'm a Terran," said Harrison with suitable dignity. "What's more, all the folk who originally settled this planet were Terrans."

"You trying to teach me history?" He gave a harsh laugh. "You're wrong. There was a five per cent strain of Martian."

"Even the Martians are descended from Terran settlers," riposted Harrison.

"So what? That was a devil of a long time back. Things change, in case you haven't heard. We've no Terrans or Martians on this world—except for your crowd which has come in unasked. We're all Gands here. And you nosey pokes are Antigands."

"We aren't anti-anything that I know of. Where did you get that idea?"

"Myob!" said the other, suddenly determined to refuse further agreement. He tossed his helmet to one side, spat on the floor.

"Huh?"

"You heard me. Go trundle your scooter."

Harrison gave up and did just that. He pedaled gloomily back to the ship.

His Excellency pinned him with an authoritative optic. "So you're back at last, mister. How many are coming and at what time?"

"None, sir," said Harrison, feeling kind of feeble.

"None?" August eyebrows rose up. "Do you mean that they have refused my invitation?"

"No, sir."

The ambassador waited a moment, then said, "Come out with it, mister. Don't stand there gawping as if your push-and-puff contraption has just given birth to a roller skate. You say they haven't refused my invitation—but nobody is coming. What am I to make of that?"

"I didn't ask anyone."

"So you didn't ask!" Turning, he said to Grayder, Shelton and the others, "He didn't ask!" His attention came back to Harrison. "You forgot all about it, I presume? Intoxicated by liberty and the power of man over machine, you flashed around the town at nothing less than eighteen miles per hour, creating consternation among the citizenry, tossing their traffic laws into the ash can, putting persons in peril of their lives, not even troubling to ring your bell or—"

"I haven't got a bell, sir," denied Harrison, inwardly resenting this list of enormities. "I have a whistle operated by rotation of the rear wheel."

"There!" said the ambassador, like one abandoning all hope. He sat down, smacked his forehead several times. "Somebody's going to get a bubble-pipe." He pointed a tragic finger. "And *he's* got a whistle."

"I designed it myself, sir," Harrison told him, very informatively.

"I'm sure you did. I can imagine it. I would expect it of you." The ambassador got a fresh grip on himself. "Look, mister, tell me something in strict confidence, just between you and me." He leaned forward, put the question in a whisper that ricocheted seven times around the room. "*Why* didn't you ask anyone?"

"Couldn't find anyone to ask, sir. I did my level best but they didn't seem to know what I was talking about. Or they pretended they didn't."

"Humph!" His Excellency glanced out of the nearest port, consulted his wrist watch. "The light is fading already. Night will be upon us pretty soon. It's getting too late for further action." An annoyed grunt. "Another day gone to pot. Two days here and we're still fiddling around." His eye was jaundiced as it rested on Harrison. "All right, mister, we're wasting time anyway so we might as well hear your story in full. Tell us what happened in complete detail. That way, we may be able to dig some sense out of it."

Harrison told it, finishing, "It seemed to me, sir, that I could go on for weeks trying to argue it out with people whose brains are oriented east-west while mine points north-south. You can talk with them from now to doomsday, even get real friendly and enjoy the conversation—without either side knowing what the other is jawing about."

"So it seems," commented the ambassador, dryly. He turned to Captain Grayder. "You've been around a lot and seen many new worlds in your time. What do you make of all this twaddle, if anything?"

"A problem in semantics," said Grayder, who had been compelled by circumstances to study that subject. "One comes across it on almost every world that has been long out of touch, though usually it has not developed far enough to get really tough." He paused reminiscently. "First guy we met on Basileus said, cordially and in what he fondly imagined was perfect English, 'Joy you unboot now!' "

"Yeah? What did that mean?"

"Come inside, put on your slippers and be happy. In other words, welcome! It wasn't difficult to get, your Excellency, especially when you expect that sort of thing." Grayder cast a thoughtful glance at Harrison, went on, "Here, things appear to have developed to a greater extreme. The language remains fluent, retains enough surface similarities to conceal deeper changes, but meanings have been altered, concepts discarded, new ones substituted, thought-forms re-angled—and, of course, there is the inevitable impact of locally developed slang."

"Such a 'myob'," offered His Excellency. "Now there's a queer word without recognizable Earth root. I don't like the way they use it. Sounds downright insulting. Obviously it has some sort of connection with these obs they keep batting around. It means 'my obligation' or something like that, but the significance beats me."

"There is no connection, sir," Harrison contradicted. He hesitated, saw they were waiting for him, plunged boldly on. "Coming back I met the lady who directed me to Baines' place. She asked whether I'd found him and I said yes, thank you. We chatted a bit. I asked her what 'myob' meant. She said it was initial-slang." He stopped at that point.

"Keep going," advised the ambassador. "After some of the sulphurous comments I've heard coming out the Blieder-room ventilation-shaft, I can stomach anything. What does it mean?"

"M-y-o-b," informed Harrison, blinking. "Mind your own business."

"So!" His Excellency gained color. "So that's what they've been telling me all along?"

"I'm afraid so, sir."

"Evidently they've a lot to learn." His neck swelled with sudden undiplomatic fury, he smacked a large hand on the table and said, loudly, "And they are going to learn it!"

"Yes, sir" agreed Harrison, becoming more uneasy and wanting out. "May I go now and attend to my bicycle?"

"Get out of my sight!" shouted the ambassador. He made a couple of meaningless gestures, turned a florid face on Captain Grayder. "Bicycle! Does anyone on this vessel own a slingshot?"

"I doubt it, your Excellency, but I will make inquiries, if you wish."

"Don't be an imbecile," ordered His Excellency. "We have our full quota of hollow-heads already."

Postponed until early morning, the next conference was relatively short and sweet. His Excellency took a seat, harumphed, straightened his vest, frowned around the table.

"Let's have another look at what we've got. We know that this planet's mules call themselves Gands, don't take much interest in their Terran origin and insist on referring to us as Antigands. That implies an education and resultant outlook inimical to ourselves.

They've been trained from childhood to take it for granted that whenever we appeared upon the scene we would prove to be against whatever they are for."

"And we haven't the remotest notion of what they're for," put in Colonel Shelton, quite unnecessarily. But it served to show that he was among those present and paying attention.

"I am grimly aware of our ignorance in that respect," indorsed the ambassador. "They are maintaining a conspiracy of silence about their prime motivation. We've got to break it somehow." He cleared his throat, continued, "They have a peculiar nonmonetary economic system which, in my opinion, manages to function only because of large surpluses. It won't stand a day when overpopulation brings serious shortages. This economic set-up appears to be based on co-operative techniques, private enterprise, a kindergarten's honor system and plain unadorned gimme. That makes it a good deal crazier than that food-in-the-bank wackidoo they've got on the four outer planets of the Epsilon system."

"But it works," observed Grayder, pointedly.

"After a fashion. That flap-eared engineer's bicycle works—and so does he! A motorized job would save him a lot of sweat." Pleased with this analogy, the ambassador mused it a few seconds. "This local scheme of economics—if you can call it a scheme—almost certainly is the end result of the haphazard development of some hick eccentricity brought in by the original settlers. It is overdue for motorizing, so to speak. They know it but don't want it because mentally they're three hundred years behind the times. They're afraid of change, improvement, efficiency—like most backward peoples. Moreover, some of them have a vested interest in keeping things as they are." He sniffed loudly to express his contempt. "They are antagonistic toward us simply because they don't want to be disturbed."

His authoritative stare went round the table, daring one of them to remark that this might be as good a reason as any. They were too disciplined to fall into that trap. None offered comment, so he went on.

"In due time, after we've got a grip on affairs, we are going to have a long and tedious task on our hands. We'll have to overhaul their entire educational system with a view to eliminating anti-Terran prejudices and bringing them up to date on the facts of life. We've had to do that on several other planets, though not to anything like the same extent as will be necessary here."

"We'll cope," promised someone.

Ignoring him, the ambassador finished, "However, all of that is in the future. We've a problem to solve in the present. It's in our laps right now, namely, where are the reins of power and who's holding them? We've got to solve that before we can make progress. How're we going to do it?" He leaned back in his chair, added, "Get your wits working and let me have some bright suggestions."

Captain Grayder stood up, a big, leather-bound book in his hands. "Your Excellency, I don't think we need exercise our minds over new plans for making contact and gaining essential information. It looks as if the next move is going to be imposed upon us."

"How do you mean?"

"There are a good many old-timers in my crew. Space lawyers, every one of them." He tapped the book. "They know official Space Regulations as well as I do. Sometimes I think they know too much."

"And so—?"

Grayder opened the book. "Regulation 127 says that on a hostile world a crew serves on a war-footing until back in space. On a nonhostile world, they serve on a peace-footing."

"What of it?"

"Regulation 131A says that on a peace-footing, the crew—with the exception of a minimum number required to keep the vessel's essential services in trim—is entitled to land-leave immediately after unloading of cargo or within seventy-two Earth hours of arrival, whichever period is the shorter." He glanced up. "By midday the men will be all set for land-leave and itching to go. There will be ructions if they don't get it."

"Will there now?" said the ambassador, smiling lopsidedly. "What if I say this world is hostile? That'll pin their ears back, won't it?"

Impassively consulting his book, Grayder came with, "Regulation 148 says that a hostile world is defined as any planet that systematically opposes Empire citizens by force." He turned the next page. "For the purpose of these regulations, force is defined as any course of action calculated to inflict physical injury, whether or not said action succeeds in its intent."

"I don't agree." The ambassador registered a deep frown. "A world can be psychologically hostile without resorting to force. We've an example right here. It isn't a friendly world."

"There are no friendly worlds within the meaning of Space Regulations," Grayder informed. "Every planet falls into one of two classifications: hostile or nonhostile." He tapped the hard leather cover. "It's all in the book."

"We would be prize fools to let a mere book boss us around or allow the crew to boss us, either. Throw it out of the port. Stick it into the disintegrator. Get rid of it any way you like—and forget it."

"Begging your pardon, your Excellency, but I can't do that." Grayder opened the tome at the beginning. "Basic regulations 1A, 1B and 1C include the following: whether in space or in land, a vessel's personnel remain under direct command of its captain or his nominee who will guided entirely by Space Regulations and will be responsible only to the Space Committee situated upon Terra. The same applies to all troops, officials and civilian passengers aboard a space-traversing vessel, whether in flight or grounded—regardless of rank or authority they are subordinate to the captain or his nominee. A nominee is defined as a ship's officer performing the duties of an immediate superior when the latter is incapacitated or absent."

"All that means you are king of your castle," said the ambassador, none too pleased. "If we don't like it, we must get off the ship."

"With the greatest respect to yourself, I must agree that that is the position. I cannot help it—regulations are regulations. And the men know it!" Grayder dumped the book, poked it away from him. "Ten to one the men will wait to midday, pressing their pants, creaming their hair and so forth. They will then make approach to me in proper manner to which I cannot object. They will request the first mate to submit their leave-roster for my approval." He gave a deep sigh. "The worst I could do would be to quibble about certain names on the roster and switch a few men around—but I couldn't refuse leave to a full quota."

"Liberty to paint the town red might be a good thing after all," suggested Colonel Shelton, not averse to doing some painting himself. "A dump like this wakes up when the fleet's in port. We ought to get contacts by the dozens. That's what we want, isn't it?"

"We want to pin down this planet's leaders," the ambassador pointed out. "I can't see them powdering their faces, putting on their best hats and rushing out to invite the yoohoo from a bunch of hungry sailors." His plump features quirked. "We have got to find the needles in this haystack. That job won't be done by a gang of ratings on the rampage."

Grayder put in, "I'm inclined to agree with you, your excellency, but we'll have to take a chance on it. If the men want to go out, the circumstances deprive me of power to prevent them. Only one thing can give me the power."

"And what is that?"

"Evidence enabling me to define this world as hostile within the meaning of Space Regulations."

"Well, can't we arrange that somehow?" Without waiting for a reply, the ambassador continued, "Every crew has its incurable trouble-maker. Find yours, give him a double shot of Venusian cognac, tell him he's being granted immediate leave—but you doubt whether he'll enjoy it because these Gands view us as reasons why people dig up the drains. Then push him out of the lock. When he comes back with a black eye and a boastful story about the other fellow's condition, declare this world hostile." He waved an expressive hand. "And there you are. Physical violence. All according to the book."

"Regulation 148A, emphasizing that opposition by force must be systematic, warns that individual brawls may not be construed as evidence of hostility."

The ambassador turned an irate face upon the senior civil servant: "When you get back to Terra—if ever you do get back—you can tell the appropriate department how the space service is balled up, hamstrung, semi-paralyzed and generally handicapped by bureaucrats who write books."

Before the other could think up a reply complimentary to his kind without contradicting the ambassador, a knock came at the door. First Mate Morgan entered, saluted smartly, offered Captain Grayder a sheet of paper.

"First liberty roll, sir. Do you approve it?"

Four hundred twenty men hit the town in the early afternoon. They advanced upon it in the usual manner of men overdue for the bright lights, that is to say, eagerly, expectantly, in buddy-bunches of two, three, six or ten.

Gleed attached himself to Harrison. They were two odd rankers, Gleed being the only sergeant on leave, Harrison the only tenth engineer. They were also the only two fish out of water since both were in civilian clothes and Gleed missed his uniform while Harrison felt naked without his bicycle. These trifling features gave them enough in common to justify at least one day's companionship.

"This one's a honey," declared Gleed with immense enthusiasm. "I've been on a good many liberty jaunts in my time but this one's a honey. On all other trips the boys ran up against the same problem—what to use for money. They had to go forth like a battalion of Santa Clauses, loaded up with anything that might serve for barter. Almost always nine-tenths of it wasn't of any use and had to be carted back again."

"On Persephone," informed Harrison, "a long-shanked Milik offered me a twenty-karat, blue-tinted first-water diamond for my bike."

"Jeepers, didn't you take it?"

"What was the good? I'd have had to go back sixteen light-years for another one."

"You could do without a bike for a bit."

"I can do without a diamond. I can't ride around on a diamond."

"Neither can you sell a bicycle for the price of a sportster Moon-boat."

"Yes I can. I just told you this Milik offered me a rock like an egg."

"It's a crying shame. You'd have got two hundred to two fifty thousand credits for that blinder, if it was flawless." Sergeant Gleed smacked his lips at the thought of so much moola stacked on the head of a barrel. "Credits and plenty of them—that's what I love. And that's what makes this trip a honey. Every other time we've gone out, Grayder has first lectured us about creating a favorable impression, behaving in a space-manlike manner, and so forth. This time, he talks about credits."

"The ambassador put him up to that."

"I liked it, all the same," said Gleed. "Ten credits, a bottle of cognac and double liberty for every man who brings back to the ship an adult Gand, male or female, who is sociable and willing to talk."

"It won't be easily earned."

"One hundred credits to whoever gets the name and address of the town's chief civic dignitary. A thousand credits for the name and accurate location of the world's capitol city." He whistled happily, added, "Somebody's going to be in the dough and it won't be Bidworthy. He didn't come out of the hat. I know—I was holding it."

He ceased talking, turned to watch a tall, lithe blonde striding past. Harrison pulled at his arm.

"Here's Baines' place that I told you about. Let's go in."

"Oh, all right." Gleed followed with much reluctance, his gaze still down the street.

"Good afternoon," said Harrison, brightly.

"It ain't," contradicted Jeff Baines. "Trade's bad. There's a semi-final being played and it's taken half the town away. They'll think about their bellies after I've closed. Probably make a rush on me tomorrow and I won't be able to serve them fast enough."

"How can trade be bad if you don't take money even when it's good?" inquired Gleed, reasonably applying what information Harrison had given him.

Jeff's big moon eyes went over him slowly, then turned to Harrison. "So he's another bum off your boat. What's he talking about?"

"Money," said Harrison. It's stuff we use to simplify trade. It's printed stuff, like documentary obs of various sizes."

"That tells me a lot," Jeff Baines observed. "It tells me a crowd that has to make a printed record of every ob isn't to be trusted—because they don't even trust each other." Waddling to his high stool, he squatted on it. His breathing was labored and wheezy. "And that confirms what our schools have always taught—that an Antigand would swindle his widowed mother."

"Your schools have got it wrong." assured Harrison.

"Maybe they have." Jeff saw no need to argue the point. "But we'll play safe until we know different." He looked them over. "What do you two want, anyway?"

"Some advice," shoved in Gleed, quickly. "We're out on a spree. Where's the best places to go for food and fun?"

"How long you got?"

"Until nightfall tomorrow."

"No use." Jeff Baines shook his head sorrowfully. "It'd take you from now to then to plant enough obs to qualify for what's going. Besides, lots of folk wouldn't let any Antigand dump an ob on them. They're kind of particular, see?"

"Look," said Harrison. "Can't we get so much as a square meal?"

"Well, I dunno about that." Jeff thought it over, rubbing several chins. "You might manage so much—but I can't help you this time. There's nothing I want of you, so you can't use any obs I've got planted."

"Can you make any suggestions?"

"If you were local citizens, it'd be different. You could get all you want right now by taking on a load of obs to be killed sometime in the future as and when the chances come along. But I can't see anyone giving credit to Antigands who are here today and gone tomorrow."

"Not so much of the gone tomorrow talk," advised Gleed. "When an Imperial Ambassador is sent it means that Terrans will be here for keeps."

"Who says so?"

"The Empire says so. You're part of it, aren't you?"

"Nope," said Jeff. "We aren't part of anything and don't want to be, either. What's more, nobody's going to make us part of anything."

Gleed leaned on the counter and gazed absently at a large can of pork. "Seeing I'm out of uniform and not on parade, I sympathize with you though I still shouldn't say it. I wouldn't care to be taken over body and soul by other-world bureaucrats, myself. But you folk are going to have a tough time beating us off. That's the way it is."

"Not with what we've got," Jeff opined. He seemed mighty self-confident.

"You ain't got so much," scoffed Gleed, more in friendly criticism than open contempt. He turned to Harrison. "Have they?"

"It wouldn't appear so," ventured Harrison.

"Don't go by appearances," Jeff advised. "We've more than you'd care to guess at."

"Such as what?"

"Well, just for a start, we've got the mightiest weapon ever thought up by mind of man. We're Gands, see? So we don't need ships and guns and suchlike playthings. We've got something better. It's effective. There's no defense against it."

"I'd like to see it." Gleed challenged. Data on a new and exceptionally powerful weapon should be a good deal more valuable than the mayor's address. Grayder might be sufficiently overcome by the importance thereof to increase the take to five thousand credits. With a touch of sarcasm, he added, "But, of course, I can't expect you to give away secrets."

"There's nothing secret about it." said Jeff, very surprisingly. "You can have it for free any time you want. Any Gand would give it you for the asking. Like to know why?"

"You bet."

"Because it works one way only. We can use it against you—but you can't use it against us."

"There's no such thing. There's no weapon inventable which the other guy can't employ once he gets his hands on it and knows how to operate it."

"You sure?"

"Positive," said Gleed, with no hesitation whatever. "I've been in the space-service troops for twenty years and can't fiddle around that long without learning all about weapons from string bows to H-bombs. You're trying to kid me—and it won't work. A one-way weapon is impossible."

"Don't argue with him," Harrison suggested to Baines. "He'll never be convinced until he's shown."

"I can see that." Jeff Baines' face creased in a slow grin. "I told you that you could have our wonder-weapon for the asking. Why don't you ask?"

"All right, I'm asking." Gleed put it without much enthusiasm. A weapon that would be presented on request, without even the necessity of first planting a minor ob, couldn't be so mighty after all. His imaginary five thousand credits shrank to five, thence to none. "Hand it over and let me try it."

Swiveling heavily on his stool, Jeff reached to the wall, removed a small, shiny plaque from its hook, passed it across the counter.

"You may keep it," he informed. "And much good may it do you."

Gleed examined it, turning it over and over between his fingers. It was nothing more than an oblong strip of substance resembling ivory. One side was polished and bare. The other bore three letters deeply engraved in bold style:

F—I.W.

Glancing up, his features puzzled, he said, "Call this a weapon?"

"Certainly."

"Then I don't get it." He passed the plaque to Harrison. "Do you?"

"No." Harrison had a good look at it, spoke to Baines. "What does this F—I.W. mean?"

"Initial-slang," informed Baines. "Made correct by common usage. It has become a world-wide motto. You'll see it all over the place, if you haven't noticed it already."

"I have spotted it here and there but attached no importance to it and thought nothing of it. I remember now I've seen it inscribed in several places, including Seth's and the fire depot."

"It was on the sides of that bus we couldn't empty," added Gleed. "Didn't mean anything to me."

"It means plenty," said Jeff. *"Freedom—I Won't!"*

"That kills me," Gleed told him. "I'm stone dead already. I've dropped in my tracks." He watched Harrison thoughtfully pocketing the plaque. "A bit of abracadabra. What a weapon!"

"Ignorance is bliss," remarked Baines, strangely certain of himself. "Especially when you don't know that what you're playing with is the safety catch of something that goes bang."

"All right," challenged Gleed, taking him up on that. "Tell us how it works."

"I won't." The grin reappeared. Baines seemed highly satisfied about something.

"That's a fat lot of help." Gleed felt let down, especially over those momentarily hoped-for credits. "You boast about a one-way weapon, toss across a slip of stuff with three letters on it and then go dumb. Any guy can talk out the back of his neck. How about backing up your talk?"

"I won't," said Baines, his grin becoming broader than ever. He favored the onlooking Harrison with a fat, significant wink.

It made something spark vividly inside Harrison's mind. His jaw dropped, he took the plaque from his pocket, stared at it as if seeing it for the first time.

"Give it back to me," requested Baines, watching him.

Replacing it in his pocket, Harrison said very firmly, "I won't."

Baines chuckled. "Some folk catch on quicker than others."

Resenting that remark, Gleed held his hand out to Harrison. "Let's have another look at that thing."

"I won't," said Harrison, meeting him eye for eye.

"Hey, that's not the way—" Gleed's protesting voice died out. He stood there a moment, his optics slightly glassy while his brain performed several loops. Then, in hushed tones, he said, "Good grief!"

"Precisely," approved Baines. "Grief, and plenty of it. You were a bit slow on the uptake."

"Overcome by the flood of insubordinate ideas now pouring upon him, Gleed said hoarsely to Harrison. "Come on, let's get out of here. I gotta think. I gotta think some place quiet."

There was a tiny park with seats and lawns and flowers and a little fountain around which a small bunch of children were playing. Choosing a place facing a colorful carpet of exotic un-Terran blooms, they sat and brooded a while.

In due course, Gleed commented, "For one solitary guy it would be martyrdom, but for a whole world—" His voice drifted off, came back. "I've been taking this about as far as I can make it go and the results give me the leaping fantods."

Harrison said nothing.

"F'rinstance," Gleed continued, "supposing when I go back to he ship that snorting rhinoceros Bidworthy gives me an order. I give him the frozen wolliker and say, 'I won't!' He either drops dead or throws me in the clink."

"That would do you a lot of good."

"Wait a bit—I ain't finished. I'm in the clink, but the job still needs doing. So Bidworthy picks on someone else. The victim, being a soul-mate of mine, also donates the icy optic and says, 'I won't!' In the clink he goes and I've got company. Bidworthy tries again. And again. There's more of us warming the jug. It'll only hold twenty. So they take over the engineer's mess."

"Leave our mess out of this," Harrison requested.

"They take the mess," Gleed insisted, thoroughly determined to penalize the engineers. "Pretty soon it's crammed to the roof with I-won'ters. Bidworthy's still raking 'em in as fast as he can go—if by that time he hasn't burst a dozen blood vessels. So they take over the Blieder dormitories."

"Why keep picking on my crowd?"

"And pile them with bodies ceiling-high," Gleed said, getting sadistic pleasure out of the notion. "Until in the end Bidworthy has to get buckets and brushes and go down on his knees and do his own deck-scrubbing while Grayder, Shelton and the rest act as clink guards. By that time, His Loftiness the ambassador is in the galley busily cooking for you and me, assisted by a disconcerted bunch of yes-ing pen-pushers." He had another somewhat awed look at the picture and finished, "Holy smoke!"

A colored ball rolled his way, he stooped, picked it up and held on to it. Promptly a boy of about seven ran up, eyed him gravely.

"Give me my ball, please."

"I won't," said Gleed, his fingers firmly around it.

There was no protest, no anger, no tears. The child merely registered disappointment, turned to go away.

"Here you are, sonny." He tossed the ball.

"Thanks." Grabbing it, the other ran off.

Harrison said, "What if every living being in the Empire, all the way from Prometheus to Kaldor Four, across eighteen hundred light-years of space, gets an income-tax demand, tears it up and says, 'I won't!'? What happens then?"

"We'd need a second universe for a pen and a third one to provide the guards."

"There would be chaos," Harrison went on. He nodded toward the fountain and the children playing around it. "But it doesn't look like chaos here. Not to my eyes. So that means they don't overdo this blank refusal business. They apply it judiciously on some mutually recognized basis. What that basis might be beats me completely."

"Me, too."

An elderly man stopped near them, surveyed them hesitantly, decided to pick on a passing youth.

"Can you tell me where I can find the roller for Martinstown?"

"Other end of Eighth," informed the youth. "One every hour. They'll fix your manacles before they start."

"Manacles?" The oldster raised white eyebrows. "Whatever for?"

"That route runs past the spaceship. The Antigands may try to drag you out."

"Oh, yes, of course." He ambled on, glanced again at Gleed and Harrison, remarked in passing, "These Antigands—such a nuisance."

"Definitely," indorsed Gleed. "We keep telling them to get out and they keep on saying, 'We won't.'"

The old gentleman missed a step, recovered, gave him a peculiar look, continued on his way.

"One or two seem to cotton on to our accents," Harrison remarked. "Though nobody noticed mine when I was having that feed in Seth's."

Gleed perked up with sudden interest. "Where you've had one feed you can get another. C'mon, let's try. What have we got to lose?"

"Our patience," said Harrison. He stood up. "We'll pick on Seth. If he won't play, we'll have a try at someone else. And if nobody will play, we'll skin out fast before we starve to death."

"Which appears to be exactly what they want us to do," Gleed pointed out. He scowled to himself. "They'll get their way over my dead body."

"That's how," agreed Harrison. "Over your dead body."

Matt came up with a cloth over one arm. "I'm serving no Antigands."

"You served me last time," Harrison told him.

"That's as maybe. I didn't know you were off that ship. But I know now!" He flicked the cloth across one corner of the table. "No Antigands served by me."

"Is there any other place where we might get a meal?"

"Not unless somebody will let you plant an ob on them. They won't do that if they're wise to you, but there's a chance they might make the same mistake I did." Another flick across the corner. "I don't make them twice."

"You're making another right now," said Gleed, his voice tough and authoritative. He nudged Harrison. "Watch this!" His hand came out of a side pocket holding a tiny blaster. Pointing it at Matt's middle, he continued, "Ordinarily, I could get into trouble for this, if those on the ship were in the mood to make trouble.

But they aren't. They're soured up on you two-legged mules." He motioned the weapon. "Get walking and bring us two full plates."

"I won't," said Matt, firming his jaw and ignoring the gun.

Gleed thumbed the safety catch which moved with an audible click. "It's touchy now. It'd go off at a sneeze. Start moving."

"I won't," insisted Matt.

Gleed disgustedly shoved the weapon back into his pocket. "I was only kidding you. It isn't energized."

"Wouldn't have made the slightest difference if it had been," Matt assured. "I serve no Antigands, and that's that!"

"Suppose I'd gone haywire and blown you in half?"

"How could I have served you then?" he inquired. "A dead person is of no use to anyone. Time you Antigands learned a little logic."

With that parting shot he went away.

"He's got something there," observed Harrison, patently depressed. "What can you do with a waxie one? Nothing whatever! You'd have put him clean out of your own power."

"Don't know so much. A couple of stiffs lying around might sharpen the others. They'd get really eager."

"You're thinking of them in Terran terms," Harrison said. "It's a mistake. They're not Terrans, no matter where they came from originally. They're Gands." He mused a moment. "I've no notion of just what Gands are supposed to be but I reckon they're some kind of fanatics. Terra exported one-track-minders by the millions around the time of the Great Explosion. Look at that crazy crowd they've got on Hygeia."

"I was there once and I tried hard not to look," confessed Gleed, reminiscently. "Then I couldn't stop looking. Not so much as a fig leaf between the lot. They insisted that we were obscene because we wore clothes. So eventually we had to take them off. Know what I was wearing at the time we left?"

"A dignified poise," Harrison suggested.

"That and an identity disk, cupro-silver, official issue, spacemen, for the use of," Gleed informed. "Plus three wipes of greasepaint on my left arm to show I was a sergeant. I looked every inch a sergeant—like hell I did!"

"I know. I had a week in that place."

"We'd a rear admiral on board," Gleed went on. "As a fine physical specimen he resembled a pair of badly worn suspenders. He couldn't overawe anyone while in his birthday suit. Those Hygeians cited his deflation as proof that they'd got real democracy, as distinct from our fake version." He clucked his tongue. "I'm not so sure they're wrong."

"The creation of the Empire has created a queer proposition," Harrison meditated. "Namely, that Terra is always right while sixteen hundred and forty-two planets are invariably wrong."

"You're getting kind of seditious, aren't you?"

Harrison said nothing. Gleed glanced at him, found his attention elsewhere, followed his gaze to a brunette who had just entered.

"Nice," approved Gleed. "Not too young, not too old. Not too fat, not too thin. Just right."

"I know her." Harrison waved to attract her attention.

She tripped lightly across the room, sat at their table. Harrison made the introduction.

"Friend of mine. Sergeant Gleed."

"Arthur," corrected Gleed, eating her.

"Mine's Elissa," she told him. "What's a sergeant supposed to be?"

"A sort of over-above underthing," Gleed informed. "I pass along the telling to the guys who do the doing."

Her eyes widened. "Do you mean that people really allow themselves to be told?"

"Of course. Why not?"

"It sounds crazy to me." Her gaze shifted to Harrison. "I'll be ignorant of *your* name forever, I suppose?"

He hastened to repair the omission, adding, "But I don't like James. I prefer Jim."

"Then we'll let it be Jim." She examined the place, looking over the counter, the other tables. "Has Matt been to you two?"

"Yes. He refuses to serve us."

She shrugged warm shoulders. "It's his right. Everyone has the right to refuse. That's freedom, isn't it?"

"We call it mutiny," said Gleed.

"Don't be so childish," she reproved. She stood up, moved away. "You wait here. I'll go see Seth."

"I don't get this," admitted Gleed, when she had passed out of earshot. "According to that fat fella in the delicatessen, their technique is to give us the cold shoulder until we run away in a huff. But this dame acts friendly. She's . . . she's—" He stopped while he sought for a suitable word, found it and said, "She's un-Gandian."

"Not so," Harrison contradicted. "They've the right to say, 'I won't.' She's practising it."

"By gosh, yes! I hadn't thought of that. They can work it any way they like, and please themselves."

"Sure." He dropped his voice. "Here she comes."

Resuming her seat, she primped her hair, said, "Seth will serve us personally."

"Another traitor," remarked Gleed with a grin.

"On one condition," she went on. "You two must wait and have a talk with him before you leave."

"Cheap at the price," Harrison decided. A thought struck him and he asked, "Does this mean you'll have to kill several obs for all three of us?"

"Only one for myself."

"How come?"

"Seth's got ideas of his own. He doesn't feel happy about Antigands any more than does anyone else."

"And so?"

"But he's got the missionary instinct. He doesn't agree entirely with the idea of giving all Antigands the ghost-treatment. He thinks it should be reserved only for those too stubborn or stupid to be converted." She smiled at Gleed, making his top hairs quiver. "Seth thinks that any intelligent Antigand is a would-be Gand."

"What is a Gand, anyway?" asked Harrison.

"An inhabitant of this world, of course."

"I mean, where did they dig up the name?"

"From Gandhi," she said.

Harrison frowned in puzzlement. "Who the deuce was he?"

"An ancient Terran. The one who invented The Weapon."

"Never heard of him."

"That doesn't surprise me," she remarked.

"Doesn't it?" He felt a little irritated. "Let me tell you that these days we Terrans get as good an education as—"

"Calm down, Jim." She made it more soothing by pronouncing it "Jeem." "All I mean is that ten to one he's been blanked out of your history books. He might have given you unwanted ideas, see? You couldn't be expected to know what you've been deprived of the chance to learn."

"If you mean that Terran history is censored, I don't believe it," he asserted.

"It's your right to refuse to believe. That's freedom, isn't it?"

"Up to a point. A man has duties. He's no right to refuse those."

"No?" She raised tantalizing eyebrows, delicately curved. "Who defines those duties—himself, or somebody else?"

"His superiors, most times."

"No man is superior to another. No man has the right to define another man's duties." She paused, eyeing him speculatively. "If anyone on Terra exercises such idiotic power, it is only because idiots permit him. They fear freedom. They prefer to be told. They like being ordered around. What men!"

"I shouldn't listen to you," protested Gleed, chipping in. His leathery face was flushed. "You're as naughty as you're pretty."

"Afraid of your own thoughts?" she jibed, pointedly ignoring his compliment.

He went redder. "Not on your life. But I—" His voice tailed off as Seth arrived with three loaded plates and dumped them on the table.

"See you afterward," reminded Seth. He was medium-sized, with thin features and sharp, quick-moving eyes. "Got something to say to you."

Seth joined them shortly after the end of the meal. Taking a chair, he wiped condensed steam off his face, looked them over.

"How much do you two know?"

"Enough to argue about it," put in Elissa. "They are bothered about duties, who defines them, and who does them."

"With good reason," Harrison riposted. "You can't escape them yourselves."

"Meaning—?" asked Seth.

"This world runs on some strange system of swapping obligations. How will any person kill an ob unless he recognizes his duty to do so?"

"Duty has nothing to do with it," said Seth. "And if it did happen to be a matter of duty, every man would recognize it for himself. It would be outrageous impertinence for anyone else to remind him, unthinkable to anyone to order him."

"Some guys must make an easy living," interjected Gleed. "There's nothing to stop them that I can see." He studied Seth briefly before he continued, "How can you cope with a citizen who has no conscience?"

"Easy as pie."

Elissa suggested, "Tell them the story of Idle Jack."

"It's a kid's yarn," explained Seth. "All children here know it by heart. It's a classic fable like . . . like—" He screwed up his face. "I've lost track of the Terran tales the first comers brought with them."

"Red Riding Hood," offered Harrison.

"Yes." Seth seized on it gratefully. "Something like that one. A nursery story." He licked his lips, began, "This Idle Jack came from Terra as a baby, grew up in our new world, studied our economic system and thought he'd be mighty smart. He decided to become a scratcher."

"What's a scratcher?" inquired Gleed.

"One who lives by taking obs and does nothing about killing them or planting any of his own. One who accepts everything that's going and gives nothing in return."

"I get it. I've known one or two like that in my time."

"Up to age sixteen, Jack got away with it. He was a kid, see. All kids tend to scratch to a certain extent. We expect it and allow for it. After sixteen, he was soon in the soup."

"How?" urged Harrison, more interested than he was willing to show.

"He went around the town gathering obs by the armful. Meals, clothes and all sorts for the mere asking. It's not a big town. There are no big ones on this planet. They're just small enough for everyone to know everyone—and everyone does plenty of gabbing. Within three or four months the entire town knew Jack was a determined scratcher."

"Go on," said Harrison, getting impatient.

"Everything dried up," said Seth. "Wherever Jack went, people gave him the 'I won't'. That's freedom, isn't it? He got no meals, no clothes, no entertainment, no company, nothing! Soon he became terribly hungry, busted into someone's larder one night, gave himself the first square meal in a week."

"What did they do about that?"

"Nothing. Not a thing."

"That would encourage him some, wouldn't it?"

"How could it?" Seth asked, with a thin smile. "It did him no good. Next day his belly was empty again. He had to repeat the performance. And the next day. And the next. People became leery, locked up their stuff, kept watch on it. It became harder and harder. It became so unbearably hard that it was soon a lot easier to leave the town and try another. So Idle Jack went away."

"To do the same again," Harrison suggested.

"With the same results for the same reasons," retorted Seth. "On he went to a third town, a fourth, a fifth, a twentieth. He was stubborn enough to be witless.

"He was getting by," Harrison observed. "Taking all at the mere cost of moving around."

"No he wasn't. Our towns are small, like I said. And folk do plenty of visiting from one to another. In town number two Jack had to risk being seen and talked about by someone from town number one. As he went on it got a whole lot worse. In the twentieth he had to take a chance on gabby visitors from any of the previous nineteen." Seth leaned forward, said with emphasis, "He never got to town number twenty-eight."

"No?"

"He lasted two weeks in number twenty-five, eight days in twenty-six, one day in twenty-seven. That was almost the end."

"What did he do then?"

"Took to the open country, tried to live on roots and wild berries. Then he disappeared—until one day some walkers found him swinging from a tree. The body was emaciated and clad in rags. Loneliness and self-neglect had killed him. That was Idle Jack, the scratcher. He wasn't twenty years old."

"On Terra," informed Gleed, "we don't hang people merely for being lazy."

"Neither do we," said Seth. "We leave them free to go hang themselves." He eyed them shrewdly, went on, "But don't let it worry you. Nobody has been driven to such drastic measures in my lifetime, leastways, not that I've heard about. People honor their obs as a matter of economic necessity and not from any sense of duty. Nobody gives orders, nobody pushes anyone around, but there's a kind of compulsion built into the circumstances of this planet's way of living. People play square—or they suffer. Nobody enjoys suffering—not even a numbskull."

"Yes, I suppose you're right," put in Harrison, much exercised in mind.

"You bet I'm dead right!" Seth assured. "But what I wanted to talk to you two about is something more important. It's this: What's your real ambition in life?"

Without hesitation, Gleed said, "To ride the spaceways while remaining in one piece."

"Same here," Harrison contributed.

"I guessed that much. You'd not be in the space service if it wasn't your choice. But you can't remain in it forever. All good things come to an end. What then?"

Harrison fidgeted uneasily. "I don't care to think of it."

"Some day, you'll have to," Seth pointed out. "How much longer have you got?"

"Four and a half Earth years."

Seth's gaze turned to Gleed.

"Three Earth years."

"Not long," Seth commented. "I didn't expect you would have much time left. It's a safe bet that any ship penetrating this deeply into space has a crew composed mostly of old-timers getting near the end of their terms. The practiced hands get picked for the awkward jobs. By the day your boat lands again on Terra it will be the end of the trail for many of them, won't it?"

"It will for me," Gleed admitted, none too happy at the thought.

"Time—the older you get the faster it goes. Yet when you leave the service you'll still be comparatively young." He registered a faint, taunting smile. "I suppose you'll then obtain a private space vessel and continue roaming the cosmos on your own?"

"Impossible," declared Gleed. "The best a rich man can afford is a Moon-boat. Puttering to and fro between a satellite and its primary is no fun when you're used to Bliederzips across the galaxy. The smallest space-going craft is far beyond reach of the wealthiest. Only governments can afford them."

"By 'governments' you mean communities?"

"In a way."

"Well, then, what are you going to do when your space-roving days are over?"

"I'm not like Big Ears here." Gleed jerked an indicative thumb at Harrison. "I'm a trooper and not a technician. So my choice is limited by lack of qualifications." He rubbed his chin, looked wistful. "I was born and brought up on a farm. I still know a good deal about farming. So I'd like to get a small one of my own and settle down."

"Think you'll manage it?" asked Seth, watching him.

"On Falder or Hygeia or Norton's Pink Heaven or some other undeveloped planet. But not on Terra. My savings won't extend to that. I don't get half enough to meet Earth costs."

"Meaning you can't pile up enough obs?"

"I can't," agreed Gleed, lugubriously. "Not even if I saved until I'd got a white beard four feet long."

"So there's Terra's reward for a long spell of faithful service—forego your heart's desire or get out?"

"Shut up!"

"I won't," said Seth. He leaned nearer. "Why do you think two hundred thousand Gands came to this world, Doukhobors to Hygeia, Quakers to Centauri B, and all the others to their selected haunts? Because Terra's reward for good citizenship was the peremptory order to knuckle down or get out. So we got out."

"It was just as well, anyway," Elissa interjected. "According to our history books, Terra was badly overcrowded. We went away and relieved the pressure."

"That's beside the point," reproved Seth. He continued with Gleed. "You want a farm. It can't be on Terra much as you'd like it there. Terra says, 'No! Get out!' So it's got to be some place else." He waited for that to sink in, then, "Here, you can have one for the mere taking." He snapped his fingers. "Like that!"

"You can't kid me," said Gleed, wearing the expression of one eager to be kidded. "Where are the hidden strings?"

"On this planet, any plot of ground belongs to the person in possession, the one who is making use of it. Nobody disputes his claim so long as he continues to use it. All you need do is look around for a suitable piece of unused territory—of which there is plenty—and start using it. From that moment it's yours. Immediately you cease using it and walk out, it's anyone else's, for the taking."

"Zipping meteors!" Gleed was incredulous.

"Moreover, if you look around long enough and strike really lucky," Seth continued, "you might stake first claim to a farm someone else has abandoned because of death, illness, a desire to move elsewhere, a chance at something else he liked better, or any other excellent reason. In that case, you would walk into ground already part-prepared, with farmhouse, milking shed, barns and the rest. And it would be yours, all yours."

"What would I owe the previous occupant?" asked Gleed.

"Nothing. Not an ob. Why should you? If he isn't buried, he has got out for the sake of something else equally free. He can't have the benefit both ways, coming and going."

"It doesn't make sense to me. Somewhere there's a snag. Somewhere I've got to pour out hard cash or pile up obs."

"Of course you have. You start a farm. A handful of local folk help you build a house. They dump heavy obs on you. The carpenter wants farm produce for his family for the next couple of years. You give it, thus killing that ob. You continue giving it for a couple of extra years, thus planting an ob on *him*. First time you want fences mending, or some other suitable task doing, along he comes to kill *that* ob. And so with all the rest, including the people who supply your raw materials, your seeds and machinery, or do your trucking for you."

"They won't all want milk and potatoes," Gleed pointed out.

"Don't know what you mean by potatoes. Never heard of them."

"How can I square up with someone who may be getting all the farm produce he wants from elsewhere?"

"Easy," said Seth. "A tinsmith supplies you with several churns. He doesn't want food. He's getting all he needs from another source. His wife and three daughters are overweight and dieting. The mere thought of a load from your farm gives them the horrors."

"Well?"

"But this tinsmith's tailor, or his cobbler, have got obs on him which he hasn't had the chance to kill. So he transfers them to you. As soon as you're able, you give the tailor or cobbler what they need to satisfy the obs, thus doing the tinsmith's killing along with your own." He gave his usual half-smile, added, "And everyone is happy."

Gleed stewed it over, frowning while he did it. "You're tempting me. You shouldn't ought to. It's a criminal offense to try to divert a spaceman from his allegiance. It's sedition. Terra is tough with sedition."

"Tough my eye!" said Seth, sniffing contemptuously. "We've Gand laws here."

"All you have to do," suggested Elissa, sweetly persuasive, "is say to yourself that you've got to go back to the ship, that it's your duty to go back, that neither the ship nor Terra can get along without you." She tucked a curl away. "Then be a free individual and say, 'I won't!' "

"They'd skin me alive. Bidworthy would preside over the operation in person."

"I don't think so," Seth offered. "This Bidworthy—whom I presume to be anything but a jovial character—stands with you and the rest of your crew at the same junction. The road before him splits two ways. He's got to take one or the other and there's no third alternative. Sooner or later he'll be hell-bent for home, eating his top lip as he goes, or else he'll be running around in a truck delivering your milk—because, deep inside himself, that's what he's always wanted to do."

"You don't know him like I do," mourned Gleed. "He uses a lump of old iron for a soul."

"Funny," remarked Harrison, "I always thought of *you* that way—until today."

"I'm off duty,' said Gleed, as though that explained everything. "I can relax and let the ego zoom around outside of business hours." He stood up, firmed his jaw. "But I'm going back on duty. Right now!"

"You're not due before sundown tomorrow," Harrison protested.

"Maybe I'm not. But I'm going back all the same."

Elissa opened her mouth, closed it as Seth nudged her. They sat in silence and watched Gleed march determinedly out.

"It's a good sign," commented Seth, strangely self-assured. "He's been handed a wallop right where he's weakest." He chuckled low down, turned to Harrison. "What's *your* ultimate ambition?"

"Thanks for the meal. It was a good one and I needed it." Harrison stood up, manifestly embarrassed. He gestured toward the door. "I'm going to catch him up. If he's returning to the ship, I think I'll do likewise."

Again Seth nudged Elissa. They said nothing as Harrison made his way out, carefully closing the door behind him.

"Sheep," decided Elissa, disappointed for no obvious reason. "One follows another. Just like sheep."

"Not so," Seth contradicted. "They're humans animated by the same thoughts, the same emotions, as were our forefathers who had nothing sheeplike about them." Twisting round in his chair, he beckoned to Matt. "Bring us two shemaks." Then to Elissa. "My guess is that it won't pay that ship to hang around too long."

The battleship's caller-system bawled imperatively, "Fanshaw, Folsom, Fuller, Garson, Gleed, Gregory, Haines, Harrison, Hope—" and down through the alphabet.

A trickle of men flowed along the passages, catwalks and alleyways toward the fore chartroom. They gathered outside it in small clusters, chattering in undertones and sending odd scraps of conversation echoing down the corridor.

"Wouldn't say anything to us but, 'Myob!' Got sick and tired of it after a while."

"You ought to have split up, like we did. That show place on the outskirts didn't know what a Terran looks like. I just walked in and took a seat."

"Hear about Meakin? He mended a leaky roof, chose a bottle of double dith in payment and mopped the lot. He was dead flat when we found him. Had to be carried back."

"Some guys have all the luck. We got the brush-off wherever we showed our faces. It gets you down."

"You should have separated, like I said."

"Half the mess must be still lying in the gutter. They haven't turned up yet."

"Grayder will be hopping mad. He'd have stopped this morning's second quota if he'd known in time."

Every now and again First Mate Morgan stuck his head out of the chartroom door and uttered a name already voiced on the caller. Frequently there was no response.

"Harrison!" he yelled.

With a puzzled expression, Harrison went inside. Captain Grayder was there, seated behind a desk and gazing moodily at a list lying before him. Colonel Shelton was stiff and erect to one side, with

Major Hame slightly behind him. Both wore the pained expressions of those tolerating a bad smell while the plumber goes looking for the leak.

His Excellency was tramping steadily to and fro in front of the desk, muttering deep down in his chins. "Barely five days and already the rot has set in." He turned as Harrison entered, fired off sharply, "So it's you, mister. When did you return from leave?"

"The evening before last, sir."

"Ahead of time, eh? That's curious. Did you get a puncture or something?"

"No, sir. I didn't take my bicycle with me."

"Just as well," approved the ambassador. "If you had done so, you'd have been a thousand miles away by now and still pushing hard."

"Why, sir?"

"Why? He asks me why! That's precisely what I'd like to know—*why*?" He fumed a bit, then inquired, "Did you visit this town by yourself, or in company?"

"I went with Sergeant Gleed, sir."

"Call him," ordered the ambassador, looking at Morgan.

Opening the door, Morgan obediently shouted, "Gleed! Gleed!"

No answer.

He tried again, without result. They put it over the caller-system again. Sergeant Gleed refused to be among those present.

"Has he booked in?"

Grayder consulted his list. "In early. Twenty-four hours ahead of time. He may have sneaked out again with the second liberty quota this morning and omitted to book it. That's a double crime."

"If he's not on the ship, he's off the ship, crime or no crime."

"Yes, your Excellency." Captain Grayder registered slight weariness.

"GLEED!" howled Morgan, outside the door. A moment later he poked his head inside, said, "Your Excellency, one of the men says Sergeant Gleed is not on board because he saw him in town quite recently."

"Send him in." The ambassador made an impatient gesture at Harrison. "Stay where you are and keep those confounded ears from flapping. I've not finished with you yet."

A long, gangling grease-monkey came in, blinked around, a little awed by high brass.

"What do you know about Sergeant Gleed?" demanded the ambassador.

The other licked his lips, seemed sorry that he had mentioned the missing man. "It's like this, your honor, I—"

"Call me 'sir.'"

"Yes, sir." More disconcerted blinking. "I went out with the second party early this morning, came back a couple of hours ago because my stomach was acting up. On the way, I saw Sergeant Gleed and spoke to him."

"Where? When?"

"In town, sir. He was sitting in one of those big long-distance coaches. I thought it a bit queer."

"Get down to the roots, man! What did he tell you, if anything?"

"Not much, sir. He seemed pretty chipper about something. Mentioned a young widow struggling to look after two hundred acres. Someone had told him about her and he thought he'd take a peek." He hesitated, backed away a couple of paces, added, "He also said I'd see him in irons or never."

"One of *your* men," said the ambassador to Colonel Shelton. "A trooper, allegedly well-disciplined. One with long service, three stripes, and a pension to lose." His attention returned to the informant. "Did he say exactly where he was going?"

"No, sir. I asked him, but he just grinned and said, 'Myob!' So I came back to the ship."

"All right. You may go." His Excellency watched the other depart, then continued with Harrison. "You were with that first quota."

"Yes, sir."

"Let me tell you something, mister. Four hundred twenty men went out. Only two hundred have returned. Forty of those were in various stages of alcoholic turpitude. Ten of them are in the clink yelling, 'I won't!' in steady chorus. Doubtless they'll go on yelling until they've sobered up."

He stared at Harrison as if that worthy were personally responsible, then went on, "There's something paradoxical about this. I can understand the drunks. There are always a few individuals who blow their tops first day on land. But of the two hundred who have condescended to come back, about half returned before time, the same as you did. Their reasons were identical—the town was unfriendly, everyone treated them like ghosts until they'd had enough."

Harrison made no comment.

"So we have two diametrically opposed reactions," the ambassador complained. "One gang of men say the place stinks so much that they'd rather be back on the ship. Another gang finds it so hospitable that either they get filled to the gills on some stuff called double dith, or they stay sober and desert the service. I want an explanation. There's got to be one somewhere. You've been twice in this town. What can you tell us?"

Carefully, Harrison said, "It all depends on whether or not you're spotted as a Terran. Also on whether you meet Gands who'd rather convert you than give you the brush-off." He pondered a moment, finished, "Uniforms are a give-away."

"You mean they're allergic to uniforms?"

"More or less, sir."

"Any idea why?"

"Couldn't say for certain, sir. I don't know enough about them yet. As a guess, I think they may have been taught to associate uniforms with the Terran regime from which their ancestors escaped."

"Escaped nothing!" scoffed the ambassador. "They grabbed the benefit of Terran inventions, Terran techniques and Terran manufacturing ability to go some place where they'd have more elbow room." He gave Harrison the sour eye. "Don't any of them wear uniforms?"

"Not that I could recognize as such. They seem to take pleasure in expressing their individual personalities by wearing anything they fancy, from pigtails to pink boots. Oddity in attire is the norm among the Gands. Uniformity is the real oddity—they think it's submissive and degrading."

"You refer to them as Gands. Where did they dig up that name?"

Harrison told him, thinking back to Elissa as she explained it. In his mind's eye he could see her now. And Seth's place with the tables set and steam rising behind the counter and mouth-watering smells oozing from the background. Now that he came to visualize the scene again, it appeared to embody an elusive but essential something that the ship had never possessed.

"And this person," he concluded, "invented what they call The Weapon."

"Hm-m-m! And they assert he was a Terran? What does he look like? Did you see a photograph or a statue?"

"They don't erect statues, sir. They say no person is more important than another."

"Bunkum!" snapped the ambassador, instinctively rejecting that viewpoint. "Did it occur to you to ask at what period in history this wonderful weapon was tried out?"

"No, sir," Harrison confessed. "I didn't think it important."

"You wouldn't. Some of you men are too slow to catch a Callistrian sloth wandering in its sleep. I don't criticize your abilities as spacemen, but as intelligence-agents you're a dead loss."

"I'm sorry, sir," said Harrison.

Sorry? You louse! whispered something deep within his own mind. *Why should you be sorry? He's only a pompous fat man who couldn't kill an ob if he tried. He's no better than you. Those raw boys prancing around on Hygeia would maintain that he's not as good as you because he's got a pot belly. Yet you keep looking at his pot belly and saying, "Sir" and, "I'm sorry". If he tried to ride your bike, he'd fall off before he'd gone ten yards. Go spit in his eye and say, "I won't". You're not scared, are you?*

"No!" announced Harrison, loudly and firmly.

Captain Grayder glanced up. "If you're going to start answering questions before they've been asked, you'd better see the medic. Or have we a telepath on board?"

"I was thinking," Harrison explained.

"I approve of that," put in His Excellency. He lugged a couple of huge tomes out of the wall-shelves, began to thumb rapidly through them. "Do plenty of thinking whenever you've the chance and it will become a habit. It will get easier and easier as time rolls on. In fact, a day may come when it can be done without pain."

He shoved the books back, pulled out two more, spoke to Major Hame who happened to be at his elbow. "Don't pose there glassy-eyed like a relic propped up in a military museum. Give me a hand with this mountain of knowledge. I want Gandhi, anywhere from three hundred to a thousand Earth-years ago."

Hame came to life, started dragging out books. So did Colonel Shelton. Captain Grayder remained at his desk and continued to mourn the missing.

"Ah, here it is, four-seventy years back." His Excellency ran a plump finger along the printed lines. "Gandhi, sometimes called Bapu, or Father. Citizen of Hindi. Politico-philosopher. Opposed authority by means of an ingenious system called civil disobedience. Last remnants disappeared with the Great Explosion, but may still persist on some planet out of contact."

"Evidently it does," commented Grayder, his voice dry.

"Civil disobedience," repeated the ambassador, screwing up his eyes. He had the air of one trying to study something which was topsy-turvy. "They can't make *that* a social basis. It just won't work."

"It does work," asserted Harrison, forgetting to put in the "sir".

"Are you contradicting me, mister?"

"I'm stating a fact."

"Your Excellency," Grayder began, "I suggest—"

"Leave this to me." His color deepening, the ambassador waved him off. His gaze remained angrily on Harrison. "You're very far from being an expert on socio-economic problems. Get that into your head, mister. Anyone of your caliber can be fooled by superficial appearances."

"It works," persisted Harrison, wondering where his own stubbornness was coming from.

"So does your tomfool bicycle. You've a bicycle mentality."

Something snapped, and a voice remarkably like his own said, "Nuts!" Astounded by this phenomenon, Harrison waggled his ears.

"What was that, mister?"

"Nuts!" he repeated, feeling that what has been done can't be undone.

Beating the purpling ambassador to the draw, Captain Grayder stood up and exercised his own authority.

"Regardless of further leave-quotas, if any, you are confined to the ship until further notice. Now get out!"

He went out, his mind in a whirl but his soul strangely satisfied. Outside, First Mate Morgan glowered at him.

"How long d'you think it's going to take me to work through this list of names when guys like you squat in there for a week?" He grunted with ire, cupped hands round his mouth and bellowed, "Hope! Hope!"

No reply.

"Hope's been abandoned," remarked a wit.

"That's funny," sneered Morgan. "Look at me shaking all over." He cupped again, tried the next name. "Hyland! Hyland!"

No response.

Four more days, long, tedious, dragging ones. That made nine in all since the battleship formed the rut in which it was still sitting.

There was trouble on board. The third and fourth leave-quotas, put off repeatedly, were becoming impatient, irritable.

"Morgan showed him the third roster again this morning. Same result. Grayder admitted this world can't be defined as hostile and that we're entitled to run free."

"Well, why the hell doesn't he keep to the book? The Space Commission could crucify him for disregarding it."

"Same excuse. He says he's not denying leave, he's merely postponing it. That's a crafty evasion, isn't it? He says he'll grant it immediately the missing men come back."

"That might be never. Damn him, he's using them as an excuse to gyp me out of my time."

It was a strong and legitimate complaint. Weeks, months, years of close confinement in a constantly trembling bottle, no matter how large, demands ultimate release if only for a comparatively brief period. Men need fresh air, the good earth, the broad, clear-cut horizon, bulkfood, femininity, new faces.

"He *would* ram home the stopper just when we've learned the best way to get around. Civilian clothes and act like Gands, that's the secret. Even the first-quota boys are ready for another try."

"Grayder daren't risk it. He's lost too many already. One more quota cut in half and he won't have enough crew to take off and get back. We'd be stuck here for keeps. How'd you like that?"

"I wouldn't cry about it."

"He could train the bureaucrats. Time those guys did some honest work."

"It'd take three years. That's how long it took to train you, wasn't it?"

Harrison came along holding a small envelope. Three of them picked on him at sight.

"Look who sassed Hizonner and got confined to ship—same as us!"

"That's what I like about it," Harrison observed. "Better to get fastened down for something than for nothing."

"It won't be long, you'll see! We're not going to hang around bellyaching for ever. Mighty soon we'll *do* something."

"Such as what?"

"We're thinking it over," evaded the other, not liking to be taken up so fast. He noticed the envelope. "What have you got there? The day's mail?"

"Exactly that," Harrison agreed.

"Have it your own way. I wasn't being nosey. I thought maybe you'd got some more snafu. You engineers usually pick up that paper-stuff first."

"It *is* mail," said Harrison.

"G'wan, nobody has letters in this neck of the cosmos."

"I do."

"How did you get it?"

"Worrall brought it from town an hour back. Friend of mine gave him dinner, let him bring the letter to kill the ob." He pulled a large ear. "Influence, that's what you boys need."

Registering annoyance, one demanded, "What's Worrall doing off the boat? Is he privileged?"

"Sort of. He's married, with three kids."

"So what?"

"The ambassador figures that some people can be trusted more than others. They're not so likely to disappear, having too much to lose. So a few have been sorted out and sent into town to seek information about the missing men."

"They found out anything?"

"Not much. Worrall says it's a waste of time. He found a few of our men here and there, tried to persuade them to return, but each said, 'I won't'. The Gands all said, 'Myob!' And that's that."

"There must be something in it," decided one of them, thoughtfully. "I'd like to go see for myself."

"That's what Grayder's afraid of."

"We'll give more than that to worry about if he doesn't become reasonable soon. Our patience is evaporating."

"Mutinous talk," Harrison reproved. He shook his head, looked sad. "You shock me."

He continued along the corridor, reached his own cabin, eyed the envelope. The writing inside might be feminine. He hoped so. He tore it open and had a look. It wasn't.

Signed by Gleed, the missive read, "Never mind where I am or what I'm doing—this might get into the wrong hands. All I'll tell you is that I'll be fixed up topnotch providing I wait a decent interval to improve acquaintance. The rest of this concerns *you*."

"Huh?" He leaned back on his bunk, held the letter nearer the light.

"I found a little fat guy running an empty shop. He just sits there, waiting. Next, I learn that he's established possession by occupation. He's doing it on behalf of a factory that makes two-ball rollers—those fan-driven cycles. They want someone to operate the place as a local roller sales and service depot. The little fat man has had four applications to date, but none with any engineering ability. The one who eventually gets this place will plant a functional-ob on the town, whatever that means. Anyway, this joint is yours for the taking. Don't be stupid. Jump in—the water's fine."

"Zipping meteors!" said Harrison. His eyes traveled on to the bottom.

"P.S. Seth will give you the address. P.P.S. This burg is your brunette's home town and she's thinking of coming back. She wants to live near her sister—and so do I. Said sister is a honey!"

He stirred restlessly, read it through a second time, got up and paced around his tiny cabin. There were twelve hundred occupied worlds within the scope of the Empire. He'd seen about one-tenth of them. No spaceman could live long enough to get a look at the lot. The service was divided into cosmic groups, each dealing with its own sector.

Except by hearsay, of which there was plenty and most of it highly colored, he would never know what heavens or pseudo-heavens existed in other sectors. In any case, it would be a blind gamble to pick an unfamiliar world for landbound life on someone else's recommendation. Not all think alike, or have the same tastes. One man's meat may be another's man's poison.

The choice for retirement—which was the unlovely name for beginning another, different but vigorous life—was high-priced Terra or some more desirable planet in his own sector. There was the Epsilon group, fourteen of them, all attractive providing you could suffer the gravity and endure lumbering around like a tired elephant. There was Norton's Pink Heaven if, for the sake of getting by in peace, you could pander to Septimus Norton's rajah-complex and put up with his delusions of grandeur.

Up on the edge of the Milky Way was a matriarchy run by blonde Amazons, and a world of wizards, and a Pentecostal planet, and a globe where semisentient vegetables cultivated themselves under the direction of human masters; all scattered across forty light-years of space but readily accessible by Blieder-drive.

There were more than a hundred known to him by personal experience, though merely a tithe of the whole. All offered life and that company which is the essence of life. But this world, Gand, had something the others lacked. It had the quality of being present. It was part of the existing environment from which he drew data on which to build his decisions. The others were not. They lost virtue by being absent and faraway.

Inobtrusively, he made his way to the Blieder-room lockers, spent an hour cleaning and oiling his bicycle. Twilight was approaching when he returned. Taking a thin plaque from his pocket, he hung it on the wall, lay on his bunk and stared at it.

F—I.W.

The caller-system clicked, cleared its throat, announced, "All personnel will stand by for general instructions at eight hours tomorrow."

"I won't," said Harrison. He closed his eyes.

Seven-twenty in the morning, but nobody thought it early. There is little sense of earliness or lateness among space-roamers—to regain it they have to be landbound a month, watching a sun rise and set.

The chartroom was empty but there was much activity in the control cabin. Grayder was there with Shelton, Hame, Navigators Adamson, Werth and Yates and, of course, His Excellency.

"I never thought the day would come," groused the latter, frowning at the star map over which the navigators pored. "Less than a couple of weeks, and we get out, admitting defeat."

"With all respect, your Excellency, it doesn't look that way to me," said Captain Grayder. "One can be defeated only by enemies. These people are not enemies. That's precisely where they've got us by the short hairs. They're not definable as hostile."

'That may be. I still say it's defeat. What else could you call it?"

"We've been outwitted by awkward relations. There's not much we can do about it. A man doesn't beat up his nieces and nephews merely because they won't speak to him."

"That's your viewpoint as a ship's commander. You're confronted by a situation that requires you to go back to base and report. It's routine. The whole service is hidebound with routine." The ambassador again eyed the star map as if he found it offensive. "My own status is different. If I get out, it's a diplomatic defeat, an insult to the dignity and prestige of Terra. I'm far from sure that I ought to go. It might be better if I stayed put—though that would give them the chance to offer further insults."

"I would not presume to advise you what to do for the best," Grayder said. "All I know is this: we carry troops and armaments for any policing or protective purposes that might be found necessary here. But I can't use them offensively against these Gands because they've provided no pretext and because, in any case, our full strength isn't enough to crush twelve millions of them. We need an armada for that. We'd be fighting at the extreme of our reach—and the reward of victory would be a useless world."

"Don't remind me. I've stewed it until I'm sick of it."

Grayder shrugged. He was a man of action so long as it was action in space. Planetary shenanigans were not properly his pigeon. Now that the decisive moment was drawing near, when he would be back in his own attenuated element, he was becoming phlegmatic. To him, Gand was a visit among a hundred such, with plenty more to come.

"Your Excellency, if you're in serious doubt whether to remain or come with us, I'd be favored if you'd reach a decision fairly soon. Morgan has given me the tip that if I haven't approved the third leave-quota by ten o'clock the men are going to take matters into their own hands and walk off."

"That would get them into trouble of a really hot kind, wouldn't it?"

"Some," agreed Captain Grayder, "but not so hot. They intend to turn my own quibbling against me. Since I have not officially forbidden leave, a walk-out won't be mutiny. I've merely been postponing leave. They could plead before the Space Commission that I've deliberately ignored regulations. They might get away with it if the members were in the mood to assert their authority."

"The Commission ought to be taken on a few long flights," opined His Excellency. "They'd discover some things they'll never learn behind a desk." He eyed the other in mock hopefulness. "Any chance of accidentally dropping our cargo of bureaucrats overboard on the way back? A misfortune like that might benefit the spaceways, if not humanity."

"That idea strikes me as Gandish," observed Grayder.

"They wouldn't think of it. Their technique is to say no, no, a thousand times no. That's all—but judging by what has happened here, it is enough." The ambassador pondered his predicament, reached a decision. "I'm coming with you. It goes against the grain because it smacks of surrender. To stay would be a defiant gesture, but I've got to face the fact that it won't serve any useful purpose at the present stage."

"Very well, your Excellency." Grayder went to a port, looked through it toward the town. "I'm down about four hundred men. Some of them have deserted, for keeps. The rest will come back if I wait long enough. They've struck lucky, got their legs under somebody's table and gone A.W.O.L. and they're likely to extend their time for as long as the fun lasts on the principle that they may as well be hung for sheep as lambs. I get that sort of trouble on every long trip. It's not so bad on short ones." A pause while moodily he surveyed a terrain bare of returning prodigals. "But we can't wait for them. Not here."

"No, I reckon not."

"If we hang around any longer, we're going to lose another hundred or two. There won't be enough skilled men to take the boat up. Only way I can beat them to the draw is to give the order to prepare for takeoff. They all come under flight regulations from that moment." He registered a lopsided smile. "That will give the space lawyers something to think about!"

"As soon as you like," approved the ambassador. He joined the other at the port, studied the distant road, watched three Gand coaches whirl along it without stopping. He frowned, still upset by the type of mind which insists on pretending that a mountain isn't there. His attention shifted sidewise, toward the tail-end. He stiffened and said, "What are those men doing outside?"

Shooting a swift glance in the same direction, Grayder grabbed the caller-mike and rapped, "All personnel will prepare for take-off at once!" Juggling a couple of switches, he changed lines, said, "Who is that? Sergeant Major Bidworthy? Look, Sergeant Major, there are half a dozen men beyond the midship lock. Get them in immediately—we're lifting as soon as everything's ready."

The fore and aft gangways had been rolled into their stowage spaces long before. Some fast-thinking quartermaster prevented further escapes by operating the midship ladder-wind, thus trapping Bidworthy along with more would-be sinners.

Finding himself stalled, Bidworthy stood in the rim of the lock and glared at those outside. His mustache not only bristled, but quivered. Five of the offenders had been members of the first leave-quota. One of them was a trooper. That got his rag out, a trooper. The sixth was Harrison, complete with bicycle polished and shining.

Searing the lot of them, the trooper in particular, Bidworthy rasped, "Get back on board. No arguments. No funny business. We're taking off."

"Hear that?" asked one, nudging the nearest. "Get back on board. If you can't jump thirty feet, you'd better flap your arms and fly."

"No sauce from you," roared Bidworthy. "I've got my orders."

"He takes orders," remarked the trooper. "At his age."

"Can't understand it," commented another, shaking a sorrowful head.

Bidworthy scrabbled the lock's smooth rim in vain search of something to grasp. A ridge, a knob, a projection of some sort was needed to take the strain.

"I warn you men that if you try me too—"

"Save your breath, Biddy," interjected the trooper. "From now on, I'm a Gand." With that, he turned and walked rapidly toward the road, four following.

Getting astride his bike, Harrison put a foot on a pedal. His back tire promptly sank with a loud *whee-e-e*.

"Come back!" howled Bidworthy at the retreating five. He made extravagant motions, tried to tear the ladder from its automatic grips. A siren keened thinly inside the vessel. That upped his agitation by several ergs.

"Hear that?" With vein-pulsing ire, he watched Harrison tighten the rear valve and apply his hand pump. "We're about to lift. For the last time—"

Again the siren, this time in a quick series of shrill toots. Bidworthy jumped backward as the seal came down. The lock closed. Harrison again mounted his machine, settled a foot on a pedal but remained watching.

The metal monster shivered from nose to tail then rose slowly and in utter silence. There was stately magnificence in the ascent of such enormous bulk. It increased its rate of climb gradually, went faster, faster, became a toy, a dot and finally disappeared.

For just a moment, Harrison felt a touch of doubt, a hint of regret. It soon passed away. He glanced toward the road.

The five self-elected Gands had thumbed a coach which was picking them up. That was co-operation apparently precipitated by the ship's disappearance. Quick on the uptake, these people. He saw it move off on huge rubber balls, bearing the five with it. A fan-cycle raced in the opposite direction, hummed into the distance.

"Your brunette," Gleed had described her. What gave him that idea? Had she made some remark which he'd construed as complimentary because it made no reference to outsize ears?

He had a last look around. The earth to his left bore a great curved rut one mile long by twelve feet deep. Two thousand Terrans had been there.

Then about eighteen hundred.

Then sixteen hundred.

Less five.

"One left—me!" he said to himself.

Giving a fatalistic shrug, he put the pressure on and rode to town.

And then there were none.

BABY IS THREE

by Theodore Sturgeon

I finally got in to see this Stern. He wasn't an old man at all. He looked up from his desk, flicked his eyes over me once, and picked up a pencil. "Sit over there, Sonny."

I stood where I was until he looked up again. Then I said, "Look, if a midget walks in here, what do you say—sit over there, Shorty?"

He put the pencil down again and stood up. He smiled. His smile was as quick and sharp as his eyes. "I was wrong," he said, "but how am I supposed to know you don't want to be called Sonny?"

That was better, but I was still mad. "I'm fifteen and I don't have to like it. Don't rub my nose in it."

He smiled again and said okay, and I went and sat down.

"What's your name?"

"Gerard."

"First or last?"

"Both," I said.

"Is that the truth?"

I said, "No. And don't ask me where I live either."

He put down his pencil. "We're not going to get very far this way."

"That's up to you. What are you worried about? I got feelings of hostility? Well, sure I have. I got lots more things than that wrong with me or I wouldn't be here. Are you going to let that stop you?"

"Well, no, but—"

"So what else is bothering you? How you're going to get paid?" I took out a thousand-dollar bill and laid it on the desk. "That's so you won't have to bill me. *You* keep track of it. Tell me when it's used up and I'll give you more. So you don't need my address. Wait," I said, when he reached toward the money. "Let it lay there. I want to be sure you and I are going to get along."

He folded his hands. "I don't do business this way, Son—I mean, Gerard."

"Gerry," I told him. "You do, if you do business with me."

"You make things difficult, don't you? Where did you get a thousand dollars?"

"I won a contest. Twenty-five words or less about how much fun it is to do my daintier underthings with Sudso." I leaned forward. "This time it's the truth."

"All right," he said.

I was surprised. I think he knew it, but he didn't say anything more. Just waited for me to go ahead.

"Before we start—if we start," I said, "I got to know something. The things I say to you—what comes out while you're working on me—is that just between us, like a priest or a lawyer?"

"Absolutely," he said.

"No matter what?"

"No matter what."

I watched him when he said it. I believed him.

"Pick up your money," I said. "You're on."

He didn't do it. He said, "As you remarked a minute ago, that is up to me. You can't buy these treatments like a candy bar. We have to work together. If either one of us can't do that, it's useless. You can't walk in on the first psychotherapist you find in the phone book and make any demand that occurs to you just because you can pay for it."

I said tiredly, "I didn't get you out of the phone book and I'm not just guessing that you can help me. I winnowed through a dozen or more head-shrinkers before I decided on you."

"Thanks," he said, and it looked as if he was going to laugh at me, which I never like. "Winnowed, did you say? Just how?"

"Things you hear, things you read. You know. I'm not saying, so just file that with my street address."

He looked at me for a long time. It was the first time he'd used those eyes on me for anything but a flash glance. Then he picked up the bill.

"What do I do first?" I demanded.

"What do you mean?"

"How do we start?"

"We started when you walked in here."

So then I had to laugh. "All right, you got me. All I had was an opening. I didn't know where you would go from there, so I couldn't be there ahead of you."

"That's very interesting," Stern said. "Do you usually figure everything out in advance?"

"Always."

"How often are you right?"

"All the time. Except—but I don't have to tell you about no exceptions."

He really grinned this time. "I see. One of my patients has been talking."

"One of your ex-patients. Your patients don't talk."

"I ask them not to. That applies to you, too. What did you hear?"

"That you know from what people say and do what they're about to say and do, and that sometimes you let'm do it and sometimes you don't. How did you learn to do that?"

He thought a minute. "I guess I was born with an eye for details, and then let myself make enough mistakes with enough people until I learned not to make too many more. How did you learn to do it?"

I said, "You answer that and I won't have to come back here."

"You really don't know?"

"I wish I did. Look, this isn't getting us anywhere, is it?"

He shrugged. "Depends on where you want to go." He paused, and I got the eyes full strength again. "Which thumbnail description of psychiatry do you believe at the moment?"

"I don't get you."

Stern slid open a desk drawer and took out a blackened pipe. He smelled it, turned it over while looking at me. "Psychiatry attacks the onion of the self, removing layer after layer until it gets down to the little silver of unsullied ego. Or: psychiatry drills like an oil well, down and sidewise and down again, through all the muck and rock, until it strikes a layer that yields. Or: psychiatry grabs a handful of sexual motivations and throws them on the pinball-machine of your life, so they bounce on down against episodes. Want more?"

I had to laugh. "That last one was pretty good."

"That last one was pretty bad. They are all bad. They all try to simplify something which is complex by its very nature. The only thumbnail you'll get from me is this: no one knows what's really wrong with you but you; no one can find a cure for it but you; no one but you can identify it as a cure; and once you find it, no one but you can do anything about it."

"What are *you* here for?"

"To listen."

"I don't have to pay somebody no day's wage every hour just to listen."

"True. But you're convinced that I listen selectively."

"Am I?" I wondered about it. "I guess I am. Well, don't you?"

"No, but you'll never believe that."

I laughed. He asked me what that was for. I said, "You're not calling me Sonny."

"Not you." He shook his head slowly. He was watching me while he did it, so his eyes slid in their sockets as his head moved. "What is it you want to know about yourself, that made you worried I might tell people?"

"I want to find out why I killed somebody," I said right away.

It didn't faze him a bit. "Lie down over there."

I got up. "On that couch?"

He nodded.

As I stretched out self-consciously, I said, "I feel like I'm in some damn cartoon."

"What cartoon?"

"Guy's built like a bunch of grapes," I said, looking at the ceiling. It was pale gray.

"What's the caption?"

"'I got trunks full of 'em.'"

"Very good," he said quietly.

I looked at him carefully. I knew then he was the kind of guy who laughs way down deep when he laughs at all.

He said, "I'll use that in a book of case histories some time. But it won't include yours. What made you throw that in?" When I didn't answer, he got up and moved to a chair behind me where I couldn't see him. "You can quit testing, Sonny. I'm good enough for your purposes."

I clenched my jaws so hard, my back teeth hurt. Then I relaxed. I relaxed all over. It was wonderful. "All right," I said, "I'm sorry." He didn't say anything, but I had that feeling again that he was laughing. Not at me, though.

"How old are you?" he asked me suddenly.

"Uh—fifteen."

"Uh—fifteen," he repeated. "What does the 'uh' mean?"

"Nothing. I'm fifteen."

"When I asked your age, you hesitated because some other number popped up. You discarded that and substituted 'fifteen'."

"The hell I did! I *am* fifteen!"

"I didn't say you weren't." His voice came patiently. "Now what was the other number?"

I got mad again. "There wasn't any other number! What do you want to go pryin' my grunts apart for, trying to plant this and that and make it mean what you think it ought to mean?"

He was silent.

"I'm fifteen," I said defiantly, and then, "I don't like being only fifteen. You know that. I'm not trying to insist I'm fifteen."

He just waited, still not saying anything.

I felt defeated. "The number was eight."

"So you're eight. And your name?"

"Gerry." I got up on one elbow, twisting my neck around so I could see him. He had his pipe apart and was sighting through the stem at the desk lamp. "Gerry, without no 'uh!' "

"All right," he said mildly, making me feel real foolish.

I leaned back and closed my eyes.

Eight, I thought. Eight.

"It's cold in here," I complained.

Eight. Eight, plate, state, hate. I ate from the plate of the state and I hate. I didn't like any of that and I snapped my eyes open. The ceiling was still gray. It was all right. Stern was somewhere behind me with his pipe, and he was all right. I took two deep breaths, three, and then let my eyes close. Eight. Eight years old. Eight, hate. Years, fears. Old, cold. *Damn* it! I twisted and twitched on the couch, trying to find a way to keep the cold out. I ate from the plate of the—

I grunted and with my mind I took all the eights and all the rhymes and everything they stood for, and made it all black. But it wouldn't stay black. I had to put something there, so I made a great big luminous figure eight and just let it hang there. But it turned on its side and inside the loops it began to shimmer. It was like one of those movie shots through binoculars. I was going to have to look through whether I liked it or not.

Suddenly I quit fighting it and let it wash over me. The binoculars came close, closer, and then I was there.

Eight. Eight years old, cold. Cold as a bitch in the ditch. The ditch was by a railroad. Last year's weeds were scratchy straw. The ground was red, and when it wasn't slippery, clingy mud, it was frozen hard like a flowerpot. It was hard like that now, dusted with hoar-frost, cold as the winter light that pushed up over the hills. At night the lights were warm, and they were all in other people's houses. In the daytime the sun was in somebody else's house too, for all the good it did me.

I was dying in that ditch. Last night it was as good a place as any to sleep, and this morning it was as good a place as any to die. Just as well. Eight years old, the sick-sweet taste of porkfat and wet bread from somebody's garbage, the thrill of terror when you're stealing a gunnysack and you hear a footstep.

And I heard a footstep.

I'd been curled up on my side. I whipped over on my stomach because sometimes they kick your belly. I covered my head with my arms and that was as far as I could get.

After a while I rolled my eyes up and looked without moving. There was a big shoe there. There was an ankle in the shoe, and another shoe close by. I lay there waiting to get tromped. Not that I cared much any more, but it was such a damn shame. All these months on my own, and they'd never caught up with me, never even come close, and now this. It was such a shame I started to cry.

The shoe took me under the armpit, but it was not a kick. It rolled me over. I was so stiff from the cold, I went over like a plank. I just kept my arms over my face and head and lay there with my eyes closed. For some reason I stopped crying. I think people only cry when there's a chance of getting help from somewhere.

When nothing happened, I opened my eyes and shifted my forearms a little so I could see up. There was a man standing over me and he was a mile high. He had on faded dungarees and an old Eisenhower jacket with deep sweat-stains under the arms. His face was shaggy, like the guys who can't grow what you could call a beard, but still don't shave.

He said, "Get up."

I looked down at his shoe, but he wasn't going to kick me. I pushed up a little and almost fell down again, except he put his big hand where my back would hit it. I lay against it for a second because I had to, and then got up to where I had one knee on the ground.

"Come on," he said. "Let's go."

I swear I felt my bones creak, but I made it. I brought a round white stone up with me as I stood. I hefted the stone. I had to look at it to see if I was really holding it, my fingers were that cold. I told him, "Stay away from me or I'll bust you in the teeth with this rock."

His hand came out and down so fast, I never saw the way he got one finger between my palm and the rock, and flicked it out of my grasp. I started to cuss at him, but he just turned his back and walked up the embankment toward the tracks. He put his chin on his shoulder and said, "Come on, will you?"

He didn't chase me, so I didn't run. He didn't talk to me, so I didn't argue. He didn't hit me, so I didn't get mad. I went along after him. He waited for me. He put out his hand to me and I spit at it. So he went on, up to the tracks, out of my sight. I clawed my way up. The blood was beginning to move in my hands and feet and they felt like four point-down porcupines. When I got up to the roadbed, the man was standing there waiting for me.

The track was level just there, but as I turned my head to look along it, it seemed to be a hill that was steeper and steeper and turned over above me. And next thing you know, I was lying flat on my back looking up at the cold sky.

The man came over and sat down on the rail near me. He didn't try to touch me. I gasped for breath a couple of times, and suddenly felt I'd be all right if I could sleep for a minute—just a little minute. I closed my eyes. The man stuck his finger in my ribs, hard. It hurt.

"Don't sleep," he said.

I looked at him.

He said, "You're frozen stiff and weak with hunger. I want to take you home and get you warmed up and fed. But it's a long haul up that way, and you won't make it by yourself. If I carry you, will that be the same to you as if you walked it?"

"What are you going to do when you get me home?"

"I told you."

"All right," I said.

He picked me up and carried me down the track. If he'd said anything else in the world, I'd of laid right down where I was until I froze to death. Anyway, what did he want to ask me for, one way or the other? I couldn't of done anything.

I stopped thinking about it and dozed off.

I woke up once when he turned off the right of way. He dove into the woods. There was no path, but he seemed to know where he was going. The next time I woke from a crackling noise. He was carrying me over a frozen pond and the ice was giving under his feet. He didn't hurry. I looked down and saw the white cracks raying out under his feet, and it didn't seem to matter a bit. I bleared off again.

He put me down at last. We were there. "There" was inside a room. It was very warm. He put me on my feet and I snapped out of it in a hurry. The first thing I looked for was the door. I saw it and jumped over there and put my back against the wall beside it, in case I wanted to leave. Then I looked around.

It was a big room. One wall was rough rock and the rest was logs with stuff shoved between them. There was a big fire going in the rock wall, not in a fireplace, exactly; it was a sort of hollow place. There was an old auto battery on a shelf opposite, with two yellowing electric light bulbs dangling by wires from it. There was a table, some boxes and a couple of three-legged stools. The air had a haze of smoke and such a wonderful, heartbreaking, candy-and-crackling smell of food that a little hose squirted inside my mouth.

The man said, "What have I got here, Baby?"

And the room was full of kids. Well, three of them, but somehow they seemed to be more than three kids. There was a girl about my age—eight, I mean—with blue paint on the side of her face. She had an easel and a palette with lots of paints and a fistful of brushes, but she wasn't using the brushes. She was smearing the paint on with her hands. Then there was a little Negro girl about five with great big eyes who stood gaping at me. And in a wooden crate, set up on two saw-horses to make a kind of bassinet, was a baby. I guess about three or four months old. It did what babies do, drooling some, making small bubbles, waving its hands around very aimless, and kicking.

When the man spoke, the girl at the easel looked at me and then at the baby. The baby just kicked and drooled.

The girl said, "His name's Gerry. He's mad."

"What's he mad at?" the man asked. He was looking at the baby.

"Everything," said the girl. "Everything and everybody."

"Where'd he come from?"

I said, "Hey, what is this?" but nobody paid any attention. The man kept asking questions at the baby and the girl kept answering. Craziest thing I ever saw.

"He ran away from a state school," the girl said. "They fed him enough, but no one bleshed with him."

That's what she said—"bleshed".

I opened the door then and cold air hooted in. "You louse," I said to the man, "you're from the school."

"Close the door, Janie," said the man. The girl at the easel didn't move, but the door banged shut behind me. I tried to open it and it wouldn't move. I let out a howl, yanking at it.

"I think you ought to stand in the corner," said the man. "Stand him in the corner, Janie."

Janie looked at me. One of the three-legged stools sailed across to me. It hung in mid-air and turned on its side. It nudged me with its flat seat. I jumped back and it came after me. I dodged to the side, and that was the corner. The stool came on. I tried to bat it down and just hurt my hand. I ducked and it went lower than I did. I put one hand on it and tried to vault over it, but it just fell and so did I. I got up again and stood in the corner, trembling. The stool turned right side up and sank to the floor in front of me.

The man said, "Thank you, Janie." He turned to me. "Stand there and be quiet, you. I'll get to you later. You shouldn'ta kicked up all that fuss." And then, to the baby, he said, "He got anything we need?"

And again it was the little girl who answered. She said, "Sure. He's the one."

"Well," said the man. "What do you know!" He came over. "Gerry, you can live here. I don't come from the school. I'll never turn you in."

"Yeah, huh?"

"He hates you," said Janie.

"What am I supposed to do about that?" he wanted to know.

Janie turned her head to look into the bassinet. "Feed him." The man nodded and began fiddling around the fire.

Meanwhile, the little Negro girl had been standing in the one spot with her big eyes right out on her cheekbones, looking at me. Janie went back to her painting and the baby just lay there same as always, so I stared back at the little Negro girl. I snapped, "What the devil are you gawking at?"

She grinned at me. "Gerry ho-ho," she said, and disappeared. I mean she really disappeared, went out like a light, leaving her clothes where she had been. Her little dress billowed in the air and fell in a heap where she had been, and that was that. She was gone.

"Gerry hee-hee," I heard. I looked up, and there she was, stark naked, wedged in a space where a little outcropping on the rock wall stuck out just below the ceiling. The second I saw her she disappeared again.

"Gerry ho-ho," she said. Now she was on top of the row of boxes they used as storage shelves, over on the other side of the room.

"Gerry hee-hee!" Now she was under the table. "Gerry ho-ho!" This time she was right in the corner with me, crowding me.

I yelped and tried to get out of the way and bumped the stool. I was afraid of it, so I shrank back again and the little girl was gone.

The man glanced over his shoulder from where he was working at the fire. "Cut it out, you kids," he said.

There was a silence, and then the girl came slowly out from the bottom row of shelves. She walked across to her dress and put it on.

"How did you do that?" I wanted to know.

"Ho-ho," she said.

Janie said, "It's easy. She's really twins."

"Oh," I said. Then another girl, exactly the same, came from somewhere in the shadows and stood beside the first. They were identical. They stood side by side and stared at me. This time I let them stare.

"That's Bonnie and Beanie," said the painter. "This is Baby and that—" she indicated the man—"that's Lone. And I'm Janie."

I couldn't think of what to say, so I said, "Yeah".

Lone said, "Water, Janie." He held up a pot. I heard water trickling, but didn't see anything. "That's enough," he said, and hung the pot on a crane. He picked up a cracked china plate and brought it over to me. It was full of stew with great big lumps of meat in it, and thick gravy and dumplings and carrots. "Here, Gerry. Sit down."

I looked at the stool. "On that?"

"Sure."

"Not me," I said. I took the plate and hunkered down against the wall.

"Hey," he said after a time. "Take it easy. We've all had chow. No one's going to snatch it away from you. Slow down!"

I ate even faster than before. I was almost finished when I threw it all up. Then for some reason my head hit the edge of the stool. I dropped the plate and spoon and slumped there. I felt real bad.

Lone came over and looked at me. "Sorry, kid," he said. "Clean up, will you, Janie?"

Right in front of my eyes, the mess on the floor disappeared. I didn't care about that or anything else just then. I felt the man's hand on the side of my neck. Then he tousled my hair.

"Beanie, get him a blanket. Let's all go to sleep. He ought to rest a while."

I felt the blanket go around me, and I think I was asleep before he put me down.

I don't know how much later it was when I woke up. I didn't know where I was and that scared me. I raised my head and saw the dull glow of the embers in the fireplace. Lone was stretched out on it in his clothes. Janie's easel stood in the reddish blackness like some great preying insect. I saw the baby's head pop up out of the bassinet, but I couldn't tell whether he was looking straight at me or away. Janie was lying on the floor near the door and the twins were on the old table. Nothing moved except the baby's head, bobbing a little.

I got to my feet and looked around the room. Just a room, only the one door. I tiptoed toward it. When I passed Janie, she opened her eyes.

"What's the matter?" she whispered.

"None of your business," I told her. I went to the door as if I didn't care, but I watched her. She didn't do anything. The door was as solid tight closed as when I'd tried it before.

I went back to Janie. She just looked up at me. She wasn't scared. I told her, "I got to go to the john."

"Oh," she said. "Why'n't you say so?"

Suddenly I grunted and grabbed my guts. The feeling I had I can't begin to talk about. I acted as if it was a pain, but it wasn't. It was like nothing else that ever happened to me before.

"Okay," Janie said. "Go on back to bed."

"But I got to—"

"You got to what?"

"Nothing." It was true. I didn't have to go no place.

"Next time tell me right away. I don't mind."

I didn't say anything. I went back to my blanket.

"That's all?" said Stern. I lay on the couch and looked up at the gray ceiling. He asked, "How old are you?"

"Fifteen," I said dreamily. He waited until, for me, the gray ceiling acquired walls and a floor, a rug and lamps and a desk and a chair with Stern in it. I sat up and held my head a second, and then I looked at him. He was fooling with his pipe and looking at me. "What did you do to me?"

"I told you. I don't do anything here. You do it."

"You hypnotized me."

"I did not." His voice was quiet, but he really meant it.

"What was all that, then? It was . . . it was like it was happening for real all over again."

"Feel anything?"

"Everything." I shuddered. "*Every* damn thing. What was it?"

"Anyone doing it feels better afterward. You can go over it all again now any time you want to, and every time you do, the hurt in it will be less. You'll see."

It was the first thing to amaze me in years. I chewed on it and then asked, "If I did it by myself, how come it never happened before?"

"It needs someone to listen."

"Listen? Was I talking?"

"A blue streak."

"Everything that happened?"

"How can I know? I wasn't there. You were."

"You don't believe it happened, do you? Those disappearing kids and the footstool and all?"

He shrugged. "I'm not in the business of believing or not believing. Was it real to you?"

"Oh, hell, yes!"

"Well, then, that's all that matters. Is that where you live, with those people?"

I bit off a fingernail that had been bothering me. "Not for a long time. Not since Baby was three." I looked at him. "You remind me of Lone."

"Why?"

"I don't know. No, you don't," I added suddenly. "I don't know what made me say that." I lay down abruptly.

The ceiling was gray and the lamps were dim. I heard the pipe-stem click against his teeth. I lay there for a long time.

"Nothing happens," I told him.

"What did you expect to happen?"

"Like before."

"There's something there that wants out. Just let it come."

It was as if there was a revolving drum in my head, and on it were photographed the places and things and people I was after. And it was as if the drum was spinning very fast, so fast I couldn't tell one picture from another. I made it stop, and it stopped at a blank segment. I spun it again, and stopped it again.

"Nothing happens," I said.

"Baby is three," he repeated.

"Oh," I said. "That." I closed my eyes.

That might be it. Might, sight, night, light. I might have the sight of a light in the night. Maybe the baby. Maybe the sight of the baby at night because of the light . . .

★

There was night after night when I lay on that blanket, and a lot of nights I didn't. Something was going on all the time in Lone's house. Sometimes I slept in the daytime. I guess the only time everybody slept at once was when someone was sick, like me the first time I arrived there. It was always sort of dark in the room, the same night and day, the fire going, the two old bulbs *hanging* yellow by their wires from the battery. When they got too dim, Janie fixed the battery and they got bright again.

Janie did everything that needed doing, whatever no one else felt like doing. Everybody else did things, too. Lone was out a lot. Sometimes he used the twins to help him, but you never missed them, because they'd be here and gone and back again *bing!* like that. And Baby, he just stayed in his bassinet.

I did things myself. I cut wood for the fire and I put up more shelves, and then I'd go swimming with Janie and the twins sometimes. And I talked to Lone. I didn't do a thing that the others couldn't do, but they all did things I couldn't do. I was mad, mad all the time about that. But I wouldn't of known what to do with myself if I wasn't mad all the time about something or other. It didn't keep us from bleshing. Bleshing, that was Janie's word. She said Baby told it to her. She said it meant everyone all together being something, even if they all did different things. Two arms, two legs, one body, one head, all working together, although a head can't walk and arms can't think. Lone said maybe it was a mixture of "blending" and "meshing," but I don't think he believed that himself. It was a lot more than that.

Baby talked all the time. He was like a broadcasting station that runs twenty-four hours a day, and you can get what it's sending any time you tune in, but it'll keep sending whether you tune in or not. When I say he talked, I don't mean exactly that. He semaphored mostly. You'd think those wandering, vague movements of his hands and arms and legs and head were meaningless, but they weren't. It was semaphore, only instead of a symbol for a sound, or such like, the movements were whole thoughts.

I mean spread the left hand and shake the right high up, and thump with the left heel, and it means, "Anyone who thinks a starling is a pest just don't know anything about how a starling thinks" or something like that.

Lone couldn't read the stuff and neither could I. The twins could, but they didn't give a damn. Janie used to watch him all the time. He always knew what you meant if you wanted to ask him something, and he'd tell Janie and she'd say what it was. Part of it, anyway. Nobody could get it all, not even Janie. Lone once told me that all babies know that semaphore. But when nobody receives it, they quit doing it and pretty soon they forget. They *almost* forget. There's always some left. That's why certain gestures are funny the world over, and certain others make you mad. But like everything else Lone said, I don't know whether he believed it or not.

All I know is Janie would sit there and paint her pictures and watch Baby, and sometimes she'd bust out laughing, and sometimes she'd get the twins and make them watch and they'd laugh, too, or they'd wait till he was finished what he was saying and then they'd creep off to a corner and whisper to each other about it. Baby never grew any. Janie did, and the twins, and so did I, but not Baby. He just lay there.

Janie kept his stomach full and cleaned him up every two or three days. He didn't cry and he didn't make any trouble. No one ever went near him.

Janie showed every picture she painted to Baby, before she cleaned the boards and painted new ones. She had to clean them because she only had three of them. It was a good thing, too, because I'd hate to think what that place would of been like if she'd kept them all; she did four or five a day. Lone and the twins were kept hopping getting turpentine for her. She could shift the paints back into the little pots on her easel without any trouble, just by looking at the picture one color at a time, but turps was something else again. She told me that Baby remembered all her pictures and that's why she didn't have to keep them. They were all pictures of machines and gear-trains and mechanical linkages and what looked like electric circuits and things like that. I never thought too much about them.

I went out with Lone to get some turpentine and a couple of picnic hams, one time. We went through the woods to the railroad track and down a couple of miles to where we could see the glow of a town. Then the woods again, and some alleys, and a back street.

Lone was like always, walking along, thinking, thinking.

We came to a hardware store and he went up and looked at the lock and came back to where I was waiting, shaking his head. Then we found a general store. Lone grunted and we went and stood in the shadows by the door. I looked in.

All of a sudden, Beanie was in there, naked like she always was when she traveled like that. She came and opened the door from the inside. We went in and Lone closed it and locked it.

"Get along home, Beanie," he said, "before you catch your death."

She grinned at me and said, "Ho-ho," and disappeared.

We found a pair of fine hams and a two-gallon can of turpentine. I took a bright yellow ballpoint pen and Lone cuffed me and made me put it back.

"We only take what we need," he told me.

After we left, Beanie came back and locked the door and went home again. I only went with Lone a few times, when he had more to get than he could carry easily.

I was there about three years. That's all I can remember about it. Lone was there or he was out, and you could hardly tell the difference. The twins were with each other most of the time. I got to like Janie a lot, but we never talked much. Baby talked all the time, only I don't know what about.

We were all busy and we bleshed.

I sat up on the couch suddenly.

Stern said, "What's the matter?"

"Nothing's the matter. This isn't getting me any place."

"You said that when you'd barely started. Do you think you've accomplished anything since then?"

"Oh, yeah, but—"

"Then how can you be sure you're right this time?" When I didn't say anything, he asked me, "Didn't you like this last stretch?"

I said angrily, "I didn't like or not like. It didn't mean nothing. It was just—just talk."

"So what was the difference between this last session and what happened before?"

"My gosh, plenty! The first one, I felt everything. It was all really happening to me. But this time—nothing."

"Why do you suppose that was?"

"I don't know. You tell me."

"Suppose," he said thoughtfully, "that there was some episode so unpleasant to you that you wouldn't dare relive it."

"Unpleasant? You think freezing to death isn't unpleasant?"

"There all kinds of unpleasantness. Sometimes the very thing you're looking for—the thing that'll clear up your trouble—is so revolting to you that you won't go near it. Or you try to hide it. Wait," he said suddenly, "maybe 'revolting' and 'unpleasant' are inaccurate words to use. It might be something very desirable to you. It's just that you don't want to get straightened out."

"I *want* to get straightened out."

He waited as if he had to clear something up in his mind, and then said, "There's something in that 'Baby is three' phrase that bounces you away. Why is that?"

"Damn if I know."

"Who said it?"

"I dunno . . . uh . . ."

He grinned. "Uh?"

I grinned back at him. "I said it."

"Okay. When?"

I quit grinning. He leaned forward, then got up.

"What's the matter?" I asked.

"I didn't think anyone could be that mad." I didn't say anything. He went over to his desk. "You don't want to go on any more, do you?"

"No."

"Suppose I told you you want to quit because you're right on the very edge of finding out what you want to know?"

"Why don't you tell me and see what I do?"

He just shook his head. "I'm not telling you anything. Go on, leave if you want to. I'll give you back your change."

"How many people quit just when they're on top of the answer?"

"Quite a few."

"Well, I ain't going to." I lay down.

He didn't laugh and he didn't say, "Good," and he didn't make any fuss about it. He just picked up his phone and said, "Cancel everything for this afternoon," and went back to his chair, up there out of my sight.

It was very quiet in there. He had the place soundproofed.

I said, "Why do you suppose Lone let me live there so long when I couldn't do any of the things that the other kids could?"

"Maybe you could."

"Oh, no," I said positively. "I used to try. I was strong for a kid my age and I knew how to keep my mouth shut, but aside from those two things I don't think I was any different from any kid. I don't think I'm any different right now, except what difference there might be from living with Lone and his bunch."

"Has this anything to do with 'Baby is three'?"

I looked up at the gray ceiling. "Baby is three. Baby is three. I went up to a big house with a winding drive that ran under a sort of theater-marquee thing. Baby is three. Baby . . ."

"How old are you?"

"Thirty-three," I said, and the next thing you know I was up off that couch like it was hot, and heading for the door.

"Don't be foolish," Stern said. "Want me to waste a whole afternoon?"

"What's that to me? I'm paying for it."

"All right, it's up to you."

I went back. "I don't like any part of this," I said.

"Good. We're getting warm then."

"What made me say 'Thirty-three'? I ain't thirty-three. I'm fifteen. And another thing . . ."

"Yes?"

"It's about that 'Baby is three'. It's me saying it, all right. But when I think about it—it's not my voice."

"Like thirty-three's not your age?"

"Yeah," I whispered.

"Gerry," he said warmly, "there's nothing to be afraid of."

I realized I was breathing too hard. I pulled myself together. I said, "I don't like remembering saying things in somebody else's voice."

"Look," he told me. "This head-shrinking business, as you called it a while back, isn't what most people think. When I go with you into the world of your mind—or when you go yourself, for that matter—what we find isn't so very different from the so-called real world. It seems so at first, because the patient comes out with all sorts of fantasies and irrationalities and weird experiences. But everyone lives in that kind of world. When one of the ancients coined the phrase 'truth is stranger than fiction,' he was talking about that.

"Everywhere we go, everything we do, we're surrounded by symbols, by things so familiar we don't ever look at them or don't see them if we do look. If anyone ever could report to you exactly what he saw and thought while walking ten feet down the street, you'd get the most twisted, clouded, partial picture you ever ran across. And nobody ever looks at what's around him with any kind of attention until he gets into a place like this. The fact that he's looking at past events doesn't matter; what counts is that he's seeing clearer than he ever could before, just because, for once, he's trying.

"Now—about this 'thirty-three' business. I don't think a man could get a nastier shock than to find he has someone else's memories. The ego is too important to let slide that way. But consider: all your thinking is done in code and you have the key to only about a tenth of it. So you run into a stretch of code which is abhorrent to you. Can't you see that the only way you'll find the key to it is to stop avoiding it?"

"You mean I'd started to remember with . . . with somebody else's mind?"

"It looked like that to you for a while, which means something. Let's try to find out what."

"All right." I felt sick. I felt tired. And I suddenly realized that being sick and being tired was a way of trying to get out of it.

"Baby is three," he said.

Baby is maybe. Me, three, thirty-three, me, you Kew you.

"Kew!" I yelled. Stern didn't say anything. "Look, I don't know why, but I think I know how to get to this, and this isn't the way. Do you mind if I try something else?"

"You're the doctor," he said.

I had to laugh. Then I closed my eyes.

There, through the edges of the hedges, the ledges and wedges of windows were shouldering up to the sky. The lawns were sprayed-on green, neat and clean, and all the flowers looked as if they were afraid to let their petals break and be untidy.

I walked up the drive in my shoes. I'd had to wear shoes and my feet couldn't breathe. I didn't want to go to the house, but I had to.

I went up the steps between the big white columns and looked at the door. I wished I could see through it, but it was too white and thick. There was a window the shape of a fan over it, too high up, though, and a window on each side of it, but they were all crudded up with colored glass. I hit on the door with my hand and left dirt on it.

Nothing happened, so I hit it again. It got snatched open and a tall, thin colored woman stood there. "What you want?"

I said I had to see Miss Kew.

"Well, Miss Kew don't want to see the likes of you," she said. She talked too loud. "You got a dirty face."

I started to get mad then. I was already pretty sore about having to come here, walking around near people in the daytime and all. I said, "My face ain't got nothin' to do with it. Where's Miss Kew? Go on, find her for me."

She gasped. "You can't speak to me like that!"

I said, "I didn't want to speak to you like any way. Let me in." I started wishing for Janie. Janie could of moved her. But I had to handle it by myself. I wasn't doing so hot, either. She slammed the door before I could so much as curse at her.

So I started kicking on the door. For that, shoes are great. After a while, she snatched the door open again so sudden I almost went on my can. She had a broom with her. She screamed at me, "You get away from here, you trash, or I'll call the police!" She pushed me and I fell.

I got up off the porch floor and went for her. She stepped back and whupped me one with the broom as I went past, but anyhow I was inside now. The woman was making little shrieking noises and coming for me. I took the broom away from her and then somebody said, "Miriam!" in a voice like a grown goose.

I froze and the woman went into hysterics. "Oh, Miss Kew, look out! He'll kill us all. Get the police. Get the—"

"Miriam!" came the honk, and Miriam dried up.

There at the top of the stairs was this prune-faced woman with a dress on that had lace on it. She looked a lot older than she was, maybe because she held her mouth so tight. I guess she was about thirty-three—*thirty-three*. She had mean eyes and a small nose.

I asked, "Are you Miss Kew?"

"I am. What is the meaning of this invasion?"

"I got to talk to you, Miss Kew."

"Don't say 'got to'. Stand up straight and speak out."

The maid said, "I'll get the police."

Miss Kew turned on her. "There's time enough for that, Miriam. Now, you dirty little boy, what do you want?"

"I got to speak to you by yourself," I told her.

"Don't you let him do it, Miss Kew," cried the maid.

"Be quiet, Miriam. Little boy, I told you not to say 'got to'. You may say whatever you have to say in front of Miriam."

"Like hell." They both gasped. I said, "Lone told me not to."

"Miss Kew, are you goin' to let him—"

"Be quiet, Miriam! Young man, you will keep a civil—" Then her eyes popped up real round. "*Who* did you say . . ."

"Lone said so."

"Lone." She stood there on the stairs looking at her hands. Then she said, "Miriam, that will be all." And you wouldn't know it was the same woman, the way she said it.

The maid opened her mouth, but Miss Kew stuck out a finger that might as well of had a riflesight on the end of it. The maid beat it.

"Hey," I said, "here's your broom." I was just going to throw it, but Miss Kew got to me and took it out of my hand.

"In there," she said.

★

She made me go ahead of her into a room as big as our swimming hole. It had books all over and leather on top of the tables, with gold flowers drawn into the corners.

She pointed to a chair. "Sit there. No, wait a moment." She went to the fireplace and got a newspaper out of a box and brought it over and unfolded it on the seat of the chair. "Now sit down."

I sat on the paper and she dragged up another chair, but didn't put no paper on it.

"What is it? Where is Lone?"

"He died," I said.

She pulled in her breath and went white. She stared at me until her eyes started to water.

"You sick?" I asked her. "Go ahead, throw up. It'll make you feel better."

"Dead? Lone is dead?"

"Yeah. There was a flash flood last week and when he went out the next night in that big wind, he walked under a old oak tree that got gullied under by the flood. The tree come down on him."

"*Came* down on him," she whispered. "Oh, no . . . it's not true."

"It's true, all right. We planted him this morning. We couldn't keep him around no more. He was beginning to st—"

"Stop!" She covered her face with her hands.

"What's the matter?"

"I'll be all right in a moment," she said in a low voice. She went and stood in front of the fireplace with her back to me. I took off one of my shoes while I was waiting for her to come back. But instead she talked from where she was. "Are you Lone's little boy?"

"Yeah. He told me to come to you."

"Oh, my dear child!" She came running back and I thought for a second she was going to pick me up or something, but she stopped short and wrinkled up her nose a little bit. "Wh-what's your name?"

"Gerry," I told her.

"Well, Gerry, how would you like to live with me in this nice big house and—and have new clean clothes—and everything?"

"Well, that's the whole idea. Lone told me to come to you. He said you got more dough than you know what to do with, and he said you owed him a favor."

"A favor?" That seemed to bother her.

"Well," I tried to tell her, "he said he done something for you once and you said some day you'd pay him back for it if you ever could. This is it."

"What did he tell you about that?" She'd got her honk back by then.

"Not a damn thing."

"Please don't use that word," she said, with her eyes closed. Then she opened them and nodded her head. "I promised and I'll do it. You can live here from now on. If—if you want to."

"That's got nothin' to do with it. Lone *told* me to."

"You'll be happy here," she said. She gave me an up-and-down. "I'll see to that."

"Okay. Shall I go get the other kids?"

"*Other* kids—children?"

"Yeah. This ain't for just me. For all of us—the whole gang."

"Don't say 'ain't'." She leaned back in her chair, took out a silly little handkerchief and dabbed her lips with it, looking at me the whole time. "Now tell me about these—these other children."

"Well, there's Janie, she's eleven like me. And Bonnie and Beanie are eight, they're twins, and Baby. Baby is three."

"Baby is three," she said.

I screamed. Stern was kneeling beside the couch in a flash, holding his palms against my cheeks to hold my head still; I'd been whipping it back and forth.

"Good boy," he said. "You found it. You haven't found out *what* it is, but now you know *where* it is."

"But for sure," I said hoarsely. "Got water?"

He poured me some water out of a thermos flask. It was so cold it hurt. I lay back and rested, like I'd climbed a cliff. I said, "I can't take anything like that again."

"You want to call it quits for today?"

"What about you?"

"I'll go on as long as you want me to."

I thought about it. "I'd like to go on, but I don't want no thumping around. Not for a while yet."

"If you want another of those inaccurate analogies," Stern said, "psychiatry is like a road map. There are always a lot of different ways to get from on place to another place."

"I'll go around by the long way," I told him. "The eight-lane highway. Not that track over the hill. My clutch is slipping. Where do I turn off?"

He chuckled. I liked the sound of it. "Just past that gravel driveway."

"I been there. There's a bridge washed out."

"You've been on this whole road before," he told me. "Start at the other side of the bridge."

"I never thought of that. I figured I had to do the whole thing, every inch."

"Maybe you won't have to, maybe you will, but the bridge will be easy to cross when you've covered everything else. Maybe there's nothing of value on the bridge and maybe there is, but you can't get near it till you've looked everywhere else."

"Let's go." I was real eager, somehow.

"Mind a suggestion?"

"No."

"Just talk," he said. "Don't try to get too far into what you're saying. That first stretch, when you were eight—you really lived it. The second one, all about the kids, you just talked about. Then, the visit when you were eleven, you felt that. Now just talk again."

"All right."

He waited, then said quietly, "In the library. You told her about the other kids."

I told her about . . . and then she said . . . and something happened, and I screamed. She confronted me and I cussed at her.

But we're not thinking about that now. We're going on.

In the library. The leather, the table, and whether I'm able to do with Miss Kew what Lone said.

What Lone said was, "There's a woman lives up on the top of the hill on the Heights section, name of Kew. She'll have to take care of you. You got to get her to do that. Do everything she tells you, only stay together. Don't you ever let any one of you get away from the others, hear? Aside from that, just you keep Miss Kew happy and she'll keep you happy. Now you do what I say." That's what Lone said. Between every word there was a link like steel cable, and the whole thing made something that couldn't be broken. Not by me it couldn't.

Miss Kew said, "Where are your sisters and the baby?"

"I'll bring 'em."

"Is it near here?"

"Near enough." She didn't say anything to that, so I got up. "I'll be back soon."

"Wait," she said. "I—really, I haven't had time to think. I mean—I've got to get things ready, you know."

I said, "You don't need to think and you are ready. So long."

From the door I heard her saying, louder and louder as I walked away, "Young man, if you're to live in this house, you'll learn to be a good deal better mannered—" and a lot more of the same.

I yelled back at her, "Okay, *okay*!" and went out.

The sun was warm and the sky was good, and pretty soon I got back to Lone's house. The fire was out and Baby stunk. Janie had knocked over her easel and was sitting on the floor by the door with her head in her hands. Bonnie and Beanie were on a stool with their arms around each other, pulled up together as close as they could get, as if it was cold in there, although it wasn't.

I hit Janie in the arm to snap her out of it. She raised her head. She had gray eyes—or maybe it was more a kind of green—but now they had a funny look about them, like water in a glass that had some milk left in the bottom of it.

I said, "What's the matter around here?"

"What's the matter with what?" she wanted to know.

"All of yez," I said.

She said, "We don't give a damn, that's all."

"Well, all right," I said, "but we got to do what Lone said. Come on."

"No." I looked at the twins. They turned their backs on me. Janie said, "They're hungry."

"Well, why not give 'em something?"

She just shrugged. I sat down. What did Lone have to go get himself squashed for?

"We can't blesh no more," said Janie. It seemed to explain everything.

"Look," I said, "I've got to be Lone now."

Janie thought about that, and Baby kicked his feet. Janie looked at him. "You can't," she said.

"I know where to get the heavy food and the turpentine," I said. "I can find that springy moss to stuff in the logs, and cut wood, and all."

But I couldn't call Bonnie and Beanie from miles away to unlock doors. I couldn't just say a word to Janie and make her get water and blow up the fire and fix the battery. I couldn't make us blesh.

We all stayed like that for a long time. Then I heard the bassinet creak. I looked up. Janie was staring into it.

"All right," she said. "Let's go."

"Who says so?"

"Baby."

"Who's running things now?" I said, mad. "Me or Baby?"

"Baby," Janie said.

I got up and went over to bust her one in the mouth, and then I stopped. If Baby could make them do what Lone wanted, then it would get done. If I started pushing them all around, it wouldn't. So I didn't say anything. Janie got up and walked out the door. The twins watched her go. Then Bonnie disappeared. Beanie picked up Bonnie's clothes and walked out. I got Baby out of the bassinet and draped him over my shoulders.

It was better when we were all outside. It was getting late in the day and the air was warm. The twins flitted in and out of the trees like a couple of flying squirrels, and Janie and I walked along like we were going swimming or something. Baby started to kick, and Janie looked at him a while and got him fed, and he was quiet again.

When we came close to town, I wanted to get everybody close together, but I was afraid to say anything. Baby must of said it instead. The twins came back to us and Janie gave them their clothes and they walked ahead of us, good as you please. I don't know how Baby did it. They sure hated to travel that way.

We didn't have no trouble except one guy we met on the street near Miss Kew's place. He stopped in his tracks and gaped at us, and Janie looked at him and made his hat go so far down over his eyes that he like had to pull his neck apart getting it back up again.

What do you know, when we got to the house somebody had washed off all the dirt I'd put on the door. I had one hand on Baby's arm and one on his ankle and him draped over my neck, so I kicked the door and left some more dirt.

"There's a woman here name of Miriam," I told Janie. "She says anything, tell her to go to hell."

The door opened and there was Miriam. She took one look and jumped back six feet. We all trailed inside. Miriam got her wind and screamed, "Miss Kew! Miss Kew!"

"Go to hell," said Janie, and looked at me. I didn't know what to do. It was the first time Janie ever did anything I told her to.

Miss Kew came down the stairs. She was wearing a different dress, but it was just as stupid and had just as much lace. She opened her mouth and nothing came out, so she just left it open until something happened. Finally she said, "Dear gentle Lord preserve us!"

The twins lined up and gawked at her. Miriam sidled over to the wall and sort of slid along it, keeping away from us, until she could get to the door and close it. She said, "Miss Kew, if those are the children you said were going to live here, I quit."

Janie said, "Go to hell."

Just then, Bonnie squatted down on the rug. Miriam squawked and jumped at her. She grabbed hold of Bonnie's arm and went to snatch her up. Bonnie disappeared, leaving Miriam with one small dress and the damnedest expression on her face. Beanie grinned enough to split her head in two and started to wave like mad. I looked where she was waving, and there was Bonnie, naked as a jaybird, up on the banister at the top of the stairs.

Miss Kew turned around and saw her and sat down plump on the steps. Miriam went down, too, like she'd been slugged. Beanie picked up Bonnie's dress and walked up the steps past Miss Kew and handed it over. Bonnie put it on. Miss Kew sort of lolled around and looked up. Bonnie and Beanie came back down the stairs hand in hand to where I was. Then they lined up and gaped at Miss Kew.

"What's the matter with her?" Janie asked me.

"She gets sick every once in a while."

"Let's go back home."

"No," I told her.

Miss Kew grabbed the banister and pulled herself up. She stood there hanging on to it for a while with her eyes closed. All of a sudden she stiffened herself. She looked about four inches taller. She came marching over to us.

"Gerard," she honked.

I think she was going to say something different. But she sort of checked herself and pointed. "What in heaven's name is *that*?" And she aimed her finger at me.

I didn't get it right away, so I turned around to look behind me. "What?"

"That! That!"

"Oh!" I said. "That's Baby."

I slung him down off my back and held him up for her to look at. She made a sort of moaning noise and jumped over and took him away from me. She held him out in front of her and moaned again and called him a poor little thing, and ran and put him down on a long bench thing with cushions under the colored-glass window. She bent over him and put her knuckle in her mouth and bit on it and moaned some more. Then she turned to me.

"How long has he been like this?"

I looked at Janie and she looked at me. I said, "He's always been like he is."

She made a sort of cough and ran to where Miriam was lying flaked on the floor. She slapped Miriam's face a couple of times back and forth. Miriam sat up and looked us over. She closed her eyes and shivered and sort of climbed up Miss Kew hand over hand until she was on her feet.

"Pull yourself together," said Miss Kew between her teeth. "Get a basin with some hot water and soap. Washcloth. Towels. Hurry!" She gave Miriam a big push. Miriam staggered and grabbed at the wall, and then ran out.

Miss Kew went back to Baby and hung over him, titch-titching with her lips all tight.

"Don't mess with him," I said. "There's nothin' wrong with him. We're hungry."

She gave me a look like I punched her. "Don't speak to me!"

"Look," I said, "we don't like this any more'n you do. If Lone hadn't told us to, we wouldn't never have come. We were doing all right where we were."

"Don't say 'wouldn't never'," said Miss Kew. She looked at all of us, one by one. Then she took that silly little hunk of handkerchief and pushed it against her mouth.

"See?" I said to Janie. "All the time gettin' sick."

"Ho-ho," said Bonnie.

Miss Kew gave her a long look. "Gerard," she said in a choked sort of voice, "I understood you to say that these children were your sisters."

"Well?"

She looked at me as if I was real stupid. "We don't have little colored girls for sisters, Gerard."

Janie said, "*We* do."

Miss Kew walked up and back, real fast. "We have a great deal to do," she said, talking to herself.

Miriam came in with a big oval pan and towels and stuff on her arm. She put it down on the bench thing and Miss Kew stuck the back of her hand in the water, then picked up Baby and dunked him right in it. Baby started to kick.

I stepped forward and said, "Wait a minute. Hold on now. What do you think you're doing?"

Janie said, "Shut up, Gerry. He says it's all right."

"All right? She'll drown him."

"No, she won't. Just shut up."

Working up a froth with the soap, Miss Kew smeared it on Baby and turned him over a couple of times and scrubbed at his head and like to smothered him in a big white towel. Miriam stood gawking while Miss Kew lashed up a dishcloth around him so it come out pants. When she was done, you wouldn't of known it was the same baby. And by the time Miss Kew finished with the job, she seemed to have a better hold on herself. She was breathing hard and her mouth was even tighter. She held out the baby to Miriam.

"Take this poor thing," she said, "and put him—"

But Miriam backed away. "I'm sorry, Miss Kew, but I am leaving here and I don't care."

Miss Kew got her honk out. "You can't leave me in a predicament like this! These children need help. Can't you see that for yourself?"

Miriam looked me and Janie over. She was trembling. "You ain't safe, Miss Kew. They ain't just dirty. They're crazy!"

"They're victims of neglect, and probably no worse than you or I would be if we'd been neglected. And don't say 'ain't'. Gerard!"

"What?"

"Don't say—oh, dear, we have so much to do. Gerard, if you and your—these other children are going to live here, you shall have to make a great many changes. You cannot live under this roof and behave as you have so far. Do you understand that?"

"Oh, sure. Lone said we was to do whatever you say and keep you happy."

"Will you do whatever I say?"

"That's what I just said, isn't it?"

"Gerard, you shall have to learn not to speak to me in that tone. Now, young man, if I told you to do what Miriam says, too, would you do it?"

I said to Janie, "What about that?"

"I'll ask Baby." Janie looked at Baby and Baby wobbled his hands and drooled some. She said, "It's okay."

Miss Kew said, "Gerard, I asked you a question."

"Keep your pants on," I said. "I got to find out, don't I? Yes, if that's what you want, we'll listen to Miriam, too."

Miss Kew turned to Miriam. "You hear that, Miriam?"

Miriam looked at Miss Kew and at us and shook her head. Then she held out her hands a bit to Bonnie and Beanie.

They went right to her. Each one took hold of a hand. They looked up at her and grinned. They were probably planning some sort of hellishness, but I guess they looked sort of cute. Miriam's mouth twitched and I thought for a second she was going to look human. She said, "All right, Miss Kew."

Miss Kew walked over and handed her the baby and she started upstairs with him. Miss Kew herded us along after Miriam. We all went upstairs.

They went to work on us then and for three years they never stopped.

"That was hell," I said to Stern.

"They had their work cut out."

"Yeah, I s'pose they did. So did we. Look, we were going to do exactly what Lone said. Nothing on earth could of stopped us from doing it. We were tied and bound to doing every last little thing Miss Kew said to do. But she and Miriam never seemed to understand that. I guess they felt they had to push every inch of the way. All they had to do was make us understand what they wanted, and we'd of done it. That's okay when it's something like telling me not to climb into bed with Janie.

"Miss Kew raised holy hell over that. You'd of thought I'd robbed the Crown Jewels, the way she acted. But when it's something like, 'You must behave like little ladies and gentlemen,' it just doesn't mean a thing. And two out of three orders she gave us were like that. 'Ah-ah!' she'd say. 'Language, language!' For the longest time I didn't dig that at all. I finally asked her what the hell she meant, and then she finally came out with it. But you see what I mean."

"I certainly do," Stern said. "Did it get easier as time went on?"

"We only had real trouble twice, once about the twins and once about Baby. That one was real bad."

"What happened?"

"About the twins? Well, when we'd been there about a week or so we began to notice something that sort of stunk. Janie and me, I mean. We began to notice that we almost never got to see Bonnie and Beanie. It was like that house was two houses, one part for Miss Kew and Janie and me, and the other part for Miriam and the twins. I guess we'd have noticed it sooner if things hadn't been such a hassle at first, getting us into new clothes and making us sleep all the time at night, and all that. But here was the thing: We'd all get turned out in the side yard to play, and then along comes lunch, and the twins got herded off to eat with Miriam while we ate with Miss Kew. So Janie said, 'Why don't the twins eat with us?'

" 'Miriam's taking care of them, dear,' Miss Kew says.

"Janie looked at her with those eyes. 'I know that. Let 'em eat here and I'll take care of 'em.'

"Miss Kew's mouth got all tight again and she said, 'They're little colored girls, Jane. Now eat your lunch.'

"But that didn't explain anything to Janie or me, either. I said, 'I want 'em to eat with us. Lone said we should stay together.'

" 'But you *are* together,' she says. 'We all live in the same house. We all eat the same food. Now let us not discuss the matter.'

"I looked at Janie and she looked at me, and she said, 'So why can't we all do this livin' and eatin' right here?'

"Miss Kew put down her fork and looked hard. 'I have explained it to you and I have said that there will be no further discussion.'

"Well, I thought that was real nowhere. So I just rocked back my head and bellowed, 'Bonnie! Beanie!' And *bing*, there they were.

"So all hell broke loose. Miss Kew ordered them out and they wouldn't go, and Miriam come steaming in with their clothes, and she couldn't catch them, and Miss Kew got to honking at them and finally at me. She said this was too much. Well, maybe she had had a hard week, but so had we. So Miss Kew ordered us to leave.

"I went and got Baby and started out, and along came Janie and the twins. Miss Kew waited till we were all out the door and next thing you know she ran out after us. She passed us and got in front of me and made me stop. So we all stopped.

" 'Is this how you follow Lone's wishes?' she asked.

"I told her yes. She said she understood Lone wanted us to stay with her. And I said, 'Yeah, but he wanted us to stay together more.'

"She said come back in, we'd have a talk. Janie asked Baby and Baby said okay, so we went back. We had a compromise. We didn't eat in the dining room no more. There was a side porch, a sort of verandah thing with glass windows, with a door to the dining room and a door to the kitchen, and we all ate out there after that. Miss Kew ate by herself.

"But something funny happened because of that whole cockeyed hassle."

"What was that?" Stern asked me.

I laughed. "Miriam. She looked and sounded like always, but she started slipping us cookies between meals. You know, it took me years to figure out what all that was about. I mean it. From what I've learned about people, there seems to be two armies fightin' about race. One's fightin' to keep 'em apart, and one's fightin' to get 'em together. But I don't see why both sides are so *worried* about it! Why don't they just forget it?"

"They can't. You see, Gerry, it's necessary for people to believe they are superior in some fashion. You and Lone and the kids—you were a pretty tight unit. Didn't you feel you were a little better than all of the rest of the world?"

"Better? How could we be better?"

"Different, then."

"Well, I suppose so, but we didn't think about it. Different, yes. Better, no."

"You're a unique case," Stern said. "Now go on and tell me about the other trouble you had. About Baby."

"Baby. Yeah. Well, that was a couple of months after we moved to Miss Kew's. Things were already getting real smooth, even then. We'd learned all the 'yes, ma'am, no, ma'am' routines by then and she'd got us catching up with school—regular periods morning and afternoons, five days a week. Janie had long ago quit taking care of Baby, and the twins walked to wherever they went. That was funny. They could pop from one place to another right in front of Miss Kew's eyes and she wouldn't believe what she saw. She was too upset about them suddenly showing up bare. They quit doing it and she was happy about it. She was happy about a lot of things. It had been years since she'd seen anybody—years. She'd even had the meters put outside the house so no one would ever have to come in. But with us there, she began to liven up. She quit wearing those old-lady dresses and began to look halfway human. She ate with us sometimes, even.

"But one fine day I woke up feeling real weird. It was like somebody had stolen something from me when I was asleep, only I didn't know what. I crawled out of my window and along the ledge into Janie's room, which I wasn't supposed to do. She was in bed. I went and woke her up. I can still see her eyes, the way they opened a little slit, still asleep, and then popped up wide. I didn't have to tell her something was wrong. She knew, and she knew what it was.

" 'Baby's gone!' she said.

"We didn't care then who woke up. We pounded out of her room and down the hall and into the little room at the end where Baby slept. You wouldn't believe it. The fancy crib he had, and the white chest of drawers, and all that mess of rattles and so on, they were gone, and there was just a writing desk there. I mean it was as if Baby had never been there at all.

"We didn't say anything. We just spun around and busted into Miss Kew's bedroom. I'd never been in there but once and Janie only a few times. But forbidden or not, this was different. Miss Kew was in bed, with her hair braided. She was wide awake before we could get across the room. She pushed herself back and up until she was sitting against the headboard. She gave the two of us the cold eye.

" 'What is the meaning of this?' she wanted to know.

" 'Where's Baby?' I yelled at her.

" 'Gerard,' she says, 'there is no need to shout.'

"Janie was a real quiet kid, but she said, 'You better tell us where he is, Miss Kew,' and it would of scared you to look at her when she said it.

"So all of sudden Miss Kew took off the stone face and held out her hands to us. 'Children,' she said, 'I'm sorry. I really am sorry. But I've just done what is best. I've sent Baby away. He's gone to live with some children like him. We could never make him really happy here. You know that.'

"Jane said, 'He never told us he wasn't happy.'

"Miss Kew brought out a hollow kind of laugh. 'As if he could talk, the poor little thing!'

" 'You better get him back here,' I said. 'You don't know what you're fooling with. I told you we wasn't ever to break up.'

"She was getting mad, but she held on to herself. 'I'll try to explain it to you, dear,' she said. 'You and Jane here and even the twins are all normal, healthy children and you'll grow up to be fine men and women. But poor Baby's—different. He's not going to grow very much more, and he'll never walk and play like other children.'

" 'That doesn't matter,' Jane said. 'You had no call to send him away.'

"And I said, 'Yeah. You better bring him back, but quick.'

"Then she started to jump salty. 'Among the many things I have taught you is, I am sure, not to dictate to your elders. Now, then, you run along and get dressed for breakfast, and we'll say no more about this.'

"I told her, nice as I could, 'Miss Kew, you're going to wish you brought him back right now. But you're going to bring him back soon. Or else.'

"So then she got up out of her bed and ran us out of the room."

I was quiet a while, and Stern asked, "What happened?"

"Oh," I said, "she brought him back." I laughed suddenly. "I guess it's funny now, when you come to think of it. Nearly three months of us getting bossed around, and her ruling the roost, and then all of a sudden we lay down the law. We'd tried our best to be good according to her ideas, but, by God, that time she went too far. She got the treatment from the second she slammed her door on us. She had a big china pot under her bed, and it rose up in the air and smashed through her dresser mirror. Then one of the drawers in the dresser slid open and a glove come out of it and smacked her face.

"She went to jump back on the bed and a whole section of plaster fell off the ceiling onto the bed. The water turned on in her little bathroom and the plug went in, and just about the time it began to overflow, all her clothes fell off their hooks. She went to run out of the room, but the door was stuck, and when she yanked on the handle it opened real quick and she spread out on the floor. The door slammed shut again and more plaster come down on her. Then we went back in and stood looking at her. She was crying. I hadn't known till then that she could.

" 'You going to get Baby back here?' I asked her.

"She just lay there and cried. After a while she looked up at us. It was real pathetic. We helped her up and got her to a chair. She just looked at us for a while, and at the mirror, and at the busted ceiling, and then she whispered, 'What happened? What happened?'

" 'You took Baby away,' I said. 'That's what.'

"So she jumped up and said real low, real scared, but real strong: 'Something struck the house. An airplane. Perhaps there was an earthquake. We'll talk about Baby after breakfast.'

"I said, 'Give her more, Janie.'

"A big gob of water hit her on the face and chest and made her nightgown stick to her, which was the kind of thing that upset her most. Her braids stood straight up in the air, more and more, till they dragged her standing straight up. She opened her mouth to yell and the powder puff off the dresser rammed into it. She clawed it out.

" 'What are you doing? What are you doing?' she says, crying again.

"Janie just looked at her, and put her hands behind her, real smug. 'We haven't done anything,' she said.

"And I said, 'Not yet we haven't. You going to get Baby back?'

"And she screamed at us, 'Stop it! Stop it! Stop talking about that mongoloid idiot! It's no good to anyone, not even itself! How could I ever make believe it's mine?'

"I said, 'Get rats, Janie.'

"There was a scuttling sound along the baseboard. Miss Kew covered her face with her hands and sank down on the chair. 'Not rats,' she said. 'There are no rats here.' Then something squeaked and she went all to pieces. Did you ever see anyone really go to pieces?"

"Yes," Stern said.

"I was about as mad as I could get," I said, "but that was almost too much for me. Still, she shouldn't have sent Baby away. It took a couple of hours for her to get straightened out enough so she could use the phone, but we had Baby back before lunch time." I laughed.

"What's funny?"

"She never seemed able to rightly remember what had happened to her. About three weeks later I heard her talking to Miriam about it. She said it was the house settling suddenly. She said it was a good thing she'd sent Baby out for that medical checkup—the poor little thing might have been hurt. She really believed it, I think."

"She probably did. That's fairly common. We don't believe anything we don't want to believe."

"How much of this do you believe?" I asked him suddenly.

"I told you before—it doesn't matter. I don't want to believe or disbelieve it."

"You haven't asked me how much of it I believe."

"I don't have to. You'll make up your own mind about that."

"Are you a *good* psychotherapist?"

"I think so," he said. "Whom did you kill?"

The question caught me absolutely off guard. "Miss Kew," I said. Then I started to cuss and swear. "I didn't mean to tell you that."

"Don't worry about it," he said. "What did you do it for?"

"That's what I came here to find out."

"You must have really hated her."

I started to cry. Fifteen years old and crying like that!

He gave me time to get it all out. The first part of it came out in noises, grunts and squeaks that hurt my throat. Much more than you'd think came out when my nose started to run. And finally—words.

"Do you know where I came from? The earliest thing I can remember is a punch in the mouth. I can still see it coming, a fist as big as my head. Because I was crying. I been afraid to cry ever since. I was crying because I was hungry. Cold, maybe. Both. After that, big dormitories, and whoever could steal the most got the most. Get the hell kicked out of you if you're bad, get a big reward if you're good. Big reward: they let you alone. Try to live like that. Try to live so the biggest, most wonderful thing in the whole damn world is just to have 'em let you alone!

"So a spell with Lone and the kids. Something wonderful: you belong. It never happened before. Two yellow bulbs and a fireplace and they light up the world. It's all there is and all there ever has to be.

"Then the big change: clean clothes, cooked food, five hours a day school; Columbus and King Arthur and a 1925 book on Civics that explains about septic tanks. Over it all a great big square-cut lump of ice, and you watch it melting and the corners curve, and you know it's because of you, Miss Kew . . . hell, she had too much control over herself ever to slobber over us, but it was there, that feeling. Lone took care of us because it was part of the way he lived. Miss Kew took care of us, and none of it was the way she lived. It was something she wanted to do.

"She had a weird idea of 'right' and a wrong idea of 'wrong,' but she stuck to them, tried to make her ideas do us good. When she couldn't understand, she figured it was her own failure . . . and there was an almighty lot she didn't understand and never could. What went right was our success. What went wrong was her mistake. That last year, that was . . . oh, good."

"So?"

"So I killed her. Listen," I said. I felt I had to talk fast. I wasn't short of time, but I had to get rid of it. "I'll tell you all I know about it. The one day before I killed her. I woke up in the morning and the sheets crackly clean under me, the sunlight coming in through white curtains and bright red-and-blue drapes. There's a closet full of my clothes—mine, you see; I never had anything that was really mine before—and downstairs Miriam clinking around with breakfast and the twins laughing. Laughing with *her*, mind you, not just with each other like they always did before.

"In the next room, Janie moving around, singing, and when I see her, I know her face will shine inside and out. I get up. There's *hot* water and the toothpaste bites my tongue. The clothes fit me and I go downstairs and they're all there and I'm glad to see them and they're glad to see me, and we no sooner get around the table when Miss Kew comes down and everyone calls out to her at once.

"And the morning goes by like that, school with a recess, there in the big long living room. The twins with the ends of their tongues stuck out, drawing the alphabet instead of writing it, and then Janie, when it's time, painting a picture, a real picture of a cow with trees and a yellow fence that goes off into the distance. Here I am lost between the two parts of a quadratic equation, and Miss Kew bending close to help me, and I smell the sachet she has on her clothes. I hold up my head to smell it better, and far away I hear the shuffle and klunk of filled pots going on the stove back in the kitchen.

"And the afternoon goes by like that, more school and some study and boiling out into the yard, laughing. The twins chasing each other, running on their two feet to get where they want to go; Janie dappling the leaves in her picture, trying to get it just the way Miss Kew says it ought to be. And Baby, he's got a big play-pen. He don't move around much any more, he just watches and dribbles some, and gets packed full of food and kept as clean as a new sheet of tinfoil.

"And supper, and the evening, and Miss Kew reading to us, changing her voice every time someone else talks in the story, reading fast and whispery when it embarrasses her, but reading every word all the same.

"And I had to go and kill her. And that's all."

"You haven't said why," Stern said.

"What are you—stupid?" I yelled.

Stern didn't say anything. I turned on my belly on the couch and propped up my chin in my hands and looked at him. You never could tell what was going on with him, but I got the idea that he was puzzled.

"I said why," I told him.

"Not to me."

I suddenly understood that I was asking too much of him. I said slowly, "We all woke up at the same time. We all did what somebody else wanted. We lived through a day someone else's way, thinking someone else's thoughts, saying other people's words. Janie painted someone else's pictures. Baby didn't talk to anyone, and we were all happy with it. Now do you see?"

"Not yet."

"God!" I said. I thought for a while. "We didn't blesh."

"Blesh? Oh. But you didn't after Lone died, either."

"That was different. That was like a car running out of gas, but the car's there—there's nothing wrong with it. It's just waiting. But after Miss Kew got done with us, the car was taken all to pieces, see?"

It was his turn to think a while. Finally he said, "The mind makes us do funny things. Some of them seem completely reasonless, wrong, insane. But the cornerstone of the work we're doing is this: there's a chain of solid, unassailable logic in the things we do. Dig deep enough and you find cause and effect as clearly in this field as you do in any other. I said *logic*, mind; I didn't say 'correctness' or 'rightness' or 'justice' or anything of the sort. Logic and truth are two very different things, but they often look the same to the mind that's performing the logic.

"When that mind is submerged, working at cross-purposes with the surface mind, then you're all confused. Now in your case, I can see the thing you're pointing at—that in order to preserve or to rebuild that peculiar bond between you kids, you had to get rid of Miss Kew. But I don't see the logic. I don't see that regaining that 'bleshing' was worth destroying this new-found security which you admit was enjoyable."

I said, desperately, "Maybe it wasn't worth destroying it."

Stern leaned forward and pointed his pipe at me. "It *was* because it made you do what you did. After the fact, maybe things look different. But when you were moved to do it, the important thing was to destroy Miss Kew and regain this thing you'd had before. I don't see why and neither do you."

"How are we going to find out?"

"Well, let's get right to the most unpleasant part, if you're up to it."

I lay down. "I'm ready."

"All right. Tell me everything that happened just before you killed her."

I fumbled through that last day, trying to taste the food, hear the voices. A thing came and went and came again: it was the crisp feeling of the sheets. I thrust it away because it was at the beginning of that day, but it came back again, and I realized it was at the end, instead.

I said, "What I just told you, all that about the children doing things other people's way instead of their own, and Baby not talking, and everyone happy about it, and finally that I had to kill Miss Kew. It took a long time to get to that, and a long time to start doing it. I guess I lay in bed and thought for four hours before I got up again. It was dark and quiet. I went out of the room and down the hall and into Miss Kew's bedroom and killed her."

"How?"

"That's all there is!" I shouted, as loud as I could. Then I quieted down. "It was awful dark . . . it still is. I don't know. I don't want to know. She did love us. I know she did. But I had to kill her."

"All right, all right," Stern said. "I guess there's no need to get too gruesome about this. You're—"

"What?"

"You're quite strong for your age, aren't you, Gerard?"

"I guess so. Strong enough, anyway."

"Yes," he said.

"I still don't see that logic you were talking about." I began to hammer on the couch with my fist, hard, once for each word: "Why—did—I—have—to—go—and—do—that?"

"Cut that out," he said. "You'll hurt yourself."

"I ought to get hurt," I said.

"Ah?" said Stern.

I got up and went to the desk and got some water. "What am I going to do?"

"Tell me what you did after you killed her, right up until the time you came here."

"Not much," I said. "It was only last night. I went back to my room, sort of numb. I put all my clothes on except my shoes. I carried them. I went out. Walked a long time, trying to think, went to the post office when it opened. Miss Kew used to let me go for the mail sometimes. Found this check waiting for me for the contest. Cashed it at the bank, opened an account, took eleven hundred bucks. Got the idea of getting some help from a psychiatrist, spent most of the day looking for one, came here. That's all."

"Didn't you have any trouble cashing the check?"

"I never have any trouble making people do what I want them to do."

He gave a surprised grunt.

"I know what you're thinking—I couldn't make Miss Kew do what I wanted."

"That's part of it," he admitted.

"If I had of done that," I told him, "she wouldn't of been Miss Kew any more. Now the banker—all I made him do was be a banker."

I looked at him and suddenly realized why he fooled with that pipe all the time. It was so he could look down at it and you wouldn't be able to see his eyes.

"You killed her," he said—and I knew he was changing the subject—"and destroyed something that was valuable to you. It must have been less valuable to you than the chance to rebuild this thing you used to have with the other kids. And you're not sure of the value of that." He looked up. "Does that describe your main trouble?"

"Just about."

"You know the single thing that makes people kill?" When I didn't answer, he said, "Survival. To save the self or something which identifies with the self. And in this case that doesn't apply, because your set-up with Miss Kew had far more survival value for you, singly and as a group, than the other."

"So maybe I just didn't have a good enough reason to kill her."

"You had, because you did it. We just haven't located it yet. I mean we have the reason, but we don't know why it was important enough. The answer is somewhere in you."

"Where?"

He got up and walked some. "We have a pretty consecutive life-story here. There's fantasy mixed with the fact, of course, and there are areas in which we have no detailed information, but we have a beginning and a middle and an end. Now, I can't say for sure, but the answer may be in that bridge you refused to cross a while back. Remember?"

I remembered, all right. I said, "Why that? Why can't we try something else?"

He quietly pointed out, "Because you just said it. Why are you shying away from it?"

"Don't go making big ones out of little ones," I said. Sometimes the guy annoyed me. "That bothers me. I don't know why, but it does."

"Something's lying hidden in there, and you're bothering *it* so it's fighting back. Anything that fights to stay concealed is very possibly the thing we're after. Your trouble is concealed, isn't it?"

"Well, yes," I said, and I felt that sickness and faintness again, and again I pushed it away. Suddenly I wasn't going to be stopped any more. "Let's go get it." I lay down.

He let me watch the ceiling and listen to silence for a while, and then he said, "You're in the library. You've just met Miss Kew. She's talking to you; you're telling her about the children."

I lay very still. Nothing happened. Yes, it did; I got tense inside, all over, from the bones out, more and more. When it got as bad as it could, still nothing happened.

I heard him get up and cross the room to the desk. He fumbled there for a while; things clicked and hummed. Suddenly I heard my own voice:

"Well, there's Jane, she's eleven like me. And Bonnie and Beanie are eight, they're twins, and Baby. Baby is three."

And the sound of my own scream—

And nothingness.

Sputtering up out of the darkness, I came flailing out with my fists. Strong hands caught my wrists. They didn't check my arms; they just grabbed and rode. I opened my eyes. I was soaking wet. The thermos lay on its side on the rug. Stern was crouched beside me, holding my wrists. I quit struggling.

"What happened?"

He let me go and stood back watchfully. "Lord," he said, "what a charge!"

I held my head and moaned. He threw me a hand-towel and I used it. "What hit me?"

"I've had you on tape the whole time," he explained. "When you wouldn't get into that recollection, I tried to nudge you into it by using your own voice as you recounted it before. It works wonders sometimes."

"It worked wonders this time," I growled. "I think I blew a fuse."

"In effect, you did. You were on the trembling verge of going into the thing you don't want to remember, and you let yourself go unconscious rather than do it."

"What are you so pleased about?"

"Last-ditch defense," he said tersely. "We've got it now. Just one more try."

"Now hold on. The last-ditch defense is that I drop dead."

"You won't. You've contained this episode in your subconscious mind for a long time and it hasn't hurt you."

"Hasn't it?"

"Not in terms of killing you."

"How do you know it won't when we drag it out?"

"You'll see."

I looked up at him sideways. Somehow he struck me as knowing what he was doing.

"You know a lot more about yourself now than you did at the time," he explained softly. "You can apply insight. You can evaluate it as it comes up. Maybe not completely, but enough to protect yourself. Don't worry. Trust me. I can stop it if it gets too bad. Now just relax. Look at the ceiling. Be aware of your toes. Don't look at your toes. Look straight up. Your toes, your big toes. Don't move your toes, but feel them. Count outward from your big toes, one count for each toe. One, two, three. Feel that third toe. Feel the toe, feel it, feel it go limp, go limp, go limp. The toe next to it on both sides gets limp. So limp because your toes are limp, all of your toes are limp—"

"What are you doing?" I shouted at him.

He said in the same silky voice, "You trust me and so do your toes trust me. They're all limp because you trust me. You—"

"You're trying to hypnotize me. I'm not going to let you do that."

"You're going to hypnotize yourself. You do everything yourself. I just point the way. I point your toes to the path. Just point your toes. No one can make you go anywhere you don't want to go, but you want to go where your toes are pointed, where your toes are limp, where your . . ."

On and on and on. And where was the dangling gold ornament, the light in the eyes, the mystic passes? He wasn't even sitting where I could see him. Where was the talk about how sleepy I was supposed to be? Well, he knew I wasn't sleepy and didn't want to be sleepy. I just wanted to be toes. I just wanted to be limp, just a limp toe. No brains in a toe, a toe to go, go, go eleven times, eleven, I'm eleven . . .

I split in two, and it was all right, the part that watched the part that went back to the library, and Miss Kew leaning toward me, but not too near, me with newspaper crackling under me on the library chair, me with one shoe off and my limp toes dangling . . . and I felt a mild surprise at this. For this was hypnosis, but I was quite conscious, quite altogether there on the couch with Stern droning away at me, quite able to roll over and sit up and talk to him and walk out if I wanted to, but I just didn't want to. Oh, if this was what hypnosis was like, I was all for it. I'd work at this. This was all right.

There on the table I'm able to see that the gold will unfold on the leather, and whether I'm able to stay by the table with you, with Miss Kew, with Miss Kew . . .

". . . and Bonnie and Beanie are eight, they're twins, and Baby. Baby is three."

"Baby is three," she said.

There was a pressure, a stretching apart, and a . . . a breakage. And with a tearing agony and a burst of triumph that drowned the pain, it was done.

And this is what was inside. All in one flash, but all this.

Baby is three? My baby would be three if there were a baby, which there never was . . .

Lone, I'm open to you. Open, is this open enough?

His irises like wheels. I'm sure they spin, but I never catch them at it. The probe that passes invisibly from his brain, through his eyes, into mine. Does he know what it means to me? Does he care? He doesn't care, he doesn't know; he empties me and I fill as he directs me to; he drinks and waits and drinks again and never looks at the cup.

When I saw him first, I was dancing in the wind, in the wood, in the wild, and I spun about and he stood there in the leafy shadows, watching me. I hated him for it. It was not my wood, not my gold-spangled fern-tangled glen. But it was my dancing that he took, freezing it forever by being there. I hated him for it, hated the way he looked, the way he stood, ankle-deep in the kind wet ferns, looking like a tree with roots for feet and clothes the color of earth. As I stopped he moved, and then he was just a man, a great ape-shouldered, dirty animal of a man, and all my hate was fear suddenly and I was just as frozen.

He knew what he had done and he didn't care. Dancing . . . never to dance again, because never would I know the woods were free of eyes, free of tall, uncaring, dirty animal men. Summer days with the clothes choking me, winter nights with the precious decencies round and about me like a shroud, and never to dance again, never to remember dancing without remembering the shock of knowing he had seen me. How I hated him! Oh, how I hated him!

To dance alone where no one knew, that was the single thing I hid to myself when I was known as Miss Kew, that Victorian, older than her years, later than her time; correct and starched, lace and linen and lonely. Now indeed I would be all they said, through and through, forever and ever, because he had robbed me of the one thing I dared to keep secret.

He came out into the sun and walked to me, holding his great head a little on one side. I stood where I was, frozen inwardly and outwardly and altogether by the core of anger and the layer of fear. My arm was still out, my waist still bent from my dance, and when he stopped, I breathed again because by then I had to.

He said, "You read books?"

I couldn't bear to have him near me, I couldn't move. He put out his hard hand and touched my jaw, turned my head up until I had to look into his face. I cringed away from him, but my face would not leave his hand, though he was not holding it, just lifting it. "You got to read some books for me. I got no time to find them."

I asked him, "Who are you?"

"Lone," he said. "You going to read books for me?"

"No. Let me go, let me go!"

He laughed at me. He wasn't holding me.

"What books?" I cried.

He thumped my face, not very hard. It made me look up a bit more. He dropped his hand away. His eyes, the irises were going to spin . . .

"Open up in there," he said. "Open way up and let me see."

There were books in my head, and he was looking at the titles . . . he was not looking at the titles, for he couldn't read. He was looking at what I knew of the books. I suddenly felt terribly useless, because I had only a fraction of what he wanted.

"What's that?" he barked.

I knew what he meant. He'd gotten it from inside my head. I didn't know it was in there, even, but he found it.

"Telekinesis," I said.

"How is it done?"

"Nobody knows if it can be done. Moving physical objects with the mind!"

"It can be done," he said. "This one?"

"Teleportation. That's the same thing—well, almost. Moving your own body with mind power."

"Yeah, yeah, I see it," he said gruffly.

"Molecular interpenetration. Telepathy and clairvoyance. I don't know anything about them. I think they're silly."

"Read about 'em. It don't matter if you understand or not. What's this?"

It was there in my brain, on my lips. "*Gestalt.*"

"What's that?"

"Group. Like a cure for a lot of diseases with one kind of treatment. Like a lot of thoughts expressed in one phrase. The whole is greater than the sum of the parts."

"Read about that, too. Read a whole lot about that. That's the *most* you got to read about. That's important."

He turned away, and when his eyes came away from mine it was like something breaking, so that I staggered and fell to one knee. He went off into the woods without looking back. I got my things and ran home. There was anger, and it struck me like a storm. There was fear, and it struck me like a wind. I knew I would read the books, I knew I would come back, I knew I would never dance again.

So I read the books and I came back. Sometimes it was every day for three or four days, and sometimes, because I couldn't find a certain book, I might not come back for ten. He was always there in the little glen, waiting, standing in the shadows, and he took what he wanted of the books and nothing of me. He never mentioned the next meeting. If he came there every day to wait for me, or if he only came when I did, I have no way of knowing.

He made me read books that contained nothing for me, books on evolution, on social and cultural organization, on mythology, and ever so much on symbiosis. What I had with him were not conversations; sometimes nothing audible would pass between us but his grunt of surprise or small, short hum of interest.

He tore the books out of me the way he would tear berries from a bush, all at once; he smelled of sweat and earth and the green juices his heavy body crushed when he moved through the wood.

If he learned anything from the books, it made no difference in him.

There came a day when he sat by me and puzzled something out.

He said, "What book has something like this?" Then he waited for a long time, thinking. "The way a termite can't digest wood, you know, and microbes in the termite's belly can, and what the termite eats is what the microbe leaves behind. What's that?"

"Symbiosis," I remembered. I remembered the words. Lone tore the content from words and threw the words away. "Two kinds of life depending upon one another for existence."

"Yeah. Well, is there a book about four-five kinds doing that?"

"I don't know."

Then he asked, "What about this? You got a radio station, you got four-five receivers, each receiver is fixed up to make something different happen, like one digs and one flies and one makes noise, but each one takes orders from the one place. And each one has its own power and its own thing to do, but they are all apart. Now: is there life like that, instead of radio?"

"Where each organism is a part of the whole, but separated? I don't think so . . . unless you mean social organizations, like a team, or perhaps a gang of men working, all taking orders from the same boss."

"No," he said immediately, "not like that. Like one single animal." He made a gesture with his cupped hand which I understood.

I asked, "You mean a *gestalt* life-form? It's fantastic."

"No book has about that, huh?"

"None I ever heard of."

"I got to know about that," he said heavily. "There is such a thing. I want to know if it ever happened before."

"I can't see how anything of the sort could exist."

"It does. A part that fetches, a part that figures, a part that finds out, and a part that talks."

"Talks? Only humans talk."

"I know," he said, and got up and went away.

I looked and looked for such a book, but found nothing remotely like it. I came back and told him so. He was still a very long time, looking off to the blue-on-blue line of the hilly horizon. Then he drove those about-to-spin irises at me and searched.

"You learn, but you don't think," he said, and looked again at the hills.

"This all happens with humans," he said eventually. "It happens piece by piece right under folks' noses, and they don't see it. You got mindreaders. You got people can move things with their mind. You got people can move themselves with their mind. You got people can figure anything out if you just think to ask them. What you ain't got is the one kind of person who can pull 'em all together, like a brain pulls together the parts that press and pull and feel heat and walk and think and all the other things.

"I'm one," he finished suddenly. Then he sat still for so long, I thought he had forgotten me.

"Lone," I said, "what do you do here in the woods?"

"I wait," he said. "I ain't finished yet." He looked at my eyes and snorted in irritation. "I don't mean 'finished' like you're thinking. I mean I ain't—completed yet. You know about a worm when it's cut, growin' whole again? Well, forget about the cut. Suppose it just grew that way, for the first time, see? I'm getting parts. I ain't finished. I want a book about that kind of animal that is me when I'm finished."

"I don't know of such a book. Can you tell me more? Maybe if you could, I'd think of the right book or a place to find it."

He broke a stick between his huge hands, put the two pieces side by side and broke them together with one strong twist.

"All I know is I got to do what I'm doing like a bird's got to nest when it's time. And I know that when I'm done I won't be anything to brag about. I'll be like a body stronger and faster than anything there ever was, without the right kind of head on it. But maybe that's because I'm one of the first. That picture you had, the caveman . . ."

"Neanderthal."

"Yeah. Come to think of it, he was no great shakes. An early try at something new. That's what I'm going to be. But maybe the right kind of head'll come along after I'm all organized. Then it'll be something."

He grunted with satisfaction and went away.

I tried, for days I tried, but I couldn't find what he wanted. I found a magazine which stated that the next important evolutionary step in man would be a psychic rather than a physical direction, but it said nothing about a—shall I call it a *gestalt* organism? There was something about slime molds, but they seem to be more a hive activity of amoebae than even a symbiosis.

To my own unscientific, personally uninterested mind, there was nothing like what he wanted except possibly a band marching together, everyone playing different kinds of instruments with different techniques and different notes, to make a single thing move along together. But he hadn't meant anything like that.

So I went back to him in the cool of an early fall evening, and he took what little I had in my eyes, and turned from me angrily with gross word I shall not permit myself to remember.

"You can't find it," he told me. "Don't come back."

He got up and went to a tattered birch and leaned against it, looking out and down into the wind-tossed crackling shadows. I think he had forgotten me already. I know he leaped like a frightened animal when I spoke to him from so near. He must have been completely immersed in whatever strange thoughts he was having, for I'm sure he didn't hear me coming.

I said, "Lone, don't blame me for not finding it. I tried."

He controlled his startlement and brought those eyes down to me. "Blame? Who's blamin' anybody?"

"I failed you," I told him, "and you're angry."

He looked at me so long I became uncomfortable.

"I don't know what you're talkin' about," he said.

I wouldn't let him turn away from me. He would have. He would have left me forever with not another thought; he didn't care! It wasn't cruelty or thoughtlessness as I have been taught to know those things. He was as uncaring as a cat is of the bursting of a tulip bud.

I took him by the upper arms and shook him, it was like trying to shake the front of my house. "You *can* know!" I screamed at him. "You know what I read. You must know what I think!"

He shook his head.

"I'm a person, a woman," I raved at him. "You've used me and used me and you've given me nothing. You've made me break a lifetime of habits—reading until all hours, coming to you in the rain and on Sunday—you don't talk to me, you don't look at me, you don't know anything about me and you don't care. You put some sort of a spell on me that I couldn't break. And when you're finished, you say, 'Don't come back'."

"Do I have to give something back because I took something?"

"People do."

He gave that short interested hum. "What do you want me to give you? I ain't got anything."

I moved away from him. I felt . . . I don't know what I felt. After a time I said, "I don't know."

He shrugged and turned. I fairly leaped at him, dragging him back. "I want you to—"

"Well, damn it, what?"

I couldn't look at him; I could hardly speak. "I don't know. There's something, but I don't know what it is. It's something that—I couldn't say if I knew it." When he began to shake his head, I took his arms again. "You've read the books out of me; can't you read the . . . the *me* out of me?"

"I ain't never tried." He held my face up, and stepped close. "Here," he said.

His eyes projected their strange probe at me and I screamed. I tried to twist away. I hadn't wanted this, I was sure I hadn't. I struggled terribly. I think he lifted me right off the ground with his big hands. He held me until he was finished, and then let me drop. I huddled to the ground, sobbing. He sat down beside me. He didn't try to touch me. He didn't try to go away. I quieted at last and crouched there, waiting.

He said, "I ain't going to do much of that no more."

I sat up and tucked my skirt close around me and laid my cheek on my updrawn knees so I could see his face. "What happened?"

He cursed. "Damn mishmash inside you. Thirty-three years old—what you want to live like that for?"

"I live very comfortably," I said with some pique.

"Yeah," he said. "All by yourself for ten years now 'cept for someone to do your work. Nobody else."

"Men are animals, and women . . ."

"You really hate women. They all know something you don't."

"I don't want to know. I'm quite happy the way I am."

"Hell you are."

I said nothing to that. I despise that kind of language.

"Two things you want from me. Neither makes no sense." He looked at me with the first real expression I have ever seen in his face: a profound wonderment. "You want to know all about me, where I came from, how I got to be what I am."

"Yes, I do want that. What's the other thing I want that you know and I don't?"

"I was born some place and growed like a weed somehow," he said, ignoring me. "Folks who didn't give even enough of a damn to try the orphanage routine. I lived with some other folks for a while, tried school, didn't like it. Too small a town for them special schools for my kind, retarded, y'know. So I just ran loose, sort of in training to be the village idiot. I'da made it if I'd stayed there, but I took to the woods instead."

"Why?"

He wondered why, and finally said, "I guess because the way people lived didn't make no sense to me. I saw enough up and down, back and forth, to know that they live a lot of different ways, but none of 'em was for me. Out here I can grow like I want."

"How is that?" I asked over one of those vast distances that built and receded between him and me so constantly.

"What I wanted to get from your books."

"You never told me."

For the second time he said, "You learn, but you don't think. There's a kind of—well, *person*. It's all made of separate parts, but it's all one person. It has like hands, it has like legs, it has like a talking mouth, and it has like a brain. That's me, a brain for that person. Damn feeble, too, but the best I know of."

"You're mad."

"No, I ain't," he said, unoffended and completely certain. "I already got the part that's like hands. I can move 'em anywhere and they do what I want, though they're too young yet to do much good. I got the part that talks. That one's real good."

"I don't think you talk very well at all," I said. I cannot stand incorrect English.

He was surprised. "I'm not talking about me! She's back yonder with the others."

"She?"

"The one that talks. Now I need one that thinks, one that can take anything and add it to anything else and come up with a right answer. And once they're all together, and all the parts get used together often enough, I'll be that new kind of thing I told you about. See? Only—I wish it had a better head on it than me."

My own head was swimming. "What made you start doing this?"

He considered me gravely. "What made you start growing hair in your armpits?" he asked me. "You don't figure a thing like that. It just happens."

"What is that . . . that thing you do when you look in my eyes?"

"You want a name for it? I ain't got one. I don't know how I do it. I know I can get anyone I want to do anything. Like you're going to forget about me."

I said in a choked voice, "I don't want to forget about you."

"You will." I didn't know then whether he meant I'd forget, or I'd *want* to forget. "You'll hate me, and then after a long time you'll be grateful. Maybe you'll be able to do something for me some time. You'll be that grateful that you'll be glad to do it. But you'll forget, all right, everything but a sort of . . . feeling. And my name, maybe."

I don't know what moved me to ask him, but I did, forlornly. "And no one will ever know about you and me?"

"Can't," he said. "Unless . . . well, unless it was the head of the animal, like me, or a better one." He heaved himself up.

"Oh, wait, wait!" I cried. He mustn't go yet, he mustn't. He was a tall, dirty beast of a man, yet he had enthralled me in some dreadful way. "You haven't given me the other . . . whatever it was."

"Oh," he said. "Yeah, that."

He moved like a flash. There was a pressure, a stretching apart, and a . . . a breakage. And with a tearing agony and a burst of triumph that drowned the pain, it was done.

I came up out of it, through two distinct levels:

I am eleven, breathless from shock from a transferred agony of that incredible entrance into the ego of another. And:

I am fifteen, lying on the couch while Stern drones on, ". . . quietly, quietly limp, your ankles and legs as limp as your toes, your belly goes soft, the back of your neck is as limp as your belly, it's quiet and easy and all gone soft and limper than limp . . ."

I sat up and swung my legs to the floor. "Okay," I said.

Stern looked a little annoyed. "This is going to work," he said, "but it can only work if you co-operate. Just lie—"

"It did work," I said.

"What?"

"The whole thing. A to Z." I snapped my fingers. "Like that."

He looked at me piercingly. "What do you mean?"

"It was right there, where you said. In the library. When I was eleven. When she said, 'Baby is three.' It knocked loose something that had been boiling around in her for three years, and it all came blasting out. I got it, full force; just a kid, no warning, no defenses. It had such a—a pain in it, like I never knew could be."

"Go on," said Stern.

"That's really all. I mean that's not what was in it; it's what it did to me. What it was, a sort of hunk of her own self. A whole lot of things that happened over about four months, every bit of it. She knew Lone."

"You mean a whole *series* of episodes?"

"That's it."

"You got a series all at once? In a split second?"

"That's right. Look, for that split second I *was* her, don't you see? I was her, everything she'd ever done, everything she'd ever thought and heard and felt. Everything, everything, all in the right order if I wanted to bring it out like that. Any part of it if I wanted it by itself. If I'm going to tell you about what I had for lunch, do I have to tell you everything else I've ever done since I was born? No. I tell you I *was* her, and then and forever after I can remember anything she could remember up to that point. In just that one flash."

"A *gestalt*," he murmured.

"Aha!" I said, and thought about that. I thought about a whole lot of things. I put them aside for a moment and said, "Why didn't I know all this before?"

"You had a powerful block against recalling it."

I got up excitedly. "I don't see why. I don't see that at all."

"Just natural revulsion," he guessed. "How about this? You had a distaste for assuming a female ego, even for a second."

"You told me yourself, right at the beginning, that I didn't have that kind of a problem."

"Well, how does this sound to you? You say you felt pain in that episode. So—you wouldn't go back into it for fear of re-experiencing the pain."

"Let me think, let me think. Yeah, yeah, that's part of it—that thing of going into someone's mind. She opened up to me because I reminded her of Lone. I went in. I wasn't ready; I'd never done it before, except maybe a little, against resistance. I went all the way in and it was too much; it frightened me away from trying it for years. And there it lay, wrapped up, locked away. But as I grew older, the power to do that with my mind got stronger and stronger, and still I was afraid to use it. And the more I grew, the more I felt, down deep, that Miss Kew had to be killed before she killed the . . . what I am. My God!" I shouted. "Do you know what I am?"

"No," he said. "Like to tell me about it?"

"I'd like to," I said. "Oh, yes, I'd like that."

He had that professional open-minded expression on his face, not believing or disbelieving, just taking it all in. I had to tell him, and I suddenly realized that I didn't have enough words. I knew the things, but not the names for them.

Lone took the meanings and threw the words away.

Further back: *"You read books. Read books for me."*

The look of his eyes. That—"opening up" thing.

I went over to Stern. He looked up at me. I bent close. First he was startled, then he controlled it, then he came even closer to me.

"My God," he murmured. "I didn't look at those eyes before. I could have sworn those irises spun like wheels . . ."

Stern read books. He'd read more books than I ever imagined had been written. I slipped in there, looking for what I wanted.

I can't say exactly what it was like. It was like walking in a tunnel, and in this tunnel, all over the roof and walls, wooden arms stuck out at you, like the thing at the carnival, the merry-go-round, the thing you snatch the brass rings from. There's a brass ring on the end of each of these arms, and you can take any one of them you want to.

Now imagine you make up your mind which rings you want, and the arms hold only those. Now picture yourself with a thousand hands to grab the rings off with. Now just suppose the tunnel is a zillion miles long, and you can go from one end of it to the other, grabbing rings, in just the time it takes you to blink once. Well, it was like that, only easier.

It was easier for me to do than it had been for Lone.

Straightening up, I got away from Stern. He looked sick and frightened.

"It's all right," I said.

"What did you do to me?"

"I needed some words. Come on, come on. Get professional."

I had to admire him. He put his pipe in his pocket and gouged the tips of his fingers hard against his forehead and cheeks. Then he sat up and he was okay again.

"I know," I said. "That's how Miss Kew felt when Lone did it to her."

"What *are* you?"

"I'll tell you. I'm the central ganglion of a complex organism which is composed of Baby, a computer; Bonnie and Beanie, teleports; Jane, telekineticist; and myself, telepath and central control. There isn't a single thing about any of us that hasn't been documented: the teleportation of the Yogi, the telekinetics of some gamblers, the idio-savant mathematicians, and most of all, the so-called poltergeist, the moving about of household goods through the instrumentation of a young girl. Only in this case every one of my parts delivers at peak performance.

"Lone organized it, or it formed around him; it doesn't matter which. I replaced Lone, but I was too underdeveloped when he died, and on top of that I got an occlusion from that blast from Miss Kew. To that extent you were right when you said the blast made me subconsciously afraid to discover what was in it. But there was another good reason for my not being able to get in under that 'Baby is three' barrier.

"We ran into the problem of what it was I valued more than the security Miss Kew gave us. Can't you see now what it was? My *gestalt* organism was at the point of death from that security. I figured she had to be killed or it—I—would be. Oh, the parts would live on: two little colored girls with a speech impediment, one introspective girl with an artistic bent, one mongoloid idiot, and me—ninety per cent short-circuited potentials and ten per cent juvenile delinquent." I laughed. "Sure, she had to be killed. It was self-preservation for the *gestalt*."

Stern bobbled around with his mouth and finally got out: "I don't—"

"You don't need to," I laughed. "This is wonderful. You're fine, hey, fine. Now I want to tell you this, because you can appreciate a fine point in your specialty. You talk about occlusions! I couldn't get past the 'Baby is three' thing because in it lay the clues to what I really am. I couldn't find that out because I was afraid to remember that I had failed in the thing I had to do to save the *gestalt*. Ain't that purty?"

"Failed? Failed how?"

"Look. I came to love Miss Kew, and I'd never loved anything before. Yet I had reason to kill her. She *had* to be killed; I *couldn't* kill her. What does a human mind do when presented with imperative, mutually exclusive alternatives?"

"It—it might simply quit. As you phrased it earlier, it might blow a fuse, retreat, refuse to function in that area."

"Well, I didn't do that. What else?"

"It might slip into a delusion that it had already taken one of the courses of action."

I nodded happily. "I didn't kill her. I decided I must; I got up, got dressed—and the next thing I knew I was outside, wandering, very confused. I got my money—and I understand now, with super-empathy, how I can win *anyone's* prize contest—and I went looking for a head-shrinker. I found a good one."

"Thanks," he said dazedly. He looked at me with a strangeness in his eyes. "And now that you know, what's solved? What are you going to do?"

"Go back home," I said happily. "Reactivate the superorganism, exercise it secretly in ways that won't make Miss Kew unhappy, and we'll stay with her as long as we know it pleases her. And we'll please her. She'll be happy in ways she's never dreamed about until now. She rates it, bless her strait-laced, hungry heart."

"And she can't kill your—*gestalt* organism?"

"Not a chance. Not now."

"How do you know it isn't dead already?"

"How?" I echoed. "How does your head know your arm works?"

He wet his lips. "You're going home to make a spinster happy. And after that?"

I shrugged. "After that?" I mocked. "Did the Peking man look at Homo Sap walking erect and say, 'What will he do after that?' We'll live, that's all, like a man, like a tree, like anything else that lives. We'll feed and grow and experiment and breed. We'll defend ourselves." I spread my hands. "We'll just do what comes naturally."

"But what can you do?"

"What can an electric motor do? It depends on where we apply ourselves."

Stern was very pale. "But you're the only such organism . . ."

"Are we? I don't know. I don't think so. I've told you the parts have been around for ages—the telepaths, the *poltergeists*. What was lacking was the ones to organize, to be heads to the scattered bodies. Lone was one, I'm one; there must be more. We'll find out as we mature."

"You—aren't mature yet?"

"Lord, no!" I laughed. "We're an infant. We're the equivalent of about a three-year-old child. So you see, there it is again, and this time I'm not afraid of it; Baby is three." I looked at my hands. "Baby is three," I said again, because the realization tasted good. "And when this particular group-baby is five, it might want to be a fireman. At eight, maybe a cowboy or maybe an FBI man. And when it grows up, maybe it'll build a city, or perhaps it'll be President."

"Oh, God!" he said. "God!"

I looked down at him. "You're afraid," I said. "You're afraid of *Homo Gestalt*."

He made a wonderful effort and smiled. "That's bastard terminology."

"We're a bastard breed," I said. I pointed. "Sit over there."

He crossed the quiet room and sat at the desk. I leaned close to him and he went to sleep with his eyes open. I straightened up and looked around the room. Then I got the thermos flask and filled it and put it on the desk. I fixed the corner of the rug and put a clean towel at the head of the couch. I went to the side of the desk and opened it and looked at the tape recorder.

Like reaching out a hand, I got Beanie. She stood by the desk, wide-eyed.

"Look here," I told her. "Look good, now. What I want to do is erase all this tape. Go ask Baby how."

She blinked at me and sort of shook herself, and then leaned over the recorder. She was there—and gone—and back, just like that. She pushed past me and turned two knobs, moved a pointer until it clicked twice. The tape raced backward past the head swiftly, whining.

"All right," I said, "beat it."

She vanished.

I got my jacket and went to the door. Stern was still sitting at the desk, staring.

"A *good* head-shrinker," I murmured. I felt fine.

Outside I waited, then turned and went back in again.

Stern looked up at me. "Sit over there, Sonny."

"Gee," I said. "Sorry, sir. I got in the wrong office."

"That's all right," he said.

I went out and closed the door. All the way down to the store to buy Miss Kew some flowers, I was grinning about how he'd account for the loss of an afternoon and the gain of a thousand bucks.

FIREWATER

William Tenn

The hairiest, dirtiest, and oldest of the three visitors from Arizona scratched his back against the plastic of the webfoam chair. "Insinuations are lavender nearly," he remarked by way of opening the conversation.

His two companions—the thin young man with dripping eyes, and the woman whose good looks were marred chiefly by incredibly decayed teeth—giggled and relaxed. The thin young man said "Gabble, gabble, honk!" under his breath, and the other two nodded emphatically.

Greta Seidenheim looked up from the tiny stenographic machine resting on a pair of the most exciting knees her employer had been able to find in Greater New York. She swiveled her blond beauty at him. "That too, Mr. Hebster?"

The president of Hebster Securities, Inc., waited until the memory of her voice ceased to tickle his ears; he had much clear thinking to do. Then he nodded and said resonantly, "That too, Miss Seidenheim. Close phonetic approximations of the gabble-honk and remember to indicate when it sounds like a question and when like an exclamation."

He rubbed his recently manicured fingernails across the desk drawer containing his fully loaded Parabellum. Check. The communication buttons with which he could summon any quantity of Hebster Securities personnel up to the nine hundred working at present in the Hebster Building lay some eight inches from the other hand. Check. And there were the doors here, the doors there, behind which his uniformed bodyguard stood poised to burst in at a signal which would blaze before them the moment his right foot came off the tiny spring set in the floor. *And* check.

Algernon Hebster could talk business—even with Primeys.

Courteously, he nodded at each one of his visitors from Arizona; he smiled ruefully at what the dirty shapeless masses they wore on their feet were doing to the calf-deep rug that had been woven specially for his private office. He had greeted them when Miss Seidenheim had escorted them in. They had laughed in his face.

"Suppose we rattle off some introductions. You know me. I'm Hebster, Algernon Hebster—you asked for me specifically at the desk in the lobby. If it's important to the conversation, my secretary's name is Greta Seidenheim. And you, sir?"

He had addressed the old fellow, but the thin young man leaned forward in his seat and held out a taut, almost transparent hand. "Names?" he inquired. "Names are round if not revealed. Consider names. How many names? Consider names, *reconsider* names!"

The woman leaned forward too, and the smell from her diseased mouth reach Hebster even across the enormous space of his office. "Rabble and reaching and all the upward clash," she intoned, spreading her hands as if in agreement with an obvious point. "Emptiness derogating itself into infinity—"

"Into duration," the older man corrected.

"Into infinity," the woman insisted.

"Gabble, gabble, honk?" the young man queried bitterly.

"Listen!" Hebster roared. "When I asked for—"

The communicator buzzed and he drew a deep breath and pressed a button. His receptionist's voice boiled out rapidly, fearfully: "I remember your orders, Mr. Hebster, but those two men from the UM Special Investigating Commission are here again and they look as if they mean business. I mean, they look as if they'll make trouble."

"Yost and Funatti?"

"Yes, sir. From what they said to each other, I think they know you have three Primeys in there. They asked me what are you trying to do—deliberately inflame the Firsters? They said they're going to invoke full supranational powers and force an entry if you don't—"

"Stall them."

"But, Mr. Hebster, the *UM Special Investigating*—"

"Stall them, I said. Are you a receptionist or a swinging door? Use your imagination, Ruth. You have a nine-hundred-man organization and a multi-million-dollar corporation at your disposal. You can stage any kind of farce in that outer office you want—up to and including the deal where some actor made up to look like me walks in and drops dead at their feet. Stall them and I'll nod a bonus at you. *Stall them.*" He clicked off, looked up.

His visitors, at least, were having a fine time. They had turned to face each other in a reeking triangle of gibberish. Their voices rose and fell argumentatively, pleadingly, decisively; but all Algernon Hebster's ears could register of what they said were very many sounds similar to *gabble* and an occasional, indisputable *honk!*

His lips curled contempt inward. Humanity prime! *These* messes? Then he lit a cigarette and shrugged. Oh, well. Humanity prime. And business is business.

Just remember they're not supermen, he told himself. They may be dangerous, but they're not supermen. Not by a long shot. Remember that epidemic of influenza that almost wiped them out, and how you diddled those two other Primeys last month. They're not supermen, but they're not humanity either. They're just different.

He glanced at his secretary and approved. Greta Seidenheim clacked away on her machine as if she were recording the curtest, the tritest of business letters. He wondered what system she was using to catch the intonations. Trust Greta, though, she'd do it.

"Gabble, honk! Gabble, gabble, gabble, honk, honk. Gabble, honk, gabble, gabble, honk? Honk."

What had precipitated all this conversation? He'd only asked for their names. Didn't they use names in Arizona? Surely, they knew that it was customary here. They claimed to know at least as much as he about such matters.

Maybe it was something else that had brought them to New York this time—maybe something about the Aliens? He felt the short hairs rise on the back of his neck and he smoothed them down self-consciously.

Trouble was it was so *easy* to learn their language. It was such a very simple matter to be able to understand them in these talkative moments. Almost as easy as falling off a log—or jumping off a cliff.

Well, his time was limited. He didn't know how long Ruth could hold the UM investigators in his outer office. Somehow he had to get a grip on the meeting again without offending them in any of the innumerable, highly dangerous ways in which Primeys could be offended.

He rapped the desk top—gently. The gabble-honk stopped short at the hyphen. The woman rose slowly.

"On this question of names," Hebster began doggedly, keeping his eyes on the woman, "since you people claim—"

The woman writhed agonizingly for a moment and sat down on the floor. She smiled at Hebster. With her rotted teeth, the smile had all the brilliance of a dead star.

Hebster cleared his throat and prepared to try again.

"If you want names," the older man said suddenly, "you can call me Larry."

The president of Hebster Securities shook himself and managed to say "Thanks" in a somewhat weak but not too surprised voice. He looked at the thin young man.

"You can call me Theseus." The young man looked sad as he said it.

"Theseus? Fine!" One thing about Primeys when you started clicking with them, you really moved along. But *Theseus!* Wasn't that just like a Primey? Now the woman, and they could begin.

They were all looking at the woman, even Greta with a curiosity which had sneaked up past her beauty-parlor glaze.

"Name," the woman whispered to herself. "Name a name."

Oh, no, Hebster groaned. *Let's not stall here.*

Larry evidently had decided that enough time had been wasted. He made a suggestion to the woman. "Why not call yourself Moe?"

The young man—Theseus, it was now—also seemed to get interested in the problem. "Rover's a good name," he announced helpfully.

"How about Gloria?" Hebster asked desperately.

The woman considered. "Moe, Rover, Gloria," she mused. "Larry, Theseus, Seidenheim, Hebster, me." She seemed to be running a total.

Anything might come out, Hebster knew. But at least they were not acting snobbish any more: they were talking down on his level now. Not only no gabble-honk, but none of this sneering double-talk which was almost worse. At least they were making sense—of a sort.

"For the purposes of this discussion," the woman said at last, "my name will be . . . will be—My name *is* S.S. Lusitania."

"Fine!" Hebster roared, letting the word he'd kept bubbling on his lips burst out. "That's a *fine* name. Larry, Theseus, and . . . er, S.S. Lusitania. Fine bunch of people. Sound. Let's get down to business. You came here on business, I take it?"

"Right," Larry said. "We heard about you from two others who left home a month ago to come to New York. They talked about you when got back to Arizona."

"They did, eh? I hoped they would."

Theseus slid off his chair and squatted next to the woman who was making plucking motions at the air. "They talked about you," he repeated. "They said you treated them very well, that you showed them as much respect as a thing like you could generate. They also said you cheated them."

"Oh, well, Theseus," Hebster spread his manicured hands. "I'm a businessman."

"You're a businessman," S.S. Lusitania agreed, getting to her feet stealthily and taking a great swipe with both hands at something invisible in front of her face. "And here, in this spot, at this moment, so are we. You can have what we've brought, but you'll pay for it. And don't think you can cheat *us*."

Her hands, cupped over each other, came down to her waist. She pulled them apart suddenly and a tiny eagle fluttered out. It flapped toward the fluorescent panels glowing in the ceiling. Its flight was hampered by the heavy, striped shield upon its breast, by the bunch of arrows it held in one claw, by the olive branch it grasped with the other. It turned its miniature bald head and gasped at Algernon Hebster, then began to drift rapidly down to the rug. Just before it hit the floor, it disappeared.

Hebster shut his eyes, remembering the strip of bunting that had fallen from the eagle's beak when it had turned to gasp. There had been words printed on the bunting, words too small to see at the distance, but he was sure the words would have read "*E Pluribus Unum*." He was as certain of that as he was of the necessity of acting unconcerned over the whole incident, as unconcerned as the Primeys. Professor Kleimbocher said Primeys were mental drunkards. But why did they give everyone else the D.T.'s?

He opened his eyes. "Well," he said, "what have you to sell?"

Silence for a moment. Theseus seemed to forget the point he was trying to make; S.S. Lusitania stared at Larry.

Larry scratched his right side through heavy, stinking cloth.

"Oh, an infallible method for defeating anyone who attempts to apply the *reductio ad absurdum* to a reasonable proposition you advance." He yawned smugly and began scratching his left side.

Hebster grinned because he was feeling so good. "No. Can't use it."

"Can't use it?" The old man was trying hard to look amazed. He shook his head. He stole a sideways glance at S.S. Lusitania.

She smiled again and wriggled to the floor. "Larry still isn't talking a language you can understand, Mr. Hebster," she cooed, very much like a fertilizer factory being friendly. "We came here with something we know you need badly. Very badly."

"Yes?" *They're like those two Primeys last month*, Hebster exulted: *they don't know what's good and what isn't. Wonder their masters would know. Well, and if they did—who does business with Aliens?*

"We . . . have," she spaced the words carefully, trying pathetically for a dramatic effect, "a new shade of red, but not merely that. Oh, *no*! A new shade of red, and a full set of color values derived from it! A complete set of color values derived from this one shade of red, Mr. Hebster! Think what a non-objectivist painter can do with such a—"

"Doesn't sell me, lady. Theseus, do you want to have a go now?"

Theseus had been frowning at the green foundation of the desk. He leaned back, looking satisfied. Hebster realized abruptly that the tension under his right foot had disappeared. Somehow, Theseus had become cognizant of the signal-spring set in the floor; and, somehow, he had removed it.

He had disintegrated it without setting off the alarm to which it was wired.

Giggles from three Primey throats and a rapid exchange of "gabble-honk". Then they all knew what Theseus had done and how Hebster had tried to protect himself. They weren't angry, though—and they didn't sound triumphant. Try to understand Primey behavior!

No need to get unduly alarmed—the price of dealing with these characters was a nervous stomach. The rewards, on the other hand—

Abruptly, they were businesslike again.

Theseus snapped out his suggestion with all the finality of a bazaar merchant making his last, absolutely the last offer. "A set of population indices which can be correlated with—"

"No, Theseus," Hebster told him gently.

Then, while Hebster sat back and enjoyed, temporarily forgetting the missing coil under his foot, they poured out more, desperately, feverishly, weaving in and out of each other's sentences.

"A portable neutron stabilizer for high altit—"

"More than fifty ways of saying 'however' without—"

". . . So that every housewife can do an *entrechat* while cook—"

". . . Synthetic fabric with the drape of silk and manufactura—"

". . . Decorative pattern for bald heads using the follicles as—"

". . . Complete and utter refutation of all pyramidologists from—"

"All right!" Hebster roared, "*All right*! That's enough!"

Greta Seidenheim almost forgot herself and sighed with relief. Her stenographic machine had been sounding like a centrifuge.

"Now," said the executive. "What do you want in exchange?"

"One of those we said is the one you want, eh?" Larry muttered. "Which one—the pyramidology refutation? That's it, I betcha."

S.S. Lusitania waved her hands contemptuously. "Bishop's miters, you fool! The new red color values excited him. The new—"

Ruth's voice came over the communicator. "Mr. Hebster, Yost and Funatti are back. I stalled them, but I just received word from the lobby receptionist that they're back on their way upstairs. You have two minutes, maybe three. And they're so mad they almost look like Firsters themselves!"

"Thanks. When they climb out of the elevator, do what you can without getting too illegal." He turned to his guests. "Listen—"

They had gone off again.

"Gabble, gabble, honk, honk, honk? Gabble, honk, *gabble*, gabble! Gabble, honk, gabble, honk, gabble, honk, honk."

Could they honestly make sense out of these throat-clearings and half-sneezes? Was it really a language as superior to all previous languages of man as . . . as the Aliens were supposed to be to man himself? Well, at least they could communicate with the Aliens by means of it. And the Aliens, the Aliens—

He recollected abruptly the two angry representatives of the world state who were hurtling towards his office.

"Listen, friends. You came here to sell. You've shown me your stock, and I've seen something I'd like to buy. *What* exactly is immaterial. The only question now is what you want for it. And let's make it fast. I have some other business to transact."

The woman with the dental nightmare stamped her foot. A cloud no larger than a man's hand formed near the ceiling, burst, and deposited a pailful of water on Hebster's fine custom-made rug.

He ran a manicured forefinger around the inside of his collar so that his bulging neck veins would not burst. Not right now, anyway. He looked at Greta and regained confidence from the serenity with which she waited for more conversation to transcribe. There was a model of business precision for you. The Primeys might pull what one of them had in London two years ago, before they were barred from all metropolitan areas—increased a housefly's size to that of an elephant—and Greta Seidenheim would go on separating fragments of conversation into the appropriate shorthand symbols.

With all their power, why didn't they *take* what they wanted? Why trudge wearisome miles to cities and attempt to smuggle themselves into illegal audiences with operators like Hebster, when most of them were caught easily and sent back to the reservation and those that weren't were cheated unmercifully by the "straight" humans they encountered? Why didn't they just blast their way in, take their weird and pathetic prizes and toddle back to their masters? For that matter, why didn't their masters—But Primey psych was Primey psych—not for this world, nor of it.

"We'll tell you what we want in exchange," Larry began in the middle of a honk. He held up a hand on which the length of the fingernails was indicated graphically by the grime beneath them and began to tot up the items, bending a digit for each item. "First, a hundred paper-bound copies of Melville's *Moby Dick*. Then, twenty-five crystal radio sets, with earphones; two earphones for each set. Then, two Empire State Buildings or three Radio Cities, whichever is more convenient. We want those with foundations intact. A reasonably good copy of the 'Hermes' statue by Praxiteles. And an electric toaster, *circa* 1941. That's about all, isn't it, Theseus?"

Theseus bent over until his nose rested against his knees.

Hebster groaned. The list wasn't as bad as he'd expected—remarkable the way their masters always yearned for the electric gadgets and artistic achievements of Earth—but he had so little time to bargain with them. *Two* Empire State Buildings!

"Mr. Hebster," his receptionist chattered over the communicator. "Those SIC men—I managed to get a crowd out in the corridor to push toward their elevator when it came to this floor, and I've locked the . . . I mean I'm trying to . . . but I don't think—Can you—"

"Good girl! You're doing fine!"

"Is that all we want, Theseus?" Larry asked again. "Gabble?"

Hebster heard a crash in the outer office and footsteps running across the floor.

"See here, Mr. Hebster," Theseus said at last, "if you don't want to buy Larry's *reductio ad absurdum* exploder, and you don't like my method of decorating bald heads for all its innate artistry, how about a system of musical notation—"

Somebody tried Hebster's door, found it locked. There was a knock on the door, repeated most immediately with more urgency.

"He's *already* found something he wants," S.S. Lusitania snapped. "Yes, Larry, that was the complete list."

Hebster plucked a handful of hair from his already receding forehead. "Good! Now, look, I can give you everything but the two Empire State Buildings and the three Radio Cities."

"*Or* the three Radio Cities," Larry corrected. "Don't try to cheat us! Two Empire State Buildings *or* three Radio Cities. Whichever is more convenient. Why . . . isn't it worth that to you?"

"Open this door!" a bull-mad voice yelled. "Open this door in the name of United Mankind!"

"Miss Seidenheim, open the door," Hebster said loudly and winked at his secretary who rose, stretched, and began a thoughtful, slow-motion study in the direction of the locked panel. There was a crash as of a pair of shoulders being thrown against it. Hebster knew that his office door could withstand a medium-sized tank. But there was a limit even to delay when it came to fooling around with the UM Special Investigating Commission. Those boys knew their Primeys and their Primey-dealers; they were empowered to shoot first and ask questions afterwards—as the questions occurred to them.

"It's not a matter of whether it's worth my while," Hebster told them rapidly as he shepherded them to the exit behind his desk. "For reasons I'm sure you aren't interested in, I just can't give away two Empire State Buildings and/or three Radio Cities with foundations intact—not at the moment. I'll give you the rest of it, and—"

"Open this door or we start blasting it down!"

"Please, gentlemen, please," Greta Seidenheim told them sweetly. "You'll kill a poor working girl who's trying awfully hard to let you in. The lock's stuck." She fiddled with the door-knob, watching Hebster with a trace of anxiety in her fine eyes.

"And to replace those items," Hebster was going on. "I will—"

"What I mean," Theseus broke in, "is this. You know the greatest single difficulty composers face in the twelve-tone technique?"

"I can offer you," the executive continued doggedly, sweat bursting out of his skin like spring freshets, "complete architectural blueprints of the Empire State Building and Radio City, plus five . . . no, I'll make it ten . . . scale models of each. And you get the rest of the stuff you asked for. That's it. Take it or leave it. Fast!"

They glanced at each other, as Hebster threw the exit door open and gestured to the five liveried bodyguards waiting near his private elevator. "*Done*," they said in unison.

"Good!" Hebster almost squeaked. He pushed them through the doorway and said to the tallest of the five men: "Nineteenth floor!"

He slammed the exit shut just as Miss Seidenheim opened the outer office door. Yost and Funatti, in the battle-green police uniform of the UM, charged through. Without pausing, they ran to where Hebster stood and plucked the exit open. They could all hear the elevator descending.

Funatti, a little, olive-skinned man, sniffed. "Primeys," he muttered. "He had Primeys here, all right. Smell that unwash, Yost?"

"Yeah," said the bigger man. "Come on. The emergency stairway. We can track that elevator!"

They holstered their service weapons and clattered down the metal-tipped stairs. Below, the elevator stopped.

Hebster's secretary was at the communicator. "Maintenance!" She waited. "Maintenance, automatic locks on the nineteenth-floor exit until the party Mr. Hebster just sent down gets to a lab somewhere else. And keep apologizing to those cops until then. Remember, they're SIC."

"Thanks, Greta," Hebster said, switching to the personal now that they were alone. He plumped into his desk chair and blew out gustily: "There must be easier ways of making a million."

She raised two perfect blond eyebrows. "Or of being an absolute monarch right inside the parliament of man?"

"If they wait long enough," he told her lazily. "I'll *be* the UM, modern global government and all. Another year or two might do it."

"Aren't you forgetting one Vandermeer Dempsey? His huskies also want to replace the UM. Not to mention their colorful plans for you. And there are an awful, awful lot of them."

"They don't worry me, Greta. *Humanity First* will dissolve overnight once that decrepit old demagogue gives up the ghost." He stabbed at the communicator button. "Maintenance! Maintenance, that party I sent down arrived at a safe lab yet?"

"No, Mr. Hebster. But everything's going all right. We sent them up to the twenty-fourth floor and got the SIC men rerouted downstairs to the personnel levels. Oh, Mr. Hebster—about the SIC. We take your orders and all that, but none of us wants to get in trouble with the Special Investigating Commission. According to the latest laws, it's practically a capital offense to obstruct 'em."

"Don't worry," Hebster told him. "I've never let one of my employees down yet. 'The boss fixes everything' is the motto here. Call me when you've got those Primeys safely hidden and ready for questioning."

He turned back to Greta. "Get that stuff typed before you leave and into Professor Kleimbocher's hands. He thinks he may have a new angle on their gabble-honk."

She nodded. "I wish you could use recording apparatus instead of making me sit over an old-fashioned click-box."

"So do I. But Primeys enjoy reaching out and putting a hex on electrical apparatus—when they aren't collecting it for the Aliens. I had a raft of wire and tape recorders busted in the middle of Primey interviews before I decided that human stenos were the only answer. And a Primey may get around to bollixing them some day."

"Cheerful thought. I must remember to dream about the possibility some cold night. Well, I should complain," she muttered as she went into her own little office. "Primey hexes built this business and pay my salary as well as supply me with the sparkling little knickknacks I love so well."

That was not quite true, Hebster remembered as he sat waiting for the communicator to buzz the news of his recent guests' arrival in a safe lab. Something like ninety-five per cent of Hebster Securities had been built out of Primey gadgetry extracted from them in various fancy deals, but the base of it all had been the small investment bank he had inherited from his father, back in the days of the Half-War—the days when the Aliens had first appeared on Earth.

The fearfully intelligent dots swirling in their variously shaped multicolored bottles were completely outside the pale of human understanding. There had been no way at all to communicate with them for a time.

A humorist had remarked back in those early days that the Aliens came not to bury man, not to conquer or enslave him. They had a truly dreadful mission—to ignore him!

No one knew, even today, what part of the galaxy the Aliens came from. Or why. No one knew what the total of their small visiting population came to. Or how they operated their wide-open and completely silent spaceships. The few things that had been discovered about them on the occasions when they deigned to swoop down and examine some human enterprise, with the aloof amusement of the highly civilized tourist, had served to confirm a technological superiority over Man that strained and tore the capacity of his richest imagination. A sociological treatise Hebster had read recently suggested that they operated from concepts as far in advance of modern science as a meteorologist sowing a drought-struck area with dry ice was beyond the primitive agriculturist blowing a ram's horn at the heavens in a frantic attempt to wake the slumbering gods of rain.

Prolonged, infinitely dangerous observation had revealed, for example, that the dots-in-bottles seemed to have developed past the need for prepared tools of any sort. They worked directly on the material itself, shaping it to need, evidently creating and destroying matter at will!

Some humans had communicated with them—

They didn't stay human.

Men with superb brains had looked into the whirring, flickering settlements established by the outsiders. A few had returned with tales of wonders they had realized dimly and not quite seen. Their descriptions always sounded as if their eyes had been turned off at the most crucial moments or a mental fuse had blown just this side of understanding.

Others—such celebrities as a President of Earth, a three-time winner of the Nobel Prize, famous poets—had evidently broken through the fence somehow. These, however, were the ones who didn't return. They stayed in the Alien settlements in the Gobi, the Sahara, the American Southwest. Barely able to fend for themselves, despite newly-acquired and almost unbelievable powers, they shambled worshipfully around the outsiders speaking, with weird writhings of larynx and nasal passage, what was evidently a human approximation of their masters' language—a kind of pidgin Alien. Talking with a Primey, someone had said, was like a blind man trying to read a page of Braille originally written for an octopus.

And that these bearded, bug-ridden, stinking derelicts, these chattering wrecks drunk and sodden on the logic of an entirely different life-form, were the heavy yellow cream of the human race didn't help people's egos any.

Humans and Primeys despised each other almost from the first; humans for Primey subservience and helplessness in human terms, Primeys for human ignorance and ineptness in Alien terms. And, except when operating under Alien orders and through barely legal operators like Hebster, Primeys didn't communicate with humans any more than their masters did.

When institutionalized, they either gabble-honked themselves into an early grave or, losing patience suddenly, they might dissolve a path to freedom right through the walls of the asylum and any attendants who chanced to be in the way. Therefore the enthusiasm of sheriff and deputy, nurse and orderly, had waned considerably, and the forcible incarceration of Primeys had almost ceased.

Since the two groups were so far apart psychologically as to make mating between them impossible, the ragged miracle-workers had been honored with the status of a separate classification:

Humanity Prime. Not better than humanity, not necessarily worse—but different, and dangerous.

What made them that way? Hebster rolled his chair back and examined the hole in the floor from which the alarm spring had spiraled. Theseus had disintegrated it—*how*? With a thought? Telekinesis, say, applied to all the molecules of the metal simultaneously, making them move rapidly and at random. Or possibly he had merely moved the spring somewhere else. Where? In space? In hyperspace? In time? Hebster shook his head and pulled himself back to the efficiently smooth and sanely useful desk surface.

"Mr. Hebster?" the communicator inquired abruptly, and he jumped a bit, "this is Margritt of General Lab 23B. Your Primeys just arrived. Regular check?"

Regular check meant drawing them out on every conceivable technical subject by the nine specialists in the general laboratory. This involved firing questions at them with the rapidity of a police interrogation, getting them off balance, and keeping them there in the hope that a useful and unexpected bit of scientific knowledge would drop.

"Yes," Hebster told him. "Regular check. But first let a textile man have a whack at them. In fact let him take charge of the check."

A pause. "The only textile man in this section is Charlie Verus."

"Well?" Hebster asked in mild irritation. "Why put it like that? He's competent, I hope. What does personnel say about him?"

"Personnel says he's competent."

"Then there you are. Look, Margritt, I have the SIC running around my building with blood in its enormous eye. I don't have time to muse over your departmental feuds. Put Verus on."

"Yes, Mr. Hebster. Hey, Bert! Get Charlie Verus. Him."

Hebster shook his head and chuckled. These technicians! Verus was probably brilliant and nasty.

The box crackled again: "Mr. Hebster? Mr. Verus." The voice expressed boredom to the point of obvious affectation. But the man was probably good despite his neuroses. Hebster Securities, Inc., had a first-rate personnel department.

"Verus? Those Primeys, I want you to take charge of the check. One of them knows how to make a synthetic fabric with the drape of silk. Get that first and then go after anything else they have."

"Primeys, Mr. Hebster?"

"I said Primeys, Mr. Verus. You are a textile technician, please to remember, and not the straight or ping-pong half of a comedy routine. Get jumping. I want a report on that synthetic fabric by tomorrow. Work all night if you have to."

"Before we do, Mr. Hebster, you might be interested in a small piece of information. There is *already* in existence a synthetic which falls better than silk—"

"I know," his employer told him shortly. "Cellulose acetate. Unfortunately, it has a few disadvantages: low melting-point, tends to crack; separate and somewhat inferior dye-stuffs have to be used for it; poor chemical resistance. Am I right?"

There was no immediate answer, but Hebster could feel the dazed nod. He went on. "Now, we also have protein fibers. They dye well and fall well, have the thermoconductivity control necessary for wearing apparel, but don't have the tensile strength of synthetic fabrics. An *artificial* protein fiber might be the answer: it would drape as well as silk, might be we could use the acid dyestuffs we use on silk which result in shades that dazzle female customers and cause them to fling wide their pocketbooks. There are a lot of *ifs* in that, I know, but one of those Primeys said something about a synthetic with the drape of silk, and I don't think he'd be sane enough to be referring to cellulose acetate. Nor nylon, orlon, vinyl chloride, or anything else we already have and use."

"You've looked into textile problems, Mr. Hebster."

"I have. I've looked into everything to which there are big gobs of money attached. And now suppose you go look into those Primeys. Several million women are waiting breathlessly for the secrets concealed in their beards. Do you think, Verus, that with the personal and scientific background I've just given you it's possible you might now get around to doing the job you are paid to do?"

"Um-m-m. Yes."

Hebster walked to the office closet and got his hat and coat. He liked working under pressure; he liked to see people jump up straight whenever he barked. And now, he liked the prospect of relaxing.

He grimaced at the webfoam chair that Larry had used. No point in having it resquirted. Have a new one made.

"I'll be at the University," he told Ruth on his way out. "You can reach me through Professor Kleimbocher. But don't, unless it's very important. He gets unpleasantly annoyed when he's interrupted."

She nodded. Then, very hesitantly: "Those two men—Yost and Funatti—from the Special Investigating Commission? They said no one would be allowed to leave the building."

"Did they now?" he chuckled. "I think they were angry. They've been that way before. But unless and until they can hang something on me—And Ruth, tell my bodyguard to go home, except for the man with the Primeys. He's to check with me, wherever I am, every two hours."

He ambled out, being careful to smile benevolently at every third executive and fifth typist in the large office. A private elevator and entrance were all very well for an occasional crisis, but Hebster liked to taste his successes in as much public as possible.

It would be good to see Kleimbocher again. He had a good deal of faith in the linguistic approach; grants from his corporation had tripled the size of the university's philology department. After all, the basic problem between man and Primey, as well as man and Alien, was one of communication. Any attempt to learn their science, to adjust their mental processes and logic into safer human channels, would have to be preceded by understanding.

It was up to Kleimbocher to find that understanding, not him. "I'm Hebster," he thought. "I *employ* the people who solve problems. And then I make money off them."

Somebody got in front of him. Somebody else took his arm. "I'm Hebster," he repeated automatically, but out loud. "*Algernon* Hebster."

"Exactly the Hebster we want," Funatti said, holding tightly on to his arm. "You don't mind coming along with us?"

"Is this an arrest?" Hebster asked the larger Yost who now moved aside to let him pass. Yost was touching his holstered weapon with dancing fingertips.

The SIC man shrugged. "Why ask such questions?" he countered. "Just come along and be sociable, kind of. People want to talk to you."

He allowed himself to be dragged through the lobby ornate with murals by radical painters and nodded appreciation at the doorman who, staring right through his captors, said enthusiastically, "Good *afternoon*, Mr. Hebster." He made himself fairly comfortable on the back seat of the dark-green SIC car, a late model Hebster Monowheel.

"Surprised to see you minus your bodyguard." Yost, who was driving, remarked over his shoulder.

"Oh, I gave them the day off."

"As soon as you were through with the Primeys? No," Funatti admitted, "we never did find out where you cached them. That's one big building you own, mister. And the UM Special Investigating Commission is notoriously understaffed."

"Not forgetting it's also notoriously underpaid," Yost broke in.

"I couldn't forget that if I tried," Funatti assured him. "You know, Mr. Hebster, I wouldn't have sent my bodyguard off if I'd been in your shoes. Right now there's something about five times as dangerous as Primeys after you. I mean Humanity Firsters."

"Vandermeer Dempsey's crackpots? Thanks, but I think I'll survive."

"That's all right. Just don't give any long odds on the proposition. Those people have been expanding fast and furious. *The Evening Humanitarian* alone has a tremendous circulation. And when you figure their weekly newspapers, their penny booklets, and throw-away handbills, it adds up to an impressive amount of propaganda. Day after day they bang away editorially at the people who're making money off the Aliens and Primeys. Of course, they're really hitting at the UM, like always, but if an ordinary Firster met you on the street, he'd be as likely to cut your heart out as not. Not interested? Sorry. Well, maybe you'll like this. *The Evening Humanitarian* has a cute name for you."

Yost guffawed. "Tell him, Funatti."

The corporation president looked at the little man inquiringly.

"They call you," Funatti said with great savoring deliberation, "they call you an interplanetary pimp!"

Emerging at last from the crosstown underpass, they sped up the very latest addition to the strangling city's facilities—the East Side Air-Floating Super-Duper Highway, known familiarly as Dive-Bomber Drive. At the Forty-Second Street offway, the busiest road exit in Manhattan, Yost failed to make a traffic signal. He cursed absent-mindedly, and Hebster found himself nodding the involuntary passenger's agreement. They watched the elevator section dwindling downward as the cars that were to mount the highway spiraled up from the right. Between the two, there rose and fell the steady platforms of harbor traffic while, stacked like so many decks of cards, the pedestrian stages awaited their turn below.

"Look! Up there, straight ahead! See it?"

Hebster and Funatti followed Yost's long, waggling forefinger with their eyes. Two hundred feet north of the offway and almost a quarter of a mile straight up, a brown object hung in obvious fascination. Every once in a while a brilliant blue dot would enliven the heavy murk imprisoned in its bell-jar shape only to twirl around the side and be replaced by another.

"Eyes? You think they're eyes?" Funatti asked, rubbing his small dark fists against each other futilely. "I know what the scientists say—that every dot is equivalent to one person and the whole bottle is like a family or a city, maybe. But how do they know? It's a theory, a guess. *I* say they're eyes."

Yost hunched his great body half out of the open window and shaded his vision with his uniform cap against the sun. "Look at it," they heard him say, over his shoulder. A nasal twang, long-buried, came back into his voice as heaving emotion shook out its cultivated accents. "A-setting up there, a-staring and a-staring. So all-fired interested in how we get on and off a busy highway! Won't pay us no never mind when we try to talk to it, when we try to find out what it wants, where it comes from, who it is. Oh, no! It's too superior to talk to the likes of us! But it can watch us, hours on end, days without end, light and dark, winter and summer; it can watch us going about our business; and every time we dumb two-legged animals try to do something *we* find complicated, along comes a blasted "dots-in-bottle" to watch and sneer and—"

"Hey there, man," Funatti leaned forward and tugged at his partner's green jerkin. "Easy! We're SIC, on business."

"All the same," Yost grunted wistfully, as he plopped back into his seat and pressed the power button, "I wish I had Daddy's little old M-1 Garand right now." They bowled forward, smoothed into the next long elevator section and started to descend. "It would be worth the risk of getting *pinged*."

And this was a UM man, Hebster reflected with acute discomfort. Not only UM, at that, but member of a special group carefully screened for their lack of anti-Primey prejudice, sworn to enforce the reservation laws without discrimination and dedicated to the proposition that Man could somehow achieve equality with Alien.

Well, how much dirt-eating could people do? People without a business sense, that is. His father had hauled himself out of the pick-and-shovel brigade hand over hand and raised his only son to maneuver always for greater control, to search always for that extra percentage of profit.

But others seemed to have no such abiding interest, Algernon Hebster knew regretfully.

They found it impossible to live with achievements so abruptly made inconsequential by the Aliens. To know with certainty that the most brilliant strokes of which they were capable, the most intricate designs and clever careful workmanship, could be duplicated—and surpassed—in an instant's creation by the outsiders and was of interest to them only as a collector's item. The feeling of inferiority is horrible enough when imagined; but when it isn't feeling but *knowledge*, when it is inescapable and thoroughly demonstrable, covering every aspect of constructive activity, it becomes unbearable and maddening.

No wonder men went berserk under hours of unwinking Alien scrutiny—watching them as they marched in a colorfully uniformed lodge parade, or fished through a hole in the ice, as they painfully maneuvered a giant transcontinental jet to a noiseless landing or sat in sweating, serried rows chanting to a single, sweating man to "knock it out of the park and sew the whole thing up!" No wonder they seized rusty shotgun or gleaming rifle and sped shot after vindictive shot into a sky poisoned by the contemptuous curiosity of a brown, yellow, or vermilion "bottle".

Not that it made very much difference. It did give a certain release to nerves backed into horrible psychic corners. But the Aliens didn't notice, and that was most important. The Aliens went right on watching, as if all this shooting and uproar, all these imprecations and weapon-wavings, were all part of the self-same absorbing show they had paid to witness and were determined to see through it for nothing else than the occasional amusing fluff some member of the inexperienced cast might commit.

The Aliens weren't injured, and the Aliens didn't feel attacked. Bullets, shells, buckshot, arrows, pebbles from a slingshot—all Man's miscellany of anger passed through them like the patient and eternal rain coming in the opposite direction. Yet the Aliens had solidity somewhere in their strange bodies. One could judge that by the way they intercepted light and heat. And also—

Also by the occasional *ping*.

Every once in a while, someone would evidently have hurt an Alien slightly. Or more probably just annoyed it by some unknown concomitant of rifle-firing or javelin-throwing.

There would be the barest suspicion of a sound—as if a guitarist had lunged at a string with his fingertip and decided against it one motor impulse too late. And, after this delicate and hardly heard *ping* quite unspectacularly, the rifleman would be weaponless. He would be standing there sighting stupidly up along his empty curled fingers, elbow cocked out and shoulder hunched in, like a large oafish child who had forgotten when to end the game. Neither his rifle nor a fragment of it would ever be found. And—gravely, curiously, intently—the Alien would go on watching.

The *ping* seemed to be aimed chiefly at weapons. Thus, occasionally, a 155 mm. howitzer was *pinged*, and, also occasionally, unexpectedly, it might be a muscular arm, curving back with another stone, that would disappear to the accompaniment of a tiny elfin note. And yet sometimes—could it be that the Alien, losing interest, had become careless in its irritation?—the entire man, murderously violent and shrieking, would *ping* and be no more.

It was not as if a counter-weapon was being used, but a thoroughly higher order of reply, such as a slap to an insect bite. Hebster, shivering, recalled the time he had seen a black tubular Alien swirl its amber dots over a new substreet excavation, seemingly entranced by the spectacle of men scrabbling at the earth beneath them.

A red-headed Sequoia of Irish labor had looked up from Manhattan's stubborn granite just long enough to shake the sweat from his eyelids. So doing, he had caught sight of the dot-pulsing observer and paused to snarl and lift his pneumatic drill, rattling it in noisy, if functionless, bravado at the sky. He had hardly been noticed by his mates, when the long, dark, speckled representative of a race beyond the stars turned end over end once and *pinged*.

The heavy drill remained upright for a moment, then dropped as if it had abruptly realized its master was gone. Gone? Almost, he had never been. So thorough had his disappearance been, so rapid, with so little flicker had he been snuffed out—harming and taking with him nothing else—that it had amounted to an act of gigantic and positive noncreation.

No, Hebster decided, making threatening gestures at the Aliens was suicidal. Worse, like everything else that had been tried to date, it was useless. On the other hand, wasn't the *Humanity First* approach a complete neurosis? What *could* you do?

He reached into his soul for an article of fundamental faith, found it. "I can make money," he quoted to himself. "That's what I'm good for. That's what I can always do."

As they spun to a stop before the dumpy, brown-brick armory that the SIC had appropriated for its own use, he had a shock. Across the street was a small cigar store, the only one on the block. Brand names which had decorated the plate-glass window in all the colors of the copyright had been supplanted recently by great gilt slogans. Familiar slogans they were by now—but this close to a UM office, the Special Investigating Commission itself?

At the top of the window, the proprietor announced his affiliation in two huge words that almost screamed their hatred across the street:

HUMANITY FIRST!

Underneath these, in the exact center of the window, was the large golden initial of the organization, the wedded letters HF arising out of the huge, symbolic safety razor.

And under that, in straggling script, the theme repeated, reworded, and sloganized: "*Humanity first, last, and all the time!*"

The upper part of the door began to get nasty: "*Deport the Aliens! Send them back to wherever they came from!*"

And the bottom of the door made the store-front's only concession to business: "*Shop here! Shop Humanitarian!*"

"*Humanitarian!*" Funatti nodded bitterly beside Hebster. "Ever see what's left of a Primey if a bunch of Firsters catch him without SIC protection? Just about enough to pick up with a blotter. I don't imagine you're too happy about boycott-shops like that?"

Hebster managed a chuckle as they walked past the saluting, green-uniformed guards. "There aren't very many Primey inspired gadgets having to do with tobacco. And if there were, one *Shop Humanitarian* outfit isn't going to break me."

But it is, he told himself disconsolately. It is going to break me—if it means what it seems to. Organization membership is one thing and so is planetary patriotism, but business is something else.

Hebster's lips moved slowly, in half-remembered catechism: Whatever the proprietor believes in or does not believe in, he has to make a certain amount of money out of that place if he's going to keep the door free of bailiff stickers. He can't do it if he offends the greater part of his possible clientele.

Therefore, since he's still in business and, from all outward signs, doing quite well, it's obvious that he doesn't have to depend on across-the-street UM personnel. Therefore, there must be a fairly substantial trade to offset this among entirely transient customers who not only don't object to his Firstism but are willing to forgo the interesting new gimmicks and lower prices in standard items that Primey technology is giving us.

Therefore, it is entirely possible—from this one extremely random but highly significant sample—that the newspapers I read have been lying and the socio-economists I employ are incompetent. It is entirely possible that the buying public, the only aspect of the public in which I have the slightest interest, is beginning a shift in general viewpoint which will profoundly affect its purchasing orientation.

It is possible that the entire UM economy is now at the top of a long slide into Humanity First domination, the secure zone of fanatic blindness demarcated by men like Vandermeer Dempsey. The highly usurious, commercially speculative economy of Imperial Rome made a similar transition in the much slower historical pace of two millennia ago and became, in three brief centuries, a static unbusinesslike world in which banking was a sin and wealth which had not been inherited was gross and dishonorable.

Meanwhile, people may already have begun to judge manufactured items on the basis of morality instead of usability, Hebster realized, as dim mental notes took their stolid place beside forming conclusions. He remembered a folderful of brilliant explanation Market Research had sent up last week dealing with unexpected consumer resistance to the new Evvakleen dishware. He had dismissed the pages of carefully developed thesis—to the effect that women were unconsciously associating the product's name with a certain Katherine Evvakios who had recently made the front page of every tabloid in the world by dint of some fast work with a breadknife on the throats of her five children and two lovers—with a yawning smile after examining its first brightly colored chart.

"Probably nothing more than normal housewifely suspicion of a radically new idea," he had muttered, "after washing dishes for years, to be told it's no longer necessary! She can't believe her Evvakleen dish is still the same after stripping the outermost film of molecules after a meal. Have to hit that educational angle a bit harder—maybe tie it in with the expendable molecules lost by the skin during a shower."

He'd penciled a few notes on the margin and flipped the whole problem onto the restless lap of Advertising and Promotion.

But then there had been the seasonal slump in furniture—about a month ahead of schedule. The surprising lack of interest in the Hebster Chubbichair, an item which should have revolutionized men's sitting habits.

Abruptly, he could remember almost a dozen unaccountable disturbances in the market recently, and all in consumer goods. That fits, he decided; any change in buying habits wouldn't be reflected in heavy industry for at least a year. The machine tools plants would feel it before the steel mills; the mills before the smelting and refining combines; and the banks and big investment houses would be the last of the dominoes to topple.

With its capital so thoroughly tied up in research and new production, his business wouldn't survive even a temporary shift of this type. Hebster Securities, Inc., could go like a speck of lint being blown off a coat collar.

Which is a long way to travel from a simple little cigar store. Funatti's jitters about growing Firstist sentiment are contagious! he thought.

If only Kleimbocher could crack the communication problem! If we could talk to the Aliens, find some sort of place for ourselves in their universe. The Firsters would be left without a single political leg!

★

Hebster realized they were in a large, untidy, map-spattered office and that his escort was saluting a huge, even more untidy man who waved their hands down impatiently and nodded them out of the door. He motioned Hebster to a choice of seats. This consisted of several long walnut-stained benches scattered about the room.

P. Braganza, said the desk nameplate with ornate Gothic flow. P. Braganza had a long, twirlable, and tremendously thick mustache. Also, P. Braganza needed a haircut badly. It was as if he and everything in the room had been carefully designed to give the maximum affront to Humanity Firsters. Which, considering their crew-cut, closely-shaven, "Cleanliness is next to Manliness" philosophy, meant that there was a lot of gratuitous unpleasantness in this office when a raid on a street demonstration filled it with jostling fanatics, antiseptically clean and dressed with bare-bone simplicity and neatness.

"So you're worrying about Firster effect on business?"

Hebster looked, startled.

"No, I don't read your mind," Braganza laughed through tobacco-stained teeth. He gestured at the window behind his desk. "I saw you jump just the littlest bit when you noticed that cigar store. And then you stared at it for two full minutes. I knew what you were thinking about."

"Extremely perceptive of you," Hebster remarked dryly.

The SIC official shook his head in a violent negative. "No, it wasn't. It wasn't a bit perceptive. I knew what you were thinking about because I sit up here day after day staring at that cigar store and thinking exactly the same thing. Braganza, I tell myself, that's the end of your job. That's the end of scientific world government. Right there on that cigar-store window."

He glowered at his completely littered desk top for a moment. Hebster's instincts woke up—there was a sales talk in the wind. He realized the man was engaged in the unaccustomed exercise of looking for a conversational gambit. He felt an itch of fear crawl up his intestines. Why should the SIC, whose power was almost above law and certainly above governments, be trying to dicker with him?

Considering his reputation for asking questions with the snarling end of a rubber hose, Braganza was being entirely too gentle, too talkative, too friendly. Hebster felt like a trapped mouse into whose disconcerted car a cat was beginning to pour complaints about the dog upstairs.

"Hebster, tell me something. What are your goals?"

"I beg your pardon?"

"What do you want out of life? What do you spend your days planning for, your nights dreaming about? Yost likes the girls and wants more of them. Funatti's a family man, five kids. He's happy in his work because his job's fairly secure, and there are all kinds of pensions and insurance policies to back up his life."

Braganza lowered his powerful head and began a slow, reluctant pacing in front of the desk.

"Now, I'm a little different. Not that I mind being a glorified cop. I appreciate the regularity with which the finance office pays my salary, of course; and there are very few women in this town who can say that I have received an offer of affection from them with outright scorn. But the one thing for which I would lay down my life is United Mankind. *Would* lay down my life? In terms of blood pressure and heart strain you might say I've already done it! 'Braganza,' I tell myself, 'you're a lucky dope. You're working for the first world government in human history. Make it count.' "

He stopped and spread his arms in front of Hebster. His unbuttoned green jerkin came apart awkwardly and exposed the black slab of hair on his chest. "That's me. That's basically all there is to Braganza. Now if we're to talk sensibly I have to know as much about you. I ask—what are your goals?"

The President of Hebster Securities, Inc., wet his lips. "I'm afraid I'm even less complicated."

"That's all right," the other man encouraged. "Put it any way you like."

"You might say that before everything else I am a businessman. I am interested chiefly in becoming a better businessman, which is to say a bigger one. In other words, I want to be richer than I am."

Braganza peered at him intently. "And that's all?"

"All? Haven't you ever heard it said that money isn't everything, but that what it isn't it can buy?"

"It can't buy me."

Hebster examined him coolly. "I don't know if you're a sufficiently desirable commodity. I buy what I need, only occasionally making an exception to please myself."

"I don't like you." Braganza's voice had become thick and ugly. "I never liked your kind and there's no sense being polite. I might as well stop trying. I tell you straight out—I think your guts stink."

Hebster rose. "In that case, I believe I should thank you for—"

"Sit *down*! You were asked here for a reason. I don't see any point to it, but we'll go through the motions. Sit down."

Hebster sat. He wondered idly if Braganza received half the salary he paid Greta Seidenheim. Of course, Greta was talented in many different ways and performed several distinct and separately useful services. No, after tax and pension deductions, Braganza was probably fortunate to receive one third of Greta's salary.

He noticed that a newspaper was being proffered him. He took it. Braganza grunted, clumped back behind his desk, and swung his swivel chair around to face the window.

It was a week-old copy of *The Evening Humanitarian*. The paper had lost the "voice-of-a-small-but-highly-articulate-minority" look, Hebster remembered from his last reading of it, and acquired the feel of publishing big business. Even if you cut in half the circulation claimed by the box in the upper left-hand corner, that still gave them three million paying readers.

In the upper right-hand corner, a red-bordered box exhorted the faithful to "*Read Humanitarian*! A green streamer across the top of the first page announced that "*Making sense is human—to gibber, Prime*!"

But the important item was in the middle of the page. A cartoon.

Half-a-dozen Primeys wearing long, curved beards and insane, tongue-lolling grins, sat in a rickety wagon. They held reins attached to a group of straining and portly gentlemen dressed—somewhat simply—in high silk hats. The fattest and ugliest of these, the one in the lead, had a bit between his teeth. The bit was labeled "*crazy-money*" and the man, "Algernon Hebster".

Crushed and splintering under the wheels of the wagon were such varied items as a "Home Sweet Home" framed motto with a piece of wall attached, a clean-cut youngster in a Boy Scout uniform, a streamlined locomotive, and a gorgeous young woman with a squalling infant under each arm.

The caption inquired starkly: "Lords of Creation—or *Serfs?*"

"This paper seems to have developed into a fairly filthy scandal sheet," Hebster mused out loud. "I shouldn't be surprised if it makes money."

"I take it then," Braganza asked without turning around from his contemplation of the street, "that you haven't read it very regularly in recent months?"

"I am happy to say I have not."

"That was a mistake."

Hebster stared at the clumped locks of black hair. "Why?" he asked carefully.

"Because it *has* developed into a thoroughly filthy and extremely successful scandal sheet. You're its chief scandal." Braganza laughed. "You see, these people look upon Primey-dealing as more of a sin than a crime. And, according to that morality, you're close to Old Nick himself!"

Shutting his eyes for a moment, Hebster tried to understand people who imagined such a soul-satisfying and beautiful concept as profit to be a thing of dirt and crawling maggots. He sighed. "I've thought of Firstism as a religion myself."

That seemed to get the SIC man. He swung around excitedly and pointed with both forefingers. "I tell you that you are right! It crosses all boundaries—incompatible and warring creeds are absorbed into it. It is willful, witless denial of a highly painful fact—that there are intellects abroad in the universe which are superior to our own. And the denial grows in strength every day that we are unable to contact the Aliens. If, as seems obvious, there is no respectable place for humanity in this galactic civilization, why, say men like Vandermeer Dempsey, then let us preserve our self-conceit at the least. Let's stay close to and revel in the things that are undeniably human. In a few decades, the entire human race will have been sucked into this blinkered vacuum."

He rose and walked around the desk again. His voice has assumed a terribly earnest, tragically pleading quality. His eyes roved Hebster's face as if searching for a pin-point of weakness, an especially thin spot in the frozen calm.

"Think of it," he asked Hebster. "Periodic slaughters of scientists and artists who, in the judgment of Dempsey, have pushed out too far from the conventional center of so-called humanness. An occasional *auto-da-fé* in honor of a merchant caught selling Primey goods—"

"I shouldn't like that," Hebster admitted, smiling. He thought a moment. "I see the connection you're trying to establish with the cartoon in *The Evening Humanitarian.*"

"Mister, I shouldn't have to. They want your head on the top of a long stick. They want it because you've become a symbol of dealing successfully for your own ends, with these stellar foreigners, or at least their human errand-boys and chambermaids. They figure that maybe they can put a stop to Primey-dealing generally if they put a bloody stop to you. And I tell you this—maybe they are right!"

"What exactly do you propose?" Hebster asked in a low voice.

"That you come in with us. We'll make an honest man of you—officially. We want you directing our investigation; except that the goal will not be an extra buck but all-important interracial communication and eventual interstellar negotiation."

The president of Hebster Securities, Inc., gave himself a few minutes on that one. He wanted to work out a careful reply. And he wanted time—above all, he wanted time!

He was so close to a well-integrated and world-wide commercial empire! For ten years, he had been carefully fitting the component industrial kingdoms into place, establishing suzerainty in this production network and squeezing a little more control out of that economic satrapy. He had found delectable tidbits of power in the dissolution of his civilization, endless opportunities for wealth in the shards of his race's self-esteem. He required a bare twelve months now to consolidate and co-ordinate. And suddenly—with the open-mouthed shock of a Jim Fiske who had cornered gold on the Exchange only to have the United States Treasury defeat him by releasing enormous quantities from the Government's own hoard—suddenly, Hebster realized he wasn't going to have the time. He was too experienced a player not to sense that a new factor was coming into the game, something outside his tables of actuarial figures, his market graphs, and cargo-loading indices.

His mouth was clogged with the heavy nausea of unexpected defeat. He forced himself to answer:

"I'm flattered. Braganza, I *really* am flattered. I see that Dempsey has linked us—we stand or fall together. But—I've always been a loner. With whatever help I can buy, I take care of myself. I'm not interested in any goal but the extra buck. First and last, I'm a businessman."

'Oh, stop it!" the dark man took a turn up and down the office angrily. "This is a planet-wide emergency. There are times when you can't be a businessman."

"I deny that. I can't conceive of such a time."

Braganza snorted. "You can't be a businessman if you're strapped to a huge pile of blazing faggots. You can't be a businessman, if people's minds are so thoroughly controlled that they'll stop eating at their leader's command. You can't be a businessman, my slavering, acquisitive friend, if demand is so well in hand that it ceases to exist."

"That's impossible!" Hebster had leaped to his feet. To his amazement, he heard his voice climbing up the scale to hysteria. "There's *always* demand. Always! The trick is to find what new form it's taken and then fill it!"

"Sorry! I didn't mean to make fun of your religion."

Hebster drew a deep breath and sat down with infinite care. He could almost feel his red corpuscles simmering.

Take it easy, he warned himself, take it easy! This is a man who must be won, not antagonized. They're changing the rules of the market, Hebster, and you'll need every friend you can buy.

Money won't work with this fellow. But there are *other* values—

"Listen to me, Braganza. We're up against the psycho-social consequences of an extremely advanced civilization hitting a comparatively barbarous one. Are you familiar with Professor Kleimbocher's Firewater Theory?"

"That the Alien's logic hits us mentally in the same way as whisky hit the North American Indian? And the Primeys, representing our finest minds, are the equivalent of those Indians who had the most sympathy with the white man's civilization? Yes. It's a strong analogy. Even carried to the Indians who, lying sodden with liquor in the streets of frontier towns, helped create the illusion of the treacherous, lazy, kill-you-for-a-drink aborigines while being so thoroughly despised by their tribesmen that they didn't dare go home for fear of having their throats cut. I've always felt—"

"The only part of that I want to talk about," Hebster interrupted, "is the firewater concept. Back in the Indian villages, an ever-increasing majority became convinced that firewater and gluttonous paleface civilization were synonymous, that they must rise and retake their land forcibly, killing in the process as many drunken renegades as they came across. This group can be equated with the Humanity Firsters. Then there was a minority who recognized the white man's superiority in numbers and weapons, and desperately tried to find a way of coming to terms with his civilization—terms that would not include his booze. For them read the UM. Finally, there was my kind of Indian."

Braganza knitted voluminous eyebrows and hitched himself up to a corner of the desk. "Hah?" he inquired. "What kind of Indian were *you*, Hebster?"

"The kind who had enough sense to know that the paleface had not the slightest interest in saving him from slow and painful cultural anemia. The kind of Indian, also, whose instincts were sufficiently sound so that he was scared to death of innovations like firewater and wouldn't touch the stuff to save himself from snake bite. But the kind of Indian—"

"Yes? Go on!"

"The kind who was fascinated by the strange transparent container in which the firewater came! Think how covetous an Indian potter might be of the whisky bottle, something which was completely outside the capacity of his painfully acquired technology. Can't you see him hating, despising, and terribly afraid of the smelly amber fluid, which toppled the most stalwart warriors, yet wistful to possess a bottle minus contents? That's about where I see myself, Braganza—the Indian whose greedy curiosity shines through the murk of hysterical clan politics and outsiders' contempt like a lambent flame. I want the new kind of container somehow separated from the firewater."

Unblinkingly, the great dark eyes stared at his face. A hand came up and smoothed each side of the arched mustachio with long, unknowing twirls. Minutes passed.

"Well. Hebster as our civilization's noble savage," the SIC man chuckled at last, "it almost feels right. But what does it mean in terms of the over-all problem?"

"I've told you," Hebster said wearily, hitting the arm of the bench with his open hand, "that I haven't the slightest interest in the over-all problem."

"And you only want the bottle. I heard you. But you're not a potter, Hebster—you haven't an elementary particle of craftsman's curiosity. All of that historical romance you spout—you don't care if your world drowns in its own agonized juice. You just want a profit."

"I never claimed an altruistic reason. I leave the general solution to men whose minds are good enough to juggle its complexities—like Kleimbocher."

"Think somebody like Kleimbocher could do it?"

"I'm almost certain he will. That was our mistake from the beginning—trying to break through with historians and psychologists. Either they've become limited by the study of human societies or—well, this is personal, but I've always felt that the science of the mind attracts chiefly those who've already experienced grave psychological difficulty. While they might achieve such an understanding of themselves in the course of their work as to become better adjusted, eventually, than individuals who had less problems to begin with, I'd still consider them too essentially unstable for such an intrinsically shocking experience as establishing *rapport* with an Alien. Their internal dynamics inevitably make Primeys of them."

Braganza sucked at a tooth and considered the wall behind Hebster. "And all this, you feel, wouldn't apply to Kleimbocher?"

'No, not a philology professor. He has no interest, no intellectual roots in personal and group instability. Kleimbocher's a comparative linguist—a technician, really—a specialist in basic communication. I've been out to the university and watched him work. His approach to the problem is entirely in terms of his subject—communicating with the Aliens instead of trying to understand them. There's been entirely too much intricate speculation about Alien consciousness, sexual attitudes, and social organization, about stuff from which we will derive no tangible and immediate good. Kleimbocher's completely pragmatic."

"All right. I follow you. Only he went Prime this morning."

Hebster paused, a sentence dangling from his dropped jaw. "Professor Kleimbocher? *Rudolf* Kleimbocher?" he asked idiotically. "But he was so close . . . he almost had it . . . an elementary signal dictionary . . . he was about to—"

"He *did*. About nine forty-five. He'd been up all night with a Primey one of the psych professors had managed to hypnotize and gone home unusually optimistic. In the middle of his first class this morning, he interrupted himself in a lecture on medieval Cyrillic to . . . to gabble-honk. He sneezed and wheezed at the students for about ten minutes in the usual Primey pattern of initial irritation, then, abruptly giving them up as hopeless, worthless idiots, he leviated himself in that eerie way they almost always do at first. Banged his head against the ceiling and knocked himself out. I don't know what it was, fright, excitement, respect for the old boy perhaps, but the students neglected to tie him up before going for help. By the time they'd come back with the campus SIC man, Kleimbocher had revived and dissolved one wall of the Graduate School to get out. Here's a snapshot of him about five hundred feet in the air, lying on his back with his arms crossed behind his head, skimming west at twenty miles an hour."

The executive studied the little paper rectangle with blinking eyes. "You radioed the air force to chase him, of course."

"What's the use? We've been through *that* enough times. He'd either increase his speed and generate a tornado, drop like a stone and get himself smeared all over the countryside, or materialize stuff like wet coffee grounds and gold ingots inside the jets of the pursuing plane. Nobody's caught a Primey yet in the first flush of . . . whatever they do feel at first. And we might stand to lose anything from a fairly expensive hunk of aircraft, including pilot, to a couple of hundred acres of New Jersey topsoil."

Hebster groaned. "But the eighteen years of research that he represented!"

"Yeah. That's where we stand. Blind alley umpteen hundred thousand or thereabouts. Whatever the figure is, it's awfully close to the end. If you can't crack the Alien on a straight linguistic basis, you can't crack the Alien at all, period, end of paragraph. Our most powerful weapons affect them like bubble pipes, and our finest minds are good for nothing better than to serve them in low, fawning idiocy. But the Primeys are all that's left. We might be able to talk sense to the Man if not the Master."

"Except that Primeys, by definition, don't talk sense."

Braganza nodded. "But since they were human—*ordinary* human—to start with, they represent a hope. We always knew we might some day have to fall back on our only real contact. That's why the Primey protective laws are so rigid; why the Primey reservation compounds surrounding Alien settlements are guarded by our military detachments. The lunch spirit has been evolving into the pogrom spirit as human resentment and discomfort have been growing. Humanity First is beginning to feel strong enough to challenge United Mankind. And honestly, Hebster, at this point neither of us knows which would survive a real fight. But you're one of the few who have talked to Primeys, worked with them—"

"Just on business."

"Frankly, that much of a start is a thousand times further along than the best that we've been able to manage. It's so blasted ironical that the only people who've had any conversation at all with the Primeys aren't even slightly interested in the imminent collapse of civilization! Oh, well. The point is that in the present political picture, you sink with us. Recognizing this, my people are prepared to forget a great deal and document you back into respectability. How about it?"

"Funny," Hebster said thoughtfully. "It can't be knowledge that makes miracle-workers out of fairly sober scientists. They all start shooting lightnings at their families and water out of rocks far too early in Primacy to have had time to learn new techniques. It's as if by merely coming close enough to the Aliens to grovel, they immediately move into position to tap a series of cosmic laws more basic than cause and effect."

The SIC man's face slowly deepened into purple. "Well, are you coming in, or aren't you? Remember, Hebster, in these times, a man who insists on business as usual is a traitor to history."

"I think Kleimbocher *is* the end," Hebster nodded to himself. "Not much point in chasing Alien mentality if you're going to lose your best men on the way. I say let's forget all this nonsense of trying to live as equals in the same universe with Aliens. Let's concentrate on human problems and be grateful that they don't come into our major population centers and tell us to shove over."

The telephone rang. Braganza had dropped back into his swivel chair. He let the instrument squeeze out several piercing sonic bubbles while he clicked his strong square teeth and maintained a carefully-focused glare at his visitor. Finally, he picked it up, and gave it the verbal minima:

"Speaking. He is here. I'll tell him. 'Bye."

He brought his lips together, kept them pursed for a moment and then, abruptly, swung around to face the window.

"Your office, Hebster. Seems your wife and son are in town and have to see you on business. She the one you divorced ten years ago?"

Hebster nodded at his back and rose once more. "Probably wants her semi-annual alimony dividend bonus. I'll have to go. Sonia never does office morale any good."

This meant trouble, he knew. "Wife-and-son" was executive code for something seriously wrong with Hebster Securities, Inc. He had not seen his wife since she had been satisfactorily maneuvered into giving him control of his son's education. As far as he was concerned, she had earned a substantial income for life by providing him with a well-mothered heir.

"Listen!" Braganza said sharply as Hebster reached the door. He still kept his eyes studiously on the street. "I tell you this: You don't want to come in with us. All right! You're a businessman first and a world citizen second. All right! But keep your nose clean, Hebster. If we catch you the slightest bit off base from now on, you'll get hit with everything. We'll not only pull the most spectacular trial this corrupt old planet has ever seen, but somewhere along the line, we'll throw you and your entire organization to the wolves. We'll see to it that *Humanity First* pulls the Hebster Tower down around your ears."

Hebster shook his head, licked his lips. "*Why*? What would that accomplish?"

"Hah! It would give a lot of us here the craziest kind of pleasure. But it would also relieve us temporarily of some of the mass pressure we've been feeling. There's always the chance that Dempsey would lose control of his hotter heads, that they'd go on a real gory rampage, make with the sound and the fury sufficiently to justify full deployment of troops. We could knock off Dempsey and all of the big-shot Firsters then, because John Q. United Mankind would have seen to his own vivid satisfaction and injury what a dangerous mob they are."

"This," Hebster commented bitterly, 'is the idealistic, legalistic world government!"

Braganza's chair spun around to face Hebster and his fist came down on the desk top with all the crushing finality of a magisterial gavel. "No, it is not! It is the SIC, a plenipotentiary and highly practical bureau of the UM, especially created to organize a relationship between Alien and human. Furthermore, it's the SIC in a state of the greatest emergency when the reign of law and world government may topple at a demagogue's belch. Do you think"—his head snaked forward belligerently, his eyes slitted to thin lines of purest contempt—"that the career and fortune, even the life, let us say, of as openly selfish a slug as you, Hebster, would be placed above that of the representative body of two billion *socially* operating human beings?"

The SIC official thumped his sloppily buttoned chest. "'Braganza,' I tell myself now, 'you're lucky he's too hungry for his blasted profit to take you up on that offer. Think how much fun it's going to be sink a hook into him when he makes a mistake at last! To drop him onto the back of *Humanity First* so that they'll run amuck and destroy themselves!' Oh, get out, Hebster. I'm through with you."

He had made a mistake, Hebster reflected as he walked out of the armory and snapped his fingers at a gyrocab. The SIC was the most powerful single government agency in a Primey-infested world; offending them for a man in his position was equivalent to a cab driver delving into the more uncertain aspects of a traffic cop's ancestry in the policeman's popeyed presence.

But what could he do? Working with the SIC would mean working under Braganza—and since maturity, Algernon Hebster had been quietly careful to take orders from no man. It would mean giving up a business which, with a little more work and a little more time, might somehow still become the dominant combine on the planet. And worst of all, it would mean acquiring a social orientation to replace the calculating businessman's viewpoint which was the closest thing to a soul he had ever known.

The doorman of his building preceded him at a rapid pace down the side corridor that led to his private elevator and flourished aside for him to enter. The car stopped on the twenty-third floor. With a heart that had sunk so deep as to have practically foundered, Hebster picked his way along the wide-eyed clerical stares that lined the corridor. At the entrance to General Laboratory 23B, two tall men in the gray livery of his personal bodyguard moved apart to let him enter. If they had been recalled after having been told to take the day off, it meant that a full-dress emergency was being observed. He hoped that it had been declared in time to prevent any publicity leakage.

It had, Greta Seidenheim assured him. "I was down here applying the clamps five minutes after the fuss began. Floors twenty-one through twenty-five are closed off and all outside lines are being monitored. You can keep your employees an hour at most past five o'clock—which gives you a maximum of two hours and fourteen minutes."

He followed her green-tipped fingernail to the far corner of the lab where a body lay wrapped in murky rags. Theseus. Protruding from his back was the yellowed ivory handle of quite an old German S. S. dagger, 1942 edition. The silver swastika on the hilt had been replaced by an ornate symbol—an HF. Blood had soaked Theseus' long matted hair into an ugly red rug.

A dead Primey, Hebster thought, staring down hopelessly. In *his* building, in the laboratory to which the Primey had been spirited two or three jumps ahead of Yost and Funatti. This was capital offense material—if the courts ever got a chance to weigh it.

"Look at the dirty Primey-lover!" a slightly familiar voice jeered on his right. "He's scared! Make money out of *that*, Hebster!"

The corporation president strolled over to the thin man with the knobby, completely shaven head who was tied to an unused steampipe. The man's tie, which hung outside his laboratory smock, sported an unusual ornament about halfway down. It took Hebster several seconds to identify it. A miniature gold safety razor upon a black "3."

"He's a third echelon official of *Humanity First*!"

"He's also Charlie Verus of Hebster Laboratories," an extremely short man with a corrugated forehead told him. "My name is Margritt, Mr. Hebster, Dr. J. H. Margritt. I spoke to you on the communicator when the Primeys arrived."

Hebster shook his head determinedly. He waved back the other scientists who were milling around him self-consciously. "How long have third echelon officials, let alone ordinary members of *Humanity First*, been receiving salary checks in my laboratories?"

"I don't know." Margritt shrugged up at him. "Theoretically, no Firsters can be Hebster employees. Personnel is supposed to be twice as efficient as the SIC when it comes to sifting background. They probably are. But what can they do when an employee joins *Humanity First after* he's passed his probationary period? These proselyting times you'd need a complete force of secret police to keep tabs on all the new converts!"

"When I spoke to you earlier in the day, Margritt, you indicated disapproval of Verus. Don't you think it was your duty to let me know I had a Firster official about to mix it up with Primeys?"

The little man beat a violent negative back and forth with his chin. "I'm paid to supervise research, Mr. Hebster, not to co-ordinate your labor relations nor vote your political ticket!"

Contempt—the contempt of the creative researcher for the businessman-entrepreneur who paid his salary and was now in serious trouble—flickered behind every word he spoke. Why, Hebster wondered irritably, did people so despise a man who made money? Even the Primeys back in his office, Yost and Funatti, Braganza, Margritt—who had worked in his laboratories for years. It was his only talent. Surely, as such, it was as valid as a pianist's?

"I've never liked Charlie Verus," the lab chief went on, "but we never had reason to suspect him of Firstism! He must have hit the third echelon rank about a week ago, eh, Bert?"

"Yeah," Bert agreed from across the room. "The day he came in an hour late, broke every Florence flask in the place, and told us all dreamily that one day we might be very proud to tell our grandchildren that we'd worked in the same lab with Charles Bolop Verus."

"Personally," Margritt commented, "I thought he might have just finished writing a book which proved that the Great Pyramid was nothing more than a prophecy in stone of our modern textile designs. Verus was that kind. But it probably was his little safety razor that tossed him up so high. I'd say he got the promotion as a sort of payment in advance for the job he finally did today."

Hebster ground his teeth at the carefully hairless captive who tried, unsuccessfully, to spit in his face; he hurried back to the door where his private secretary was talking to the bodyguard who had been on duty in the lab.

Beyond them, against the wall, stood Larry and S.S. Lusitania conversing in a low-voiced and anxious gabble-honk. They were evidently profoundly disturbed. S.S. Lusitania kept plucking tiny little elephants out of her rags which, kicking and trumpeting tinnily, burst like malformed bubbles as she dropped them on the floor. Larry scratched his tangled beard nervously as he talked, periodically waving a hand at the ceiling which was already studded with fifty or sixty replicas of the dagger buried in Theseus. Hebster couldn't help thinking anxiously of what could have happened to his building if the Primeys had been able to act human enough to defend themselves.

"Listen, Mr. Hebster," the bodyguard began, "I was told not to—"

"Save it," Hebster rapped out. "This wasn't your fault. Even Personnel isn't to blame. Me and my experts deserve to have our necks chopped for falling so far behind the times. We can analyze any trend but the one which will make us superfluous. Greta! I want my roof helicopter ready to fly and my personal stratojet at LaGuardia alerted. Move, girl! And *you* . . . Williams is it?" he queried, leaning forward to read the bodyguard's name on his badge, "Williams, pack these two Primeys into my helicopter upstairs and stand by for a fast take-off."

He turned. "Everyone else!" he called. "You will be allowed to go home at six. You will be paid one hour's overtime. Thank you."

Charlie Verus started to sing as Hebster left the lab. By the time he reached the elevator, several of the clerks in the hallway had defiantly picked up the hymn. Hebster paused outside the elevator as he realized that fully one-fourth of the clerical personnel, male and female, were following Verus' cracked and mournful but terribly earnest tenor.

We will overturn the cesspool where the Primey slime is born,
We'll be wearing cleanly garments as we face a human morn—
The First are on the march!
Glory, glory, halleluiah,
Glory, glory, halleluiah . . .

If it was like this in Hebster Securities, he thought wryly as he came into his private office, how fast was *Humanity First* growing among the broad masses of people? Of course, many of those singing could be put down as sympathizers rather than converts, people who were suckers for choral groups and vigilante posses—but how much more momentum did an organization have to generate to acquire the name of political juggernaut?

The only encouraging aspect was the SIC's evident awareness of the danger and the unprecedented steps they were prepared to take as a countermeasure.

Unfortunately, the unprecedented steps would take place upon Hebster.

He now had a little less than two hours, he reflected, to squirm out of the most serious single crime on the books of present World Law.

He lifted one of his telephones. "Ruth," he said. "I want to speak to Vandermeer Dempsey. Get me through to him personally."

She did. A few moments later he heard the famous voice, as rich and slow and thick as molten gold. "Hello, Hebster, Vandermeer Dempsey speaking." He paused as if to draw breath, then went on sonorously: "*Humanity—may it always be ahead, but, ahead or behind, Humanity*!" He chuckled. "Our newest. What we call our telephone toast. Like it?"

"Very much," Hebster told him respectfully, remembering that this former video quizmaster might shortly be church and state combined. "Er . . . Mr. Dempsey, I notice you have a new book out, and I was wondering—"

"Which one? *Anthropolitics*?"

"That's it. A fine study! You have some very quotable lines in the chapter headed, 'Neither More Nor Less Human'."

A raucous laugh that still managed to bubble heavily. "Young man, I have quotable lines in every chapter of every book! I maintain a writer's assembly line here at headquarters that is capable of producing up to fifty-five memorable epigrams on any subject upon ten minutes' notice. Not to mention their capacity for political metaphors and two-line jokes with sexy implications! But you wouldn't be calling me to discuss literature, however good a job of emotional engineering I have done in my little text. What is it about, Hebster? Go into your pitch."

"Well," the executive began, vaguely comforted by the Firster chieftain's cynical approach and slightly annoyed at the openness of his contempt, "I had a chat today with your friend and my friend, P. Braganza."

"I know."

"You do? How?"

Vandermeer Dempsey laughed again, the slow, good-natured chortle of a fat man squeezing the curves out of a rocking chair. "Spies, Hebster, *spies*. I have them everywhere practically. This kind of politics is twenty per cent espionage, twenty per cent organization, and sixty per cent waiting for the right moment. My spies tell me everything you do."

"They didn't by any chance tell you what Braganza and I discussed?"

"Oh, they did, young man, they did!" Dempsey chuckled a carefree scale exercise. Hebster remembered his pictures: the head like a soft and enormous orange, gouged by a brilliant smile. There was no hair anywhere on the head—all of it, down to the last eyelash and follicled wart, was removed regularly through electrolysis. "According to my agents, Braganza made several strong representations on behalf of the Special Investigating Commission which you rightly spurned. Then, somewhat out of sorts, he announced that if you were henceforth detected in the nefarious enterprises which everyone knows have made you one of the wealthiest men on the face of the Earth, he would use you as bait for our anger. I must say I admire the whole ingenious scheme immensely."

"And you're not going to bite," Hebster suggested. Greta Seidenheim entered the office and made a circular gesture at the ceiling. He nodded.

"On the contrary, Hebster, we *are* going to bite. We're going to bite with just a shade more vehemence than we're expected to. We're going to swallow this provocation that the SIC is devising for us and go on to make a world-wide revolution out of it. We *will*, my boy."

Hebster rubbed his left hand back and forth across his lips. "Over my dead body!" He tried to chuckle to himself and managed only to clear his throat. "You're right about the conversation with Braganza, and you may be right about how you'll do when it gets down to paving stones and baseball bats. But, if you'd like to have the whole thing a lot easier, there is a little deal I have in mind—"

"Sorry, Hebster my boy. No deals. Not on this. Don't you see we really *don't* want to have it easier? For the same reason, we pay our spies nothing despite the risks they run and the great growing wealth of *Humanity First*. We found that the spies we acquired through conviction worked harder and took many more chances than those forced into our arms by economic pressure. No, we desperately need *l'affaire Hebster* to inflame the populace. We need enough excitement running loose so that it transmits to the gendarmerie and the soldiery, so that conservative citizens who normally shake their heads at a parade will drop their bundles and join the rape and robbery. Enough such citizens and Terra goes *Humanity First*."

"Heads you win, tails I lose."

The liquid gold of Dempsey's laughter poured. "I see what you mean, Hebster. Either way, UM or HF, you wind up a smear-mark on the sands of time. You had your chance when we asked for contributions from public-spirited businessmen four years ago. Quite a few of your competitors were able to see the valid relationship between economics and politics. Woodran of the

Underwood Investment Trust is a first echelon official today. Not a single one of *your* top executives wears a razor. But, even so, whatever happens to you will be mild compared to the Primeys."

"The Aliens may object to their body-servants being mauled."

"There are no Aliens!" Dempsey replied in a completely altered voice. He sounded as if he had stiffened too much to be able to move his lips.

"No Aliens? Is that your latest line? You don't mean that!"

"There are only Primeys—creatures who have resigned from human responsibility and are therefore able to do many seemingly miraculous things, which real humanity refuses to do because of the lack of dignity involved. But there are no Aliens. Aliens are a Primey myth."

Hebster grunted. "That is the ideal way of facing an unpleasant fact. Stare right through it."

"If you insist on talking about such illusions as Aliens," the rustling and angry voice cut in, "I'm afraid we can't continue the conversation. You're evidently going Prime, Hebster."

The line went dead.

Hebster scraped a finger inside the mouthpiece rim. "He believes his own stuff!" he said in an awed voice. "For all of the decadent urbanity, he has to have the same reassurance he gives his followers—the horrible, superior thing just isn't there!"

Greta Seidenheim was waiting at the door with his briefcase and both their coats. As he came away from the desk, he said, "I won't tell you not to come along, Greta, but—"

"Good," she said, swinging along behind him. "Think we'll make it to—wherever we're going?"

"Arizona. The first and largest Alien settlement. The place our friends with the funny names come from."

"What can you do there that you can't do here?"

"Frankly, Greta, I don't know. But it's a good idea to lose myself for a while. Then again, I want to get in the area where all this agony originates and take a close look. I'm an off-the-cuff businessman; I've done all of my important figuring on the spot."

There was bad news waiting for them outside the helicopter. "Mr. Hebster," the pilot told him tonelessly while cracking a dry stick of gum, "the stratojet's been seized by the SIC. Are we still going? If we do it in this thing, it won't be very far or very fast."

"We're still going," Hebster said after a moment's hesitation.

They climbed in. The two Primeys sat on the floor in the rear, sneezing conversationally at each other. Williams waved respectfully at his boss. "Gentle as lambs," he said. "In fact, they made one. I had to throw it out."

The large pot-bellied craft climbed up its rope of air and started forward from the Hebster Building.

"There must have been a leak," Greta muttered angrily. "They heard about the dead Primey. Somewhere in the organization there's a leak that I haven't been able to find. The SIC heard about the the dead Primey and now they're hunting us down. Real efficient, I am!"

Hebster smiled at her grimly. She was very efficient. So were Personnel and a dozen other subdivisions of the organization. So was Hebster himself. But these were functioning members of a normal business designed for stable times. *Political* spies! If Dempsey could have spies and saboteurs all over Hebster Securities, why couldn't Braganza? They'd catch him before he had even started running; they'd bring him back before he could find a loophole.

They'd bring him back for trial, perhaps, for what in all probability would be known to history as the Bloody Hebster Incident. The incident that had precipitated a world revolution.

"Mr. Hebster, they're getting restless," Williams called out. "Should I relax 'em out, kind of?"

Hebster sat up sharply, hopefully. "No," he said. "Leave them alone!" He watched the suddenly agitated Primeys very closely. This was the odd chance for which he'd brought them along! Years of haggling with Primeys had taught him a lot about them. They were good for other things than sheer gimmick-craft.

Two specks appeared on the windows. They enlarged sleekly into jets with SIC insignia.

"Pilot!" Hebster called, his eyes on Larry who was pulling painfully at his beard. "Get away from the controls! Fast! Did you hear me? That was an *order! Get away from those controls!*"

The man moved off reluctantly. He was barely in time. The control board dissolved into rattling purple shards behind him. The vanes of the gyro seemed to flower into indigo saxophones. Their ears rang with supersonic frequencies as they rose above the jets on a spout of unimaginable force.

Five seconds later they were in Arizona.

They piled out of their weird craft into a sage-cluttered desert.

"I don't ever want to know what my windmill was turned into," the pilot commented, "or what was used to push it along—but how did the Primey come to understand the cops were after us?"

"I don't think he knew that," Hebster explained, "but he was sensitive enough to know he was going home, and that somehow those jets were there to prevent it. And so he functioned, in terms of his interests, in what was almost a human fashion. He protected himself."

"Going home," Larry said. He'd been listening very closely to Hebster, dribbling from the right-hand corner of his mouth as he listened. "Haemostat, hammersdarts, hump. Home is where the hate is. Hit is where the hump is. Home and locks the door."

S.S. Lusitania had started on one leg and favored them with her peculiar fleshy smile. "Hindsight," she suggested archly, "is no more than home site. Gabble, honk?"

Larry started after her, some three feet off the ground. He walked the air slowly and painfully as if the road he traveled were covered with numerous small boulders, all of them pitilessly sharp.

"Goodbye, people," Hebster said. "I'm off to see the wizard with my friends in greasy gray here. Remember, when the SIC catches up to your unusual vessel—stay close to it for that purpose, by the way—it might be wise to refer to me as someone who forced you into this. You can tell them I've gone into the wilderness looking for a solution, figuring that if I went Prime I'd still be better off than as a punching bag whose ownership is being hotly disputed by such characters as P. Braganza and Vandermeer Dempsey. I'll be back with my mind or on it."

He patted Greta's cheek on the wet spot; then he walked deftly away in pursuit of S.S. Lusitania and Larry. He glanced back once and smiled as he saw them looking curiously forlorn, especially Williams, the chunky young man who earned his living by guarding other people's bodies.

The Primeys followed a route of sorts, but it seemed to have been designed by someone bemused by the motions of an accordion. Again and again it doubled back upon itself, folded across itself, went back a hundred yards, and started all over again.

This was Primey country—Arizona, where the first and largest Alien settlement had been made. There were very few humans in this corner of the southwest any more—just the Aliens and their coolies.

"Larry," Hebster called as an uncomfortable thought struck him. "Larry! Do . . . do your masters know I'm coming?"

Missing his step as he looked up at Hebster's peremptory question, the Primey tripped and plunged to the ground. He rose, grimaced at Hebster, and shook his head. "You are not a businessman," he said. "Here there can be no business. Here there can only be humorous what-you-might-call-worship. The movement to the universal, the inner nature— The realization, complete and eternal, of the partial and evanescent that alone enables . . . that alone enables—" His clawed fingers writhed into each other, as if he were desperately trying to pull a communicable meaning out of the palms. He shook his head with a slow rolling motion from side to side.

Hebster saw with a shock that the old man was crying. Then going Prime had yet another similarity to madness! It gave the human an understanding of something thoroughly beyond himself, a mental summit he was constitutionally incapable of mounting. It gave him a glimpse of some psychological promised land, then buried him, still yearning, in his own inadequacies. And it left him at last bereft of pride in his realizable accomplishments with a kind of myopic half-knowledge of where he wanted to go but with no means of getting there.

"When I first came," Larry was saying haltingly, his eyes squinting into Hebster's face, as if he knew what the businessman was thinking, "when first I tried to know . . . I mean the charts and textbooks I carried here, my statistics, my plotted curves were so useless. All playthings I found, disorganized, based on shadow-thought. And then, Hebster, to watch real-thought, real-control! You'll see the joy— You'll serve beside us, you will! Oh, the enormous lifting—"

His voice died into angry incoherencies as he bit into his fist. S.S. Lusitania came up, still hopping on one foot. "Larry," she suggested in a very soft voice, "gabble-honk Hebster away?"

He looked surprised, then nodded. The two Primeys linked arms and clambered laboriously back up to the invisible road from which Larry had fallen. They stood facing him for a moment, looking like a weird, ragged, surrealistic version of Tweedledee and Tweedledum.

Then they disappeared and darkness fell around Hebster as if it had been knocked out of the jar. He felt under himself cautiously and sat down on the sand which retained all the heat of daytime Arizona.

Now!

Suppose an Alien came. Suppose an Alien asked him point-blank what it was that he wanted. That would be bad. Algernon Hebster, businessman extraordinary—slightly on the run, at the moment, of course—didn't know what he wanted; not with reference to Aliens.

He didn't want them to leave, because the Primey technology he had used in over a dozen industries was essentially an interpretation and adaptation of Alien methods. He didn't want them to stay because whatever was orderly in his world was dissolving under the acids of their omnipresent superiority.

He also knew that he personally did not want to go Prime.

What was left then? Business? Well, there was Braganza's question. What does a businessman do when demand is so well controlled that it can be said to have ceased to exist?

Or what does he do in a case like the present, when demand might be said to be nonexistent, since there was nothing the Aliens seemed to want of Man's puny hoard?

"He *finds* something they want," Hebster said out loud.

How? *How*? Well, the Indian still sold his decorative blankets to the paleface as a way of life, as a source of income. And he insisted on being paid in cash—not firewater. If *only*, Hebster thought, he could somehow contrive to meet an Alien he'd find out soon enough what its needs were, what was basically desired.

And then as the retort-shaped, the tube-shaped, the bell-shaped bottles materialized all around him, he understood! They had been forming the insistent questions in his mind. And they weren't satisfied with the answers he had found thus far. They liked answers. They liked answers very much indeed. If he was interested, there was always a way—

A great dots-in-bottle brushed his cortex and he screamed. "No! I don't *want* to!" he explained desperately.

Ping! went the dots-in-bottle and Hebster grabbed at his body.

His continuing flesh reassured him. He felt very much like the girl in Greek mythology who had begged Zeus for the privilege of seeing him in the full regalia of his godhood. A few moments after her request had been granted, there had been nothing left of the inquisitive female but a fine feathery ash.

The bottles were swirling in and out of each other in a strange and intricate dance from which there radiated emotions vaguely akin to curiosity, yet partaking of amusement and rapture.

Why rapture? Hebster was positive he had caught that note, even allowing for the lack of similarity between mental patterns. He ran a hurried dragnet through his memory, caught a few corresponding items, and dropped them after a brief, intensive examination. What was he trying to remember—what was his supremely efficient businessman's instincts trying to remind him of?

The dance became more complex, more rapid. A few bottles had passed under his feet, and Hebster could see them, undulating and spinning some ten feet below the surface of the ground as if their presence had made the Earth a transparent as well as permeable medium. Completely unfamiliar with all matters Alien as he was, not knowing—nor caring!—whether they danced as an expression of the counsel they were taking together, or as a matter of necessary social ritual, Hebster was able none the less to sense an approaching climax. Little crooked lines of green lightning began to erupt between the huge bottles. Something exploded near his left ear. He rubbed his face fearfully and moved away. The bottles followed, maintaining him in the imprisoning sphere of their frenzied movements.

Why *rapture*? Back in the city, the Aliens had had a terribly studious air about them as they hovered, almost motionless, above the works and lives of mankind. They were cold and careful scientists and showed not the slightest capacity for . . . for—

So he had something. At last he had something. But what do you do with an idea when you can't communicate it and can't act upon it yourself?

Ping!

The previous invitation was being repeated, more urgently. *Ping! Ping! Ping*!

"No!" he yelled and tried to stand. He found he couldn't. "I'm not . . . I don't want to go Prime!"

There was detached, almost divine laughter.

He felt that awful scrabbling inside his brain as if two or three entities were jostling each other within it. He shut his eyes hard and thought. He was close, he was very close. He had an idea, but he needed time to formulate it—a little while to figure out just exactly what the idea was and just exactly what to do with it!

Ping, ping, ping! Ping, ping, ping!

He had a headache. He felt as if his mind were being sucked out of his head. He tried to hold on to it. He couldn't.

All right, then. He relaxed abruptly, stopped trying to protect himself. But with his mind and his mouth, he yelled. For the first time in his life and with only a partially formed conception of whom he was addressing the desperate call to, Algernon Hebster screamed for help.

"I can do it!" he alternately screamed and thought. "Save money, save time, save whatever it is you want to save, whoever you are and whatever you call yourself—I can help you save! Help me, *help me*—*We* can do it—but *hurry*. Your problem can be solved—Economize. The balance-sheet—*Help*—"

The words and frantic thoughts spun in and out of each other like the contracting rings of Aliens all around him. He kept screaming, kept the focus on his mental images, while, unbearably, somewhere inside him, a gay and jocular force began to close a valve on his sanity.

Suddenly, he had absolutely no sensation. Suddenly, he knew dozens of things he had never dreamed he could know and had forgotten a thousand times as many. Suddenly, he felt that every nerve in his body was under control of his forefinger. Suddenly, he—

Ping, ping, ping! Ping! Ping! PING! PING! PING! PING!

". . . like that," someone said.

"What, for example?" someone else asked.

"Well, they don't even lie normally. He's been sleeping like a human being. They twist and moan in their sleep, the Primeys do, for all the world like habitual old drunks. Speaking of moans, here comes our boy."

Hebster sat up on the army cot, rattling his head. The fears were leaving him, and, with the fears gone, he would no longer be hurt. Braganza, highly concerned and unhappy, was standing next to his bed with a man who was obviously a doctor. Hebster smiled at both of them, manfully resisting the temptation to drool out a string of nonsense syllables.

"Hi, fellas," he said. "Here I come ungathering nuts in May."

"You don't mean to tell me you communicated!" Braganza yelled. "You communicated and didn't go Prime!"

Hebster raised himself on an elbow and glanced out past the tent flap to where Greta Seidenheim stood on the other side of a port-armed guard. He waved his fist at her, and she nodded a wide-open smile back.

"Found me lying in the desert like a waif, did you?"

"*Found* you!" Braganza spat. "You were brought in by Primeys, man. First time in history they ever did that. We've been waiting for you to come to in the serene faith that once you did, everything would be all right."

The corporation president rubbed his forehead. "It will be, Braganza, it will be. Just Primeys, eh? No Aliens helping them?"

"*Aliens*?" Braganza swallowed. "What led you to believe—What gave you reason to hope that . . . that *Aliens* would help the Primeys bring you in?"

"Well, perhaps I shouldn't have used the word 'help'. But I did think there would be a few Aliens in the group that escorted my unconscious body back to you. Sort of an honor guard, Braganza. It would have been a real nice gesture, don't you think?"

The SIC man looked at the doctor who had been following the conversation with interest. "Mind stepping out for a minute?" he suggested.

He walked behind the man and dropped the tent flap into place. Then he came around to the foot of the army cot and pulled on his mustache vigorously. "Now, see here, Hebster, if you keep up this clowning, so help me I will slit your belly open and snap your intestines back in your face! *What happened*?"

"What happened?" Hebster laughed and stretched slowly, carefully, as if he were afraid of breaking the bones of his arm. "I don't think I'll ever be able to answer that question completely. And there's a section of my mind that's very glad that I won't. This much I remember clearly: I had an idea. I communicated it to the proper and interested party. We concluded—this party and I—a tentative agreement as agents, the exact terms of the agreement to be decided by our principals and its complete ratification to be contingent upon their acceptance. Furthermore, we—All right, Braganza, all right! I'll tell it straight. Put down that folding chair. Remember, I've just been through a pretty unsettling experience!"

"Not any worse than the world is about to go through," the official growled. "While you've been out on your three-day vacation, Dempsey's been organizing a full-dress revolution every place at once. He's been very careful to limit it to parades and verbal fireworks so that we haven't been able to make with the riot squads, but it's pretty evident that he's ready to start using muscle. Tomorrow might be it; he's spouting on a world-wide video hookup and it's the opinion of the best experts we have available that his tag line will be the signal for action. Know what their slogan is? It concerns Verus who's been indicted for murder; they claim he'll be a martyr."

"And you were caught with your suspicions down. How many SIC men turned out to be Firsters?"

Braganza nodded. "Not too many, but more than we expected. More than we could afford. He'll do it, Dempsey will, unless you've hit the real thing. Look, Hebster," his heavy voice took on a pleading quality, "don't play with me any more. Don't hold my threats against me; there was no personal animosity in them, just a terrible, fearful worry over the world and its people and the government I was supposed to protect. If you still have a gripe against me, I, Braganza, give you leave to take it out of my hide as soon as we clear this mess up. But let me know where we stand first. A lot of lives and a lot of history depend on what you did out there in that patch of desert."

Hebster told him. He began with the extraterrestrial *Walpurgis Nacht*. "Watching the Aliens slipping in and out of each other in that cock-eyed and complicated rhythm, it struck me how different they were from the thoughtful dots-in-bottles hovering over our busy places, how different all creatures are in their home environments—and how hard it is to get to know them on the basis of their company manners. And then I realized that this place wasn't their home."

"Of course. Did you find out which part of the galaxy they come from?"

"That's not what I mean. Simply because we have marked this area off—and others like it in the Gobi, in the Sahara, in Central Australia—as a reservation for those of our kind whose minds have crumbled under the clear, conscious, and certain knowledge of inferiority, we cannot assume that the Aliens around whose settlements they have congregated have necessarily settled themselves."

"*Huh?*" Braganza shook his head rapidly and batted his eyes.

"In other words, we had made an assumption on the basis of the Aliens' very evident superiority to ourselves. But that assumption—and therefore that superiority—was in our own terms of what is superior and inferior, and not the Aliens'. And it especially might not apply to those Aliens on . . . the reservation."

The SIC man took a rapid walk around the tent. He beat a great fist into an open sweaty palm. "I'm beginning to, just beginning to—"

"That's what I was doing at that point, just beginning to. Assumptions that don't stand up under the structure they're supposed to support have caused the ruin of more close-thinking businessmen than I would like to face across any conference table. The four brokers, for example, who, after the market crash of 1929—"

"All right," Braganza broke in hurriedly, taking a chair near the cot. "Where did you go from there?"

"I still couldn't be certain of anything; all I had to go on were a few random thoughts inspired by extrasubstantial adrenalin secretions and, of course, the strong feeling that these particular Aliens weren't acting the way I had become accustomed to expect Aliens to act. They reminded me of something, of somebody. I was positive that once I got that memory tagged, I'd have most of the problem solved. And I was right."

"How were you right? What was the memory?"

"Well, I hit it backwards, kind of. I went back to Professor Kleimbocher's analogy about the paleface inflicting firewater on the Indian. I've always felt that somewhere in that analogy was the solution. And suddenly, thinking of Professor Kleimbocher and watching those powerful creatures writhing their way in and around each other, suddenly I knew what was wrong. Not the analogy, but our way of using it. We'd picked it up by the hammer head instead of the handle. The paleface gave firewater to the Indian all right—but he got something in return."

"What?"

"Tobacco. Now there's nothing very much wrong with tobacco if it isn't misused, but the first white men to smoke probably went as far overboard as the first Indians to drink. And both booze and tobacco have this in common—they make you awfully sick if you use too much for your initial experiment. See, Braganza? These Aliens out here in the desert reservation are *sick*. They have hit something in our culture that is as psychologically indigestible to them as . . . well, whatever they have that sticks in our mental gullet and causes ulcers among us. They've been put into a kind of isolation in our desert areas until the problem can be licked."

"Something that's as indigestible psychologically—What could it be, Hebster?"

The businessman shrugged irritably. "I don't know. And I don't want to know. Perhaps it's just that they can't let go of a problem until they've solved it—and they can't solve the problems of mankind's activity because of mankind's inherent and basic differences. Simply because we can't understand them, we had no right to assume that they could and did understand us."

"That wasn't all, Hebster. As the comedians put it—everything we can do, they can do better."

"Then why did they keep sending Primeys in to ask for those weird gadgets and impossible gimcracks?"

"They could duplicate anything we made."

"Well, maybe that is it," Hebster suggested. "They could duplicate it, but could they design it? They show every sign of being a race of creatures who never had to make very much for themselves; perhaps they evolved fairly early into animals with direct control over matter, thus never having had to go through the various stages of artifact design. This, in our terms, is a tremendous advantage; but it inevitably would have concurrent disadvantages. Among other things, it would mean a minimum of art forms and a lack of basic engineering knowledge of the artifact itself, if not of the directly activated and altered material. The fact is I was right, as I found out later.

For example. Music is not a function of theoretical harmonics, of complete scores in the head of a conductor or composer—these come later, much later. Music is first and foremost a function of the particular instrument, the reed pipe, the skin drum, the human throat—it is a function of tangibles which a race operating upon electrons, positrons, and mesons would never encounter in the course of its construction. As soon as I had that, I had the other flaw in the analogy—the assumption itself."

"You mean the assumption that we are necessarily inferior to the Aliens?"

"Right, Braganza. They can do a lot that we can't do, but vice very much indeed versa. How many special racial talents we possess that they don't is a matter of pure conjecture—and may continue to be for a good long time. Let the theoretical boys worry that one a century from now, just so they stay away from it at present."

Braganza fingered a button on his green jerkin and stared over Hebster's head. "No more scientific investigation of them, eh?"

"Well, we can't right now and we have to face up to that mildly unpleasant situation. The consolation is that they have to do the same. Don't you see? It's not a basic inadequacy. We don't have enough facts and can't get enough at the moment through normal channels of scientific observation because of the implicit psychological dangers to both races. Science, my forward-looking friend, is a complex of interlocking theories, *all derived from observation.*

"Remember, long before you had any science of navigation you had coast-hugging and river-hopping traders who knew how the various currents affected their leaky little vessels, who had learned things about the relative dependability of the moon and the stars—without any interest at all in integrating these scraps of knowledge into broader theories. Not until you have a sufficiently large body of these scraps, and are able to distinguish the preconceptions from the actual observations, can you proceed to organize a science of navigation without running the grave risk of drowning while you conduct your definitive experiments.

"A trader isn't interested in theories. He's interested only in selling something that glitters for something that glitters even more. In the process, painlessly and imperceptibly, he picks up bits of knowledge which gradually reduce the area of unfamiliarity. Until one day there are enough bits of knowledge on which to base a sort of preliminary understanding, a working hypothesis. And then, some Kleimbocher of the future, operating in an area no longer subject to the sudden and unexplainable mental disaster, can construct meticulous and exact laws out of the more obviously valid hypotheses."

"I might have known it would be something like this, if you came back with it, Hebster! So their theorists and our theorists had better move out and the traders move in. Only how do we contact their traders—if they have any such animals?"

The corporation president sprang out of bed and began dressing. "They have them. Not a Board of Directory type perhaps—but a business-minded Alien. As soon as I realized that the dots-in-bottles were acting, relative to their balanced scientific colleagues, very like our own high IQ Primeys, I knew I needed help. I needed someone I could tell about it, someone on their side who had as great a stake in an operating solution as I did. There had to be an Alien in the picture somewhere who was concerned with profit and loss statements, with how much of a return you get out of a given investment of time, personnel, material, and energy. I figured with him I could talk—*business*. The simple approach: What have you got that we want and how little of what we have will you take for it. No attempts to understand completely incompatible philosophies. There had to be that kind of character somewhere in the expedition. So I shut my eyes and let out what I fondly hoped was a telepathic *yip* channeled to him. I was successful.

"Of course, I might not have been successful, if he hadn't been searching desperately for just that sort of *yip*. He came buzzing up in a rousing United States Cavalry-routs-the-redskins type of rescue, stuffed my dripping psyche back into my subconscious, and hauled me up into some sort of never-never-ship. I've been in this interstellar version of Mohammed's coffin, suspended between Heaven and Earth, for three days, while he alternately bargained with me and consulted the home office about developments.

"We dickered the way I do with Primeys—by running down a list of what each of us could offer and comparing it with what we wanted; each of us trying to get a little more than we gave to the other guy, in our own terms, of course. Buying and selling are intrinsically simple processes; I don't imagine our discussions were very much different from those between a couple of Phoenician sailors and the blue-painted Celtic inhabitants of early Britain."

"And this . . . this business-Alien never suggested the possibility of taking what they wanted—"

"By force? No, Braganza, not once. Might be they're too civilized for such shenanigans. Personally I think the big reason is that they don't have any idea of what it is they do want from us. We represent a fantastic enigma to them—a species which uses matter to alter matter, producing objects which, while intended for similar functions, differ enormously from each other. You might say that we ask the question '*how*' about their activities; and they want to know the '*why*' about ours. Their investigators have compulsions even greater than ours. As I understand it, the intelligent races they've encountered up to this point are all comprehensible to them since they derive from parallel evolutionary paths. Every time one of their researchers get close to the answer of why we wear various colored clothes even in climates where clothing is unnecessary, he slips over the edges and splashes.

"Of course, that's why this opposite number of mine was so worried. I don't know his exact status—he may be anything from the bookkeeper to the business-manager of the expedition—but it's his bottle-neck if the outfit continues to be uneconomic. And I gathered that not only has his occupation kind of barred him from doing the investigation his unstable pals were limping back from into the asylums he's constructed here in the deserts, but those of them who've managed to retain their sanity constantly exhibit a healthy contempt for him. They feel, you see, that their function is that of the expedition. He's strictly supercargo. Do you think it bothers them one bit," Hebster snorted, "that he has a report to prepare, to show how his expedition stood up in terms of a balance sheet—"

"Well, you did manage to communicate on that point, at least," Braganza grinned. "Maybe traders using the simple, earnestly chiseling approach will be the answer. You've certainly supplied us with more basic data already than years of heavily subsidized research. Hebster, I want you to go on the air with this story you told me and show a couple of Primey Aliens to the video public."

"Uh-uh. You tell 'em. You can use the prestige. I'll think a message to my Alien buddy along the private channel he's keeping open for me, and he'll send you a couple of human-happy dots-in-bottles for the telecast. I've got to whip back to New York and get my entire outfit to work on a really encyclopedic job."

"Encyclopedic?"

The executive pulled his belt tight and reached for a tie. "Well, what else would you call the first edition of the Hebster Interstellar Catalogue of all Human Activity and Available Artifacts, prices available upon request with the understanding that they are subject to change without notice?"

THE ALLEY MAN

Philip José Farmer

"The man from the puzzle factory was here this morning," said Gummy, "While you was out fishin."

She dropped the piece of wiremesh she was trying to tie with string over a hole in the rusty window screen. Cursing, grunting like a hog in a wallow, she leaned over and picked it up. Straightening, she slapped viciously at her bare shoulder.

"Figurin skeeters! Must be a million outside, all tryin to get away from the burnin garbage."

"Puzzle factory?" said Deena. She turned away from the battered kerosene-burning stove over which she was frying sliced potatoes and perch and bullheads caught in the Illinois River, half a mile away.

"Yeah!" snarled Gummy. "You heard Old Man say it. Nuthouse. Booby hatch. So . . . this cat from the puzzle factory was named John Elkins. He gave Old Man all those tests when they had im locked up last year. He's the skinny little guy with a moustache 'n never lookin you in the eye 'n grinnin like a skunk eatin a shirt. The cat who took Old Man's hat away from him 'n wun't give it back to him until Old Man promised to be good. Remember now?"

Deena, tall, skinny, clad only in a white terrycloth bathrobe, looked like a surprised and severed head stuck on a pike. The great purple birthmark on her cheek and neck stood out hideously against her paling skin.

"Are they going to send him back to the State hospital?" she asked.

Gummy, looking at herself in the cracked full-length mirror nailed to the wall, laughed and showed her two teeth. Her frizzy hair was a yellow brown, chopped short. Her little blue eyes were set far back in tunnels beneath two protruding ridges of bone; her nose was very long, enormously wide, and tipped with a brokenveined bulb. Her chin was not there, and her head bent forward in a permanent crook. She was dressed only in a dirty once-white slip that came to her swollen knees. When she laughed, her huge breasts, resting on her distended belly quivered like bowls of fermented cream. From her expression, it was evident that she was not displeased with what she saw in the broken glass.

Again she laughed. "Naw, they din't come to haul him away. Elkins just wanted to interduce this chick he had with him. A cute little brunette with big brown eyes behint real thick glasses. She looked just like a collidge girl, 'n she was. This chick has got a B.M. or something in sexology . . ."

"Psychology?"

"Maybe it was societyology . . ."

"Sociology?"

"Umm. Maybe. Anyway, this foureyed chick is doin a study for a foundation. She wants to ride aroun with Old Man, see how he collects his junk, what alleys he goes up 'n down, what his, uh, habit patterns is, 'n learn what kinda bringing up he had . . ."

"Old Man'd never do it!" burst out Deena. "You know he can't stand the idea of being watched by a False Folker!"

"Umm. Maybe. Anyway, I tell em Old Man's not goin to like their slummin on him, 'n they say quick they're not slummin, it's for science. 'N they'll pay him for his trouble. They got a grant from the foundation. So I say maybe that'd make Old Man take another look at the color of the beer, 'n they left the house . . ."

"You *allowed* them in the house? Did you hide the birdcage?"

"Why hide it? His hat wasn't in it."

Deena turned back to frying her fish, but over her shoulder she said, "I don't think Old Man'll agree to the idea, do you? It's rather degrading."

"You *kiddin*? Who's lower'n Old Man? A snake's belly, maybe. Sure, he'll agree. He'll have a eye for the foureyed chick, sure."

"Don't be absurd," said Deena. "He's a dirty stinking one-armed middle-aged man, the ugliest man in the world."

"Yeah, it's the uglies he's got, for sure. 'N he smells like a goat that fell in a outhouse. But it's the smell that gets em. It got me, it got you, it got a whole stewpotfull a others, includin that high-society dame he used to collect junk off of . . ."

"Shut up!" spat Deena. "This girl must be a highly refined and intelligent girl. She'd regard Old Man as some sort of ape."

"You know them apes," said Gummy, and she went to the ancient refrigerator and took out a cold quart of beer.

Six quarts of beer later, Old Man had still not come home. The fish had grown cold and greasy, and the big July moon had risen. Deena, like a long lean dirty-white nervous alley cat on top of a backyard fence, patrolled back and forth across the shanty. Gummy sat on the bench made of crates and hunched over her bottle. Finally, she lurched to her feet and turned on the battered set. But, hearing a rattling and pounding of a loose motor in the distance, she turned it off.

The banging and popping became a roar just outside the door. Abruptly, there was a mighty wheeze, like an old rusty robot coughing with double pneumonia in its iron lungs. Then, silence.

But not for long. As the two women stood paralyzed, listening apprehensively, they heard a voice like the rumble of distant thunder.

"Take it easy, kid."

Another voice, soft, drowsy, mumbling.

"Where . . . we?"

The voice like thunder, "Home, sweet home, where we rest our dome."

Violent coughing.

"It's this smoke from the burnin' garbage, kid. Enough to make a maggot puke, ain't it? Lookit! The smoke's risin t'wards the full moon like the ghosts a men so rotten even their spirits're carrin the contamination with em. Hey, li'l chick, you didn't know Old Man knew them big words like contamination, didja? That's what livin on the city dump does for you. I hear that word all a time from the big shots that come down inspectin the stink here so they kin get away from the stink a City Hall. I ain't no illiterate. I got a TV set. Hor, hor, hor!"

There was a pause, and the two women knew he was bending his knees and tilting his torso backwards so he could look up at the sky.

"Ah, you lovely lovely moon, bride a The Old Guy In The Sky! Some day to come, rum-a-dum-a-dum, one day I sear it, Old Woman a The Old Guy In The Sky, if you help me find the longlost headpiece a King Paley that I and my fathers been lookin' for for fifty thousand years, so help me, Old Man Paley'll spread the freshly spilled blood a a virgin a the False Folkers out across the ground for you, so you kin lay down in it like a red carpet or a new red dress and wrap it aroun you. And then you won't have to crinkle up your lovely shinin nose at me and spit your silver spit on me. Old Man promises that, just as sure as his good arm is holdin a daughter a one a the Falsers, a virgin, I think, and bringin her to his home, however humble it be, so we shall see . . ."

"Stone out a his head," whispered Gummy.

"My God, he's bringin a girl in here!" said Deena. "*The* girl!"

"Not the *collidge* kid?"

"Does the idiot want to get lynched?"

The man outside bellowed, "Hey, you wimmen, get off your fat asses and open the door 'fore I kick it in! Old Man's home with a fistfull a dollars, a armful a sleepin lamb, and a gutfull a beer! Home like a conquerin hero and wants service like one, too!"

Suddenly unfreezing, Deena opened the door.

Out of the darkness and into the light shuffled something so squat and blocky it seemed more a tree trunk come to life than a man. It stopped, and the eyes under the huge black homburg hat blinked glazedly. Even the big hat could not hide the peculiar lengthened-out breadloaf shape of the skull. The forehead was abnormally low; over the eyes were bulging arches of bone. These were tufted with eyebrows like Spanish moss that made even more cavelike the hollows in which the little blue eyes lurked. Its nose was very long and very wide and flaring-nostrilled. The lips were thin but pushed out by the shoving jaws beneath them. Its chin was absent, and head and shoulders joined almost without intervention from a neck, or so it seemed. A corkscrew forest of rusty-red hairs sprouted from its open shirt front.

Over his shoulder, held by a hand wide and knobbly as a coral branch, hung the slight figure of a young woman. He shuffled into the room in an odd bent-kneed gait, walking on the sides of his thick-soled engineer's boots. Suddenly, he stopped again, sniffed deeply, and smiled, exposing teeth thick and yellow, dedicated to biting.

"Jeez, that smells good. It takes the old garbage stink right off. Gummy! You been sprinklin yourself with that perfume I found in a ash heap up on the bluffs?"

Gummy, giggling, looked coy.

Deena said, sharply, "Don't be a fool, Gummy. He's trying to butter you up so you'll forget he's bringing this girl home."

Old Man Paley laughed hoarsely and lowered the snoring girl upon an Army cot. There she sprawled out with her skirt around her hips. Gummy cackled, but Deena hurried to pull the skirt down and also to remove the girl's thick shellrimmed glasses.

"Lord," she said, "how did this happen? What'd you do to her?"

"Nothin," he growled, suddenly sullen.

He took a quart of beer from the refrigerator, bit down on the cap with teeth thick and chipped as ancient gravestones, and tore it off. Up went the bottle, forward went his knees, back went his torso as he leaned away from the bottle, and down went the amber liquid, gurgle, gurgle, glub. He belched, then roared. "There I was, Old Man Paley, mindin' my own figurin business, packin a bunch a papers and magazines I found, and here comes a blue fifty-one Ford sedan with Elkins, the doctor jerk from the puzzle factory. And this little foureyed chick here, Dorothy Singer. And . . ."

"Yes," said Deena. "We know who they are, but we didn't know they went after you."

"Who asked you? Who's tellin this story? Anyway, they tole me what they wanted. And I was gonna say no, but this little collidge broad says if I'll sign a paper that'll agree to let her travel around with me and even stay in our house a couple a evenins, with us actin natural, she'll pay me fifty dollars. I says yes! Old Guy In The Sky! That's a hundred and fifty quarts a beer! I got principles, but they're washed away in a roarin foamin flood of beer.

"I says yes, and the cute little runt give me the paper to sign, then advances me ten bucks and says I'll get the rest seven days from now. Ten dollars in my pocket! So she climbs up into the seat a my truck. And then this figurin Elkins parks his Ford and he says he thinks he ought to go with us to check on if everything's gonna be O.K.

"He's not foolin Old Man. He's after Little Miss Foureyes. Everytime he looks at her, the lovejuice runs out a his eyes. So, I collect junk for a couple a hours, talkin all the time. And she is scared a me at first because I'm so figurin ugly and strange. But after a while she busts out laughin. Then I pulls the truck up in the alley back a Jack's Tavern on Ames Street. She asks me what I'm doin. I says I'm stoppin for a beer, just as I do every day. And she says she could stand one, too. So . . ."

"You actually went inside with her?" asked Deena.

"Naw. I was gonna try, but I started gettin the shakes. And I hadda tell her I coun't do it. She asks me why. I say I don't know. Ever since I quit bein a kid, I kin't. So she says I got a . . . something like a fresh flower, what is it?"

"Neurosis?" said Deena.

"Yeah. Only I call it a taboo. So Elkins and the little broad go into Jack's and get a cold six-pack, and bring it out, and we're off . . ."

"So?"

"So we go from place to place, though always stayin in alleys, and she thinks it's funnier'n hell gettin loaded in the backs a taverns.

Then I get to seein double and don't care no more and I'm over my fraidies, so we go into the Circle Bar. And get in a fight there with one a the hillbillies in his sideburns and leather jacket that hangs out there and tries to take the foureyed chick home with him."

Both the women gasped, "Did the cops come?"

"If they did, they was late to the party. I grab this hillbilly by his leather jacket with my one arm—the strongest arm in this world—and throw him clean acrosst the room. And when his buddies come after me, I pound my chest like a figurin gorilla and make a figurin face at em, and they all of a sudden get their shirts up their necks and go back to listen to their hillbilly music. And I pick up the chick—she's laughin so hard she's chokin—and Elkins, white as a sheet out a the laundromat, after me, and away we go, and here we are."

"Yes, you fool, here you are!" shouted Deena. "Bringing that girl here in that condition! She'll start screaming her head off when she wakes up and sees you!"

"Go figure youself!" snorted Paley. "She was scared a me at first, and she tried to stay upwind a me. But she got to *likin* me. I could tell. And she got so she liked my smell, too. I knew she would. Don't all the broads? These False wimmen kin't say no once they get a whiff of us. Us Paleys got the gift in the blood."

Deena laughed and said. "You mean you have it in the head. Honest to God, when are you going to quit trying to force feed me with that bull? You're insane!"

Paley growled. "I tole you not never to call me nuts, not never!" and he slapped her across the cheek.

She reeled back and slumped against the wall, holding her face and crying, "You ugly stupid stinking ape, you hit me, the daughter of people whose boots you aren't fit to lick. *You* struck *me*!"

"Yeah, and ain't you glad I did," said Paley in tones like a complacent earthquake. He shuffled over to the cot and put his hand on the sleeping girl.

"Uh, feel that. No sag there, you two flabs."

"You beast!" screamed Deena. "Taking advantage of a helpless little girl!"

Like an alley cat, she leaped at him with claws out.

Laughing hoarsely, he grabbed one of her wrists and twisted it so she was forced to her knees and had to clench her teeth to keep from screaming with pain. Gummy cackled and handed Old Man a quart of beer. To take it, he had to free Deena. She rose, and all three, as if nothing had happened, sat down at the table and began drinking.

★

About dawn a deep animal snarl awoke the girl. She opened her eyes but could make out the trio only dimly and distortedly. Her hands, groping around for her glasses, failed to find them.

Old Man, whose snarl had shaken her from the high tree of sleep, growled again. "I'm tellin' you, Deena, I'm tellin' you, don't laugh at Old Man, don't laugh at Old Man, and I'm tellin' you again, three times, don't laugh at Old Man!"

His incredible bass rose to a high-pitched scream of rage.

"Whassa matta wi your figurin brain? I show you proof after proof, 'n you sit there in all your stupidity like a silly hen that sits down too hard on its eggs and breaks em but won't get up 'n admit she's squattin on a mess. I—I—Paley—Old Man Paley—kin prove I'm what I say I am, a Real Folker."

Suddenly, he propelled his hand across the table towards Deena.

"Feel them bones in my lower arm! Them two bones ain't straight and dainty like the arm bones a you False Folkers. They're thick as flagpoles, and they're curved out from each other like the backs a two tomcats outbluffing each other over a fishhead on a garbage can. They're built that way so's they kin be real strong anchors for my muscles, which is bigger'n False Folkers'. Go ahead, feel em.

"And look at them brow ridges. Like the tops a those shellrimmed spectacles all them intellekchooalls wear. Like the spectacles this collidge chick wears.

"And feel the shape a my skull. It ain't a ball like yours but a loaf a bread."

"Fossilized bread!" sneered Deena. "Hard as a rock, through and through."

Old Man roared on, "Feel my neck bones if you got the strength to feel through my muscles! They're bent forward, not—"

"Oh, I know you're an ape. You can't look overhead to see if that was a bird or just a drop of rain without breaking your back."

"Ape, hell! I'm a Real Man! Feel my heel bone! Is it like yours? No, it ain't! It's built different, and so's my whole foot!"

"Is that why you and Gummy and all those brats of yours have to walk like chimpanzees?"

"Laugh, laugh, laugh!"

"I am laughing, laughing, laughing. Just because you're a freak of nature, a monstrosity whose bones all went wrong in the womb, you've dreamed up this fantastic myth about being descended from the Neanderthals . . ."

"Neanderthals!" whispered Dorothy Singer. The walls whirled about her, looking twisted and ghostly in the half-light, like a room in Limbo.

". . . all this stuff about the lost hat of Old King," continued Deena, "and how if you ever find it you can break the spell that keeps you so-called Neanderthals on the dumpheaps and in the alleys, is garbage, and not very appetizing . . ."

"And you," shouted Paley, "are headin for a beatin!"

"Thass wha she wants," mumbled Gummy. "Go ahead. Beat her. She'll get her jollies off, 'n quit needin you. 'N we kin all git some shuteye. Besides, you're gonna wake up the chick."

"That chick is gonna get a wakin up like she never had before when Old Man gits his paws on her," rumbled Paley. "Guy In The Sky, ain't it somethin she should a met me and be in this house? Sure as an old shirt stinks, she ain't gonna be able to tear herself away from me.

"Hey, Gummy, maybe she'll have a kid for me, huh? We ain't had a brat around here for ten years. I kinda miss my kids. You gave me six that was Real Folkers, though I never was sure about that Jimmy, he looked too much like O'Brien. Now you're all dried up, dry as Deena always was, but you kin still raise em. How'd you like to raise the collidge chick's kid?"

Gummy grunted and swallowed beer from a chipped coffee mug. After belching loudly, she mumbled, "Don know. You'e crazier'n even I think you are if you think this cute little Miss Foureyes'd have anything to do wi you. 'N even if she was out a her head nough to do it, what kind a life is this for a brat? Get raised in a dump? Have a ugly old maw 'n paw? Grow up so ugly nobody's have nothin to do wi him 'n smellin so strange all the dogs'd bite him?"

Suddenly, she began blubbering.

"It ain't only Neanderthals has to live on dumpheaps. It's the crippled 'n the stupid 'n the queer in the head that has to live here. 'N they become Neanderthals just as much as us Real Folk. No diff'rence, no diff'rence. We're all ugly 'n hopeless 'n rotten. We're all Neander . . ."

Old Man's fist slammed the table.

"Name me no names like that! That's a *G'Yaga* name for us Paleys—Real Folkers. Don't let me never hear that other name again! It don't mean a man; it means somethin like a high-class gorilla."

"Quit lookin in the the mirror!" shrieked Deena.

There was more squabbling and jeering and roaring and confusing and terrifying talk, but Dorothy Singer had closed her eyes and fallen asleep again.

★

Some time later, she awoke. She sat up, found her glasses on a little table beside her, put them on, and stared about her.

She was in a large shack built of odds and ends of wood. It had two rooms, each about ten feet square. In the corner of one room was a large kerosene-burning stove. Bacon was cooking in a huge skillet; the heat from the stove made sweat run from her forehead and over her glasses.

After drying them off with her handkerchief, she examined the furnishings of the shack. Most of it was what she had expected, but three things surprised her. The bookcase, the photograph on the wall, and the birdcage. The bookcase was tall and narrow and of some dark wood, badly scratched. It was crammed with comic books, Blue Books, and Argosies, some of which she supposed must be at least twenty years old. There were a few books whose ripped backs and waterstained covers indicated they'd been picked out of ash heaps. Haggard's *Allan and the Ice Gods*, *Wells's Outline of History*, Vol. I, and his *The Croquet Player*. Also *Gog and Magog, A Prophecy of Armageddon* by the Reverend Caleb G. Harris. Burroughs' *Tarzan the Terrible* and *In the Earth's Core*. Jack London's *Beyond Adam*.

The framed photo on the wall was that of a woman who looked much like Deena and must have been taken around 1890. It was very large, tinted in brown, and showed an aristocratic handsome woman of about thirty-five in a high-busted velvet dress with a high neckline. Her hair was drawn severely back to a knot on top of her head. A diadem of jewels was on her breast.

The strangest thing was the large parrot cage. It stood upon a tall support which had nails driven through its base to hold it to the floor. The cage itself was empty, but the door was locked with a long narrow bicycle lock.

Her speculation about it was interrupted by the two women calling to her from their place by the stove.

Deena said, "Good morning, Miss Singer, How do you feel?"

"Some Indian buried his hatchet in my head," Dorothy said. "And my tongue is molting. Could I have a drink of water, please?"

Deena took a pitcher of cold water out of the refrigerator, and from it filled up a tin cup.

"We don't have any running water. We have to get our water from the gas station down the road and bring it here in a bucket."

Dorothy looked dubious, but she closed her eyes and drank.

"I think I'm going to get sick," she said. "I'm sorry."

"I'll take you to the outhouse," said Deena, putting her arm around the girl's shoulder and heaving her up with surprising strength.

"Once I'm outside," said Dorothy faintly, "I'll be all right."

"Oh, I know," said Deena. "It's the odor. The fish, Gummy's cheap perfume, Old Man's sweat, the beer. I forgot how it first affected me. But it's no better outside."

Dorothy didn't reply, but when she stepped through the door, she murmured, "Ohh!"

"Yes, I know," said Deena. "It's awful, but it won't kill you."

Ten minutes later, Deena and a pale and weak Dorothy came out of the ramshackle outhouse.

They returned to the shanty, and for the first time Dorothy noticed that Elkins was sprawled face up on the seat of the truck. His head hung over the end of the seat, and the flies buzzed around his open mouth.

"This is horrible," said Deena. "He'll be very angry when he wakes up and finds out where he is. He's such a respectable man."

"Let the heel sleep it off," said Dorothy. She walked into the shanty, and a moment later Paley clomped into the room, a smell of stale beer and very peculiar sweat advancing before him in a wave.

"How you feel?" he growled in a timbre so low the hairs on the back of her neck rose.

"Sick. I think I'll go home."

"Sure. Only try some a the hair."

He handed her a half-empty pint of whiskey. Dorothy reluctantly downed a large shot chased with cold water. After a brief revulsion, she began feeling better and took another shot. She then washed her face in a bowl of water and drank a third whiskey.

"I think I can go with you now," she said. "But I don't care for breakfast."

"I ate already," he said. "Let's go. It's ten-thirty according to the clock on the gas station. My alley's prob'ly been cleaned out by now. Them other ragpickers are always moochin in on my territory when they think I'm stayin home. But you kin bet they're scared out a their pants every time they see a shadow cause they're afraid it's Old Man and he'll catch em and squeeze their gut out and crack their ribs with this one good arm."

Laughing a laugh so hoarse and unhuman it seemed to come from some troll deep in the caverns of his bowels, he opened the refrigerator and took another beer.

"I need another to get me started, not to mention what I'll have to give that damn balky bitch, Fordiana."

As they stepped outside, they saw Elkins stumble towards the outhouse and then fall headlong through the open doorway. He lay motionless on the floor, his feet sticking out of the entrance. Alarmed, Dorothy wanted to go after him, but Paley shook his head.

"He'sa big boy; he kin take care a hisself. We got to git Fordiana up and goin."

Fordiana was the battered and rusty pick-up truck. It was parked outside Paley's bedroom window so he could look out at any time of the night and make sure no one was stealing parts or even the whole truck.

"Not that I ought a worry about her," grumbled Old Man. He drank three fourths of the quart in four mighty gulps, then uncapped the truck's radiator and poured the rest of the beer down it.

"She knows nobody else'll give her beer, so I think that if any a these robbin figurers that live on the dump or at the shacks aroun the bend was to try to steal anything off'n her, she'd honk and backfire and throw rods and oil all over the place so's her Old Man could wake up and punch the figurin shirt off a the thievin figurer. But maybe not. She's a female. And you can't trust a figurin female."

He poured the last drop down the radiator and roared, "There! Now don't you dare *not* turn over. You're robbin me a the good beer I could be havin! If you so much as backfire, Old Man'll beat hell out a you with a sledge hammer!"

Wide-eyed but silent, Dorothy climbed onto the ripped open front seat beside Paley. The starter whirred, and the motor sputtered.

"No more beer if you don't work!" shouted Paley.

There was a bang, a fizz, a sput, a *whop, whop, whop*, a clash of gears, a monstrous and triumphant showing of teeth of Old Man, and they were bumpbumping over the rough ruts.

"Old Man knows how to handle all them bitches, flesh or tin, two-legged, four-legged, wheeled. I sweat beer and passion and promise em a kick in the tailpipe if they don't behave, and that gets em all. I'm so figurin ugly I turn their stomachs. But once they git a whiff a the out-a-this-world stink a me, they're done for, they fall prostrating at my big hairy feet. That's the way it's always been with us Paley men and the *G'yaga* wimmen. That's why their menfolks fear us, and why we got into so much trouble."

Dorothy did not say anything, and Paley fell silent as soon as the truck swung off the dump and onto U.S. Route 24. He seemed to fold up into himself, to be trying to make himself as inconspicuous as possible. During the three minutes it took the truck to get from the shanty to the city limits, he kept wiping his sweating palm against his blue workman's shirt.

But he did not try to release the tension with oaths. Instead, he muttered a string of what seemed to Dorothy nonsense rhymes.

"Eenie, meenie, minie, moe. Be a good Guy, help me go. Hoola boola, teenie weenie, ram em, damn em, figure em, duck em, watch me go, don't be a shmoe. Stop em, block em, sing a go go go."

Not until they had gone a mile into the city of Onaback and turned from 24 into an alley did he relax.

"Whew! That's torture, and I been doin it ever since I was sixteen, some years ago. Today seems worse'n ever, maybe cause you're along. *G'yaga* men don't like it if they see me with one a their wimmen, specially a cute chick like you."

Suddenly, he smiled and broke into a song about being covered all over "with sweet violets, sweeter than all the roses." He sang other songs, some of which made Dorothy turn red in the face, though at the same time she giggled. When they crossed a street to get from one alley to another, he cut off his singing, even in the middle of a phrase, and resumed it on the other side.

Reaching the west bluff, he slowed the truck to a crawl while his little blue eyes searched the ash heaps and garbage cans at the rears of the houses. Presently, he stopped the truck and climbed down to inspect his find.

"Guy In The Sky, we're off to a flyin start! Look!—some old grates from a coal furnace. And a pile a Coke and beer bottles, all redeemable. Get down, Dor'thy—if you want a know how us ragpickers make a livin, you gotta get in and and sweat and cuss with us. And if you come across any hats, be sure to tell me."

Dorothy smiled. But when she stepped down from the truck, she winced.

"What's the matter?"

"Headache."

"The sun'll boil it out. Here's how we do this collectin, see? The back end a the truck is boarded up into five sections. This section here is for the iron and the wood. This, for the paper. This, for the cardboard. You get a higher price for the cardboard. This, for rags. This, for bottles we can get a refund on. If you find any int'restin books or magazines, put em on the seat. I'll decide if I want to keep em or throw em in with the old paper."

They worked swiftly, and then drove on. About a block later,they were interrupted at another heap by a leaf of a woman, withered and blown by the winds of time. She hobbled out from the back porch of a large three-storied house with diamond-shaped panes in the windows and doors and cupolas at the corners. In a quavering voice she explained that she was the widow of a wealthy lawyer who had died fifteen years ago. Not until today had she made up her mind to get rid of his collection of law books and legal papers. These were all neatly cased in cardboard boxes not too large to be handled.

Not even, she added, her pale watery eyes flickering from Paley to Dorothy, not even by a poor one-armed man and a young girl.

Old Man took off his homburg and bowed.

"Sure, ma'am, my daughter and myself'd be glad to help you out in your housecleanin."

"Your daughter?" croaked the old woman.

"She don't look like me a tall," he replied. "No wonder. She's my fosterdaughter, poor girl, she was orphaned when she was still fillin her diapers. My best friend was her father. He died savin my life, and as he laid gaspin his life away in my arms, he begged me to take care a her as if she was my own. And I kept my promise to my dyin friend, may his soul rest in peace. And even if I'm only a poor ragpicker, ma'am, I been doin my best to raise her to be a decent Godfearin obedient girl."

Dorothy had to run around to the other side of the truck where she could cover her mouth and writhe in an agony of attempting to smother her laughter. When she regained control, the old lady was telling Paley she'd show him where the books were. Then she started hobbling to the porch.

But Old Man instead of following her across the yard, stopped by the fence that separated the alley from the backyard. He turned around and gave Dorothy a look of extreme despair.

"What's the matter?" she said. "Why're you sweating so? And shaking? And you're so pale."

"You'd laugh if I told you, and I don't like to be laughed at."

"Tell me. I won't laugh."

He closed his eyes and began muttering, "Never mind, it's in the mind. Never mind, you're just fine." Opening his eyes, he shook himself like a dog just come from the water.

"I kin do it. I got the guts. All them books're a lotta beer money I'll lose if I don't go down into the bowels a hell and get em. Guy In The Sky, give me the guts a a goat and the nerve a a pork dealer in Palestine. You know Old Man ain't got a yellow streak. It's the wicked spell a the False Folkers workin on me. Come on, let's go, go, go."

And sucking in a deep breath, he stepped through the gateway. Head down, eyes on the grass at his feet, he shuffled towards the cellar door where the old lady stood peering at him.

Four steps away from the cellar entrance, he halted again. A small black spaniel had darted from around the corner of the house and begun yapyapping at him.

Old Man suddenly cocked his head to one side, crossed his eyes, and deliberately sneezed.

Yelping, the spaniel fled back around the corner, and Paley walked down the steps that led to the cool dark basement. As he did so, he muttered, "That puts the evil spell on em figurin dogs."

When they had piled all the books in the back of the truck, he took off his homburg and bowed again.

"Ma'am, my daughter and myself both thank you from the rockbottom a our poor but humble hearts for this treasure trove you give us. And if ever you've anythin else you don't want, and a strong back and a weak mind to carry it out . . . well, please remember we'll be down this alley every Blue Monday and Fish Friday about time the sun is three-quarters acrosst the sky. Providin it ain't rainin cause the Old Guy In The Sky is cryin in his beer over us poor mortals, what fools we be."

Then he put his hat on, and the two got into the truck and chugged off. They stopped by several other promising heaps before he announced that the truck was loaded enough. He felt like celebrating; perhaps they should stop off behind Mike's Tavern's and down a few quarts. She replied that perhaps she might manage a drink if she could have a whiskey. Beer wouldn't set well.

"I got some money," rumbled Old Man, unbuttoning with slow clumsy fingers his shirtpocket and pulling out a roll of worn tattered bills while the truck's wheels rolled straight in the alley ruts.

"You brought me luck, so Old Man's gonna pay today through the hose, I mean, nose, har, har, har!"

He stopped Fordiana behind a little neighborhood tavern. Dorothy, without being asked, took the two dollars he handed her and went into the building. She returned with a can opener, two quarts of beer, and a halfpint of V.O.

"I added some of my money. I can't stand cheap whiskey."

They sat on the running board of the truck, drinking, Old Man doing most of the talking. It wasn't long before he was telling her of the times when the Real Folk, the Paleys, had lived in Europe and Asia by the side of the wooly mammoths and the cave lion.

"We worshipped the Guy In The Sky who says what the thunder says and lives in the east on the tallest mountain in the world. We face the skulls a our dead to the east so they could see the Old Guy when he came to take them to live with him in the mountain.

"And we was doin fine for a long time. Then, out a the east come them motherworshippin False Folk with their long straight legs and long straight necks and flat faces and thundermug round heads and their bows and arrows. They claimed they was sons a the goddess Mother Earth, who was a virgin. But we claimed the truth was that a crow with stomach trouble sat on a stump and when it left the hot sun hatched em out.

"Well, for a while we beat them hands-down because we was stronger Even one a our wimmen could tear their strongest man to bits. Still, they had that bow and arrow, they kept pickin us off, and movin in and movin in, and we kept movin back slowly, till pretty soon we was shoved with our backs against the ocean.

"Then one day a big chief among us got a bright idea. 'Why don't we make bows and arrows, too?' he said. And so we did, but we was clumsy at makin and shootin em cause our hands was so big, though we could draw a heavier bow'n em. So we kept gettin run out a the good huntin grounds.

"There was one thing might a been in our favor. That was, we bowled the wimmen a the Falsers over with our smell. Not that we smell good. We stink like a pig that's been making love to a billy goat on a manure pile. But, somehow, the wimmen folk a the Falser was all mixed up in their chemistry, I guess you'd call it, cause they got all excited and developed roundheels when they caught a whiff a us. If we'd been left alone with em, we could a Don Juan'd them alsers right off a the face a the earth. We would a mixed our blood with theirs so much that after a while you coun't tell the difference. Specially since the kids lean to their pa's side in looks. Paley blood is so much stronger.

"But that made sure there would always be war tween us. Specially after our king, Old King Paley, made love to the daughter a the Falser king, King Raw Boy, and stole her away.

"Gawd, you shou'd a seen the fuss then! Raw Boy's daughter flipped over Old King Paley. And it was her give him the bright idea a calling in every able-bodied Paley that was left and organizin em into one big army. Kind a puttin all our eggs in one basket, but it seemed a good idea. Every man big enough to carry a club went out in the big mob on Operation False Folk Massacree. And we ganged up on every little town a them motherworshippers we found. And kicked hell out a em. And roasted the men's hearts and ate em. And every now and then took a snack off the wimmen and kids, too.

"Then, all of a sudden, we come to a big plain. And there's a army a them False Folk, collected by Old King Raw Boy. They outnumber us, but we feel we kin lick the world. Specially since the magic strength a the *G'yaga* lies in their wimmen folk, cause they worship a woman god, the Old Woman In The Earth. And we've got their chief priestess Raw Boy's daughter.

"All our own personal power is collected in Old King Paley's hat—his magical headpiece. All a us Paleys believed that a man's strength and his soul was in his headpiece.

"We bed down the night before the big battle. At dawn there's a cry that'd wake up the dead. It still sends shivers down the necks a us Paleys fifty thousand years later. It's King Paley roarin and cryin. We ask him why. He says that that dirty little sneakin little hoor, Raw Boy's daughter, has stole his headpiece and run off with it to her father's camp.

"Our knees turn weak as nearbeer. Our manhood is in the hands a our enemies. But out we go to battle, our witch doctors out in front rattlin their gourds and whirlin their bullroarers and prayin. And here come the *G'yaga* medicine men doin the same. Only thing, their hearts is in their work cause they got Old King's headpiece stuck on the end a a spear.

"And for the first time they use dogs in war, too. Dogs never did like us any more'n we like em.

"And then we charge into each other. Bang! Wallop! Crash! Smash! Whack! Owwwrrroooo! And they kick hell out a us, do it to us. And we're never again the same, done forever. They had Old King's headpiece and with it our magic, cause we'd all put the soul a us Paleys in that hat.

"The spirit and power a us Paleys was prisoners cause that headpiece was. And life became too much for us Paleys. Them as wasn't slaughtered and eaten was glad to settle down on the garbage heaps a the conquerin Falsers and pick for a livin with the chickens, sometimes comin out second best.

"But we knew Old King's headpiece was hidden somewhere, and we organized a secret society and swore to keep alive his name and to search for the headpiece if it took us forever. Which it almost has, it's been so long.

"But even though we was doomed to live in shantytowns and stay off the streets and prowl the junkpiles in the alleys, we never gave up hope. And as time went on some a the no-counts a the *G'yaga* came down to live with us. And we and they had kids. Soon, most a us had disappeared into the bloodstream a the low class *G'yaga*. But there's always been a Paley family that tried to keep their blood pure. No man kin do no more, kin he?"

He glared at Dorothy. "What d'ya think a that?"

Weakly, she said, "Well, I've never heard anything like it."

"Gawdamighty!" snorted Old Man. "I give you a history longer'n a hoor's dream, more'n fifty thousand years a history, the secret story a a long lost race. And all you kin say is that you never heard nothin like it before."

He leaned towards her and clamped his huge hand over her thigh.

"Don't finch from me!" he said fiercely. "Or turn you head away. Sure, I stink, and I offend your dainty figurin nostrils and upset your figurin delicate little guts. But what's a minute's whiff a me on your part compared to a lifetime on my part a havin all the stinkin garbage in the universe shoved up my nose, and my mouth filled with what you woun't say if your mouth was full a it? What do you say to that, huh?"

Coolly, she said, "Please take your hand off me."

"Sure, I didn't mean nothin by it. I got carried away and forgot my place in society."

"Now, look here," she said earnestly. "That has nothing at all to do with your so-called social position. It's just that I don't allow anybody to take liberties with my body. Maybe I'm being ridiculously Victorian, but I want more than just sensuality. I want love, and—"

"O.K. I get the idea."

Dorothy stood up and said, "I'm only a block from my apartment. I think I'll walk on home. The liquor's given me a headache."

"Yeah," he growled. "You sure it's the liquor and not me?"

She looked steadily at him. "I'm going, but I'll see you tomorrow morning. Does that answer your question?"

"O.K.," he grunted. "See you. Maybe."

She walked away very fast.

Next morning, shortly after dawn, a sleepy-eyed Dorothy stopped her car before the Paley shanty. Deena was the only one home. Gummy had gone to the river to fish, and Old Man was in the outhouse. Dorothy took the opportunity to talk to Deena, and found her, as she had suspected, a woman of considerable education. However, although she was polite, she was reticent about her background. Dorothy, in an effort to keep the conversation going, mentioned that she had phoned her former anthropology professor and asked him about the chances of Old Man being a genuine Neanderthal. It was then that Deena broke her reserve and eagerly asked what the professor had thought.

"Well," said Dorothy, "he just laughed. He told me it was an absolute impossibility that a small group, even an inbred group isolated in the mountains, could have kept their cultural and genetic indentity for fifty thousand years.

"I argued with him. I told him Old Man insisted he and his kind had existed in the village of Paley in the mountains of the Pyrenees until Napoleon's men found them and tried to draft them. Then they fled to America, after a stay in England. And his group was split up during the Civil War, driven out of the Great Smokies. He, as far as he knows, is the last purebreed, Gummy being a half or quarter-breed.

"The professor assured me that Gummy and Old Man were cases of glandular malfunctioning, of acromegaly. That they may have a superficial resemblance to the Neanderthal man, but a physical anthropologist could tell the difference at a glance. When I got a little angry and asked him if he wasn't taking an unscientific and prejudiced attitude, he became rather irritated. Our talk ended somewhat frostily.

"But I went down to the university library that night and read everything on what makes *Homo Neanderthalensis* different from *Homo Sapiens*."

"You almost sound as if you believe Old Man's private little myth is the truth," said Deena.

"The professor taught me to be convinced only by the facts and not to say anything is impossible," replied Dorothy. "If he's forgotten his own teachings, I haven't."

"Well, Old Man is a persuasive talker," said Deena. "He could sell the devil a harp and halo."

Old Man, wearing only a pair of blue jeans, entered the shanty. For the first time Dorothy saw his naked chest, huge, covered with long red-gold hairs so numerous they formed a matting almost as thick as an orangutang's. However, it was not his chest but his bare feet at which she looked most intently. Yes, the big toes were widely separated from the others, and he certainly tended to walk on the outside of his feet.

His arm, too, seemed abnormally short in proportion to his body.

Old Man grunted a good morning and didn't say much for a while. But after he had sweated and cursed and chanted his way through the streets of Onaback, and had arrived safely at the alleys of the west bluff, he relaxed. Perhaps he was helped by finding a large pile of papers and rags.

"Well, here we go to work, so don't you dare to shirk. Jump, Dor'thy! By the sweat a your brow, you'll earn your brew!"

When that load was on the truck, they drove off. Paley said, "How you like this life without no strife? Good, huh? You like alleys, huh?"

Dorothy nodded. "As a child, I liked alleys better than streets. And they still preserve something of their first charm for me. They were more fun to play in, so nice and cozy. The trees and bushes and fences leaned in at you and sometimes touched you as if they had hands and liked to feel your face to find out if you'd been there before, and they remembered you. You felt as if you were sharing a secret with the alleys and the things of the alleys. But streets, well, streets were always the same, and you had to watch out the cars didn't run over you, and the windows in the houses were full of faces and eyes, poking their noses into your business, if you can say that eyes had noses."

Old Man whooped and slapped his thigh so hard it would have broke if it had been Dorothy's.

"You must be a Paley! We feel that way, too! We ain't allowed to hang around streets, so we make our alleys into little kingdoms. Tell me, do you sweat just crossin a street from one alley to the next?"

He put his hand on her knee. She looked down at it but said nothing, and he left it there while the truck putputted along, its wheels following the ruts of the alley.

"No, I don't feel that way at all."

"Yeah? Well, when you was a kid, you wasn't so ugly you hadda stay off the streets. But I still wasn't too happy in the alleys because a them figurin dogs. Forever and forever they was barkin and bitin at me. So I took to beatin the bejesus out a them with a big stick I always carried. But after a while I found I only had to look at em in a certain way. Yi, yi, yi, they'd run away yapping, like that old black spaniel did yesterday. Why? Cause they knew I was sneezin evil spirits at em. It was then I began to know I wasn't human. A course, my old man had been telling me that ever since I could talk.

"As I grew up I felt every day that the spell a the *G'yaga* was gettin stronger. I was gettin dirtier and dirtier looks from em on the streets. And when I went down the alleys, I felt like I really *belonged* there. Finally, the day came when I coun't cross a street without gettin sweaty hands and cold feet and a dry mouth and breathin hard. That was cause I was becomin a full-grown Paley, and the curse a the *G'yaga* gets more powerful as you get more hair on your chest."

"Curse?" said Dorothy. "Some people call it a neurosis."

"It's a curse."

Dorothy didn't answer. Again, she looked down at her knee, and this time he removed his hand. He would have had to do it, anyway, for they had come to a paved street.

On the way down to the junk dealer's, he continued the same theme. And when they got to the shanty, he elaborated upon it.

During the thousands of years the Paleys lived on the garbage piles of the *G'yaga*, they were closely watched. So, in the old days, it had been the custom for the priests and warriors of the False Folk to descend on the dumpheap dwellers whenever a strong and obstreperous Paley came to manhood. And they had gouged out an eye or cut off his hand or leg or some other member to ensure that he remembered what he was and where his place was.

"That's why I lost this arm," Old Man growled, waving the stump. "Fear a the *G'yaga* for the Paleys did this to me."

Deena howled with laughter and said, "Dorothy, the truth is that he got drunk one night and passed out on the railroad tracks, and a freight train ran over his arm."

"Sure, sure, that's the way it was. But it coun't a happened if the Falsers din't work through their evil black magic. Nowadays, stead a cripplin us openly, they use spells. They ain't got the guts anymore to do it themselves."

Deena laughed scornfully and said, "He got all those psychopathic ideas from reading those comics and weird tale magazines and those crackpot books and from watching that TV program, *Alley Oop and the Dinosaur*. I can point out every story from which he's stolen an idea."

"You're a liar!" thundered Old Man.

He struck Deena on the shoulder. She reeled away from the blow, then leaned back toward him as if into a strong wind. He struck her again, this time across her purple birthmark. Her eyes glowed, and she cursed him. And he hit her once more, hard enough to hurt but not to injure.

Dorothy opened her mouth as if to protest, but Gummy lay a fat sweaty hand on her shoulder and lifted her finger to her own lips.

Deena fell to the floor from a particularly violent blow. She did not stand up again. Instead, she got to her hands and knees and crawled toward the refuge behind the big iron stove. His naked foot shoved her rear so that she was sent sprawling on her face, moaning, her long stringy black hair falling over her face and birthmark.

Dorothy stepped forward and raised her hand to grab Old Man. Gummy stopped her, mumbling, "'S all right. Leave em alone."

"Look a that figurin female being happy!" snorted Old Man.

"You know why I *have* to beat the hell out a her, when all I want is peace and quiet? Cause I look like a figurin caveman, and they're suppose to beat their hoors silly. That's why she took up with me."

"You're an insane liar," said Deena softly from behind the stove, slowly and dreamily nursing her pain like the memory of a lover's caresses. "I came to live with you because I'd sunk so low you were the only man that'd have me."

"She's a retired high-society mainliner, Dor'thy," said Paley. "You never seen her without a longsleeved dress on. That's cause her arms're full a holes. It was me that kicked the monkey off a her back. I cursed her with the wisdom and magic a the Real Folk, where you coax the evil spirit out by talkin it out. And she's been living with me ever since. Can't get rid a her.

"Now, you take that toothless bag there. I ain't never hit her. That shows I ain't no womanbeatin bastard, right? I hit Deena cause she likes it, wants it, but I don't ever hit Gummy. . . . Hey, Gummy, that kind a medicine ain't what you want, is it?"

And he laughed his incredibly hoarse *hor, hor, hor.*

"You're a figurin liar," said Gummy, speaking over her shoulder because she was squatting down, fiddling with the TV controls. "You're the one knocked most a my teeth out."

"I knocked out a few rotten stumps you was gonna lose anyway. You had it comin cause you was running around with that O'Brien in his green shirt."

Gummy giggled and said, "Don't think for a minute I quit goin with that O'Brien in his green shirt just cause you slapped me around a little bit. I quite cause you was a better man 'n him."

Gummy giggled again. She rose and waddled across the room towards a shelf which held a bottle of her cheap perfume. Her enormous brass earrings swung, and her great hips swung back and forth.

"Look a that," said Old Man. "Like two bags a mush in a windstorm."

But his eyes followed them with kindling appreciation, and, on seeing her pour the reeking liquid over her pillowsized bosom, he hugged her and buried his huge nose in the valley of her breasts and sniffed rapturously.

"I feel like a dog that's found an old bone he buried and forgot till just now," he growled. "Arf, arf, arf!"

Deena snorted and said she had to get some fresh air or she'd lose her supper. She grabbed Dorothy's hand and insisted she take a walk with her. Dorothy, looking sick, went with her.

The following evening, as the four were drinking beer around the kitchen table, Old Man suddenly reached over and touched Dorothy affectionately. Gummy laughed, but Deena glared. However, she did not say anything to the girl but instead began accusing Paley of going too long without a bath. He called her a flat-chested hophead and said that she was lying, because he had been taking a bath every day. Deena replied that, yes he had, ever since Dorothy had appeared on the scene. An argument raged. Finally, he rose from the table and turned the photograph of Deena's mother so it faced the wall.

Wailing, Deena tried to face it outward again. He pushed her away from it, refusing to hit her despite her insults—even when she howled at him that he wasn't fit to lick her mother's shoes, let alone blaspheme her portrait by touching it.

Tired of the argument, he abandoned his post by the photograph and shuffled to the refrigerator.

"If you dare turn her around till I give the word, I'll throw her in the creek. And you'll never see her again."

Deena shrieked and crawled onto her blanket behind the stove and there lay sobbing and cursing him softly.

Gummy chewed tobacco and laughed while a brown stream ran down her toothless jaws. "Deena pushed him too far that time."

"Ah, her and her figurin mother," snorted Paley. "Hey, Dor'thy, you know how she laughs at me cause I think Fordiana's got a soul. And I put the evil eye on them hounds? And cause I think the salvation a us Paleys'll be when we find out where Old King's hat's been hidden?

"Well, get a load a this. This here intellekshooal purple-faced dragon, this retired mainliner, this old broken-down nag for a monkey-jockey, she's the sooperstishus one. She thinks her mother's a god. And she prays to her and asks forgiveness and asks what's gonna happen in the future. And when she thinks nobody's around, she talks to her. Here she is, worshippin her mother like the Old Woman In The Earth, who's The Old Guy's enemy. And she knows that makes the Old Guy sore. Maybe that's the reason he ain't allowed me to find the longlost headpiece a Old King, though he knows I been lookin in every ash heap from here to godknowswhere, hopin some fool *G'yaga* would throw it away never realizin what it was.

"Well, by all that's holy, that pitcher stays with its ugly face to the wall. Aw, shut up, Deena, I wanna watch Alley Oop."

Shortly afterwards, Dorothy drove home. There she again

phoned her sociology professor. Impatiently, he went into more detail. He said that one reason Old Man's story of the war between the Neanderthals and the invading *Homo Sapiens* was very unlikely was that there was evidence to indicate that *Homo Sapiens* might have been in Europe before the Neanderthals—it was very possible the *Homo Neanderthalensis* was the invader.

"Not invader in the modern sense," said the professor. "The influx of a new species of race or tribe into Europe during the Paleolithic would have been a sporadic migration of little groups, an immigration which might have taken a thousand to ten thousand years to complete.

"And it is more than likely that *Neanderthalensis* and *Sapiens* lived side by side for millennia with very little fighting between them because both were too busy struggling for a living. For one reason or another, probably because he was outnumbered, the Neanderthal was absorbed by the surrounding peoples. Some anthropologists have speculated that the Neanderthals were blonds and that they had passed their light hair directly to North Europeans.

"Whatever the guesses and surmises," concluded the professor, "it would be impossible for such a distinctly different minority to keep its special physical and cultural characteristics over a period of half a hundred millennia. Paley has concocted this personal myth to compensate for his extreme ugliness, his inferiority, his feelings of rejection. The elements of the myth came from the comic books and TV.

"However," concluded the professor, "in view of your youthful enthusiasm and naiveté, I will reconsider my judgment if you bring me some physical evidence of this Neandethaloid origin. Say you could show me that he had a taurodont tooth. I'd be flabbergasted, to say the least."

"But, professor," she pleaded, "why can't you give him a personal examination? One look at Old Man's foot would convince you, I'm sure."

"My dear, I am not addicted to wild goose chases. My time is valuable."

That was that. The next day, she asked Old Man if he had ever lost a molar tooth or had an X-ray made of one.

"No," he said, "I got more sound teeth than brains. And I ain't gonna lose them. Long as I keep my headpiece, I'll keep my teeth and my digestion and my manhood. What's more, I'll keep my good sense, too. The loosescrew tighteners at the State Hospital really gave me a good goin-over, fore and aft, up and down, in and out, all night long, don't never take a hotel room right by the elevator.

And they proved I wasn't hatched in a cuckoo clock. Even though they tore their hair and said something must be wrong. Specially after we had that row about my hat. I woun't let them take my blood for a test, you know because I figured they was goin to mix it with—water—*G'yaga* magic—and turn my blood to water. Somehow, that Elkins got wise that I hadda wear my hat—cause I woun't take it off when I undressed for the physical, I guess—and he snatched my hat. And I was done for. Stealin it was stealin my soul; all Paleys wears their souls in their hats. I hadda get it back. So I ate humble pie; I let them poke and pry all over and take my blood."

There was a pause while Paley breathed in deeply to get power to launch another verbal rocket. Dorothy, who had been struck by an idea, said, "Speaking of hats, Old Man, what does this hat that the daughter of Raw Boy stole from King Paley look like? Would you recognize it if you saw it?"

Old Man stared at her with wide blue eyes for a moment before he exploded.

"Would I recognize it? Would the dog that sat by the railroad tracks recognize his tail after the locomotive cut it off? Would you recognize your own blood if somebody stuck you in the guts with a knife and if pumped out with every heartbeat? Certainly, I would recognize the hat a Old King Paley! Every Paley at his mother's knee gits a detailed description a it. You want a hear about the hat? Well, hang on, chick, and I'll describe every hair and bone a it."

Dorothy told herself more than once that she should not be doing this. If she was trusted by Old Man, she was, in one sense, a false friend. But, she reassured herself, in another sense she was helping him. Should he find the hat, he might blossom forth, actually tear himself loose from the taboos that bound him to the dumpheap, to the alleys, to fear of dogs, to the conviction he was an inferior and oppressed citizen. Moreover, Dorothy told herself, it would aid her scientific studies to record his reaction.

The taxidermist she hired to locate the necessary materials and fashion them into the desired shape was curious, but she told him it was for an anthropological exhibit in Chicago and that it was meant to represent the headpiece of the medicine man of an Indian secret society dedicated to phallic mysteries. The taxidermist sniggered and said he'd give his eyeteeth to see those ceremonies.

Dorothy's intentions were helped by the run of good luck Old Man had in his alleypicking while she rode with him. Exultant, he swore he was headed for some extraordinary find; he could feel his good fortune building up.

"It's gonna hit," he said, grinning with his huge widely-spaced grave-stone teeth. "Like lightning."

Two days later, Dorothy rose even earlier than usual and drove to a place behind the house of a well-known doctor. She had read in the society column that he and his family were vacationing in Alaska, so she knew they wouldn't be wondering at finding a garbage can already filled with garbage and a big cardboard box full of cast-off clothes. Dorothy had brought the refuse from her own apartment to make it seem as if the house were occupied. The old garments, with one exception, she had purchased at a Salvation Army store.

About nine that morning, she and Old Man drove down the alley on their scheduled route.

Old Man was first off the truck; Dorothy hung back to let him make the discovery. Old Man picked the garments out of the box one by one.

"Here's a velvet dress Deena kin wear. She's been complainin she hasn't had a new dress in a long time. And here's a blouse and skirt big enough to wrap around an elephant. Gummy kin wear it. And here . . ."

He lifted up a tall conical hat with a wide brim and two balls of felted horsemane attached to the band. It was a strange headpiece, fashioned of roan horsehide over a ribwork of split bones. It must have been the only one of its kind in the world, and it certainly looked out of place in the alley of a mid-Illinois city.

Old Man's eyes bugged out. Then they rolled up, and he fell to the ground as if shot. The hat, however, was still clutched in his hand.

Dorothy was terrified. She had expected any reaction but this. If he had suffered a heart-attack, it would, she thought, be her fault.

Fortunately, Old Man had only fainted. However, when he regained consciousness, he did not go into ecstasies as she had expected. Instead, he looked at her, his face grey, and said, "It kin't be! It must be a trick the Old Woman In The Earth's playing on me so she kin have the last laugh on me. How could it be the hat a Old King Paley's? Woun't the *G'yaga* that been keepin it in their famley all these years know what it is?"

"Probably not," said Dorothy. "After all, the *G'yaga*, as you call them, don't believe in magic any more. Or it might be that the present owner doesn't even know what it is."

"Maybe. More likely it was thrown out by accident during housecleaning. You know how stupid them wimmen are. Anyway, let's take it and get going. The Old Guy In The Sky might a had a hand in fixing up this deal for me, and if he did, it's better not to ask questions. Let's go."

Old Man seldom wore the hat. When he was home, he put it in the parrot cage and locked the cage door with the bicycle lock. At nights, the cage hung from the stand; days, it sat on the seat of the truck. Old Man wanted it always where he could see it.

Finding it had given him a tremendous optimism, a belief he could do anything. He sang and laughed even more than he had before, and he was even able to venture out onto the streets for several hours at a time before the sweat and shakings began.

Gummy, seeing the hat, merely grunted and made a lewd remark about its appearance. Deena smiled grimly and said, "Why haven't the horsehide and bone rotted away long ago?"

"That's just the kind a question a *G'yaga* dummy like you'd ask," said Old Man, snorting. "How kin the hat rot when there's a million Paley souls crowded into it, standing room only? There ain't even elbow room for germs. Besides, the horsehide and the bones're jampacked with the power and the glory a all the Paleys that died before our battle with Raw Boy, and all the souls that died since. It's seething with soul-energy, the lid held on it by the magic a the *G'yaga*."

"Better watch out it don't blow up 'n wipe us all out," said Gummy, sniggering.

"Now you have the hat, what are you going to do with it?" asked Deena.

"I don't know. I'll have to sit down with a beer and study the situation."

Suddenly, Deena began laughing shrilly.

"My God, you've been thinking for fifty thousand years about this hat, and now you've got it, you don't know what to do about it! Well, I'll tell you what you'll do about it! You'll get to thinking big, a right! You'll conquer the world, rid it of all False Folk, all right! You fool! Even if your story isn't the raving of a lunatic, it would still be too late for you! You're alone! The last! One against two billion! Don't worry, World, this ragpicking Rameses, this alley Alexander, this junkyard Julius Caesar, he isn't going to conquer you! No, he's going to put on his hat, and he's going forth! To do what?

"To become a wrestler on TV, that's what! That's the height of his halfwit ambition—to be billed as the one-Armed Neanderthal, the Awful Apeman. That is the culmination of fifty thousand years, ha, ha, ha!"

The others looked apprehensively at Old Man, expecting him to strike Deena. Instead, he removed the hat from the cage, put it on, and sat down at the table with a quart of beer in his hand.

"Quit your cackling, you old hen," he said. "I got my thinking cap on."

The next day Paley, despite a hangover, was in a very good mood. He chattered all the way to the west bluff and once stopped the truck so he could walk back and forth on the street and show Dorothy he wasn't afraid.

Then, boasting he could lick the world, he drove the truck up an alley and halted it by the backyard of a huge but somewhat rundown mansion. Dorothy looked at him curiously. He pointed to the jungle-thick shrubbery that filled a corner of the yard.

"Looks like a rabbit coun't get in there, huh? But Old Man knows things the rabbit don't. Folly me."

Carrying the caged hat, he went to the shrubbery, dropped to all threes, and began inching his way through a very narrow passage. Dorothy stood looking dubiously into the tangle until a hoarse growl came from its depths.

"You scared? Or is your fanny too broad to get through here?"

"I'll try anything once," she announced cheerfully. In a short time she was crawling on her belly, then had come suddenly into a little clearing. Old Man was standing up. The cage was at his feet, and he was looking at a red rose in his hand.

She sucked in her breath. "Roses! Peonies! Violets!"

"Sure, Dor'thy," he said, swelling out his chest. "Paley's Garden a Eden, his secret hothouse. I found this place a couple a years ago, when I was looking for a place to hide if the cops was looking for me or I just wanted a place to be alone from everybody, including myself.

"I planted these rosebushes in here and these other flowers. I come here every now and then to check on em, spray them, prune them. I never take any home, even though I'd like to give Deena some. But Deena ain't no dummy, she'd know I wasn't getting them out a garbage pail. And I just din't want to tell her about this place. Or anybody."

He looked directly at her as if to catch every twitch of a muscle in her face, every repressed emotion.

"You're the only person besides myself knows about this place." He held out the rose to her. "Here. It's yours."

"Thank you. I am proud, really proud, that you've shown this place to me."

"Really are? That makes me feel good. In fact, great."

"It's amazing. This, this spot of beauty. And . . . and . . . and . . ."

"I'll finish it for you. You never thought the ugliest man in the world, a dumpheaper, a man that ain't even a man or a human bein, a—I hate that word—a Neanderthal, could appreciate the beauty of a rose. Right? Well, I growed these because I loved em.

"Look, Dor'thy. Look at this rose. It's round, not like a ball but a flattened roundness . . ."

"Oval."

"Sure. And look at the petals. How they fold in on one another, how they're arranged. Like one ring a red towers protectin the next ring a red towers. Protectin the gold cup on the inside, the precious source a life, the treasure. Or maybe that's the golden hair a the princess a the castle. Maybe. And look at the bright green leaves under the rose. Beautiful, huh? The Old Guy knew what he was doing when he made these. He was an artist then.

"But he must a been sufferin from a hangover when he shaped me, huh? His hands was shaky that day. And he gave up after a while and never bothered to finish me but went on down to the corner for some a the hair a the dog that bit him."

Suddenly, tears filled Dorothy's eyes.

"You shouldn't feel that way. You've got beauty, sensitivity, a genuine feeling, under . . ."

"Under this?" he said, pointing his finger at his face. "Sure. Forget it. Anyway, look at these green buds on these baby roses. Pretty, huh? Fresh with promise a the beauty to come. They're shaped like the breasts a young virgins."

He took a step towards her and put his arm around her shoulders.

"Dor'thy."

She put both her hands on his chest and gently tried to shove herself away.

"Please," she whispered, "please, don't. Not after you've shown me how fine you really can be."

"What do you mean?" he said, not releasing her. "Ain't what I want to do with you just as fine and beautiful a thing as this rose here? And if you really feel for me, you'd want to let your flesh say what your mind thinks. Like the flowers when they open up for the sun."

She shook her head. "No. It can't be. Please. I feel terrible because I can't say yes. But I can't. I—you—there's too much diff—"

"Sure, we're diff'runt. Goin in diff'runt directions and then, comin round the corner—bam!—we run into each other, and we wrap our arms around each other to keep from fallin."

He pulled her to him so her face was pressed against his chest.

"See!" he rumbled. "Like this. Now, breathe deep. Don't turn your head. Sniff away. Lock yourself to me, like we was glued and nothing could pull us apart. Breathe deep. I got my arm around you, like these trees round these flowers. I'm not hurtin you; I'm givin you life and protectin you. Right? Breathe deep."

"Please," she whimpered. "Don't hurt me. Gently . . ."

"Gently it is. I won't hurt you. Not too much. That's right, don't hold yourself stiff against me, like you're stone. That's right, melt like butter I'm not forcin you, Dor'thy, remember that. You want this, don't you?"

"Don't hurt me," she whispered. "You're so strong, oh my God, so strong."

For two days, Dorothy did not appear at the Paleys'. The third morning, in an effort to fire her courage, she downed two double shots of V.O. before breakfast. When she drove to the dumpheap, she told the two women that she had not been feeling well. But she had returned because she wanted to finish her study, as it was almost at an end and her superiors were anxious to get her report.

Paley, though he did not smile when he saw her, said nothing. However, he kept looking at her out of the corners of his eyes when he thought she was watching him. And though he took the hat in its cage with him, he sweated and shook as before while crossing the streets. Dorothy sat staring straight ahead, unresponding to the few remarks he did make. Finally, cursing under his breath, he abandoned his effort to work as usual and drove to the hidden garden.

"Here we are," he said. "Adam and Eve returnin to Eden."

He peered from beneath the bony ridges of his brows at the sky. "We better hurry in. Looks as if the Old Guy got up on the wrong side a the bed. There's gonna be a storm."

"I'm not going in there with you," said Dorothy. "Not now or ever."

"Even after what we did, even if you said you loved me, I still make you sick?" he said. "You din't act then like Old Ugly made you sick."

"I haven't been able to sleep for two nights," she said tonelessly. "I've asked myself a thousand times why I did it. And each time

I could only tell myself I didn't know. Something seemed to leap from you to me and take me over. I was powerless."

"You certainly wasn't paralyzed," said Old Man, placing his hand on her knee. "And if you was powerless, it was because you wanted to be."

"It's no use talking," she said. "You'll never get a chance again. And take your hand off me. It makes my flesh crawl."

He dropped his hand.

"All right. Back to business. Back to pickin people's piles a junk. Let's get out a here. Fergit what I said. Fergit this garden, too. Fergit the secret I told you. Don't tell nobody. The dumpheapers'd laugh at me. Imagine Old Man Paley, the one-armed candidate for the puzzle factory, the fugitive from the Old Stone Age, growin peonies and roses! Big, laugh, huh?"

Dorothy did not reply. He started the truck, and as they emerged onto the alley, they saw the sun disappear behind the clouds. The rest of the day, it did not come out, and Old Man and Dorothy did not speak to each other.

As they were going down Route 24 after unloading at the junkdealer's, they were stopped by a patrolman. He ticketed Paley for not having a chauffeur's license and made Paley follow him downtown to court. There Old Man had to pay a fine of twenty-five dollars. This, to everybody's amazement, he produced from his pocket.

As if that weren't enough, he had to endure the jibes of the police and the courtroom loafers. Evidently he had appeared in the police station before and was known as *King Kong*, *Alley Oop*, or just plain Chimp. Old Man trembled, whether with suppressed rage or nervouness Dorothy could not tell. But later, as Dorothy drove him home, he almost frothed at the mouth in a tremendous outburst of rage. By the time they were within sight of his shanty, he was shouting that his life savings had been wiped out and that it was all a plot by the *G'yaga* to beat him down to starvation.

It was then that the truck's motor died. Cursing, Old Man jerked the hood open so savagely that one rusty hinge broke. Further enraged by this, he tore the hood completely off and threw it away into the ditch by the roadside. Unable to find the cause of the breakdown, he took a hammer from the tool-chest and began to beat the sides of the truck.

"I'll make her go, go, go!" he shouted. "Or she'll wish she had! Run, you bitch, purr, eat gasoline, rumble your damn belly and eat gasoline but run, run, run! Or your ex-lover, Old Man, sells you for junk, I swear it!"

Undaunted, Fordiana did not move.

Eventually, Paley and Dorothy had to leave the truck by the ditch and walk home. And as they crossed the heavily traveled highway to get to the dumpheap, Old Man was forced to jump to keep from getting hit by a car.

He shook his fist at the speeding auto.

"I know you're out to get me!" he howled. "But you won't! You been tryin for fifty thousand years, and you ain't made it yet! We're still fightin!"

At that moment, the black sagging bellies of the clouds overhead ruptured. The two were soaked before they could take four steps. Thunder bellowed, and lightning slammed into the earth on the other end of the dumpheap.

Old Man growled with fright, but seeing he was untouched, he raised his fist to the sky.

"O.K., O.K., so you got it in for me, too. I get it. O.K., OK!"

Dripping, the two entered the shanty, where he opened a quart of beer and began drinking. Deena took Dorothy behind a curtain and gave her a towel to dry herself with and one of her white terrycloth robes to put on. By the time Dorothy came out from behind the curtain, she found Old Man opening his third quart. He was accusing Deena of not frying the fish correctly, and when she answered him sharply, he began accusing her of every fault, big or small, real or imaginary, of which he could think. In fifteen minutes, he was nailing the portrait of her mother to the wall with its face inwards. And she was whimpering behind the stove and tenderly stroking the spots where he had struck her. Gummy protested, and he chased her out into the rain.

Dorothy at once put her wet clothes on and announced she was leaving. She'd walk the mile into town and catch the bus.

Old Man snarled, "Go! You're too snotty for us, anyway. We ain't your kind, and that's that."

"Don't go," pleaded Deena. "If you're not here to restrain him, he'll be terrible to us."

"I'm sorry," said Dorothy. "I should have gone home this morning."

"You sure should," he growled. And then he began weeping, his pushed-out lips fluttering like a bird's wings, his face twisted like a gargoyle's.

"Get out before I fergit myself and throw you out," he sobbed.

Dorothy, with pity on her face, shut the door gently behind her.

★

The following day was Sunday. That morning, her mother phoned her she was coming down from Waukegan to visit her. Could she take Monday off?

Dorothy said yes, and then, sighing, she called her supervisor. She told him she had all the data she needed for the Paley report and that she would begin typing it out.

Monday night, after seeing her mother off on the train, she decided to pay the Paleys a farewell visit. She could not endure another sleepless night filled with fighting the desire to get out of bed again and again, to scrub herself clean, and the pain of having to face Old Man and the two women in the morning. She felt that if she said goodbye to the Paleys, she could say farewell to those feelings, too, or at least, time would wash them away more quickly.

The sky had been clear, star-filled, when she left the railroad station. By the time she had reached the dumpheap clouds had swept out from the west, and a blinding rainstorm was deluging the city. Going over the bridge, she saw by the lights of her headlamps that the Kickapoo Creek had become a small river in the two days of heavy rains. Its muddy frothing current roared past the dump and down to the Illinois River, a half mile away.

So high had it risen that the waters lapped at the doorsteps of the shanties. The trucks and jaloppies parked outside them were piled high with household goods, and their owners were ready to move at a minute's notice.

Dorothy parked her car a little off the road, because she did not want to get it stuck in the mire. By the time she had walked to the Paley shanty, she was in stinking mud up to her calves, and night had fallen.

In the light streaming from a window stood Fordiana, which Old Man had apparently succeeded in getting started. Unlike the other vehicles, it was not loaded.

Dorothy knocked on the door and was admitted by Deena. Paley was sitting in the ragged easy chair. He was clad only in a pair of faded and patched blue jeans. One eye was surrounded by a big black, blue, and green bruise. The horsehide hat of Old King was firmly jammed onto his head, and one hand clutched the neck of a quart of beer as if he were choking it to death.

Dorothy looked curiously at the black eye but did not comment on it. Instead, she asked him why he hadn't packed for a possible flood.

Old Man waved the naked stump of his arm at her.

"It's the doins a the Old Guy In The Sky. I prayed to the old idiot to stop the rain, but it rained harder'n ever. So I figure it's really the

Old Woman In The Earth who's kickin up this rain. The Old Guy's too feeble to stop her. He needs strength. So . . . I thought about pouring out the blood a a virgin to him, so he kin lap it up and get his muscles back with that. But I give that up, cause there ain't no such thing any more, not within a hundred miles a here, anyway.

"So . . . I been thinkin about going outside and doin the next best thing, that is pourin a quart or two a beer out on the ground for him. What the Greeks call pourin a liberation to the Gods . . . "

"Don't let him drink none a that cheap beer," warned Gummy. "This rain fallin on us is bad enough. I don't want no god pukin all over the place."

He hurled the quart at her. It was empty, because he wasn't so far gone he'd waste a full or even half-full bottle. But it was smashed against wall, and since it was worth a nickel's refund, he accused Gummy of malicious waste.

"If you'd a held still, it woun't a broke."

Deena paid no attention to the scene. "I'm pleased to see you, child," she said. "But it might have been better if you had stayed home tonight."

She gestured at the picture of her mother, still nailed face inwards. "He's not come out of his evil mood yet."

"You kin say that again," mumbled Gummy. "He got a pistol-whippin from the young Limpy Doolan who lives in that packinbox house with the Jantzen bathing suit ad pasted on the side, when Limpy tried to grab Old King's hat off a Old Man's head jist for fun."

"Yeah, he tried to grab it," said Paley. "But I slapped his hand hard. Then he pulls a gun out a his coat pocket with the other hand and hit me in this eye with its butt. That don't stop me. He sees me comin at him like I'm late for work, and he says he'll shoot me if I touch him again. My old man didn't raise no silly sons, so I don't charge him. But I'll get him sooner or later. And he'll be limpin in both legs, if he walks at all.

"But I don't know why I never had nothin but bad luck ever since I got this hat. It ain't supposed to be that way. It's supposed to be bringing me all the good luck the Paleys ever had."

He glared at Dorothy and said, "Do you know what? I had good luck until I showed you that place, you know, the flowers. And then, after you know what, everything went sour as old milk. What did you do, take the power out a me by doin what you did? Did the Old Woman In The Earth send you to me so you'd draw the muscle and luck and life out a me if I found the hat when Old Guy placed it in my path?"

He lurched up from the easy chair, clutched two quarts of beer from the refrigerator to his chest, and staggered towards the door.

"Kin't stand the smell in here. Talk about *my* smell. I'm sweet violets, compared to the fish a some a you. I'm goin out where the air's fresh. I'm goin out and talk to the Old Guy In The Sky, hear what the thunder has to say to me. He understand me; he don't give a damn if I'm a ugly ole man that's ha'f-ape."

Swiftly, Deena ran in front of him and held out her claws at him like a gaunt, enraged alley cat.

"So that's it! You've had the indencency to insult this young girl! You evil beast!"

Old Man halted, swayed, carefully deposited the two quarts on the floor. Then he shuffled to the picture of Deena's mother and ripped it from the wall. The nails screeched; so did Deena.

"What are you going to do?"

"Somethin I been wantin to do for a long long time. Only I felt sorry for you. Now I don't. I'm gonna throw this idol a yours into the creek. Know why? Cause I think she's a delegate a the Old Woman In The Earth, Old Guy's enemy. She's been sent here to watch on me and report to Old Woman on what I was doin. And you're the one brought her in this house."

"Over my dead body you'll throw that in the creek!" screamed Deena.

"Have it your own way," he growled, lurching forward and driving her to one side with his shoulder.

Deena grabbed at the frame of the picture he held in his hand, but he hit her over the knuckles with it. Then he lowered it to the floor, keeping it from falling over with his leg while he bent over and picked up the two quarts in his huge hand. Clutching them, he squatted until his stump was level with the top part of the frame. The stump clamped down over the upper part of the frame, he straightened, holding it tightly, lurched towards the door, and was gone into the driving rain and crashing lightning.

Deena stared into the darkness for a moment, then ran after him.

Stunned, Dorothy watched them go. Not until she heard Gummy mumbling, "They'll kill each other," was Dorothy able to move.

She ran to the door, looked out, turned back to Gummy.

"What's got into him?" she cried. "He's so cruel, yet I know he has a soft heart. Why must he be this way?"

"It's you," said Gummy. "He thought it din't matter how he looked, what he did, he was still a Paley. He thought his sweat would git you like it did all them chicks he was braggin about, no matter how uppity the sweet young thing was. 'N you hurt him when you din't dig him. Specially cause he thought more a you'n anybody before.

"Why'd you think life's been so miserable for us since he found you? What the hell, a man's a man, he's always got the eye for the chicks, right? Deena din't see that. Deena hates Old Man. But Deena can't do without him, either . . ."

"I have to stop them," said Dorothy, and she plunged out into the black and white world.

Just outside the door, she halted, bewildered. Behind her, light streamed from the shanty, and to the north was a dim glow from the city of Onaback. But elsewhere was darkness. Darkness, except when the lightning burned away the night for a dazzling frightening second.

She ran around the shanty towards the Kickapoo, some fifty yards away—she was sure that they'd be somewhere by the bank of the creek. Halfway to the stream, another flash showed her a white figure by the bank.

It was Deena in her terrycloth robe, Deena now sitting up in the mud, bending forward, shaking with sobs.

"I got down on my knees," she moaned. "To him, to him. And I begged him to spare my mother. But he said I'd thank him later for freeing me from worshipping a false goddess. He said I'd kiss his hand."

Deena's voice rose to a scream. "And then he did it! He tore my blessed mother to bits! Threw her in the creek! I'll kill him! I'll kill him!"

Dorothy patted Deena's shoulder. "There, there. You'd better get back to the house and get dry. It's a bad thing he's done, but he's not in his right mind. Where'd he go?"

"Towards that clump of cottonwoods where the creek runs into the river."

"You go back," said Dorothy. "I'll handle him. I can do it."

Deena seized her hand.

"Stay away from him. He's hiding in the woods now. He's dangerous, dangerous as a wounded boar. Or as one of his ancestors when they were hurt and hunted by ours."

"Ours?" said Dorothy. "You mean you believe his story?"

"Not all of it. Just part. That tale of his about the mass invasion of Europe and King Paley's hat is nonsense. Or, at least it's been distorted through God only knows how many thousands of years. But it's true he's at least part Neanderthal. Listen! I've fallen low, I'm only a junkman's whore. Not even that, now—Old Man never touches me any more, except to hit me. And that's not his fault, really. I ask for it; I want it.

"But I'm not a moron. I got books from the library, read what they said about the Neanderthal. I studied Old Man carefully. And I *know* he must be what he says he is. Gummy too—she's at least a quarter-breed."

Dorothy pulled her hand out of Deena's grip.

"I have to go. I have to talk to Old Man, tell him I'm not seeing him any more."

"Stay away from him," pleaded Deena, again seizing Dorothy's hand. "You'll go to talk, and you'll stay to do what I did. What a score of others did. We let him make love to us because he isn't human. Yet, we found Old Man as human as any man, and some of us stayed after the lust was gone because love had come in."

Dorothy gently unwrapped Deena's fingers from her hand and began walking away.

Soon she came to the group of cottonwood trees by the bank where the creek and the river met and there she stopped.

"Old Man!" she called in a break between the rolls of thunder. "Old Man! It's Dorothy!"

A growl as of a bear disturbed in his cave answered her, and a figure like a tree trunk come to life stepped out of the inkiness between the cottonwoods.

"What you come for?" he said, approaching so close to her that his enormous nose almost touched hers. "You want me just as I am, Old Man Paley, descendant a the Real Folk—Paley, who loves you? Or you come to give the batty old junkman a tranquilizer so you kin take him by the hand like a lamb and lead him back to the slaughterhouse, the puzzle factory, where they'll stick a ice pack back a his eyeball and rip out what makes him a man and not an ox."

"I came . . ."

"Yeah?"

"For this!" she shouted, and she snatched off his hat and raced away from him, towards the river.

Behind her rose a bellow of agony so loud she could hear it even above the thunder. Feet splashed as he gave pursuit.

Suddenly, she slipped and sprawled face down in the mud. At the same time, her glasses fell off. Now it was her turn to feel despair, for in this halfworld she could see nothing without her glasses except the lightning flashes. She must find them. But if she delayed to hunt for them, she'd lose her headstart.

She cried out with joy, for her groping fingers found what they sought. But the breath was knocked out of her, and she dropped the glasses again as a heavy weight fell upon her back and half-stunned her. Vaguely, she was aware that the hat had been taken away from her. A moment later, as her senses came back into focus, she realized she was being raised into the air. Old Man was holding her in the crook of her arm, supporting part of her weight on his bulging belly.

"My glasses. Please, my glasses. I need them."

"You won't be needin em for a while. But don't worry about em. I got em in my pants pocket. Old Man's takin care a you."

His arm tightened around her so she cried out with pain.

Hoarsely, he said, "You was sent down by the *G'yaga* to get that hat, wasn't you? Well, it din't work cause the Old Guy's stridin the sky tonight, and he's protectin his own."

Dorothy bit her lip to keep from telling him that she had wanted to destroy the hat because she hoped that that act would also destroy the guilt of having made it in the first place. But she couldn't tell him that. If he knew she had made a false hat, he would kill her in his rage.

"No. Not again," she said. "Please. Don't. I'll scream. They'll come after you. They'll take you to the State Hospital and lock you up for life. I swear I'll scream."

"Who'll hear you? Only the Old Guy, and he'd get a kick out a seeing you in this fix cause you're a Falser and you took the stuffin right out a my hat and me with your Falser Magic. But I'm gettin back what's mine and his, the same way you took it from me. The door swings both ways."

He stopped walking and lowered her to a pile of wet leaves.

"Here we are. The forest like it was in the old days. Don't worry. Old Man'll protect you from the cave bear and the bull o' the woods. But who'll protect you from Old Man, huh?"

Lightning exploded so near that for a second they were blinded and speechless. Then Paley shouted, "The Old Guy's whoopin it up tonight, just like he used to do! Blood and murder and wickedness're ridin the howlin night air!"

He pounded his immense chest with his huge fist.

"Let the Old Guy and the Old Woman fight it out tonight. They ain't going to stop us, Dor'thy. Not unless that hairy old god in the clouds is goin to fry me with his lightnin, jealous a me cause I'm havin what he can't."

Lightning rammed against the ground from the charged skies, and lightning leaped up to the clouds from the charged earth. The rain fell harder than before, as if it were being shot out of a great pipe from a mountain river and pouring directly over them. But for some time the flashes did not come close to the cottonwoods. Then, one ripped apart the night beside them, deafened and stunned them.

And Dorothy, looking over Old Man's shoulder, thought she would die of fright because there was a ghost standing over them. It was tall and white, and its shroud flapped in the wind, and its arms were raised in a gesture like a curse.

But it was a knife that it held in its hand.

Then, the fire that rose like a cross behind the figure was gone, and night rushed back in.

Dorothy screamed. Old Man grunted, as if something had knocked the breath from him.

He rose to his knees, gasped something unintelligible, and slowly got to his feet. He turned his back to Dorothy so he could face the thing in white. Lightning flashed again. Once more Dorothy screamed, for she saw the knife sticking out of his back.

Then the white figure had rushed towards Old Man. But instead of attacking him, it dropped to its knees and tried to kiss his hand and babbled for forgiveness.

No ghost. No man. Deena, in her white terrycloth robe.

"I did it because I love you!" screamed Deena.

Old Man, swaying back and forth, was silent.

"I went back to the shanty for a knife, and I came here because I knew what you'd be doing, and I didn't want Dorothy's life ruined because of you, and I hated you, and I wanted to kill you. But I don't really hate you."

Slowly, Paley reached behind him and gripped the handle of the knife. Lightning made everything white around him, and by its brief glare the women saw him jerk the blade free of his flesh.

Dorothy moaned, "It's terrible, terrible. All my fault, all my fault."

She groped through the mud until her fingers came across the old Man's jeans and its backpocket, which held her glasses. She put the glasses on, only to find that she could not see anything because of the darkness. Then, and not until then, she became concerned about locating her own clothes. On her hands and knees she searched through the wet leaves and grass. She was about to give up and go back to Old Man when another lightning flash showed the heap to her left. Giving a cry of joy, she began to crawl to it.

But another stroke of lightning showed her something else. She screamed and tried to stand up but instead slipped and fell forward on her face.

Old Man, knife in hand, was walking slowly towards her.

"Don't try to run away!" he bellowed. "You'll never get away! The Old Guy'll light things up for me so you kin't sneak away in the dark. Besides, your white skin shines in the night, like a rotten toadstool. You're done for. You snatched away my hat so you could get me out here defenseless, and then Deena could stab me in the back. You and her are Falser witches, I know damn well!"

"What do you think you're doing?" asked Dorothy. She tried to rise again but could not. It was as if the mud had fingers around her ankles and knees.

"The Old Guy's howlin for the blood a *G'yaga* wimmen. And he's gonna get all the blood he wants. It's only fair. Deena put the knife in me, and the Old Woman got some a my blood to drink. Now it's your turn to give the Old Guy some a yours."

"Don't!" screamed Deena. Dorothy had nothing to do with it! And you can't blame me, after what you were doing to her!"

"She's done everything to me. I'm gonna make the last sacrifice to Old Guy. Then they kin do what they want to me. I don't care. I'll have had one moment a bein a real Real Folker."

Deena and Dorothy both screamed. In the next second, lightning broke the darkness aroud them. Dorothy saw Deena hurl herself on Old Man's back and carry him downward. Then, night again.

There was a groan. Then, another blast of light. Old Man, bent almost double but not bent so far Dorothy could not see the handle of the knife that was in his chest.

"Oh, Christ!" wailed Deena. "When I pushed him, he must have fallen on the knife. I heard the bone in his chest break. Now he's dying!"

Paley moaned. "Yeah, you done it now, you sure paid me back didn't you? Paid me back for my taking the monkey off a your back and supportin you all these years."

"Oh, Old Man," sobbed Deena, "I didn't mean to do it. I was just trying to save Dorothy and save you from yourself. Please! Isn't there anything I can do for you?"

"Sure you kin. Stuff up the two big holes in my back and chest. My blood, my breath, my real soul's flowin out a me. Guy In The Sky, what a way to die! Kilt by a crazy woman!"

"Keep quiet," said Dorothy. "Save your strength. Deena, you run to the service station. It'll still be open. Call a doctor."

"Don't go, Deena," he said. "It's too late. I'm hanging on to my soul by its big toe now; in a minute, I'll have to let go, and it'll jump out a me like a beagle after a rabbit.

"Dor'thy, Dor'thy, was it the wickedness a the Old Woman put you up to this? I must a meant somethin to you . . . under the flowers . . . maybe it's better . . . I felt like a god, then . . . not what I really am . . . a crazy old junkman . . . a alley man . . . Just think a it . . . fifty thousand years behint me . . . older'n Adam and Eve by far . . . now, this . . ."

Deena began weeping. He lifted his hand, and she seized it.

"Let loose," he said faintly. "I was gonna knock hell otta you for blubberin . . . just like a Falser bitch . . . kill me . . . then cry . . . you never did 'preciate me . . . like Dor'thy . . ."

"His hand's getting cold," murmured Deena.

"Deena, bury that damn hat with me . . . least you kin do . . . Hey, Deena who you goin to for help when you hear that monkey chitterin outside the door, huh? Who . . .?"

Suddenly, before Dorothy and Deena could push him back down, he sat up. At the same time, lightning hammered into the earth nearby and it showed them his eyes, looking past them out into the night.

He spoke, and his voice was stronger, as if his life had drained back into him through the holes in his flesh.

"Old Guy's givin me a good send-off. Lightning and thunder. The works. Nothin cheap about him, huh? Why not? He knows this is the end a the trail fer me. The last a his worshippers . . . last a the Paleys . . ."

He choked on his own blood and sank back and spoke no more.